Belinda Alexandra is the author of nine bestselling novels and has been published around the world, including in the United States, Spain, France, Germany, the United Kingdom, Turkey, Hungary and Poland. She is the daughter of a Russian mother and an Australian father and has been an intrepid traveller since her youth. Belinda is the patron of the World League for the Protection of Animals (Australia) and lives in Sydney with her three rescue cats, Valentino, Versace and Gucci, and a garden full of interesting wildlife.

BelindaAlexandraAuthor
belinda_alexandra_author
belinda_alexandra_author
www.belinda-alexandra.com

Also by Belinda Alexandra

White Gardenia

Wild Lavender

Silver Wattle

Golden Earrings

Sapphire Skies

Southern Ruby

The Invitation

The Mystery Woman

Non Fiction

The Divine Feline: A Chic Cat Lady's Guide to Woman's Best Friend

TUSCAN ROSE

BELINDA ALEXANDRA

HarperCollins*Publishers*

HarperCollins*Publishers*

Australia • Brazil • Canada • France • Germany • Holland • Hungary
India • Italy • Japan • Mexico • New Zealand • Poland • Spain • Sweden
Switzerland • United Kingdom • United States of America

First published in Australia in 2010
This edition published in 2021
by HarperCollins*Publishers* Australia Pty Limited
Level 13, 201 Elizabeth Street, Sydney NSW 2000
ABN 36 009 913 517
harpercollins.com.au

A catalogue record for this book is available from
the National Library of Australia.

ISBN 978 1 4607 6007 9 (paperback)
ISBN 978 0 7304 4602 6 (ebook)

Cover design by Michelle Zaiter, HarperCollins Design Studio
Cover images: Woman © Ildiko Neer / Trevillion Images; background
© Barbara Prasnowska / Arcangel
Author photographs by Elizabeth Allnutt (front) and Paul Wesley (back)
Typeset in Sabon 10.5/12.5 by Kirby Jones
Printed and bound in Australia by McPherson's Printing Group
The papers used by HarperCollins in the manufacture of this book are a
natural, recyclable product made from wood grown in sustainable plantation
forests. The fibre source and manufacturing processes meet recognised
international environmental standards, and carry certification.

For my family and friends
— thank you for your love and support

PROLOGUE

Florence, 1914

The man pauses in a doorway, swaying on his feet, before lunging again along the crooked street in the direction of the river. The distance he has covered across the city leaves him panting. But the fate of the infant he has hidden in the folds of his coat depends on him, and he is terrified that if he does not deliver her to safety, and return before his absence raises suspicion, they will both be lost.

The sound of hoofs on the cobblestones makes the hairs on his neck bristle. He twists to challenge his pursuer but sees only a merchant's carriage laden with candles and bags of flour. He leaps into a passageway between two houses. The breeze is chilly but the infant cradled against his chest warms his skin. He pushes back his coat and glimpses her face. 'God be praised for the deep sleep of babes,' the man mutters, caressing the child's cheek with his gloveless, calloused hand. He turns to the sky and tries to shut away the images of the last few hours, shivering when he remembers the bloodless face of the mother ... and the screams: so terrifying he could not have imagined they came from a human being.

He creeps along the street and comes upon a group of youths loitering around a fountain. One of them catches his eye and breaks away from the others: an emaciated adolescent with a moth-eaten scarf knotted at his throat. The man licks his lips and bares his teeth, but thinks better of the challenge and turns into a laneway. '*E allora!*' the youth calls out after him but makes no move to follow. The boy may have only wanted a match for his cigarette, but Florence is on edge with the threat of war and this is not the time to take chances.

The man emerges from the laneway. The slow-moving Arno glitters before him in the setting sun. The Ponte Vecchio is golden in the rays. He remembers the first time he saw Florence and how he was sure that it was the most beautiful city in the world. But he was too naïve then to know that beauty has two faces and that a splendid façade can hide a putrid soul.

The man lopes along the bridge, ignoring the calls of the jewellers who are packing away their wares and hoping for a last-minute sale. He tracks along the banks of the Arno before his prematurely greying hair and bulky coat make him conspicuous amongst the young lovers on their evening strolls. He darts into a street of narrow houses before turning back onto Via Maggio and at last to the piazza that smells of coal fires and damp stone. A wind is swirling the leaves around the cobblestones. He stands before the high walls of the convent. Darkness is falling and he peers at the stones, hoping to see a *ruota*, a foundling wheel. There isn't one. The convent in the town he grew up in had a *ruota*: a revolving door in the wall where a child could be deposited with the nuns without them seeing the bearer's face. But the medieval practice has fallen out of favour in Italy's current spirit of liberalism and he has no choice but to rap on the door. There is no response and he strikes the wood with more force.

Footsteps scurry inside and the grate is flung aside. He is aware of being looked at but it is too dark to see the observer's face. The door scrapes open and he squints at the black-robed figure before him. He senses the nun's hesitation. It is not the custom of the sisters to welcome strange men in the night.

'I have a child,' he says.

He fears the nun will send him away. There is the Ospedale degli Innocenti for foundlings, but he knows it is overcrowded and the babies often die from poor hygiene. The infant's best chance is the convent. To his relief, the nun holds out a lamp over the steps and indicates for him to come inside. The man glances over his shoulder then follows her into the vestibule. The door thuds behind him, shutting out the encroaching night. The sound of singing drifts on the air: the sisters at vespers. The nun leads him to a parlour and turns on the light. She is young, no more than twenty, with a pleasant face. Her eyes pass over him and he sees the kindness in them. Suddenly all the strength it has taken him to steal the child to safety drains from him. Tears blur his vision.

'Come,' she says, directing him to a chair. His keen sense of smell detects the scents of rosemary and thyme on her sleeves. Does she work in the convent garden? Or the kitchen?

He unfolds his coat to reveal the child. She has woken up. Her fists are clenched into balls and her mouth is open in a silent cry.

The nun's eyes glisten when he passes the child into her arms. 'Shh! Shh!' the nun comforts her. 'You are hungry, aren't you, little one?'

The nun turns to him. 'The mother?' she asks delicately. 'Can she come to nurse her?'

'No,' the man answers, unable to hold the nun's gaze. He realises she has assumed the child is his and grimaces. He lost his family long ago. Will she think his wife has died in confinement? Or that she has left him? Or simply that they are too poor and sick to feed another mouth, like so many others in the city?

'A wet nurse is staying here to feed a baby whose mother is ill,' the nun says. 'We won't have to send this little one to a *balia*.'

The man has heard stories of the *balie*: women who take care of the abandoned infants for the convents and not always under hygienic conditions. It seems the child is doubly blessed and the man marvels at her turn in fate. He can see that the nun, beneath her robes, has a well-formed figure. She is the kind of woman, had she not been married to Christ, who would have made an excellent mother. The child is in good hands.

'Will you visit her?' the nun asks him.

The man shakes his head and the nun flinches. He watches her brush her finger over the child's dusky-rose skin. She is a fine child, born to better things, he thinks. Now she will be poor. But better poor than …

The nuns start singing again. The uplifting sound touches the man's heart. He has achieved what he set out to do.

'If you change your mind, you can come back. I'll remember you,' the nun says.

The man doesn't answer her and for a while they are silent. Then he says: 'It's best that she remains anonymous. Without her birth name and history she will be safe.'

The nun pales. She has the right to demand the mother's name but he sees that she has understood there is danger in saying anything more.

The man strides back to the vestibule. The nun follows him. He takes the handle and swings the door open, admitting a cold gust of wind. He turns for one last glimpse of the nun and the child. As he does so, he notices the only painting that adorns the white-washed wall behind them: the Madonna and the Christ child.

'May they watch over you both,' he says.

'And over you,' the nun replies.

The man nods before rushing out into the night.

*

The nun takes the child to the refectory, where a warm fire is burning. Placing the child on her lap, she feels her wrappings to see if they are wet. Something protrudes from the baby's thigh. The nun slips her hand into the wrappings and pulls out the object: a tiny silver key.

'It's magic,' the nun says under her breath. She told the stranger that she would remember him and she is certain that she will. With his watchful eyes and grizzled appearance ... he was a wolf in human form. But not the epitome of evil that the animal represented in legends. No, this wolf was kind — and badly in need of redemption.

Part One

ONE

Rosa Bellocchi was dying by inches. Her life was about to change and everything familiar was slipping from her grasp. She sat in the convent kitchen with Suor Maddalena as she had every morning since she had finished her formal education at the Convent of Santo Spirito. The kitchen was terracotta-tiled with a wooden bench running down the centre of it, and overlooked the courtyard and the statue of Sant'Agostino. Despite the fire in the cast-iron stove, the early spring air had a chill to it and the women had moved their chairs into the patch of sunlight streaming through the window. Suor Maddalena peeled potatoes while Rosa sat with her flute in her lap, her spine stiff and her stomach stretched taut. She pretended to study the phrasing of the hymn perched on her music stand but her mind was racing.

Will today be the last time we sit together like this? she asked herself.

Suor Maddalena sang when she worked in the kitchen. The convent was a place for meditation, but the cavernous halls and maze of corridors acted like echo chambers and each morning the duet of Suor Maddalena's perfect pitch and the sweet tones of Rosa's flute would reach even the remotest parts of the convent. The nuns working in the vegetable garden lifted their heads and strained to hear the heavenly music, and the older ones, allowed to rest in their cells after breakfast, dreamed of angels. But that morning Suor Maddalena was silent, absorbed in a grief her faith would not allow her to show. Rosa's heart ached to think that she would soon be separated from the woman who was the closest person to a mother she had known. Their intimate relationship, the bond that had developed during their years in the kitchen, would cease and all future conversations would take place in the formal parlour through the grille with a 'listening nun' in attendance.

I will be on the outside of the only home I have known, Rosa thought.

Her eyes took in the words of the hymn — *The greatest joy is sacrificing one's self for others* — and she was reminded of her interview with the Badessa, the convent's Mother Superior, a few days before.

'Although the outside world thinks our life is plain, we are content,' the Badessa had told her. 'Our faith is full of wonder and our community shares an understanding lacking in many families. But to live this life one must be called to it ... and, Rosa, you have not been called.'

Rosa, whose blue-black eyes had been fixed on the painting of the Ascension on the wall behind the Badessa's desk, opened her mouth to speak but closed it again. She had tried to feel 'called' but had never heard the still voice that the nuns spoke of with rapture.

'I do feel called,' she told the Badessa, 'to something.'

The Badessa took off her glasses and rubbed her eyes before putting the glasses back on. 'With your intelligence and wit I have no doubt that God has a great purpose for you, Rosa. But it is not here within the walls of the convent. It is not with us that you will fulfil it.'

Rosa's heart beat violently. She had known this moment would come, but now it was here she was not prepared for it. The older girls who had been schooled at the convent had been sent into marriages with good Florentine families. But that would not be possible for Rosa because she was an orphan.

'I have spoken with Don Marzoli,' the Badessa continued. 'And our priest agrees that you would be a good governess and is making enquiries with our patron families to see if such a position is available. After all, you have excelled in mathematics and music and can speak English, French and German.'

'I could teach here ... at the school,' Rosa blurted out.

The sight of the Badessa's raised eyebrows stopped her. It would be impossible to continue to live at the convent unless she were a nun. And she could not pretend she had been called, even though it meant she would be sent away.

'When you become a nun you are still a mother and a bride, just in a different way,' Suor Maddalena had once told her. 'The day I was consecrated, my family was present and I wore a white veil.' Some of the nuns had brothers and sisters who visited them in the parlour on festivals and special occasions, but their siblings' lives were a world apart from the cloistered existence of the convent. Suor Maddalena had only been allowed to visit her family home once, when her mother was dying. Despite the Badessa's assurances that the convent was a whole life, Rosa could not fathom giving away the good fortune of having been born into a family and having a proper name.

Suor Maddalena coughed, bringing Rosa's thoughts from her interview with the Badessa back into the kitchen. Silent tears were falling down Suor Maddalena's cheeks. The sight of them brought tears to Rosa's own eyes.

'Don Marzoli will find you a good position,' Suor Maddalena said, half to Rosa and half to herself. 'Not too far away. You can still come and see me.'

The tremble in the nun's voice pinched Rosa's heart. When she was a child, it had been Suor Maddalena who had soothed her nightmares and held her hand on the few occasions the pair was allowed to leave the convent together. The Badessa often warned the nuns about forming too close an attachment to the orphans: 'They are like little birds that have been blown out of their nests in a storm. We feed them, keep them warm and educate them, but one day we must let them go.' Rosa knew that Suor Maddalena would be lonely when her 'little bird' had flown and she would not be able to show it. Rosa glanced at her hands and thought of her birth mother. She had no memory of her and imagined her to be a woman dressed in an azure robe with a beatific smile, like the painting of the Madonna holding the Christ child in the vestibule.

'What are you thinking?' Suor Maddalena asked. 'Why don't you play? It will make us both feel better.'

Rosa brought the flute to her lips but she couldn't produce any sound. She had a sudden desire to cling to anything she and Suor Maddalena had shared.

'Tell me again the story of how I came to the convent,' she said.

Suor Maddalena shredded sprigs of rosemary and did not answer.

'Please.'

When she was a child, Rosa had often pestered Suor Maddalena to tell her the story of the night the stranger had brought her to the convent. After each telling she would puzzle over who the man had been. Her father? A servant? But the mystery could not be solved and, when she grew up, Rosa had stopped asking.

'Tell me,' she begged Suor Maddalena now. 'I need to hear it one last time. Tell me about the Wolf.'

A few days later Suor Maddalena developed a fever and was ordered to stay in bed by the Badessa. Suor Dorotea and Suor Valeria took charge of supervising the cooking and their inane chatter sent Rosa fleeing to the chapel with her flute. Unlike with her piano practice, Rosa never had to discipline herself to play her second instrument. The pure notes of the flute transported her to the heavenly realm as surely as the nuns' prayers delivered them to it. To skip practising was the same as going hungry: it left her tight in the stomach and moody.

Rosa was in the midst of Handel's Largo when she heard a car pull up in the courtyard. She glanced out the window expecting to see Don Marzoli's Fiat but instead caught sight of a black Bugatti coming to a stop near the statue. It was unprecedented for anyone except Don Marzoli or the doctor to bring a car into the convent and she wondered who had arrived to disturb the peace. She strained to see past the ilex tree and presently a chauffeur stepped out of the car and opened the rear door. First a man in a hat and with an overcoat hung on his arm appeared. He had a sportsman's physique and a tanned face. There was somebody else in the car behind him but Rosa's view was obscured by a branch moving in the breeze. All she glimpsed was a silver brocade sleeve and a white hand on the gentleman's arm.

A few minutes later, a novice nun hovered at the chapel door. 'The Badessa requires your presence immediately.'

Rosa swallowed and packed away her flute. It was her habit to take care with the task, careful not to press on the keys or force the pieces apart, because she knew how much the nuns had sacrificed to buy the instrument for her. But the thought that the man in the hat had come to claim her for employment made Rosa's hands shake. She dropped the headpiece, denting it. The damage to her most precious possession would normally have distressed her but she barely registered the accident.

Rosa followed the novice to the Badessa's office. Her bladder suddenly seemed full to the point of bursting. She excused herself to use the lavatory but when she sat down on the latrine she could not make herself pass water. If she tried longer she would test the Badessa's patience by keeping her waiting. She stood up and adjusted her stockings, with no sense of relief and a sharp pain jabbing her side.

The Badessa was sitting at her desk. The man Rosa had seen emerge from the Bugatti was there but not the woman. He was striking, with a square jaw and heavy eyebrows. He had a fresh complexion for his age, which Rosa guessed to be about forty, and would have appeared younger if not for the lines etched on his forehead and around his eyes. From the man's expensive silk suit and the gold signet ring on his finger, Rosa guessed he was someone of importance.

The Badessa spoke slowly as if to stress the significance of the occasion. 'Rosa, I introduce to you the Marchese Scarfiotti.'

A marchese? Rosa was taken aback by the noble title. She curtseyed.

'The Marchese Scarfiotti and his wife are looking for a governess for their daughter,' the Badessa explained. 'They are impressed by your accomplishments in music and your gift for languages.'

'My mother and grandmother both attended the school here and were fine musicians,' the Marchese said, crossing his legs and resting his elbow on his knee. 'Although my sister was schooled at home, she also took music lessons here as a child. Our family has always prided itself on our musical accomplishments. I want my daughter to carry on that tradition.'

'Perhaps you could play something for the Marchese now,' the Badessa said to Rosa.

Rosa clutched her flute case to her chest and squeezed her legs together. Her bladder was excruciatingly full. But she dutifully took out her flute and played the Handel piece she had been practising. Despite her discomfort, she played the piece better than she ever had before. When she finished she could see that the Marchese was pleased.

'The interpretation was sublime,' he said. 'Don Marzoli did not exaggerate your talents.' The Marchese's manner was almost fatherly and he had a pleasantly modulated voice.

'The Scarfiotti family are generous patrons of music and

art in Florence,' the Badessa said, looking steadily at Rosa. 'It is a great honour they have taken an interest in you.'

It was well known at the convent that Don Marzoli thought highly of Rosa, whom he considered advanced for her age. He must have gone to some lengths to find her a position with the Scarfiotti family. While Rosa was flattered she didn't want to leave so to whom she was sent was of little consequence.

The Badessa nodded to the novice nun and Rosa realised that she was being dismissed. Her fate had already been decided. The Marchese must have made up his mind before coming and had only wanted to hear her play out of curiosity.

Rosa returned to the chapel and knelt in a pew. She stared at the painting behind the altar of Christ on the Cross and felt like a condemned prisoner waiting for a stay of execution. Was it possible some miracle would occur, some change of policy, and she would be allowed to stay? Yet interest mingled with her despair. A marchese? Where did he live — in a castle or a villa? And why had his wife not accompanied him to the interview? Surely a mother would be keen to approve or disapprove of a governess for her daughter?

Rosa stood and went to the window. The Marchese's car was still in the courtyard. He must be completing the final details with the Badessa. Rosa opened her flute case and assembled the instrument, intending to play *Ave Maria*. The sound of the flute would soothe her, she thought, but when she placed the mouthpiece to her lips she found herself out of breath and unable to play, as she had a few days ago in the kitchen. Her thumb touched the dint in the headpiece and she sighed, longing to tell Suor Maddalena what had passed. She was panicked by the thought of being separated from her.

Rosa packed away her flute and hurried to Suor Maddalena's cell, but when she arrived she found it empty. Suor Eugenia was standing in the corridor.

'The doctor came this morning and ordered Suor Maddalena be moved to the convalescent room.'

'The infirmary?' cried Rosa, knowing only the most ill nuns were sent there. 'I must see her.'

Suor Eugenia shook her head. 'It's forbidden for anyone to go near her. There is a danger of pneumonia.'

'Pneumonia?'

'Suor Maddalena has an infection in her chest and must not be upset in any way.'

The blood drained from Rosa's face. What if she didn't get to say goodbye to Suor Maddalena at all? She rushed to her own cell and gave a cry when she saw the novice nun packing her clothes into a small suitcase.

'You are leaving this morning,' the novice told her. 'The Marchese is waiting for you in the courtyard. The Badessa said she will meet you there.'

'But Suor Maddalena is sick. I can't leave now.'

The novice touched Rosa's arm. 'Be brave,' she said.

Rosa rushed to the desk and scribbled a note for Suor Maddalena before taking her suitcase from the novice and running out to the courtyard. The Badessa was standing by the car with the Marchese. He seemed impatient to be on his way. Rosa had known for several days now that she would be leaving the convent, but everything was happening too fast.

'Please, Reverenda Madre,' she said, 'would you give this letter to Suor Maddalena? I've had no time to say goodbye to her or anyone else. I will come and see her as soon as she is better.'

The Badessa averted her eyes. 'Suor Maddalena will be pleased that you have obtained such a prestigious position. She made sure you received the best education possible.'

Rosa's heart fell with the Badessa's words. Was it possible that Suor Maddalena was not as sick as Suor Eugenia had claimed? Was she purposely being kept from Rosa's departure? Rosa wanted to ask if she might speak to Suor Maddalena through the infirmary window but the Marchese handed his hat and overcoat to the chauffeur and the Badessa nudged her towards the car.

'Don't keep your new employer waiting,' she whispered. 'Behave well and work hard, Rosa. That is the finest gratitude you can show Suor Maddalena.'

The chauffeur, a small, middle-aged man, took Rosa's bag from her but the latch was not properly secured and her clothes and books spilled out.

'I beg your pardon, signorina,' said the chauffeur, bending to retrieve the fallen items. He picked up a dress and something fell out of the pocket. It was a folded piece of paper. Rosa scooped it up before anyone saw it, and slipped it into her sleeve cuff, wondering if it was a note from Suor Maddalena.

The chauffeur opened the door for Rosa and she climbed inside. The car smelled of jasmine. She gave a start when she saw the woman in the brocade coat sitting there already. The woman was pretty, with creamy skin and strawberry-blonde curls poking out from her hat. She stared at Rosa then smiled.

'Here,' she said, spreading the ermine wrap she held on her knees so that it covered Rosa's legs as well.

Rosa cringed but resisted the urge to shove the wrap off herself. The touch of fur when it was lifeless repulsed her. She only liked it when it was warm and on a living animal. She saw the origin of things when others saw only the object. A fox stole slung over the shoulder of a woman in the convent's parlour had once sent her heart racing with fear, as if she were the hunted animal running for its life through the woods. The leather-bound Bible in the chapel nauseated her whenever Don Marzoli opened it: she pictured the leather worker scraping off animal tissue while others saw only the Word of God.

The Marchese seated himself next to the woman and Rosa pushed herself into the corner to give him room. 'This is Signora Corvetto,' he said. 'She is accompanying me today.' He gave no further explanation.

So the woman wasn't the Marchesa. Then who was she? Her clothes were elegant and she had pearls layered around her neck and emerald rings on her fingers. Could she be the Marchese's secretary?

The car started to move and Rosa waved goodbye to the Badessa. She was surprised when the old nun, who had always been formal with her, blew her a kiss. The spectacle of the Badessa against the backdrop of the only world Rosa had known brought tears to her eyes.

'So you have lived in a convent all your life?' Signora Corvetto asked her.

'Yes, signora.'

Signora Corvetto lit a cigarette and looked through the smoke at Rosa. 'You are a fine musician, I've heard. Clementina loves music.'

Signora Corvetto gave the impression that she was going to ask something else but changed her mind. Her blue eyes were sad. The Marchese slipped his hand into Signora Corvetto's. Rosa shifted in her seat and glanced back at the convent, which was disappearing into the distance. She might have lived a sheltered life but she was beginning to suspect that Signora Corvetto was not the Marchese's secretary.

The chauffeur took them along the Arno to the Ponte Santa Trinita, which was the furthest Rosa could remember travelling from the convent. The other side of the river was a Florence that she had seen only in the distance and now she was in the middle of it. She temporarily forgot her heartache and looked at the narrow streets, gloomy because of the shadows cast by the houses. Some of them were no more than alleys and passageways. The chauffeur had to manoeuvre with care through the main streets to avoid colliding with trams, bread carts and maids carrying baskets of vegetables on their heads. Every so often the sun burst upon the car when they passed a piazza. Rosa could not believe the riches displayed by the vendors whose stores bordered the open spaces: the antiques dealers and framers; the perfumers with ribbed glass bottles and gold filigree hand mirrors in their windows; the boxes stacked with asparagus, carrots, artichokes and beets in the doorways of the grocers'. Never before had Rosa seen such abundance. The convent prided itself on simplicity and self-sufficiency. The nuns pressed their own oils and wove their own cloth. Life there had always been frugal.

The Marchese slipped his hand into his pocket, took out a silver cigarette case and leaned across Signora Corvetto.

'Do you care to smoke?' he asked Rosa.

Rosa was taken aback by his sudden familiarity. She shook her head.

'There is the Duomo,' he said, pointing out the window. 'I doubt you've seen it this close before, Signorina Bellocchi? Some of Italy's greatest talents have worked on this grand monument: Giotto, Orcagna, Gaddi.'

Rosa turned to where he was indicating and saw the Basilica di Santa Maria del Fiore, known by the Florentines as the Duomo. It towered over the other buildings and she was dazzled by the walls tiled in pink and green marquetry and Brunelleschi's famous red dome. She had only ever seen the church in a black-and-white picture.

'The white tiles are from Carrara, the green from Prato and the red from Siena,' the Marchese told her, pushing back his hair. 'Some think it is excessive, but you can see that there is harmony between the cathedral, belltower and baptistry.'

The Marchese's face became flushed as he described the difficulties the various artists had encountered at each stage of the construction process and how Brunelleschi was once removed by ushers after a disagreement with the building committee. When the Marchese spoke about the artistic merits and the history of the building he became a different person: less restrained. Rosa found herself warming to him.

The chauffeur brought the car to a stop and opened the door for the Marchese and Signora Corvetto to alight. He gave no indication that Rosa should follow. The Marchese turned and dipped his head into the car.

'Giuseppe will take you on to the villa,' he said, nodding towards the chauffeur. 'I trust you will be happy in your position.'

Before Rosa had a chance to absorb what was happening, the chauffeur shut the door, returned to his seat and reversed the car. Rosa looked through the rear window to see the Marchese and Signora Corvetto strolling across the piazza, heads close together in conversation. She didn't know what to make of the situation.

'Are you comfortable there, Signorina Bellocchi?' Giuseppe asked.

'Yes, thank you.'

Rosa would have liked to ask the chauffeur about the Scarfiotti family, because she had been told so little, but she was overcome by shyness and remained quiet. Giuseppe turned his attention back to driving. Rosa took out the piece of paper she had hidden in her sleeve. She unfolded it and discovered inside a tiny silver key with a heart-shaped bow on the end of it. She checked to see if Suor Maddalena had written an explanation on the paper, but there was nothing. Rosa held the key in the palm of her hand, imagining what it might open. It was too light for a door or a wardrobe. Perhaps it fitted into the lock of a small case? She rewrapped the key and tucked it back into her sleeve.

A while later, the car passed a sign that read: *To Fiesole*.

'Ah, the English,' said Giuseppe, pointing to a gathering of women with irises in their arms outside a cemetery. Their blonde hair, lace dresses and sensible shoes reminded Rosa of her English-language tutor at the convent, Mrs Richards, who had helped the students with pronunciation when the nuns could not.

'The English are everywhere on Via Tornabuoni,' said Giuseppe. 'You will see. It's like being in London.'

I will see, thought Rosa. There was no doubt that her old life was diminishing and a new one was opening up before her. Despite her apprehension, she began to feel a tingle of excitement.

The car sped uphill and magnificent villas came into sight alongside the road, each one more elaborate than the last. Rosa noticed a sprawling villa with pietra serena columns and a loggia overlooking a garden of magnolia and olive trees, and then another with an ornate tower and windows with stone surrounds and corbels. Was this how the Scarfiotti family lived, she wondered. They passed some more villas and then some fields, and Rosa glimpsed the view of Florence below.

Giuseppe glanced over his shoulder. 'Would you like to see it?' he asked.

Rosa told him that she would and he pulled the car to the side of the road and opened the door for her. A breeze tickled the grass around her knees as she inched her way towards the slope. Florence in all its magnificence stretched out before her. The clusters of red-roofed buildings, churches and convents huddled together with the Basilica and Brunelleschi's dome towering above them all. Although she could not see the convent she could hear the bells of the city's churches ringing and she knew the nuns would be going to their prayers. It was hard to believe that she had been playing her flute in the convent's chapel only a few hours ago. Tears pricked her eyes when she realised that she would never play there again.

'You will miss the nuns, yes?' asked Giuseppe, looking at her sympathetically.

'Yes,' she replied.

He nodded but said nothing more. Rosa found it odd that he didn't try to reassure her by telling her how pleasant life would be with the Scarfiotti family.

They returned to the car and, a short while later, entered a road bordered on either side by stone walls. Rosa stretched her neck to see trees or other features of the landscape over the walls but could glimpse nothing. She felt as if the car was barrelling down a tunnel. The sensation lasted until they came to a wrought-iron gate with stone mastiffs either side of it and a gatehouse set back from the fence and surrounded by a tall hedge. Giuseppe sounded the horn. The door to the gatehouse opened and an unshaven man with shoulder-length grey hair and wearing a shirt and vest peered out. He headed towards the gates and fixed his large hands on the lock to open them so Giuseppe could drive through. Despite the man's rumpled appearance, his posture was strong and erect. Giuseppe eased the car forward. Rosa looked at the gatekeeper, intrigued by his air of dignity, but he kept his eyes averted.

The drive to the villa was through a wood. Suddenly the trees gave way and the Villa Scarfiotti came into view. The house was four storeys high, with the central section set back from the wings. From each floor eight windows looked out over the lawns. The railings and trimmings were covered with verdigris, and the bluish-green patina was repeated on the fountain at the centre of the driveway and the pillars and ornamental urns that bordered the steps leading to the imposing bronze doors. Dozens of classical statues dotted the lawns: maidens with urns and men with swords. Each statue seemed frozen in its activity, as if it had once been a real person whom an enchantress had turned to stone. There were no lemon trees in terracotta pots or flowerbeds bursting with zinnias and white stocks such as Rosa had seen on the terraces of the villas lining the road. The garden of the Villa Scarfiotti was a sudden cutting away of the woods with only box hedges and oleanders to soften it. The other villas Rosa had passed had been graceful, smaller in scale and in harmony with the surrounding countryside. The Villa Scarfiotti was imposing, as if the original designer had intended to make those who approached it feel daunted rather than welcomed.

Giuseppe brought the car to a stop, took out Rosa's flute case and bag and opened the door for her. Rosa heard the locks on the twelve-foot-high doors open and waited on the stone steps with Giuseppe, bracing herself to meet the Marchesa. But it was not a noblewoman who appeared before them but a housekeeper in a black uniform.

'Where's the Marchese?' the housekeeper asked Giuseppe, a scowl on her face.

'He is still in the city.'

The woman's fierce eyes fixed on Giuseppe. She had blonde-grey hair pulled severely back from her face and skin like crepe paper. 'Who is this?' she asked him, indicating Rosa.

'The new governess.'

The wrinkles around the housekeeper's mouth twitched. 'What's she doing here? The Marchesa won't be back until tomorrow. They are still in Venice.'

Rosa's feelings of anticipation at seeing the Villa Scarfiotti faded with the housekeeper's sharpness. She wondered if Don Marzoli and the Badessa had any idea of the chaotic arrangements of the Scarfiotti household. Then a troubling thought occurred to her: now she was out of the convent, Don Marzoli and the Badessa were no longer responsible for her welfare. She was on her own.

'The Marchese thought it would be more convenient if Signorina Bellocchi came here today,' Giuseppe told the woman. 'To settle in.'

A shrewish look passed over the housekeeper's face at the mention of Rosa's name. It meant 'beautiful eyes' and the nuns had chosen it for Rosa because she had no parents to give her their own surname. Even though Innocenti and Nocentini were the names usually given to foundlings, Rosa could tell the curious name had aroused the housekeeper's suspicions and she cringed inwardly. The suggestion that she was an orphan, or, even worse, illegitimate, would only make the woman despise her more. Rosa recalled that the Marchese had told her she would report directly to him and she felt grateful that her position was not overseen by the housekeeper.

'Convenient for whom?' the woman replied to Giuseppe. 'No one has told me which room to give her.'

'Put her in the nursemaid's room,' he suggested.

Giuseppe spoke calmly but the twinkle in his eye made Rosa think he enjoyed baiting the woman.

'That's on the fourth floor,' said the housekeeper with emphasis. 'I won't do that without the Marchesa's instructions. She can sleep in the scullery maid's room until I'm told otherwise.'

Giuseppe glanced at Rosa and shrugged.

'Come then,' the housekeeper said to Rosa, jerking her head towards the door. 'You will have to make up your own room. I am the only one here today. You are not above that, I hope, Signorina *Bellocchi*.'

Rosa followed the housekeeper dutifully. She was used to the contempt people showed towards orphans, and had suffered taunts from the paying students at the convent, especially when the teaching nuns refused to put her at the back of the classroom where they and their parents thought foundlings belonged. 'You are by far the brightest pupil,' Suor Maddalena had explained to her. 'Suor Camilla and Suor Grazia want the others to follow your example, not the other way around.'

Rosa forgot the housekeeper's hostility the moment she entered the house. The villa's exterior was Renaissance in style with some Baroque additions, but the interior was ultra-modern and glittering. Flashes of light dazzled her eyes. The floor of the entrance hall was white marble and extended to a sweeping staircase. The walls were amethyst purple with wall lights of rock crystals illuminated from within. There were mirrors of every shape, size and description: square mirrors with pearl-veneered frames; round ones with silver filigree trimmings; and dozens of oval ones that were shaped like eyes. Rosa cried out when she caught her reflection in a grand gilded mirror: she had never seen herself so clearly before. Mirrors were forbidden at the convent as symbols of vanity, and she had only glimpsed shadowy images of herself in window glass or in the rippled pool of the fountain. She was taken aback by her coal-black hair and oblong face, and her startled eyes. She was taller than the housekeeper and much longer-limbed. They looked like a deer and a hedgehog standing together.

'Shh! Do you have to make such a noise?' the housekeeper scolded her. The woman's scowl transformed into a snigger. 'Where do you come from? Haven't you seen such fine things before?'

Rosa was too overcome by the sight of herself to answer.

'Bellocchi. Is that your real name?' the housekeeper persisted.

Rosa recovered herself and saw where the conversation was headed. The sight of her reflection had not only startled her but had awakened her too. She peered at herself again. No, on second glance she did not look like an innocent deer at all. That was only how she felt on the inside. Her outer appearance suggested the contrary. Although her dark eyes were large with long lashes, the blueness in them was savage. Her limbs were long and she was muscly with sloping shoulders, like a panther.

'Yes,' she answered. 'Bellocchi is my family name.'

The housekeeper stiffened. 'Bellocchi is my family name, *Signora Guerrini*.'

'Pardon?'

'You must call me Signora Guerrini. Or didn't they teach you manners wherever you came from?' The housekeeper sniffed before fixing her eyes on the flute case Rosa held in her hand along with her bag. 'And don't think that you will be able to play that here. The Marchesa is sensitive to any kind of noise.'

Some of the older nuns at the convent had been crotchety and the Badessa had been stern, but Rosa had never before encountered anyone with such a bad temper as Signora Guerrini. No, the housekeeper's not a cute hedgehog either, she thought. She's quite something else.

Rosa followed Signora Guerrini to the grand staircase and then beyond it to a door. When the housekeeper opened it, Rosa saw a stairwell leading to the cellar. Was that where the scullery maid slept? Her skin prickled when Signora Guerrini led her down the stairs and into a dungeon-like space. The chilly stone floor bit through the soles of her shoes. Through the curtains of spider webs she could see hundreds of dusty bottles on the wrought-iron racks. Signora Guerrini reached a door that led to a corridor, which then opened into an enclave with a bed and a set of drawers. To Rosa's relief the space was pleasant. The lemon-blossom-patterned wallpaper was bordered by a strip of sunflowers that matched the cover on the iron bed. The golden theme continued to the ceiling where it culminated in a star-shaped ceiling rose. The wallpaper disguised an inbuilt cupboard, which Signora Guerrini opened and indicated for Rosa to place her bag and flute on the shelf inside. She pulled a set of sheets from the cupboard and tossed them on the bed.

'You can make it up yourself,' she said. 'I have things to do and you weren't expected.'

'Thank you, Signora Guerrini,' Rosa said, noticing the charcoal bedwarmer the housekeeper took from the cupboard and placed under the bed. Perhaps she did not despise Rosa as much as Rosa thought. 'The room is very pleasant.'

Signora Guerrini pulled aside a curtain to reveal a view of the kitchen garden. 'Yes, they made it so, didn't they?' she said, a malicious grin forming on her face. 'It used to be the hospital room. They brought servants here when they caught the plague. The scullery maid won't stay here. She says it's haunted.'

Signora Guerrini left Rosa alone to unpack her things, which were so few that the task was completed within minutes. She tucked in the sheets and then sat on the bed, thinking over the day that had passed. That morning she had awoken in her cell at the convent, and now she was here in this room, which, while much prettier, put her ill at ease.

Behind a screen she found a sink and a bucket with a wooden seat. She turned on the tap. The water was freezing and smelled of slime. She let it run then rinsed her mouth and splashed her face before returning to sit on the bed. She longed to play her flute to quiet her mind but did not wish to arouse any further ill will in Signora Guerrini.

She held an imaginary flute to her lips and lost herself in playing Bach's Allemande and other pieces from memory.

The afternoon passed by this way and evening fell. Rosa waited for Signora Guerrini to return to call her to dinner or to show her around, but once the moon rose and the room turned cold she understood that this would not happen. She took the warmer from under the bed and held it in her lap. Without coals from a fire it was useless. She remembered the charcoal warmer that Suor Maddalena had given her in winter when she was a child. The gentle heat that emanated from it had filled her with happiness.

She took out the key from her sleeve and tucked it into her flute case. A shiver passed down her spine and she undressed with the light still burning. It was not so much the thought of ghosts that made her afraid but the rats she could hear scratching in the cellar. She knelt by her bed to pray but the words she had said before bedtime all her life, which had touched her with comfort and peace, felt empty and hollow. Climbing into bed, Rosa wondered if her inability to pray was because she had been so abruptly separated from Suor Maddalena, or if it was because she was now somewhere that God couldn't hear her.

TWO

Rosa awoke the next morning with a jolt. She scanned the room, searching for something familiar. Where was the crucifix? Where was the chest of drawers? When the golden flowers on the wallpaper and the decorative ceiling came into focus she knew she was no longer at the convent. She climbed out of bed and pulled aside the curtain. The sun shone brightly. There was no clock in the room but Rosa realised that she had slept later than usual. She sat back down on the bed. Even the mattress was an anomaly. It was soft like a cloud, whereas her mattress at the convent had been filled with dried maize leaves that crackled whenever she moved.

Her life at the convent had been governed by bells: for prayer, for work, for meals and every other activity of the day. The quiet here was unnerving. Rosa hummed the Allemande to reassure herself but the sense of being cut adrift returned to her. She tried to conjure the image of herself as a panther again but she felt more like a scared kitten. She stopped, listening. Someone was walking in the room above her. They dragged something across the floor. The footsteps faded and silence returned.

Rosa quickly dressed. She'd had nothing to eat since breakfast the previous day and her mouth was dry. She opened the door to the cellar. There was a shaft of light from a high window that allowed her to find her way. She was about to climb the staircase back to the entrance hall when she noticed another set of stairs next to a pantry service lift. There had been a similar device at the convent to transport dishes from the kitchen to the refectory. Rosa assumed the stairs led to the villa's kitchen. Her instinct was right and at the top of them she found a door leading to a storeroom stocked with olives, dried tomatoes, artichokes in oil, eggs, almonds, chestnuts and pine nuts. There were bunches of rosemary and strings of garlic hanging from the ceiling and sacks of wheat, rice and saffron stacked on the floor. The door at the far end was open, revealing a kitchen with a double fireplace and terracotta tiles. Rosa was surprised to find that the kitchen was much larger than the one at the convent where Suor Maddalena had worked with her assistants. It was modern too, with a hot water tank and two large ceramic sinks. Light poured in from the floor-to-ceiling windows onto the massive table in the middle of the room. On the walls hung saucepans of every size and description. Near the door were shelves stacked with mortars and pestles, bowls and ceramic cooking pots. Rosa wondered how many people lived at the villa to justify such a large space; surely not more than the nuns and pupils at the convent?

'Good morning,' she called, hoping whoever she had heard earlier was still close by.

No-one answered.

There was a loaf of bread on a cutting board on the table along with a block of goat's cheese. Rosa's hunger overcame her timidity and she tore off a piece of the bread. The crust had a sweet flavour and, although she was famished, she chewed it slowly, letting the taste linger in her mouth. When she bit the creamy white interior, the flavour changed to a pleasant sourness on the back of her tongue. She found herself in the fields where the wheat used for the bread had grown. Her eyes drank in the crop's golden heads shimmering in the breeze and ripe for harvest. Rosa looked at the bread on the table. She had sensed the origin of things all her life, but this vision of the wheat field was more vivid. She had actually felt the sun on her back and smelt the grassy scent of the crop.

Growing in boldness, Rosa took another piece of bread along with a slice of goat's cheese. The cheese's velvety texture and the tangy flavour were a contrast to the bread and she relished the sensation in her mouth. Although the bread and cheese were satisfying, she explored the storeroom, grabbing a handful of almonds and losing herself in their sweet milkiness. If the Scarfiotti family had employed her, they should feed her too, she thought, reaching up for another handful of nuts. A shrill scream sounded from the garden, causing her to drop the nuts. They scattered over the floor. She rushed to the kitchen door but could see no-one in the kitchen garden. The scream came again. It sounded as though a woman was being murdered. Rosa ran along the path in the direction of the cry.

The grounds beyond the vegetable plot and terrace garden were wild and verdant. Box hedges held back a forest of scrub oak, pine and maple. Roses, not yet in bloom, clambered over a stone wall that led to a gravelled path into the woods. Rosa crept her way through the trees, her ears straining to every sound. She found a pool with a fountain and was startled to see a bride standing there with a long white veil hanging down her back. In a blink, she realised that the figure was not a woman but a white peacock perched on a stand with its tail feathers draping to the ground. It was the most beautiful creature she had ever seen. It turned on her approach and uttered its blood-curdling call. Rosa laughed at how wrong her impression had been. The cry was not that of a woman being murdered, simply a bird calling for its mate.

Enchanted by the lush woods, Rosa continued along the path, which followed a slope bordered by birch trees. The dappled light was charming and she walked until she came upon a stone chapel with a cemetery next to it. Both were in a state of neglect, which surprised her given the grandeur of the rest of the villa. The cemetery garden was a jungle of periwinkles, irises and violets. Ivy grew over everything and even seemed to be creeping into the cracks of the graves as if it intended to break them apart. Assuming that the cemetery must be ancient, Rosa pushed aside the ivy to read the headstones. Most of the plots belonged to ancestors of the Scarfiotti clan. The family seemed to have lived in the area for at least two centuries. There were other graves with less elaborate stones, which Rosa deduced belonged to servants.

At the far end of the cemetery she found a tomb with a tall surround that, from the thickness of the ivy that covered it, she supposed must be as old as the others. Pulling aside the vine she was surprised to see that the foliage had merely formed a loose blanket over the stone and had not damaged it. On top of the tomb was the sculptured life-size figure of a woman lying in repose. The monument was tall and so Rosa could only see the face in profile, but the details of the nose and chin and the folds of the figure's dress were so realistic it looked as if the woman had been captured at the moment of her death and frozen into stone. There was no name or date on the grave, only the inscription: *Buona notte, mia cara sorella*. Goodnight, my dear sister.

Next to the woman knelt a statue of a babe with wings, her tiny hands clasped in desperate prayer. The angel's grief tore at Rosa's heart and she had to sit down by the grave and wipe away her tears. Never before had a statue so moved her. Her thoughts drifted to her own mother. Was she still alive? And if she was, why had she been forced to abandon her?

It took Rosa a few minutes to recover from her emotions. When she did, she tugged the ivy back over the grave as if she were covering an intimate scene she should not have laid eyes upon. Something brushed against her leg and she glanced down to see a tortoiseshell cat with one ear missing looking up at her.

'Hello, pussy cat,' she said, bending down to stroke the feline's back. The cat purred when Rosa scratched her chin.

A chill ran down Rosa's spine and she lifted her eyes. At first she could see nothing but the dark woods. Then she caught her breath. The gatekeeper was standing between two trees and staring at her. She sensed that she had done something forbidden in entering the cemetery.

'Good morning,' she called out to him, her voice hoarse with guilt.

The gatekeeper didn't answer her. The shadows between the trees shifted. Rosa peered into the woods again. There was no-one there. She turned towards the cat. It was scampering away from her into some bushes. The blood thumped in Rosa's ears and terror seized her. She hurried back in the direction of the house, sure that some presence was watching her. The gatekeeper? Or something else?

She took the wrong direction on the path and, instead of returning to the terrace garden, ran through a passageway of hedges and found herself in an orchard. The entrancing scent of the plum and peach blossoms washed over her and her fear vanished. Besides the fruit trees there were giant gnarled figs and blackberry bushes sent up their thorny shoots between the neatly planted rows. Although Rosa had eaten the bread and cheese, she found herself ravenous again. She picked an apple, admiring the intense crimson colour of its skin before biting the crisp, sweet flesh. What was it about the food at the Villa Scarfiotti? It put you under a spell. Rosa had been terrified a few moments ago but now she was filled by a sense of contentment.

Suddenly a hand seized her wrist and squeezed it like a tourniquet. She cried out in pain and dropped the apple. A face with pale eyes and red-veined cheeks loomed in front of her.

'So you're the thief who stole food from the kitchen!' the woman hissed between clenched teeth.

Rosa could not make any sound. Not only did the woman frighten her but the words 'thief' and 'stole' cut her to the core. Suor Maddalena would be so ashamed.

'No,' stammered Rosa. 'I'm the new governess ...'

The woman released her grip and laughed. 'Yes, I assumed so. I suppose that old hag Signora Guerrini didn't take you the supper I prepared for you last night?'

Rosa was confused by the woman's sudden change of mood. Despite her worn and scrubbed appearance there was something of the joy and freshness of youth in her manner. She bent down to retrieve the apple she had knocked out of Rosa's hand, rubbed it on her sleeve and took a bite.

'Hmm, they must have ripened this morning,' she said, her mouth full of fruit. 'I can make an apple cake for the little girl.' The woman chewed thoughtfully for a few moments before another idea crossed her mind. 'We'd better return to the house,' she said. 'The Marchesa and her daughter are arriving at eleven. You've met them, haven't you, in Florence?'

Rosa shook her head. 'Only the Marchese Scarfiotti,' she replied. 'He collected me from the convent yesterday.'

The woman's eyes widened. 'Truly!' she said, plucking another apple from the tree and handing it to Rosa. 'This family is like no other.' She shook her head. 'The little girl, Clementina, is a wonder, but her mother ... well, you'd best avoid her as much as you can, that would be my advice. Keep to your work and mind your own business — that's how I've managed here. I'm Ada Mancini but only the Marchese calls me Signora Mancini. Everyone else calls me Ada.'

Rosa discerned the woman was the villa's cook. Her clothes and apron smelled of rosemary and other herbs just as Suor Maddalena's did. Rosa's mind drifted back to the convent. Was it only yesterday she was there? It seemed like years ago that she was sitting in the chapel. She swallowed the last bite of her apple and walked beside Ada along the path back to the house, praying silently for Suor Maddalena's return to good health.

Two swallows sped past the women, skimming so quickly over Rosa's shoulder that she heard the whoosh of their wings in her ears. The birds swooped over the garden before ascending to the sky.

'A sure sign of spring,' said Ada, shading her eyes and following the birds' path. She turned back to Rosa and a scrutinising look came to her face. 'They are heading north,' she said softly. 'The gods of fate and chance are at work today.'

The villa, when Rosa and Ada approached it, was alive with activity. An army of maids was sweeping the terraces and wiping down the garden furniture. Signora Guerrini was with them, barking out orders and tugging the maids' ears when they didn't obey quickly enough. Where had everyone appeared from, Rosa wondered. The maids heard the women's footsteps on the gravel path and looked up briefly before returning to their work.

Rosa followed Ada into the kitchen where a woman in an apron was lighting the fire. 'Come on,' the woman muttered, crossing her bony arms. 'No mischief today.' She turned and caught herself when she saw Ada come in with Rosa.

'This is Paolina, my assistant,' Ada said to Rosa.

Paolina stood up and brushed her skirt, giving Rosa a nod before taking another poke at the fire. She was about twenty years of age with a lanky figure and prominent cheekbones.

Ada turned to Rosa. 'Now, you'd best return to your room and prepare yourself for the Marchesa's arrival. She's particular so make sure your hair is tidy and your nails scrupulously clean. She's also sensitive to noise — it brings on her tension headaches — so be careful to speak softly.'

Rosa thanked Ada for her advice and headed towards the storeroom.

Ada shrieked with laughter. 'Where are you going? Are you still hungry?'

Rosa blushed. 'My room is downstairs. In the cellar.'

Paolina looked up and exchanged a glance with Ada.

'Signora Guerrini put you in the room downstairs?' Paolina asked.

Before Rosa could answer, Ada strode to the kitchen door and called out to one of the maids. 'Maria, take Signorina Bellocchi to the room set aside for her — the one opposite the schoolroom.'

A girl with wispy blonde hair tucked under her cap and pale, freckled skin rushed inside. She opened a door at the far end of the kitchen and indicated for Rosa to follow her.

'Be careful,' Ada told Rosa. 'Remember what I said.'

Rosa nodded and followed Maria into the dark passageway.

'So you are the governess?' Maria asked, her baby-blue eyes settling on Rosa's face. 'You can't be much older than me. Clementina will be thrilled. I think she's expecting a crone.'

Rosa laughed. Maria giggled too before leading the way up the servants' staircase. It was spiral shaped with a wrought-iron balustrade. The walls of the corridors that led off it were papered in brown damask and highlighted by pink glass wall sconces.

'How long have you been here?' Rosa asked Maria.

'Six months. But it seems like years. There aren't many of us young ones.'

'The villa is much grander than anything I'm used to,' Rosa confided. 'I don't know how I'll fit in.'

Maria glanced over her shoulder and smiled. 'It's grander than what most of the world is used to — and a bit strange as well.'

'What do you mean?'

The nursemaid's room was on the top floor, but when they reached the third floor Maria stopped and opened the door leading into the main part of the house.

'This is the Marchesa's quarters,' she whispered, urging Rosa to follow her. 'Only the older maids are allowed on this floor on account of the artefacts.'

Rosa found that she and Maria were standing in a corridor decorated with bronze Nubian slaves brandishing massive candelabra. At the end of it stood a life-size figure in an Egyptian dancing costume with a serpent twined around her leg. The serpent's zircon eyes glowed in the darkness.

'The Marchesa has Egyptian blood,' Maria explained. 'Come, look at this ... before anyone arrives.'

Maria pushed open a set of gilded doors and ushered Rosa into a room where the walls were covered in pictures. The light through the shutters fell across the Peking rug and left the artworks in shadow. Rosa approached an oil painting of a woman with a long torso and neck clutching a ruffled fan to her breast. The woman's pale face and blood-red lips held Rosa's attention before she turned to the china ink drawing next to it. A naked woman with lean hips stood with her arms stretched skyward and her face upturned. At her feet lay a slain bear. Further along the wall was a photograph of a woman dressed in sheer black lace with a greyhound by her side. The kohl around the woman's eyes, along with her death-like pallor, made her seem other-worldly. Rosa's gaze drifted to a marble bust sitting on a walnut cabinet. The blank eyes seemed to peer at her. All the works gleamed with a life of their own, and in that moment she realised that the subject of each piece was the same. She took in the mystery of the room before turning to Maria.

'The Marchesa?'

'They say she is very beautiful,' Maria whispered. 'That she captivates men. But I find her rather ghoulish ...' Maria stopped herself. There was a noise in the hall. 'Quick, this way,' she said, digging her nails into Rosa's arm and pulling her towards a door at the end of the room.

Rosa followed her through it and once again found

herself in the servants' corridor. She caught a glimpse of a maid with a duster hurrying into the room. Maria quietly closed the door.

'Too close,' she whispered. 'I've shown you the room but you must not go there again. It's our secret.'

Maria led the way up the stairs to the floor above. While the rest of the house was ultra-modern, the room assigned to Rosa belonged to the previous century. The walls and ceilings were adorned with frescoes of angels floating in an azure heaven together with garlands of flowers. The bedroom was mostly taken up by the canopied bed, but there was also a sitting room, similarly decorated, a bathroom and a dressing room with a round mirror in a scrolled frame above a chest of drawers. The schoolroom, which was across the hall, was sparsely furnished with a large wooden desk and a wall of bookshelves. The style of the rooms on the fourth floor was so different from the exotic décor of the Marchesa's quarters that Rosa thought she could have stepped into another villa.

'I'll fetch your things from downstairs,' Maria said, leaving Rosa alone in the bedroom.

Rosa looked at the salmon pink bed linens, the hand-carved armoire and the desk inlaid with lapis lazuli. The room was more elegant than the scullery maid's room in the cellar and more luxurious than anything she could have imagined while living at the convent. She glanced at the clock on the wall; she had an hour before the Marchesa was due to arrive. The stationery shelf on the writing desk was well supplied with paper. Rosa sat down and began to compose a letter to Suor Maddalena, to let her know that she had arrived safely. But she stopped after a few sentences, unable to rid herself of the image of those dark eyes all around the Marchesa's room, which seemed to have burnt into her soul.

An hour later, Maria knocked on the door. 'The Marchesa's cars are approaching,' she said. 'You must join with the others to greet her.'

Remembering Ada's advice, Rosa quickly tidied her hair and collar before following Maria down the stairs. The household staff were gathered on the steps outside, ranked by order. Maria joined the maids while the butler, who Rosa had not seen before, ushered her to the bottom step to stand next to Giuseppe.

'I am Eugenio Bonizzoni,' the butler said, lifting his chin and looking at Rosa with weary eyes. 'Stand up straight.'

Ada and Paolina were waiting to the right with the scullery maid. Ada caught Rosa's eye and winked.

'Here he is,' Rosa heard Maria whisper with a giggle.

The maids exchanged glances and smoothed their skirts when the Marchese hurried down the stairs. He was wearing a speckled-grey suit and his golden waves were slicked back from his forehead. He must have arrived just now, Rosa thought. Signora Corvetto was not with him, confirming Rosa's suspicion that she was his mistress.

The rumble of motors had everyone standing to attention. Rosa was bemused when one of the older maids crossed herself. Two touring cars, one with tortoiseshell side panels, appeared through the trees and headed towards the house, coming to a stop at the bottom of the steps. From where Rosa was standing, it appeared that the first car contained only luggage. But, to her surprise, the chauffeur stepped out and opened the door on the opposite side.

'Babbo!' cried a tiny voice. A girl came rushing around the back of the car and ran straight towards the Marchese, reaching up and throwing her arms around his waist. The Marchese bent down and hoisted the child onto his hip, kissing her cheeks. His serious expression disappeared and he laughed joyfully. Clementina, who Rosa guessed to be about eight years old, had inherited her father's wavy hair but not his chiselled looks. The red-blonde ringlets that framed her face emphasised her pouch-like cheeks and when she smiled she revealed only her bottom teeth. Yet she had a vitality about her that was instantly appealing.

'Oh, Babbo, we saw so many things,' Clementina gushed. 'Great pyramids and men swallowing fire while riding bicycles.' The girl pressed her cheek to her father's. 'But it would have been so much better if you had been there,' she confided to him. 'Mamma is not much fun. That's why I travelled with Rinaldo in the luggage car.'

'You prefer the company of a junior chauffeur to your mother and uncle?' asked the Marchese. He frowned but Rosa could see from the sparkle in his eyes that it was a mock scolding.

Signor Bonizzoni instructed the menservants to remove the luggage from the car. Rosa watched with amazement as trunks, hatboxes and suitcases were retrieved by the servants and spirited into the house. One of the hatboxes slipped and landed near her feet. It was embossed with the crest of a human-headed hawk. The cuoio grasso leather made her shiver. She saw the doomed veal calf from which it had been made: it was crying for its mother and awaiting its grim death in a dark, cramped stall. Rosa was so disturbed by the image that at first she did not notice the figures emerging from the second car. She turned to see a man in jackboots and a black shirt make his way towards the Marchese. The man was in his thirties but his hair was already receding, revealing a long scar from his left eyebrow to his temple. He had a martial air about him and the coldest eyes Rosa had ever seen. The smile vanished from the Marchese's face when the man approached although he returned the straight-armed salute the man delivered. Rosa's gaze fell to the skull-and-crossbones insignia on the man's shirt. She knew little about the fascists, only that they had marched on Rome in 1922 and seized power over the government and that the nuns had prayed against them. He must be Clementina's uncle, Rosa thought. But whose brother was he — the Marchese's or the Marchesa's?

Rosa forgot the fascist, however, when she saw the Marchesa's gloved hand emerge from the car. The chauffeur took it and helped her down the step. The Marchesa was the image of the painting Rosa had seen on the third floor that morning. Her face was a death mask of white powder and her eyes were rimmed thickly in kohl. Her willowy frame was wrapped in a fitted dress and around her swan-like neck dangled a scarab necklace. Her ebony hair was hidden under a velvet hat and the whole outfit was finished with a pair of cyclamen pink pumps with heels so high and narrow it was impractical for her to walk on the gravel and her chauffeur had to carry her to the steps. The Marchesa was not so much beautiful as she was striking, Rosa thought.

When the chauffeur placed her on the steps, the Marchesa looked around at the staff as if noticing them for the first time. She seemed astonished to find herself before an audience. Any charm she might have possessed was muted by her hostile stare. 'The eyes of Il Duce are on all of you,' she said in a low, languid voice.

Il Duce was Mussolini. It was a strange greeting to give her staff, Rosa thought, but no-one seemed surprised.

'Welcome home, dear,' the Marchese said. 'It sounds as though your visit with Il Duce was a success. What a trip you've had: Ancient Egypt and the Holy Roman Empire. You must be exhausted.'

The Marchese's manner was all concern over his wife but his comment was sarcastic. Mussolini saw himself as the new Roman emperor.

'Don't try to be funny,' the Marchesa replied flatly. 'You know that only little people get tired.'

Rosa glanced at the staff gathered on the steps. She understood that by 'little people' the Marchesa had not been referring to children, like Clementina, but to all of them.

The Marchesa turned and noticed Rosa. Her eyes seemed to pierce the young woman's skin. Rosa's stomach knotted. 'And who is this person?' the Marchesa asked her husband. 'I don't believe I've seen her before.'

'That is Signorina Bellocchi, the governess I have chosen for Clementina,' the Marchese replied. 'I will introduce you formally this afternoon.'

The Marchesa waved her hand dismissively. 'Bellocchi! What sort of a name is that? Well, I hope our daughter will be properly looked after.' She turned and continued towards the villa's entrance with her unhurried, regal step.

Rosa felt a cold shadow fall over her. Only Clementina, who turned and smiled at her, gave her any sense of encouragement.

After the Marchese and his wife, Clementina and the fascist had retired to the drawing room, the rest of the staff returned to the house, not through the main entrance but by a side passage near the kitchen. Only Rosa was allowed to follow Signor Bonizzoni through the main doors.

'Wait here,' he told her, ushering her into a reception room and indicating a chair before turning to go. 'The Marchese will let me know when he wishes to speak to you.'

Rosa looked about the room. The walls were marbled rose-pink with mouldings in gold. The curtains were silver satin and the chairs and sofas had been upholstered in a matching fabric. In the centre of the room was a table fashioned from an amber-coloured wood Rosa had never seen before. The spider-like legs ended in brass accents. Rosa's gaze fell to a side table on which sat a vase of orchids and a cast-iron clock. It was already midday and the scents of roasting garlic and fennel wafted from the kitchen. She caught a whiff of sage and found herself lost in a memory, wandering through the garden at the convent with Suor Maddalena, picking the herbs as the dew was disappearing and before the day became too hot.

Opening her eyes, she was astonished to find water droplets on her fingertips. She stared at them in wonder before lifting her hands to her face and discovering that tears were running down her cheeks. She wiped them away with the heels of her palms, sensing that the Villa Scarfiotti was not a place to show weakness.

An hour later, she heard the squeak of Signor Bonizzoni's shoes. He entered the reception room. 'Lunch is served,' he said, bowing slightly. A reflection from one of the lamps gleamed on his bald patch.

Rosa stood up and followed him, disappointed that her meeting with the Marchese and his family had been delayed. She was surprised when Signor Bonizzoni led her across the foyer rather than down the steps to the kitchen and ushered her into the dining room. The Marchese sat at the head of a purple-tinted beechwood table, with his wife and Clementina's uncle on his right. Clementina sat on his left. The adults were in deep discussion and no-one except Clementina, who glanced in Rosa's direction, acknowledged her when Signor Bonizzoni showed her to a setting further down the table.

Is this to be my place? Rosa wondered. Not with the servants but not quite with the family either?

'We should imitate Il Duce alone,' Clementina's uncle was saying, 'We should have no other example except him. I could have found you a girl from a good family to instruct my niece.'

The Marchese looked annoyed but shrugged off the comment. 'Even Il Duce approves of the Catholic Church these days, doesn't he, my good Vittorio? And Signorina Bellocchi comes from the same convent that educated my mother and grandmother. Her musicianship is quite extraordinary. I doubt I could find someone at her level anywhere in Florence, good family or not. I want Clementina to have a solid education, not to flit about with embroidery.'

'Like American women with their egalitarian illusions,' Vittorio sneered. 'Childbirth is to a woman what war is to a man. It is their purpose. The character of the Italians must change if we are to become a great race again. We need to be more serious, harder ... more —'

'Militaristic?' The Marchese finished the sentence.

Vittorio tossed his head in the direction of Rosa. 'Women should not be learning Latin and philosophy. Such study taxes their brains.'

The Marchesa brushed her fingers over her neck. Rosa noticed that she had a profusion of fine hair on her arms. She turned and smiled at Vittorio. 'You are quite right, my dear brother. Women should have fun. Men should be worrying about those things.'

Vittorio smiled but seemed unsure whether the Marchesa meant what she said.

Rosa glanced nervously around the room — at the marquetry sideboards and the strange beaten copper discs, like shields, hanging on the walls. Was it normal to talk about someone this way when they were in the room? Rosa remembered what Ada had said about the Scarfiotti family being strange. She understood now that Vittorio was the Marchesa's brother. They were both as odd as each other. She coughed softly into her fist with some vain hope that maybe the Marchese hadn't noticed her enter the room. But the conversation turned back to Mussolini.

'Italy needs a man like Il Duce,' the Marchesa said, crossing her arms and shivering although the room wasn't cold. 'He has the touch of an artist but also the mind of a warrior. He is a leader who loves his people but is prepared to bend them if required.'

The Marchese seemed about to disagree but the conversation ended when Signor Bonizzoni directed three servants into the room. The servants carried trays with such an abundance of food stacked on them that Rosa was sure other guests must be joining the party. It was more food than she had seen in her life. But no-one else appeared and the servants set out the dishes on the table.

The appetiser was a platter of *crostini* smeared with chicken liver pâté and some slices of salami. Rosa was ravenous and bit into the warm bread slice. Suddenly the platter of *crostini* began to shake and wobble before her eyes. Three chickens emerged from it and walked across the table, poking around the dishes and clucking to each other. One of them jumped onto the soup urn and looked at her inquisitively. The salami slices swelled and took on the form of a sow lying on her side with piglets sucking at her teats and wiggling their curly tails. Something began to tickle and scratch Rosa's throat. She gagged and turned away, spitting the mouthful of food she had been chewing into her table napkin. She gasped when she looked at it and saw a fluffy yellow chick cheeping at her before gradually fading away.

Rosa turned back to the table. The chickens and the pig were gone and the others were discussing the latest work of the poet D'Annunzio as if nothing had happened.

The next dish was a plate of fish soup accompanied by a calamari salad. Signor Bonizzoni served the soup and passed a bowl to one of the servants who placed it before Rosa. It smelled salty like the liver. Rosa steeled herself and ventured a few mouthfuls. She placed her spoon in the bowl and saw a school of anchovies swimming around it, flashing their silver bellies at her. The anchovies disappeared and a squid emerged from the bottom of the soup. As Rosa watched it propel itself around the bowl a feeling of sadness washed over her. A shadow seemed to fall over the room. She heard the moan of a cow and looked up to see that the first-course dishes had been cleared and one of the servants had placed before her a slice of steak on a bed of white beans and roasted potatoes.

She glanced up at the others. The Marchese, Vittorio and Clementina were eating their steaks with an accompaniment of steamed vegetables. The Marchesa, however, ate the meat on its own. Her plate was bloody and it seemed to Rosa that she was cutting her steak into smaller and smaller pieces until eventually she was putting only the slightest shreds of raw flesh into her mouth.

A feeling of dread fingered its way up Rosa's spine. The apple and the almonds she had eaten that morning had been living foods, but everything on the table before her now had died in pain and fear. Waves of heat burned her neck and cheeks. She reached for her glass of water, her hand trembling. Suddenly her stomach wrenched and she vomited onto her plate a bloody mess of sinews and muscles. The horror of it made her cry out. She looked at the others but no-one noticed. She threw up again, this time whole anchovies, squids and chicks. She struggled to stand up and rushed from the room.

Somehow, despite the pounding in her head and the weakness in her legs, she managed to climb to the fourth floor and run to her room. She headed towards the bed, intending to lie down, but her bowels rumbled. She managed to reach the bathroom and lift her skirt before foul-smelling faeces exploded from her. She tried to stand up but cramps seized her again and she expelled more diarrhoea. It was as if her body was trying to purge itself of some evil she had ingested. Chills and heat ran alternately over her skin. Rosa clasped her hands around her knees, weeping from the pain and humiliation. A moment later she passed out.

'Have a sip of this,' a woman's voice said.

Rosa struggled to open her eyes. She glimpsed two blurry figures bending over her. One was pressing a cup of warm liquid to her lips.

'She's still weak,' the other woman said.

Rosa recognised the voices: Ada and Paolina. She blinked and her vision cleared. She was lying in her bed and the windows were open. She managed to take a sip of the chamomile tea Ada was offering her. Reaching down her leg, Rosa realised she was in her chemise. A scent of pine tickled her nostrils. There was no trace of the intestinal carnage she had experienced before she passed out.

'What happened?' she asked.

'You fainted at the table,' Ada told her. 'I'm not surprised. The food was too rich for you. I know nuns prefer to eat simply.'

Rosa thought of her meals at the convent: bread with olive oil and salt, a little wine mixed with water, bean soups and vegetables freshly picked from the garden. Very rarely any meat.

She tried to lift her head but it felt too heavy. 'I sense the origin of things,' she said. 'I've always done it.' She recalled the vision of the wheat field she had experienced that morning and the veal calf she had seen crying in its stall. 'But I'm feeling the images much more strongly than before,' she said. 'It's as though being here —'

'Hush now,' said Ada, pressing the cup of tea to Rosa's lips again. 'Rest now and you will feel better in the morning.'

Rosa's eyelids grew heavy and she sank into a sleep of feverish dreams. She saw Ada slip into the room and place a clove of garlic on her chest. 'Something is in the wind,' she heard Paolina whisper. 'The witches are returning to the Villa Scarfiotti. I feel them everywhere. It was impossible to get the fire started this morning.'

'They are playing at mischief to gain our attention,' Ada replied. 'Or maybe to gain *her* attention.'

Early the following morning, Ada arrived with a tray of warm cornmeal porridge for Rosa. 'This will settle your stomach,' she said, placing the tray on the bedside table and propping the pillows so that Rosa could sit up. 'In the future I'll make sure that you are given simple meals when you eat with the family.'

Rosa's hand fell to her chest. There was no clove of garlic. She had been dreaming. The conversation she'd thought she'd heard between Ada and Paolina had not taken place.

'I'm so embarrassed I fainted at lunch,' she said. 'The Marchese wanted to formally introduce me to his wife. I must apologise. Do you think they will dismiss me?'

Ada shook her head and grinned. 'I don't think they even noticed. Signor Bonizzoni saw you weren't eating and realised what had happened. He carried you up here with the assistance of one of the servants.'

Rosa remembered the way the family had spoken about her as if she wasn't present, and realised that the idea that they may not have seen her faint wasn't so incredible at all.

The porridge restored her strength. Warmth flooded through her with each spoonful. She felt the sensation of sunlight on her skin and imagined herself playing her flute in a corn field, each note of *Jesu, Joy of Man's Desiring* floating away on the breeze.

After Ada left, Rosa climbed out of bed. The sight of herself in the bathroom mirror surprised her and she instinctively looked away. She filled the sink with water and lathered the castile soap in her hands. Only then did she turn back to her reflection. Like an artist studying her subject, she viewed her features. So this is what I look like, she thought, observing the slight upward slant of her eyes framed by dark eyebrows, her long narrow nose pinched slightly at the tip, her bow-like lips. She massaged the soap over her cheeks and forehead before plunging her hands into the water and rinsing the residue away. She threw back her head. Streams of water ran down her long neck and onto her chemise. She reached for the washcloth hanging by the bath, soaked it in the sudsy water and pressed it under her arms before brushing it over her shoulders and then through the armholes of her chemise to wash her chest and back. The water droplets made the material of the chemise transparent.

Rosa stared at herself then reached up, her hands hovering over her chest. She slowly slid the chemise straps down over her shoulders. Her breasts bounced up like two moons. The large nipples startled her. She had never observed her body this way before; the way someone else would see it. As long as she could remember she had always bathed in her chemise and had never looked down. It was a sin to admire one's body. 'Modesty is a woman's most precious quality,' Don Marzoli preached. 'A woman who loses it, loses everything.'

A feeling of shame bit at Rosa's stomach but her curiosity was stirred. She had understood that faces were all different but bodies too? It was liberating to feel the air on her skin, and her fingers and toes tingled with the pleasure. Despite the guilt gnawing at her, she was buoyant. She drew a breath and walked back from the mirror so that she could see herself at full length. Slowly, she slid the chemise down over her torso to her hips. The flesh over her ribs was firm under her fingertips. She caressed her stomach and touched the beauty spot near her navel. The chemise slipped. She tugged it down her pear-shaped thighs, tattooed with fine lines where her skin had stretched during puberty.

When she saw the mound of black hair that grew between her legs, a memory returned to her. The morning when she was thirteen and had found flecks of blood on her underwear. She had been reassured when Suor Maddalena explained to her that she was not hurt, she had simply become a woman. Rosa had been so thrilled by the transformation that she had told everyone she met that day, including Don Marzoli, about her new status. But when the Badessa was informed, she took Rosa aside and whispered to her, 'You must never speak of this to anyone. It is each woman's shame to bear; a reminder that we led Adam into sin.'

The joy Rosa had been experiencing in discovering her body in the mirror disappeared and a sickening fear gripped her. She hurriedly covered herself with the chemise again. Her skin prickled with shame. 'Forgive me, Father,' she prayed. She hung a towel over the mirror and hurried to her dressing room, where she hastily pulled on her dress and stockings.

Despite Ada's assurance that the Marchese and his wife had not noticed her faint during lunch the previous day, Rosa thought that she should apologise to her employers as soon as possible. She wondered where she would find them. But when she walked out of her room she noticed Clementina waiting in the schoolroom opposite. It was just after seven o'clock.

'Good morning, Signorina Bellocchi,' the girl said. 'I hope you are feeling better today.'

'I am, thank you,' Rosa replied. 'But aren't you early for lessons? Have you had breakfast yet?'

Clementina beamed at her. 'I'm too excited to eat. I've never had a governess before. Only a silly nursemaid who didn't know much, and Babbo.'

Rosa smiled at her young student. There was a pile of books and papers on the desk and Rosa examined some of them: a mathematics textbook; a comprehension exercise written out in a masculine hand; and a book on the theory of teaching. She opened the theory book and found that some of the text had been underlined: *It is the teacher's responsibility to encourage the student to work. Discipline should arise out of interest, not obedience or fear.*

'Your father is very interested in your education,' Rosa said, pulling up a chair and sitting beside Clementina. 'Shall we begin with some fractions and decimals?'

Rosa had been good at mathematics but had not particularly liked the subject. She had preferred music, languages and biology. Clementina, on the other hand, attacked her sums with gusto. She was advanced for her years and Rosa was amazed at how quickly she worked out problems. As they progressed, Rosa began to feel less apprehensive about her new life. If Clementina approached all her lessons with such enthusiasm, it would be a pleasure to teach her. Clementina's rhythmic recital of the times tables lulled Rosa into a sense of calm, and she glanced out of the window at the green hills in the distance and wondered what the future would hold. Would she always be a governess? Or would she marry one day and have children of her own? She realised that she had not considered such possibilities while she had been living at the convent.

Clementina finished her tables. Rosa took out the comprehension exercise but before they could begin she looked up to see the Marchese standing in the doorway with a frown on his face.

'You've started very early,' he said. 'I didn't anticipate any lessons until nine. You should have consulted me before taking things into your own hands.'

Rosa was stung by the rebuff. The ease she had been feeling dissolved. She stood up and stammered an apology, both for starting the lessons early and for fainting at lunch the previous day. Before she could finish, Clementina ran to her father.

'It was my idea, Babbo,' she said, pressing herself against his arm. 'I wanted to start early. I want to learn everything that Signorina Bellocchi has to teach me.'

'I see,' the Marchese said, stroking his daughter's cheek. He glanced in Rosa's direction. 'I had planned that Clementina would study with you from nine until four,' he said. 'You can then have some time to yourself before joining us for dinner, unless the Marchesa and I have guests. At those times, you and Clementina will have supper together. And you will need to supervise her going to bed until I choose a suitable nursemaid for that.'

'Yes,' Rosa said.

The apologetic tone of his voice soothed her, although, after what had happened the previous day, she was not thrilled at the idea of dining with the family. She was also surprised at his request that she put Clementina to bed. Why wasn't the Marchesa going to perform that task? When Rosa was Clementina's age, she had fantasised that she had a mother who tucked her into bed and listened to her prayers every night.

'Clementina will study from Monday to Saturday and on Wednesday afternoons you must take her to Piccole Italiane,' the Marchese continued. 'While Clementina is there you will run some errands for me in Florence.'

Rosa nodded. She had the vague idea that Piccole Italiane was a fascist organisation for children. From the look of disdain on the Marchese's face when he said the name, she gathered it was his wife's idea. Perhaps it was his compromise for not sending Clementina to a fascist private school. The Marchese's eyes swept over Rosa's faded cotton dress. She blushed. It was the better of the two dresses she owned but its worn appearance stood out more at the villa than it had at the convent.

'I will ask the staff dressmaker to sew something suitable for you to wear to the city,' the Marchese said.

Before he left, he asked Rosa to make a list of books she thought Clementina might need. 'I will obtain them,' he said. 'We also have a library here that you are welcome to use any time you wish.' With a kind smile he added, 'I noticed a dent in your flute when you played for me at the convent.' He took a piece of paper out of his pocket and scribbled down an address before handing it to Rosa. 'When you are in Florence, take it to this repair shop and they will fix it. Tell them to put it on the villa account.'

The offer to fix her flute was an unexpected courtesy. It was impossible for Rosa to forget that the Marchese was an adulterer but in her eyes he now had two redeeming characteristics: he was kinder than his aloof manners conveyed; and he loved his daughter.

As the Marchese left the schoolroom, Rosa saw something about him that she hadn't noticed before: a dark mist seemed to be shadowing him. It was another reminder of how her perception of things seemed to be heightened at the villa. She remembered her dream of the previous evening in which Ada had said that witches were trying to gain her attention. Rosa shivered. It was a sin even to consider such a possibility. But what about the things that were happening to her? The shadow around the Marchese; the visions she had seen during the lunch that had made her faint? Did they come from God or somewhere else?

'Signorina Bellocchi, are you feeling all right?'

Rosa turned to see Clementina looking at her with her china blue eyes. 'Yes,' she said. 'I'm all right. Let's get started on French.'

When the morning's lessons were over, Maria brought up a tray for lunch. Rosa sensed there was something different about the maid and then noticed that her hair was pulled back into a sleek roll. She caught a whiff of lavender water on Maria's skin when she brushed by her to place the tray on a table next to the window. Ada had warned Rosa that the Marchesa was particular about grooming and she wondered if that was the reason the Marchese had wanted her to have a new dress.

When Maria left the room, Rosa sat down with Clementina to eat. She gingerly lifted the covers from the dishes and was relieved to see that Ada had made them a white bean soup with sage and tomato, served with fresh bread.

'My favourite soup,' said Clementina. 'Have you tried it before, Signorina Bellocchi?'

Rosa shook her head and breathed in the aroma of the sage before dipping her spoon into the hearty stew. The beans were tender and the snappy taste of the cheese was softened by the sweetness of the garlic and tomato. Rosa imagined a bean shoot bursting through the dark soil and into the brilliant light. She closed her eyes, envisaging dozens of green globes on vines slowly turning red in the sun before women with wrinkled hands and scarves on their heads picked the tomatoes. The food was full of the earth's energy. Rosa opened her eyes again and saw that Clementina was looking at her curiously.

'I like to imagine where my food has come from. It is my way of saying grace,' Rosa explained, which wasn't quite true because her visions of the sources of things were not a voluntary response.

The villa's driveway and the woods were visible from the schoolroom window. Rosa thought the statues in the garden resembled chess pieces in the midst of a complicated game. There was a clearing in the woods, not far from the villa, with a summerhouse and parterre garden. Rosa saw a glimmer in the trees and noticed a car parked near the summerhouse. A chauffeur was leaning against the bonnet, but it wasn't Giuseppe or either of the Marchesa's drivers.

Clementina stood up and leaned towards the window to see what had captured Rosa's attention. The French doors of the summerhouse suddenly flew open and a woman in a moss green suit and a silk turban rushed out. Rosa thought it was the Marchesa but then realised the woman was older.

The Marchesa and Vittorio also emerged from the summerhouse and the three became engaged in a lively conversation. The stranger shrugged her shoulders and threw her hands in the air.

'That's my grandmother,' said Clementina. 'She visits once a year.'

'Oh,' said Rosa, taken aback. 'Would you like to greet her?'

Clementina shook her head. 'Babbo doesn't allow it.'

Rosa saw the chauffeur open the car door for Clementina's grandmother. Why would the Marchese forbid his daughter from seeing her? Rosa watched the black saloon emerge from the trees and head down the driveway. The car was surrounded by a gloomy presence. That's the shadow, Rosa thought. That woman has something to do with the darkness I saw around the Marchese. But why him and no-one else?

That evening, the Marchese and his wife had guests for dinner, so Clementina and Rosa ate a supper of rosemary pancakes and rice pudding torte together in Clementina's room. Rosa was charmed by her young charge's cheerful chatter about her recent trip to Egypt and France, and the lilies, honeysuckle and hydrangeas that would soon be planted in the garden borders in honour of her ninth birthday.

'Babbo has promised me a pony,' Clementina said. 'You can ride her any time you wish, Signorina Bellocchi.'

'Thank you,' Rosa laughed. She thought her charge was as bright as a sunbeam.

Clementina's room was yellow-themed with frescoes on the walls of chickens and roosters, palm trees and a giant sun. On a shelf that ran the length of one wall was a display of miniature theatre sets replicating scenes from famous operas. Rosa had never been to the opera but she could guess from the pieces of music she'd studied that the set with the pyramid was a scene from *Aida*; that the Paris street scene was from *La Bohème*; and that the grand staircase was from *Eugene Onegin*. She admired the detail of the houses and the miniature furniture.

'My aunt made them,' Clementina said.

One of the sets wasn't from an opera that Rosa could recognise and yet it seemed familiar. Then she realised that she was looking at a replica of the Villa Scarfiotti. The house was as imposing in miniature as it was in real life. The grounds included the woods and even the cemetery. Rosa saw that the graves had been accurately depicted, except the tomb with the tall surround and statue. That had not been included.

'Where does your aunt live?' Rosa asked Clementina. 'She's a talented artist.'

The girl bit her lip and shrugged. 'She died before I was born.'

Rosa sensed from the way Clementina averted her eyes that it was not a subject she should pursue. *Buona notte, mia cara sorella*. The grave with the surround must belong to Clementina's aunt. That's why it wasn't included in the replica.

'Come, let's get you into your nightdress,' Rosa said.

The Marchese had instructed Rosa to have Clementina asleep by eight o'clock. After listening to the girl's prayers and tucking her into bed, Rosa returned to her own room. While she undressed and brushed her hair she thought about the strange atmosphere at the villa and the increased intensity of her visions, the shadow around the Marchese, and the oddness of his wife and Vittorio. Maybe there is some sinister force at work here, she thought, climbing into bed. Then she remembered Ada's advice — *Keep to your work and mind your own business — that's how I've managed here* — and decided she would do her utmost to follow it. But when she laid her head on the pillow and pulled the covers over her, her eyes closing with drowsiness, a deeper intuition told her that she was being drawn into something over whose outcome she had little control.

THREE

The following Wednesday Giuseppe drove Rosa and Clementina into Florence. The branch of Piccole Italiane that Clementina belonged to met near the Piazza della Repubblica. The seriousness of Clementina's uniform — a white blouse and black pleated skirt worn with long socks and a beret — matched the expression on her face.

'The boys' club is much better,' Clementina confided in Rosa. 'They do rowing and cycling. We have to do dumb rhythm dancing and embroidery.'

Giuseppe pulled the car up in front of a gymnasium. Strung across the front of it was a banner that read: *The Piccole Italiane follow the orders of Il Duce for the cause of the Fascist Revolution.*

Rosa accompanied Clementina inside. Rows of girls were performing star jumps and sit-ups. Others danced around a pole or exercised with hoops. Some older girls passed a doll wrapped like a baby to each other. 'Support his head, don't let it droop,' their instructress told them. 'Il Duce needs you to produce good soldiers.'

'That's my group,' said Clementina, pointing to a cluster of girls the same age as herself. A woman with slicked-back hair was calling out a roll. The hard look in her eyes reminded Rosa of Signora Guerrini.

'You'd better hurry,' Rosa said, nudging Clementina.

She watched the girl take her place with the others and was seized by an impulse to snatch her back again. What sort of mother would entrust her child to these zealots? Their regimental discipline would destroy Clementina's spirit.

The woman with the severe hair finished the roll and flicked her wrists, indicating that the girls were to sing. Rosa recognised the *Giovinezza*, its original lyrics adapted by Mussolini to glorify war. She watched the girls with their baby faces and innocent eyes singing without understanding the implications of the words. I have to get Clementina out of here, she thought. Then she noticed that Clementina was singing the loudest of all, stretching her mouth to enunciate every word with uninhibited enthusiasm. It's the influence of that fanatical mother and uncle of hers, thought Rosa. It's not her fault.

But then she realised that Clementina's voice was shrill, not at all the lovely sound Rosa had heard when she accompanied her on the piano during their music lessons together. Clementina turned and winked at Rosa, and Rosa had to suppress a smile when she realised the girl was making fun of the anthem. Perhaps Clementina's spirit was not in any danger, after all.

The address of the instrument repairer the Marchese had given Rosa was in Via Tornabuoni. Giuseppe drove her to the top end of the street.

'I'll wait for you here,' he said, pulling into a side street. Other chauffeurs had gathered there, leaning on their employers' Bugattis and Alfa Romeos while talking and smoking with each other. 'We don't have to pick up Signorina Scarfiotti for another three hours.'

Via Tornabuoni was bordered by Renaissance palaces,

the ground floors of which housed jewellers, perfumeries, florists and stores selling silks and tapestries. Rosa understood why the Marchese could not allow a representative of the Villa Scarfiotti to walk around Florence in shabby clothes. She was pleased with the new dress that had been made for her, and relished the softness of the jersey against her skin and the way the neckline sat loosely on her collarbone. It was a far cry from the scratchy dresses with Peter Pan collars she had brought with her from the convent. She was still wearing her old hat and shoes, but the Marchese had given her the address of a milliner and a shoemaker to purchase new items. He was paying for everything.

Rosa was amazed to see English signs everywhere: doctors, dentists, chemists, banks. Giuseppe had said that walking down Via Tornabuoni was like being in London and now she could see what he had meant. There were shops selling mackintoshes, croquet sets and tweeds. She passed an English-language bookshop and a tea-house with scones and seedcake on the menu. She admired the ladies' crinoline hats and the men's grey flannel suits and Oxford shoes and the way the patrons sipped their tea as if they had all day to do so. Even the cocker spaniels and beagles lying at their masters' feet looked relaxed. Rosa glanced at the T-bar straps on the shoes of a young woman reading the newspaper and savouring a glass of tomato juice. How beautiful those shoes were compared to Rosa's heavy clogs.

She noticed a shoe store across the way. It wasn't the one the Marchese had written down for her, but she couldn't resist inspecting it. She saw a forlorn-looking monkey sitting in the store window, then blinked and realised there wasn't a monkey there at all, only a pair of shoes made from black suede and monkey fur. Next to them was a pair of evening slippers finished in green silk with mother-of-pearl buckles, and on the shelf below was a pair of ankle boots fashioned from leopard fur and leather. Something moved behind the glass and Rosa stepped back, terrified she might find herself face to face with a big cat from the jungle. But it was only a man with a pencil moustache. He glared at her and made a shooing gesture with his hands. Rosa blushed, wondering what she had done to offend him. But she forgot the sales clerk when she caught sight of a woman wearing a satin bolero jacket and a hat sprouting crimson plumes entering the store. She was holding the diamond-encrusted leash of a poodle dyed the same colour as the feathers in her hat. The flamboyant Florentine woman left the conservative English women in her wake. A few minutes later, a woman came out of the store wearing a magenta suit with eyes embroidered over it. Her platform shoes were five inches high.

If only Suor Maddalena could see this, thought Rosa. I wonder what she would she say? Rosa had not received any word from the convent about Suor Maddalena's health. The Marchese had informed Rosa that she was to have one weekday off a month, with the first one due after three months of service. That left her with only Sundays free, when it was impossible to visit the convent. She would have no choice but to wait until the Badessa or Suor Maddalena herself sent some news.

She watched another client step out of her chauffeur-driven Rolls-Royce. The woman wore a black rayon suit, and the Pomeranian that pattered along by her feet was fitted with a sequined cape. Compared to the previous two women, her outfit was conservative, but when the woman turned to enter the shop Rosa saw that the back of the woman's suit was embroidered to look like the X-ray of a skeleton.

'No servant girls,' said the sales clerk, striding out of the store and waving his hands at Rosa. 'Don't you have something to do?'

Rosa moved away. She was too amazed by what she had seen to worry about asserting her right to stand on a public street. The realisation that she was no longer in the sheltered community of the convent or even the confines of the villa suddenly hit her. I am out in the world, she thought. She turned and came face to face with a street sweeper who had witnessed the sales clerk's rebuff.

'They say that Mussolini will ban newspapers from printing pictures of those skinny-hipped whores and their dogs,' he whispered. 'It is an affront to Italian motherhood!'

Was the whole of Florence like this, Rosa wondered. From one extreme to the other?

The haughtiness of the sales clerk led her to think of the Marchesa, who she had seen only twice since the fateful lunch. The woman displayed no interest in Clementina, and from the way she looked through Rosa it seemed that she had no interest in 'little people' either.

Further along the street, Rosa found herself outside a clockmaker's shop. She was dazzled by the dozens of faces all telling the same time. There were marble carriage clocks, brass cuckoo clocks and longcase clocks. Some of the clocks were shaped like hot air balloons while others were shaped like banjos or lanterns. There were statues of angels and Roman soldiers with clock faces embedded in their stomachs. Rosa's gaze settled on a clock in the shape of a swan and she noticed what time it showed. One hour had already slipped away! She would have to hurry if she was to complete all her errands.

The millinery shop that the Marchese had recommended was called Signora Lucchesi's. It was not as prestigious as those further up on Via Tornabuoni but the display of satin berets, pillbox hats, cocktail hats, skullcaps and tulle bridesmaids' hats seemed luxurious to Rosa. The store was stocked for spring and the hat displays resembled bouquets of tulips, sunflowers, hyacinths and peach blossoms. Rosa's eye fell on a flamingo pink hat with clusters of silk roses on the brim. It was the most beautiful hat she had ever seen. She brushed her fingertip over the fabric and felt a sea breeze kiss her face.

'*Buon giorno, Signorina*. It's parabuntal, a fine straw made from the leaves of a palm tree.'

Rosa turned to see a shopgirl in a tailored black dress approaching her. The girl had porcelain skin and glossy hair. She was smiling but her expression changed when she laid eyes on Rosa's old cloche hat.

'You are the governess from the Villa Scarfiotti, yes?' the shopgirl said, lifting her chin. 'The Marchesa's housekeeper telephoned to say you were coming. This way, please.'

The shopgirl did not touch Rosa but steered her past the satin and organza creations using nothing more than her erect head and stiff manner. She opened a curtain at the back of the shop and ushered Rosa into a chair. The booth was full of boxes and unused hat trees. Rosa didn't think it could be where the shop's clientele usually tried on their hats; it was too dark. The shopgirl whipped off Rosa's hat and tossed it into a basket of material scraps and loose threads before Rosa had time to protest. She then lifted a box from a shelf and took out a slouch hat. 'Here,' she said, dropping the hat onto Rosa's head and holding up a mirror.

The hat was black felt with no ribbons or adornments. It was finer quality than the hat Rosa had been wearing and she would have thought it very becoming if she hadn't seen the other headwear in the store. She lifted her chin to get a better look at herself in the mirror and the hat slipped.

'It's too big,' she said.

The shopgirl sighed and grabbed a tape measure from her pocket and wrapped it around Rosa's head. 'I will get one of the apprentices to narrow the band for you,' she said. 'Wait here.'

Rosa wondered how long the resizing would take. She still had to visit the shoe store and music repair shop. She noticed a gap in the curtains next to her and peered into a room with burgundy wallpaper, scrolled mirrors and two armchairs. A woman was there in a dress with a ruffled collar that emphasised her enormous bosom. She held a cluster of wax cherries to the brim of a floppy sunhat perched on a block, before trying some silk flowers. She sighed, obviously having a hard time deciding between the two. She turned and caught sight of Rosa spying on her.

'Ah!' she said, placing her hand on her hip. 'Our governess from the Villa Scarfiotti. How generous of the Marchese to send you to us.'

Rosa guessed the woman must be the shop owner, Signora Lucchesi. But her angry tone made Rosa wary. What had she done to provoke such a reaction?

'The Old Marchese thought I was good enough to dress the heads of all the women of the Scarfiotti family,' Signora Lucchesi said, her eyes narrowing like a cat about to scratch. 'Not so the *Marchesa Milanese*. Only Paris will do for her. She doesn't approve of our Tuscan ways. That's why she took that beautiful villa and turned the interior into some hideous statement of modern art.'

Rosa's brain ticked. Signora Lucchesi was talking about the Marchesa Scarfiotti. So she was originally from Milan?

'She does strut her title,' said the shopgirl, returning to take another measurement of Rosa's head. 'They say her mother is an Egyptian princess.'

'I don't know anything about her mother,' replied Signora Lucchesi. 'But my husband tells me that her father, Generale Caleffi, was charming and brilliant.'

A milliner walked into the room carrying a natural straw hat with velvet ribbon woven through it. It seemed she was intending to show it to Signora Lucchesi but became caught up in the conversation. 'I heard that the Marchesa is covered in make-up like a ... well, you know what.'

'It's probably to hide the wrinkles,' laughed Signora Lucchesi, who had a few of her own. 'She's probably older than she says.'

The milliner put the hat down and leaned against one of the chairs. 'The Marchese must have been very much in love —'

'Until they married?' Signora Lucchesi finished her sentence. 'Yes, I'm afraid so. I heard from a reliable source that they dismissed their latest nursemaid for the same reason all the others were packed off home. The Marchesa took her daughter away with her to avoid a scandal.'

Rosa was embarrassed to be listening to the gossip even though she wasn't contributing to it. She didn't like the Marchesa but the woman was still her mistress. Rosa realised that she had been sitting on her hands and they had gone to sleep. She shook her palms in front of her, trying to rid herself of the painful pins and needles and at the same time separate herself from the conversation.

'Surely not?' sniggered the milliner. 'Not someone so below his station?'

'What's wrong with the man? He's a dish and he's rich. He could have any woman he wants,' said the shopgirl, before disappearing into the workroom again. Rosa wished whoever was adjusting her hat would hurry.

The milliner sent her a glance. 'Perhaps the Marchesa is too demanding? And I have heard that she has lovers of her own.'

It was an invitation for Rosa to join in the gossip. But apart from the fact she had nothing to add, she liked her position and wanted to keep it. What if word got back to the Marchesa about what these women were saying and that Rosa had been involved?

'You know, it is very strange,' said Signora Lucchesi. 'I knew the Marchese as a boy. He was so jealous. He'd break your fingers if you even so much as touched one of his toys. I saw him slap his sister once … and he adored her. Yet he turns a blind eye to his wife's dalliances.'

The shopgirl returned and thrust the adjusted hat onto Rosa's head. 'There, perfect,' she said.

The band cut into Rosa's forehead. She felt as though her scalp was being squeezed into a jar. 'It's tight,' she told the girl.

'It will stretch.'

The shopgirl urged Rosa out of the booth. 'Never cross a milliner,' she told her. 'They are intimate with your head. It's like being unfaithful to your husband.'

Rosa could see that from the vehemency of the gossip about the Scarfiotti family.

'You're from a convent, aren't you?' the shopgirl asked.

Rosa wondered where she'd obtained her information. Then she remembered Signora Guerrini had called to say she would be coming.

The shopgirl directed Rosa to the door. 'Their last nursemaid was a pretty French girl. I guess after the scandal they wanted someone more ... plain.'

Plain? It was probably a vengeful comment for not participating in the gossip, but it stung Rosa all the same. It reminded her of how the paying students at the convent used to refer to her as 'No Name' when out of earshot of the nuns. Rosa glanced at the flamingo pink hat on the stand when she passed by. One day I am going to wear a hat as beautiful as that one, she told herself. And I'll show that girl that I'm not plain.

Out on Via Tornabuoni again, Rosa caught her breath. She was going to have to hurry to buy new shoes and drop off her flute to be repaired. She couldn't imagine the Marchese being sympathetic if she didn't manage to finish her errands, especially as they were all for her. But she couldn't help looking at the beautiful things in the windows. Not the furs and leathers — they disgusted her because she was aware of the suffering that was the source of them — but she fell in love with some tourmaline filigree earrings in the jeweller's window, and the etched vases and Raffaellesco ceramics in the glassware shop. She understood why the nuns of Santo Spirito rarely ventured from the convent and never looked at themselves in mirrors. There was too much vanity everywhere. And now she was caught up in it. 'Plain' would have been considered a virtue by Suor Maddalena, but the idea of being nothing special bit Rosa to the core. She stopped for a moment to admire a glass-topped table in the window of a shop called Parigi's Antiques and Fine Furniture, then, seeing the smooth opaline vase next to it, could not resist the temptation to venture inside.

The shop was attractively laid out with tapestries and etchings on the walls. The armoires were polished to a high shine and the armchairs and sofas were accented with silk cushions. An arrangement of Murano glassware drew Rosa's eye to a chestnut table with turned legs in the centre of the store. She inhaled, breathing in the rich mix of scents: beeswax, wood, incense, linen and coffee. There wasn't a hint of dust in the air, which she thought unusual. The furniture and carpets at the convent always smelled musty.

The elegantly dressed sales clerk was talking to a woman with a florid complexion and her stooped husband. The clerk was tall with a high-domed forehead and the deep-set blue eyes of a northern Italian. Rosa admired his dove grey suit and the white gardenia in his buttonhole. He glanced in her direction and nodded. 'I will be with you in a moment, signorina.'

He turned back to his customers. 'You must consider these chairs for your reception room. They will complete the feeling we have been working towards.' His voice had a calm, persuasive tone that was charming and definite. Rosa tried to guess his accent. Venetian? And his age? She put it somewhere between twenty-five and thirty. The pieces he referred to were a pair of upholstered rectangular seats with swan-shaped armrests and outward-scrolling feet.

The male customer blinked behind his spectacles and grudgingly touched the chairs. 'They are very fine, Signor Parigi, but ...'

Rosa realised her mistake. The elegant man was not a sales clerk but the owner of the store. He was young to have such a sophisticated establishment, she thought.

'They are unique,' said Signor Parigi, crossing his arms.

The woman sniffed and peered at the chairs. 'We are looking for something more ... modern.'

'But that's the trick,' replied Signor Parigi. 'To place something worth talking about in a room that is otherwise stripped to the essentials.'

The man shook his head. 'We don't see the point of

investing in old furniture when we have purposely sought out the latest materials.'

Signor Parigi's mouth tightened but his manner remained courteous. 'Then come this way,' he said, directing the couple towards a pair of leather armchairs.

Rosa sensed his irritation. Compared to his clients, he exuded style. His suit jacket sat perfectly on his shoulders with a hint of shirt showing beneath the sleeve cuffs, while his client's suit, although made of fine wool, was slouchy and his sleeves hung to his knuckles. The woman had pulled up her hair under her hat in a way that did nothing to flatter her face and emphasised the pouches under her eyes.

Rosa couldn't resist looking at the upholstered chairs Signor Parigi had been keen to persuade the couple to purchase. She admired the dark grain of the wood and ran her fingers over the swan necks. A vibration buzzed through her hand. She saw a tropical forest running down to the sea. Colourful parrots squawked in the trees. The sound of wood being chopped rang in the air. She heard someone singing in a language that sounded similar to her own but not quite. A sweet fragrance tickled her nostrils. It was as if she were flipping over the pages of the past. A bearded man in an imperial uniform appeared on one of the chairs. On the other chair sat a young woman with melancholic eyes and sloping shoulders. Rosa shivered. She had seen animals before but never people. Who were they? The man pressed his hand on top of the young woman's. 'I leave you free to choose, but to refuse will bring misfortune upon our family and country,' he said.

The pair faded. Rosa's heart pounded in her chest. Her head felt as if it might burst. 'This rosewood came from a forest in Brazil,' she said aloud. 'The tree was over two hundred years old when it was felled and had been home to many birds. The chairs were fashioned by a furniture maker in Sardinia who loved nothing more than the fragrance of cut wood, the oily texture of it under his fingers, and to sing while he worked. They are the very chairs in which Victor

Emmanuel sat with his beloved daughter Maria Clotilde in 1858 when he told her that she must marry the repulsive Prince Napoleon to secure the future of Italy. The chairs were sold to a merchant when the king's private quarters were redecorated after the Risorgimento.'

The couple and Signor Parigi turned to Rosa and stared. She half-expected them to accuse her of witchcraft or trickery or at least to hustle her out of the store. Instead, the woman's eyes filled with tears. She rushed back to take another look at the chairs. It seemed as though she were imagining every word and gesture of that awful conversation between a daughter whose happiness was about to be sacrificed and the father who would go on to be the first king of a united Italy.

'Agostino,' the woman said to her husband, 'perhaps Signor Parigi is correct. These chairs would make an interesting statement.'

Her husband joined her, a greedy look flickering in his eyes. 'Why didn't you ask your assistant to explain their history sooner?' he said to Signor Parigi. Rosa wondered if he was considering how much the chairs would impress his friends and acquaintances.

The couple's new enthusiasm had manifested itself so unexpectedly that Signor Parigi took a moment to collect himself.

'Of course I am right,' he said, with a smile and a wink to Rosa. 'Look at the berried cresting and the charming glaze on the swan heads.'

'We must take these chairs immediately,' the man said.

'Certainly. Please, come this way and we will make the arrangements,' Signor Parigi said, ushering the couple towards his office at the rear of the shop.

He returned to Rosa, reached into his pocket and slipped some notes into her hand. She was too surprised to refuse them.

'Are you looking for work?' he asked, his eyes sweeping over her face. 'You dated that furniture accurately. How did you become so knowledgeable? You don't look a day over fifteen.'

He stood so close that Rosa could admire his fine skin and high cheekbones. She could even smell the lemony scent of his cologne. She was glad for her new dress and hat. She hoped he wouldn't look down at her clogs.

'No,' she said.

Signor Parigi smiled. 'No, you aren't looking for work? Or no, you aren't a day over fifteen? Which is it? If you are looking for work, I'll hire you on the spot. You're a charming saleswoman.'

Rosa blushed. She felt an unfamiliar tingle in her stomach. She'd never been so close to a man before, and certainly not one as attractive as Signor Parigi.

'I have a job,' she told him, realising that he thought she had made the story up. 'I must go now. I'm late.'

Signor Parigi looked puzzled. Rosa guessed he was wondering what she was doing in his shop if she wasn't after a job, and would have asked her if he wasn't so keen to get back to his clients before they changed their minds about the chairs. He cocked his eyebrow and smiled at her with his perfect teeth. 'Well, just come back then,' he said. 'You don't need a reason. I like people who know their furniture.'

Rosa's face turned hot and she couldn't make herself meet his eyes. She found it easier to back towards the door. When she reached it, she finally lifted her gaze to Signor Parigi and saw that he was looking at her with an amused expression on his face.

'I'm not fifteen,' she told him. 'I'm fifteen and a half.'

With that, she ran back onto the street. Dallying had cost her precious time. She decided to go to the shoe store next, then drop into the music repair shop on her way back to Giuseppe and the car.

The shoe store the Marchese had selected was a sombre affair compared to the shops she had seen on Via Tornabuoni. The shoes were stacked on floor-to-ceiling shelves and the only colours available were brown, black and navy. It was obviously a place where servants were outfitted.

The sales clerk was the same age as Rosa and as thin as a string bean. He measured her feet with care and traced their outlines. His friendly manner put her at ease.

'What beautiful feet you have,' he said. 'Perfect dimensions. The second toe is longer than the first, the sign of an independent female.'

Rosa grinned. The nuns at the convent used to say that it was the sign of an aristocratic heritage. But Rosa knew it was merely hereditary. When she was younger she used to think she would recognise her mother by her longer second toe. The idea amused her now.

The sales clerk lifted some boxes from the shelves and selected shoes in black and navy.

'Is it possible to have something that's not leather or suede?' Rosa asked, dreading seeing some poor creature running around her room each time she took off her shoes. 'It irritates my skin.'

'Of course,' said the sales clerk. 'I'll check what we have in the storeroom.'

He disappeared for a few moments before returning with a pair of shoes made of satin with rubber soles. An embroidered strap crossed the top of the foot. They were much prettier than the standard shoes in the boxes. Rosa caught sight of the price tag. They were more expensive too.

'Don't worry about that,' said the sales clerk. 'The Villa Scarfiotti sends all their staff here to be outfitted. We can make a generous discount for you.'

Rosa tried on the shoes. They fitted perfectly and were more comfortable than her clogs. She paraded around the room. The shoes were so light she thought she could dance in them, if she knew how to dance.

'You don't think the Marchese Scarfiotti will be displeased that I haven't bought standard shoes?'

'The Marchese doesn't have to wear the shoes. You do,' replied the sales clerk, his face breaking into a grin.

His cheekiness was contagious and Rosa couldn't help smiling too.

Rosa reached the music store on Via Tornabuoni with only a quarter of an hour to spare before she had to return to Giuseppe. She was disappointed she had lingered so long at the other places because the music store enchanted her. It reeked of dust, wood varnish, mildew and old brass. Her new shoes padded on the scuffed wooden floor as she wandered between the display cases, first studying a rare Stradivarius violin before spotting a Spanish guitar with the sun painted around the sound hole. She stopped to admire a mandolin inlaid with opals and noticed there was a gilded harp in the corner of the store. She was heading towards it when she saw something move in the corner of her eye. A grey-striped cat was sitting on a wonky bookshelf. Rosa blinked in case it was another illusion but the cat yawned and curled up to sleep.

It's a real cat, she thought with a smile.

'*Desidera, signorina?*'

Rosa saw an old man standing in a doorway at the rear of the shop, behind the counter. She caught a glimpse of a younger man in an apron sitting in a workshop behind him. He was replacing cork on a clarinet.

'The sales clerk has gone home,' said the old man, stroking his walrus moustache. 'Only the repair shop is open now.'

'I have come to have my flute fixed,' said Rosa, placing her case on the counter and opening it.

'Ah, then I will introduce myself,' said the old man. 'I am Ernesto Morelli. I oversee the repairs in the shop.'

He hobbled towards Rosa and picked up the headpiece to examine the dent.

'It shouldn't be too difficult to fix,' Signor Morelli said, looking over the top of his glasses at Rosa. 'We will need two days. Can you come back on Friday afternoon?'

Rosa had not been without her flute since the nuns had given it to her when she was seven years old. She would miss it, although she had not dared to play it at the villa yet for fear of inducing one of the Marchesa's migraines.

'I can't come back until next week,' she replied.

'My assistant will deliver it to you then,' said Signor Morelli, indicating the man in the workshop. He opened a drawer in the counter and took out a notebook. 'Where do you live?'

'The Marchese Scarfiotti sent me here,' Rosa told him. 'I'm the governess at his villa in Fiesole. Is that too far to come?'

A change passed over Signor Morelli's face. Rosa saw the assistant in the workshop put down the clarinet and begin polishing a French horn. She was sure he was listening. After a moment's hesitation, Signor Morelli said, 'I know the villa very well. Have you seen the Bösendorfer piano in the music room?'

From the reverence in the man's tone, Rosa was sure he was not referring to the upright piano she and Clementina played in the alcove of the schoolroom, and only when the Marchesa was out for the afternoon. He must be referring to one of the rooms off the ballroom. She had caught a glimpse of the French doors that led from the grand ballroom onto a loggia one day when she and Clementina were walking in the gardens. She shook her head in response to his question.

'Never?' Curiosity seemed to be struggling with courtesy on Signor Morelli's face. 'It's a pity, because if you like music that piano is one of the most beautiful instruments a person could hear in their lifetime. I used to tune it for the Marchese's sister when she gave recitals. The piano suited her style perfectly: dramatic, rich and full-bodied.'

Rosa's interest was piqued by the mention of Clementina's aunt. 'You used to tune her piano?' She had two minutes left in which to race to the car but she wanted to know more about the woman who had made the exquisite opera sets and — it now seemed — had been an accomplished musician.

'She died too young,' Signor Morelli lamented. 'It surprised us all. She was so robustly healthy. But then her husband had been killed in an uprising in Libya. Perhaps it was the shock.'

Signor Morelli attached a ticket to Rosa's flute case and wrote her a receipt. He was about to hand it to her when he hesitated again. 'They say the Marchese has never got over his sister's death, that he mourns for her still?'

This time Rosa was sure from the lift of the old man's eyebrow that he was waiting for her to confirm or deny his assertion. The merchants she had visited on Via Tornabuoni seemed to have a keen interest in what went on at the villa.

'I don't know the Marchese well enough,' she explained. 'I have only been governess there for a week.'

From the corner of her eye, Rosa saw the assistant put down the French horn. He was not even trying to hide his interest. 'And how does poor Giovanni fare these days?' he called out to her.

'Giovanni?'

'Giovanni Taviani. The gatekeeper. He used to be the estate manager —'

The bell on the shop door rang and a woman rushed inside, dragging a boy in a shorts suit towards the counter. The boy was carrying a violin with a broken neck. He looked pleased with himself.

'Excuse me, signore,' the woman said in Italian but with an English accent. 'This is a disaster. His music examination is tomorrow afternoon.'

Signor Morelli nodded to the woman and guided Rosa towards the door. 'We have a trumpet to return to Fiesole on Friday. My assistant will take your flute too.'

Out on the street, Rosa was relieved to see that Giuseppe had spotted her and was manoeuvring the car towards the shop. She adjusted her hat to bring back the circulation to her head while Giuseppe turned into a side street so she could get into the car. When Rosa entered the street, she passed under the window of the music workshop.

'I'll go as far as the gatehouse,' she heard the assistant tell Signor Morelli. 'No further. Witches were burnt at the Villa Scarfiotti in the days of the Inquisition. They say the place is haunted.'

The reference to witches at the villa made Rosa shiver. She hurried towards where Giuseppe had stopped the car and almost tripped over a beggar woman sitting in a doorway. Lying across the woman's patched apron was an infant swaddled in rags. The child's cheeks were sunken with hunger and it seemed to Rosa that its eyes looked up at her in despair. If the Wolf had not taken her to the convent all those years ago, she could have shared the same fate.

The woman stretched out her wasted arm. '*Per favore, signorina?*'

Something prickled Rosa's palm. She looked down at her hand and remembered the notes that Signor Parigi had placed there. She reached into her pocket and counted them out. They came to more than she would make as Clementina's governess in a week. Those chairs Signor Parigi had sold the couple must have been worth a fortune. But it was more money than Rosa needed. She was clothed and fed. It didn't occur to her that she should keep some of the money for the future. She pressed the notes into the woman's hand and continued towards the car, not stopping to take in the stunned expression on the beggar woman's face.

FOUR

In early May, after Rosa had been at the Villa Scarfiotti for two months, a garden party was held in honour of Clementina's ninth birthday. It was a birthday party in name only because from the small number of children invited compared to the adult guests, it seemed more an opportunity for the Marchesa to show off the Nile green dress she had bought in Paris and her Ferragamo red suede shoes. The guests were from the nearby villas. Some of them were Tuscans but most were foreigners. The men turned from their female companions and stood transfixed when the Marchesa moved through the gathering to greet her guests. The other women in their silk ensembles and georgette princess dresses paled in comparison. The Marchesa was like an ocean liner leaving all in her wake. Rosa followed with Clementina, whose position of honour on the day was overshadowed by her mother.

'We will see you and the Baron at the ball next month, won't we?' the Marchesa asked a blonde woman with high cheekbones.

The woman was wearing a dress with silk hibiscus flowers sewn on it and transparent nylon shoes. She carried a dachshund with a hibiscus on its collar and was the only rival to the Marchesa's striking fashion sense. 'But of course,' she replied with a French accent. 'We already have our costumes.'

The Marchesa grinned. 'Baroness Derveaux, you Parisians are more original than the conventional Florentines. If it were not for you I would kill myself.'

Baroness Derveaux threw back her head and laughed, showing her rows of pearly-white teeth. Rosa remembered the women she had seen in Via Tornabuoni. If *they* were conventional what must the Parisians be like?

The Marchesa, with Clementina and Rosa in tow, moved on to greet the other guests. Rosa was surprised to see Signora Corvetto. She was wearing a gunmetal satin dress and standing next to a white-haired man in a wheelchair. His sun-spotted hands and sagging face were such a contrast to Signora Corvetto's beauty that Rosa assumed the man was her grandfather. She was taken aback when the Marchesa greeted him and she realised that he was Signora Corvetto's husband. Rosa was even more surprised when the Marchesa did not act like the cat that got the cream around Signora Corvetto, as she had the other women. Although her husband's mistress was younger and prettier, perhaps the Marchesa did not feel outclassed by her rival. The other guests went to great lengths to speak with Signor Corvetto, who was partially deaf, but turned their faces from his wife. It was obvious they considered her below themselves socially. The snubs Rosa had received at the convent from the paying students were on a smaller social scale, but she felt Signora Corvetto's embarrassment just the same. Clementina, unconcerned with social mores, threw her arms around Signora Corvetto and embraced her without reservation.

'*Buon compleanno*! Happy birthday!' Signora Corvetto said, returning Clementina's kisses. 'Nine today! You're a big girl!'

Signora Corvetto's eyes filled with tears and Rosa wondered why Clementina's growing up would make her sad.

'Come on,' the Marchesa urged Clementina. 'Lunch will be served soon.'

Clementina squeezed Rosa's hand and whispered, 'Signora Corvetto is nice. She comes to see me every birthday.'

Rosa noticed a young man with a cowlick and disgruntled eyes standing on the edge of the gathering. His gaze did not leave the Marchesa's face but she paid him no attention. When they reached the jasmine-covered gazebo where a string quartet was playing, the Marchesa leaned over and blew air kisses on Clementina's cheeks before turning to Rosa. 'You can take her to play with the other children now.'

'Yes, Signora Marchesa,' Rosa replied in a calm voice that did not betray the rage she felt at the Marchesa's indifference to her daughter. The Marchese's mistress displayed more affection towards Clementina than her own mother! It amazed Rosa that the girl possessed a cheerful disposition despite her mother's neglect. Perhaps it was her father's love that saved her. Rosa looked around for the Marchese but he had disappeared the same time his wife had started parading around the gathering.

Maria and Rosa had been charged with taking care of Baroness Derveaux's twin boys and the seven other children of guests as well as Clementina. To help them, the twins' English governess, Miss Butterfield, had been enlisted. Miss Butterfield was in her fifties with slim ankles and a generous bosom. She was so top-heavy she looked as though she could topple over at any moment. While Rosa and Maria set about organising the children into games of octopus and beautiful queen, the effort of watching the children play seemed to exhaust Miss Butterfield. She sat down in a wicker chair and began fanning herself. Rosa was concerned that she might be ill. The Tuscan climate did not always agree with the English, Mrs Richards had told her. They were prone to all sorts of maladies: sunstroke, diarrhoea, fevers. Rosa poured a glass of lemon water and offered it to the governess.

'I wasn't cut out for this life of servitude,' Miss Butterfield told Rosa. 'My father was a gentleman in the King's service and had inherited acres in the Lake District, but alas his trickster cousin swindled him out of it all.'

Miss Butterfield launched into a litany of ills that had befallen her since she came into the world. She had three brothers and two sisters who had ill-treated her as a child and no longer spoke with her. 'A guilty conscience needs no accuser,' she sniffed. Her mother had suffered arthritis all her life and now Miss Butterfield, who looked robustly healthy to Rosa, seemed destined to suffer the same. 'How my knees throbbed this winter,' she said. 'I thought I might perish with the pain.' There were problems with sore teeth, a weak chest, aching bones and constipation. Miss Butterfield's greatest disappointment was her 'beloved' suitor who in the end married her younger sister. 'She stole him away, right from under my nose. Like a thief in the night. Gone! All my hopes for a happy life!'

Rosa tried to show concern but realised it was only encouraging Miss Butterfield to continue. She was relieved when she saw Ada and Paolina bringing platters of fruit tarts, slices of *castagnaccio* and *cenci* dusted in sugar down the path towards them. A manservent and maid followed behind, carrying jugs of fruit punch and glasses.

'Look! They are bringing the treats,' Rosa said, standing up. She organised the children to each take a napkin and to sit on the carpet that had been laid out for them.

The maid with the fruit punch sidled up to Maria. 'The men are very dashing today,' she said to her. 'Especially him.'

'He's *always* dashing,' Maria giggled.

Rosa glanced towards the adult party, wondering who the maids were talking about. The Marchese was still nowhere to be seen. The young man with the cowlick was continuing to follow the Marchesa's every move with his blazing eyes. His features were even but his expression was like that of a man fixed on a problem. Rosa could not imagine him ever laughing. The only other man under forty was Vittorio and surely the maids couldn't be referring to him. The Marchesa's brother was strutting among the guests in his jackboots and black shirt. His only concession to the celebration was a gardenia in his buttonhole. Rosa thought he was the most unattractive human being she had ever seen and the most stupid. Once, at one of the torturous dinners she shared with the Scarfiotti family, she had heard him claim, 'War is not an unfortunate necessity but an expression of man's virility', and a few moments later whine like an infant because his soup was cold. Paolina had told her that Vittorio had participated in D'Annunzio's daring expedition to Fiume and that the scar on his forehead was from a raid with the *squadristi* on a communist meeting. 'But one day when he discovered a boil on his back, he took to bed and moaned as if he had been visited by the Black Death,' she said.

Ada showed more sympathy for Vittorio. 'He took a blow to the head in battle and has been having trouble adjusting to a quiet life since he came back from the war,' she explained. 'Signora Guerrini said that he is suffering a form of amnesia and can't remember anything of his childhood or youth. All he knows is how to fight.'

Rosa watched Vittorio give some Austrian guests the fascist salute. Even in the short time she had known him, he seemed to be deteriorating further into madness.

Ada nudged Rosa. 'Those girls have men on the brain,' she said, indicating Maria and the maid. 'Mind you don't go the same way. They aren't worth it.'

The children finished their sweets and licked their fingers. They wiped their icing-sugar-covered hands on their smock dresses and sailor suits and bustled around Rosa, urging her to let them play a game of ice witch. Rosa turned to ask

Maria to assist her but the maid had disappeared. She assumed she had returned to the house with Ada to help in the kitchen.

'They pay me a meagre allowance for clothes,' said Miss Butterfield, after Rosa had settled the children into their game and sat down to watch them. 'They say it is because the Baroness gives me her mother's dresses after they have been worn only a few times. Can you imagine? Hand-me-downs! What an insult! Look at this one, for instance: it's almost threadbare!'

Miss Butterfield's dress was made of mulberry crepe and was the slip-on type with an overblouse front that looked fashionable. It was nicer than anything Rosa owned. She began to feel impatient with Miss Butterfield's complaining. Perhaps the true reason her suitor had preferred her sister was because he had discerned there would be no pleasing her.

A shrill laugh pierced the air. It startled Rosa. The Marchesa was talking with a man whose wide girth hung over his pants. She was sucking on a cigarette in a holder and blowing the smoke flirtatiously in the man's direction. Rosa saw the man with the cowlick turn and flee towards the house.

'You Italians create fantasies and everyone else believes them,' Miss Butterfield sneered. 'The Marchesa Scarfiotti! Oh, she loves the title, doesn't she? The villa. The clothes. Everyone believes that preposterous story about her mother being an Egyptian princess! What a load of codswallop!'

Rosa drew back at Miss Butterfield's remark. She wasn't fond of the Marchesa but she was growing tired of the gossip. She felt it was wrong to take wages from the Scarfiottis then talk about them behind their backs. Suor Maddalena had often quoted from Proverbs: *Only a liar listens to gossip*. Rosa turned away, hinting that she was not interested in any sordid details Miss Butterfield wished to share about her mistress, but the governess pressed on as if she hadn't noticed.

'One of my cousins was posted in Egypt. He knew Generale Caleffi. The Marchesa's mother danced in a bar in Cairo. She tricked the general into marrying her and his family had to make something up to avoid the scandal.'

Rosa drew a breath through clenched teeth. The Marchese was obviously proud of his family name and she doubted he would have chosen a wife who would sully it. Her mind turned back to the woman in the turban she had seen outside the summerhouse. Still, what Miss Butterfield said would explain why the Marchese would not allow Clementina to speak with her grandmother.

Seeing that she had struck some interest in Rosa, Miss Butterfield became animated. 'The Marchesa's mother is ruthless. Why, my cousin used to say that the old general never died of dysentery. She —'

Miss Butterfield was cut off by the appearance of Maria hurrying towards them from the direction of the loggia. Rosa was thankful. She did not like the direction Miss Butterfield's story was taking.

'I'm so sorry,' said Maria. 'I remembered I had to see the gardener about roses for the bomboniere. They are making them up in the house now.'

Maria's cap was askew and her chin was red. Rosa reached up to help her straighten the cap and noticed a sour smell about her — like body odour and bleach. It struck Rosa as strange because Maria was fastidious about her grooming. It must have been because it was a warm day and she had been running.

'It's all right,' said Rosa. 'I was about to set the children up for the sack race.'

Applause sounded through the gathering. The children began to cheer. Rosa and Maria turned to where everyone was looking. The Marchese was walking down the path leading a grey pony with a white mane. The pony's pink saddle and bridle were engraved with stars and a pink plume was perched on its head. Clementina's eyes grew wide with excitement. She rushed towards her father.

'She's come all the way from Scotland especially for you,' the Marchese told her.

'She's beautiful,' said Clementina, nestling her cheek to the pony's flank. 'What's her name?'

'Bonnie Lass,' replied the Marchese in a mock Scottish accent that made the children laugh.

The Marchese's usual aloofness gave way to a face alive with love and pride when he led his daughter around the garden on the pony. After Clementina's parade, he helped the other children take turns in riding it. He threw back his head and laughed when one boy asked if the pony was real or whether it was two servants dressed up. Rosa had heard that ponies could be bad-tempered, but the little horse behaved docilely, even with the children hopping and skipping alongside it.

Baron Derveaux, a man with gangly legs and winged eyebrows, joined in to help. His tender manner when he lifted the children into the saddle made him seem like an agreeable man. Rosa wondered why Miss Butterfield found so much in her employers to complain about.

'A complete disaster,' said Miss Butterfield, shaking her head. 'What a lack of decorum! Baron Derveaux is like a child himself. It's the French, they never grow up.'

Rosa dismissed Miss Butterfield as someone with a pessimistic view of the world. She thought the Derveaux twins were lovely and their parents seemed charming. She recalled a quote from the English poet John Milton: *The mind can make a heaven out of hell or a hell out of heaven.* Miss Butterfield would do well to listen to her countryman. The story about the Marchesa's mother dancing in a bar probably wasn't true at all.

When the party was over and the guests were ready to leave, Signor Bonizzoni instructed Rosa and Maria to assist him with the bomboniere because the Marchesa's personal maid was busy with the guest book and Signora Guerrini was organising the other maids to tidy up. The two young women passed the packages to the Marchese and Marchesa to give out as their guests departed. The men received a silver pen with Clementina's name and the date engraved on it, while the women were given crystal perfume bottles etched with the same. The children received tulle bags of sugared almonds. Clementina curtseyed gracefully to each parting guest.

Rosa noticed the bomboniere were tied with violet posies. 'It's a pity the gardener didn't have the roses ready. They would have been so elegant,' she said to Maria.

Spots of colour came to Maria's cheeks and she averted her eyes. Rosa realised that she had embarrassed her without understanding why. She saw the Marchese glance in Maria's direction and wondered if he had noticed her crumpled skirt. She hoped the maid would not be reprimanded.

Baron and Baroness Derveaux were the last guests to leave. Rosa reached to take a pen to pass to the Marchese and when she turned back she saw the Baron was staring at her with a puzzled expression on his face.

'I beg your pardon, Mademoiselle,' he said. 'But have I seen you somewhere before?'

The Marchese raised his eyebrows. 'It's impossible, François. She was cloistered in a convent until she came here.'

The Baron nodded apologetically.

'Perhaps it was on Via Tornabuoni,' offered Rosa. 'I was there a few weeks ago having my flute repaired. Or somewhere else in the city? I run errands there on Wednesdays.'

'Ah, but I never go to the city if I can help it,' said the Baron, a wry smile coming to his face. 'My wife loves Florence but I can't abide it. Too many Florentines to tell me that theirs is the most beautiful language, the finest wine, the purest olive oil, the loveliest art. They will even tell you the best walking canes are made in Florence! I spend my time within the grounds of our villa here in Fiesole whenever we are in Italy. I did that as a child when my family came to holiday here.'

The Marchesa turned and studied Rosa. It was the first time Rosa thought she had really looked at her. 'Who does she remind you of, François?' the Marchesa asked.

The Baron was quiet for a moment before he answered. 'It's when she turned a certain way ... Well, perhaps it is a trick of the light.'

'Or a trick of the champagne,' laughed the Baroness, linking her arm with her husband's.

The Baron smiled but Rosa could see he was perplexed.

The Baron's driver brought his Alfa Romeo to the front steps and opened the doors. Signor Bonizzoni sent Maria away to help the other maids and returned into the house himself. The Marchese and Marchesa, with Clementina and Rosa behind, stood on the steps to witness the departure of the Derveaux family. The Baron and Baroness entered the car followed by their twins. The Baron glanced at Rosa again. She blinked and saw a vision of a young boy and girl standing by a pond. She knew from the gangly legs and winged eyebrows that the boy was the young Baron. But who was the dark-haired girl? Her face was turned away and she was crouching, as if she were about to skim stones across the water. The image was the picture of innocence and yet it filled Rosa with sadness.

Rosa's attention was pulled back to the present as the Baron's driver manoeuvred the vehicle around the fountain and headed down the driveway.

'*Au revoir, mes chéris*,' the Baroness shouted from the car window. 'We will see you at the ball.'

After the car had disappeared into the woods, the Marchese returned to the house without a word to his wife. The Marchesa walked down the steps towards the driveway. Clementina followed some distance behind, sensing adventure. Rosa, who had not been dismissed for the day, had no choice but to go with Clementina.

'We shouldn't be following your mother,' she told the child. 'She may wish to be alone.'

'She goes somewhere in the woods,' Clementina replied without a hint of guilt. 'I want to know where.'

It was late afternoon and the light glistened on the trees. The Marchesa took a turn into the woods, oblivious to Clementina and Rosa scampering after her or the damage the earthen path was doing to her shoes. The path took them past the cemetery before curving again in the direction of the gatehouse. The shimmery light through the leaves was beautiful but there was something eerie about the forest. It was as if the trees and birds were waiting and watching for something. Rosa shivered when she remembered the conversation she had overheard outside the music repair shop. Had witches truly been burnt here during the Inquisition?

They were only a short distance from the gatehouse when the man with the cowlick stepped out from behind a tree. He had a closed wicker basket in his hand and put it down beside his feet. Rosa and Clementina hid behind some bushes. The Marchesa was not surprised by the man's appearance and Rosa wondered if she had gone there to meet him.

'I left everything for you,' the man said to the Marchesa.

'I didn't ask you to,' she replied.

'You said you would come away with me.'

The Marchesa let out a sharp laugh. 'I said it because I'd had too much to drink. We both know it was only a pleasure of the flesh, nothing more.'

Rosa blushed and tugged Clementina's arm. 'It's time to go back,' she told her. 'This is a conversation between adults.'

Clementina looked at her with shining eyes, oblivious to the meaning of the conversation. 'But I want to see what's in the basket.'

'Hello!' the man called. Rosa looked up and realised that he had spotted her and Clementina.

'I brought a present for you, Clementina,' the man said, opening the wicker basket. He pulled out a Weimaraner puppy.

'She doesn't want it,' the Marchesa told him.

'Yes, she does,' the man said, placing the wriggling puppy on the ground.

The dog scrambled towards Clementina who ran to meet it. She picked it up and laughed when it licked her face. There was a dark patch in the dog's fur, near its muzzle. It would have been a blemish in a pedigree, but Rosa thought the puppy was even more adorable for it.

'I'm sorry, Signora Marchesa,' Rosa said, gesturing to Clementina to bring the dog and follow her. 'We didn't mean to intrude.'

The Marchesa flashed Rosa a derisive look. 'You don't have much control of my daughter,' she said.

'No, Signora Marchesa,' Rosa replied, feeling herself grow hot with embarrassment. 'I don't usually have to exercise discipline. She's normally obedient.'

The Marchesa shrugged then turned back to the man, obviously dismissing Rosa from her mind. 'Did you think I would leave this?' she asked him, indicating the grounds and villa. 'To become the wife of some dusty university scholar?' She beat her chest with her fist. 'You don't know what I've paid for it! What I've had to give up to become the Marchesa Scarfiotti!'

The blood drained from Rosa's face. Clementina, who was having trouble getting the excited puppy to follow her, was out of earshot. But she wasn't. Did the Marchesa intend for her to hear this conversation? Or did she simply not care?

'So it was all lies?' the man asked.

The Marchesa shrugged.

The man staggered backwards as if he had been shot. 'You told me you loved me,' he said, shaking his head.

'You were stupid enough to believe it.'

The man stared at the Marchesa. The confusion on his face was palpable. 'You were a different person when … you were different.'

'We are all different when we want to be,' the Marchesa told him. 'We all act our parts. Well, the show is over now.'

The man groaned. The Marchesa's eyes gleamed. It seemed to Rosa that she was enjoying the pain she inflicted. She was like a vampire, drawing strength from another human's weakness. Rosa was sickened. If the man loved the Marchesa, then he loved unwisely. She didn't love anybody, not even her husband and daughter. The man gave one last look to the Marchesa before he turned and fled into the woods like a wounded animal. A few moments later a car engine started.

The Marchesa stared after the man for a moment then she spun around and fixed her eyes on Rosa and then Clementina and the puppy. A menacing look fell over her face. 'I'll teach you both to spy on me,' she said.

'Clementina, come this way and bring the dog,' she called, walking in the direction of the gatehouse. 'We'll show it to Signor Taviani.'

Clementina picked up the puppy and ran after her mother, unaware that she was about to be punished. Rosa followed. Goose bumps broke out over her skin.

'He's so beautiful, Mamma!' Clementina sang out, kissing the puppy who licked her in return. 'So beautiful!'

Signor Taviani was standing at the rear of the gatehouse, chopping wood. He frowned when he saw the women and Clementina approaching. The Marchesa grabbed the dog from Clementina by the scruff of its neck and thrust it at Signor Taviani who caught it in his arm.

'Kill it!' the Marchesa said.

Clementina screamed. Rosa was too stunned to speak. The puppy wriggled from the gatekeeper's grasp and ran back to Clementina. She threw her body over it and protected it with her arms.

'We are not keeping that dog,' the Marchesa said. Her voice was no longer languid and arrogant. It was high-pitched and hysterical.

'No, Mamma! No!' Clementina cried.

The puppy peeked out from Clementina's arms. The sight of its wagging tail was too much for Rosa. 'It's only a puppy,

Signora Marchesa,' she said. 'Perhaps we can give it to one of the servants. For their children.'

The Marchesa snapped her head in Rosa's direction. The whites of her eyes were showing, like a horse about to bite. 'God, you're a classless little stray, aren't you? How my husband ever thought you were suitable for this house, I don't know! Look at the mark near its nose, you stupid girl! It's deformed!'

'No, it isn't!' shouted Clementina. 'And don't be rude to Signorina Bellocchi! She's smarter than you!'

The Marchesa raised her hand. Rosa stepped in front of Clementina, terrified she was about to slap the girl.

'I can't stand malformed things!' the Marchesa raged, lowering her arm. 'They disgust me!'

Clementina broke into sobs. Rosa tried to steady her own nerves. She had thought the Marchesa wanted the dog destroyed because it had been given to Clementina by her lover, or to teach them a lesson for following her. What sort of deformity was a dark patch on a dog's nose? Rosa's mind was a throng of confusion. Only a while ago she had been presiding over children at a party — and now this? The Marchesa was mad, Rosa was sure of it.

The Marchesa turned to Signor Taviani. 'Kill it!' she said. 'I don't care how. Drown it. Shoot it. Use that axe you were holding a moment ago.'

Clementina let out a wail. Rosa prayed that someone back at the villa would hear her cry and come to investigate.

Signor Taviani glanced from Rosa to the Marchesa. 'Not in front of the child,' he said.

Rosa was taken aback by his voice. It wasn't the rough dialect she had been expecting; it sounded refined and calm. Then she remembered that he had not always been a gatekeeper; he had once managed the estate. She considered appealing to his mercy but there was something formidable in his face that stopped her. Even the Marchesa seemed wary of him.

'All right,' the Marchesa said to him, brushing her hand

through her hair. She gave a short laugh and waved in the direction of Clementina and Rosa. 'They don't understand. They're too stupid. But you understand, Signor Taviani. *I know you do.* One has to make difficult choices if one is to be great. Not everyone has the strength to make those choices. That's why they stay little people all their meagre lives.'

The Marchesa turned and grabbed Clementina's arm and twisted it. The girl struggled but lost her balance. 'You'll shut up now, Clementina,' the Marchesa told her. 'Or I'll get rid of your governess too.'

The Marchesa didn't wait for Clementina to regain her footing but dragged her through the undergrowth on her backside towards the driveway. Rosa was too shocked to react. Never in her life could she have imagined a mother doing that to her child. When she came to her senses a wave of anger washed over her. She didn't care about her position, she cared about Clementina. Could she run fast enough to the villa to alert the Marchese? Surely he would put a stop to this insanity.

Rosa broke into a sprint, thrusting past the Marchesa and Clementina. Her breath hurt in her chest and her legs cramped, but she fought through the pain. She had reached the driveway and the villa was in sight when she heard the shot ring through the air. It sent birds into the sky from fright. Rosa fell to the ground and clasped her knees, agonisingly trying to regain her breath. A sick feeling rose in her stomach. There was no use running any more. It was too late. Clementina's puppy was dead.

That night, Rosa was woken by the sound of Clementina crying. She rushed to the girl's room to find her bathed in sweat and rocking in her sleep. Rosa lifted her into a sitting position and embraced her. Clementina opened her eyes and stared at Rosa. Her lips were trembling.

'It's all right,' Rosa told her. 'I'm here.'

She had written her letter of resignation before going to bed but now realised she could not present it. If she left, who would take care of Clementina? Certainly not her sadistic mother! Even the Marchese was preoccupied by other things. Rosa had searched for him after the incident that afternoon and had not been able to find him. Only when one of the maids brought her dinner did Rosa learn that he had retired to his study with the strict instruction that he was not to be disturbed. It was probably just as well Rosa hadn't been able to speak to him. She would have said things about the Marchesa that couldn't be retracted.

Clementina began to sob again. Rosa wondered why Maria, who had been appointed the girl's nursemaid, hadn't appeared. She'd been informed that afternoon by Signora Guerrini of her new position, which was to start immediately. Rosa soothed Clementina until the girl's breathing calmed and her twitching subsided. Rosa knew it was the slaughter of the puppy that had distressed her. It had disturbed Rosa too. But she didn't think that talking about it would make either of them feel better.

'Shall we read something together?' she asked instead.

Clementina blinked away her tears. '*Le tigri di Mompracem*?' she sniffed.

It made Rosa smile to think that Clementina preferred Salgari's swashbuckling pirate adventure story over *Sleeping Beauty* or *Snow White*.

'Ah, well, you had better read it to me then,' she told the little girl. 'So I can hide under the blankets during the fight scenes.'

'All right,' Clementina answered, opening the well-worn pages of the book.

Rosa pressed her cheek to Clementina's and tried to block out her memory of the Badessa's warning to the nuns about becoming too attached to their charges: *They are like little birds that have been blown out of their nests in a storm. We feed them, keep them warm and educate them, but one day we must let them go.*

I won't let her go, thought Rosa. She needs me.

It was the early hours of the morning before Clementina

finally fell asleep. Rosa pulled the covers around her before returning to her own room. In the hallway she caught a glimpse of Maria sneaking up the stairs and slipping into the nursemaid's room. Where had she been all this time?

Rosa tried to sleep, but found herself unable to settle down. She kept seeing the scene with the puppy before her again and again. *I can't stand malformed things!* the Marchesa had said. *They disgust me!*

Rosa was lonely at the villa. Her position as a governess put her in limbo. She wasn't part of the family and at the same time she didn't belong in the hierarchy of the other servants. At Villa Scarfiotti this wasn't necessarily a disadvantageous situation, however: apart from Clementina she would rather be distant from the family; and she was glad that she wasn't under the thumb of Signora Guerrini. Rosa passed much of her spare time in the villa's extensive library. Although they lived in enclosure, the nuns of Santo Spirito were great scholars as well as musicians. They had imparted to Rosa a love of study and she continued her education at the villa by reading works as far-reaching in range as Tolstoy and Ralph Waldo Emerson. Still, she had been brought up in a close community and longed for human contact. She climbed out of bed and dressed again, and wandered down to the kitchen where she knew Ada and Paolina would be making an early start. She found them trimming artichokes. They invited Rosa to sit by the fire while they continued working.

'How long have you been at the villa?' Rosa asked Ada.

Ada clucked her tongue. 'I came here in 1914, when the Scarfiottis turned away their cook of thirty years. I sent for Paolina when she was sixteen. She's my niece.'

'Why did they get rid of their cook?' asked Rosa.

'I don't know,' Ada said. 'The woman was the third generation in her family to be in charge of the food at the villa. The Marchese pensioned her off, but, with no husband or children and only old age to look forward to, I heard she died of despair.'

That sort of callous behaviour wouldn't have surprised Rosa if it had come from the Marchesa. But the Marchese? Rosa had known him to be generous, even if somewhat aloof. Why had he done that?

'Clementina's aunt must have still been alive when you came here,' Rosa said.

'Yes. But I never laid eyes on the woman,' Ada said. 'She had recently returned from Libya where her husband had been killed and she was pregnant and ill. Only Signora Guerrini was allowed anywhere near her.'

'Signor Morelli at the music repair shop said she was beautiful.'

Ada nodded. 'I believe so. Well, she certainly was in the portraits I saw of her. She was as beautiful as Giorgione's *Sleeping Venus*: full-figured as a woman should be, with a round, gentle face. A natural beauty without artifice.'

Rosa thought that Clementina's aunt sounded the opposite of the Marchesa. 'What was her name?' she asked.

'I believe Cristina was her baptismal name,' said Ada. 'But I never heard anyone use that. Everyone called her Nerezza.'

The unusual name struck Rosa. It meant 'darkness'. Clementina's aunt must have been a brunette.

'I haven't seen a portrait of a full-figured woman anywhere in the house,' she said.

Ada sighed. 'The Marchese had them taken down after her death. It was the grief and … guilt.'

'Guilt?'

'The Marchese was away on his honeymoon in Egypt when his sister returned here. She died a few weeks after the birth of her child from an infection. He only made it back in time for the funeral. The war slowed down his travel.'

'Was the Marchese close to his sister?' asked Rosa, thinking of the grave and inscription: *Buona notte, mia cara sorella*.

Ada nodded. 'She was his elder sister and had practically brought him up after their mother was killed in a hunting accident. They were twin souls. Well, until the Marchesa came along, apparently.'

'I heard it was the Marchesa who convinced the Marchese not to hurry home,' Paolina said. 'Nerezza was supposed to be as strong as an ox. Illnesses that felled other members of the family never touched her. No-one expected her to die.'

Rosa thought about that piece of information. Signor Morelli had said the same thing. It seemed Nerezza had been known for her vital constitution. 'I guess that's why the Marchese and Marchesa don't get along together,' Rosa said. 'He probably blames her for his not being with his sister when she needed him.'

Ada and Paolina nodded. 'Apparently there was no love lost between the Marchesa and her sister-in-law,' said Ada. 'The rumour was that they hated each other.'

'What happened to the child?' Rosa asked.

Paolina glanced at her aunt. Ada's chin quivered and tears came to her eyes. Rosa was taken aback by the cook's show of emotion.

'She was a beautiful child,' Ada said. 'Despite her mother's illness she was as plump as a dumpling. Signora Guerrini would bring her to me each morning to bathe. I would weigh her on my scales and give her a little diluted goat's milk and thin gruel to make her stronger. I told Signora Guerrini we should find a wet nurse but she said Nerezza insisted on feeding the infant herself. Some idea she had got in Paris. Well, the mother's milk must have been infected too. The little angel survived only a short while after her mother's death, despite the help of the wet nurse we eventually employed when I noticed she was losing weight. The infant died the day the Marchese returned.'

The women fell silent.

'What a terrible tragedy,' Rosa said. She felt for the Marchese, no matter his faults. His sister's child might have been a comfort to him had she survived.

Ada and Paolina prepared to make breakfast and Rosa offered to help them. It was like being back at the convent again, working with Suor Maddalena. She ground chestnuts to make flour and thought about what Ada and Paolina had told her. The Marchese had loved his sister but had married a woman who hated her. There were things about the Scarfiotti family that didn't make sense. The fire began to die and Paolina picked up the poker to stir the coals. She stopped mid-action, as if she had seen something that puzzled her.

'Three spirits of fate,' she said. 'They are weaving a garment and have almost completed it.'

Rosa remembered the dream she'd had where Ada and Paolina were talking about witches. The Bible said that magic was of the devil. But there was nothing malevolent about Ada and Paolina.

'Are you *streghe*?' Rosa asked the women. 'Are you witches?'

Ada chuckled. 'All women are witches,' she said, brushing her hands down her apron. 'Only some of us are more aware of it than others.'

'I'm not a witch,' said Rosa.

'Oh, yes, you are,' said Paolina. 'I saw the power in you the first time you walked into the kitchen. You can see things that others can't.'

Rosa was taken aback. What Paolina said was true. She did see things differently from others. When one person saw a piece of meat, Rosa saw a cow munching grass.

'That doesn't make me a witch,' she protested. 'Witches are evil.'

Ada raised her eyebrows. 'Do you think Paolina and I are evil?'

Rosa swallowed her words. Of course they weren't evil. She found herself thinking back to what she had read in the Bible. Perhaps she had taken it too literally. Even Suor Maddalena had displayed an open mind to philosophies besides Catholicism. *If one can't understand others' beliefs how can one argue for one's own?* she used to say. Rosa often found her in the convent library looking up Plato and

Pythagoras and passing it off as an interest in mathematics and science. What did witches believe? She remembered Suor Maddalena had explained to her that while many women who were called witches had been persecuted with false charges such as human sacrifice and evil deeds, their basic belief was that no matter how complicated the world seemed, everything was made up of the same four elements: earth, air, fire and water. *Rather than being separate entities, they believe we are all parts of the same body*, Suor Maddalena had said. Was that so far-fetched, Rosa wondered now.

'Is is true that witches were burnt in the woods here?' she asked Ada and Paolina. 'During the Inquisition?'

Ada glanced at her. 'So you've heard the story of Orsola Canova?'

Rosa shook her head. 'I only overhead someone saying that the woods are haunted.'

Ada placed the breakfast rolls in the oven before turning back to Rosa. 'Then let me explain,' she said. 'In the time of the Medicis, Francesco Canova spoke out against the ruling classes' corrupt ways. He was banished from Florence and his properties were divided amongst the elite. Only his youngest daughter, Orsola, remained in the city with her aunt and cousin. Most women were not taught to read then, but Orsola's relations were scholars and she grew into an educated girl, but one with no respect for the powerful families. The women had an interest in medicine, and would secretly visit people in their homes to cure them of illnesses. The Scarfiottis had a son who fell in love with Orsola. She did nothing to encourage him, but the young man's infatuation became so embarrassing for the Scarfiotti family that they claimed Orsola had used magic to make him fall in love with her. The authorities searched her aunt's house and found phials and books on anatomy. Orsola, her aunt and cousin were brought before the tribunal and accused of sins against the church. They were burnt here in the woods.'

'What a horrible death,' Rosa said, shaking her head. 'I'm glad that humankind has progressed since those times.'

'Do you think so?' Ada asked, looking at her uncertainly. 'They say that when the pyre was lit, Orsola swore that she would return and haunt the Scarfiottis.'

Rosa remembered the queer feeling of being watched she had experienced in the woods. 'Do you think Orsola is still here?'

'You can't kill a witch like Orsola,' Ada replied. 'Her spirit will remain here until her vow is accomplished.'

'That's what I saw in the fire,' said Paolina. 'The Fates have decided. Orsola and her companions are ready.'

'For what?' Rosa asked.

Paolina peered into the smouldering ashes before turning back to Rosa. 'I can't tell. But you coming here has stirred them up, that much I know.'

The weeks before the ball were a flurry of activity. The French doors to the ballroom were flung open and maids busied themselves dusting paintings and polishing the mirrors and floorboards. Rosa caught a glimpse of the Bösendorfer piano when it was moved into the ballroom to make space in the music room for the card games. 'Dramatic, rich and full-bodied' had been the description given to both the piano's sound and Nerezza. Rosa stood in the doorway for a moment, trying to imagine the woman sitting at the keyboard. She recalled the profile of the statue on the grave. Nerezza had been a skilled artist and musician. She was beautiful and had died young and unexpectedly. Her husband had been killed in Libya. Rosa felt her interest in Clementina's aunt grow with each new fact she learned about her. But Nerezza wasn't the only person Rosa was curious about at the villa.

The Marchesa hurried past with Signora Guerrini, discussing the flowers for the ball. Rosa turned away. Although the Marchesa had not changed her behaviour towards Rosa after the incident with the puppy, Rosa found it difficult to hide her repulsion for the Marchesa. Why is she so cruel? Rosa wondered. And how can I protect Clementina — and myself — against her? She no longer had any qualms about uncovering the Marchesa's dark secrets. She needed to understand them for her own self-defence. Miss Butterfield had said that the Marchesa's mother was not an Egyptian princess as she claimed but had been a dancer in a Cairo bar. Paolina had implied that the Marchese blamed his wife for his not being with his sister when she died. Rosa would have once dismissed such comments as gossip, but now she wanted the truth.

Two weeks before the ball, Clementina was sent on a camp with the Piccole Italiane, the Marchesa arranged to visit Baroness Derveaux at her villa, and the Marchese was away in Florence, presumably with Signora Corvetto. Rosa knew that with everyone away at the same time, this would be her only chance to investigate the Marchesa's quarters.

The day the Scarfiottis departed for their individual destinations, she waited until the servants were at their evening meal before descending the staff staircase to the Marchesa's quarters. A surge of panic overtook her when she reached for the door. If she was discovered, she would be dismissed. To her dismay, the door to the Marchesa's floor was locked. She hesitated, wondering if it was a sign from God that she should abandon her perilous undertaking. What was she expecting from pitting herself against such a powerful woman? And what was it she was hoping to find? The Marchesa hadn't been embarrassed to have a scene with her lover in front of Rosa. Perhaps it was futile to try and have something over someone who was shameless?

Rosa inhaled a breath and steeled herself. Knowledge and a better understanding of the woman she was dealing with was her way of combating her helplessness. She continued down the staircase to the lower floor, and opened a door, which she found led onto the main landing where she was as exposed as a rabbit caught between two hollows.

Distant clinks of cutlery and voices rose from the servants' dining room below. She would be seen if Signor Bonizzoni or another servant walked out into the foyer. Rosa swallowed and crossed the open area to another set of stairs that gave access to the third floor. She willed that the door to the Marchesa's quarters would be unlocked from that approach, and breathed a sigh of relief when she turned the doorknob without resistance. She slipped inside to the inner corridor she had seen with Maria. A wedge of twilight lit the Nubian slaves and the Egyptian dancer with the serpent entwined around her leg. Rosa had read somewhere that Egyptian artefacts were supposed to contain the spirits of the beings they represented. She turned away from the serpent's zircon eyes and entered the parlour of paintings and sculptures of the Marchesa. Why was it necessary for a woman to have so many representations of herself? It had to be more than vanity alone.

There was a door at the opposite end of the parlour. Rosa opened it and found herself inside the Marchesa's bedroom. The canopied bed sat on a platform. Rosa's gaze followed the gold posts and tasselled steel blue curtains up to the gold crown pinnacle of the bed. A matching chaise longue was placed near the marble fireplace. The walls were papered in black-and-gold damask. Next to the bed was a *prie-dieu* inlaid with emeralds. Did the Marchesa pray? Rosa could not imagine it. The overblown palazzo atmosphere of the room was at odds with the Marchesa's slick personality. Rosa remembered the first time she had seen the Marchesa eating the bloody steak, and the way the woman had fed off the vulnerability of the man with the cowlick. Perhaps the funereal colour scheme suited the Marchesa's vampiric nature.

Rosa strained her ears to listen for anyone approaching the Marchesa's quarters before moving on to the next room. The space had no windows. She flicked on the light. Floor-to-ceiling shelves stored the Marchesa's array of hats and purses, while her Schiaparelli and Mainbocher dresses dangled on hangers in the open wardrobe. The dressing room was more in keeping with the style she expected of the Marchesa. Rosa cast her eye over the gold tray ceiling, triple-mirrored walnut dresser and coromandel screens. She glanced at the clock on the dresser and realised she only had a quarter of an hour before the staff would start returning to their posts.

Attached to the dressing room was a bathroom decorated in black-and-white porcelain with gold trimmings. Beyond that was another door. Rosa opened it and found herself looking into a bare room with unpolished floorboards. It might have been a cupboard except that there were no shelves, only a window covered by a red curtain at the far end of the room. Rosa was curious to find out what could be seen from the window. She pulled the curtain aside and discovered not a window but a metal door. She supposed it was a safe and expected it to be locked, but to her surprise the latch sprang open when she touched it. She stared into the darkness. It wasn't a safe but another room from which a spicy smell emanated. There was no light switch near the door but she noticed a cord dangling from the ceiling and tugged it. Two lamps set on either side of a stone altar were illuminated. Rosa found herself staring at a huge eye painted on the wall. Next to it was a gold figure of a vulture with a plumed head and the claws of a lion. She was so hypnotised by it that it took her a few moments to notice the other objects in the room. Propped on shelves and stools were figurines of beetles, scorpions, bears, lions and crocodiles. There were hundreds of stones, gems and crystals spilling out of ivory chests and bowls: green basalt, granite, marble, jasper, bloodstone and haematite. Hieroglyphics covered one wall. It was as if Rosa had walked into the tomb of an Egyptian queen. The collection looked ancient and must have been worth a fortune. Miss Butterfield was wrong — the Marchesa's mother had to be a princess. How else could the Marchesa have acquired all these things?

On the stone table was a gold coiled serpent with ruby eyes and a slab of lapis lazuli next to a larger stone. On the lapis lazuli something had been written in gold. Rosa picked it up and held it under the light to get a better view. The words were in Italian: *Otterrò il controllo del mio cuore. I shall gain mastery over my heart.*

She replaced the slab and picked up the other stone, which was white and semi-transparent. On it was written: *My heart is triumphant. I have gained power over it and will not be judged according to what I have done.*

Rosa reread the mysterious message. She heard a bell ring downstairs, which was the signal that dinner was over and the staff would be returning to their posts. She turned to go, and spotted a gold-leaf etching of an Egyptian king and queen on the adjacent wall. The queen was nursing a baby on her lap. There was a handle at her feet and Rosa realised that the etching was a cupboard set into the wall. She opened it and found a glass jar on a shelf inside. There was something inside the jar but she couldn't see it clearly. She lifted the jar and discovered it was full of liquid. She held it to the light to see what it contained. At first she only registered that the pale object was about the size of a small pear. There were dozens of metal pins stuck into it. Then a sickening realisation hit her and her stomach heaved. She managed to put the jar back into the cupboard and close it before lurching towards the bathroom. She dry-retched over the sink. The blood roared in her ears. There was no mistaking what the object was: she had sketched it many times while studying Leonardo da Vinci's drawings, only this one was smaller. A heart.

Rosa would have to hurry out of the Marchesa's quarters or be discovered. By sheer force of will she managed to stand upright. But when she had fled the third floor and hidden herself in her own room, she could not rid herself of the vision of the faded organ of life floating in the formalin. A pain seared through her head from her eyes to the back of her skull. From the size of the heart Rosa guessed it had belonged to a child, maybe even an infant. One question ran around and around her head: whose heart was it?

FIVE

When Rosa's first day off came, three months after her arrival at the villa, she was glad to get away from the Marchesa. Although she didn't see the woman daily, images of the child's heart with pins in it haunted her dreams. She had no doubt that the Marchesa was a practitioner of black magic and the words she had seen on the lapis lazuli and white stone were demonic incantations. One afternoon, while Clementina practised her scales on the piano, Rosa had searched through an anatomy book in the library. Perhaps the heart belonged to a lamb or a calf? But when she found the section on the heart, the pictures were too close to what she had seen in the jar. Where could the Marchesa have obtained the heart? Was she a graverobber? Rosa closed her eyes and tried to discover the owner of the heart by willing a vision of its origin. She could see nothing but the dead flesh floating in the jar.

She had been tempted to tell Ada and Paolina about her discovery but the atmosphere of the villa made her suspicious of everybody. They seemed like good women but she didn't know what they truly thought of the Scarfiottis. They might be indignant that she had invaded their employer's private quarters, and might even tell the Marchesa.

On her day off Rosa planned to visit Suor Maddalena. She had heard nothing from her despite having sent several letters. The estate manager, Signor Collodi, was driving into Florence to pick up supplies and offered to take Rosa with him. His truck wasn't as luxurious as the Marchese's car and reeked of oil and mouldy grass but it was better than waiting for the tram or walking.

The truck rattled and bumped down the driveway. The wildflowers on the side of the road were in full bloom. 'The bees love the flowering mallow,' Signor Collodi told Rosa. 'We will have good honey this year.'

When they reached the end of the driveway, Signor Taviani came out to open the gate for them. Rosa averted her eyes. Signor Collodi worked a toothpick around his mouth while they waited. He looked as ill at ease as Rosa felt. Signor Taviani strode towards the gates, unlocked them, then remained by the gatepost until the truck had passed through. Although Rosa still didn't look at him, she shivered, sure that he was staring at her.

When they were some distance down the road, Signor Collodi ran his fingers over his moustache and turned to Rosa. 'My father took over Giovanni's job so I'm uncomfortable around him. He was the big man on the estate when the Old Marchese was alive. The Marchese trusted him completely. But he had some trouble ... I think the young Marchese keeps him here out of respect for his late father. Signor Taviani won't allow anyone near his lodge. He once threw a rock at the gardener when the man tried to trim the gatehouse's hedge.'

Rosa couldn't feel sympathy for the gatekeeper, no matter what his troubles had been. When she thought of him, all she saw was the innocent puppy he had slaughtered.

The road levelled out and the engine ran more quietly. Signor Collodi asked Rosa how she was finding the villa.

Rosa answered that she enjoyed teaching Clementina and then asked Signor Collodi about the preparations for the ball, which she knew were extensive.

'We are all working at a pace,' he told her. 'They haven't had a ball at the villa since the Marchese's sister married. That was before the Great War.'

Rosa remembered the way the Marchesa had strutted about at Clementina's birthday party. 'I'm surprised to hear that,' she said. 'I thought the Marchesa was partial to social gatherings.'

'I believe she is too but she prefers to host them in Paris. Perhaps she doesn't think that Florentines are up to her standards.'

Signor Collodi brushed his hair across his pate with one hand while holding onto the wheel with the other. Rosa sensed his wounded Tuscan pride. She decided to use it to her advantage to glean more information.

'Why has she changed her mind this time?' she asked.

Signor Collodi shrugged. 'Can you imagine anywhere more beautiful to have a ball than here? The villa was always lit up in the days of Nerezza Scarfiotti. Her social events were famous. Perhaps somebody has said something like that to the Marchesa and it has finally prompted her into action. After all these years.'

'I heard Nerezza Scarfiotti was a great beauty and an accomplished musician,' Rosa said. 'And that she and the Marchesa didn't get along.'

She realised that she was walking on dangerous ground, speaking so personally about her employer. She affected a casual tone, but she was digging for dark secrets and wondered if Signor Collodi would notice it.

He merely nodded. 'I was only a boy when Nerezza Scarfiotti was alive. But I do remember sneaking a look at her one evening when she hosted a soirée. She was a magnificent woman ... and not only an accomplished musician but an excellent linguist and conversationalist as well. The whole of Florence was enamoured of her.'

'I guess it would be enough to make any woman jealous?' Rosa fished.

Signor Collodi shrugged. 'If you mean the Marchesa Scarfiotti ... well, there might have been some jealousy but perhaps more on Nerezza Scarfiotti's part. She was proud of her family's name. Whoever her brother married would become mistress of their home. I'm not sure she thought the Marchesa was suitable for the role.'

A truck appeared before them on a steep part of the road and Signor Collodi had to concentrate on the gears. While he was occupied, Rosa considered what he had said. It was true that it was hard to imagine the Marchesa feeling inferior to anyone, but Nerezza had been of noble birth, beautiful and accomplished. Perhaps the Marchesa didn't like to give parties at the villa because Florence's elite shared Nerezza's opinion that she wasn't good enough to have married into the Scarfiotti family. That would explain her strutting about at Clementina's birthday party. Perhaps the Marchesa had wanted to punish the women for their snobbery by enchanting their husbands.

Signor Collodi let Rosa out near the Ponte Santa Trinita. The sun was high in the sky and Rosa knew Suor Maddalena would have some free time before she began the afternoon's chores. As she passed through the Piazza de' Frescobaldi and the fountain of Bernardo Buontalenti, she smiled at the artist's nickname, 'good talents', and thought how it was as improbable as her own name. The houses of the quarter had their shutters closed against the heat, and Rosa dabbed her face with her handkerchief as she made her way along the streets and lanes to her destination. When she reached the convent, she stared at the walls, never having seen the place where she had passed nearly all of her life from that aspect. She gazed up at the sky; the expanse of blue was the link between the outside world and those inside the convent.

There was a shiny bell near the convent door. Was it new? Rosa grabbed the clanger and rang it. Suor Daria, the portress nun, appeared. She didn't recognise Rosa in her well-cut dress and new hat.

'Ah, Rosa,' she laughed, when the young woman gave her name. 'How you have changed in such a short time.'

A short time? Rosa felt as though she had been away for years. Her life had changed completely.

Suor Daria ushered her into the vestibule and led her towards the parlour. The smell of incense and beeswax brought memories of prayers and schoolrooms flooding back to Rosa. The blue-and-white parlour was a jolt to her. She stared at the carved chairs and the oil painting of Jesus drinking with the sinners and remembered the faces of the parents she had seen sitting in the room while she ran errands for the nuns. How many mothers had she witnessed trying to look proud of their daughters while being devastated that their child had chosen God over family?

'Suor Maddalena will be here in a moment,' Suor Daria told Rosa, closing the parlour door and taking a seat next to it. The elderly nun did her best to be discreet but Rosa knew her role was to listen in on the conversation.

She heard the doors from the inner convent open, and Suor Daria pushed a buzzer to indicate that the doors to the outside world were closed. Rosa knew that only when that was ascertained would the wooden shutter behind the grille rise. Within a second it did, and Rosa found herself face to face with Suor Maddalena. She was so moved by the sight of the dear face that she had not seen in months that it took all her effort not to burst into tears.

'How are you, my child?' Suor Maddalena asked. 'You seem well. Are you keeping up with your flute?'

The nun's formality cut Rosa to the core. Suor Maddalena was thinner than when she had last seen her but otherwise appeared to be in good health. Why hadn't she replied to any of Rosa's letters? Rosa did her best to answer Suor Maddalena's questions cheerfully but she felt as though her heart was in her feet. Surely not even the bars between them, nor Suor Daria's presence, could have curbed Suor

Maddalena's motherly affection towards her. What had changed? Had another orphan taken Rosa's place in the nun's heart?

'I haven't had a chance to play my flute much, but I am hoping to practise every day again now that things are settling down into a routine,' Rosa replied.

Her life at the convent had been governed by routine. She recalled the sense of inner restlessness she had felt then. The Badessa had been right when she said that Rosa was not suited to the religious life. Rosa bit her lip and wished that she had not come. She had happy memories of her life at the convent and now they were ruined. Her head began to swim and spots flickered before her eyes. She was about to get up and make some excuse to leave when the door behind Suor Maddalena opened and Suor Dorotea slipped a grey spotted cat onto the nun's lap. 'I thought Rosa might like to see Michelangelo,' she giggled, before disappearing again.

Suor Maddalena's face broke into a smile and her shoulders relaxed. She held the cat up to the grille. 'They gave me Michelangelo to keep mice away from the kitchen. But the mice scare him.'

The cat rubbed against the grille. Rosa poked her fingers through the bars and scratched its chin. Suor Maddalena took Rosa's finger and squeezed it. The gesture was an opening between them. Suddenly the resentment Rosa had been feeling melted away.

'Thank you for your letters,' Suor Maddalena told her. 'I've kept every one. But the Badessa said that I had best not reply until you were settled into your new place. Now I see that you are, I hope you will visit often and continue to write.'

There were tears in Suor Maddalena's eyes and Rosa felt her own eyes well up. The nuns of the Augustine order were not as strictly enclosed as the Carmelites and Poor Clares. There were certain occasions when they were allowed out of the convent. Perhaps at such a time Rosa and Suor Maddalena would be able to talk without bars between them. But that wasn't likely to happen in the near future unless there was a war or an earthquake or some other disaster that would bring the nuns out of the convent to help the injured and sick.

Rosa told Suor Maddalena about the pleasant things at the villa and about Clementina. 'She's a bright girl; she learns everything so quickly.'

'Just like you,' said Suor Maddalena.

Rosa glanced over her shoulder and saw that Suor Daria had nodded off to sleep. She took the opportunity to slip the silver key from her pocket and show it to Suor Maddalena.

'It was in your wrappings when you came here as a baby,' Suor Maddalena whispered. 'The women in my village used a charm like that to protect a child from harm.'

'You mean witches?' Rosa asked, her eyes wide. She was surprised Suor Maddalena wasn't offended by the charm if that was the case.

Suor Maddalena gave a wise smile. 'There are many ways to the Almighty, Rosa,' she said. 'I simply think the Catholic Church is the most direct one. We have our symbols and charms too, after all.'

Rosa didn't know whether to be proud or shocked that the most religious person she knew was also the most open-minded. Wasn't what Suor Maddalena was saying a kind of heresy? Ada had claimed that all women were witches. By that definition, nuns were witches too. Rosa thought about that idea for a moment: was there really such a difference between prayers and spells? Weren't both appeals to the Almighty? She was about to tell Suor Maddalena that the cooks at the villa were *streghe*, but Suor Daria stirred and coughed into her hand, signalling the visit was over and that Suor Maddalena needed to attend to her chores.

'I will come next month,' Rosa said.

Suor Maddalena nodded. 'I would like that.'

Out in the sunshine again, Rosa walked to the Pitti Palace and Boboli Gardens. Although she had lived in the area, she had never seen them. She stood in front of the severe façade of the enormous palace and thought about how one powerful family could fall and be replaced by another. Luca Pitti had ordered the building of the palace in 1457, to outrival the Medici family with a display of wealth and grandeur. The irony was that the cost of the building bankrupted the Pitti heirs and the palace was bought by the Medicis in 1550. The Medicis eventually fell too, as did the rulers who lived in the palace after them. Now it was an art gallery. Would the Scarfiotti family also fade to oblivion in the future? Rosa recalled her conversation with Signor Collodi. Was that why Nerezza had feared her brother marrying beneath himself?

The sun was hot and Rosa walked into the gardens and along a path lined with cypress trees until she came to an artificial lake where she sat down on a bench in the shade. A young couple were standing near a fountain. They spoke with their heads close together. Suddenly the man seized the girl and kissed her passionately. Rosa felt her toes tingle. What was it like to kiss someone, she wondered. She thought of Signor Parigi at the antiques store on Via Tornabuoni and hoped that the first man she kissed was as handsome as him.

She felt in her pocket and took out the silver key. So a witch had put the charm in her wrappings to protect her. Was it her mother? Was that why Rosa had grown up with the power to see the source of things?

She unclasped the chain around her neck that held her crucifix and added the key to it, then tucked the chain back under her collar. What was the witch trying to protect me from? she wondered, then sighed when she realised that no matter how many questions she asked herself, her origins would always be a mystery.

The night of the ball, the villa took on the appearance of a mauve-tinted underworld. The colour theme for the evening was purple and the house and the statues had been lit in the regal colour. The cut flowers were arrangements of violet roses, hyacinths, lilies and tulips, while the driveway and paths were lined with urns sprouting damson-coloured sweet peas, lavender, anemones and dahlias. The menservants were dressed in plum-coloured livery and the musicians of the thirty-six-piece string ensemble in the ballroom wore aubergine purple jackets. Round tables covered in mauve linens had been set up in the garden. On the loggia was a buffet. Extra kitchen staff had been hired to help Ada and the permanent staff prepare the extravagant dishes. Paolina had shown Rosa the menu a few weeks before. It included cold cucumber and cream soup, prawn risotto, artichoke frittata, trout basted with oil and herbs, and zucchini flowers cooked in a wafer-thin batter. Dessert was to be *fragoline nelle ceste*, baskets of spun sugar filled with strawberries, hazelnut mousse and mascarpone.

Clementina was permitted to attend the first hour to see the guests arrive before Rosa put her to bed. The girl couldn't contain her excitement when people began to appear in their Rolls-Royces, Bugattis and Alfa Romeos. A few months prior to the ball, modernist lampposts had been imported from Barcelona to light the driveway and Signor Collodi had inserted tinted globes for the evening, so the guests looked as though they were appearing through a tunnel of purple light. Chauffeurs opened the doors and out spilled women in lilac taffeta gowns, men in evening suits and lavender shirts, and lap-dogs dyed violet for the occasion. When one group of guests alighted from their car, Rosa jumped at the sight of monkeys and an antelope leaping out with them. She was surprised that no-one else reacted until she realised it was an illusion. One of the women was wearing a purple cape trimmed in monkey fur, while another strode forward in antelope-skin shoes.

The Marchesa's outfit was the most striking of all and had been made specially for her by Schiaparelli in Paris. It was a grape-coloured sequined evening gown with a fishtail hem, a low-cut back and a plunging V-neckline that left little to the imagination. Through the deep armholes Rosa could see the Marchesa's ribs protruding through her pale skin, and the skirt of the dress was tight enough that the Marchesa's hipbones showed through. It occurred to Rosa that the woman might be sick. She hardly ate anything as it was, but in the last few weeks before the ball she had not even come to dinner. But the guests were too mesmerised by the boa constrictor dangling around the Marchesa's shoulders to notice her weight loss. The Marchesa had brought the snake with her from her last trip to France, where the Parisian social set were ditching their Pekineses and poodles for more exotic animals like cheetahs and lions.

'What an amazing atmosphere you have created,' Baroness Derveaux exclaimed to the Marchese and Marchesa. The Baroness was wearing a lilac Delphos dress with a gold hairband, while her husband had donned an embroidered suit.

'Well, they say one's greatest enemy is boredom and we certainly don't want that,' the Marchesa replied, turning to her husband.

The Marchese, looking dapper in a wine-coloured damask evening suit, smiled uneasily. He was standing with Vittorio, who was dressed in his fascist uniform. When the Baroness raised her eyebrows, Vittorio pulled back his cuff to reveal a purple watchband.

Once the guests had arrived and were being ushered to their tables, Rosa and Clementina went to retire for the night.

As they passed by the buffet table, Signor Bonizzoni touched Rosa's arm. 'Maria is not well this evening,' he said. 'I need all hands on deck. After you have put the little one to bed go and see Signora Guerrini. You'll have to help with clearing the tables.'

Rosa, who had been hoping to play her flute when it was too noisy for anyone in the house to notice, was disappointed but had no choice but to agree to the request. She took Clementina to her room, helped her to wash and tucked her into bed. What was wrong with Maria? The nursemaid had seemed peaky lately but Rosa had put it down to the strain the ball preparations had placed on the staff. She returned downstairs where Signora Guerrini was waiting for her with a maid's uniform.

'Now you have come down from your ivory tower, you can see how real people earn their living,' the housekeeper told her gruffly.

Rosa stepped into the garden as a commotion was erupting amongst the guests. A Hispano-Suiza car had pulled up with what looked like a gypsy wagon trailing behind it. The chauffeur opened the door of the car and out stepped a bald man in a Chinoiserie silk suit. He waved a flourish at the watching guests and some of them cheered. The chauffeur assisted a woman wearing a dress with puffed sleeves out of the car. She was probably no older than forty but something in her eyes made her seem hard, Rosa thought, or perhaps the chunky amethyst earrings and choker she was wearing aged her.

'Signor Castelletti and Contessa Pignatello! How delightful!' said the Marchesa, greeting the late arrivals with kisses on their cheeks. 'What have you brought for us?'

The guests and servants waited with necks stretched to see what would emerge from the wagon. The back ramp was lowered and out stepped a swarthy man in a grubby hat and vest. He was holding a chain, and something large and black lumbered after him. Rosa realised it was an animal. The man said something to the beast and it rose to its full height on its back feet. Some of the guests gasped but others stepped forward to get a better view. The animal was a black bear with a moonlike crescent on its chest.

'It's quite tame,' said Signor Castelletti. 'Its mother was killed by hunters and this man raised it from a cub.'

The gypsy gave a tug on the chain, which was attached to a ring in the bear's nose. The animal flinched but began to dance, lolling from side to side and turning. The audience clapped and cheered. The Marchesa seemed delighted but the Marchese curled his top lip with disgust. Rosa could feel the animal's humiliation. A scene flashed before her eyes. Her toes turned icy and she realised she was standing in a forest. The vegetation was lush and moist. Voices shouted in a strange language. Russian? There was a crash through the trees and she saw a mother bear and her two cubs running. Then gunshots …

'Where are we going to keep a bear?' the Marchese asked his wife.

'Oh, he will be fine in the cage I have brought,' said Signor Castelletti, indicating the wagon. 'That's what he has lived in most of his life. And if one of your guests makes you unhappy tonight, you can feed him to the bear for dinner.'

The guests laughed at Signor Castelletti's joke.

'I think it would prefer bark and berries, you fool,' the Marchese muttered under his breath.

Signor Collodi was called. He looked perturbed when the Marchesa instructed him to find a place for the cage and the bear somewhere in the garden. Rosa was worried about Clementina: it was in the girl's nature to try to pat a wild animal. She looked at the bear as it passed by with its tamer. It had sores on its knees and was missing fur on its snout. It might kill a human from sheer frustration, Rosa thought. She couldn't blame it. But someone like Clementina would be a misdirected target.

'It's a fine beast,' said Vittorio, after the bear had been led away. 'But not as efficient as a cannon or a machine gun.'

Contessa Pignatello smiled, assuming that Vittorio was joking. But Rosa thought about what Ada had said. Vittorio *was* having difficulty adjusting to normal life after the war and he seemed to be getting worse.

Signor Castelletti and his companion were welcomed by the guests and Signor Bonizzoni was called to direct them to their table. Before Signor Castelletti departed, he leaned towards the Marchese and whispered loud enough for Rosa to hear, 'What do you think of my companion?'

'She's very charming,' answered the Marchese politely.

Signor Castelletti laughed. 'Young and beautiful she may not be, but when a rich and lonely woman makes herself available to be used, it would be most unchivalrous of me not to oblige, don't you agree?'

The Marchese stiffened with what Rosa guessed was revulsion and she couldn't blame him. She turned away and began collecting used dishes from those tables whose guests had entered the ballroom. She caught Baron Derveaux staring at her but pretended not to notice.

'What's your fascination with that girl?' the Baroness asked her husband. 'Are you looking for a young lover? We agreed that neither of us was to take another until we were both over fifty.'

The Baron laughed at his wife's joke then said something in response, which Rosa didn't hear. The ensemble began to play a Viennese waltz and many more guests left their tables for the ballroom. Rosa moved around the empty tables, clearing them of cutlery and china. Another maid came to help her and they worked together.

'How is Maria?' the maid asked her.

'I don't know,' said Rosa. 'I didn't see her.'

The maid glanced towards where the Marchese and Vittorio were in conversation. 'Stupid fool. Did she think *he* would marry her?'

'What do you mean?' Rosa asked.

The maid raised her eyebrow. 'Maria has a lover,' she whispered. 'Surely you must have noticed? When you turn around to speak to her and she's not there, you can be sure she's snuck off to be with him.'

Rosa was dumbfounded. Maria was running around with the Marchese? She couldn't believe her employer would behave that way with his daughter's nursemaid! Then she recalled the gossip of the women in the millinery shop and their comments about why the previous nursemaid had left.

'Signorina Bellocchi, could you help with the buffet?' Signor Bonizzoni called to Rosa.

Rosa put the used cutlery on a trolley and hurried to the loggia where she began removing empty platters so the menservants could replace them with new ones. The Marchesa was leaning against a column talking with a plump woman who was holding a papillon spaniel with a mauve ribbon around its neck.

'If you are from Milan you must know the Trivulzio family,' the woman said.

The Marchesa shrugged. The noncommittal gesture might have meant that she didn't know the family or that she did know them but didn't think highly of them. The woman was taken aback but continued on, perhaps hoping to impress the Marchesa.

'They have a butler,' she said, 'who runs the tightest ship. He can sniff out a speck of dust from yards away. But he is blind. *Completely blind*. Yet he is the best butler you could imagine. And, as I'm sure you know, good butlers are not so easy to find. They must know everything about the family but never breathe a word.'

The woman laughed and patted the Marchesa's arm. The Marchesa shrank back against the column. Rosa assumed she was cringing because of the woman's reference to the butler's 'deformity'. She wondered what the woman would think if she knew that the Marchesa had ordered a puppy destroyed simply because it had a splodge on its nose.

On her way to the kitchen, Rosa overheard Contessa Pignatello talking with Baroness Derveaux.

'The Marchese is an egotist but charming. I can't say so much for his wife. She's as cold as a fish,' the Contessa said.

The Baroness came to the Marchesa's defence. 'Oh, I have pity for her. I believe her father was a powerful and sometimes cruel man. And do you know what her mother was once heard to say? "A wise woman doesn't give anyone anything. Not even sympathy." How could Luisa have grown up any other way but to be standoffish? I believe under that hard exterior there is a fine human being.'

Rosa was surprised by the Baroness's words. Either she was generous in attributing good qualities to people whether they deserved them or not, or she knew something about the Marchesa that nobody else did. She certainly seemed to be the Marchesa's only true supporter.

The ensemble stopped playing and the guests gathered around the sides of the ballroom. Rosa was blocked from the kitchen and had no choice but to pause for a moment too. Baron Derveaux had seated himself at the Bösendorfer piano and indicated to the musicians that he intended to play something. He had been smoking a cigarette and placed it, still smouldering, on the lid of the piano. He would have to remove it soon otherwise it would damage the wood. Rosa cringed; as a musician she would never treat an instrument with such irreverence. The Marchesa followed the other guests into the ballroom. When she saw the Baron at the piano and the cigarette on the lid, a look passed over her face that made Rosa shiver. Her eyes narrowed as if she intended kill him. But why was the Marchesa reacting that way? Shouldn't she be pleased? The Bösendorfer had belonged to her rival.

The guests fell silent in anticipation of being entertained by the Baron. The Marchesa wove her way between them, her spine arched and her eyes like slits.

'What will you play?' Signor Castelletti shouted to the Baron.

'Liszt.'

The Marchesa slipped through the guests and made a line straight for the piano. The Baron didn't see her coming. He brought his hands over the keyboard and hit the first chord. The piano was out of tune. The guests burst into laughter. The Baron smiled but was put out at having his moment of fun thwarted.

'Luisa,' he said, picking up his cigarette just as the Marchesa reached for it. 'Has no-one tuned this thing in years?'

'*Nobody* plays it,' she said.

'One day Clementina might,' said the Baron, missing the Marchesa's meaning. She was giving a warning, not making a statement. Rosa sensed it. For a moment she saw something: a flash of light; a sheet of music. But no vision came.

'We haven't heard truly fine music in Fiesole since Nerezza passed away,' said one elderly man.

The guests murmured amongst themselves.

'Fiesole? I haven't heard such playing anywhere. Not in Paris nor Vienna,' exclaimed a matronly woman.

The Marchesa pursed her lips. Rosa could almost see the goose bumps prickling the woman's skin. Rosa had gathered from her conversation with Signor Collodi that this party was meant to outshine those hosted by Nerezza, not be compared to them.

'Well, there will only ever be one Nerezza,' said Baron Derveaux, shrugging his shoulders. 'That sort of woman comes once a century.'

The Marchesa's eyes flared. Rosa could only imagine what she was thinking. The guests could not be aware of how much rivalry had existed between the women otherwise they would have been more careful not to insult their hostess. Baroness Derveaux and the Marchese, who was trying to make his way through the guests towards his wife, seemed to be the only two people besides Rosa who had noticed the Marchesa's agitation. The Baroness took her husband's arm and ushered him away to the garden.

'Come and see what they have done with the fountain. It's truly magnificent,' she said.

The Marchese indicated for the ensemble to play and entreated his guests to move to the dance floor once again. He then took the Marchesa's arm. It was the first time Rosa had seen him touch her with any sort of tenderness.

'Come on,' he said. 'Our guests expect us to dance.'

Once the guests took to the dance floor again, Rosa was able to manoeuvre through them to the kitchen. She sensed that there was a lot riding on the success of the evening for the Marchesa, and that nothing had better ruin it.

*

Before dessert was served, the Marchese called the guests together and announced that a scavenger hunt had been arranged. A flurry of excitement rushed through the gathering. There was no-one present who was less than twenty years of age, but the guests hopped and skipped into their groups with all the excitement of children at a birthday party. A leader was chosen for each team and Signor Bonizzoni handed them an envelope.

'You have one hour to return here,' the Marchese said, indicating an hourglass that Signor Bonizzoni was about to turn. 'The winners will each get a prize but the losers will have to perform a dare of the winners' choosing.'

The threat brought bursts of laughter and exclamations from the guests. The men checked their watches while the women patted their flushed faces with handkerchiefs. The atmosphere of the party had shifted from one of refinement to one of gay abandon. Signor Bonizzoni turned the glass and the guests scattered like marbles, running into the garden to count the statues or the number of windows on the upper storey. Rosa had never seen adults behave that way.

Signor Bonizzoni clapped his hands and the servants, including Rosa, hurried about the tables, changing any soiled cloths and napkins or melted candles and resetting the tables for dessert.

'They'll be gone an hour,' said the maid helping Rosa with the cutlery. 'We should finish this task quickly and then put our feet up for a bit. It's been non-stop this evening.'

Rosa was about to agree with her when a woman's scream pierced the air. The cry was one of such terror that people came rushing from all over the villa to see what had happened. Rosa's first thought was that somebody had got too close to the bear but then she realised the sound had come from the direction of the driveway. The Marchese shouted to Signor Collodi to grab his gun. It was unlikely but possible that a wolf had wandered onto the property. There were wild boars in the region but they tended to avoid human contact. Rosa thought of witches, but then reminded herself that neither Ada nor Suor Maddalena thought witches were evil. The other guests didn't wait to consider the possibilities; they charged towards the sound, oblivious to any danger.

'Signorina Bellocchi, come with me,' said the Marchese, grabbing Rosa's arm and moving in the direction of the driveway. 'In case the woman is in need of female assistance.'

The Marchese and Rosa managed to overtake the other guests. Baron Derveaux, whose team had been busy sketching the coat of arms in the foyer, caught up with the Marchese. 'The women should stay back,' he said. 'There may be a ravisher in the woods.'

The Marchese stopped and related what the Baron had said. Reluctantly the women turned back. Signor Collodi appeared with his gun.

'What was the question in this direction?' the Marchese asked him.

'A very simple one. To count the number of lampposts before the lion statues.'

Rosa recalled that the statues were only a short way down the drive, where the wall ended. They turned a bend and found one of the party's teams gathered around a lamppost, staring at something like people in a trance. A woman was lying in a faint on the ground, with another woman fanning her. An older man was dry-retching into the bushes.

Signor Castelletti, who had been part of the group, rushed towards the Marchese. 'Tell the others to stay back. It's horrible! Too horrible!'

The Marchese called to his guests that they had best return to the villa. Some of them did, but many continued on, intrigued by what ghoulish sight might await them. Rosa ran towards the prostrate woman to see if she could be of assistance. But before she reached her, the huddle moved aside to let the Marchese through and she glimpsed something hanging from the lamppost. She moved a step forward then stopped. The purple light had muted the object. What on earth ...? Rosa suddenly realised what it was and reeled back. A dead man was dangling from a rope.

The Marchesa arrived in her car. She had driven herself and slammed the door when she got out. The glare of the headlights illuminated the victim's swollen face, which had previously been in the shadows. New cries of horror rose from the onlookers at the sight of the man's blue tongue and bulging eyes.

'Who is it?' Baron Derveaux asked.

'I'm not sure,' said the Marchese.

Rosa turned to the Marchesa. The woman's face was twitching; it was the first time Rosa had seen her genuinely shocked. The Marchesa's eyes met Rosa's and she glowered. At that moment Rosa realised who the dead man was. It was the man with the cowlick.

SIX

After the disastrous end to the ball, the Villa Scarfiotti went into retreat. Signor Collodi and the estate hands removed the decorations the next day so that by the following evening the house had returned to its daunting atmosphere. The servants spoke in hushed tones, and Ada and Paolina replaced the usual menu with simpler meals. Rosa only managed morning or afternoon lessons with Clementina because the girl was forever being whisked off by her father somewhere. Although he had been concerned about Clementina's education, it seemed that in this time of crisis the Marchese dreaded being alone. His wife, the cause of his vexations, was of no use to him. She withdrew to her quarters after the body had been identified and stayed there. The scandal was not so much that a jilted lover of the Marchesa's had hanged himself in the villa's driveway, but rather that what had promised to be the party of the decade had come to a startlingly grim end. The evening was supposed to finish with a display of fireworks. Not with a death. None of the festivities Nerezza Scarfiotti had presided over had concluded so ignobly. That, Rosa thought, was where the real sting for the Marchesa lay.

Rosa recalled what the man with the cowlick had told the Marchesa that afternoon in the woods: *I left everything for you.* She wondered what he had meant. A wife? Children? His position? She noticed that the lamppost where he had hanged himself retained its purple globe. Perhaps no-one wanted to touch it. Rosa didn't blame them. She couldn't pass that section of the driveway without a shiver running down her spine. Or perhaps the purple globe was a tribute from the estate hands to the young man so he wouldn't be forgotten. Possibly that was what he had wanted? To be imprinted on the Marchesa's mind forever.

One afternoon, when Clementina was out with the Marchese, Rosa was returning to the schoolroom from the library with a selection of books she had chosen to study. She was halfway up the servants' staircase when she heard the strains of music. She was surprised because she had never heard music played in the villa, except for the ball and garden party. Signora Guerrini had been definite that music brought on migraines in the Marchesa. Rosa and Clementina only practised their instruments when they were sure the Marchesa was out for the day.

She continued up the stairs and the music grew louder. She recognised the piece. It was the Intermezzo from the opera *Cavalleria Rusticana* by Mascagni. She realised the sound was coming from the fourth floor. Rosa passed Clementina's room on her way to the schoolroom and gave a start when she saw the Marchesa standing there. A disc was playing on a gramophone and the Marchesa was gazing at the opera sets Nerezza had made. She sensed Rosa's presence and turned to her. Rosa flinched, expecting a reprimand for sneaking up on her, and instead was shocked to see tears in the Marchesa's eyes. She quickly blinked them away.

'When a Sicilian challenges another to a duel,' she said, fixing her gaze on Rosa, 'the one who accepts bites his opponent's ear to draw blood, demonstrating he understands that the fight is to the death. When two opponents meet, there can only be one winner.'

Rosa remained silent. She knew there was a duel in *Cavalleria Rusticana* and that the story was set in Sicily, but she wasn't sure that was what the Marchesa was talking about. The Marchesa looked almost ... bereft. But the impression lasted only a few seconds before the woman's face formed into its severe angles again. She took the disc from the gramophone, stared at it for a moment, then handed it to Rosa before brushing past her and disappearing down the stairs.

Rosa stood in the doorway of Clementina's room with the disc in her hand, bemused by the Marchesa's odd behaviour. She only hoped that the gesture hadn't meant the Marchesa was challenging her to some sort of duel.

The following afternoon, a van arrived at the villa. Rosa, who had been walking in the garden, saw two men loading the Bösendorfer piano into it. She noticed the Marchese's car in the garage and hurried towards the house to see if Clementina would like a lesson that afternoon. When she approached the loggia, she caught sight of the Marchese standing in the doorway weeping. Taken aback by his tears, Rosa ducked behind a trellis to avoid being seen. Through the gaps in the jasmine she glimpsed the Marchesa approach her husband.

'She's dead, Emilio,' she said flatly. 'We have to stop living with her ghost.'

Rosa was shocked. The Marchese had adored his sister. How could his wife expect him to part with Nerezza's most treasured possession? The Baroness Derveaux could say what she liked, Rosa thought, but the Marchesa was surely the cruellest woman alive, especially to her own husband. Was she still carrying on the rivalry with his sister even though she was dead? Was that what she had been talking about in Clementina's room the previous day? Was the 'duel' still being fought?

*

On the afternoons when Clementina was out with her father, Rosa visited the bear, whom Ada had named Dono. Rosa learned from the encyclopaedia that the crescent on his chest meant he was a moon bear. Signor Collodi had set up Dono's cage under some trees at the back of the kitchen garden and fed the bear fruit and bread gingerly through the sliding door at the bottom of the cage. The spot Signor Collodi had chosen was cool and pleasant but the cage was too small for an animal born to wander mountain ranges and climb trees. The bear paced in the limited space and Rosa realised the injury to his snout was caused by his banging his head against the bars. Despite his ill treatment by humans, the bear was not as aggressive as Rosa expected. When she approached him, he looked at her with melancholy eyes. If the Marchesa was away, Rosa would play her flute near his cage. The music seemed to calm the bear and often lulled him into restful sleep. One day, after he had eaten a pear Rosa had given him, Dono licked his paws and looked at her intently. A wave of warmth washed over her and Rosa realised that the bear had communicated his gratitude for her kindness. She was touched that he had 'spoken' to her. Gentleness was not what he was used to from humans; he had no reason to trust them.

She remembered overhearing the Marchese saying that bears liked to eat bark and berries, so she left her flute by Dono's cage and walked into the woods to see if she could find any juniper or blackberries. It was the height of summer and the woods seemed less eerie than they had in the spring. The heat penetrated through the trees and insects hummed in an incessant chorus. Rosa's dress stuck to her back and her skin smelled salty. The blackberries she found were not ripe, so she continued along the path to look for some others. She came across a tree with sap dripping down its bark and had stopped to take a piece when a rustling sound caught her attention. Something was moving through the leaf litter.

She glimpsed an animal bounding between the trees. Her first thought was that it was a boar or a rabbit, but its movement had a loping action that suggested longer limbs. Rosa lost sight of the animal. She listened then caught a flash of silver-grey fur. It was a dog. No-one at the villa had a dog because the Marchese had forbidden hunting on his property and the Marchesa seemed to prefer snakes to poodles.

The dog rushed towards the driveway and Rosa ran after it. Once they were both clear of the trees she could see it was a Weimaraner. The dog turned its head to her playfully and she stopped in her tracks. It had a brown splodge on its muzzle. It wasn't a chubby puppy any more, but it was still young, and Rosa was sure it was the same dog the man with the cowlick had given to Clementina and which the Marchesa had told Signor Taviani to destroy.

'Come here,' she called softly.

The dog hesitated then took off again. Rosa was compelled to chase after it.

A man's gruff voice called in the woods. 'Marcellino!'

Rosa recognised the voice as belonging to Signor Taviani. She realised she was near the gatekeeper's house and crouched down in the bushes and watched as the dog ran to Signor Taviani and jumped up against his legs. The gatekeeper affectionately rubbed the dog's head.

'Marcellino,' he said in his sonorous voice, 'you mustn't run off again. It is dangerous for you to do that.'

The gatekeeper led the dog back into his house and closed the door. Rosa blinked. Sitting in the window at the back of the house was the tortoiseshell cat with one ear that she had seen on her first morning at the villa. A strange feeling ran through her and she nearly swooned. She wondered if she was becoming heat-dazed.

She inched her way towards the house and crept past the hedge. By standing on a rock, she managed to peep in the window. The cat had moved and was on Signor Taviani's lap. The gatekeeper was sitting in a chair with his back to Rosa. At his feet was the Weimaraner, chewing on a ball, and another dog, a greyhound with mottled fur on its face that suggested it was old. In a cage hanging from the wall was a parrot with one foot and in another cage a squirrel-like animal was chewing on some lettuce.

The Marchesa had instructed Signor Taviani to kill the puppy. Rosa had heard the shot herself, hadn't she? Was he collecting the animals the Marchesa told him to destroy, she wondered. The dizziness returned. It felt as though she had been given a piece of a puzzle but didn't know where it fitted. Signor Taviani was taking a risk, keeping those animals against the Marchesa's orders, and it changed Rosa's view of him. She remembered reading that Leonardo da Vinci had felt compassion for animals and had refused to eat them. Taking life unnecessarily was abhorrent to him. He had been known to buy birds from the market simply to set them free. Perhaps Signor Taviani was someone like that.

The stone Rosa was standing on wobbled under her feet. She lost her balance and fell to the ground. The greyhound barked. Before Signor Taviani could catch sight of her, Rosa ran as fast as she could into the woods.

When she neared the house, she saw the Marchese's car drive past and come to a stop outside the villa. Clementina jumped out. Rosa knew the girl would head straight to the schoolroom, eager for a lesson, so she quickened her pace. She picked up her flute before entering the house via the kitchen and straightened her dress and hair, which had become dishevelled in her rush through the woods.

Ada walked out of the storeroom, a string of garlic dangling from her hand, and smiled at Rosa. 'Will you want lunch in the schoolroom today?' she asked. 'I can make you —' She stopped and gave a cry, staring at something on Rosa's collarbone.

Rosa grabbed for her chest, thinking she had picked up a spider in the woods. She had seen black ones living in the garden walls. She looked down and saw there was nothing there. Her chain with the cross and silver key had simply fallen out of her neckline.

Ada pointed to the silver key. 'Where did you get that?' she asked, stepping closer and examining it. Her face was as white as a sheet and she was shaking from head to foot.

'It was in my wrappings when a stranger brought me to the convent as an infant.'

Rosa wanted to add what Suor Maddalena had said about witches, but she was perturbed by Ada's stricken expression. The cook's lips were trembling and beads of sweat rose up on her forehead. Rosa thought she was in danger of fainting and helped her into a chair. Ada rubbed her face.

'When was that?' she asked.

'December 1914. Before Italy joined the Great War.'

Ada swallowed and stared at Rosa as if she was searching for something in her face. Finally she shook her head. 'I knew it,' she said. 'I sensed it. All those signs of fate and destiny since you arrived. But I was sure the babe had …' Her eyes suddenly grew wide and her fists clenched. She stood up and grabbed Rosa's shoulders. 'There is something I must tell you,' she said.

The dizziness that had struck Rosa in the woods when she saw Signor Taviani with the dog returned to her. Out of the corner of her eye she saw flecks of dust swirling in a sunbeam. She was sure they formed into a woman's face.

'What?' she asked Ada.

'Signorina Bellocchi! Signorina Bellocchi!' Clementina's voice called from the corridor.

'You had better go,' Ada told Rosa. 'But come to me tonight. I will tell you everything. You are in great danger here.'

Clementina and Rosa had been studying geography in their sporadic lessons together and Clementina's choice of country to concentrate on was China. Rosa was pleased with her selection. Suor Grazia had been fascinated by the work of Christian missionaries in Asia so Rosa was well read on Chinese culture and history. Clementina had meticulously pasted the newspaper articles that Rosa had collected for her into a scrapbook and sketched detailed drawings of sampans and women in straw hats working in rice fields. This afternoon, Rosa tried to listen with enthusiasm while Clementina read out loud about the Manchurian Chinese Eastern Railway and the conflicts Chiang Kai-shek had had with Russia, but her mind kept wandering to the conversation with Ada. What did the cook have to tell her? Why was she in danger?

'What's feng shoo-ee?' asked Clementina.

'Pardon?' Rosa's attention came back to her student. She realised she hadn't heard anything Clementina had read in the past five minutes.

Clementina pointed to the photograph of a Buddhist temple that accompanied the article she was reading. 'This journalist says the Chinese in Harbin built the Temple of Bliss because they were concerned that buildings erected by the Russians were negatively affecting the feng shoo-ee of the city.'

Rosa corrected Clementina's pronunciation. '*Feng shui* — you say it *fung schway*.' She pulled out the chair next to Clementina and sat down. 'The Chinese believe in *chi*,' she explained. 'A vital energy that exists everywhere and in everything. Certain elements in the design of a city or building can block its flow.'

Clementina was satisfied with Rosa's answer and turned to the next article, which was on Chinese opera. Rosa thought about the strange feelings and visions she had experienced at the Villa Scarfiotti. Maybe there was something to the Chinese belief that there was an omnipresent energy contained in all things. She thought about Signor Taviani and his animals and the heart she had seen in the Marchesa's quarters. She felt as though energy was somehow trapped in the villa and was building up, ready to blow at any moment.

After the geography lesson, Clementina and Rosa revised some mathematics problems and then practised French. It was the longest time they had spent together since the ball and Rosa half-expected the Marchese to burst in at any moment and call Clementina away. But he didn't appear. He must have gone to Florence; perhaps to find solace with Signora Corvetto instead. Rosa would have been delighted for the extended time if she wasn't so anxious to speak with Ada.

Six o'clock came and Maria didn't appear to take over as nursemaid and organise Clementina's dinner.

'Do you know where Maria is?' Rosa asked.

'No,' said Clementina. 'I didn't see her last night either. I put myself to bed.'

Rosa was shocked. 'What? Why didn't you come and tell me?'

Clementina shrugged.

Rosa was growing impatient with life at the villa. She could see that Clementina was becoming used to the lack of routine. The Marchese took off with her whenever he felt like it and now Maria was growing careless. She had no right to ignore her responsibilities to her young charge.

'Wait here,' she told Clementina.

She walked down the hall to Maria's room and knocked on the door. There was no answer. Rosa was turning to go when she noticed a glimmer of light under the door. She knocked again. 'Maria?' She pushed open the door. The light was coming from a lamp on a writing desk. Next to it was Maria's armoire with her nursemaid's uniform dangling from a hanger on the door. If she wasn't wearing her uniform, where had she gone? Clementina said that she hadn't seen Maria the previous evening.

The room was neat with buttercup yellow walls and a Chinese rug on the floorboards. There was a strange smell: a sour stink like flowers that had been left in the vase too long. The room needed airing. The bed was in an alcove behind a drawn curtain. Rosa didn't think Maria was there and was about to leave when she heard a moan.

'Maria?'

She hesitated then moved towards the curtain. Her eye

caught something in the washbasin: a bloodied towel. She pulled aside the curtain and reeled back. Maria was curled up on the bed with her knees to her chest. She was covered in sweat and shaking. Rosa reached for the bedside lamp and turned it on. Her stomach heaved. The bedding was soaked in blood.

'Maria!' she cried. 'What's happened?'

'I've committed a sin,' the girl wept. 'God is punishing me.'

Rosa took Maria's hand and was shocked to feel her pulse pounding like a hammer under her skin. She could see it too in the raised veins on Maria's neck. Her own hands started to tremble and she had to struggle to think clearly. Then her eye caught something on the floor. It was a bloodied piece of metal that resembled an umbrella rib. Rosa remembered many years before when a young girl had come to the convent for help in the middle of the night. She had died in agony, her screams reaching the dormitory where Rosa and the other girls lay shivering in their beds. Rosa later overheard the Badessa telling Suor Maddalena that the girl had haemorrhaged after using a knitting needle to abort the child she was carrying.

'Oh, Maria,' cried Rosa. 'Who did this to you?'

Maria's lips were blue. 'It's not his fault,' she said through clenched teeth. 'I love him. I'd have left if I thought it was better, but there is no work out there for pregnant maids. I thought if I got rid of the ... it ... I could stay and he wouldn't get into trouble.'

Rosa's head was pounding. Did Maria mean the Marchese? Surely if he had any decency he would have sent Maria to a convent until she'd had the baby.

A spasm shook Maria. She clutched her stomach and tried to sit up. A clot the size of an egg passed between her legs. The horror of it shocked Rosa into action. She raced to the schoolroom where Clementina was still waiting.

'Get Signor Bonizzoni! Quickly!' she said to the girl. 'Tell him Maria needs a doctor. Urgently!'

Rosa returned to Maria's side and fell to her knees, praying for the nursemaid. Maria was gasping for air. Despite her agony, a strange smile came to her face. 'Vittorio,' she whispered. 'Vittorio.'

The name hit Rosa like a slap. Vittorio? Her mind raced to make sense of things. Pictures of the Marchesa's brother at Clementina's birthday party and the ball flashed into her mind. Yes, he was always at the villa while the Marchese was often not. *He* was the one Maria had been seeing.

Maria sat up again and struggled for another breath. It was her last. She fell back on the pillow and her eyes glazed over. Rosa stood up and crossed herself. She heard footsteps in the hall and covered Maria's lower half with a sheet and tried to arrange her into a more dignified position. But when she straightened Maria's legs more blood flowed out of her and onto the floor.

'Good God!'

Rosa looked up to see Signor Bonizzoni standing in the doorway. Signora Guerrini was with him. The housekeeper was the last person Rosa would have called for assistance but, as the maids were her responsibility, Signor Bonizzoni must have asked her to come along too.

Signora Guerrini glared at the umbrella rib on the floor then looked at Rosa. 'What have you done?' she demanded.

Rosa glanced down and saw the front of her dress and shoes were covered in blood. Her hands too. It seemed that she could even taste blood in her mouth. 'I've done nothing,' she said. 'I found her like this when I came to look for her after Clementina's lesson. The poor girl is dead.'

'We'd best go see the Marchesa,' said Signor Bonizzoni. 'She'll have to call the police.'

The Marchesa was sitting with Vittorio in the parlour. They were smoking and playing cards.

'What is it?' she asked when the butler ushered Rosa and Signora Guerrini into the room. She caught sight of the blood on Rosa's dress. Disgust pinched the corners of her mouth. 'What's happened?'

'A most terrible incident,' said Signor Bonizzoni. 'The young maid Maria is dead.'

Rosa's brain had clamped up and she couldn't think at all. Not even to defend herself when Signora Guerrini insinuated that she had helped in Maria's botched abortion. Signor Bonizzoni, who did not seem to think Rosa was the culprit, suggested the police should be called to investigate the matter.

The Marchesa jumped from her seat. 'Police?' she repeated, her voice turning shrill. 'Another scandal! After what we have just been through!'

'The girl is dead, Signora Marchesa,' said Signor Bonizzoni. 'We can't hush such a thing up. The girl will have relatives and the younger servants will talk.'

Rosa's stomach turned. Maria was being reduced to a pile of dirt to be swept under the carpet. 'Little people' the Marchesa had called her staff on the first day Rosa had laid eyes on her.

Vittorio was tapping his fingers and singing under his breath. He had heard the discussion but seemed indifferent to the fact that a young woman he had defiled was dead. Rosa was filled with disgust. Vittorio had used Maria like an old rag and she had been starry-eyed enough to believe she was in love with him.

The Marchesa launched herself at Rosa.

'Who is the father?' she demanded. 'Who made the girl pregnant?'

Rosa had no time to think. She involuntarily turned in Vittorio's direction. Signora Guerrini let out a gasp. Vittorio leaped out of his seat and backed away towards the fireplace.

'A spoil of war! Little slut!' he said, jerking his head nervously.

Oh, Maria, Rosa thought.

The Marchesa glared at Rosa. A sharp pain jabbed inside Rosa's skull. It was as if the Marchesa had pierced her mind and was able to see what she was thinking. Understanding dawned on the Marchesa's face. Rosa was no longer inconsequential to her: she was the enemy.

'Abortion is a crime,' the Marchesa said, turning to Signor Bonizzoni. 'Mussolini says it is a crime against the integrity and health of the race. It must come with the severest penalties.' She caught her breath as an idea crossed her mind. 'I will call Il Duce myself,' she said. 'He will send someone here to deal with the matter.'

Signor Bonizzoni cleared his throat. 'Very well, Signora Marchesa,' he said. 'But I don't believe Signorina Bellocchi had anything to do with what's happened.'

The Marchesa threw her head back. Rosa had a vision of her as a dragon sending out an explosion of fire; she felt it burn her feet, singe her clothes and melt her insides. The peculiar dizziness that had struck her with both Signor Taviani and Ada that afternoon gripped her again. The triangle was complete: Signor Taviani; Ada; and the Marchesa. But what did it mean? Rosa sensed that she had faced the Marchesa as her adversary some time in the past. And then, just as now, she had been helpless in her grasp.

'Of course she helped,' the Marchesa spat. 'Those servant girls are all the same. They stick together. Take her downstairs and keep a watch on her.'

Signor Bonizzoni and Rosa stood motionless. Even Signora Guerrini hadn't expected such a reaction. They waited to see if the Marchesa would continue, but she simply turned away from them and said, 'That will be all.'

Rosa was taken to the laundry room where she waited with Signora Guerrini. The housekeeper wrung her hands and her eyes flickered to the window every few minutes. Rosa could tell she was worried that her insinuations would result in more grievous consequences than she had anticipated and that she might be implicated too. Half an hour later Rosa heard Signor Bonizzoni and Signor Collodi speaking as they came down the stairs. The men walked past the laundry window, carrying Maria's body on a stretcher towards the garage. They had wrapped the corpse in a blanket but a pool of blood was seeping through it. The body looked diminutive, like a child's. The sight gave Rosa the strength to speak finally.

'I was with Clementina all afternoon. You can ask her yourself,' she told Signora Guerrini. 'And before that I was playing my flute near the bear. Ada saw me.'

'Yes, yes, I'm sure it will be sorted out,' said Signora Guerrini, twisting her apron in her hands. 'That stupid, stupid girl. She's brought trouble on all of us.'

Rosa tried to recall anyone who might be able to help her. She remembered the maid who had spoken with Maria at the garden party. The girl had obviously known that Vittorio was Maria's lover. But what would be the point of involving her? She would become another innocent person caught up in the mess. Rosa realised that the only hope for her to keep her position at the Villa Scarfiotti would be if the Marchese arrived before whoever Mussolini was sending and intervened on her behalf. Otherwise she was sure she was going to be sent back to the convent and would never see Clementina again.

When Rosa heard a car coming down the driveway just after nine o'clock, she prayed it was the Marchese. Her heart fell to her feet when Signor Bonizzoni walked into the room followed by two men in fascist uniforms. The shorter of the two was in his thirties and seemed agitated. He kept taking a handkerchief from his pocket and wiping it across his sweaty brow and cheeks. The taller man was older with piercing eyes and pockmarks on his cheeks. Signora Guerrini gave a cry, stood up and rushed towards the other side of the room, as if Rosa had a contagious disease.

'Is this her?' the man with the pockmarks asked, pointing to Rosa.

Signor Bonizzoni gave a cautious glance in Rosa's direction, then averted his eyes and nodded.

'I had nothing to do with the matter,' Rosa said.

'Well, a tribunal will decide that,' the short fascist said.

He grabbed Rosa by the arm and handcuffed her. There was no use struggling so she let herself be jostled out of the exterior door and around the side of the house. Parked in front of the villa was a van with mesh on the windows. Her legs gave beneath her when she realised she wasn't being sent back to the convent; she was being taken to prison.

Ada was out the front of the house, running up and down the steps like a crazed animal. The Marchesa was also there with Vittorio.

'Rosa, Rosa. What's happened?' Ada called. She tried to reach Rosa but the pockmarked fascist pushed her back.

'I didn't do anything wrong,' Rosa told her. 'I didn't do what Signora Guerrini said. I found Maria dying when I went to search for her after she didn't show up to look after Clementina.'

'I know, I know,' said Ada. Her eyes met Rosa's. She had to be careful because the Marchesa was watching. 'Remember the key,' she said under her breath. 'It will keep you safe as it did for so many years.'

The short fascist opened the door to the van and pushed Rosa inside. Although she didn't resist him he punched her in the breast for good measure. She collapsed backwards in pain. The motor started up, the van pulled away and Rosa felt her freedom vanishing from her. She thought of Dono the bear; now she was caged and humiliated too. She looked back at the villa and caught a glimpse of someone at the schoolroom window. Clementina! The girl was rubbing her face and crying.

The van picked up speed. Flashes of light illuminated the interior as it passed each lamppost. Rosa shivered when a purple flash flickered over her. She understood then that she was being sacrificed to save Vittorio and avoid another scandal. The Marchesa saw her as expendable; just like the man with the cowlick.

Part Two

SEVEN

The prison where Rosa was taken was a former convent. It retained the medieval look of a religious institution although it housed another kind of cloistered community now. The van stopped and the pockmarked fascist opened the doors. He bundled Rosa into the admissions room while his accomplice waited outside.

The fascist pushed Rosa towards a wooden bench. 'Sit!' he told her.

The prison warden appeared at the reception desk, tucking his shirt into his pants and smoothing his hair over his pate, as if he'd just woken from a nap. The fascist and the warden spoke in undertones. When they were finished, the warden picked up the telephone and barked some instructions. A guard and a nun, who was dressed entirely in white, appeared a few minutes later. The nun was stout with alabaster skin and thick eyebrows. Rosa's eyes darted from the nun to the damp-stained walls of the room. This isn't happening, she thought. The fascist seized her arm and forced her to stand in front of the reception desk. Then he left. Rosa heard the van's motor start up and the vehicle sped away.

The warden lit a cigarette and let it dangle from his lips when he spoke. 'Name?' he asked Rosa. 'Date of birth?'

He spoke with the same rhythm as the typewriter he was using to complete Rosa's form. She could almost hear the 'ding' at the end of each of his questions; then a slight pause before he rattled off the next one.

The warden turned to the guard. 'Section A,' he said. 'She's not been sentenced yet.'

'Sentenced?' asked Rosa, struggling to think clearly. 'What's the charge?'

The warden shuffled through the paperwork on his desk and exchanged a look with the guard. 'You'll be informed when you appear before the tribunal,' he told her.

'When will that be?' Rosa could barely get the words out, she was breathing so hard. Her stomach was a tight knot. Sentenced? Tribunal? *She hadn't done anything wrong.*

The warden shrugged, taking the cigarette from his lips and holding it in his fingertips. The nun cleared her throat and raised her caterpillar eyebrows. The warden took the hint and noticed that Rosa's dress was covered in blood.

'Fetch her a uniform, please, Suor Gabriella,' he said.

The nun took a prison tunic from a cupboard and led Rosa to a screen in the corner. 'You wouldn't normally have to wear this until you have been sentenced but I have nothing else to give you,' she said, biting her lip. She was diminutive, barely reaching Rosa's waist. The compassion in her voice made Rosa want to cry.

The guard undid Rosa's handcuffs so she could change her clothes. He noticed the chain with the cross and key around her neck and nodded to Suor Gabriella.

'I'm sorry,' the nun said to Rosa. 'You'll have to give that to me.'

'No, please!' cried Rosa. She felt as if she was being stripped of everything. The key was meant to keep her safe.

'Enough!' shouted the warden. 'This isn't a hotel! You do what you're told!'

'I'll put it in a safety box for you until you are released,'

Suor Gabriella assured her. Their eyes met and Rosa realised that the nun understood that several steps in the justice procedure were being overlooked.

Rosa stood behind the screen to change her clothes. The encrusted blood on her dress pulled her skin when she tugged it off, but the prison tunic was even rougher. It smelled like mouldy bread.

Rosa wasn't fingerprinted, photographed or searched. The guard threw her dress into a sack of rubbish when it should have been kept as evidence. It was clear that instead of recording her existence at the prison, the warden was doing his best to erase it.

'Take her,' the warden told the guard.

Rosa nearly swooned. The guard grabbed her arm to stop her falling. His sweaty fingertips squeezed her skin. 'Come on,' he said, flicking his tongue across his lips. 'It's not that bad. You'll be all right. The nuns are good here.'

With each set of gates they passed through, Rosa felt the walls closing further in on her. The blood pounded in her ears. This is a nightmare, she thought. This can't be real. They passed a dormitory where several women were asleep on wooden bunks with infants tucked up with them. Rosa wasn't put in there. She was taken to a row of single cells with steel doors. The cell she was allocated was fifteen feet long, seven feet wide, eight feet high. It was the same size as her room at the convent had been but there were bars on the window. Above the bed was a faded outline of a crucifix and some bent screws in the wall. It looked as though somebody had ripped the crucifix off with their fingers.

Rosa collapsed on the bunk and listened to the guard snap the lock shut. The finality of the situation hit her. She dropped her head into her hands and wept.

Rosa didn't sleep that night. She jumped at every sound in the corridor. She longed to have her flute with her; playing it would have given voice to her anxiety and bitterness. Why did Maria have to get involved with Vittorio? She was a pretty girl. Any of the male servants would have loved to have married her. Now she was dead and Rosa was in prison. Rosa lifted her hands and imagined her beloved instrument in them. It was at the villa and lost to her. She prayed that Clementina might find it and play it. It would be the only link between them now.

The following day Rosa had contact with no-one except a bad-tempered nun whose rotund body resembled a water-logged sponge. She lumbered into the cell with a bowl of thin broth, stale bread and wine diluted with water. The wine tasted sour but Rosa drank it anyway because she was thirsty.

'When will I be sentenced?' she asked the nun.

The nun's face pinched. 'I don't know! Don't speak to me! I know nothing!'

The nun left and Rosa's mood plummeted further. She remembered Ada's instruction to hold onto the key: *It will keep you safe as it did for so many years*. In the light of what had happened, Rosa could not see any significance in the key or what Ada had wished to tell her. All she could think about was surviving this terrible dream.

When she still had not been charged three days later, a stark fear churned in her belly. The Marchesa was personal friends with Mussolini. Maybe there was never going to be any charge or hearing. Maybe she had simply been locked away.

'Can I write a letter?' she asked the obese nun when she brought her supper. She wanted to contact Don Marzoli. Surely he would be able to help her.

'No!' the nun said, turning away. 'Stop asking me. You plotted against the state. You're not allowed any contact.'

Rosa stared at the nun in disbelief. Plotting against the state was a serious crime committed by intellectuals and revolutionaries — people like the activists Antonio Gramsci and Camilla Ravera — not humble governesses like herself. Even if abortion was against the law, Maria had not been thinking of the state when she tried to get rid of her child.

The nun left and Rosa felt ill, not with a physical disorder but with an attack of nerves. She paced the cell like Dono paced his cage, and swung from feeling sorry for Maria to berating the dead girl for her stupidity.

Rosa was kept in the cell on her own for the next three weeks. She did none of the things she had read about prisoners in novels doing: scratching out the days on the wall of her cell or tapping messages to other prisoners. She had no idea who occupied the other cells. She only heard movements behind the steel doors when one of the nuns led her down the corridor to empty her chamber pot. There was no hollering of desperate captives, no drifting of broken voices. If she hadn't seen her own excrement mix with that of other human beings when she emptied her pot into the pit, she might have thought she was the only prisoner there. She passed her days as if in a trance, trying not to think of anything: not the future, nor the present nor the past.

Then one morning a guard woke her early. 'Hurry up!' he said. 'Someone is here to see you!'

Rosa was groggy with sleep but slipped on her prison clogs and followed the guard to a room that contained a table and two chairs. One of the chairs was occupied by a man in a fascist uniform. He had sunken cheeks and lifeless eyes. His mouth narrowed to a slit when he saw Rosa. The spite in his gaze chilled her blood.

'You are accused of a crime of the most serious nature,' he said. 'You have set yourself up as an enemy of the state.'

The second time Rosa heard that accusation was almost as much of a shock as the first. 'When is the trial?' she asked, her voice barely audible.

A look of distaste filled the official's face. 'Trial? There is no trial. You stay here until you are reformed.'

Rosa found the courage to speak up. 'There are witnesses at the Villa Scarfiotti who know that I had nothing to do with the death of Maria Melossi,' she said.

The official pursed his lips. 'If I were you,' he said coldly, 'I wouldn't mention the Scarfiotti family. You have never heard of them. Never worked for them. Say nothing of your time there. Until we are sure of your silence, you stay here.'

When the guard was taking Rosa back to her cell, they passed a nun leading an elderly prisoner towards the infirmary. The prisoner walked with tiny, pigeon-toed steps and she leaned heavily on the nun. She glanced at Rosa with world-weary eyes and Rosa wondered what kind of judge would send such a frail old woman to prison. Then it occurred to her that the prisoner might have been sentenced when she was a young woman and had been in prison all her life. I'm finished, Rosa thought. *I've been buried alive.*

Back in her cell, she wept bitterly. She could be in prison for years without any way to present her case. The Marchesa had more influence with Mussolini than Rosa had anticipated. And Il Duce, it seemed, was not above circumventing the due processes of the law.

'What's wrong?'

Rosa looked up to see a guard peering at her through the window in the door.

'I'm fifteen! I'm innocent!' she cried. 'I don't belong in prison! I swear before God I've done nothing wrong!'

She heard the key turn in the lock and the door opened. The guard stepped inside her cell. He was the guard who had been in the admissions area the night she had arrived at the prison. She remembered him by his fastidiously combed hair and five-o'clock shadow. He had even features and could have been handsome but somehow wasn't.

'Only fifteen?' he said, hitching up his pants a little higher. 'That's too bad. But in my opinion they are simply trying to scare you. They send the real anti-fascists to Trani or Ponza, which are much harsher places than this. The Madre Superiora here is sympathetic to political prisoners, although she has to be careful not to antagonise the Blackshirts.'

Rosa's tears dried. These were the first words of encouragement she had heard in weeks. The guard smiled at her. His teeth were straight but yellow. The guard's uniform was neat but he had sweat stains under his arms. There was something incongruous about him that Rosa couldn't put her finger on. Yet he seemed to mean well.

'How do you know so much about the other prisons?' she asked.

'I've worked in most of them,' he replied. 'I move around.' Then, scratching his head, the guard asked Rosa, 'Don't you have any family? Someone who can write to Mussolini for a pardon on your behalf?'

'No,' said Rosa, looking at her hands.

'No family?' said the guard, his voice rising a pitch. 'No-one to look out for you?'

Rosa shook her head. 'The priest for the convent where I was brought up would help, but I'm not allowed to write letters.'

The guard clucked his tongue. 'There are ways around that. I'll bring you some writing materials and I'll give your letter to the Madre Superiora. As long as she approves, it will be sent out with the prison mail.'

The glimmer of hope the guard gave Rosa hit her heart like a sunbeam. 'Thank you,' she said.

'See,' he said, 'you're much prettier when you smile. I told you things are not so bad here.'

Rosa wrote a letter to Don Marzoli, begging him to come and see her at the prison. She gave it to the guard, whose name, she learned, was Osvaldo. Then she lay on her bunk with her hand over her eyes and imagined that she was back in the schoolroom with Clementina. She recalled the details of their lessons together: the sound of Clementina's pen scratching out her sums; the smell of gorgonzola wafting from the tray of food Ada had prepared for lunch; Clementina's small hands over the piano keyboard when she practised her scales. Rosa decided that when she was released she would return to the convent and take holy vows. Somehow she would convince the Badessa that she was meant for the life of a nun. *I'm not made for the outside* world, that's for sure, she thought, recalling the fleeting pleasures she had experienced on her first day on Via Tornabuoni. She remembered the strange fashions, the joy of new shoes and the dashing Signor Parigi. None of those things meant anything now.

As well as having to remain in her cell at mealtimes, Rosa was sent by herself to the exercise yard. She heard other prisoners moving along the corridor to spend time in the yard for several minutes each day but she was allowed into the yard only twice a week and was often left there for hours at a time, sometimes under the watch of a guard and sometimes under the supervision of Suor Gabriella. Rosa sensed there was something different about Suor Gabriella: she was not hard like the other nuns. She would have liked to turn to her for solace, but contact beyond basic communication was forbidden for political prisoners. It was as if Rosa wasn't a person any more. Not even a prisoner. She had become a ghost.

She did not hear back from Don Marzoli.

'Ah, the Madre Superiora has contacted him herself,' Osvaldo reassured her when she asked if there had been a reply. 'Together they are working to get you released. But you have to be patient. These things take time.'

Rosa agreed to be patient but asked if Osvaldo would deliver another letter for her. This time she wrote to Suor Maddalena, pouring out her sorrows to her former guardian and asking for her prayers.

Tears trickled down Rosa's face when she handed the letter to Osvaldo. 'The letter will be sent soon, won't it?' she asked.

'Of course,' he said, taking the envelope and slipping it into his pocket. 'I told you that I would help you. I'll keep my promise.'

At the beginning of autumn, Rosa was taken to the exercise yard and was surprised to see another prisoner standing at the far end.

'You are not to speak to her,' Osvaldo warned Rosa. 'We have to put you in together to save watch time.'

The yard was a narrow enclosure with a bench at either end. The only exercise that could be performed in it was to walk up and down its short length. When Rosa and the other prisoner passed each other, they exchanged glances but then quickly looked away. The woman was about forty years old. Rosa could tell from the noble line of her neck that she'd once been handsome, but time had ravaged her beauty. The woman's skin was covered in fine wrinkles and age-spotted by the sun. Rosa assumed that because she and the woman were not allowed to speak with each other, and because they were alone in the yard, that she was a political prisoner too.

The next time they were in the exercise yard, the women held each other's gaze for longer. Rosa thought the other woman seemed gentle. The impression surprised her because there was nothing gentle about being in prison.

One day, when Suor Gabriella was on duty, the woman spoke to Rosa when they passed each other.

'Are you a political prisoner too?' she asked.

Rosa's heart beat like thunder in her chest. Having had no-one to talk to for so long, her voice had dried up. She simply nodded. For weeks now, she had lived in her head, but the woman had taken a risk in communicating with her and Rosa wanted to share it.

The next time they passed each other, Rosa asked, 'Why are you here?'

'I protested against female teachers being paid less than men, and not being able to teach science and maths,' the woman replied. 'I've been in prison for two years.'

Rosa walked on and the other prisoner did the same. So the woman was a teacher. Rosa was thrilled by the idea that they had something in common.

When they passed each other again, Rosa hurriedly whispered, 'I was a governess. My name is Rosa.'

'Sibilla,' answered the woman, coughing into her hand to avoid being seen talking. 'I'm pleased to make your acquaintance.'

The conversation ended when another guard arrived with a group of prisoners to take the women's place in the yard. But when they were called to return to their cells, Rosa and Sibilla exchanged secret smiles.

The next time Rosa was taken to the exercise yard, her heart leaped with joy when she saw Sibilla was there again. 'My husband was a university professor,' Sibilla explained to Rosa in successive passes. 'He wouldn't join the fascists and spoke against them. They were going to arrest him but he fled to Paris and has been living there in exile for four years. I've been under watch ever since. Then they finally found a reason to imprison me.'

'They don't always need a reason,' said Rosa.

Sibilla frowned. Rosa looked up and saw that Suor Gabriella had seen them talking. Her stomach lurched. Her fear wasn't so much that her sentence would be extended for talking to Sibilla but that the brief exchange of words she shared with another human being would be terminated. The fascists were achieving their aim of turning her into a ghost. Talking with Sibilla was the only way she had of resisting them. Suor Gabriella turned her back on the women.

Sibilla sighed with relief. 'She's all right, that one. Sometimes I think she feels sorry for those of us imprisoned for our ideals.'

'I can't imagine how you've lasted two years,' Rosa said. 'I've only been here a few months and I think I'm going mad. They don't allow me to speak to anyone. I'm only referred to as a number.'

Sibilla nodded grimly. 'You have to fight the battle for your mind. You must think constantly about what you will do when you get out of here. That will pull you through.'

'Is that what you do?' asked Rosa, feeling grateful for Sibilla's encouragement.

A troubled expression clouded Sibilla's eyes, but then she smiled. 'I think of Pythagoras when things get to me. He's my hero.'

'Pythagoras!' Rosa exclaimed, then checked herself for speaking too loudly. 'The nun who raised me loved to study Pythagoras from the books in the convent library,' she whispered, feeling a warmth as she remembered Suor Maddalena's regard for the Greek philosopher.

'Isn't that unusual for a nun?' Sibilla asked, raising her eyebrows. 'Pythagoras believed in reincarnation.'

'He taught the immortality of the soul and asceticism,' Rosa said, remembering her own reading. 'But the nuns studied him because of his theories of music, astronomy and mathematics rather than his philosophies.'

Sibilla nodded approvingly. 'It sounds like you were brought up by cultured nuns.'

'I was,' agreed Rosa. 'They were cloistered but they weren't ignorant. I was lucky.'

'Well, then,' said Sibilla, checking over Rosa's shoulder to see if they were being watched, 'Pythagoras believed one's highest purpose was to pursue enlightenment and knowledge, to become the fullest person one can be. For some reason we've been given this experience to realise that.'

'What have you learnt?' Rosa asked, hungry to take in every piece of wisdom she could from Sibilla.

Her companion raised her eyes and smiled. 'I've learnt that if the soul is immortal, then one never has to fear death.'

Rosa sensed Sibilla would like to say more but Suor Gabriella turned around and they quickly separated. The nun might be more lenient than the other guards but they still had to be careful.

The next time Rosa was in the exercise yard with Sibilla it was under the watch of Osvaldo and, as he was in the habit of staring at them, they couldn't talk. But even though they couldn't speak, they exchanged looks that were full of warmth and friendship. They would have to wait patiently for another chance to share their ideas.

*

A few days later, Rosa was lying on her bunk when Osvaldo arrived at her cell, grinning ear to ear. She'd been trying to follow Sibilla's advice about fighting for her mind by recalling everything she knew about Pythagoras. She remembered that he'd been in prison too, in Babylon.

'I have arranged something special for you,' Osvaldo said.

'What?' asked Rosa, standing. Had Don Marzoli finally come to see her?

'Come this way,' he said, unlocking the door to let her out.

Osvaldo led her past the exercise yard to a workroom where rows of prisoners sat at knitting equipment and electrically powered sewing machines.

'Usually political prisoners are not allowed out of their cells,' he said. 'But I have permission from the Madre Superiora for you to work here.'

The workroom supervisor set Rosa to the task of braiding straw for wine casks. The chore was a disappointment in comparison to the visit from Don Marzoli she had been hoping for, but Osvaldo was right: it was better than sitting in her cell and doing nothing.

'The money you earn will be held for your release,' Osvaldo told her.

Rosa's task was a solitary one but at least she had the chance to *see* the other prisoners. They were a mix of ages. Some looked depressed, while others looked resigned to making the best of their lot. Rosa tried to match the crime to the woman: murder, theft, prostitution. But she would never know if her guesses were correct. She couldn't have spoken with anyone even if she wasn't in a corner on her own. The guards in the workroom were vigilant; they had to be with so many sharp objects in the prisoners' hands. When Osvaldo was on duty he was forever sneaking glances and smiles in Rosa's direction. Rosa returned his smiles because he had been kind to her, but she couldn't help feeling obligated to him in a way that made her uncomfortable. She wondered why Sibilla was never in the workroom. Surely she should be allowed to earn money for her release too? Protesting unfair wages couldn't be any worse a crime than the one Rosa had been accused of.

Winter arrived and the air through the cell window was cold. Whenever Osvaldo was on duty in solitary confinement, Rosa begged him for news from Don Marzoli. His answer was always the same: 'He is waiting for an appointment to be fixed with the Fascist Party officials in Florence. You must be patient. These things take time.'

Despite the cold, Rosa was still sent to the exercise yard twice a week. The contact with Sibilla was a lifeline. Usually when she returned to her cell after being with Sibilla, Rosa felt better than when she had left it, but sometimes she felt worse. She would have to harden herself again until the next time she met her friend. Rosa constantly feared that Sibilla might be swapped with another prisoner, but by some grace that hadn't happened yet. Then, a few days before Christmas, Sibilla and Rosa experienced a miracle. They were walking in the yard, stamping their feet and beating their arms to keep warm, when the prison alarm sounded. They looked at each other.

'Someone's escaped,' said Sibilla.

The guard who was watching them locked the gate to the exercise yard and fled to join the search. They were left alone and unsupervised. Such a thing had never happened before.

'Come,' Sibilla said to Rosa, taking her by the arm. 'Let's huddle in the corner. We can pretend we had to stay together to keep warm after we were abandoned.'

It was freezing and the women only had their prison clogs on their feet and a padded jacket over their thin tunics. It wouldn't take much to pretend they were cold. But Rosa was thankful for the precious time together; she couldn't be happier even if she were sitting in the full rays of the sun. Sibilla and Rosa spoke of everything they had longed to share for the past months. They told each other about their favourite foods, music, paintings and even smells and times of the day — all the things that they had not spoken about for so long and which they had almost forgotten themselves. Rosa told Sibilla about her visions and how she saw the source of things.

Sibilla's eyes grew wide. 'Those visions are a sign,' she said. 'I believe you have them because you have a supernatural sympathy with animals. That's why when you see leather or fur or meat you see it for what it really is: something murdered. Pythagoras did too.'

Rosa considered what Sibilla had said. 'Yes,' she agreed. 'That makes sense to me — that animals have souls. They have spirits. *Just like us*. I'm seeing the spirits of the animals that have been killed to satisfy people's gluttony and vanity.'

It was a revelation to Rosa. The Church taught that animals didn't have souls or personalities; which was why Christians didn't have any qualms about killing them.

'What you are saying is against everything I have been taught,' Rosa said. 'I believe in God yet I'm starting to question some of the Church's teachings. But that's a sin, isn't it?'

Sibilla shook her head. 'Questioning things makes you a complete human being. If God created you, wouldn't He take delight in you being a full person? The Pythagorists believed that the earth's soil provides everything we need to eat and there was no need to inflict suffering on animals by slaughtering them for food. They believed humans and animals were linked spiritually and the harm mankind did to animals was what brought all sorts of troubles onto humans — like wars, plagues and disease.'

The women went on to talk about their interests. Rosa was in awe to discover that Sibilla had read the Greek philosophers who had been influenced by Pythagoras too — Socrates, Aristotle, Plato.

'And you speak French, English and German?' exclaimed Sibilla. 'How can you hold so many languages in your head?'

'There weren't a lot of distractions at the convent,' Rosa explained. 'For me, learning each new language was like exploring the world from my classroom. Once I'd mastered French, I couldn't stop "travelling".'

'Not having learnt French is my greatest regret,' said Sibilla. 'After not having children with my husband before he went into exile. French is the language of romance.'

'I can teach you,' Rosa offered. 'When we pass each other in the yard ... I can give you a phrase at a time.'

Sibilla laughed and hugged Rosa. It was the first time anyone had embraced her since she had been with Clementina. It warmed her.

'Yes, that would be wonderful,' said Sibilla. 'Sometimes at night I imagine I am there with Alberto in Paris. I can speak to him in French in my dreams.'

The women fell silent for a moment. Their lips were turning blue and their feet were frozen. Yet neither of them wished for their time together outside to end.

'How did you meet your husband?' Rosa asked through chattering teeth.

Sibilla pulled her tunic over her legs as far as it would go. 'We were in an astronomy class together at university. We fell in love gazing at Venus.'

Rosa's toes tingled. She thought of the couple she had seen kissing in the Boboli Gardens and then, to her surprise, she thought of Signor Parigi. 'It must be nice to be in love,' she said.

'Stand up!' a voice shouted.

The women jumped apart at the command. The guard had returned. He was about to shout something else but one look at their pale faces and blue lips and he decided against it. He'd been negligent in his duties. Any longer in the cold and they might both have come down with pneumonia.

'Move this way,' he said, ordering them out of the yard.

*

July, the month of her incarceration, came around again and Rosa remained in prison. She tried to take consolation in Osvaldo's assurances that Don Marzoli and the Madre Superiora were making progress on her case, but she was frustrated.

'Why doesn't Don Marzoli come to see me?' Rosa asked Osvaldo one day.

'Perhaps he feels it would compromise your case. Perhaps he wants to appear impartial.'

Osvaldo's reasoning made no sense to Rosa. 'I'm not allowed to go to chapel,' she said. 'I can't take communion. I'm not only being cut off from life and other human beings but from God.'

'You are full of complaints today,' said Osvaldo, looking at Rosa disapprovingly. 'Don't you appreciate what I'm doing for you? I'm taking risks to help you.'

'Of course I appreciate it,' Rosa was quick to reassure him. She didn't want to offend Osvaldo, he was her only hope of contact with the outside world.

'I'm glad you do,' he said, placing his hand on her shoulder. Rosa cringed. Something about Osvaldo revolted her, but she couldn't say what.

Rosa was more genuinely appreciative of Suor Gabriella who, she had discovered, was in charge of the exercise yard timetables. Rosa and Sibilla had been caught talking more than once, but they were still put in the exercise yard together twice a week. Suor Gabriella was obviously turning a blind eye. Could such kindness exist in a place like this? Rosa's snatched conversations with Sibilla, now imbued with French phrases and mathematical questions, were what was keeping her mind alive. She was sure she would not have survived prison for a year without Sibilla's friendship.

Late one night, long after lights out, Rosa was tossing in her bed from a bad dream when she heard the latch on her cell door click open. She sat up and saw Osvaldo in the light from the corridor. He closed the door behind him.

'What is it?' Rosa asked, rubbing the sleep from her face.

Osvaldo put his finger to his lips. He sat next to her on the bunk. His close proximity made her uncomfortable. She shifted.

'I have a letter for you from Don Marzoli,' he said.

Rosa's groggy mind pulled in several directions. 'A letter?' She swung her legs to the floor and stood up. 'May I see it?'

Osvaldo passed her his torch and she switched it on. He didn't have any letter in his hands. In the dim light Rosa could see that his eyes were bloodshot. He reeked of alcohol.

'Let me see it?' she pleaded. 'I've waited for a year.'

Osvaldo raised his hand and placed it on Rosa's hip. Her blood turned cold and she yanked herself free.

'Let me touch you,' he whispered.

'No,' said Rosa, backing away. She didn't understand what Osvaldo wanted but she knew something was wrong. Every nerve in her body was charged. She would have run for the door if it wasn't locked.

'Don't tease me,' he said, standing up. 'After the way you've been making eyes at me. Let me touch you.'

'No!' Rosa said again, trying not to cry. Making eyes at him? What did he mean? She couldn't get the air in and out of her lungs fast enough — the room seemed to be spinning.

Osvaldo lunged at her and crushed her to his chest, his fingers travelling down her back. Rosa shoved him away and he staggered off balance. He lurched at her again, this time grabbing her more fiercely.

'Don't struggle,' he said, his breathing agitated.

'Please, leave me alone,' Rosa begged.

Osvaldo pressed his mouth hard against hers. His tongue rubbed against her teeth. It revolted her so much she thought she might be sick. She writhed in an attempt to free herself but Osvaldo was too strong. He grabbed her by the arm and flung her on the bunk. She fell on her stomach and tried to get up but he pinned her down with one hand, leaning his weight on her back. With his other hand he pulled Rosa's tunic up to her waist and tore at her underwear. Rosa remembered Don Marzoli's sermon about a woman who lost her modesty losing everything. Was this what he had meant? She felt Osvaldo push himself against her and began to weep.

'Don't make a sound,' Osvaldo said, clamping his hand over her mouth. 'Don't be scared. I've been patient enough, waiting all this time for you. Now you're sixteen, you can take it.'

Pain pierced Rosa between the thighs and she knew something terrible had happened. Her mouth opened in a mute scream. Osvaldo thrust into her so forcefully that she passed out from the pain. When she regained consciousness he had turned her over and was thrusting from the front. His twisted face panting and sweating over her made Rosa cry out but the sound was muffled by his hand on her mouth. She felt that she was being torn in two.

Then it was over. Osvaldo sat back and tugged up his pants.

'Next time it won't hurt so much,' he said to her.

He tried to kiss her again but she turned away from him, curling into a ball. She heard him lock the door behind him when he left. Something sticky and hot leaked from the raw spot between her legs. She remembered Maria and wondered if her insides were coming out. In that case, she hoped she would die quickly — or at least that she would never see the morning.

A few hours later, she heard a voice and felt a hand touching her shoulder. She opened her eyes, terrified that Osvaldo had returned. The cell was full of light. Sunlight was streaming through the bars of the window. Suor Gabriella was standing over her.

'Good gracious,' she said, looking Rosa over and covering her with the blanket. 'Good gracious.'

The obese nun, Suor Chiara, was standing in the

doorway. 'Go tell the Madre Superiora,' Suor Gabriella said to her. 'We have to take her to the infirmary.'

'What's happened to her?' Suor Chiara asked. 'Why has she torn her clothes?'

'Go tell the Madre Superiora now!' Suor Gabriella hissed between her teeth. 'This poor girl needs help. She's been violated.'

EIGHT

Rosa never saw Osvaldo again. The Madre Superiora had him removed from the prison when she learned what had happened. Rosa thought she might die of the shame. Her world, already dark after being put in prison, grew darker. She stopped eating. Suor Gabriella brought her food not available to the other prisoners to tempt her to eat again: roasted aubergines and tomatoes, cucumbers and pears. But Rosa barely touched them. No matter how many times she washed herself she couldn't get rid of the musky stink of Osvaldo. He had raped her so violently that a week after the attack she still bled when she urinated. Rumours were running rife in the prison, and Rosa was kept out of sight. She wasn't taken to the workroom any more or to the exercise yard, although the person she yearned to see most was Sibilla.

One morning, several weeks after the attack, Suor Chiara arrived at Rosa's cell and told her to get up. Rosa thought she was being sent to the infirmary because, now she was eating again, she was throwing up her food. But instead she was taken to a room with bars running down the centre of it. On either side of the bars were chairs. When they entered the room, Rosa saw someone dressed in black rise to meet her.

'Rosa?'

It was Don Marzoli.

In other circumstances the sight of the priest would have filled her with joy. Instead, when Rosa saw the shock on his face, she felt only humiliation. She understood how she must appear to him — emaciated, her hair cut short … soiled. She was no longer the bright young woman he had sent to be a governess at the Villa Scarfiotti.

'It's taken me all this time to find out where you were,' Don Marzoli said, after he had recovered himself. 'Otherwise I would have come straightaway. When Suor Maddalena raised her concerns that you hadn't come to visit, we contacted the Villa Scarfiotti and they said they didn't know where you were. That you had simply left.'

Rosa blinked. 'You didn't get my letters?' she asked. 'Didn't the Madre Superiora contact you?'

Don Marzoli shook his head.

Rosa felt nauseated. Osvaldo had lied. For getting her hopes up for nothing, he may as well have raped her again.

Don Marzoli glanced at his hands before turning back to Rosa. 'My child, the prison director says you are here because … because you helped a woman lose her baby. Rosa, this can't be true. You know that the murder of an infant is a terrible crime against God.'

The questioning look in his eyes hurt Rosa. He was searching in her face for her innocence, something of the former Rosa to take back to Suor Maddalena. She tried to find some emotion inside herself. For so long it had not mattered that she was innocent.

'Rosa?'

She stared at her lap, trying to think. She saw things differently now from how she had when she'd thought Osvaldo was helping her. If she told Don Marzoli she was innocent, he would move heaven and earth to get her out of prison. He might even approach the Pope. But Mussolini himself was involved in her imprisonment. If Don Marzoli tried to free Rosa, it could cause trouble for the convent. God forbid, they might even put Suor Maddalena and the others in prison. Rosa shivered and bit her lip. A terrible image of Suor Maddalena enduring what Osvaldo had performed on her sprang into her mind. She almost cried out.

'Rosa?' Don Marzoli implored her with his eyes.

It took the last piece of hope Rosa had left in her to do it, but she realised it was better if Don Marzoli and Suor Maddalena believed she was guilty. They would pray for her, but they wouldn't try to get her out of prison. It would be up to God alone then to decide when she had suffered enough.

'I only wanted to help her,' Rosa said.

Don Marzoli's face collapsed. He bowed his head and twisted his hands. It was a few moments before he could look at Rosa again. 'You don't repent of it?'

Rosa hesitated then shook her head.

Don Marzoli stood up, unsteady on his feet. 'Then I am sorry for you, child. You are lost,' he said. The next moment he was gone.

One day, Rosa was finishing the bread she had been given for breakfast when she realised that she'd lost track of time. The air through the window was growing cool but her monthly period hadn't arrived. When had she last had it? Perhaps it's because I stopped eating for a while, she thought. She had a sudden urge to urinate but after doing so she felt heavier not lighter. Her breasts were swollen and sore and her tunic was tight across her stomach. After all that had happened, how could she have put on weight? She slumped down on her bunk. Something was wrong with her body. Maybe Osvaldo had injured her so badly inside that now she was dying.

'Come on,' said Suor Gabriella, unlocking her cell door.

Rosa looked up. 'Where am I going?' she asked.

Suor Gabriella smiled. 'To the exercise yard.'

When Rosa saw Sibilla waiting for her in the exercise yard, she was so relieved that she almost forgot everything. Sibilla gave a cry of surprise. 'I've been so worried,' she said, clutching Rosa in her arms. Suor Gabriella made no attempt to stop the women from speaking to each other.

Sibilla turned Rosa's face to hers. 'What happened?' she asked, her eyes full of anguish. 'Nobody would tell me where you were.'

Rosa swallowed and tried to speak but couldn't answer. She could not take her eyes from Sibilla's face.

'You're so pale! When did you last see the sun?' Sibilla asked. 'I thought that they'd changed the schedule. Now I can see something terrible has happened!'

Rosa's legs nearly gave way beneath her. Sibilla helped her to the bench. She did not take her eyes off Rosa when she told her, in halting sentences, about the rape. It was a few moments before Sibilla could move or speak.

'May that monster burn in hell!' she muttered finally. She clasped Rosa's hands in her own. 'He's not here any more, is he? I haven't seen him. They've got rid of him?'

Rosa nodded.

'Thank God!' she said, clutching Rosa to her again. 'You must never think of him again. You must put this terrible thing behind you.'

'I can't,' Rosa said, her voice breaking. 'He's made me sick. I think I'm going to die here and never see the outside world again.'

'Sick?'

Rosa stared at the ground and recounted her symptoms: tender breasts, dizziness and nausea. The disappearance of her monthly periods. Sibilla brought her hand to her face. Rosa's heart skipped a beat. She truly feared the worst now. Sibilla was a mature woman; she knew what was wrong with her.

'Rosa, do you understand how babies are made?' Sibilla asked.

Rosa was puzzled by the question. 'They come after a man and woman spend lots of time together.'

That was all she knew. She had gathered that it was because Maria had spent a lot of time with Vittorio that she had become pregnant. She sensed that something happened between men and women to create children, but she hadn't been able to piece everything together.

Sibilla looked at her askance. 'Tell Suor Gabriella that you must see the nurse.'

Rosa stared at Sibilla, not comprehending.

Sibilla sighed. 'I don't see to what purpose the Church keeps young women ignorant,' she said. 'Rosa, when Osvaldo put his organ inside you, he might have made you pregnant.'

'His organ?' Rosa shuddered. She remembered the terrible pain between her thighs. She couldn't contemplate that such a horrific act could make a child. 'No, no,' she said. 'That can't be true! I'm too young! I'm not married!'

Sibilla took Rosa's hand and considered her with pity. She said nothing more.

Rosa spent the next few days willing her period to come. She clung to the illusion that it was all a nightmare and she would wake up. But her period didn't come and she only grew fatter. She realised with a heavy heart that she had no choice but to see the nurse.

The prison infirmary was icy. The hissing steam heater in the corner failed to warm it. Rosa changed into the examination gown and followed the nurse barefoot across the chipped tiled floor. She stood on the scales as instructed. The nurse was a different one from the nurse who had treated Rosa after the rape. She was a colourless woman with cold hands and an even colder manner.

'You've been here since July 1930?' the nurse said. It was a rhetorical question because the information was on the sheet of paper she was checking off.

She told Rosa to lie down on the bench and listened unsympathetically to her answers to questions about symptoms. She felt Rosa's stomach and took her temperature. Then she made Rosa go behind a curtain and urinate into a bottle.

'The urine test will confirm it,' said the nurse, scribbling on her notepad. 'But it's quite obvious that you are pregnant.'

The confirmation was like a lightning strike. Was God punishing her? Any child of Osvaldo's would be a monster! Rosa remembered Maria. Sometimes Rosa hated her because of all the trouble the maid's stupidity had caused her. But today she couldn't hate her. She understood the desperation that she had felt.

'What will happen?' she asked.

The nurse clucked her tongue. 'Will the father recognise the child?'

How could Rosa say who the father was? She would never even utter his name. Never, so long as she lived. She shook her head.

The nurse's mouth turned down. 'You'll have the child with you until it is two years old and then it will be given to an orphanage. You can claim the child after you are released. *If* you are released. Now get dressed.'

Rosa did as she was told. Before she left the infirmary, the nurse grabbed her by the arm and peered into her face. 'So, you've been here for over a year and you are pregnant. What did the guard give you? A pack of cigarettes?'

Rosa did her best to hold back her tears. This was what she was now: human dirt. Anyone could abuse her. The nurse gave her a shove towards the door and called Suor Chiara to escort her back to her cell.

Before Suor Chiara arrived, the nurse glared at Rosa and said, 'You whores are all the same. You never change. Even when they stick you in here you still can't keep your legs together.'

I'm not a whore, thought Rosa. That's not why I was put in prison. But for all that's happened to me, I may as well be one.

*

The next time Rosa saw Sibilla a male guard was watching over them so they had to speak in snatches when they passed each other.

'I'll never love this child,' Rosa wept.

Sibilla's head snapped up. 'You will love the baby!'

'A child born of ... born of *that*?'

'You won't love it any less because of how it was conceived,' Sibilla whispered. On the next pass, she added: 'Each child is a miracle, a slate yet to be written on. I might not have children of my own, but I have held my nieces and nephews.'

'But the shame ...' cried Rosa.

'Shame?' exclaimed Sibilla. 'There's only one person who should feel shame and that's not you or the baby. Rosa, you might be confused now, but trust me, you will love the baby.'

It rained for the next few weeks and Rosa had no chance to discuss her troubles further with Sibilla in the yard. Her friend was convinced that she wouldn't love the baby any less because of how it was conceived. But Rosa was beginning to realise that how it was conceived was only one of the many troubles she faced. She was unmarried and in prison. Even if she was released, how would she support a child?

None of this would have happened if not for the Marchesa Scarfiotti, Rosa thought. She has ruined my life!

Rosa cried herself to sleep every night for a week.

The nuns knew how Rosa had become pregnant and when they explained the slur it was on the prison to the director he agreed to bend the rules and allow Rosa to attend chapel. She tried to find solace in God. Suor Gabriella gave her a Bible, the only book she had been given the whole time she had been in prison. Rosa looked up her favourite verse from Jeremiah, where God says his plans for his children are always for their ultimate good, not to cause them pain. But how can any good come of this? she wondered.

As time went on, Rosa found herself in a constant turmoil of love and hate: hate for Osvaldo; and, as Sibilla had predicted, love for the baby. Once she started to feel the child move inside her, Rosa decided she wasn't going to punish an innocent life for something that it had played no role in creating. She would close her eyes and imagine the baby growing in her womb. She saw its pink form, the buds of its ears, its tiny hands and feet. It occurred to her that when the child was born, she would no longer be alone in the world. She would be connected by blood with another person. 'A miracle' Sibilla had called it. Was it possible that the child was somehow *meant* to be? Rosa had thought that Osvaldo had destroyed all her chances for happiness, but when she placed her hands on her belly she began to wonder if that was true. She thought of the life inside her and found sparks of joy exploding in her heart. She began to reject the possibility that the child would have anything of Osvaldo in it. After all, it was growing inside *her*. It was her baby, not his!

'Rosa, given that the nuns told you so little, forgive me if I am stating the obvious,' Sibilla said to her one day when they were walking past each other in the yard. 'But you do know that when the baby is born it will come out from between your legs?'

'Yes, I know,' said Rosa.

At some level she had understood this; she had seen what had happened to Maria. Still, Sibilla's statement came as something of a shock. That night, Rosa placed her hand between her legs and wondered how the baby would get out. They must be tiny when they are born, she thought.

Rosa's acceptance that she was bringing a child into the world woke her from the stupor that had enveloped her since she had been put in prison. She *had* to get out. She was allowed to return to the workroom to earn money for her child's needs, and with renewed vigour she asked Suor Gabriella for an interview with the prison director. She needed to protest not her innocence, for that was a moot point, but her willingness never to approach the Scarfiotti family or even to mention them. Suor Gabriella promised her that she would pursue the matter.

By the time the interview was granted Rosa was already seven months pregnant. A guard led her to the interview room and told her to sit down.

'Signor Direttore is busy at the present,' the guard told her, locking her into the room. 'You may have to wait some time.'

Rosa sat down in a chair. Her back was hurting and she felt a tiny elbow sticking into her stomach. There was a window in the interview room and through the dirty glass she could see the blue sky. The baby kicked. Rosa rubbed her belly. 'I'll get us out of here, little one,' she whispered to it.

Despite her advanced pregnancy, Rosa felt well. She had been given a reason to help herself and she was determined that whatever it took she was going to do it. She'd plead her allegiance to Mussolini if that would get her out.

She glanced at the clock on the wall. Fifteen minutes had passed. She rubbed her belly again and stood up from the chair and stared out the window. The baby was pressing on her bladder but she would have to bear it. She remembered the day that the Marchese had come to the convent and asked her to play the flute. Her bladder had caused her discomfort then. But that was a lifetime ago. She wished that she had played badly for him, she wished she had wet her pants, she wished anything that day had gone wrong and he had not chosen her. But the past is what it is, Rosa thought. I can't change it. I must move on. She glanced back to the clock. She had been waiting forty-five minutes.

The prison director strode in the door. Rosa stood to attention, in accordance with the prison rule. It was the first time she had ever met with the man. He was buck-toothed and weedy and the buttons on his uniform were undone. Yet this slovenly official held her fate in his hands. She had rehearsed this moment many times. She would not smile but she would not be sullen either. She would be suitably serious; contrite. She would not beg. She would simply put herself in the director's — and God's — hands.

'I see that you have made a productive effort in the workroom,' the director said, glancing at a file on the desk.

'Yes, Signor Direttore,' Rosa answered. 'I am saving up to support my child.'

The director glanced at Rosa's stomach and nodded before looking back to his file. 'Yes, quite,' he said. 'Well, I see the Madre Superiora's statement on your rehabilitation. I have to submit it to the Ministry of Justice. Then we will see what happens.'

The director sounded positive but Rosa was not out of danger yet. Her heart pounded in her chest so fiercely she was sure that he would hear it. 'Thank you,' she said.

'Sibilla,' Rosa asked her friend when they were in the exercise yard again, 'you said that you were arrested for protesting against women teachers being paid less than men?'

'Yes.'

'Why do they pay women less than men?'

Rosa was too heavily pregnant to keep up the charade of waddling up and down the yard. She stood on the spot while Sibilla walked past her.

'Well, the male teachers want to protect their jobs,' Sibilla explained. 'They argue that women need less and they aren't as productive. But that's just lies. The women I worked with could run circles around the men.'

'Why do you think they are paid less?'

Sibilla sighed. 'Because women don't have the right to vote and they don't have organised unions to protect them.

Many of them still consider themselves appendages to their husbands with no right to work and support themselves.'

Rosa adjusted her stance so the baby would sit more comfortably and thought about what Sibilla had said. She imagined what it would be like to have a husband who earned money and took care of her. She pictured a nice home and food on the table. She'd forgo the right to work and vote if she could have something as simple as that for herself and the baby. Tears filled Rosa's eyes because she knew that was not going to happen. No man would want her. It was going to be a struggle, especially if women were paid less than men for the same work. She realised how different she and Sibilla were from each other. Sibilla had once had a choice whether to work or not. Rosa never had.

'I don't need less,' Rosa said, cradling her stomach. 'I need more.'

When Rosa was in her eighth month of pregnancy, she found it difficult to sleep. Her dreams were full of sinister omens. She would see herself back at the Villa Scarfiotti, heavily pregnant and running through the woods with an unseen presence chasing her. She woke up bathed in sweat. One night, she tossed and turned until she finally found a comfortable position on the bunk and fell into a stupor. In her nightmares she heard voices: Sibilla; a guard; footsteps. Something was wrong. She tried to wake up but couldn't. Her eyelids were like lead.

When she was taken to the exercise yard the following day, Sibilla wasn't there. A male guard was on duty and Rosa couldn't ask him where Sibilla was. They've separated us, she thought, regretting that she'd spoken so openly with Sibilla the last time they were together. They are still torturing me. I haven't heard back about my release and now they've taken my only friend from me.

Rosa sat on the bench. Her ankles were too swollen to continue walking. She saw Suor Gabriella approach the guard and say something. He let her into the exercise yard. Something was wrong. Was Sibilla sick?

'Here,' Suor Gabriella said, giving Rosa a slip of paper. 'She wanted me to give this to you.'

'Sibilla?' A thought occurred to Rosa: maybe Sibilla had been released!

> *Dear Rosa,*
>   *How I longed that I should live to see*
> *your child born. I was sure that the baby*
> *would be exactly like its mother and no less*
> *beautiful. Tell your child about me and teach*
> *it to love Italy and be strong. The solace you*
> *have brought me these last few months is the*
> *greatest treasure I have ever received.*
> *Goodnight, my sweet friend.*
>   *Sibilla*

A chill trembled down Rosa's spine. Her heart beat faster. 'What does this mean?' she asked Suor Gabriella.

The nun averted her eyes. 'She was a leading member of Giustizia e Libertà, a personal enemy of Il Duce. Her husband was involved in a plot to assassinate him.'

Rosa clutched the note, still not comprehending. 'Sibilla was a teacher. She was arrested for standing up for women's rights.'

Suor Gabriella sighed. She had circles under her eyes and the lacklustre air of someone who hadn't slept properly. 'She was a condemned prisoner. An enemy of the state.'

'A condemned prisoner?' repeated Rosa, swallowing. She remembered what Osvaldo had said about political prisoners usually being sent to Trani or Ponza. 'Did they move her to another prison?'

The pained expression on Suor Gabriella's face sent Rosa's thoughts into disarray. 'What?' she asked, almost shrieking. 'What's happened?'

Rosa's distress caught the guard's attention but Suor Gabriella dismissed him with a wave of her hand. 'Sibilla Ciruzzi's final appeal was denied yesterday,' she told Rosa. 'She was taken outside Florence last night and shot.'

Rosa's shoulders crumpled and she felt nauseous. She recalled Sibilla's words: *I've learnt that if the soul is immortal, then one never has to fear death*; and understood that her friend had known that she was condemned.

'Sibilla!' Rosa cried, clutching her hands to her chest as if she could close the gaping hole that was opening in her heart. 'Sibilla!' Her despair echoed throughout the prison.

'Why?' she asked Suor Gabriella through her tears. 'Why? She's been here for two years. Couldn't they just let her be?'

But the nun was unable to say anything to comfort her. Rosa understood why. The only answer was one that was forbidden to be spoken. As long as Italy was in the clutches of a madman, there would be no justice.

NINE

One morning in early May, Rosa woke with a cramping pain in her pelvis and thighs. The bed was damp. Her first thought was of the baby. She threw off the blanket, terrified she might be haemorrhaging like Maria. But there was no blood. She climbed out of bed and moved about but the ache in her abdomen remained. She sat down on her bunk and the pain subsided. It's a false alarm, she thought. It's only night sweats.

Suor Chiara arrived with Rosa's breakfast. She was hungry and tried to eat the bread but it made her retch.

'Are you all right?' Suor Chiara asked her.

Rosa was about to tell her she was fine when her abdomen tightened and she had to grip the bunk for pain. 'The baby is coming,' she said.

'I'll fetch the nurse,' Suor Chiara told her.

Rosa walked up and down the cell. The pain subsided as quickly as it had come. It was another hour before the nurse arrived with Suor Gabriella and by then the pain was worse.

No matter how Rosa stood, sat or crouched she was uncomfortable.

'Do you have birth pangs?' the nurse asked her.

Rosa nodded. She assumed that was what the pains were. It felt like someone had tied a rope around her insides and was pulling it tight.

'You'd better take her to the infirmary,' Suor Gabriella told the nurse.

'She's not having the baby here,' replied the nurse. 'I've got my hands full with a prisoner with diphtheria. She's going to Santa Caterina. I've got permission from Signor Direttore.'

Another contraction seized Rosa, this one much stronger than the others. She doubled over. The nurse told her that the pains would be mild at first and spaced apart, but the pain Rosa was feeling was not mild. Each contraction sent spasms around her body. She felt nauseous.

'Come on then,' the nurse said. 'We'd better get you to the hospital while there is still time.'

'You're not going to make her walk there?' said Suor Gabriella, her eyebrows rising in horror.

'It's only a few streets away,' the nurse replied. 'We're not getting an ambulance.'

'Nurse, this girl is not walking,' said Suor Gabriella, her fists clenched in frustration. 'I will get a stretcher.' She strode to the cell door and called for assistance.

A contraction racked Rosa's body. Beads of sweat pricked her face. A few moments later two guards arrived with a stretcher. Suor Gabriella helped Rosa onto it and placed her hand on her shoulder. 'It will be easier after the first one.'

Rosa did her best to smile. Despite her discomfort, she appreciated Suor Gabriella's consideration. Apart from Sibilla, she was the only person who had been kind to her in prison.

The guards carried Rosa down the corridor. The prisoners in the dormitory came to the door to see what was going on. Most of them gawked but a few called out 'good luck' to Rosa when they realised she was in labour.

When the guards reached the yard, the director was waiting there. 'I've just received this morning the letter from the Ministry of Justice. You were due to be released today,' he told Rosa, placing a bundle wrapped in a handkerchief in her hand. 'But I will send someone to the hospital to complete the paperwork later.'

The director's words barely registered with Rosa. She looked at the bundle he had given her. Her chain was tucked inside the handkerchief. She clutched it to her chest. The silver key was in her possession again. It's a good omen, she thought, remembering that it had been given to her to protect her from danger.

'God bless you,' said Suor Gabriella before the guards passed through the gates.

Rosa felt the sun on her face. It was a beautiful spring day. The air was fresh with the smell of jasmine and roses. She placed her hand on her belly as another pain seized her. 'It's all right, little one,' she whispered to her unborn child. 'We will see this through together.'

The Santa Caterina was a charitable lying-in hospital for unwed mothers. Rosa shut her eyes to the stares of shopkeepers and the people on the street. A priest made a point of glaring at her then looking away. Her condition and the direction she was being taken brought sneers to the onlookers' faces and one surly blacksmith whistled a catcall. But Rosa shut the taunts out of her mind. Nothing was going to spoil this special day. People could look down on her if they wanted to but she would never allow them to look down on her child.

The guards carried her into the admissions area of the hospital. The building was cool and quiet. A nurse in a white uniform with black stockings and shoes stood up when the guards came inside.

'Will you being staying?' she asked them.

'There's no need,' said the guard holding the stretcher near Rosa's feet. 'She was due to be released today and she's not dangerous.'

The nurse nodded and called to an orderly to bring a trolley. The guards and the orderly helped Rosa move from the stretcher onto it. She was wheeled down a corridor and through a set of swing doors. Compared to the calm of the admissions area, the corridor was a cacophony of wails, moans and screams. Rosa's own pains were stronger than before. She gritted her teeth until the current contraction passed. The orderly left her outside a room on the trolley. Rosa could hear a woman screaming as if her legs were being cut off. She clenched her fists and did her best to quell her fears. Women died in childbirth, she knew that, but nothing must stop her from delivering her child safely.

Despite the pains and the noise, Rosa drifted off into a restless sleep. She was woken some time later by an orderly pushing the trolley into the room. A matron and a nurse were waiting for her there. All she could see from where she lay were a washbasin and a medicine cupboard stacked with cotton swabs, thermometers, throat sticks, gloves and bottles. The air was tinged with the smell of antiseptic.

'Can you get onto the bench yourself?' the matron asked her. 'I don't want to risk you falling.'

The matron took Rosa's arm to support her while the nurse helped her slide off the trolley. Rosa felt dizzy and nearly fainted but the women had a strong grip on her. She thought how cool their flesh felt compared with hers. She was burning.

The nurse put down a stool and Rosa climbed onto it then onto the bench. When she lay down an excruciating pain pinched her back. She tried to relieve it by lying on her side but the nurses turned her on her back again and strapped her legs. The pain was stronger than ever now. Rosa felt an urge to bear down but the elevated position of her legs made it awkward. She wailed from the pain.

'You still have a while to go,' the matron told her. 'Try to stay calm.'

Rosa stared at the ceiling. Things were starting to blur. She could barely hear what the matron was telling her through the haze of pain. The nurse took her temperature and listened to her heartbeat. Some time passed. Rosa was aware that the light through the curtains had changed. There was a patter of rain. It must already be late afternoon. She heard water being poured into a basin. The nurse washed her between the legs with Lysol. A few months ago, she would have been mortified to have her private parts handled by another person. But the pain had put her beyond that. All she cared about was bringing her baby into the world. She thought of another woman seventeen years ago. It would have been winter and cold. It might have happened at home or in a hospital, but Rosa's mother had gone through these same things to bring her into the world.

A contraction seized Rosa's womb, much longer and stronger than the previous ones. She cried out and gripped the bench.

'Shh! Shh!' the matron told her. 'Be brave. You're young. This should be easy for you.'

'What have you got in your hand?' asked the nurse.

'My cross,' Rosa moaned.

'Here,' said the nurse, prising the chain from Rosa's hand. 'I will put it around your neck. If you hold it in your hand you might squeeze it when the baby comes and hurt yourself.'

'Thank you,' said Rosa.

Sibilla had warned her that the birth would be painful, but Rosa could never have imagined such violent, torturing pains. Was the nurse telling her it was going to get worse? Another long contraction seized her, followed by waves of them. Rosa tried to sit up but the nurse pushed her back down.

'We need to see the baby's head,' she told her.

Tears poured down Rosa's face and mixed with her sweat. There was such pressure in her back she thought her spine might break. A fire seared her pelvis.

'Push!' said the matron. 'Push!'

Rosa gripped the sides of the bench and pushed with all her strength. There was a burning between her legs. Then pain so terrible she screamed.

'The baby is crowning,' said the matron. 'You're lucky. This birth is moving quickly.'

Rosa bit her lip till it bled. She could not imagine enduring the agony for much longer. She cried out, sure she was being split in two. Then suddenly something moved.

'One more push,' the matron said, holding out a blanket to the nurse.

Rosa gritted her teeth and pushed. Something gushed out of her. The relief from the agony was so sudden that she jolted with the shock.

'Good,' said the nurse. 'Are you all right?'

Rosa couldn't answer her. She was trying to catch her breath. The nurse wrapped the baby in the blanket. It's supposed to cry, isn't it? thought Rosa, her heart racing. There was no sound; only a terrible silence. She attempted to sit up. She wanted to see what was going on with the baby. But she was too feeble.

'Lie back, lie back,' the nurse told her. 'You still have to deliver the afterbirth.'

'My baby ... the baby,' Rosa struggled to say. A horrible feeling stirred in her. The baby was dead. It was a cruel joke on God's part to give her this hope. She started to weep.

Suddenly a cry broke the air.

'It's a girl,' said the matron, holding up the pink-faced infant for Rosa to see. 'A nice healthy girl.'

Rosa was filled with wonder at her baby daughter. The day after she was born, Rosa's breasts flowed with milk. The child took to the nipple without difficulty. Rosa gazed in amazement at her daughter's face. It was not like a newborn baby's but slender with well-defined eyes and a rosebud mouth. Where had she inherited such beauty, Rosa wondered. In comparison to Signora Corvetto and the Baroness Derveaux, she knew herself to be only pretty in an ordinary way and certainly, to her relief, the child had nothing of Osvaldo in her. She played with the baby's fingers and toes, and whenever she finished feeding, it was only a short while before her breasts began to ache with longing for the child to be with her again. Her milk was so plentiful that the ward nurse asked if she would feed some of the other babies whose mothers were too weak after the delivery to feed them or whose milk hadn't come in yet. Rosa nursed two other babies, washing her breasts with disinfectant and hot water between feeds. Despite the multiple feedings, her breasts overflowed. The nurses had to give her three changes of nightshifts and place a wad of muslin on her chest when she slept. Rosa didn't mind. She would have nursed all the children in the hospital if they needed it, she enjoyed nurturing them so much. But with her own child it was special: she had brought her into life from her womb.

Giving birth had changed the way she viewed herself, Rosa realised. She reflected on her years at the convent and saw how tragic it was that the nuns were made to feel ashamed of their physical functions. A woman's body and all its processes was a miracle. It was a force of nature; not something to be shamefully hidden from oneself under a chemise. Although her organs were still tender, she felt the strength of them. Sibilla had said the fascists tried to control women by controlling their bodies. Perhaps, Rosa mused, society also tried to control women by making them feel there was something wrong with them. She smiled when she realised that she was starting to think like Sibilla. *Tell your child about me and teach it to love Italy and be strong*. She gazed down at the sleeping babe in her arms and knew exactly what she would call her.

In the ward where Rosa convalesced, there were eleven other women. Five days after the birth, only a few still had their babies with them. Rosa wondered what had happened to the other infants. Of the women without babies, four looked depressed, two seemed relieved and one of them wept day and night. The woman in the bed next to Rosa wasn't an unwed mother; she was a poor factory worker whose midwife had recommended that she deliver her next baby in hospital because of complications with her last pregnancy. She was missing her front upper and lower teeth. 'One for each child,' she told Rosa, cheerfully sticking her fingers into the gap in her mouth.

Although the nurses were kind, there was a sense that the unmarried mothers were in disgrace. Rosa had overheard the ward sister try to comfort the crying woman by saying, 'You have redeemed yourself by putting your baby in the arms of a couple wed before God.'

Rosa held little Sibilla and fought back her tears. She remembered the harsh looks she had received on the street when she was in labour and on her way to the hospital. 'Never,' she whispered into her daughter's ear. 'I will never give you up.' After that, Rosa dreaded it when Sibilla was taken to the hospital nursery after her feedings. She was afraid that she would never see her again.

A week after the birth, Rosa started to feel restless. She had spent so long between four walls she wanted to be out in the world. She knew she faced challenges but hiding away in a hospital wasn't going to stop them coming. The prison director had promised to send someone with her release documents so she could be discharged. Rosa planned to find a room to live in and some work she could do while taking care of Sibilla. She asked the ward sister when she might be able to leave. The sister promised she would speak to the hospital administrator.

The following day, a woman in a tailored dress with puffed sleeves came to see Rosa. She was short, and her navy blue hat with a cluster of daisies on it did little to distract from her heavy jowls. She drew the curtains around the bed although that wouldn't stop the others from overhearing the conversation. Sibilla had been brought from the nursery for her midday feeding but was still asleep in the basket by Rosa's bed. The woman gazed at Sibilla for a moment then introduced herself as Signora Cherubini, the head of the charity board that ran the hospital. She had Sibilla's registration of birth papers in her hand.

'I heard that you are doing well, Signorina Bellocchi,' she said. 'And that you have been able to assist with other babies.'

Signora Cherubini smiled but there was an undertone in her voice that put Rosa on edge. She had eyes like a falcon.

'Yes, signora. I feel well and, as the other babies I was feeding no longer need me, I would like to leave as soon as possible.'

'I see,' said Signora Cherubini, looking at the registration form. 'It says here that the father is unknown?'

Rosa hesitated. The father was known but she would not acknowledge him. It might make her sound like a loose woman, but she resented the way the women in the ward were treated as though they should be ashamed of themselves. After all, she had been wrongly put in prison and raped, although she would never mention such things. She did not want Sibilla to be stigmatised or to be seen as of less worth than a child who had been conceived in love.

'That's right,' she replied.

The smile dissolved from Signora Cherubini's face. 'Extraordinary!' she said, rolling her eyes. 'And the nurse tells me you want to keep the child?'

Rosa felt a pinch in her belly. 'Yes,' she replied.

'Well, I'm afraid that is impossible,' said Signora Cherubini, shaking her head. 'The child must go to the hospital's foundling home. That is the condition of your coming here.'

Rosa gasped. 'I was told no such thing!'

Of all the nightmares she had suffered in the past years, this was by far the worst. She instinctively put her hand on Sibilla's blanket and felt the warm body of her baby wriggle under her palm.

Signora Cherubini's eyes hardened. 'Signorina Bellocchi,' she said, 'it seems to me you have spent the majority of your life so far in a convent and the rest of it in prison. I don't think you understand what the outside world is like. Do you realise how hard it will be for you to raise a daughter? Where are you going to live? How are you going to support yourself? Who will employ an unwed mother and, if you do find work, who will take care of your baby while you do it? *Signorina* Bellocchi, have you thought seriously about these things?'

Rosa shrank under Signora Cherubini's barrage. So far she had been able to hide from the other women in the ward that she had been in prison. She was humiliated.

'I have the money I saved from sewing,' Rosa stammered. 'I will find somewhere to work where I can take Sibilla with me.'

Signora Cherubini looked at her impatiently. 'For whom? What business of any repute is going to employ a criminal?'

She paused to check if she was hitting the mark and smiled when tears pricked Rosa's eyes. 'I'm not a criminal,' Rosa said quietly.

'You are an ignorant girl indeed,' Signora Cherubini said. 'Do you know where you will end up if you persist with such foolishness? Let me not mince words, Signorina Bellocchi: you will end up selling yourself on the street!'

Rosa looked at Sibilla sleeping peacefully beside her. 'I only want what's best for her,' she said. Despite herself, she started to cry.

Signora Cherubini's expression softened. 'Look,' she said, patting Rosa's hand, 'you have a chance to put this behind you. You can begin again. And your daughter will be properly brought up. If you stay together, you will be a weight around her neck. You will sink together. Do you want that, Signorina Bellocchi? Now try to think clearly. Your daughter is not a doll to be played with. Do you want to be responsible for her downfall?'

Rosa's chest heaved with her crying. Her whole body was

racked with grief. Signora Cherubini was right. It was selfish of her to want to keep Sibilla when the baby would be better off with someone who could give her a steady life and education. She thought of Suor Maddalena. Rosa had been lovingly raised by the sisters of Santo Spirito. Wouldn't that be better for Sibilla than being raised by a 'fallen woman'?

Signora Cherubini put a form on Rosa's lap. 'Sign this,' she said. 'And all will be well. *For the both of you*. You can have a fresh start. Maybe even get married some day and start a legitimate family of your own.'

Rosa took the form and pen but hesitated.

'Sign it,' said Signora Cherubini. 'Don't drag this out for yourself ... and her.'

Rosa felt herself staring down a dark hole. 'I'll never forget her,' she wept.

Signora Cherubini smiled condescendingly. 'Yes, you will. You're still young with so much ahead of you.'

Through her blurry vision Rosa saw the title of the form: *Document of Relinquishment*. She was to surrender all claims on the child she had brought into the world.

'I love you,' she said to Sibilla through her tears. 'I love you.'

Rosa tried to steady her hand to sign the form. Before she did, she gazed once more at the angelic face of her daughter. Sibilla's eyes flickered open and she began to cry. A strange sensation stirred in Rosa's bosom. Milk welled up in her breasts. Sibilla cried more and the milk began to overflow and leak through Rosa's nightshift. 'Oh,' she said, grabbing a wad of muslin and holding it to her breasts. But she couldn't stem the flow. It rushed in streams down her nightshift and onto the form. Signora Cherubini quickly retrieved the paper before it was soaked.

'You had better feed her,' she said to Rosa. 'I'll come back with the form in an hour.'

Rosa picked up Sibilla and held her to her breast. How could she give her up any more than she could give up any other part of her body? Could she surrender her heart or her kidneys and go on living? She had been lovingly brought up by Suor Maddalena, but she was out of the convent now and on her own; rootless, without a family. At least Sibilla could know, whatever they faced, that she had a mother who loved her. Maybe it wasn't much, but maybe it was everything.

Rosa closed her eyes and prayed to San Giuseppe. He was the saint who watched over orphans and unwed mothers. 'Please help me,' she wept. 'Please.' She opened her eyes and was jolted by a bright light sweeping across her bed. A sense of peace washed over her. She was sure it was an angel.

'Speak to me,' she whispered. 'Tell me what I must do.'

'What that woman is telling you is illegal.'

Rosa started. She turned to see Suor Gabriella slipping through the curtains. She clutched a folder under her arm and carried a package wrapped in brown paper. She sat on the end of Rosa's bed.

'This hospital is supposed to be encouraging you to keep your child. That is the law,' Suor Gabriella said. 'There is no foundling home. That woman sells babies to rich women who can't have their own. The women want to pass themselves off as the birth mother, so there is never any adoption record kept. The natural mother has no hope of seeing the child again. The form she is trying to get you to sign is a bluff. She will destroy it the minute you leave here.'

Rosa stared at Suor Gabriella in horror. Adopted children had even less status than illegitimate ones, so it made sense that the adoptive parents would try to make the babies appear as their own. Still, such corruption was difficult to believe.

'But ... but this is a charity hospital,' Rosa stammered. 'They do good works.'

'Do you see any nuns here?' Suor Gabriella waved her hand at Rosa. 'This place is about profit not charity. I was shocked when I heard the nurse was sending you here. I couldn't obtain leave earlier to come and see you, and it looks like I came just in time.'

'But how will I support my baby?' asked Rosa, remembering the harsh picture Signora Cherubini had painted for her future.

'You are entitled to OMNI payments,' explained Suor Gabriella. 'You must go to the *comune* to make a claim.'

'OMNI?'

'The National Organisation for the Protection of Motherhood and Infancy,' said Suor Gabriella. 'They have a special allowance for unwed mothers.'

'I'm entitled to payments. Why?'

Suor Gabriella smiled. 'Because you gave birth to an Italian baby and you *didn't* leave it at a foundling home where mortality rates are high. Mussolini wants more healthy children. He wants a bigger army.'

Rosa cringed at the mention of Mussolini. He was the reason she had been put in prison. It wasn't her intention to be of assistance to him, especially not in producing a fascist army. 'But my child is a girl,' she said.

'Girls produce more babies, don't they?'

Suor Gabriella was most certainly the kindest of the nuns working at the prison, but now Rosa saw that the woman's diminutive stature belied a subversive nature.

Suor Gabriella opened the file she was holding and handed Rosa her release documents. 'You'll have to see Signor Direttore about collecting your work payment.' She passed Rosa the package she was holding. 'Sorry, it was the only one I could find,' she said.

Rosa opened the package and found a blue dress. It was frayed around the collar and three sizes too big for her. She wondered if it had belonged to a prisoner who had been executed and therefore didn't need it for her release. She thought of Sibilla and shivered.

Suor Gabriella stood up to leave. 'Remember, this place is run by crooks,' she said. 'I've heard of them drugging mothers to take their babies away from them. I suggest you get out of here today. Now you have the release form, discharge yourself and go.'

'Can I do that?'

'Of course you can. You are a free woman now.'

Rosa thanked Suor Gabriella for her advice and watched her leave. She remembered Signora Cherubini had said that she would be back in an hour. She was worried the woman might forcibly take her baby from her. Sibilla had finished feeding and had fallen back to sleep. Rosa changed into the dress Suor Gabriella had brought and swaddled Sibilla in her blanket. Before anyone noticed, she walked out into the hall.

She approached the nurse at the reception desk in the admissions area to discharge herself. The woman was speaking with someone on the telephone. Rosa glanced at the clock on the wall behind the desk. It was nearly the time Signora Cherubini had said she would return and she would pass by the admissions area on her way to the ward. The admissions nurse looked up at Rosa and pointed to the telephone with an apologetic expression on her face. Rosa could hear the muffled voice of the caller. Whatever they were saying it was taking too long to express it. Her heart pounded and her courage started to fail. She glanced towards the entrance doors. It occurred to her that she was no longer a prisoner and the swing doors were not locked. There was no guard to stop her. She could simply walk through them. The discharge procedure was of no consequence to her as she did not intend to return to the Santa Caterina. All she was missing was Sibilla's registration of birth and surely she could find another way to obtain a copy. Still Rosa could not move. She had been institutionalised for so long it was difficult to believe that she could walk through a door herself without someone else's permission.

The sound of high heels approaching startled her into action. She ran towards the doors and, without looking back, pushed her way through them. The afternoon sunlight hit her face.

'We are free,' she said, kissing Sibilla. She hurried down the steps and mingled with the other people on the street.

*

The prison director was surprised to see Rosa waiting for him in the interview room. He glanced at her shabby dress.

'They discharged you from the hospital so soon?' he asked. 'How long has it been? A week?'

'I'm well enough,' Rosa lied. 'They need the bed for other patients.'

He checked Rosa's release papers. She glanced over her shoulder towards the window, half-expecting to see a hysterical Signora Cherubini in pursuit of her. But there was no-one on the street outside the prison.

It had been unnerving for Rosa to re-enter the prison. She was afraid that the guards may not open the gates for her again to leave and she would be trapped there forever and Sibilla would be taken away from her. All she wanted to do was collect her money and get out.

The director seemed to take forever to calculate the figure owed for Rosa's sewing work. The procedure was further delayed because Rosa had no fixed address yet. It took over an hour before the process was completed, and by the time Rosa was allowed out through the gates with Sibilla, it was too late for her to go to the *comune*. The truth was that Rosa wasn't keen to register with OMNI. They were a government organisation, but Italy's government was fascist and its head was Mussolini. After what had happened to her friend Sibilla, Rosa felt it would somehow be disloyal. At the same time, she knew she had to put her daughter's welfare above her scruples. The best that she could do for now was to find a room for them both and something to eat.

Rosa headed in the direction of Via Giuseppe Verdi. People stared at her and she knew she was a sorry sight. The director had returned her shoes but her feet were swollen and the shoes pinched her heels and toes. She could feel blisters forming. She turned down a laneway and saw a dingy-looking hotel. It had water stains down the walls and the shutters were in need of painting, but at two lire a night, it would have to do until she found work.

The reception area was tiled with a strip of red carpet. A limp parlour palm sat in the corner. The stink of stale tobacco permeated the air and dust motes floated in the light from a frosted glass window. The desk was behind bars, with a board for keys above it. Most of the keys were on their hooks and Rosa assumed that meant there were rooms available. She rang the bell on the counter. A woman with untidily pinned hair and sullen eyes appeared from behind a door. She settled her gaze on Rosa.

'There are no rooms,' she said.

'Oh,' said Rosa, taken aback. She glanced to the board.

'The guests are out and will be returning soon. They must all leave their keys at reception.'

'Excuse me then, signora,' she said, turning to go.

Rosa continued her search for a room along Via Ghibellina. She almost wished she had her prison-issue clogs back for her feet were bleeding. Every hotel she tried told her the same thing: that there were no rooms available. Finally she asked the proprietress of one of the hotels why the sign in her window said they had rooms free if there were no vacancies.

The woman stared at Rosa. 'Oh, there are rooms free,' she said. 'But not for sluts and their *bastardi*.'

The insult stung Rosa as violently as if the woman had physically slapped her. She ran out onto the street, tears burning her eyes. She didn't care what people said about her ... but Sibilla! This is exactly how Signora Cherubini said it would be, she thought. What was she to do? She couldn't sleep on the street with her baby.

She sat on a doorstep and tried to gather her thoughts. She had pushed herself for Sibilla's sake, but she was more worn out by the birth than she had thought. She was hungry and weak. She realised that she had one place to go, but whether they would accept her she did not know.

It took Rosa several minutes before she could summon the courage to ring the bell of the Convent of Santo Spirito. The portress nun who answered the door was not one that Rosa recognised. She must be new. Rosa asked to see Suor Maddalena and was led to the parlour. She waited for an hour and when the wooden shutter behind the grille opened, it was not Suor Maddalena who sat there but the Badessa.

'Did you go to confession before coming here?' she asked Rosa.

Rosa's mouth turned dry. The Badessa's manner was courteous as usual, but there was a coldness in her stare that chilled her.

'There was no time,' Rosa explained, holding up Sibilla. 'I have just been released and I have nowhere to stay with my baby.'

The Badessa looked at the sleeping infant and raised her hand. For one terrifying moment, Rosa thought she was going to close the shutter again. She hurriedly explained that she did not want Sibilla sent to a foundling home and that she needed to obtain her birth registration. She also told the Badessa why she had not explained her innocence to Don Marzoli. But she did not mention the rape. If the Badessa knew how her daughter had been conceived, she might insist it was better for Rosa to give her up.

The Badessa shook her head. 'What became of you, Rosa? What happened to the girl who showed so much promise?'

Rosa was stung. The Badessa must have thought her guilty for so long that she hadn't heard a word of her explanation. Rosa's heart was too heavy to protest her blamelessness further. She had done that for months and it had not got her anywhere. She saw that it would be easier not to resist when people spoke down to her.

The Badessa rose from her seat. 'I will give you a place to stay here tonight,' she said. 'But, let me make this very clear. This is the last time you will ever be accepted into this convent. You must go tomorrow morning and never return.'

Rosa trembled. Weak and tired, she was no match for the Badessa's stern words. 'Doesn't God forgive our sins?' she asked.

The Badessa looked at her with weary eyes. 'If God can forgive you, then I can forgive you,' she said. 'But I am thinking of Suor Maddalena's welfare. She suffered a breakdown after Don Marzoli spoke to you in prison. I won't let you hurt her any more with your wayward behaviour.'

Rosa could bear all that had happened to her, but not to have hurt Suor Maddalena. She felt a dark void opening up inside her and started to succumb to despair. Sibilla wailed and the sound yanked her back. Her breasts were growing moist and if she didn't feed Sibilla soon the milk would leak through her dress.

The Badessa signalled to the portress nun who indicated that Rosa should follow her. She was taken to a room in the bowels of the convent, far away from the others. Rosa sank onto the bed, so exhausted she could barely keep her eyes open. She unbuttoned her dress so that Sibilla could nurse.

'I'll bring you some supper,' the portress nun said, retiring from the room.

Only after the nun had departed did Rosa let her tears fall. 'Poor Suor Maddalena,' she wept. 'My dear Suor Maddalena.' She could not bear to think that the woman who had raised her had suffered over her. Rosa was cursed, she was sure of it. The only reason she had to keep living was Sibilla. Otherwise, she would have thrown herself into the Arno.

TEN

The next morning, the portress nun brought Rosa milk and bread. She gave her a dress similar to the one Rosa had worn when she left the convent: black cotton with a Peter Pan collar. There was also a layette for Sibilla. Rosa thanked the nun for the convent's generosity. Following the Badessa's cold reception, it was unexpected.

'I also have your flute,' the nun said, handing Rosa the case.

Rosa felt the weight of her beloved instrument. She had thought it was lost to her. Having the flute back in her possession was as miraculous to Rosa as Lazarus returning from the dead. She looked up at the nun.

'A woman brought it here soon after you disappeared.'

Rosa opened the case and gazed at the flute. Ada must have retrieved it, she thought. Her heart warmed with the memory of the cook. She touched the key under her collar and saw flashes of images from that last day at the villa. Ada had wanted to warn her about the Marchesa Scarfiotti. Had she sensed that something terrible was going to happen that evening? Rosa sighed. She couldn't think of any of that now. She must put all her mind towards survival.

'Thank you,' she said to the nun. 'Please tell the Badessa that I am grateful.'

The nun stepped out of the way so that Rosa could move through the door with Sibilla and the layette, bundled in a blanket, in one arm and her flute in the other. When they reached the entrance door to the piazza, the nun blessed Rosa and Sibilla.

'Please pray for us,' Rosa said. 'I never meant to hurt Suor Maddalena. That was the last thing I wanted.'

The nun nodded. 'I'll pray for you. Have courage. You must think of your daughter now.'

After arriving at the Comune di Firenze and obtaining Sibilla's birth document, Rosa decided to also apply for OMNI's allowance for unwed mothers. Her experience at the Santa Caterina hospital had made her suspicious of charity, but if she could not find accommodation for herself, she would have to try for a place in one of the state's unwed mothers' homes. She justified her change of mind by telling herself that if Mussolini had caused her to suffer so unfairly, he should pay for her re-entry into society. She was sure her friend Sibilla would have agreed.

Rosa took a number from a clerk and waited in the crowded reception area. She noticed the colour of her ticket was different from those of the other mothers with newborn infants in their laps. When two of them sent her disapproving looks, she understood her ticket signified her marital status.

'They favour sluts like that over respectable married women like us,' said one of the women, loudly enough for everyone else to hear. 'We are poor too but they give them subsidies to feed their babies!'

'It's to stop them from abandoning them — or strangling them!' the woman's companion replied.

Most of the people waiting buried themselves deeper in

their newspapers to avoid becoming part of the brewing dispute. But several looked up with interest.

'They are building yet another special home for *them*,' a woman with a toddler added.

Rosa tried to hide herself by reading over her forms. But she could feel the eyes of the women boring into her. When she could bear it no longer she stood up to leave, but at that moment one of the clerks called her number.

'Come this way,' the female clerk said to Rosa, leading her to a desk behind the counter.

Rosa waited in the seat opposite while the woman checked the various boxes on Rosa's forms.

'So you have some means of support?' she asked Rosa, pushing back a stray lock of hair. 'Please write down the amount here.'

Rosa took the pen and form offered to her and filled in the sum of money she had earned from sewing. She could tell from the way the clerk's eyebrows lifted that it was meagre.

'Our mothers' home has a waiting list,' the clerk told her sympathetically. 'I will put your name on it. Meanwhile, I have heard that there is accommodation around the Palazzo Vecchio.' The clerk leaned forward and whispered, 'It might help if you … if you wear a wedding ring and pretend you are a widow.'

Rosa blushed for the shame but sensed that the clerk meant well. She was in her early twenties with teardrop-shaped eyes.

'You're entitled to a subsidy for nursing and accommodation,' the woman said, returning to her normal tone. She signed off the forms. 'We have a mothers' kitchen around the corner. You can have lunch there.'

Rosa was surprised that the fascists were so generous towards unwed mothers when the rest of society despised them.

'I need to have these approved by my supervisor,' the clerk told her. 'One moment, please.'

Rosa rocked Sibilla in her arms. Her courage had been strengthened. With some monetary help their lives would be easier. In her clean dress and with Sibilla's new layette, Rosa felt nothing could stop her. Her thoughts were interrupted by the sound of a man's raised voice. She turned and saw the clerk talking with another official. He was pointing to something on Rosa's documents. Her heart sank. What was it? Would she be rejected because of the *Figlia di Non Noto* that was written on her records? It didn't look good, did it? She was a foundling *and* an unwed mother.

The supervisor approached her with the red-faced clerk in tow.

'You see this number here,' he said to Rosa, thrusting the forms into her lap and hitting Sibilla in the face with them. 'You are an enemy of the state. And you have the gall to ask for help from it!'

The women in the waiting area raised their heads, keen to see what was happening.

The clerk tried to intervene. 'She's served her sentence.'

The supervisor raised his hand. 'Once a bad seed always a bad seed.'

Sibilla was agitated by the raised voices and started to wail. Rosa picked up the birth registration documents but left the other ones on the chair. Without looking at the supervisor, she headed towards the door.

'Wait!' the clerk called after her. Despite the disapproving looks given to her by the women in the waiting area, the clerk reached under the counter and handed Rosa two boxes of baby cereal and a cloth nappy.

'Thank you,' Rosa said.

The clerk nodded. Rosa would have liked to have said something more but the stares of the people in the reception area were too much for her. She rushed out onto the street. Whatever hardship befell her, Rosa promised herself that she would never turn to charity or the state again.

After walking a few blocks, she began to recover from

the shock of the scene at the *comune*. Perhaps things were not so hopeless. She had some money and her flute. The return of her instrument meant Rosa had a possible source of income other than cleaning or factory work. Once she found a place to stay and bought some decent clothes, she would advertise herself as a music teacher. She could go to the pupils' homes and take Sibilla with her. If she fed her baby before each lesson, Sibilla would sleep for a couple of hours without crying.

The streets around the Palazzo Vecchio had no footpaths. It had rained that morning and streams of water ran along the central runnels in the cobblestoned roads. Rosa cringed whenever a car or a van passed, afraid she would be splashed. She had seen rooms advertised in houses for only half a lire, but they were in the cellars and she would not take a chance on that. The city was prone to flooding and often the drains became choked and the overflow rushed into buildings. A room in a cellar could be a death trap.

Rosa introduced herself to the managers of the first two hotels she visited on Via dei Calzaiuoli as *Signora* Bellocchi, widow of the late Artemio Bellocchi, and implied that she was a music teacher, but they still refused her accommodation.

'If I take your *bambina* in here all my other guests will leave,' said the first manager. 'They will complain about the noise.'

The response of the second manager was unexpected. 'I can't have a respectable mother stay here, signora,' he whispered, staring at her with his soulful eyes. 'This is not the place for a nicely-brought-up young lady.'

Rosa was about to protest. The desperation she had felt the previous day returned. Where else was she to go? Before she had a chance to say anything a door on the first-floor landing opened. A man wearing trousers and a singlet that barely covered his hairy paunch stepped out and lit a cigarette. A few moments later a woman in a red dress and feathered hat rushed out onto the landing and down the stairs. She wore as much make-up as the Marchesa Scarfiotti but the fabric of her dress was cheap. Rosa noticed the woman's stockings were ripped. She rushed by the reception desk and Rosa caught a whiff of something that reminded her of Osvaldo.

'No, perhaps not, signore,' Rosa said, hastily withdrawing.

Around the corner and down a laneway, she found a narrow house advertising an attic room for rent. The paint was peeling from the walls and the window boxes were full of weeds. It was the most dilapidated of all the places she had seen so far but perhaps that meant the occupants wouldn't be too choosy.

'*A mali estremi, estremi rimedi,*' sighed Rosa. Desperate times need desperate measures.

There was a pile of rubbish by the doorstep. A thin ginger cat was sniffing through it. Rosa knocked on the door. A baby started crying. She heard a woman shout something but no-one answered the door. She waited a few minutes, undecided whether she should knock again or walk away. She raised her hand to try again when the door swung open and she found herself face to face with a woman with unruly hair, prematurely grey around the temples. She held a baby to her breast. The woman had large hips but the rest of her was scrawny. Three small children gathered around her skirt. The youngest one was biting his thumb and scratching his head.

'What do you want?' the woman asked. 'You're not another nosy bitch from OMNI, are you? You can see my babies are well cared for. Look! I've got one on my breast!'

'I'm looking for a room,' Rosa responded before she had a chance to think. She wanted a room but did she want one in this house? The woman's skirt had an iron burn on it; the children's clothes were smeared with food and their hair was untidy. And, it seemed, the woman had had some trouble with OMNI herself.

The frown on the woman's face relaxed. She looked Rosa up and down. 'Two lire a night,' she said. 'Lunch included.'

Rosa was caught off guard. The woman had seen Sibilla sleeping in her arms and hadn't turned her away. 'May I see the room first?' she asked. It was her last stab at dignity; she already knew that she'd have no choice but to take it.

The woman indicated for her to enter the house. The gloomy hallway was host to a wide range of odours, the strongest of which were stale coffee and dirty nappies. A man's coat and Sunday hat hung on a stand, lopsided under the weight of various scarves and shawls. The kitchen was on the ground floor and Rosa caught sight of a girl about five years of age and a boy of about seven sitting at a table and eating polenta. The terracotta tiles were covered in crumbs. Unwashed pots and pans were piled up in the sink and over the countertops. The woman placed the baby in a basket by the fireplace and told the three children to join their brother and sister at the table. While the woman buttoned up her blouse Rosa caught sight of her breasts. They sagged and were covered in red lines.

'The room is on the third floor with a view,' the woman told Rosa, leading her up the stairs.

The first and second levels were as unkempt as the ground floor, with unmade beds and toys and shoes strewn everywhere. The balustrade and doorframes were in need of new lacquer and the wallpaper was yellowing. The higher they rose, the narrower the stairs became. The heat was stifling. Rosa clutched the balustrade with one hand and Sibilla with the other, afraid she might faint.

The woman opened a door at the top of the stairs and ushered Rosa inside. Although the shutters were closed to keep out the sun, the air was oppressive. The heat seemed to be pouring down from the sloped ceiling. The room was tidier than the rest of the house but a film of dust covered the floor and bedhead. The armoire had mirrored doors and Rosa caught sight of herself. The reflection was different from the fresh-faced girl who had first seen herself at the Villa Scarfiotti. She looked tired, and, despite having recently given birth, she was thin. If Rosa had a choice of rooms, she would not have taken this one. But she had no choice. She would have to be vigilant that neither she nor Sibilla suffered heatstroke. She told the woman, who introduced herself as Signora Porretti, that she would take the room.

A wail started up downstairs followed by the sound of a toddler crying. Signora Porretti rushed down the stairs to see what had happened. Rosa sat on the bed and pressed Sibilla's face to her own. A few minutes later, she heard Signora Porretti screaming at the children to clean up the mess they'd made. 'How did you think of eating off the floor when you've got tables and chairs!'

Rosa kissed Sibilla on the top of her head. 'At least she can't complain when you cry.'

She took one of the drawers from the wardrobe and used the baby blanket to fashion it into a bed for Sibilla. She opened the window and shutters to see the view Signora Porretti had promised. She looked down into a courtyard full of rusty machine parts and lines of washing. The view was disappointing but a sign hanging from the building beyond it caused Rosa to gasp. She slammed the shutters closed, wanting to block out the memory of the night her friend Sibilla was shot. The sign proclaimed the Fascist Party slogan: *Mussolini is always right!*

'No!' said Rosa under her breath. 'Mussolini is not always right. Mussolini is a devil.'

The following morning, Rosa counted out her money. Her rent included lunch so she had enough for the room as well as bread and some groceries for three weeks. Or she had enough until the end of the week if she bought a new dress and hat and had the pads on her flute replaced. She had examined her instrument the day before and noticed that the keys were sticking. Having a nice dress and keeping her flute in good repair would increase her chances of obtaining work teaching music, which she assumed would be better paid and less arduous than cleaning. She sighed and caressed

Sibilla who was sleeping in her drawer-bed. 'I have to make a good life for us,' she whispered.

Rosa decided to take a chance on the second plan. She washed herself in the basin and tidied herself as best she could. At least Sibilla looked smart in the dress the nuns had given her. Rosa's plan was to head to the music shop on the Via Tornabuoni. She would ask Signor Morelli if he knew of anyone looking for a flute and piano teacher.

On the first-floor landing, Rosa found two of Signora Porretti's children playing with a sock puppet. They looked at her with wide eyes.

'*Buon giorno*,' she said to them.

'*Buon giorno, signora*,' they replied shyly.

Rosa noticed they had red splotches on their necks. She wondered if they had allergies from the heat and dust. 'You'd better get your mother to look at your skin,' she told them kindly.

Via Tornabuoni was as elegant as Rosa remembered it but the fashions had changed. Padded shoulders and puffed sleeves were everywhere, along with gossamer hats, wide belts and spectator shoes. Rosa was not as tempted this time to dally and look in the shop windows. The exception was when she passed Parigi's Fine Furniture and Antiques. She thought of Signor Parigi that day she had seen him in his dove grey suit with the gardenia in his buttonhole. She peered in the shop window and saw a writing desk with a blue motif on display. Next to it stood a chest of drawers in cherrywood. She looked at her hand and remembered the time that Signor Parigi had given her money. She'd had no idea then what a fortune she had received. He had offered her a job too. Would he still be interested in her?

Rosa caught a glimpse of her reflection in the glass. When she had first visited the store, she had been young and carefree. Now, the fresh look in her face was gone. She was the mother of an illegitimate child and an 'enemy of the state'. Besides, she wasn't sure that she could see the origin of things any more. She hadn't for a long time. All the magic had vanished from her life the day she was thrown in prison.

Rosa caught sight of a woman walking out of the backroom with some customers. She was attired in a figure-hugging dress with a scooped collar. Her hair was coiffed into an upswept style and her long nails were plum red. An enormous diamond ring sparkled on her finger. Signor Parigi must have got married, Rosa thought, her heart sinking. She shook her head at her foolish daydreams and continued on her way. A sophisticated woman like that was exactly the kind of woman the elegant Signor Parigi would marry. Rosa thought of the beautiful flamingo pink hat she had once desired on this same street and realised that she would never be glamorous like Signor Parigi's wife. She pressed her face to Sibilla's cheek. 'But you could be, you beautiful girl,' she told her baby.

To Rosa's relief, the music shop on Via Tornabuoni was still there and Signor Morelli was standing behind the counter when she entered. He didn't recognise her from her previous visit, which Rosa preferred. On her way she had stopped at a haberdashery and bought a gold curtain ring to wear on her left hand. It would eventually tarnish but would have to do for now. She showed him her flute and explained the repairs it needed, and then asked if he knew of anyone who was looking for a music teacher.

'Why, yes,' he said. 'I did get a request a few days ago from Signora Agarossi. She has three children. Would you like me to call her now?'

'That would be kind of you,' Rosa said, trying not to sound desperate.

Signor Morelli studied her over the top of his glasses. 'They are rather naughty children. They have worn out a few teachers.'

Rosa was not put off by Signor Morelli's warning. After all, how bad could children be? The previous evening she had heard Signora Porretti admonishing her children for various offences, none of which had sounded serious to Rosa.

'That's all right,' she reassured him. 'I'm certain we will get along.'

Signor Morelli dialled the telephone. Once he was connected to the Agarossi home and put through to the mistress, he explained there was a young woman available to give flute and piano lessons. He paused for a moment then put his hand over the receiver to talk to Rosa. 'How much do you charge?'

Rosa had given her fee some consideration. She didn't want to charge too much, but she didn't want to undersell herself either. 'Ten lire an hour,' she replied. Signor Morelli gave nothing away in his face but Rosa wondered if that was too much. It was, after all, almost a week's rent. Signor Morelli repeated the price to Signora Agarossi. Rosa heard the muffled voice on the line. Signor Morelli turned to Rosa again.

'Can you teach the three children together?' he asked.

'However Signora Agarossi prefers,' Rosa replied.

Signor Morelli conveyed this information to Signora Agarossi. He exchanged a few more words and then hung up the telephone.

'Signora Agarossi will see you on Friday at eleven o'clock,' he said, scribbling down the address for Rosa. 'You will teach the children for two hours. I can have your flute repaired by Thursday afternoon.'

Rosa thanked Signor Morelli. Compared to trying to find a place to live, obtaining work might be easy after all. She bought sheet music suitable for children and left the store buoyant with hope. Maybe Signora Agarossi had other friends who would like music lessons for their children too and would recommend her. At ten lire an hour she could do well for herself. She would soon be able to afford better accommodation.

Happy for the first time in a long time, Rosa allowed herself to enjoy the pleasures of the senses that Via Tornabuoni offered. She couldn't afford a dress or shoes from any of the stores, but she decided to treat Sibilla by buying a cake of carnation milk soap to bathe her with and a tiny bottle of orange blossom perfume for herself. She could have such small luxuries now, she reassured herself, especially if she was on her way to making ten lire an hour as a music teacher. She had been deprived of so much for so long that she wanted to drink it all up.

She still suffered faintness from the birth and stopped outside a café with the idea of having a cup of coffee and a sweet. She looked in the window, trying to decide which pastry to choose: a raspberry tart or a biscotto; a slice of panforte or a raisin square. A shadow passed over her. Rosa held Sibilla tighter. In the window's reflection, she saw a black touring car with tortoiseshell side panels gliding past on the street behind her. The car became caught in the traffic. Rosa glimpsed the dark-haired passenger and bile rose in her throat. She dared not turn around. The Marchesa Scarfiotti had not changed in the years since Rosa had last seen her. She was still an apparition with ghostly make-up and a waif-like figure. She tilted her head in that haughty manner of hers, looking down her nose at the world. Rosa struggled to catch her breath. Feelings of loathing and fear coursed through her. The car came to a halt a few yards away. For a fleeting moment, Rosa saw herself rushing towards it and opening the door. She would drag out that conceited passenger and trample her to death.

Rosa gasped, shocked at her murderous impulses. She pressed her lips to Sibilla's downy head. She could never contemplate going back to prison and leaving Sibilla alone. She was a defenceless person in the face of a powerful woman, and she could do nothing about it. Revenge would not be sweet: Sibilla would be taken from her and placed in an orphanage.

Rosa noticed that there was someone in the car with the Marchesa. She saw a flash of red hair. Clementina. Rosa remembered the forlorn face staring down at her from the schoolroom the night she was arrested. She turned to get a better look at Clementina but at that moment the traffic unfroze and the car sped away. Rosa trembled from head to foot. She turned to the café window again but her appetite had vanished.

The following Friday, Rosa prepared for her interview with Signora Agarossi. For an extra fee, Signora Porretti let Rosa use the bathroom. Once Rosa saw it, she realised that she should have charged Signora Porretti because the bath needed to be scrubbed of slime before it could be used and the floor swept of hairs, cigarette butts and toenail clippings. Rosa guessed that the cigarette butts were Signor Porretti's. He was a stout man who worked shifts on the railways. Rosa had only seen him twice. She assumed he was also responsible for the urine spills around the floor of the courtyard lavatory. Rosa was puzzled by the strong smell of vinegar and the half-dozen empty vinegar bottles under the sink. How could Signora Porretti use all that vinegar and still have such a filthy bathroom? She piled the soiled towels in a corner, hoping Signora Porretti would wash them. After bathing, she used her chemise to dry herself and put on the dress she had bought: a tailored outfit in black rayon and a matching straw hat. It was a suitable outfit for a young widow. She had bought a wicker basket in which to carry Sibilla and stopped for a moment to admire her baby before heading out the door with her.

The Agarossi family lived in an apartment near Piazza Massimo d'Azeglio. The day was hot and Rosa caught the tram part of the way then walked. She had used a lotion to set her fingercurls and now she regretted it. Her scalp was itching. She must have been sensitive to some ingredient in the lotion, but she had no choice but to ignore the discomfort until after her interview was over and she could wash the lotion out.

The Agarossis' apartment occupied two floors of a Renaissance palace. When the maid showed her inside, Rosa was taken aback by the vaulted ceilings, the frescoes and the sculptured reliefs. The apartment was not as grand as the Villa Scarfiotti but it was elegant and meticulously clean. Despite the apartment's age there were no scuffmarks on the walls or fingermarks on the mirrors, the floor and rugs were clean and the furniture was polished to a high shine. The Agarossis were obviously a houseproud family. Rosa wondered if this exactness translated into what they expected of a music teacher. She made a mental note to emphasise the importance of precision in her interview with Signora Agarossi.

Rosa was led to a drawing room with a grand piano by the window. She allowed herself to absorb the luxury of sitting in the rose-scented room with its orderly arranged paintings and cushions. Her scalp was still itching. She quickly scratched it then smoothed down her hair again. A few minutes later a blonde woman wearing a royal blue satin dress entered. She was everything Rosa might have expected of Signora Agarossi from seeing her apartment: tall, with a dancer's figure and flawless skin. Her pale eyes fell on Rosa, who stood to greet her.

'*Buon giorno*, Signora Agarossi,' Rosa said. She felt like she was back at the convent and almost curtseyed to the woman.

Signora Agarossi glanced at Sibilla who was awake but quiet in her basket. 'Your baby?'

Rosa nodded and discreetly flashed the curtain ring on her finger. She lowered her eyes. 'My husband ... he was ...'

'Oh, I see,' said Signora Agarossi, indicating for Rosa to sit down again. 'She can stay with the nursemaid during the lessons.'

'Thank you.'

Signora Agarossi glanced at Sibilla. Her face twitched. 'Your baby, she is ... disease free?'

'Yes, Signora Agarossi,' Rosa answered. She resented the question but under the circumstances she had no choice but to answer it.

'Oh, that's good,' said Signora Agarossi. 'You see,

my children are very sensitive. I don't let them play with other children. I don't like dirt brought into the house.'

Rosa wondered what sort of childhood the Agarossi offspring were experiencing if they were not allowed to play with other children. Signora Agarossi did have the appearance of a perfectionist. Her nails were scrubbed and buffed, her teeth were pearly-white and her eyebrows were groomed into arches with not a stray hair in sight.

Signora Agarossi rang a bell. Rosa wondered if she was ordering tea but a few moments later a nursemaid appeared with three children, two boys and one girl, aged from seven to twelve. The boys' shirts were starched, and the little girl wore a yellow pleated dress with a matching ribbon in her hair. All of them had inherited their mother's colouring. Signora Agarossi introduced them by their names and ages: Sebastiano was twelve, Fiorella was ten, and Marco was seven.

'What beautiful children,' Rosa exclaimed. 'They look like angels.'

Signora Agarossi instructed the nursemaid to take Sibilla to a quiet room in the apartment. Then she rose to leave herself.

'Wouldn't you like to stay for the lesson, Signora Agarossi?' Rosa asked. 'To make sure all goes to your satisfaction.'

Signora Agarossi seemed surprised by the suggestion. 'But the children will be the best judges of that,' she replied. 'Besides I will be in my sewing room. I shall hear you.'

The children bowed and curtseyed when their mother left. But once she was out of sight their decorum collapsed. Sebastiano headed for the sofa and flung himself on it. Marco pulled Fiorella's ribbon out and tugged her hair. She wailed.

'Come here, children,' Rosa said patiently. 'Which one of you would like to play first?'

'The flute is a sissy instrument,' Sebastiano sneered. 'I want to play the trombone.'

'Flutes are for girls,' Marco agreed, picking his nose.

Fiorella unpacked her flute from its case and blew on it. Her attempt was unmusical but at least she seemed willing to learn.

'Here, let me show you the correct technique,' Rosa said. She assembled her own flute and demonstrated to the girl how to hold her instrument properly.

Fiorella ignored her and continued to play random rasping notes.

Rosa sighed. Teaching one of the children would have been a challenge, but all three of them at once was a nightmare. She had no choice but to press on. She needed the money.

'If the flute is of no interest to you,' she said to Sebastiano, 'show me what you can do at the piano.'

Sebastiano stood up and strode to the piano. Rosa was glad that he was finally showing some enthusiasm for the lesson. He sat down at the keyboard and played a few elementary scales then commenced the *Moonlight Sonata* in an average way. Yet he seemed satisfied with himself when he had finished.

Rosa could see now that he was an arrogant and spoilt child who would not be corrected. So she flattered him regarding his interpretation, then played the first movement as it should be played, discreetly suggesting he might like to try improving his hand technique. To her surprise, he played the movement again and attempted to include her corrections while his brother and sister wrestled each other on the floor: a fight that ended with Marco biting Fiorella's arm and bringing her to tears.

After several further tests of her patience, Rosa managed to manoeuvre all the children into playing *Greensleeves* together. Sebastiano performed the piece on the piano and Fiorella and Marco accompanied him for a few bars on their flutes. It was at that high point in the lesson that Signora Agarossi returned along with the nursemaid and Sibilla.

'That's going well,' Signora Agarossi said.

Rosa, who was at her wits' end, was taken aback by the praise. The children had told her that they had been learning the piano for years but none of them, except for Sebastiano in the very slightest way, showed any knowledge of the instrument.

'That's the most progress I've seen them make in a while,' Signora Agarossi added. 'Perhaps you should come twice a week.'

Despite her nerves being on edge, Rosa was pleased by the suggestion. The children were difficult to teach but perhaps they would improve over time. And it was more money for her and Sibilla.

'Where did you learn to play music?' Signora Agarossi asked.

'At the Convent of Santo Spirito.'

Signora Agarossi was impressed. 'The convent has a good reputation,' she said.

Signora Agarossi asked about her education at the convent with genuine interest. Rosa did her best to answer without giving away that she was an orphan but was distracted by Fiorella and Marco giggling. They were still standing behind her while she shared the piano stool with Sebastiano.

'You can teach foreign languages too,' said Signora Agarossi, with approval. 'I will speak to my husband but I believe Fiorella would benefit from lessons in French. She picks things up so easily.'

There were more giggles from Fiorella and Marco.

'Mamma,' Sebastiano interrupted.

'What is it, darling?'

'She's got insects in her hair.'

'Who?'

'Signora Bellocchi. I saw one crawling on her neck. Here, I caught it.'

Signora Agarossi stood up in a flash. Her face turned pale. She put out her hand and Sebastiano dropped something into it. She screamed and the maid stepped forward and took whatever it was from her, dumping it into the water jug. A sick sensation gripped Rosa's stomach. Signora Agarossi looked at her in horror. 'Lice!' she screamed.

Rosa's face burned. It wasn't possible. She had washed and scrubbed herself so thoroughly. Then she remembered the bottles of vinegar in the bathroom that morning and the red welts she had seen on the Porretti children's necks. Oh my God, she thought, I caught the lice from them!

'Get away from her!' Signora Agarossi shouted to her children. They scattered to the corners of the room as if Rosa were a dangerous animal. Signora Agarossi's perfect façade was shattered. Her face twisted with disgust. She glared at Rosa. 'You brought lice into this house!' she said, her voice quivering. 'Get out! Get out now!'

Rosa grabbed Sibilla's basket and ran for the door. Signora Agarossi and the nursemaid chased after her like townsfolk running an adulteress out of their village.

'Get out! Get out!' Signora Agarossi shouted. 'And take your dirty child with you!'

Rosa sat on the banks of the Arno with Sibilla, paralysed by panic. What was she to do now? She had little money left. She had taken a chance on being hired as a music teacher and had failed. How could she find work as a maid or a cleaner as quickly as she needed to? Who would take care of Sibilla? She couldn't entrust her to Signora Porretti.

If you stay together you will be a weight around her neck. Signora Cherubini's words stung Rosa's conscience. She looked at Sibilla lying in her basket. Her attempt to save them both had sent them slipping further down the slope. Tears welled in Rosa's eyes. The only thing she could do to save her daughter was to give her up to the sisters of Santo Spirito. But how could she bear the pain of not being with her? Sibilla was all she had.

Rosa stared at the Arno and imagined sinking to the

bottom of it — the cool, muddy water engulfing her; never feeling sorrow again. No, no, no, she told herself. There must be another way. God will help us.

She lifted Sibilla out of her basket and arranged her on the blanket next to her. She pushed the basket into the sunshine to repel any lice that might be lurking there. 'I can't give you up,' she told Sibilla. 'I must stay strong.'

She assembled her flute. It had brought her peace in the past and Rosa hoped it would help her to think clearly now. She played Bach's Air from Orchestral Suite 3, letting the music express the wretchedness in her heart. She was a good-for-nothing whose own daughter would be better off without her. Rosa closed her eyes and lost herself in the sorrowful music. She did not hear the metallic ching of something landing near her. The sound repeated several times at intervals and still she did not pay attention to it.

'You play well,' a man's voice said. 'Beautifully, in fact.'

Rosa opened her eyes and saw that there were coins and notes in Sibilla's basket, at least twenty lire. The same amount she would have received if Signora Agarossi had paid her for the music lesson instead of chasing her out of the house. A woman with a pram walked by and dropped in some coins as did a man in a herringbone suit. They had mistaken her for a street entertainer. At first Rosa was ashamed to be seen to be begging but then she realised the money might be an answer to her prayer.

She looked up at the man who had spoken to her and blinked. He was standing with the sun behind him and was illuminated by its golden rays. He was in his late twenties with tanned skin and copper-brown hair with blond spun through it. He smiled and his teeth gleamed beneath his light beard. He was handsome in a rugged sort of way. He wore gabardine pants and a white shirt. His shoes were worn at the heel and unpolished and yet he looked more elegant than the best-dressed men on Via Tornabuoni. The man's grey eyes flickered to the curtain ring Rosa wore on her finger but his gaze quickly returned to her face. There was something about the way he looked at her. He had a presence Rosa had never seen in any other person.

'Thank you.' She choked on her words. 'Are you a musician too?'

'I'm the leader of a theatrical troupe,' he said. 'We need a flute player. Are you interested?'

Rosa felt light-headed. It must be the lack of food that was making her faint. She averted her eyes.

'Go on,' he said gently and laughed. It was an attractive sound, masculine and deep like his voice.

Rosa wasn't sure she could have refused him, even if she'd wanted to.

ELEVEN

The man's name was Luciano Montagnani. 'Call me Luciano or Montagnani, whichever pleases you better, but never Signor Montagnani. It makes me feel like a town official,' he said.

Luciano was on his way to book a theatre, but asked if Rosa could come to see him that evening. He scribbled out an address for an apartment in Via Ghibellina.

Rosa needed a job if Signora Cherubini's prediction about her ending up on the street wasn't to come true. But she was terrified of giving Luciano lice. Every time he stepped closer to her, she inched back.

'Not this evening,' she told him. 'I can come tomorrow night.'

Tonight she planned to soak her hair in vinegar and wash her clothes to get rid of the parasites.

Early the next evening Rosa set out to meet The Montagnani Company, carrying Sibilla in her basket. Light streamed between the houses and the heat off the cobblestones was searing. She was dazed. Her body had been in decline since she had been in prison and she was still recovering from Sibilla's birth. She wished that she could rest for a few days in bed, but there was no chance of that. She had to press on for Sibilla's sake.

Luciano's apartment building was near the corner of Via delle Casine. The shutters were closed and the door to the street was shut. Rosa was about to push it when her attention was taken by the Medusa-head door pull. She was mesmerised for a moment before she remembered that staring at a gorgon was supposed to turn you to stone. Or was that only men? She heard hammering from inside the building and smelled paint. A woman was singing the 'Ballad of Santa Zita'. The door suddenly swung open and Rosa found herself facing a man in a striped shirt with a patch over his eye.

'I saw you from the window,' he said.

At first Rosa thought the patch might have been part of a pirate costume but then she noticed the scar across the man's face.

'I'm here to audition for the troupe,' she told him.

The man puffed out his barrel chest and examined her with his good eye. 'I am Piero Montagnani,' he said. 'Come this way.'

Rosa guessed that Piero was in his early thirties. She wondered how he had got the scar. Could it have been the Great War? Piero led her into a passageway plastered with tattered theatre bills. She wanted to stop to read them but he indicated a door with some steps leading downwards.

'Our apartment is on the second floor,' he explained. 'But we rent the cellar as well. We use it for rehearsals.'

Rosa followed Piero down the stairs. The hammering grew louder. There was a crash followed by cursing and a burst of laughter. Entering the cellar, Rosa found Luciano nursing his thumb surrounded by two men and two women. His shirtsleeves were rolled up, revealing his muscled arms.

'Signora Bellocchi,' he said, smiling. 'I should have known that banging my thumb was a foretelling of your arrival.'

'If I must call you Luciano then you must call me Rosa,' she replied.

Rosa's comment brought laughter from the others. She blushed, not understanding what was so amusing. It was awkward to call a man she had just met by his Christian name. She glanced at the scenery that was being assembled: a backdrop of a garden of sunflowers and geraniums.

Luciano folded his arms and nodded towards the others. 'This is the young woman I was telling you about,' he said.

'*Che bella bambina*,' said the younger of the two women, stepping forward to admire Sibilla. 'She's so tiny.'

The woman had a fine, sculptured face that was the feminine version of Luciano's. Rosa guessed that she was his sister.

'I am Orietta,' the woman said. 'And I see that you have already met Piero.'

A youth with blond ringlets smiled at Rosa. He had a face like a cherub. 'And I am the youngest brother of all: Carlo.'

'So you are all brothers and sisters?' Rosa asked.

'Good gracious no,' said the remaining man, running his fingers through his well-groomed moustache. He had a refined actor's voice. 'Some of us have class.'

'That is the famous Benedetto Raimondo,' said the older woman, curtseying and covering her mouth to hide her laughter. There was an upright piano to the side of the cellar and the woman sat down at it and played a chord. 'Benedetto Raimondo is an actor extraordinaire. And I am Donatella Fabrizi,' she sang in an operatic voice. She was about fifty years old with a wistful look about her. Her face, while wrinkled, was attractive with finely drawn eyebrows and a flattish nose.

'We come together in the summer,' explained Luciano, pulling out a chair for Rosa. 'The rest of the year we do what we can.'

Piero opened up a piano accordion and commenced playing a tango. Luciano took up a guitar and Orietta a violin. They joined in with him.

'This year we are staging a play and we need someone who can provide music to help set the mood,' Luciano explained while playing.

Rosa realised that she wasn't at an audition — Luciano seemed to have already settled on her — rather she was meeting the others to see if they could get along together. She had played duets and trios with the nuns at the convent but had rarely played entirely by ear. Still, there was something free and dramatic in the music that urged her to join in with it.

She placed Sibilla's basket down next to her chair and felt under the blanket for her flute. She assembled it and came in on the melody with greater ease than she had expected. The music was more sensual than anything she had played before — parts of it were fiery and temperamental, while others were slow, dark and melancholic. At first she felt self-conscious and rested for a few bars to listen to the others. She glanced at Luciano. Suddenly she saw Giovanni Taviani, the gatekeeper at the Villa Scarfiotti, standing and looking at her from the woods. The vision stayed with her no more than a second but was powerful enough to leave her breathless. What did it mean?

She picked up the melody again and played well despite having been shaken by the image. The others stopped playing one by one and let Rosa continue with a solo. She moved on to Bach's Air from Orchestral Suite 3, which was the piece Luciano had heard her playing by the Arno. When she finished, the troupe applauded.

'She's very good,' said Benedetto, giving an excited laugh. 'Perhaps *too* good for us.'

'Yes, she is far too good,' Luciano agreed.

Rosa thought she saw admiration flash in his eyes. She sensed that he knew she was desperate for work but he didn't intend to use that against her.

Luciano was pleased when Rosa told him that she could also play the piano. 'Excellent,' he said. 'You can accompany Donatella and Carlo in their acts and that will leave me free to do other things.'

Carlo announced he would perform his act for Rosa. She watched, astonished, as he juggled balls, clubs and rings using not only his hands but his forehead and feet as well. She was astounded when he added pirouettes and somersaults to the routine. She had never seen anything like it. When he finished, Luciano hummed a tune and asked Rosa to follow it on the piano. She caught the tune easily. Donatella picked up a basket covered with a cloth and carried it to the centre of the room. She whistled and the corner of the cloth lifted. A black nose and two eyes appeared. The next moment a papillon spaniel jumped out and padded along the floor towards Donatella. Rosa continued to play while watching the act. The dog jumped through rings and pranced on his hind legs for Donatella. At first Rosa was reminded of the unfortunate Dono and the undignified way that the gypsy had forced him to dance. But the dog didn't give Rosa the impression of being compelled in any way. He seemed to be enjoying himself. His antics complemented Donatella's comic gestures. Whenever she bent over he took a run and propelled himself into the air off her backside. It was the funniest thing Rosa had seen and she had to cease playing for a while because she couldn't stop laughing.

'You like my act with Dante, do you?' asked Donatella, winking at Rosa. Dante leaped into her arms and gazed at her with adoration. She brought him over to Rosa, who patted his head. 'He's my darling. He's so clever,' gushed Donatella. 'I never have to use a harsh word on him.'

'So what do you think?' Luciano asked Rosa. 'Will you join our troupe? It's not an easy life, especially when we are on tour and performing three times a day as well as rehearsals.'

Rosa caught the expectant looks on the faces of the others. She could see from the tatty costumes that the troupe was poor and that she wasn't going to make a fortune playing with them. But their extroverted energy was uplifting and Luciano's beguiling charm was hard to resist. Before she realised what she was saying, she found herself agreeing to play with them. Her compliance brought whoops of joy from everyone except Luciano, who simply cocked his head in approval.

'Well, that settles it,' he said. 'Let's get something to eat.'

Rosa expected that they might have some bread with a 'C' of olive oil or make some *farinata*. But the troupe headed out to the street. She realised that if they went to a café, even a cheap one, she wouldn't be able to join them. Her rent for the month was due the following day and she needed the rest of the money she had received by the Arno for food. Besides that, Sibilla would want to be nursed soon and, although her milk flow had settled down, Rosa's breasts felt full. She was thinking of ways to excuse herself when the group came to a halt outside a restaurant. Because the evening was warm, the windows were open and some tables and chairs were set up on the cobblestones at the front. A red carpet had been put down and the area was roped off with gold braid. One look at the elegantly dressed diners and the damask table linens and Rosa knew she could not afford to eat there.

A waiter appeared with a stack of plates in his arms, piled so high he could barely see over them. He was followed by another waiter carrying a pile of bowls. Rosa wondered where they were headed. Suddenly Luciano, Carlo and Piero rushed forward and seized the waiters, snatching the plates and bowls off them. Some of the patrons screamed. Rosa felt the blood rush to her feet. They were stealing the plates and bowls! One man stood up and made fists, ready to accost them. Another called out for the police: 'Help! Thieves! Help!' Rosa froze to the spot. Was she going to be sent to prison again? She could only clutch Sibilla's basket and watch with horror as the scene unfolded.

The manager appeared and rushed at Luciano and Carlo. But the brothers were too quick for him. They made a straight line along with Orietta and Piero, while Benedetto opened up the piano accordion and starting playing *La Tarantella*. The Montagnani siblings passed the plates to each other one by one through the air in a juggling act. They slipped them underarm, overarm and spun them on the tips of their fingers. Rosa, along with the patrons, realised it was an act. The man who had challenged the brothers smiled sheepishly and returned to his seat. Donatella encouraged everyone to clap in time while the troupe passed the dishes faster and faster to each other and Dante ran in loops between their legs. As a finale, Orietta climbed on top of her brothers' shoulders and the plates were passed in a triangle formation, which earned a burst of applause from the onlookers. Donatella danced among the diners with a hat, collecting money. The manager slipped a few notes into it. He must have been in on the act. Rosa sighed with relief.

Benedetto slowed his playing and Luciano and Carlo collected the plates and bowls as they were passed back to them. They then handed the piles back to the waiters. After more applause and shouts of '*Bravo!*' the diners returned their attention to their food.

Luciano gestured for everyone to hurry to the adjacent laneway, where Donatella counted out the money into piles.

'They were generous tonight,' she said with a wide grin.

Luciano took some notes from Donatella and gave them to Rosa. She was desperate for money but she couldn't take something she hadn't earned.

'I didn't do anything,' she protested, trying to pass the money back to Luciano. 'I can't accept it.'

'*Non fare brutta figura!*' Luciano scolded her. 'Don't make a scene! It's a gift for the little one's welfare.' He spoke gruffly but Rosa sensed the kindness behind his act.

'*From each according to his ability, to each according to his need*,' said Piero. 'That's Karl Marx. The founder of communism.'

'You are communists?' Rosa asked. She liked the troupe, but if they were communists that could get her into trouble with the fascists.

Carlo burst into laughter. 'No, we're not communists,' he said, patting Rosa on the back. 'We're a family. We take care of each other. And when you join the troupe, you are part of the family too.'

The play the troupe was rehearsing was *Les Misérables*. Luciano and Benedetto had rewritten it so that it required only a small cast along with some multiple-role acting. Rosa watched the performance through to decide on the appropriate music. The subject matter was close to home: abandoned foundlings; a young girl reduced to prostitution after giving birth to an illegitimate daughter. Even the scene where Jean Valjean was turned away by the innkeeper because of his convict past was painful to Rosa. When Luciano called a break mid-afternoon, she excused herself to feed Sibilla but the truth was that she needed to be alone. She took Sibilla to the courtyard where it was quiet and undid her blouse and nursed her daughter under the lines of washing. A while later Carlo appeared with a plate of fried potatoes, mushrooms and radicchio.

'*Bambina* is growing well,' he said, placing the food next to Rosa. 'But you must take care of yourself too.'

'Thank you,' Rosa said, grateful for his thoughtfulness.

'Orietta went out early this morning to the woods,' Carlo explained. 'The mushrooms are particularly good. She said they will bring colour to your face.'

Rosa was touched by Orietta's concern for her health. She remembered what Carlo had said about everyone in the troupe being like a family. Was this what being a family was about? To have someone looking out for you?

Carlo and Rosa spoke for a while about the play and the music before he had to go back inside. Rosa switched Sibilla to her other breast and, when she was done, burped her and laid her back in her basket.

'I brought you some water.'

Rosa saw Luciano looking down at her. She blushed. How did he know that breastfeeding left the mother thirsty? She accepted the glass from him and took small sips.

'Do you like the play?' he asked, sitting down next to her.

Rosa didn't want to tell him that the themes were too close to her heart. 'How does it end?' she asked instead.

'The poor rise up against their oppressors.'

Rosa remembered the servants at the Villa Scarfiotti. She saw them lined up on the steps awaiting the arrival of the Marchesa, who referred to them as 'little people'. She thought of Maria, and the Porrettis.

'Do you think that could happen in Italy?' she asked Luciano. 'Could the poor rise up against their oppressors?'

Luciano studied her. His leg was pressing against her own, but whether he noticed or not Rosa couldn't tell. She felt the warmth of his skin through their clothes. 'They did,' he said. 'And they were crushed. You would have been too young to remember.'

'You mean the workers' strikes after the war?'

Sibilla gurgled and Luciano tickled her chin. His gesture touched Rosa. She had thought he was too masculine to be affectionate towards a baby.

'Piero fought in the Great War,' Luciano said, staring at his feet. 'The soldiers were promised a good life in return for their sacrifice — land, work, education for their children. Well, that didn't happen.'

'Did Piero receive that … I mean, was Piero injured in the war?' Rosa asked.

Luciano shook his head. 'By some miracle he came home unscathed. He lost his eye to the fascists. He took part in the strikes and had his head kicked in by a Blackshirt.'

Rosa shuddered. She had heard a little about the riots while she was at the convent, but only from the paying pupils whose fathers were rich factory owners and fascists themselves. In their recounts, it was always the workers who were to blame for the violence. Rosa realised that there was so much that she didn't know. She glanced at Luciano. She couldn't blame him for being bitter. She had suffered because of the fascists too.

'It must have been terrible,' she said.

Luciano nodded. 'I was a youth. Piero told me to stay home and take care of my mother and younger siblings. But I wanted to see ... Well, what did I see? Women beaten until their faces were pulp. A man tied to a truck and dragged along until his arms were torn off. All for asking for bread for their families and some dignity.'

'Oh, God,' said Rosa, covering her mouth in horror.

Luciano turned away and shrugged. 'I hate what Italy has turned into now. Even the peasants and workers have been convinced to think that Mussolini is a hero. Well, he's not. He'll drag us all to our doom if he isn't stopped.'

'What makes you say that?' Rosa asked.

Sibilla gurgled again. Rosa picked her up and cradled her in her arms. Luciano looked at Sibilla and fell silent. Rosa waited for him to say something further about Mussolini but he averted his gaze. Speaking ill of the dictator could lead to a lot of trouble. Perhaps he didn't trust her.

'What were you going to say?' she prompted him.

Luciano shook his head. 'Never mind,' he said, standing up. 'Play the piano, Rosa, and enjoy yourself with the troupe. Your baby needs you. The less you know what I think the better.'

Les Misérables ran for four weeks at a run-down theatre on Via del Parlascio. The audience was not as abjectly poor as the characters but carried about them an air of fatalism that their lives would be hard work until the day they died. They were factory workers; coal sellers who didn't wash before they came so that all that could be seen of them in the dark was their teeth; cobblers with blisters on their hands; blacksmiths; barbers; travelling salesmen. In the better seats at the front were those whose position in society placed them above the poor, but who knew that their situation could change with a bout of ill health or bad luck. They were the bakers and merchants, railway station masters and petty officials. On Friday nights, the estate managers and *fattori* came to see the performance after a long day of haggling with brokers and suppliers and visiting the prostitutes who waited for them in the Piazza della Signoria. Rosa wondered if she might see Signor Collodi in the audience, but she never did.

'Four weeks is a good run in Florence,' Orietta explained to Rosa. 'But we need to take the show on tour if we are to save sufficient money for the quieter months. We try to perform in the towns before August, when the big theatres send their troupes on tour.'

Rosa was glad to get away from the chaotic Porretti household and her attic room, which was proving unbearably hot as July approached. The first destination was the spa town of Montecatini Terme. To save on the cost of train fares, Luciano had arranged for the troupe to travel part of the way in two empty lorries heading towards Pistoia to pick up loads of charcoal. When Rosa saw the black dust that covered the insides of the lorries, she understood why Luciano had instructed everyone to wear dark clothes for the journey.

While they were waiting for the drivers to check over the lorries, Orietta rummaged in her bag and pulled out a package wrapped in brown paper.

'I made it for Sibilla,' she told Rosa.

Donatella and Carlo turned around, interested to see what was in the package. Benedetto and Piero were already asleep under the canopy they'd erected to provide shade while waiting. Luciano was talking with the drivers. He glanced over his shoulder then turned back to the conversation.

Rosa untied the string and opened the paper. Inside she found a cotton batiste baby dress and bonnet. The dress was decorated with pink embroidery and the bonnet was trimmed in dainty lace. Rosa was filled with gratitude.

'Thank you,' she said. 'I never expected such a lovely gift.'

Orietta squeezed Rosa's arm. 'Sibilla's a beautiful baby, she needs a nice dress.'

If Rosa had been blessed with a sister, she would have wished for one like Orietta. She admired the seams. 'The stitchwork is so fine,' she said. 'You're very talented.'

'I come from a family of tailors,' Orietta replied. 'It must be in my blood.'

Luciano shot a dark look at his sister. Carlo turned away. Orietta blushed and stopped herself from saying anything further. Rosa, sensing the tension, glanced at Donatella who shook her head. It was obviously better not to pursue that line of discussion.

Rosa carefully folded the dress and rewrapped it in the paper. 'Sibilla can wear it tonight. For our opening,' she said.

The trip to Montecatini Terme was Rosa's first so far out of Florence and she enjoyed the view of the woodlands and vineyards. A sense of adventure was stirring in her breast. 'Enclosed' had been the term used to describe life at the convent. Rosa realised that her life had been enclosed in more ways than one: the convent; the villa; and prison. Poverty was another kind of enclosure. Suddenly she felt the joy of freedom growing inside her. The troupe was a band of outsiders and Rosa was an outsider too. But she didn't mind being one as long as she was with them. None of the troupe asked her prying questions about her heritage or Sibilla's father. They didn't seem to judge her. She'd given up the farce of wearing the curtain ring on her wedding finger. Rosa wondered about Luciano's reaction to Orietta mentioning that their family had once been tailors. Perhaps they didn't pry because the Montagnani family carried secrets of their own.

The drivers made a brief stop outside Prato.

Sibilla was hungry and Rosa sat by the roadside to feed her. When she'd finished, she felt sleepy. She rolled up her bag as a pillow and lay back. Between Sibilla's feeds and working with the troupe, she'd learnt to snatch sleep whenever she could. She noticed that Orietta, Carlo and Luciano were talking with each other on the opposite side of the road. Donatella, with Dante under her arm, sidled up next to Rosa.

'It's a sore point with Luciano,' she whispered.

'What?' Rosa asked.

'Their father and how their family were once famous tailors.'

'They were?'

'Oh, yes,' said Donatella, nodding. 'They were wealthy. Their clients included dukes and marcheses.'

Rosa looked at Donatella. 'What happened?'

'Their father gambled on a risky investment and lost it all.'

'Oh,' said Rosa. She'd always been poor but she could imagine it would be a shock to be born wealthy and then suddenly have nothing.

Donatella leaned forward. 'Not only did their father lose everything but he ran away for the shame. Their mother was pregnant with Carlo and Orietta was only a baby. They were taken in by their mother's brother but after that their mother was bedridden. She died soon afterwards. Luciano won't speak of his father. Piero told me that Luciano's grief was so great that he often ran away, and Piero would find him in a field or piazza staring forlornly at the sky.'

'How old was he when this happened?' Rosa asked, surprised to find herself so curious. Why was it when someone mentioned Luciano's name she wanted to know everything about him?

'Luciano was ten. Piero was fourteen. They were only boys but they had to carry the family,' Donatella said, before adding: 'They still do.'

Rosa glanced in Luciano's direction. The contradiction of his fine profile and elegant gestures against his poverty made sense now. He laughed and joked with the troupe, but Rosa noticed the faint worry lines that marked his forehead.

It was always Luciano who was working out when and where the troupe would eat, sleep, and how to divide the earnings. Rosa imagined him as a ten-year-old boy trying to support his family and his ailing mother. The thought of it gave her a panicked feeling in her chest. No wonder he looks anxious so often, she thought.

Montecatini Terme was a picturesque town of tree-lined boulevards, and classical and Art Nouveau buildings. It had a belle-époque elegance about it. The shops were as fine as any found on Via Tornabuoni and the people promenading on the pavements were beautifully turned out in butterfly-sleeved dresses or drape-cut suits. They sported suntans, and their carefree languor reminded Rosa of the sculptured nymphs that decorated the town's fountains. Because the troupe did not have the means to perform at the new Teatro Giardino Le Terme, Luciano obtained a permit to set up the troupe's tent in the park that formed the centrepiece of the town.

When the tent was ready and chairs had been hired from a local café, Luciano, Piero, Carlo and Benedetto handed out bills for the evening's performance to people strolling and picnicking in the park. Donatella took Dante for a walk, while Rosa and Orietta prepared polenta with leeks and tomatoes. The men returned along with Donatella, who had purchased wafer biscuits made of almonds and sugar for dessert. They ate quickly before changing into their costumes and taking positions at the tent entrance to welcome the patrons. The audience consisted of spa attendants, masseurs and hotel waiters on their night off. Some tourists also came, but the serious theme of *Les Misérables* didn't sit well with them, and most left after the first act.

'Tomorrow night we'd better resort to our juggling and dog acts,' said Luciano, eyeing the pile of poster bills that would now be wasted. 'I guess that after a day of taking the waters, mudpacks and herbal massages the last thing they want is a dose of reality.'

'*Les Misérables* is far too serious for this crowd. Why don't we pull out *Gabriella*?' suggested Benedetto. 'It was a hit when I was performing with another troupe in Rome a few years ago.'

'What's *Gabriella* about?' asked Rosa. If they changed plays she was going to have to come up with a different musical accompaniment.

Benedetto spread out his hands dramatically. 'A husband goes to France to find work to support his family. He leaves behind his beautiful wife, Gabriella, and two young daughters. Although he sends them money faithfully, Gabriella takes a lover. When she learns her husband is returning, she kills her two daughters and runs away with her lover.'

'It's too gruesome for this town,' objected Donatella. 'The woman chops her daughters into pieces.'

Despite the heat, Rosa shivered.

'Rosa, are you all right?' asked Orietta, looking concerned.

Rosa knew that Benedetto was only fooling around, telling his bloodthirsty story for entertainment. But the idea disturbed her. 'A mother would never do that,' she said, tears burning her eyes. 'A mother would never kill her children.'

Benedetto raised his eyebrows. 'Italy has one of the highest infanticide rates in the world! Women kill their babies all the time — or abandon them at orphanages.'

Anger raged inside Rosa, but it wasn't directed at Benedetto. What he'd said was true: it was one of the reasons for the existence of OMNI. She couldn't understand herself why she was having such a fierce reaction. The image of Maria bleeding to death loomed up before her.

'Only when they are so desperate there is no alternative,' she said. 'Only when the life of the child will be so miserable that the mother feels she has no choice.'

Benedetto was about to say something else when Orietta tweaked his arm and he thought better of it.

Orietta looked at Rosa. 'It's all right. You are a beautiful mother, Rosa. That's why you can't believe anyone could murder their own child.'

Despite her effort to control herself, Rosa burst into tears.

'It's a stupid idea,' said Luciano, flashing an annoyed look at Benedetto. 'If the audience can't appreciate *Les Misérables* on their holidays, I can't see them flocking to see a bloodthirsty play.'

'It has a good ending,' insisted Benedetto. 'The husband returns and takes revenge on his wife and her lover. He cuts them up into pieces and then throws them in the toilet.'

'*Perfetto!*' groaned Luciano, shaking his head.

Rosa couldn't bear it any longer. She picked up Sibilla and rushed out of the tent. She found a seat under a tree and threw herself down on it, heaving with grief. Had her mother not wanted her? Was that why she had been left at the convent?

'They are exhausted. Sometimes they say stupid things.' Rosa looked up to see Luciano standing in front of her. 'Benedetto didn't mean anything by it,' he said.

Rosa nodded but couldn't bring herself to speak. Luciano sat down next to her. He took Sibilla and bounced her on his knee. The baby laughed with delight. Luciano gazed at Rosa with a mingled expression of pity and admiration.

'Orietta is right,' he said. 'It's because you are a good mother that you can't believe others could be such poor ones.'

'Thank you,' said Rosa. 'I try to be a good mother but I think you know that I was never married.'

She watched his face, expecting disapproval, but his expression was undisturbed. 'Ah, I see,' he said.

Rosa felt a fleeting moment of anxiety and wondered if she had said too much. They sat in silence for a while looking at the stars, each lost in their own thoughts. A soft light lingered in the sky.

'Well, now you know what there is to know about me,' said Rosa.

Luciano leaned back on his elbow and sighed. 'My mother was a saint,' he said. 'Despite the terrible thing my father did, she would never say a bad word about him.'

Rosa was taken aback by Luciano's sudden intimacy. Hadn't Donatella said that he never spoke about his father? She was finding herself more and more curious about him.

'We lived in a house on Via della Vigna Vecchia with parquet floors and tapestries on the walls,' Luciano continued. 'We had two cats and three dogs. I remember my father singing while he dressed to go to work in his store on Via Tornabuoni. His grandfather had started as a humble tailor in Turin and by the time my father inherited the business the family was already wealthy. He moved the store to Florence and his reputation as the finest tailor in the city grew.'

Rosa saw that Luciano's shoulders sank with the weight of his own story. The pain the memory caused him was evident on his face.

'When my father came home from work,' Luciano told her, 'he spent hours playing hand puppets with us and telling us stories. Life was as good as we could wish for, but my father wasn't happy with that. He was envious of his excessively rich clients. He wanted to be like them. He took our money and invested it in a shipping scheme, which might have gone well if the fleet hadn't sunk.'

Rosa felt a crushing sadness. 'That's terrible!' she said.

Luciano shook his head. 'It took a while to go into complete decline. It was a drawn-out slide. Then, before the creditors had taken everything except the clothes off our backs, my father decided to clear out of our lives.'

Rosa was unable to meet Luciano's pain-filled eyes. 'And your mother? She became sick?'

He hesitated before answering. '"I'm not strong," my mother would say on the mornings she couldn't get out of bed. "Don't marry a weak woman, Luciano. Marry someone strong." But it wasn't my mother who was weak.'

Rosa found Luciano's story shocking. She had always fantasised what it would be like to have grown up with a family. She'd pictured a warm home, everyone gathered around the table at meal times, and someone to kiss her goodnight. But having parents didn't guarantee the security and love Rosa had imagined it would. It certainly hadn't for Luciano and his family.

'Is your father still alive?' she asked.

Luciano shrugged. 'I suppose so. When our mother became gravely ill, he sent my uncle money for the hospital and to take care of us. But he never came back to see us.'

Rosa closed her eyes and imagined a young Luciano standing near the door of his uncle's house and looking expectantly at the street. She saw every detail of the boy, from his sailor suit to the curl that flopped over his forehead. A pain jabbed her heart. She opened her eyes and studied the hard line of Luciano's jaw. She understood that he had waited every day for his father until one day he finally gave up.

TWELVE

The troupe toured the towns and villages along the Arno, and also briefly toured Siena where they tried *Les Misérables* again and it was well received. Their last stop was Lucca, the birthplace of Puccini. The town's Roman origins lingered in the grid pattern of its streets, and the Piazza dell'Anfiteatro retained the circular shape of an ancient amphitheatre. The weather was boiling. The men erected the tent while the women sheltered in the shade with Sibilla and Dante. Donatella and Orietta repaired the costumes while Rosa sewed pillowcases for the troupe. The only accommodation they could afford was a hotel near Via Sant'Andrea. One look at it and Rosa knew it was a haven for vermin. She didn't intend to catch lice again.

'What are you doing?'

Rosa looked up to see Luciano standing before her. He was naked to the waist. The spicy smell of his perspiration tickled her nostrils. She turned away. There was something about his muscled torso and sun-bronzed skin that unsettled her.

'I'm making pillowcases for everyone,' she replied.

'I told you to help repair the costumes for this evening.'

Luciano's tone was sharp. Rosa flinched but the memory of the humiliation she had suffered at the Agarossi home helped her to hold her ground.

'It's the small things that can ruin your life,' she told him. 'Do you think people will come and see us perform if we give them lice?'

'What?'

Rosa sensed that Luciano was looking at her but kept her gaze lowered.

Donatella and Orietta giggled. 'Tell him the story,' Donatella urged Rosa.

Luciano let out an exasperated breath. 'I don't have time for this chatter. You can tell me later, Rosa. The performance is in a few hours and we are only half-ready.'

'Come on, Luciano,' said Donatella. 'Why are you being so serious? Do you have heatstroke? Rosa lost her engagement as a music teacher because the place she was staying was riddled with lice. That's what happened before you found her sitting by the Arno. It's why she wouldn't come and see us that night.'

Rosa blushed and fell into a mortified silence. She hadn't expected Donatella to repeat the story to Luciano. She should have known better than to tell her in the first place.

'Well, I hadn't thought of that,' Luciano said. 'It's not a bad idea. I was attacked by mites last summer and it was terrible. The last thing we want is to be itching and scratching on stage.'

Rosa dared to raise her eyes. Luciano was still frowning but she could see from the way his lips twitched that he was resisting a grin. Something in her stirred and she couldn't help smiling. They both quickly looked away from each other. Rosa was sure that her face must be as red as tomato paste.

'Luciano!' Benedetto called. 'Come on!'

The tent was sagging in the middle. Luciano ran towards the men. 'Quick, pull the ropes!' he shouted. 'It's going to collapse!'

Orietta glanced at Rosa. 'My brother can come across as a hard nut,' she said. 'But he has a soft centre.'

'Nilda used to call Luciano the "Amaretti biscuit",' said Donatella.

Orietta flashed Donatella a displeased look.

'Who is Nilda?' Rosa asked.

Donatella opened her mouth, about to pour out a story, but Orietta jabbed her in the ribs. 'We have to work,' she said. 'You heard Luciano. The performance is in a few hours.'

Rosa wanted to know about Nilda, but Orietta and Donatella went on with their sewing and said nothing more.

Later, when the tent was up, the women fetched water from the cistern to give to the men. Carlo and Piero looked beaten and sat with their heads hanging on their chests. Benedetto lay down on his back while Dante licked his face. Rosa handed a cup to Luciano who was perched on a stool, rolling a cigarette. He received the water with a nod and took a sip.

'I suppose I have to be grateful to lice,' he said. 'If it wasn't for them, you wouldn't be with us. You'd be teaching some brats in Florence.'

Something about the way that Luciano looked at her when he spoke both pleased Rosa and made her afraid. But she couldn't explain her reasons for either emotion.

The hour before a show was always a rush, with the performers dressing and applying their make-up while undertaking a multitude of other tasks. The first night in Lucca was no exception. Donatella ran around in her petticoat, holding ladders for Piero and Carlo so they could adjust lights. Orietta, with curlers in her hair, fixed a rip in the curtains while Benedetto, dressed as a policeman, hammered a loose board on the stage into place. Rosa would have helped but she had to time Sibilla's feeding and nappy changes so that her cries wouldn't interrupt the performance.

When Sibilla was finished nursing, Rosa laid her in the basket. She asked Orietta to keep an eye on her while she went to the toilet. Rather than make her way to the tent entrance, Rosa slid under the back of the tent to make her trip shorter. She straightened up and bumped into a woman who was standing there.

'Excuse me, signorina,' Rosa said.

The woman was statuesque with ebony hair. She carried a kitbag in her hand, and hurried away as soon as she saw Rosa. The woman's odd behaviour made her wonder if she was a fascist spy. There was nothing subversive in the troupe's repertoire, but if someone in the town had found out that she was an 'enemy of the state', they might be planning to make trouble. Rosa crept around the side of the tent and spotted the woman talking with Luciano. After a brief embrace, Luciano took the case from the woman, who then walked away towards the piazza.

Rosa returned to the dressing area in time to see Luciano slip the bag under a blanket. Neither Orietta nor Donatella, who were changing behind the ladies' modesty curtain, saw what Luciano had done. Rosa pretended not to notice.

'There's a crowd already,' Carlo said, rushing into the dressing area.

'Come,' Luciano said to Rosa. 'You start playing and I'll sell the tickets.'

That night's performance was the largest audience the troupe had attracted on the tour. They were also the most appreciative, clapping for all the tricks and laughing and crying in the right places for *Les Misérables*. Rosa played well but all the time her thoughts were about the woman and the bag. Why had Luciano hidden it from even his sister? Rosa knew it didn't contain the takings; Luciano kept those in a pouch tucked under his shirt. And the beautiful woman — who was she? Rosa pursed her lips, convinced she must be the Nilda that Donatella had mentioned. Was she Luciano's lover? Rosa experienced something she had never felt before: a strange combination of disappointment, fear, rage and yearning. It was her first attack of jealousy.

When the performance was over, the troupe packed up and prepared to go to the hotel. All except Benedetto. The men had agreed one of them would stay in the tent each night to guard the equipment. Although she was exhausted, Rosa could not quell her desire to know what was in the bag. Carlo and Luciano led the way down the street with the women following behind. Rosa slipped her chain from her neck and hid it in her pocket.

'Oh,' she said, feeling her neck. 'I left my chain on the dressing table.'

'I thought you were wearing it during the performance,' said Orietta, looking concerned.

Carlo and Luciano stopped and turned around to see what was happening.

'You go ahead,' Rosa told them, handing Sibilla's basket to Orietta. 'I'll only be a minute. I know where it is.'

Luciano frowned at her. Rosa was glad it was dark because she was sure her face was red. 'Ask Benedetto for the torch,' he said. 'We'll wait here.'

Rosa rushed back to the tent with the Church's teachings against being a busybody ringing around her head. She remembered Don Marzoli reading from the book of Peter that those who meddled in the affairs of others were as bad as murderers, thieves and other evildoers. Still, Rosa could not help herself. She found Benedetto dozing off at the entrance and slipped the torch from under his seat before running to the dressing area. Luciano would not wait more than a few minutes so she had to hurry. She moved the blanket and was relieved to see that the bag was still there. She undid the catch and opened it, shining the torch into the interior. There were papers, hundreds of them, all folded the same way. Rosa pulled one out and opened it. The words *fascismo* and *liberazione* jumped out at her. Written in bold type across the sheet was the appeal: *Don't destroy this pamphlet. Pass it on to sympathetic friends or leave it where others might find it.*

'I knew you were lying!'

Rosa spun around to see Luciano standing behind her. He switched on a light. His body was trembling with rage.

'What are these?' she asked in a low voice. 'Anti-fascist pamphlets?'

Luciano clenched his fists. 'I should not have trusted you!'

'Not trusted me?' cried Rosa. 'Don't you know that this sort of material puts the whole troupe in danger?'

'That's why none of the others know about them, except Piero!' Luciano retorted. 'What the hell are you doing snooping through my things?'

Rosa's heart thumped in her chest. She had expected to discover some secret about Luciano's lover, not to find out about his covert anti-fascist activities. 'I'm not a fascist, Luciano,' she told him. 'Believe me. But my friend ... she was executed for her involvement with Giustizia e Libertà.'

Luciano's eyes grew wide with Rosa's mention of the organisation. 'The only way to fight the fascists is to expose their lies,' he said in a calmer tone. 'This is the way I do it. Who was your friend?'

'Sibilla Ciruzzi. I named Sibilla after her.'

Luciano stepped towards Rosa. 'You knew Sibilla Ciruzzi?' He peered at her as if he was reassessing his opinion of her.

Rosa nodded. 'Did you know her too?'

Luciano shook his head. 'Only as a brave woman. Her husband is a leading member of Giustizia e Libertà.'

Rosa looked at the pamphlets. 'You distribute these? Then you are courageous yourself.'

She admired Luciano for what he was doing. The fascists had broken her.

'I won't say anything,' she told him. 'And you *are* right. It's better for the others that they don't know anything. But ignorance won't necessarily protect them. The fascists put innocent people in prison too.'

Luciano frowned. 'You sound as though you are speaking from experience?'

Rosa shrugged. One day she might tell him what had happened, but not tonight. She was too shaken by her discovery.

Luciano studied her. 'What were you doing looking through the bag anyway?'

Rosa knew that she'd made a fool of herself. How could she save the situation? 'Curiosity trapped the bird in the net,' she grinned sheepishly, quoting the Italian proverb.

'Ha!' laughed Luciano, his gaze settling on Rosa's lips. 'Well, if that's the case, the bird died nobly.'

The final evening of their stint in Lucca was stifling hot. After the performance, Rosa lay awake in the room she shared with Orietta and Donatella, fanning Sibilla. The heat had reduced her milk flow and she was worried Sibilla could become dehydrated. When things had not cooled down by three o'clock in the morning, Rosa could stand it no longer. The hotel had a courtyard and she crept down the stairs with Sibilla, hoping for some relief in the cooler air. She placed Sibilla's basket on the stones and sang softly to the baby so that she wouldn't start crying. She found a wooden tub propped against the wall and filled it with water from the cistern. She dabbed Sibilla's face and chest to soothe her. After a while she decided to try feeding her again. She pulled her nightdress down and splashed water on her breasts. She heard someone behind her and spun around.

'Who's there?'

Luciano stepped out of the shadows. He was wearing his pants with the braces hanging down and a singlet. At first Rosa didn't cover herself. Luciano had seen her breasts before when she had been feeding Sibilla. Rosa had lost the modesty the nuns had attempted to instil in her about her body and behaved as most Italian mothers did — except for the very rich who were concerned about their figures. Her breasts were for feeding her baby. But this time Luciano's gaze was different and she sensed it. Her skin prickled with goose bumps.

'It was too hot to sleep,' she said, pulling her nightdress back up and buttoning it. 'I was worried about Sibilla.'

Luciano crouched near the basket and felt Sibilla's face. 'She is warm. Has she been wetting her nappy?'

'Yes,' said Rosa. 'But I'm not sure she is getting enough milk from me.'

Luciano unknotted the cotton scarf he was wearing around his neck and soaked it under the cistern. He squeezed it out and gently patted it on Sibilla's feet.

'She'll be fine as long as you keep drinking water,' he said to Rosa. 'Tomorrow I will rise early and buy some fresh milk. My mother used to say drinking two cups of milk over a sink would make breast milk plentiful.'

'Thank you,' Rosa said.

'Why don't you sleep out here?' Luciano offered. 'I'll bring a mattress.'

'Orietta said there are rats.'

'I'll watch over you while you sleep.'

Luciano disappeared then returned with the bedding as promised. He propped himself up against one of the courtyard's pillars and lit a cigarette. Rosa lay down on the mattress with Sibilla. Her body felt weighted with exhaustion. Her eyelids drooped but she couldn't sleep. She was taken with a desire she couldn't yet fathom: for Luciano to lie next to her and hold her in his arms.

'Luciano?' she said softly.

'Yes?'

'Who is Nilda? Is she your lover?'

Luciano stared at the sky and blew out a long puff of cigarette smoke. 'Go to sleep, Rosa,' he said. 'Don't worry about Nilda. Poor Nilda is dead.'

Luciano left the hotel early the following morning to purchase milk for Rosa. When he returned, he collected the troupe's equipment and organised transport to the railway station. Once they were on the train, Luciano lay his head back and instructed Piero not to let him sleep more than a couple of hours. 'We are stopping briefly at Pistoia,' he told him. 'I want to see if the theatre there is free next August.'

Rosa was disappointed to be returning to Florence. The tour had been tiring but it had also been an adventure. She'd had a glimpse of what it was to feel truly alive for the first time in her life; to live by her wits and succeed. Now they were returning to the city, it was uncertain how much work there would be for them as entertainers. Benedetto would find roles with a theatre or on a film, while the others would have to seek odd jobs to supplement their income over the winter. Rosa knew that she would miss the camaraderie of the troupe and the sense of family. But most of all she knew she would miss Luciano.

When Luciano left to go into Pistoia, he gave some money to Piero and told him to buy everyone a meal at one of the restaurants near the station. They found a café and ate soup, spaghetti with garlic and olive oil, and *panzanella* — a salad of bread crumbled with tomatoes, onions, basil and vinegar. While they were eating, Orietta turned to Rosa.

'What do you intend to do when we are back in Florence?' she asked. 'Where will you live?'

Rosa shrugged. She had been loath to think about it. She wasn't sure that she had the confidence to be a music teacher after what had happened at the Agarossi home.

'Well,' said Orietta, sending a glance to Piero and Carlo. 'We'd like you to come and live with us.'

Rosa was too moved to speak. The Montagnanis had been like aunts and uncles to Sibilla, the closest thing Rosa could give her daughter to a family.

'Live with you? Me? Why me?' she stammered.

Carlo placed his hand on Rosa's shoulder and looked at her with his angelic eyes. 'Because I'm tired of being the youngest,' he said. 'If you come and live with us, everyone can pick on you instead.'

Benedetto laughed and ribbed Carlo: 'They don't tease you because you are the youngest.'

Rosa couldn't blink away her tears fast enough. She had never known such kindness. She and Sibilla would have a home. It was too wonderful to believe.

'Ah, Rosa,' said Piero, shaking his finger at her, 'no crying. Come and live with us and be happy.'

When the troupe arrived back in Florence, Benedetto and Donatella bade them farewell. Benedetto was returning to Rome with the promise to contact the troupe again the following summer. Donatella and Dante had found work with a circus that was touring France and Britain. Orietta took in sewing work and Carlo found a job as a porter at a hotel where the manager didn't ask for any paperwork. Piero and Luciano had the most difficulty finding jobs because, along with Carlo, they refused to obtain Fascist Party memberships. They ended up working illegally for a publisher, hawking journals and magazines door to door.

Piero took to the work philosophically but Rosa could see Luciano's pride was rankled. They were capable of something better, but without Fascist Party cards no one would employ them. Rosa thought of the Italian proverb: *A burden that one chooses is not felt.* But it seemed to her that Piero and Luciano felt theirs.

The Montagnanis agreed that Rosa didn't need to work until Sibilla was weaned, but she was determined to pay her way. Her mind drifted back to Via Tornabuoni. She no longer felt ashamed at the idea of approaching Signor Parigi. Her 'family' needed the money and the worst Signor Parigi could do was say no.

Rosa stopped a moment to admire the window display before entering Signor Parigi's store. A pair of bronze candelabra with jasperware medallions were arranged on top of a mahogany credenza. Next to the credenza was a rosewood firescreen with a peacock-motif panel. Rosa glanced through the window and saw that Signor Parigi was talking with a female customer. He was still elegant, this time in a charcoal grey suit. Rosa smiled when she remembered the infatuation she had once felt for him. Her heart now only had space for Luciano, although she had no idea how he thought about her.

Rosa entered the store and a bell on the door tinkled. She had left Sibilla with Orietta and felt 'phantom pains' not to be carrying the baby basket. She would explain about her daughter if she was offered a job.

As Signor Parigi was occupied, Rosa expected that his wife might appear to greet her. But it seemed she wasn't there. Signor Parigi made a gesture of acknowledgement to Rosa but showed no recognition of her. Disappointed, Rosa turned her attention to some etched-glass lamps but felt drawn to look again at what the customer was wearing. The woman's lithe figure was flattered by the crimson coat dress, pinched at the waist with a wide leather belt. Rosa experienced a wave of dizziness as she stared at the belt, and found herself standing on vast grasslands that were burnt yellow by the sun. An animal moved up ahead of her. It had powerful hind legs and a long thick tail. It leaped — no, hopped — through the grass, coming to a stop near a muddy waterhole before turning to look at her. It had long ears and doe-like eyes. There was a bulge in its stomach. Something moved and then a smaller version of the animal appeared from a pouch. Rosa thought it was the most beautiful vision she had ever experienced. Suddenly there was a loud *bang*! The animal fell to its side and flailed on the ground as blood burst from its neck. There was another gunshot and the baby animal's body spun through the air. Rosa gasped and found herself standing back in the store with Signor Parigi and his customer staring at her.

'You're admiring my belt,' said the woman with a smile. 'It's Schiaparelli.'

'It's kangaroo leather. From Australia,' said Rosa, shocked that her power to see the origin of things had returned with such force. She had not felt it so vividly for years.

The woman laughed with surprise. 'Very good. How did you know that? Schiap is the only one importing it into Europe. She's a genius.'

Rosa looked beyond the woman to Signor Parigi. He was beaming at her and she saw that he remembered her now.

'Concentrate, Signora Bellocchi,' said Signor Parigi, winking and placing a jewellery box in front of her. 'Tell me about this item.'

Rosa stared at the box. At first she found it difficult to see beyond the image of the tortoise whose shell had been used to decorate the lid. She had an image of the hundred-year-old reptile floating peacefully in the green sea off the New Guinea coast, unaware that his life was about to be taken by a spear thrust by a native. Sibilla had said that Rosa had a supernatural sympathy with animals. Rosa was going to have to see further than that if she was to impress Signor Parigi. She ran her gaze over the bronze-winged women on the sides of the box before opening the lid and smelling the velvet-lined interior. Suddenly in her mind's eye she saw a reflection shining back at her from the box's mirror: a young woman with blonde ringlets was checking her complexion.

'France, 1870,' Rosa said. 'The young woman who owned this box died in a carriage accident when she was seventeen. Two days before she was to be married.'

Rosa looked up at Signor Parigi and saw the surprise on his face.

'Incredible!' he said, clapping his hands. 'I don't know about the woman but the date and origin are perfect. And what about these?' He held up a pair of cherub torcheres with foliate carving.

Rosa wasn't enjoying the forced psychic readings; they left her drained. She had no control over her power to see the source of things so couldn't guarantee her ability every time. Sometimes the vibrations were so strong that she felt the animal or tree from which the object had been fashioned; other times she sensed nothing at all. Rosa glanced at Signor Parigi and understood that he did not believe in her intuition. He thought her visions were creative embellishments on a solid knowledge of antiques, but he was enjoying the 'show'. He saw it as a novel kind of salesmanship.

Rosa concentrated on the torcheres. She saw streets of water. 'They are Venetian,' she said. She had a vision of a woman kneeling by her bed and praying. 'They belonged to a pious woman.' She was about to add that she thought the woman was Signor Parigi's late mother, but decided to keep that knowledge to herself.

Signor Parigi placed the torcheres down with care. 'They are not for sale,' he said. 'I just like to have them close by.' Then, turning back to Rosa, he grinned from ear to ear. 'When can you start?'

Rosa enjoyed her work at Signor Parigi's shop. He paid her a commission on any furniture she helped to sell with her 'charming stories' and didn't mind her bringing Sibilla with her. The baby slept in the backroom and Rosa fed her when the shop was quiet.

A few days after Rosa began at the shop, Signor Parigi gave Sibilla a rattle. 'Look what Uncle Antonio has for you, eh?' he said.

The rattle was sterling silver with a whistle handle. Rosa realised that behind Signor Parigi's elegant appearance and keen business acumen lurked a warm heart. Sibilla could see it too. She responded to Signor Parigi's gift by blowing bubbles and lifting her feet to her hands for him.

Rosa thanked Signor Parigi profusely.

He waved his hand. 'It's nothing,' he said. 'But if I am Uncle Antonio for your daughter, it's silly for you to be so formal with me. Address me as Signor Parigi in front of customers. Otherwise I'd prefer it if you call me Antonio.'

Rosa bought two dress suits to wear to work, one with a wraparound jacket and the other with bell sleeves. The rest of the money she put into the communal tin at the apartment in Via Ghibellina. Within a short while, however, she was making much more than everyone else.

One morning while Rosa was getting ready for work, she walked into the kitchen to find Orietta cleaning up after breakfast and Luciano putting on his boots. He wasn't going with Piero to hawk magazines that day; he'd found a labouring job. He looked Rosa up and down.

'I hear this Signor Parigi lets you call him Antonio now,' he said, glancing at Orietta. 'Is he married?'

Luciano's tone was protective and Rosa experienced a shiver of excitement when she sensed the jealousy behind it. It wasn't that she wanted Luciano to be unhappy, she simply needed to know that he felt *something* for her. Since the end of the tour she had wondered if the attraction was all one way. He hardly ever looked at her.

'Why, yes,' she answered, trying to reassure Luciano. She harboured such tender thoughts for him, she didn't want to play games with him. 'Or at least, I think so. He hasn't mentioned his wife since I started there. Perhaps she's pregnant and not working any more. He goes home at lunchtime. Somebody must be waiting there for him.'

'A maid perhaps,' said Luciano, turning to the window.

Orietta put down the coffee cup she was washing and looked from her brother to Rosa. Guessing the reason for Luciano's mood, she smiled.

'Aren't you two going in the same direction today?' she asked, nudging her brother. 'Sibilla's getting heavy. Maybe you can carry her basket for Rosa.'

Rosa's heart lit up. She could have hugged Orietta.

'Of course,' said Luciano. He kissed Orietta goodbye and grabbed his jacket and hat before opening the door for Rosa. Together they walked out to the street. Being close to Luciano made Rosa light-headed. She kept bumping into him as they made their way. She sneaked glances at him, trying to tell what he was thinking.

Luciano stopped and turned to face her. 'Do you

remember that night in Lucca when you asked me about Nilda?'

'Yes.'

'She was the wife of a good friend of mine. He was sent to prison for his role in organising the front against fascism and she took over his work printing an anti-fascist newspaper. She was denounced by a neighbour and deported to Ponza where she was so ill-treated she died. She was only twenty.'

A chill prickled Rosa's skin. She felt sorry for Nilda, instead of jealous. It could have been her own fate.

'Did you love her?' she asked Luciano. She could tell from the way he avoided her eyes that he had. 'I'm sorry,' she said.

'Many anti-fascists use their wives and girlfriends to carry out undercover work because they aren't as conspicious,' Luciano said. 'But battles should be fought by men, not the women we are supposed to be protecting. I've lost my mother and … Nilda … and that's enough. I don't want to lose any more women that I …' Luciano stepped closer to Rosa and took her hand. 'I don't want you to be *curious* any more. Do you understand what I'm saying?'

Rosa nodded. Her skin tingled at his touch but before she could relish it too long, he let her hand go. A grim conversation was not what she had been expecting from the walk.

They reached Via Tornabuoni. 'I have to head this way,' Luciano said, pointing in the direction of the Arno and handing Sibilla's basket to Rosa. She didn't want him to go. She wanted him to stay with her and Sibilla. Something glinted in the sunlight.

'What's that?' Luciano asked, pointing to Sibilla's rattle.

'It's only a toy,' Rosa said hastily.

Luciano's mouth pursed. 'From Antonio Parigi?'

Rosa didn't want to lose the moment. But she didn't want to lie to Luciano either. 'He likes children,' she said.

A veil fell over Luciano's eyes. 'I'd better be going.' He turned away.

'Luciano!'

He looked back at her. Rosa wanted to tell him something. But what? They hardly ever talked. And yet there was a connection between them.

'What time do you finish today?' she asked him. 'Do you want to walk back with us too?'

'I would have,' he said slowly. 'But I have to meet someone this evening. Some other time?'

Rosa nodded. 'Some other time.'

She watched Luciano walk away. Was he doing something dangerous this evening? Would he be arrested? She couldn't bear to think about it. With a heavy heart, she headed in the direction of the shop.

As the weeks passed by and Antonio made no mention of a wife, Rosa began to suspect that the woman she had seen may have only been a customer after all. She was too embarrassed to reveal this possibility to Luciano. Besides, Antonio never behaved improperly towards her so Luciano had no cause to be jealous. Then, one blustery day when Rosa was polishing a Chinese cabinet, the door to the shop flung open and in swept the woman Rosa had seen. She looked chic in a turquoise dress suit with a Fabergé pendant and matching earrings. Her shoes were white pumps and she wore a marina hat on top of her finger-waved black hair. Working with fine furniture had given Rosa an appreciation of beauty and she couldn't take her attention off the vision before her. The woman's dark eyes were broody, her nose was perfectly formed, and her full mouth was sultry. She was the classic Italian beauty.

The woman glanced around the store. 'Is Antonio ... is Signor Parigi here?'

Rosa shook her head. 'He went home for lunch.'

The woman bit her lip. 'I see,' she said. 'Could you give him a message for me?'

'Of course,' said Rosa.

'Please tell him that Signora Visconti called to see him.'

'Yes, signora. My pleasure,' said Rosa, watching the beautiful woman walk out the door. Well, if she wasn't Antonio's wife, then who was she?

Rosa was the first one back that evening and lit the stove before going to the room she shared with Orietta. She slipped the pins from her hair and changed from her suit into an ordinary dress before feeding Sibilla.

'You're a good girl,' she said, tickling Sibilla's tummy. Her baby wriggled with delight and smiled at her. 'You grow more beautiful every day.'

Rosa gazed at her child, still mystified by the source of her exotic beauty. She closed her eyes and tried to see her own origins again, the same way she had with the jewellery box at the shop. But she felt and saw nothing.

Someone knocked at the bedroom door. Rosa turned to see Luciano.

'I was putting Sibilla to sleep,' she said.

Luciano stepped towards the bed and kissed Sibilla on the forehead. Rosa was moved whenever he did that. Sometimes, before she fell asleep, she fantasised that Luciano was Sibilla's father and the three of them were a family.

She tucked Sibilla into her basket and Luciano lifted it into the cot that he and Carlo had made. 'She's as beautiful as her mother,' Luciano said.

He turned to Rosa and pressed his hand against her cheek before slipping his arms around her. Rosa melted. All the nerve endings that had been deadened by prison sprang to life again. She hadn't known until Luciano pressed her to his chest how much she had yearned for him to do that. He took her hand and kissed her palm. She sighed, and his kisses grew more passionate, burning her face and neck. Waves of pleasure washed over her as she felt his warm breath caress her skin. She thought she must be dreaming. Could what she'd hoped for be happening? Did Luciano love her?

'Luciano,' she whispered. His skin smelled like fresh apples. 'What are you doing to me?'

He lifted her in his arms and carried her to the bed. He laid her down and pressed the weight of his body against her. She drank in his warm, salty breath. He sat back, his eyes on fire, before sliding his fingers down Rosa's throat to the neckline of her dress. Slowly he undid the buttons, tugging open the fabric. Her breasts lay exposed to him. She shivered when he cupped them in his hands and lowered his lips to her nipples. Her breasts were tender from feeding Sibilla but the pleasure his touch brought was greater than the discomfort.

'I want you, Rosa,' he said, before finding her mouth again and kissing her. He pressed his cheek to hers. 'Is it all right?'

'Luciano,' she whispered, stroking his face.

His fingers ran down her thigh and found the hem of her skirt. He lifted it to her waist and caressed her hip. Rosa was delirious with sensations she had never imagined. He slipped his hand between her legs.

'Does it feel nice?' he asked her.

Rosa answered with a weak moan. Her nerves were on fire. All the muscles in her stomach were drawing down, longing for some sort of relief. He lifted himself over her, rubbing himself between her legs. Suddenly Osvaldo's face appeared between them. The image was like a shock through her body. Pain and humiliation seized her. She shoved Luciano in the chest. 'No!' she screamed.

Luciano leaped back, shocked.

'Get out!' Rosa said, covering herself. 'Don't touch me!'

The moment of passion was shattered. Rosa fought the confusion in her mind but all she could remember was the excruciating pain when Osvaldo raped her.

Luciano slipped off the bed and stared at Rosa. 'I would never have laid a hand on you,' he said, 'if I hadn't thought you wanted me to.'

Rosa tried to say something but couldn't find the words. Luciano waited for her to explain her violent reaction. When she didn't, he took a step back. 'Forget this happened,' he said. 'I won't come near you again.' He turned and slammed the door behind him.

Rosa had never made an association between Luciano and Osvaldo. She hadn't linked the yearning she felt for Luciano with the despicable act Osvaldo had performed on her. Now the thing she longed for was gone. Osvaldo had won again. He had stolen her joy. Her body, on fire a moment ago, felt cold and empty.

When she heard the others arrive home a while later and ask after her, she thought, for the sake of appearances, that she had better join them for supper. She wiped her face and tidied her hair. Her cheeks were blotchy. She soaked a towel in the basin and pressed it against her eye sockets to bring down the swelling.

Luciano was sitting at the far end of the table when she walked into the kitchen. He was fidgeting with his fork and barely touching the food.

'What's wrong with you?' Piero asked him. 'Did you have a bad day?'

Luciano shook his head. 'No, I'm just tired.'

'You should go to bed early,' Orietta advised him. 'You don't want to get sick.'

The more his siblings questioned him, the further Luciano retreated. He didn't look in Rosa's direction. She stared at the fire in the stove, trying to find comfort in its glow, but only sank deeper into loneliness. Everything was ruined between her and Luciano now.

'The fire is dying down,' Luciano said. 'I'll get some more coal.'

Rosa listened to the others talk although she could think of nothing but Luciano. Carlo was making them laugh by recounting the things guests left behind in their hotel rooms. Along with the usual socks, underwear, eyeglasses and ointments he had found a suitcase full of suppositories and a jar with a tapeworm in it. Carlo's banter usually made Rosa laugh too but this evening she was engulfed in gloominess. When she couldn't stand it any more, she excused to herself to feed Sibilla but instead went down the stairs to the cellar where Luciano was collecting coal in a bucket from the pile. He looked up when she entered then turned away.

'Luciano,' Rosa said.

He didn't answer her. He continued dropping coal into the bucket.

'I have to explain.'

He shrugged his shoulders. 'There's nothing to explain.'

He wasn't making things easy for Rosa but she felt she owed him the truth. She opened her mouth to tell him about Osvaldo but found herself choking on her words.

'I was raped,' she finally managed to say. 'That's how I became pregnant with Sibilla.'

Luciano flinched. He stopped gathering the coal and looked at her.

All the horrible details flooded back to Rosa: the dank smell of Osvaldo; the stale wine on his lips; the painful tearing sensation. 'I'm so ashamed,' she said, crying into her fist.

'Who did that to you?' asked Luciano, stepping towards her and searching her face. 'Who did that to you?'

Rosa sank to her knees and Luciano crouched down with her. 'A prison guard,' she said. 'I was a virgin before that. I didn't know anything. I was brought up in a convent.'

The colour drained from Luciano's face. He wrapped his arms around her. 'Prison? Rosa, what were you doing in prison?'

'The fascists,' Rosa said. 'I was accused of helping a woman with an abortion but I was never tried. It was to cover up the mistake of one of their own.'

She gave way to tears. They shook her until she thought her ribs would break. Luciano didn't let go of her. When she calmed, he turned her face to his.

'Rosa, if you were never tried ... is there a record of your imprisonment?'

Rosa nodded. 'It's on my papers,' she said. 'Enemy of the state.'

Luciano's face didn't change expression but his eyes darkened.

'What's wrong?' she asked.

His brow furrowed. He didn't answer her. Instead he held her tighter. Despite everything that had gone wrong, Rosa felt comforted. Being with Luciano was like standing in the eye of a storm: in his arms she was safe.

THIRTEEN

The following evening when Rosa was on her way home, she found Luciano waiting on the street corner for her. He had shaved off his beard and looked young and fresh.

'I thought we could go for a walk,' he said.

Rosa smiled, thankful that the revelations of the night before hadn't left them awkward with each other. 'Yes,' she agreed.

They strolled in the direction of the Arno. The daylight was fading and the air was cool and fresh. They carried Sibilla's basket between them, one handle each. Shopkeepers smiled at them and women stopped to admire Sibilla.

'*Che bella bambina! Che bella coppia!*' they said. 'What a beautiful baby! What a beautiful couple!'

Rosa didn't know how to react to the attention. She had become used to catcalls and hostile stares. When she walked along the street it was usually with her eyes downcast. But being with Luciano made all the difference. Rosa lifted her gaze and returned the greetings with pride. Was it possible to be this happy? Was it possible to be this *normal*? She felt the black hole in her heart close a little.

Maybe she didn't know who her parents were but that didn't mean she couldn't have a family of her own.

They reached the place on the bank of the Arno where they had first met each other.

'You had the sun in your eyes,' Luciano said, bending to kiss Rosa on the forehead. She was sorry that she had destroyed his passion of the previous evening. But she knew they were both still confused by her reaction. She understood Luciano would wait for her, and that made her love him more.

Luciano and Rosa sat there with their arms linked and their heads together, speaking about insignificant things, until the moon rose. Then he stood up and extended his hand to her. 'There is something I want you to hear,' he said.

A few streets away he stopped in front of a house and told Rosa to sit with him on the doorstep. A beautiful operatic voice drifted from an open window of one of the houses on the opposite side of the street. Rosa caught a glimpse of the woman's blonde hair set against the blood-red wallpaper of the room. She was singing an aria. There were bars on the window. The leaves of a potted palm poked through them and quivered in the breeze. The effect was to make the woman appear like an exotic bird in a cage. Her voice was poignant and sweet.

'Who is she?' Rosa asked.

'A nightwatchman's wife,' he answered. 'Every evening, after her husband has left for work, she sings.'

Rosa leaned against Luciano's shoulder. The woman's voice was remarkable. They could have been sitting in the royal box at the Teatro Comunale and they would not have heard anything more magnificent.

They listened a while longer until Luciano nudged Rosa. 'Orietta will be getting dinner on the table, and we'd better take Sibilla home before it gets too cold.' He picked up Sibilla's basket and offered his arm to Rosa.

'The woman has an extraordinary voice,' Rosa said, entwining her arm with his.

'Yes, she's missed her calling.'

They walked along the streets, which were quieter now. Rosa puzzled over what Luciano had said about the nightwatchman's wife. If Luciano's father had not made the mistakes he had, Luciano would probably have gone to university or taken his place in the family business. He would not have been peddling goods door to door or labouring on building sites.

'Do you feel you've missed your calling?' she asked him.

Luciano frowned. 'Missed it? No, not missed it,' he replied. 'I am sure that it is coming to me. I'm impatient for it.'

Rosa studied his firm profile. He was not like other people. There was something dynamic about him. Rosa agreed that he must have some special destiny. He seemed marked out for it. *Didn't I also feel destined for something once?* Rosa recalled. *Now my destiny is to be a mother.* But she couldn't complain. She loved her daughter more than life and working at Antonio's shop was more a pleasure than a job.

Not long after Rosa had begun working for Antonio, he had started taking her to auctions, markets and estate sales.

'Liking a piece and understanding its history is one thing,' he told her at one pre-auction viewing. 'But appraising it is quite another. You must be confident that you will find a customer who will like it as much as you do — otherwise a dealer is in danger of filling his shop with charming but unsaleable items. I've noticed you are fascinated by ornate furniture, but our clients want pieces that are practical as well as beautiful.'

He led Rosa to a walnut armoire with rocaille crowns. It had three bevelled-mirror doors and cabriole legs. Rosa ran her hands over the French piece. 'It's lovely,' she said.

'No one will buy it unless they reduce the reserve price,' Antonio told her.

'Why not?'

'Because it's eight feet tall. Too tall for the average maid or lady of the house to reach the top shelves. Practicality as well as beauty must be our guide. There is a certain beauty in the utility of an item.' He flashed her a smile.

Rosa had thought Antonio was condescending in his cynical attitude towards her ability to see the origins of things, but he obviously respected her intelligence if he was explaining his work to her. Although they used each other's Christian names when out of the hearing of customers, their relationship was formal. Now Rosa found herself warming to him. She began to think of him as a friend.

'Now, what about this piece?' Antonio asked, pointing out a Spanish table in chestnut wood.

He reached into his pocket and took out a magnifying glass. He handed it to Rosa. She searched the piecrust edging and lyre base for chips, cracks, scratches and discolourations as he had taught her to do. She was beginning to understand which defects were of little consequence, which reduced an item's value and which enhanced it. She checked the maker's mark. The legs were original, giving no indication of having been replaced or revived. She ran her fingers over the tabletop and examined it closely.

'It's been refinished,' she said. 'The original patina has been sanded back.'

'And what does that mean?' Antonio asked, raising his eyebrows.

'Refinishing ruins the value of an antique.'

'Because?'

'Because the patina is the history of an object and shows what has happened over time. A crackled finish, a nick, a scratch — all these things give a piece character. The patina is what makes the piece a true antique. Otherwise one might as well buy new reproduction furniture.'

Antonio clapped his hands. 'Excellent! Now you are not only lovely but knowledgeable as well!'

One of Rosa's favourite tasks was to find an object that a customer had specifically requested, such as a particular style of mirror or table to finish off a room. Antonio would send her out to select possible pieces and would then examine them himself before deciding which was most suitable. She was delighted one day when he told her that he had received a request to find a unique present for a girl's twelfth birthday.

'The customer doesn't need it until spring,' Antonio explained, 'so we have some time up our sleeves. Apparently she's a bright girl who likes to write and sketch in a journal. There is a seller in Fiesole who is in the process of redecorating. We can go there tomorrow morning if you'd like to come. The family has always had a large proportion of daughters. We might find something suitable there.'

Rosa winced at the mention of Fiesole. She could leave Sibilla with Orietta for the morning, but she had a vision of pulling up with Antonio outside the Villa Scarfiotti. She had put that world out of her mind for many months now.

'What's the seller's name?' she asked.

Antonio looked at her interestedly. 'Signora Armelli. Do you know her?'

Rosa shook her head. 'I just wondered,' she said, relieved that it wasn't the Marchesa.

Signora Armelli's villa was an eighteenth-century affair with a panoramic view of the Florentine hills. When Antonio brought his van to a stop in the driveway, Rosa was surprised to see two other Fiat vans already parked there.

'Not to worry,' said Antonio, opening the door for her. 'They aren't competition. They belong to Signor Risoli, who specialises in rare books and maps, and Signor Zalli, who collects hatpins and buttons.'

Rosa and Antonio were led by the butler down a corridor to a room stacked with furniture and household items. Every surface was covered in knick-knacks. Antonio's attention was taken by a mahogany corner cabinet while Rosa stood in the doorway a moment, absorbing the scene. There were oriental rugs piled on the floor, along with wrought-iron furniture, botanical prints, chandeliers and sconces, and a pair of Venetian mirrors. She spotted a marble chessboard on an extendable table and caught a glimpse of two old men playing at it, until the vision faded away.

There were a couple of porcelain dolls and some mother-of-pearl hand mirrors, but Rosa sensed the customer seeking the birthday gift wasn't after objects like those. She looked through a drawer of lace and ivory fans before she noticed a pair of candelabra piled on an old dresser. Between them was an object half-covered by a silk table runner. Rosa moved towards the dresser, wondering what the object could be. She lifted the runner and discovered a rosewood writing box with rounded edges. It was decorated with inlaid pewter depicting deer in a forest. Inside was an embossed velvet writing surface with compartments for paper and writing instruments. Rosa felt around the box and found a spring mechanism. She released it and gave a cry of joy when she discovered a secret drawer.

She called to Antonio: 'I think I've found something for that twelve-year-old girl.'

Antonio was impressed by Rosa's find and said that he would take her to Casa dei Bomboloni, which was famous for its doughnuts, to celebrate.

'They have a rather ingenious system for making the *bomboloni*,' he told her, once they were in the van and heading back to Florence. 'They are dropped down a herringbone slide to shake off excess oil before they land in the sugar tray.'

At the Casa dei Bomboloni, Rosa and Antonio took a seat by the window. Rosa, who had never eaten a doughnut before, was lost in its sweet, doughy flavour.

'Good?' asked Antonio, reaching across the table to wipe a crumb from her chin.

'Very good,' Rosa replied, embarrassed that she'd had food on her face and not noticed.

The radio was playing a popular tune of the day:

> *When you smile, I always laugh.*
> *When you laugh, I always smile …*

The lyrics made no sense but the tune was catchy and Rosa tapped her foot in time to the beat. The song was interrupted by a blast of the *Giovinezza* and then an announcement that Il Duce was about to speak. Everyone in the Casa dei Bomboloni stood up to attention. The counter staff stopped serving customers and doughnuts no longer fell from the chute. Antonio raised himself to his feet and Rosa did likewise, although she hated herself for doing so. But to not stand up when Mussolini spoke would draw attention and could result in her being arrested. She wasn't going to risk that.

Mussolini's announcement was a long-winded explanation of his concept of fascism: 'The state is everything. The individual is only accepted as far as his interests coincide with the state's …'

When it was over, Antonio drove Rosa back to the store. She couldn't help dwelling on Mussolini's statement that no human or spiritual values existed outside of the state. Luciano would not have stood up for a proclamation like that. She felt weak for having crumbled in the face of such insipid indoctrination.

Antonio could see that something was troubling her. 'What's wrong?' he asked.

'I'm not a fascist,' Rosa told him. 'I want you to know that.'

'Good God!' he exclaimed. 'Do you think I am?'

She turned to him, relieved but not convinced. 'But you have a Fascist Party card. I've seen it in the office files.'

Antonio shrugged. 'Every businessman has one, otherwise the fascists will come and bust up the shop. We don our black shirts when necessary, wave our arms about as required, then go back to our work and leave the stupid buffoonery behind us. Besides, my grandparents were Jewish. I can't take risks.'

'I didn't know that,' Rosa said, recalling her vision about the torcheres. 'I thought your mother was Catholic.'

Antonio looked puzzled; he must have been wondering

how she knew that. 'My father converted to marry my mother,' he said. 'I was brought up Catholic. But it seems in Germany those things don't matter, and Hitler and Mussolini are too good friends for comfort.'

Rosa remembered that while the troupe was on tour, Luciano had spoken about the boycotting of Jewish businesses that was encouraged in Germany. 'Do you think that sort of racial discrimination will happen here?' she asked Antonio.

He shook his head. 'No, the Italians are *brava gente*. They are not racists like the Germans. Mussolini himself has a Jewish mistress. But the fascist thugs ... well, one always has to be cautious. They could be influenced by anybody with an agenda.'

'So you are nervous?' Rosa asked.

Antonio laughed. 'Life's too short to always be worried. I say, "Take care of this day and tomorrow will take care of itself." None of us can predict the future. Idiots like Mussolini come and go. It's been like that since the Roman Empire. Eventually the pendulum will swing back to rampant liberalism.'

At first Rosa was shocked by Antonio's pragmatism, but then she saw the sense behind it. Fascism was like a wildfire: it was too big to fight so it was better to let it burn out on its own. She leaned back in the seat. As guilty as it made her feel, she was glad to hear someone making light of Italy's politics for a change. She admired Antonio's approach to life, although she was sure Luciano would not approve of it.

Rosa often thought that her work was like a treasure hunt. She attended houses that were being redecorated and also deceased estates.

'Don't you find that macabre?' Orietta asked her one day. 'Looking through a dead person's things?'

'No,' answered Rosa. 'If you can't take your worldly goods with you, someone else may as well enjoy them. Besides, all antiques are "dead person's things".'

But there was one aspect of her work that Rosa had not been prepared for. One day, Antonio sent her to a house in Via della Pergola.

'Go and see if there is anything you think worthwhile,' he said.

The house was white with green shutters. The polished oak door and the wrought-iron balcony above it gave the house an air of elegance. Rosa shivered in anticipation of the beautiful things she hoped to find inside. She was about to cross the narrow street towards the house when a truck with an open tray pulled up in front of it. A few moments later a woman and two children appeared in the doorway, each carrying a suitcase. The boy and the girl were dressed in expensive woollen coats and the woman wore strings of pearls, but their faces were grim. The driver of the truck loaded the suitcases, and helped the children into the tray and the woman into the seat beside him. The next person out of the door was a slender man in his mid-forties. He dragged a trunk out and the driver helped him load it. The man glanced at the woman but she stiffened and turned away. He disappeared into the house again. An elderly couple peered from the window of the house next door, but the woman ignored them.

The front door opened again and this time two men in overalls came out carrying a velvet chaise longue with gold tassels. They did not put it on the truck but propped it up on the pavement. They went back into the house and returned with a pair of filigree lamps and a terracotta pot. The slender man came out with a couple of paintings. He patted the girl's cheek and touched the boy's hair. But when he turned and saw the workmen carting out a child's bed with angels carved into the headboard, his composure broke. His hands trembled and his lips quivered. It dawned on Rosa that the family was being evicted. The realisation twisted her gut and caused her physical pain.

A white spitz dog appeared at one of the downstairs windows and pressed his face to it, scratching the glass with his paw. He was joined by a white cat with black cap and saddle markings. She sat on the windowsill and peered out.

'Ambrosio! Allegra!' the girl called out. Turning to the man, she asked, 'Babbo, they are coming too, aren't they?'

Her brother, who was older, looked to his father. The man shook his head.

'No!' the girl cried. 'We can't leave them behind! Everything else but them!'

The man glanced at his feet, then quickly opened the passenger door of the truck and climbed in alongside his wife. The driver started the engine. The girl clung to the sides of the tray, her face and knuckles white. Tears rolled down her cheeks. Her dog barked desperately. The cat meowed. The truck gained speed and disappeared around the corner. Rosa stood glued to the spot. All she could think about was the Montagnanis being evicted from their home. The dreadful scene had been brought to life before her. Sobs she couldn't repress shook her.

She was about to leave when a man in a suit came out of the door and spotted her.

'Signora Bellocchi?' he called. 'I am Fabio Mirra. Signor Parigi said to watch out for you. I've saved a dining suite I think he would like.'

He must be the debt collector, Rosa thought. She couldn't believe that he could be so composed after having evicted a man and his family. He was the same age as the slender man and could have been a father himself. But he didn't have the ruthless appearance she might have expected. Rosa took a handkerchief out of her pocket and dabbed at her cheeks before stepping towards him.

Signor Mirra laid his hand on her shoulder. 'It doesn't pay to get emotionally involved,' he said in a paternal tone. 'That man was born into more wealth than you and I will ever know. But he gambled it away. It's like a disease in some people. Of course I feel sorry for his wife and children. That's the hard part.'

Rosa remembered the stricken look on the little girl's face. What did that man think when he saw his humiliated wife and distressed children? Did it affect him to know that he had brought calamity to the people who depended on him? She couldn't help thinking of Luciano's father. At least the man she had seen had stayed with his family to share their fate.

'I'm sorry,' Rosa said, composing herself as best she could. 'When Signor Parigi sent me here, I didn't know it was ...'

'An eviction?' Signor Mirra nodded sympathetically and guided Rosa into the house.

The interior was as beautiful as she had expected, with cream-and-white wallpaper, rosewood panelling and parquet floors. But it didn't hold any magic for her now.

'Does Signor Parigi often buy from evictions?' Rosa asked.

She was fond of Antonio. It pained her to think he might be a vulture, profiting from misery.

'All the dealers do, high and low,' Signor Mirra replied, leading Rosa towards the dining room, which featured a Bohemian crystal chandelier. 'You have to think, Signora Bellocchi, that you are helping these people in a way. The more you buy, the more they can repay their debts. Signor Parigi didn't tell the man to gamble his fortune away, did he?'

Rosa shook her head. 'I suppose not.'

The dining suite Signor Mirra had put aside for her to look at was as stunning as he had indicated. The table was in Louis XVI style and the matching medallion chairs were upholstered in toile depicting pastoral scenes of shepherds and shepherdesses. The chairs were slightly faded but not stained and the table had not been altered in any way. Rosa knew that its simple elegance would appeal to many customers.

'It is a fine suite, I am sure Signor Parigi will like it,' said Rosa. 'Can you hold it until this afternoon?'

'Of course,' said Signor Mirra with a slight bow.

Rosa followed him back down the corridor and heard the dog barking. 'What will happen to the animals?' she asked.

Signor Mirra shrugged. 'The cat I can let go to catch mice, but the dog ... well, it's against the law to let them onto the streets in case of rabies. I will have to take him to the police station to be ...'

'Shot?'

'Put down.'

The euphemism didn't soften the image. She remembered the shattered look on the girl's face. The cat and dog had been beloved pets. They passed by the drawing room and Rosa saw the cat sticking its paw under the door. She hesitated and looked at a Pompeii fresco on the wall.

Signor Mirra turned to her. 'Is there something else that interests you, Signora Bellocchi?' he asked.

'Yes,' she replied, straightening her coat. 'I'd like to take the dog and cat.'

Antonio looked from the cat curled up on the windowsill to the dog sitting at his heels. 'The dining suite, I understand,' he said. 'But explain to me again how I came to be the master of these noble animals?'

Allegra jumped off the windowsill and rubbed against Rosa's leg. She emitted a purr so loud that she could have been a truck starting up.

'I can't understand people who abandon their animals any more than I can understand people who give away their children,' said Rosa, bending down to scratch the cat under her chin. She looked up and saw Antonio was smiling at her and shaking his head.

'Well, the dog, I like,' he said. 'He's Italian. A *volpino italiano*. A little fox. They've been favoured by royalty for hundreds of years. Michelangelo had one. But the cat ... well, I don't like cats.'

Rosa straightened. 'You can't get rid of her ... they are like brother and sister.'

Antonio fought the faint smile that was tickling his lips. Rosa had no idea what to make of the sparkle in his eyes.

'All right, all right, she can stay,' he said. 'But you're in charge of removing cat fur and stopping her from scratching anything.'

When she returned home that evening, Rosa gave Luciano a long embrace.

'Are you all right?' he asked her.

Rosa didn't want to tell him that she had witnessed an eviction and bring up his own pain. But the look of despair on the little girl's face had burnt into her memory. Her heart ached with the suffering she had seen. The only way she felt she could relieve it was to have taken care of Allegra and Ambrosio.

'I'm just tired,' she said, placing Sibilla's basket by the stove.

'I want to show you something,' Luciano said, leading her into the corridor.

They left the building and re-entered the one next door, climbing up several flights of stairs to a one-room apartment with a view of the street. A double bed with a ruffled cover took up most of the space. A small armoire and Sibilla's cot had been placed in one corner. Luciano fluffed up the embroidered pillows on the bed.

'Lie down,' he said. 'This is our place now.' He threw himself on the bed and patted the space next to him. 'Orietta sewed all the covers.'

Rosa couldn't move. Luciano had gone to a lot of trouble to make the room appealing to her. Was he intending to marry her? Rosa's heart swelled with the idea: a husband, a child, a sweet little room. What more could she want?

'Come, Rosa,' he said. 'Lie down and rest. I can see how tired you are.'

Rosa slipped off her shoes and lay down next to him. He put his arms around her and she felt instant comfort in his strength. Although they hadn't been physically intimate yet, Rosa knew that Luciano thought of her as his woman.

'What does this mean?' she asked him.

Luciano didn't answer straightaway and Rosa's heart sank. Maybe he was like most men and didn't want to marry a woman who wasn't a virgin.

He sighed. 'I would love to marry you, Rosa, more than anything in the world.' He hesitated and slid off the bed, moving to the window and looking out.

'But?' she prompted him.

Luciano turned to her. 'Now is not the time,' he said. 'I want to marry you when I can give you and Sibilla a country free of the fascists. A real Italy.'

'That's quite a wedding gift,' said Rosa, sitting up. She was trying to make light of the situation but her heart was breaking. She knew Luciano's anti-fascist activities were important to him, but didn't see why they should interfere with their having a life together.

Luciano came back to the bed and brushed Rosa's hair from her forehead. 'Can you trust me to keep my promise?' he asked her.

She looked into his eyes. Unwed single mothers in Italy were unacceptable but unwed couples were different. Many working-class men and women lived together but didn't marry until they could afford at least a wedding bed. Rosa turned away. She loved Luciano but she wanted more. She wanted a name, a real name. She wanted to appear somewhere on someone's family tree. And she wanted a father for Sibilla. Then another thought occurred to her about why Luciano was hesitant to marry.

'Are Sibilla and I in danger? Does moving us have something to do with the pamphlets?'

Luciano's face turned grim. 'They caught that woman who delivered the pamphlets to me when we were in Lucca. She's a tough nut. I don't think she'll talk, but she might.'

'Then it's you who's in danger,' said Rosa. 'She barely took any notice of me.'

Luciano shook his head. 'The fascists use wives and children to get at the men who oppose them. I want to keep you and Sibilla safe. I have to keep you separate from me … for now. It won't always be like this, I promise.'

Rosa squeezed her hands together. Now she understood why Luciano had chosen an apartment with a view of the street — so she could escape with Sibilla if she saw he was arrested. She was torn. She loved Luciano but she feared going back to prison. But even more, she was afraid for her daughter. If Rosa was arrested, she'd be left an orphan.

The day the customer who had ordered the present for the twelve-year-old girl was due to collect it, Rosa arrived with Sibilla at the shop before her usual time. Sibilla had been too big for a basket for a while now and Antonio had given Rosa a wicker pram that he claimed to have picked up 'for nothing' at an estate sale. But Rosa could see it was made in England and the lining was new. She was embarrassed but grateful. When Luciano saw it, Rosa lied to spare his feelings. She said it was given to her by the benefactor of a deceased estate. She needed the pram: Sibilla was too heavy to carry the distance from the apartment to the shop.

That morning, Rosa headed towards the backroom and stopped in her tracks when she heard raised voices. Antonio was arguing with someone. She recognised Signora Visconti's voice.

'What has brought this on?' she shouted. 'We've been happy for years.'

'We've never been happy,' Antonio answered.

'What has your father threatened now?' Signora Visconti asked. 'That if you don't marry he will give all your inheritance to the Church?'

'I don't care if he does,' Antonio snapped back. 'That's never been the point. It's … he's getting on now and he has no grandchildren.'

'Well, marry then!' Signora Visconti said. Her tone did not sound convincing to Rosa.

'How can I? The only woman I have ever loved is you.'

Rosa could hear the pain in Antonio's voice. He was going to make someone a fine husband one day, but Rosa suspected it wouldn't be Signora Visconti.

It was far too intimate a conversation to be overhearing and Rosa retreated to her desk at the front of the shop. She took Sibilla out of her pram and placed her on the floor next to her. Sibilla was starting to walk herself by gripping onto furniture. There was a playpen in the backroom, but out in the shop Rosa had to keep an eye on Sibilla every second. As tolerant as Antonio was of Rosa bringing her child to work, and of Ambrosio and Allegra as the shop pets, she didn't think he'd be thrilled at the sight of an eleven-month-old child drooling onto a two-hundred-year-old sofa. Rosa sighed at her daughter's happy smile. Sibilla had begun to wean herself earlier than Rosa expected and was more interested in soft-boiled eggs than in Rosa's breasts. In a short while Rosa would have to leave Sibilla with Orietta, who worked from the apartment all the time now.

'But how I shall miss your pretty face,' Rosa said, kneeling to kiss Sibilla.

She took out the catalogue to update it but the voices from the backroom grew louder.

'I can't divorce Stefano and marry you. This is Florence not Hollywood!' Signora Visconti shouted.

'Why did you marry the buffoon in the first place?' Antonio hissed.

'Because he can give me things you can't!'

'A palazzo and a country house! But you don't love him!'

Signora Visconti was crying now. 'No, I love you! But I can't do it! The Church would not have it! I don't want to burn in hell!'

Rosa froze, wondering what she should do. Antonio knew little about her private life and never pried. She didn't want to learn more about his than was necessary. She stood up with the idea of taking Sibilla for a walk or to a café for a while. She was putting on her coat when a teary-eyed

Signora Visconti burst from the backroom. She ran past Rosa with barely a glance towards her and rushed out of the shop. Rosa turned to see a stricken-looking Antonio standing behind her. She averted her eyes.

'*Buon giorno*, Rosa,' he said.

'*Buon giorno*,' she replied, blushing. 'Can I get you anything? A cup of tea?'

'Thank you. I could do with a cup of tea.'

Rosa picked up Sibilla and walked to the backroom to put the kettle on the stove. Antonio sat down at his desk and began making telephone calls to customers. Both of them kept up a semblance of normality, but the air was thick with tension.

In the afternoon, Antonio went to visit some craftsmen and Rosa stayed in the shop to meet with the customer coming to collect the writing box. Antonio had provided a list of other items to consider in case the customer did not like the box, but Rosa was convinced that it was the perfect gift. She was cleaning some crystal vases when the bell to the shop tinkled. There was a swish of a skirt and the smell of orange blossoms. Rosa turned and froze to the spot. The red-blonde hair and the blue eyes were unmistakable. It was Signora Corvetto, the Marchese Scarfiotti's mistress.

'*Buon giorno, signora*,' Rosa said, trying to recover her composure.

Signora Corvetto smiled but in a puzzled way. She had recognised Rosa but seemed to be having trouble placing where she had seen her before. Memories flooded back to Rosa. She remembered the day she had left the convent. Signora Corvetto had been in the car when the Marchese had picked her up. She had thrown her ermine wrap over Rosa's knees.

'Have you come about the writing box?' Rosa managed to say.

'Yes,' answered Signora Corvetto, taking the seat Rosa offered to her. 'Signor Parigi said it is a particularly beautiful one.'

Rosa smiled to hide her inner turmoil. Signora Corvetto would recognise her eventually. Then what would happen? Would she tell Antonio? Would she tell the Marchese Scarfiotti? Rosa had kept her agreement to stay away from the Scarfiotti family and to never mention them to anybody. But it seemed the past had caught up to her, whether she wanted it to or not.

Rosa brought the box to Signora Corvetto, who gave a gasp of delight when she saw it. She ran her fingers over the rosewood then undid the latch and looked inside. 'It's beautiful,' she said. 'How clever of you to think of it.'

'It has a secret compartment,' said Rosa, demonstrating the springlock.

'It's perfect,' said Signora Corvetto. 'Would I be able to have it engraved?'

Rosa took out her notebook to write down Signora Corvetto's instructions. Antonio hated people engraving objects; it destroyed the value of the antique. But Rosa understood Signora Corvetto was looking for an exquisite gift, not for something to be resold.

'What would you like the engraving to say?' she asked.

'For Clementina. Eighth of May, 1933.'

Rosa's hand trembled but she did her best to appear calm. Darling Clementina. She remembered the garden party held in honour of her ninth birthday at the Villa Scarfiotti. *Signora Corvetto is very nice. She comes to see me every birthday,* Clementina had said. Memories Rosa had pushed down for years rose to the surface: Clementina in the schoolroom at the crack of dawn, eager for her classes; reading *Le tigri di Mompracem* together; the anxiety Rosa had felt when she had to entrust Clementina to the instructors at Piccole Italiane.

'Are you all right, Signora ...?'

Rosa recovered herself. 'Montagnani,' she said, finishing Signora Corvetto's question. 'I'm sorry, I thought I heard my daughter cry.' She nodded towards the backroom, where Sibilla was visible playing with her toys in her pen.

Signora Corvetto turned in Sibilla's direction. 'What a beautiful child,' she said. 'Can I hold her? I love children.'

Rosa led Signora Corvetto towards the backroom and picked Sibilla up for her to hold.

'Hello,' said Signora Corvetto, ticking Sibilla's nose.

Sibilla giggled in delight. With the Montagnani family always doting on her, she never shied from attention.

Signora Corvetto turned to Rosa. 'You have your daughter with you while you work?'

'Only for a short while longer,' said Rosa with a resigned shrug. 'When I was nursing her she had to be with me, but now she is becoming too active and will soon have to stay with her aunt.'

A distressed look passed over Signora Corvetto's face. 'It's not easy to give your child up to someone else,' she said. 'But sometimes you have to do it for the best.'

The women returned to the shop where Rosa wrote out a bill of sale and attached the documents giving the details of the writing box. She had not had a vision of the box's origins and now she wished she had tried. She attempted to peer into its past while she wrapped it in tissue paper to take to the engraver later, but nothing came to her. Perhaps her attachment to the future owner of the box prevented her from seeing its past ones.

Signora Corvetto paid for the box and Rosa handed her the bill of sale. When she did, their fingers touched and Rosa felt a tingle run through her.

'I recognise you now,' said Signora Corvetto. 'You were Clementina's first governess. Signorina Bellocchi.'

Rosa blushed to the roots of her hair.

'Clementina missed you terribly,' Signora Corvetto said. 'I think she still does.'

'I … I didn't leave voluntarily,' Rosa stammered.

Signora Corvetto looked at her, surprised. 'Oh,' she said, 'I didn't realise that. They told me that you'd found a placement elsewhere.'

Rosa's mind raced. She wanted to beg Signora Corvetto

not to tell anyone that she had seen her. What would happen if Antonio found out she wasn't a widow? Or the Marchesa Scarfiotti discovered she was in Florence? Although she feared that to mention anything may make matters worse, she decided to take the risk.

'The Marchesa Scarfiotti and I,' Rosa began awkwardly, 'we didn't get along.'

Signora Corvetto fixed her eyes on Rosa's face. 'I quite understand,' she said. 'It must have been difficult for a young girl like you. She can be very intimidating.'

Rosa opened the shop door for Signora Corvetto. 'Please,' she said quietly, 'don't mention to anyone that you saw me.'

Signora Corvetto nodded. 'No, of course not. You have a new life now with a husband and a baby. I wish you nothing but happiness.'

'Thank you.'

Rosa watched Signora Corvetto walk down the street. She was an elegant woman but there was something lonely about her too. Rosa's hand tingled again. She saw Signora Corvetto's face loom up before her at the garden party. It became juxtaposed with Clementina's and the revelation took Rosa's breath away. The creamy skin, the red-blonde hair, the blue eyes … Signora Corvetto was Clementina's birth mother!

Suddenly things that had happened made more sense. Now she understood why it was Signora Corvetto who had come with the Marchese to collect Rosa from the convent, and why she always visited Clementina on her birthdays. What had forced Signora Corvetto to surrender Clementina to the Marchesa? *It's not easy to give your child up to someone else. But sometimes you have to do it for the best*, she had said.

Rosa thought it must be dreadful for a mother to be in such a situation: to see her daughter grow up before her eyes and never be able to acknowledge her. But most of all Rosa felt sorry for Clementina. She thought of Signora Corvetto and Clementina embracing at the garden party. The girl had been in the arms of her real mother and not known it.

FOURTEEN

The day Sibilla said her first word Rosa had been feeding her puréed vegetables in the Montagnanis' kitchen while Carlo played peekaboo with her behind Rosa's back. Sibilla squealed with delight and dribbled food over her face.

'Carlo, I know you are there,' said Rosa, turning around. 'You're distracting Sibilla from eating.'

'I'm not distracting her from eating,' Carlo replied, pulling his lip down and waving at Sibilla. 'No one in their right mind would eat puréed broccoli.'

'She's a baby!'

'Even a baby,' said Carlo, dancing around Sibilla's high chair.

Rosa did her best to maintain a stern expression with him but it wasn't easy. Carlo was the family clown, and because of his angelic face frequently got away with it.

'Mamma!'

Rosa and Carlo looked at each other, startled. They turned to Sibilla who was watching them and wriggling her feet. She had been babbling and saying pseudo words for a few months but it was the first time she had pronounced anything clearly.

'Mamma!' she repeated, waving her arms.

Rosa pressed her lips to her daughter's hands. Of all the things in life that brought her pleasure — playing her flute, discovering a beautiful antique at a market, window shopping on Via Tornabuoni — nothing compared to the joy her daughter brought her.

'I'm back,' said Luciano, coming into the kitchen with a loaf of bread and a bag of potatoes. He sniffed the cannellini bean soup that was simmering on the stove, filling the kitchen with the aroma of sage leaves and garlic. His hair was clinging to his cheeks from the rain that had been falling that afternoon. Rosa handed him a towel.

'Sibilla said her first word,' Carlo told him.

'*Brava bambina*!' cried Luciano. 'What did she say?'

'Mamma,' replied Carlo.

Luciano laughed. 'Not Babbo?'

'Not yet,' said Rosa.

She and Luciano exchanged a glance. Although they had no plans to marry yet, they had spent many nights talking about the future. Luciano intended to adopt Sibilla and give his name to her once the fascists were out of power.

Luciano squeezed Rosa's shoulder. 'She will,' he said, kissing her cheek. 'When the time is right.'

With the warmer months approaching, Luciano began to re-form The Montagnani Company. Donatella was returning with Dante, but Benedetto was working on a film and wouldn't be able to perform with them over summer. Luciano had to find another actor.

'Come and meet Roberto Pecoraro,' Luciano said to Rosa and Orietta one day when they were painting a backdrop of a street scene in Marseilles. The new play was *The Count of Monte Cristo*.

Rosa turned around to see Luciano standing with a plump young man with a stubby nose and thinning hair. The women greeted Roberto but he returned their warmth with only the slightest hint of a smile.

'Roberto will be playing several parts,' Luciano said.

Rosa had read the play in order to plan the music. She started off trying to distance herself from the story of wrongful imprisonment as the friendship between Edmond and his doomed companion stirred up memories of her friend Sibilla. But then Edmond's escape and rise to high society were too miraculous to believe and Rosa was swept up in the fantasy of the story. Life is nothing like that, she'd thought at the end. The bad are not punished. The Marchesa Scarfiotti had got away with having Rosa sent to prison under false pretences. She was a rich and powerful woman and a friend of Mussolini's. She could get away with anything.

Luciano asked Roberto to show the women his interpretation of Abbé Faria and Baron Danglars. Roberto shrugged his agreement. Rosa and Orietta sat on upturned fruit crates to watch him. All actors with the troupe needed to be able to play several roles, but the way Roberto switched from one character to the other with effortless ease and played the intellectual priest and the greedy, evil baron with equal conviction was outstanding.

'*Bravo! Bravo!*' Rosa and Orietta shouted when he had finished.

They were sincere in their praise but Roberto barely acknowledged them. It was strange that he was extroverted when acting but so standoffish in person. Rosa studied the young man's face: those haughty eyes, that superior manner. Why did she sense Roberto spelled trouble?

Rosa had told Antonio before she accepted the job at his shop that she would be travelling with the troupe in summer. He appeared to have forgotten and she wondered how he would react when she reminded him. She arrived at the shop one morning ready to tell him that she would be leaving soon, and found him on his hands and knees under his desk.

Ambrosio was watching him with a bemused expression in his canine eyes. At first Rosa thought Antonio must be tightening a screw until she saw Allegra's white paw stretch out and grab for the roll of paper he held in his fingers.

'Missed it, kitty!' he said, poking the roll of paper around the legs of the desk again. Allegra swiped for it and this time caught the paper and chewed on it. Antonio laughed.

Rosa stared in disbelief. *He's playing with Allegra!*

'Antonio?'

He whipped his head out from under the desk. When he saw that Rosa realised what he was doing, he blushed. 'Stupid cat!' he said unconvincingly. 'She knocked my pen under there and now I can't find it.'

He sat back in his chair. Allegra jumped into his lap and snuggled there.

'It looks like she's done that a few times before,' Rosa said, laughing.

'Well,' replied Antonio with a sheepish grin, 'she has grown on me.'

When Rosa told him that she was leaving for the tour, he sighed and lifted his hands. 'Ah, so you *are* going? I thought maybe I had lured you away from your thespian friends. Never mind. I can't replace you, Rosa. Can you come back in the autumn?'

'Yes, and I can work in the mornings for another month. The rehearsals are in the late afternoon.'

Antonio's face brightened. 'So all is not lost,' he said, lifting Allegra off his lap and placing her on the floor before standing. 'I have a favour to request of you. The week after next, I am going to Venice to see a glass blower there. My elderly father lives with me. He has a nurse but he tires of her company quickly. I wondered if you would mind reading to him for an hour or so after you finish here?'

Antonio had been so generous to her and Sibilla that Rosa was pleased to have an opportunity to return the kindness. 'I could play my flute for him as well,' she told Antonio. 'Do you think he would like that?'

Antonio looked dubious. 'Rosa, I must be frank. My father is not exactly ... cultured. You won't be reading him anything highbrow. He likes adventure and mystery stories. I've just obtained a copy of *The Hound of the Baskervilles*.'

'Sherlock Holmes? In English?' asked Rosa.

'Oh, no,' Antonio laughed. 'The translation. He also likes Jules Verne and Jack London. He swears and blasphemes quite a bit too. You mustn't be offended.'

Rosa found the insight into Antonio's life intriguing: he was a closet cat lover and the debonair son of a blaspheming father. She could not have imagined it.

'My father was a plasterer,' Antonio explained, as if he had read Rosa's thoughts. 'But he did very well. He made sure I received a good education.'

Antonio's apartment was near the Piazza della Repubblica. The maid opened the door and invited Rosa inside. It was no surprise that the apartment was exquisitely decorated. The furniture was mahogany, Antonio's favourite wood, and the rooms were spacious with high ceilings. It was not grand, but there was an elegance in the way the light filtered from the tall windows onto the terracotta-tiled floors. The apartment was not overcrowded with furniture and she could see that each piece had been chosen with care. From the foyer, where the maid took Rosa's coat, she glimpsed a sitting room with a Louis XV settee and a Renaissance-style cabinet. But they were the only decorative pieces. The other furniture was unadorned. On the hall table was a framed photograph of an elderly woman with a lily in her hand who Rosa recognised from her vision with the torcheres as Antonio's late mother.

The maid led Rosa past the dining room and she noticed a pedestal dining table with six chairs and Dresden china on the sideboard. Antonio obviously didn't host large parties, but when he did have guests he entertained in good taste. Apart from an empire-style clock and a bronze horse statue, there were no vases or figurines anywhere; nothing to distract from the furniture. And yet, despite the lack of effects, Antonio's personality was present in the apartment. It had a private and serene air. There was a sense of simplicity about it that reminded Rosa of the convent.

'If it was warmer you could have sat out on the terrace,' said the maid. 'But Signor Parigi's lungs are weak and the nurse decided it's better if he stays in bed.'

The maid knocked on a door at the end of the corridor. A female voice told her to enter. The maid ushered Rosa into a dim room lit only by two bedside lamps. A nurse in a white uniform sat next to a four-poster bed where an elderly man lay with his head back on the pillow, sleeping. He was pale and breathing heavily. At first the room seemed different from the rest of the apartment only in that the curtains were dark and the furniture was ornate and carved. Then Rosa noticed a horseshoe-shaped wall mirror with a cowboy hat perched on it. A bull's skull hung from the opposite wall and on a side table sat a chessboard topped by cowboy-and-Indian pieces.

'Should I leave?' Rosa whispered to the nurse. 'Maybe Signor Parigi is too tired today?'

'It's all right,' whispered the nurse, who introduced herself as Giuseppina. 'He's drifted off. And you'd better call him Nonno. He prefers it.'

She looked furtively over her shoulder, like someone who has lulled a difficult baby to sleep and is enjoying the temporary peace. Rosa's impression was right because the next moment Nonno's eyes flew open and he sat up.

'*Che cazzo fai?*' he shouted. 'What the fuck are you doing? Your loud talking woke me up!'

Rosa blushed. She hadn't heard such language since she had been in prison.

'*Non capisci un cazzo,*' Nonno said, waving his arms at Giuseppina. 'You're as dumb as a fucking plank.' Then, looking at Rosa, he asked: 'Who's this?'

'This is Signora Bellocchi, your son's assistant.' Giuseppina explained to him. 'She has come to read to you.'

'*Porca, puttana, troia, lurida, maiala!*' shouted Nonno, a run of swearwords such as Rosa had never heard before. 'I don't need some tart to read to me. Where's my son?'

Giuseppina and the maid were calm in the face of Nonno's outburst and Rosa could only assume it was because they were used to his colourful language. But she was struck dumb. 'Nonno' meant 'grandfather', but Antonio's father was not like any grandfather Rosa had ever imagined.

Giuseppina opened the curtains and offered a seat to Rosa. 'You mustn't let his language put you off,' she whispered, squeezing Rosa's arm. 'Once you get to know him, he's charming.'

'Don't open the curtains and don't whisper!' Nonno snapped.

'Signora Bellocchi needs some more light. It's too dark in this room,' Giuseppina told him.

Nonno sat up with his arms folded, mumbling while Giuseppina and the maid left the room. Rosa took the copy of *The Count of Monte Cristo* out of her bag. She'd decided that she would leave the Sherlock Holmes for Antonio to read to his father.

Nonno glanced at her. 'What have you got there, heh?'

Rosa showed him the copy of the book. He took it from her. His hands were swollen around the knuckles and his nails were gnarled and yellow as if they still had pieces of plaster under them. They were not at all like his son's manicured hands. Nonno's eyes were the same faraway blue as Antonio's but that was where the similarity ended. His face was hard and wrinkled. He resembled a gargoyle.

'What are you staring at?' he asked, handing the book back.

'I was trying to see in what ways your son resembles you — or differs,' Rosa replied.

'He's an idiot and I'm not,' said Nonno. 'That's the difference! Now stop meddling in other people's business and read if that's what you came to do.'

Antonio had warned Rosa that his father was rough, but she had not anticipated that he would be so confronting. She thought of the days when she used to read to Clementina. It occurred to her that she was about to read bedtime stories to a foul-tempered old man. Despite herself, she started to laugh.

Nonno frowned at her. '*Cazzo!*' he said. 'My son has sent me a crazy woman.'

His comment only made Rosa laugh more.

'All right, I'll read,' she said. 'But only if you are polite.'

'Good, get on with it,' said Nonno, rolling his eyes. '*Dio buono!* Women can talk!'

Rosa read for about ten minutes with no outbursts from Nonno. She had to glance at him every few pages because he was so quiet she thought that he had fallen asleep.

'Stop staring at me and keep reading!' he said.

Rosa read on without further outbursts for another hour. She only stopped because she had to leave for rehearsals, not because Nonno wanted her to go.

'It's a good story,' he said, pursing his mouth and lifting his chin. 'Better than most of the rubbish my son reads me.'

'I'll come back tomorrow,' said Rosa, gathering her things. 'Do you want me to tell Giuseppina to come back in?'

Nonno waved his hand dismissively. 'Silly fusspot, why would I want her to come in again?'

'Well, then,' said Rosa, trying to keep a straight face. 'I'll see you the same time tomorrow.'

Rosa returned to read to Antonio's father every day while Antonio was away, as she had promised she would. On her last visit, when she finished reading, Nonno turned to her. '*Signora* Bellocchi?' he said, staring at her hand. 'But you have no ring. Are you a widow?'

Rosa nodded.

'But you're so young. Still a girl.'

'I was unlucky.'

Nonno was quiet for a moment, thinking something over. He wrapped his misshapen fingers around Rosa's wrist. 'Listen,' he said. 'You're a pretty girl. Why don't you marry my son? Antonio's nice-looking and he works hard. He'd make a good husband.'

'I don't think your son is interested in me,' Rosa said diplomatically.

'Bah!' scoffed Nonno, shaking his head. 'He's still in love with that stupid *puttana*?' He rolled his eyes. 'You know, I worked like a brute so that my son wouldn't have to; worked until my back broke so he could be educated. Those Tamaris — do you know what they are? Cheesemakers who have gone up in the world! "Signor Parigi," that *puttana*'s father told me, "I've got ambitions for my daughter." *Testa di cazzo*! Does he think she shits gold and pisses silver? My son is better than her! Better than all of them! That Visconti he married her off to has money but he has no sense!'

The more Nonno recalled Signor Tamari's rejection of his son, the more heated he became. Rosa tried to placate him. After about a quarter of an hour of listening to his woes about Antonio's lack of marital status, Rosa managed to extricate herself by promising she would do something to woo him — which, of course, she had no intention of doing.

Out in the foyer, the maid, Ylenia, helped Rosa on with her coat. 'I hope you managed today,' she said. 'He can be a handful. I've worked for him for nearly fifteen years. He turned my hair grey when I was still a young woman.'

Rosa smiled politely but her curiosity got the better of her. 'Why does Nonno have all those cowboy items in his room?'

'Oh, Nonno loves his cowboy films,' said Ylenia, with a smile. 'Before he became sick, he and Signor Parigi used to go the cinema to watch them.'

Rosa walked back to her apartment feeling worn out. Antonio obviously trusted her: his father was not somebody anyone could handle. She laughed out loud when she thought of Antonio and his father sitting in the cinema and watching westerns together. It was almost as funny as him secretly playing with Allegra. Antonio was full of surprises.

Roberto, the new member of the troupe, exasperated Rosa. For the first few rehearsals, she tried to engage him in conversation but grew tired of him looking over her head and answering her in monosyllables. She didn't like the way he bossed Carlo about, correcting his pronunciation in the middle of a scene or criticising his costume, or that he never helped with the menial tasks that needed to be done. One day Piero was rolling a cigarette when Roberto snatched it out of his hand and threw it away. 'Don't you know the tax they put on tobacco goes into building Mussolini's army?' he said. Piero clenched his jaw and looked as if he was about to punch Roberto, but thought better of it. Luciano smoothed things over when he saw them happen, but otherwise was oblivious to the tension Roberto created. Rosa wished Benedetto was coming on tour with them instead. Six weeks with Roberto was going to be unbearable.

'Roberto snubs everyone except Luciano,' Orietta told Rosa one evening when they were making pasta dough together. 'He thinks the rest of us aren't good enough for him.'

Rosa rolled her eyes. 'What does he want?' she asked, making a well in the flour and breaking the eggs into it. 'I speak three foreign languages and you read more books than anybody else I know.'

'Yes,' said Orietta, passing a fork to Rosa to mix the dough, 'but I don't read in *Greek*.'

Rosa laughed. 'Isn't he the son of a tram driver? I heard him boasting of his working-class origins to Luciano the other day.'

'Well, he sees himself and Luciano as Renaissance men and the rest of us as peasants.'

Rosa shrugged. 'He hasn't even spoken to the rest of us to tell what we are.'

Orietta took over the kneading of the dough to give Rosa a rest. 'Roberto has given me some violin pieces to play in the monologue he is doing tomorrow,' she said. 'But he won't let me rehearse with him.'

'What monologue?' asked Rosa. She brushed the flour from her apron.

'Some piece he's insisted on doing before the play,' Orietta told her. 'Luciano had to agree because we can't replace him this late in the season.'

*

To begin the tour, The Montagnani Company opened again at the theatre on Via del Parlascio. Before the play, Carlo, Donatella and Roberto were scheduled to perform a variety act each to warm up the crowd. Carlo's juggling and Donatella's routine with Dante were crowd-pleasers. Rosa was intrigued to know what Roberto had planned for his monologue. The audience of workers and shopkeepers would not stand for anything highbrow; they might even throw fruit. The idea of Roberto covered in rotten melons made Rosa smile. She was annoyed at him for having done nothing to help set up the theatre before the performance. Luciano was in the ticket office and didn't see Roberto sitting on the stage steps, reading a book on Florentine art, while everyone else hurried about around him. When Donatella suggested that Roberto could help her set up the chairs, he gave her such a disdainful look that she burst into tears.

'I don't like him,' she whispered to Rosa in the wings.

'Neither does Dante,' Rosa replied, pointing at the dog and trying not to laugh. He was piddling on one of Roberto's costumes.

When it was time for Roberto to perform, he didn't appear straightaway. The evening was warm and the audience was restless, clapping their hands and stamping their feet. Rosa glanced at Luciano who was standing with the lighting assistant. His shoulders were tensed. Rosa caught his eye and pointed to the piano, asking with her gestures if he wanted her to perform a piece to keep the audience entertained. But then there was a ripple of the curtains. The assistant turned on the spotlight. The curtain opened and Roberto was revealed, standing on the stage with his foot on a chair. He wore black pants and a black shirt with a sash across his chest. The audience fell silent. From the whimsical look on his face, Rosa anticipated Roberto was about to perform a comedy act and hoped he could pull it off. She glanced at Luciano. Was he thinking the same thing? Was that why he was looking so anxious?

Roberto turned and faced the audience. He spread his legs apart, thrust out his chest and tensed his jaw.

'*Ho sempre ragione!*' he roared, waving his right hand as if he were holding a gun. '*Credere! Obbedire! Combattere!*'

Rosa couldn't believe what she was seeing. The bulldog chin, the flashing eyes, the dramatic pauses were all Il Duce's. Roberto had transformed himself into Mussolini.

'I flew my plane, swam the Mediterranean, duelled with a villain, raced my Alfa Romeo and rode my stallion to be here,' said Roberto.

He paused a moment to mime playing the violin. The music was filled in by Orietta who, on cue from Roberto, played a few bars of Paganini's Caprice No 24, a notoriously difficult piece.

Most of the audience laughed but some of them shifted in their seats. It was standard propaganda for Mussolini to be photographed undertaking some activity: fencing, horseback riding, playing the violin, painting, skiing. He was always portrayed as valiant, fearless, heroic, cultured and masculine.

'When I visited Sicily,' Roberto continued in Mussolini's character, 'my presence stopped the flow of Mount Etna and saved hundreds of lives. Once I brought rain to a drought-ridden region. On another occasion I underwent an operation without chloroform, having trained my body to be above pain.'

Those in the audience who found Roberto's satire amusing laughed louder.

'Pressmen, if you want a photograph, then you must catch me on my *daily* walk, *daily* horse ride, *daily* car ride or *daily* swim. I read Dante every morning before playing my violin like a maestro.'

Orietta came in with the first movement of Brahms's Violin Concerto.

'In my spare time I write novels, translate books, bed women and answer the letters of the thousands of citizens who write to me each year begging me to intervene in their personal problems. All this as well as being Italy's leader and overseeing the ministries of Foreign Affairs, War and Navy and Aviation. I never sleep, and the light is always left on in my office to prove it.'

More hoots of laughter from the audience. Of course, twenty-four hours were too few for all of Mussolini's purported daily activities. But it was dangerous to publicly make fun of the dictator. What had possessed Luciano to allow Roberto to do it? His act put the troupe at risk of being arrested, Rosa thought angrily.

Piero played the accordion while Roberto sang a list of Mussolini's aphorisms from the ridiculous to the threatening. 'If you are fat, I have no pity for you: you are stealing from Italy with your greediness'; 'It is my intention to transform Italians from a race of spaghetti-munching romantics into soldiers'; and 'No-one has stopped us. No-one will stop us.'

The last statement was chilling because it was true. Roberto could laugh at Mussolini all he liked, Rosa thought, but the other politicians either sided with Mussolini or crumbled under the fascist violence.

Roberto ended his act by placing his foot on the chair again and leaning on his knee. 'I am Alexander the Great and Caesar rolled into one. I am Socrates and Plato. Machiavelli, Napoleon and Garibaldi. I am Italy's greatest hero. But … oh, how my jaw aches at night.'

The curtain dropped and the audience cheered. Rosa cast her eyes down, too frightened to look. Were they *all* cheering? She was barely able to perform the music for *The Count of Monte Cristo*. After the performance, she helped the others clean the theatre but the more she thought about Roberto's act, the more her blood boiled. What was he doing? There were fascist spies everywhere looking for subversive activity. Rosa held in her anger despite Luciano's constant glances at her. Had he known Roberto was going to satirise Mussolini?

The troupe walked back to the Montagnani family's apartment. Carlo was tired and went to bed. Rosa tucked Sibilla in her cot by the stove before joining the others at the kitchen table. Orietta sliced some bread for supper. When Roberto congratulated himself on the success of his act, Rosa could not contain herself any longer.

'How could you do that act,' she asked, 'knowing it could have us sent to prison?'

Roberto's face pinched but he didn't answer. Piero and Donatella sent Rosa looks of sympathy. Luciano shifted in his chair.

'You don't know who was in that audience,' Rosa continued. 'Just because they are workers doesn't make them all anti-fascists. Some of them are *fattori* and estate managers. Some of them are working for the fascist elite.'

Roberto scoffed. 'We need to do more than pass around little pamphlets in secret,' he said. 'Or spend our lives worrying about what sauce we put on our pasta.'

'Enough!' said Luciano, raising his hand to silence Roberto. 'I won't have you insulting Rosa. She understands what the fascists represent.'

Luciano turned to Rosa. 'We can't remain passive,' he said. 'Mussolini intends to march on Europe the same way he did on Rome. It will be a disaster for Italy. We are the artists of the city. We have to awaken public opinion. Make people aware of the propaganda they are being fed.'

An uneasy feeling stirred in Rosa's stomach. So Luciano had known about Roberto's monologue. She sensed a gulf opening up between herself and Luciano. She wanted to close it, but didn't know how. She couldn't remain silent when her child's life was being put in danger. Roberto has done this, she thought. Luciano was satisfied with his small offensive against fascism until Roberto came along. Now he is taking more dangerous risks.

'Do you know what the fascists are doing?' Roberto asked Rosa, folding his arms across his chest. 'Thousands of innocent Italians have been imprisoned without trial.'

Rosa's skin prickled. The condescending expression on Roberto's face infuriated her. 'And do you have any idea what it is like to be sent to prison by the fascists?' she retorted. 'Well, I do! It's not some marvellously heroic gesture, believe me!'

Roberto opened his mouth and then shut it again.

'I have Sibilla's welfare to consider,' she told him. 'If something happens to me she'll be left an orphan. As petty and self-centred as that might sound to you, she's my first responsibility. I'm not risking going back to prison.'

Sibilla started crying. The argument had woken her up. Rosa picked her daughter up and fled to Orietta's bedroom. 'Shh, don't cry,' she told Sibilla, sitting on the bed and cuddling her. Tears poured down Rosa's own cheeks. Her heart ached. What was happening? She loved Luciano but this would drive them apart. Was fighting Mussolini more important to him than her and Sibilla?

'Rosa?'

She looked up to see Luciano standing in the doorway. His face was drawn.

'I've told Roberto he'll have to drop his act,' he said. 'You're right. It's not fair to put you and the others in danger.'

Rosa pulled Sibilla closer to her. 'What did he say?'

'He's not happy.'

'What if he leaves? Who will play all those roles?'

Luciano shrugged. 'We'll work something out.' He sat down next to Rosa and nestled his chin into her neck. 'We'll be more careful in the future, all right?'

'All right,' said Rosa.

Her heart was full of conflicting emotions: tenderness, sorrow, fear. She couldn't help feeling that she was making Luciano sacrifice something that was important to him. Luciano drew her to his side and kissed her. But even as they embraced, Rosa felt something had changed between them.

When *The Count of Monte Cristo* finished its run in Florence, the troupe revisited the towns they had the previous season and also expanded their tour to Prato. They returned to the spa town of Montecatini Terme. One day when she was walking by the town hall, Rosa imagined how nice it would be to get married there and have a picnic with the troupe in the park afterwards. It saddened her to think that there were no wedding plans in the near future; the fascists were more entrenched in power than ever. No matter what Luciano said about being committed to her, she was not a woman married before God and that hurt her. She sometimes fantasised about turning up at the Convent of Santo Spirito with a wedding ring on her finger and redeeming herself in Suor Maddalena's eyes. Now it seemed her desire for a name and a family had been thwarted. But she had no choice: she loved Luciano and the fight against fascism was everything to him. He'd cease to be Luciano if he was any other way.

Roberto remained with the troupe but his attitude towards Rosa was cool. She no longer bothered talking to him. Once she overheard him saying to Luciano, 'Are you sure Rosa is the right woman for you? I could introduce you to my sister. Now, she's a fighter.' A split lip from Luciano meant that Roberto never made the mistake of making a comment like that again.

While Rosa was organising the music for the first performance in Montecatini Terme, she caught a glimpse of the program. Roberto was back on in the variety acts. Her mind spun. Had Luciano put Roberto back on the program to appease him? If so, it would be a betrayal of Rosa's trust in him. She felt she was in a tug of war with Roberto over Luciano's loyalty.

Rosa did her best to play well for Carlo's and Donatella's acts but she had difficulty concentrating. When Roberto appeared on stage, she glanced at Luciano but he did not look in her direction. Roberto was wearing a white shirt instead of a black one. This time he didn't swagger like Mussolini. He stretched his hands out to the audience beseechingly.

'*An Appointment with Pegasus*,' he said.

Rosa held her breath. It didn't sound like something Mussolini would say, but she couldn't be sure with Roberto. To her amazement, what followed was a lyrical poem about the winged horse from Greek mythology — wherever his hoof struck the earth, a spring burst forth. The audience was moved by the beauty of the imagery and the idea of a majestic creature bringing freedom to the people of the earth.

As the poem continued, Rosa began to read the underlying meaning. It was the disguised story of Lauro de Bosis, a young intellectual from Rome who had flown over the city and dropped leaflets urging the Italian people to throw off the rule of the fascists. Afterwards, he and his plane, *Pegasus*, were lost at sea.

'You live in a prison and pity those who are free,' said Roberto.

Roberto was treading a fine line. As well as tourists, the audience contained schoolteachers, notaries, pharmacists and doctors — people who may or may not be enthusiastic fascists. And yet this time Rosa could not be angry. Her conscience was pricked. If she had suffered, how many more thousands of innocent people were continuing to suffer?

Rosa was unable to sleep after the performance. She

tucked Sibilla under Orietta's arm and went outside the tent for some fresh air. She was surprised when she saw Luciano standing a few yards away looking at the sky.

'You had the same idea?' he said, turning to face her. 'It's too hot to sleep.'

'Let's walk for a bit,' suggested Rosa.

Luciano took her hand and they strolled down a path and into a grove of trees.

'The poem Roberto recited was beautiful,' Rosa said.

'So you are not angry at me for letting him perform it?'

Rosa shook her head. 'Not everyone will understand the double meaning, although it is still treading on dangerous ground.'

They walked on in silence.

'Luciano,' Rosa said, touching his arm, 'I wouldn't object to Roberto's anti-fascist messages if I didn't have Sibilla to think about.'

'I know,' said Luciano. 'I think of her too.'

Rosa stopped and turned to him. 'I'm also concerned about you.'

Luciano shook his head. 'I've never been able to live only for myself,' he said. 'It's never been in me. I'm not like your Antonio Parigi, able to keep a Fascist Party card in my drawer and even wear a black shirt on occasion so I can keep my business.'

'He's part Jewish,' Rosa tried to explain. 'He has an elderly father to support.'

'It's everyone thinking about themselves that has brought about the downfall of Italy,' Luciano replied. 'To be a great nation, we need to have visionaries and great thinkers. Not to be focused on what clothes we wear or how finely we furnish our houses.'

A shiver passed over Rosa. She thought of de Bosis flying over the dark ocean and realised that he had thought the same thing. His death had been noble. But Rosa didn't want to be mourning a noble man; she wanted to be caressing a living one.

'Luciano,' she said, seized by a sudden panic, 'promise me you won't do anything reckless. I don't know what I would do without you.'

Luciano turned his gaze to the stars and didn't reply. Rosa could feel him slipping away from her.

'Make love to me,' she said.

He stared at her. 'Are you sure? Here?'

Rosa nodded. She undid the buttons of her dress, slipped it over her shoulders and down her hips. She removed her chemise and underwear and stood naked before Luciano in the night air. He drank her in with his eyes before removing his shirt and pants. He picked up Rosa's dress and put their clothes together on the ground, making a cover for them to lie on. Rosa did not think of Osvaldo this time. She only thought how beautiful Luciano looked in the moonlight.

Luciano took Rosa in his arms and pressed his lips to her neck. His hand lingered over her breasts. 'Touch me,' she whispered, lying back on the clothes. She sighed when he caressed her breasts, then brushed his tongue over her nipples. His hand swept down her stomach to her thighs. She shuddered with pleasure as he pressed his lips to her sex and gripped his shoulders when a sensation like dozens of electric shocks burst over her body. She squeezed her eyes shut, struggling to catch her breath.

When she opened her eyes again, she saw Luciano lingering over her. 'Please,' she said. 'It's all right.' She saw the stars twinkling in the sky behind him. There was no pain, only a tingling pleasure that made her moan and dig her fingers into his back. She wrapped her legs around his waist wanting to cling to him like that forever. Luciano's breathing quickened.

After a few moments, they lay side by side and nestled into each other. Luciano fell asleep with his hand resting on Rosa's thigh. She told herself that she would forever associate the stars with this night and with Luciano.

FIFTEEN

When the tour was finished Rosa returned to work in Antonio's shop. Luciano told her that she didn't need to work but Rosa wanted to save money. She had ambitions of sending Sibilla to a convent school as a *paying* student, and Luciano had promised that he would set aside money from the communal tin for that purpose.

One morning at Antonio's shop, Rosa was sitting at the front desk thinking over her fears about Luciano's activities. She wanted things to go back to how they were before Roberto appeared, when Luciano was going to defeat fascism with his pamphlets and protect her and Sibilla.

Antonio returned from visiting a customer. He stopped in his tracks when he saw Rosa. She realised she must have looked miserable.

'You're deep in thought,' he said. 'Were you contemplating the new piece that arrived yesterday?' Antonio rested his hand on an oak dresser with a candle stand over the centre leg. 'What do you make of it?'

Rosa knew Antonio was trying to cheer her up but she wasn't in the mood for attempting a reading on the dresser, especially when he didn't believe in her powers to see the origins of things. She asked after his father instead.

Antonio lowered his eyes. 'He declined over the summer,' he said. 'It's difficult to witness. He used to be so strong. When I was a boy I'd watch him strutting along with several bags of plaster on his head.'

'I'm sorry,' said Rosa.

Antonio grimaced. 'I don't have any brothers and sisters. My cousins are all in Venice. So …'

He didn't finish the sentence but Rosa knew what he was trying to say. He was lonely. She realised that Signora Visconti had taken away more than his chance at marital happiness. She had stopped him enjoying children of his own. If his father passed away, Antonio would be all alone.

'Would you like me to visit him when you go back for lunch today?' she asked.

Antonio brightened. 'That's kind of you, Rosa. He often asks after you.'

Rosa could tell there was something weighing on Antonio's mind. Something he wanted to tell her. But he seemed to be having trouble raising the courage to come out with it.

'Why don't we take Allegra and Ambrosio to stay with him?' she said. 'They will be good company.'

At lunchtime, Antonio and Rosa walked to the apartment, with Ambrosio on a lead beside Antonio and Rosa carrying Allegra in a cane basket.

'Ah, what beautiful children you have,' called out a florist.

Antonio and Rosa looked at each other and laughed.

'Well, Allegra is pretty like you,' said Antonio. 'But I don't lift my leg at every statue and planter.'

Rosa was shocked to see how frail Nonno had become since she had visited him last. When Giuseppina ushered her and Antonio into Nonno's room, he could barely lift his head off the pillow. He smiled when he saw the animals. 'They are much better than people,' he said, rubbing Allegra under the chin. 'They give so much and only ask for kindness in return.' The effort of talking tired him. There would be no swearing today.

'How about a card game?' Antonio asked his father.

Nonno laughed weakly. 'You only want to play me now because you think you'll win.'

'I brought my flute,' Rosa told him. 'Antonio says you don't listen to music much, but I think you might like this.'

She assembled her flute and played Saint-Saëns's *The Swan*. She chose it because it was a tranquil piece that conjured perfectly the image of a swan gliding on water. Antonio sat down next to his father to listen. The door opened and Giuseppina and Ylenia peered inside. When they saw that Rosa was playing, they entered the room and stood either side of the bed.

'Did that please you?' Rosa asked Nonno when she had finished.

'It pleased me very much,' he said, closing his eyes. 'It eased the pain. Play me something else.'

Antonio glanced at Rosa admiringly. 'I didn't realise you were so proficient,' he said. 'You're obviously classically trained.'

Rosa played several more pieces until Nonno fell asleep. Then she and Antonio walked back to the shop in silence. It was sad seeing Nonno so feeble, like watching a great lion taking its last breaths.

They passed by the clock shop and Rosa's heart jumped when she recognised Signora Visconti through the window. Antonio's mistress was admiring gold watches with a man Rosa assumed was her husband. He was not as handsome as Antonio and much older. Antonio noticed her too. Signora Visconti saw Antonio but they didn't acknowledge each other. Rosa, however, could feel the charge of energy that passed between them when they locked eyes.

They walked on, Antonio noticeably unnerved. Rosa wondered why Signora Visconti had kept coming to see him after she had married someone else. If she really loved him, she would have left him alone to carry on with his life.

'Why don't you bring Sibilla to the shop with you any more?' Antonio suddenly asked Rosa. 'With Ambrosio and Allegra keeping my father company, it's going to be quiet.'

'She's very active,' explained Rosa. 'I'm afraid she might damage something.'

'Not in the backroom,' he answered. 'I can put locks on the cupboard doors and a gate into the shop and then Sibilla — and the furniture — should be quite safe. I miss her happy face.'

'That's kind of you,' Rosa told him.

She was grateful for his offer. Orietta was having difficulty obtaining sufficient sewing work since returning from tour. She had been offered a job in a patisserie and this way she would be able to take it.

They continued walking. Before they reached the shop, Antonio turned to Rosa. 'Listen, I don't want to pry into your private life but I'm worried about you,' he said. 'I don't know what sort of provision your late husband left for you, but if you are working I assume it wasn't enough. If you ever need anything, please ask me.'

Rosa was touched and ashamed at the same time. Antonio was a kind man and she had never confessed the truth to him that she was not a widow. If she hadn't known how deeply in love he was with Signora Visconti, she might have mistaken his generosity for something else.

The troupe had one more engagement before the winter set in: to play music together at the Festa della Rificolona. Rosa's flute was in need of maintenance and she took it to Signor Morelli at the music store. She was grateful that he remembered her from the time she'd had her flute repaired before seeing the Agarossi family but not from the time she'd been a governess at the Villa Scarfiotti. Signor Morelli had aged. He was greyer and more stooped than when she had last seen him, but just as cheerful.

'Things didn't work out with the Agarossi family, eh?' he said. 'Never mind, they are difficult children. It seems you have found a niche with the Montagnani family? I saw *The Count of Monte Cristo* in the summer and recognised you at the piano.'

'The season went well for us,' Rosa said.

Signor Morelli cocked his head. 'You're a good musician, Signora Bellocchi. I could find you work playing for weddings.'

Rosa thanked him. She was happy selling furniture but it was good to know she could do something else if she needed extra money.

'You do know the Montagnanis are the children of a famous Florentine tailor?' Signor Morelli asked Rosa.

She wasn't in the mood for hearing the tragic story over again. Anything that hurt Luciano hurt her too. But there were no other customers in the store and Signor Morelli was intent on telling it.

'Their father was tailor to the rich and famous of Florence,' said Signor Morelli. 'He used to buy his children's instruments from this store.'

'Truly?' said Rosa. A faint tingle started in her fingers and toes. It was the same feeling she experienced whenever she was about to see the origin of an object. 'I was brought up in a convent,' she explained. 'I had never heard of a famous tailor called Montagnani.'

Signor Morelli raised his eyebrows. 'Oh, his name wasn't Montagnani,' he said. 'That was the name of their uncle. They took his name when he adopted them … after their father had left.'

The tingling in Rosa's fingers and toes grew stronger. The hairs on the back of her neck prickled.

'No,' said Signor Morelli. 'His name was Taviani. Giovanni Taviani.'

Rosa didn't breathe for a few seconds. 'Giovanni Taviani? The gatekeeper at the Villa Scarfiotti?'

Signor Morelli was surprised that Rosa knew of the villa. 'Yes. Well, he originally went there as the estate manager. The Old Marchese was fond of him. They served together in the cavalry in Africa. Giovanni Taviani had saved the Old Marchese's life. But of course it was a far fall from the existence he'd been leading in Florence.'

Rosa suddenly understood the vision she had experienced the first time she had played with the Montagnani family. She walked back to the apartment in such deep thought that she took a false turn and found herself on the wrong street. All she could see before her was the image of Giovanni Taviani. She remembered his wild grey hair, his upright posture and his cultured voice. He was Luciano's father! She thought of the eviction she had witnessed in Via della Pergola and how Giovanni Taviani had gone a step further and deserted his family. Then she thought of the Weimaraner puppy and the other animals he had saved. Was it his way of trying to make amends — if not with his children then with God?

When Rosa arrived at the Montagnanis' apartment and found no-one there, she went down to the cellar. She was surprised to discover Luciano and Roberto speaking with a man she had never seen before. He had a malnourished look about him. His fringe hung over his eyes. The man was nervous and gave a start when Rosa appeared.

'It's all right,' Roberto told him. 'It's only Rosa.'

Rosa's eyes fell to a large trunk at the man's feet and a suitcase next to it. She looked at Luciano. He took her by the arm and led her up the stairs. When they were in the Montagnanis' apartment, he told her: 'Roberto is moving into the cellar.'

'What's in the trunk?' she asked.

'Parts of a printing press. We're going to produce our own anti-fascist newspaper. It's become too dangerous to get everything through France.'

'Here? In this building?' Rosa's eyes pleaded with Luciano to be more cautious. 'But your family lives here.'

'It's perfect,' he said. 'The sound doesn't travel to the hall. No-one will know it's here.'

The apartment above the cellar was occupied by an elderly couple who were both half-deaf. Luciano was probably right that they wouldn't hear the clack of the press through the solid walls and floors. The apartment next to the couple was occupied by a shifty-looking man who was possibly doing something illegal himself and was unlikely to report anybody else for doing the same. Still, Rosa wished she hadn't asked what Luciano and Roberto were planning. It was one more thing to worry about.

'Rosa?' Luciano grasped her hands. 'The anti-fascist movement has almost disappeared. People have been terrorised into silence. We mustn't cower now. We've heard that Mussolini is afraid of our small group.'

Rosa put her hand to Luciano's cheek. If Mussolini was afraid of them, he would increase the number of spies he sent out to find them. But she didn't say anything. There was nothing she could say that would stop Luciano.

'We have to continue to fight,' he told her, his eyes aflame with passion. 'Mussolini is growing less friendly with Britain and closer to Hitler. Do you understand what such an association would mean for Italy?'

Rosa put her arms around Luciano's neck and hugged him. It couldn't have been easy to obtain the printing press. It looked like it was being delivered to them in parts. She didn't want to spoil his triumph with her fears, so she hid what she felt.

'I understand,' she said.

Luciano peered into Rosa's eyes. 'I'm lucky to have you and Sibilla,' he said. 'I thank God for you every day. You give me the strength to fight.'

After Luciano had returned to the cellar, Rosa slumped into a chair in the kitchen. She admired his courage. She was the one who was weak. As much as she despised fascism, she longed for comfort and security. What she wanted most was a husband and a home, and yet every day that dream seemed to be slipping further from her. Tears rolled down her cheeks. She couldn't be anything but loyal to Luciano; he had saved her and Sibilla from the street and had been good to them. Her love for him was rooted deeply in her heart.

Rosa dried her tears and set about making supper. She thought of all the women who had loved great men: Joséphine and Napoleon; Anita Ribeiro and Garibaldi; Madame du Barry and Louis XV. She wondered if they had felt the same heights of joy and depths of fear that she did.

Nonno's health took a turn for the worse and Antonio had to spend more time at his apartment and less time at the shop. He left Rosa in charge most days. He had come to trust her judgement on furniture and if she went to an estate sale and found a piece she thought was good, he let her buy it without his checking it first.

At the same time, Luciano started writing and printing the first edition of his newspaper. The money promised by Giustizia e Libertà hadn't come through so Rosa had let him use the money they had put aside for Sibilla's education to cover the first few editions.

'They are an honest organisation,' Luciano assured her. 'You'll have the money in the next few months. The problem is, working through France.'

'I'm not worried,' Rosa told him.

She had no doubt that Giustizia e Libertà would pay if they could. Sibilla wasn't going to school for some years yet, and Rosa was doing so well selling furniture that she would replenish the money herself within a few months, even if she wasn't paid back. Rosa was proud that she could help the work of the anti-fascists in some way. The withering looks Roberto had been sending her grated on her nerves. She hadn't forgotten what he'd said to Luciano about her not being a strong partner to him.

'I'm glad to help. It makes me feel less of a coward,' she told Luciano.

Luciano frowned. 'Wherever did you get that idea?' he asked. 'I've told you I don't want you directly involved in the cause. It's too dangerous for you. But how can I honour the woman I love if I let her live in a country where the leadership is rotten to the core? I don't want you to be anyone other than yourself. I love you.'

Rosa melted. They were the most heartfelt, emotional words Luciano had ever spoken to her. She never told him she had learned where his father was because she hadn't wanted to hurt him. She knew that he would never do anything to hurt her or Sibilla. They had that trust.

That night, when she and Luciano lay in each other's arms, Rosa reflected on what he had said. But the more she relived the sentiments he'd voiced, the less peace she felt. Perhaps he knows how dangerous his life has become, she thought. There is no time for mincing words. Luciano could be snatched out of my arms at any moment and sent to prison — or shot.

The following morning when Rosa arrived at the shop with Sibilla, she was surprised to find Antonio sitting at his desk and looking pale. Had his father passed away overnight? She placed Sibilla in her cot before approaching him. But when she enquired about Nonno, Antonio puzzled her by saying that his father was better than he had been in weeks. Why did Antonio look so tired, then? Was it because of Signora Visconti that he was losing sleep?

'Please sit down, Rosa,' he said, indicating that she should take the chair opposite his desk. His expression was serious. She wondered if he hadn't liked the sideboard she had bought at an auction, or thought she'd paid too high a price for it.

Antonio stared at his hands, keeping Rosa in suspense. Finally he looked up and said, 'I have been thinking about this for some time now. We get along well, you and I. I'd like to give you and Sibilla a home and a secure life.'

Rosa stared at him. Was he offering her a share in the business? She waited for him to continue.

'Rosa?'

'I'm not sure I understand,' she said.

Antonio smiled. 'I'm asking you to be my wife.'

The statement knocked the breath out of Rosa. She struggled to regain her composure but it was impossible. She was too shocked. A marriage proposal was what she had expected from Luciano, not from Antonio! She had not seen it coming at all: not in their chats in the shop or their visits to Nonno. She enjoyed Antonio's charm, his sense of humour, his kindness. But she had never thought of him as anything other than her friend and employer.

Antonio took her silence as encouragement to continue. 'You've seen my home,' he said. 'It's not a palace but it's comfortable. If you wanted to add your own feminine touches, I think we could be very happy there. It would mean a lot to my father, especially in his last months. And, of course, I would recognise Sibilla as my stepdaughter.'

Rosa stared at the floor, overcome by unbearable remorse. How could she have let this happen? How could she have deceived a generous man like Antonio to the point he truly believed she was a good widow in need of rescuing? For surely that was what this was: a rescue. His heart, like hers, belonged elsewhere. She looked up and saw that Antonio was watching her with a bemused expression.

'Rosa, what is it?' he asked. 'Have I really surprised you so?'

Rosa clenched her fists and managed to stammer, 'But Signora Visconti? You love her, not me.'

Antonio flinched. 'I came to realise my attachment was nothing more than the vain imaginings of a young man. I am no longer that man,' he said firmly. 'I put aside my ... hopes with her some time ago.'

The turn of events had given Rosa such a shock that she began to cry. Antonio was willing to give her what she most wanted for herself and Sibilla — a name and a home. Why couldn't she have that with Luciano when she loved him so?

Rosa inhaled a breath, drawing up the courage she needed to speak.

'There's been a terrible misunderstanding,' she said. 'There's something I haven't told you.'

Antonio's brow furrowed. 'Do you mean there's someone else? That you are already engaged?'

Rosa nodded. Antonio's face turned pale. The despair she felt at hurting him made her realise she had deeper feelings for him than she'd thought.

'Oh dear,' he said, clenching his jaw. 'I'm sorry, I didn't realise ... But of course there would be a man for you, wouldn't there? You're so lovely and young.'

The pain in his voice made Rosa cry even harder.

'Please, Rosa,' he said, standing up and passing her his handkerchief. 'This is my mistake, not yours. I've made too many assumptions. Please let's put this conversation behind us.'

Rosa tried to do as Antonio suggested, to forget that he had proposed to her, but she found it impossible to continue working at the shop. Antonio spent more time than he previously had visiting suppliers and attending estate sales. He was obviously ill at ease at being around her. Rosa felt she was living dishonestly. She was disgusted with herself for having deceived Antonio, and now that he had proposed to her, she felt unfaithful to Luciano for continuing to work for him.

'What's the matter?' Luciano asked her one morning when she'd burnt the coffee for the second time. He looked at her with eyes full of concern. Rosa couldn't meet his gaze.

'You've been like this for a couple of days,' whispered Orietta, taking the burnt pan from Rosa and scrubbing it. 'Are you pregnant?'

Rosa realised that the most honourable thing she could do was to quit working for Antonio. One afternoon when he was out inspecting some furniture in Fiesole, she wrote him a letter confessing everything she could without endangering anyone. She told him about her prison sentence, alluding as tactfully as possible to the circumstances of Sibilla's conception. She told him that she was engaged to the troupe's manager, but said nothing of Luciano's clandestine activities. She wondered if it might ease Antonio's mind to know that she wasn't who he thought she was. Perhaps if he had known about her past, he wouldn't have asked her to marry him.

She left the note on Antonio's desk. 'I'm sorry I deceived you, good friend,' she whispered, before picking up Sibilla and glancing once more over the beautiful furniture. She locked the shop before heading down Via Tornabuoni, walking quickly for several blocks with no clear idea exactly where she was going.

Winter that year was bitter. Rosa had grown used to Antonio's shop, which was well heated. The apartment she shared with Luciano was icy cold. She stuffed rags into the cracks around the windows to block out the draughts and spent most of her time in the kitchen of the Montagnanis' apartment, where the stove remained warm until midday. Piero told her to put more coal in it to keep it going but Rosa knew the pile was growing low and night-time was colder. She was sorry that she was no longer bringing home the money she once did. She had told Luciano that Antonio didn't have enough work for her and he'd had to let her go. It made her feel even guiltier that he believed her without question. Signor Morelli was true to his offer to recommend Rosa to play at weddings, but not only was the pay meagre compared to what she had been earning it also seemed no-one intended to get married until the spring. Luciano found a second job. He said it was to keep things going, but Rosa suspected it was also due to his sense of honour. The money sent by Giustizia e Libertà to pay Rosa back had been stolen by the courier who was supposed to deliver it.

By three o'clock in the afternoons, it became so cold that Rosa couldn't continue with the housework. She would put on her coat and hold Sibilla tucked to her chest. They would sit like that until six when she would relight the stove and start preparing dinner. The vegetables Orietta brought home from the market were declining in quality, and Rosa had to stretch her imagination to come up with variations on the polenta, potatoes and *baccalà* that was the staple of their diet. She often went without because she couldn't bring herself to eat the dried codfish. Luciano, Carlo, Piero and Orietta arrived home in the evenings tired from working hard. Rosa understood that Roberto was running the press, but she resented his lack of contribution to the household, especially as he joined them for dinner and ate more than anybody else.

One afternoon in January, the apartment was so cold that Rosa could no longer stand it. She climbed into Orietta's bed with Sibilla to keep warm under the covers until the others came home. She woke a few hours later with a jolt. The front of her dress was damp with sweat, but when she touched her forehead, her flesh was cool. Sibilla was lying next to her, her face turned to the pillow.

'Sibilla, what's wrong?' Rosa asked, picking her up. Her skin was on fire.

'Head hurt,' Sibilla whimpered.

Rosa pressed her palm to Sibilla's forehead. The child was feverish. Rosa's throat went dry. She loosened Sibilla's nightdress to listen to her chest and noticed two spots like bruises on her skin. She heard the locks on the front door click open. Luciano had returned.

'Hurry! Get a doctor!' Rosa told him. 'Sibilla has a high fever!'

The panic in her voice sent Luciano rushing back out without delay.

Sibilla grew limper in Rosa's arms. She fainted but revived a moment later. 'Dear God, help us!' Rosa prayed, returning to the bedroom and lying Sibilla on the bed. She sat down next to her. Rosa didn't know if it was hours or minutes before Luciano returned with the doctor: a man in his thirties with heavy jowls and intense eyes.

Carlo and Orietta arrived home at the same time. As soon as they heard Sibilla was sick, Orietta put aside her own distress and set about performing practical tasks: hanging the doctor's coat; throwing coals in the stove; boiling water. Carlo sat on the bed, his head in his hands. Roberto arrived shortly afterwards, expecting dinner. Carlo told him what had happened. Roberto hovered near the bedroom door. As much as Rosa disliked him, she was touched by the concern on his face.

The doctor took Sibilla's temperature and felt her neck. Sibilla was squinting as if the light hurt her eyes. This symptom seemed to trouble the doctor more than her high fever. He took out his stethoscope and loosened Sibilla's dress so he could listen to her breathing. The spots had spread. There were more than a dozen of them now over her chest. The doctor put his stethoscope away.

'Who's the father?' he asked.

'I am,' said Luciano.

The doctor indicated for Luciano to follow him to the hallway. A sick feeling clenched Rosa's stomach. The blood pounded so loudly in her ears she couldn't hear what the doctor was saying. Luciano slumped as if he had received a blow. Sibilla lost consciousness again. The doctor returned to the room, and Luciano came with him and put his hand on Rosa's shoulder. A lump irritated her throat. She felt as if she might vomit.

'I'm sorry,' said the doctor.

Rosa couldn't speak. She found herself bargaining with God — *Take my eyes, take my legs, but don't take …*

'It's meningitis,' the doctor said.

At first Rosa thought she had misheard him. Meningitis. There was an epidemic of the disease in Florence that winter. All the babies and most of the young children who had caught it had died. Carlo let out a sob. Orietta came running from the kitchen.

'You need to prepare for the worst,' the doctor said. 'Is your daughter baptised?'

Rosa stood and nearly toppled over. Luciano grabbed her arm to steady her. This couldn't be happening. She couldn't be losing the bright star that Sibilla had been to her. Rosa wasn't going to give in like that. She had fought to keep Sibilla with her and she would fight God himself if that's what it took to keep her alive.

'No! Sibilla is strong!' she said, her fists clenched. 'They have anti-serums for this now, don't they?'

The doctor exhaled a breath. 'The central OMNI clinic may administer it. Your daughter is succumbing ... but you can try.'

'OMNI?' Rosa recollected the humiliating day at the *comune* when her application for assistance had been rejected. 'They won't accept me,' she said, a tremor in her voice. 'I am listed as an enemy of the state.'

The doctor's mouth twitched. Rosa could see he didn't approve of her record but thankfully his main concern was Sibilla. He looked to Luciano. 'What about you? Do you have party membership?'

Luciano lowered his eyes and shook his head. The doctor's face collapsed with dismay.

'There's nothing more I can do,' he said. 'You'd better send for a priest.'

Rosa's head spun. 'Isn't there a private clinic?' she asked.

The doctor raised his eyebrows. 'Yes, but ... you need money to go there. A lot of money.'

'We have money!' Rosa said. The room was turning white. Her mind was a jumble of thoughts and she struggled to make sense of them. 'Luciano,' she said. 'We have the money we were putting aside for Sibilla's education.'

Luciano looked aghast. 'Rosa,' he said, 'you know that money is gone. You know what for.'

As they locked eyes, the terrible truth dawned on Rosa. The anti-fascist paper — they had spent the money that could have saved Sibilla on fighting Mussolini.

Luciano turned to the doctor. 'I can get the money,' he said. 'But I can't get it right now.'

The doctor shook his head. 'They'll want it upfront. If you can't pay, they'll send her to a charity hospital and, frankly, it's better to keep your daughter here.'

Rosa looked at Sibilla. Her breathing was laboured. No, she thought. No, I won't let her die.

'Luciano, Orietta,' she said, pulling them both towards Sibilla. 'Watch over her for me. I know someone who will help us. I will go to him now.'

Rosa addressed the doctor. 'Do you have a car?'

'Yes.'

'Then please take my daughter to the clinic. I will meet you there with the money, I promise. I will have it in an hour.'

'Where are you going?' asked Luciano. 'I'll come with you.'

'No!' Rosa wanted to look at Luciano but she couldn't. 'I'm going to see Antonio. He loves her. He loves Sibilla. He will help us.'

The night air was freezing and Rosa hadn't dressed properly for it, with only her coat over her house dress. But she didn't feel the cold biting her skin and drying her eyes. She refused to allow herself to feel anything. She had only one purpose in mind: that she must save Sibilla. She ran through the streets like a woman gone crazy. Her head pounded and her feet hurt but she wouldn't stop. When she reached Antonio's apartment she pressed the buzzer, praying that he was at home.

Antonio answered the door instead of Ylenia. He was wearing a dressing-gown over his suit and gave a start when he saw Rosa.

'My God! It's freezing tonight. What are you doing here?' he said, pulling her inside the foyer. He turned pale when he saw the wild look on her face. 'What's the matter?'

'Sibilla!' Rosa cried, collapsing to her knees.

Antonio's eyes grew wide. 'What's happened?' he asked. 'What's happened to Sibilla?'

The tears Rosa had been forcing down burst out from her. 'Help us! Antonio! Oh God! Please help us!'

*

Rosa did not take her eyes off Sibilla that critical night in the clinic. They were alone together in the isolation room, with a nurse coming every half-hour to check Sibilla's vital signs. Rosa did not allow herself to think about what had happened in the last few hours. All her mental efforts were spent on prayers for her daughter. She did not want to remember the humiliated expression on Luciano's face when Antonio presented his Fascist Party card to the admissions nurse and handed over a wad of bills. 'Anything she needs,' he had said. 'Anything at all, I will pay for it.'

Rosa would never intentionally hurt Luciano, but all she could think about was saving Sibilla.

Only Rosa was allowed to stay with her, everyone else was sent away. The child fell unconscious after the serum was administered. Each time her daughter's condition deteriorated, Rosa felt part of herself being torn away. Yet, by some miracle, Sibilla was still breathing the next morning.

Antonio arrived and organised for a cot bed to be brought for Rosa to sleep on, and told her that he would ring a friend of his in Rome who was a children's specialist to see if there was anything else that could be done. 'Luciano and the others are waiting outside the clinic,' he said. 'They are worried senseless, but it's better they don't come in. It might jeopardise Sibilla's treatment. The head doctor is an ardent fascist.'

Sibilla's condition worsened in the afternoon. Her closed eyelids were swollen and her mouth was limp. The situation continued with minor improvements followed by deteriorations for another week.

'I'm afraid I can't let you stay overnight again,' the nurse told Rosa. 'It's against the regulations. Your husband persuaded us to bend them for you, but we've done it for as long as we can. You'll have to go home and come back in the morning.'

Rosa understood that by 'husband' the nurse meant Antonio. He came every day to the clinic, taking back news of Sibilla's progress to Luciano and his family. He brought soup for Rosa to eat. 'Ylenia made it for you. You have to stay strong for Sibilla,' he told her. 'You can't let yourself waste away.' Then he would stay and make sure that she ate it. Rosa did so to please him, not because she was hungry. She remembered what she had said to Luciano about Antonio: *He loves her. He loves Sibilla.* Yes, but Antonio also loves me, Rosa realised. She saw it in the way he cared for her. Somewhere, somehow, the affections he had held for Signora Visconti had transferred to her. His proposal had not been a rescue mission at all.

When Rosa came home each day from the clinic, she and Luciano collapsed into each other's arms but were usually too distressed to speak much. What could they say? Rosa couldn't think clearly enough to talk about anything. Her entire mind was filled with thoughts of Sibilla.

'You must hate me,' Luciano said once, his eyes brimming with pain. 'If I hadn't used the money ...'

Rosa put her fingers to his lips and shook her head. 'It was *our* decision ... and in the end, Sibilla received the serum. It's up to God now.'

The Montagnanis didn't have a telephone and Rosa dreaded going to the clinic each morning knowing that she might be greeted with the news that Sibilla had perished overnight. Although Sibilla was conscious again and eating small amounts of gruel, the doctor told Rosa that she was still in danger. But Rosa refused to give up hope.

'Come on, my little one,' she whispered to her daughter, stroking her cheek. 'Mamma wants to take you home.'

Each day on her way back from the clinic, Rosa stopped at a church to light a candle. She would sit in the silence and pray, never sure if the peace she felt came from faith or weariness.

On the fifteenth morning of Sibilla's illness, Rosa had a

dream. She was woken by a bright light. She climbed out of bed and followed it down a dark corridor with a door at the end of it. The door slowly swung open. On the other side was Sibilla in the arms of an angel. The angel had its wings tucked behind its back and cradled Sibilla, who was happy and laughing. The light grew stronger and Rosa woke up. It was already nine o'clock in the morning. She had overslept. Luciano left for work at five o'clock and would have thought that too early to wake her.

Rosa hurriedly dressed and caught the tram to the clinic. While she had been dreaming, she had felt peace. But now she was panicked. Why an angel? Had Sibilla passed away?

There wasn't anyone at the clinic's reception desk. Rosa ran straight up the stairs. When she entered the room where Sibilla had been staying, her daughter wasn't there. The sheets had been stripped from the bed. Rosa ran back into the corridor. Her heart stopped when she saw a trolley with a body lying on it covered with a sheet. The body was small: its feet only reached part of the way down the trolley. The blood drained from Rosa's face. *Help me to be strong, help me to trust*, she prayed, her legs shaking beneath her. With a trembling hand, she tugged back the sheet. A little boy with a halo of blond hair lay before her. His skin was mottled but he looked at rest, as if he were sleeping. Rosa recognised him as the boy who had fallen from his bicycle and hit his head. He had been alive the day before, but now his voice and presence were lost to his family forever. She leaned forward and kissed his forehead before covering him again.

'Your daughter is here, Signora Parigi.'

Rosa turned to see the matron standing at the end of the corridor. She was pointing to the door next to her.

Rosa's feet barely touched the floor. She ran to the room the matron indicated. Sibilla was sitting up in bed. She was pale but she wasn't struggling to breathe. She was nibbling at a plum that she held in her hand. When she saw Rosa, her face broke into a smile.

'Head don't hurt, Mamma,' she said.

Rosa threw her arms around her daughter and wept.

Rosa stopped at the church on her way home. She sat in the pew, staring at the statue of Christ. The nagging thought that she had managed to suppress during the crisis of Sibilla's illness now demanded her attention. She could no longer avoid what was obvious: her love for Luciano took her one way, but her love for Sibilla and her duty to her daughter's welfare pulled her another. She had to think of Sibilla and the sort of life into which she would be leading her if she stayed with Luciano. He was called to a greater cause and, although he would never say it, she and Sibilla were a weight holding him back. Rosa remembered the words the Badessa had said to her when she was leaving the convent: *To live this life you must be called to it* … Luciano loved them but he was no more suited to being an ordinary family man than Rosa was to being a nun. He couldn't turn away from what God had designated him to do. It was as much a part of him as Rosa's ability to see the source of things was of her.

Rosa's mind drifted to Antonio. He had offered her marriage and she had refused it because her heart belonged to Luciano. Had she given any thought to what was best for Sibilla? Antonio could give her daughter a warm home and a good education. Ballet lessons, art lessons, beautiful clothes. It could all be hers. What could Rosa give her if she stayed with Luciano? Love alone would not have saved Sibilla from meningitis.

Rosa sensed someone standing next to her. She looked up to see Luciano.

'I thought I would find you here,' he said, kneeling beside her. 'Antonio told me that Sibilla has passed the worst danger.'

Rosa stared at her hands. She was afraid to look at Luciano. She was afraid of what she might see in his eyes — or what he might see in hers.

'I didn't know he had proposed to you,' said Luciano softly. 'You didn't tell me that. He's a good man. We had a long talk. It seems you told him about your past and he's not put off by that.'

'Stop!' said Rosa.

With Luciano so near to her, his familiar arm pressed against hers, she forgot everything she had been considering. She *loved* him. She *needed* him. She was afraid of what he was going to say because she knew it was what she had been thinking. Which is easier to bear, Rosa wondered, the truth or lies?

'Will you light a candle for me, Rosa?' Luciano asked. 'Will you light a candle and pray for the cause I am pledged to?'

Rosa felt his eyes on her but she refused to meet his gaze. The aching in her chest was going to kill her. Maybe one day all that had happened would make sense and she would be able to see it from a detached point of view. But not today. There were no words for the agony she felt.

'What are you saying, Luciano?' she asked, finally mustering the courage. 'What are you trying to tell me?'

'I love you, Rosa. And I know you love me. But this isn't about us any longer. It's about what is right. I can't give you and Sibilla what Antonio Parigi can. I can't be that sort of man. You know what I am saying is true.'

And Rosa did. She knew it in her heart. She didn't feel passion for Antonio the way she did for Luciano, but she could come to love him as her husband with time. Rosa struggled against her tears and failed. They poured thick and fast down her cheeks. Luciano drew her to him. Somehow she found the strength to look into his eyes. She saw in them the night they had made love under the stars. She remembered the first time she had seen him, by the Arno. The sun had glistened on his hair and skin.

'You must go, Rosa,' he said, swallowing hard. 'We both know it is the right thing for you and Sibilla. My work is becoming more dangerous.'

Rosa couldn't tell him how much she loved him or how she was afraid she might die without him. 'When she's old enough, I will tell Sibilla —' she began instead.

'No!' said Luciano, helping her to her feet. 'It's better that she isn't confused in her loyalties.'

For a minute they gazed into each other's eyes. Was this it? Rosa wondered. Was the love they knew coming to such a sudden end? They did not move or speak. She longed to kiss Luciano but resisted the urge.

'Fight Mussolini for me and Sibilla,' she said. 'I will be with you in spirit. I will light a candle for you every evening and pray for you and the others.'

Then Luciano kissed her. A lingering kiss that warmed her lips, then left them chilled again as soon as he pulled away.

'You'll explain to Orietta?' she asked him. 'To Piero and Carlo? They have been my family.'

Luciano nodded. Rosa's heart seemed to have stopped beating. All she felt inside was a crushing pain. With one last longing look at Luciano, she turned to go. She could barely breathe from the agony but she willed herself to move away. She was a mother. She couldn't think of herself. This was what she had to do. The floor seemed to shudder beneath her as she made her way towards the church door. It was as if she were standing on the deck of a ship that was preparing to sail out to sea. She felt Luciano's eyes on her until she walked out into the sunlight. But she didn't turn around.

It's for the best, she told herself. This is how it was meant to be. But her heart ached with the idea that she had somehow failed Luciano when he needed her most.

Part Three

Part Three

SIXTEEN

'Italy, relive the glories of Rome! Empire for Italy!' the announcer bellowed from the radio in Geppetto's toy store on Via della Vigna Nuova. It was 1935, and Mussolini had just announced that the Italian army had invaded Abyssinia.

Rosa, who had been shopping for gifts for her twin sons, was jostled by customers cheering and embracing each other. The shopkeeper, a Pinocchio puppet in hand, danced a jig on the countertop. Rosa wondered how these people could be so happy when the war would result in the starvation of thousands of children. Or didn't that matter because it wouldn't be *their* children who would die? Rosa was ashamed of her countrymen. How could they call themselves 'civilised' and attack a defenceless nation? Abyssinia had no planes or anti-aircraft weapons. It could barely feed its own people.

On her way to Via Tornabuoni, Rosa stopped at an English tea-house. The story of Italy's attack on Abyssinia was reported differently in the British newspapers. The British condemned Italy for not declaring war before attacking and for bombing hospitals. Rosa looked at the picture of the barefoot Abyssinian soldiers on the cover of *The Times* and felt nauseated. The League of Nations had condemned Italy as an aggressor, and in truth Mussolini could have developed Abyssinia without conquering it. The British had tried to find a peaceful solution to Mussolini's demands, offering a strip of their own territory to Abyssinia to give it access to a port in return for ceding some land to Italy. But Mussolini was not looking for peaceful solutions. He had defined the 'Fascist State' as 'a wish for power and domination'. He wanted war, as Luciano had warned.

Rosa looked around the café. The patrons were fewer than they had been the previous month. The British were nervous. Mussolini was using the press to incite Italians against them because of their government's opposition to his expansionist policies. Most of the tourists had left and many of the expatriates were packing up. It seemed only the old ladies with no homes or families to return to in England were staying on. Italy had been their home for years and they could not leave it, no matter how feelings were turning against them.

Rosa paid for her tea and cake, filled with a sudden urge to rush home and embrace her children. The twins were in the care of Giuseppina, who had stayed on after Nonno's death. They had just started saying concrete words like 'Dog!' and 'Cat!'; and Sibilla had taken to singing them lullabies. Rosa trembled to think her children's safe world could be shattered by war. Why couldn't Mussolini concern himself with Italy's internal problems rather than dragging the country into conflict?

Eager as she was to get home, Rosa went to the furniture shop first. She stood at the door to the office a moment, watching Antonio reconciling invoices. She was overcome by the same tenderness towards him that she experienced on those mornings when she awoke to find his cheek pressed to hers.

'Did you hear the news?' she asked him.

Antonio looked up from his work and smiled. 'What news?'

'About Italy attacking Abyssinia. Everyone in the toy store cheered.'

Antonio leaned back in his chair and shrugged. 'Mussolini has made this nation stupid. Do they really think this is empire building? All that's going to happen now is the League of Nations will impose economic sanctions against us. Perhaps people won't cheer so much when they haven't food to put on the table.'

He stood and took Rosa's parcels from her before wrapping his arms around her shoulders. 'We can't worry about what we can't fix,' he said, kissing her on the top of her head. Then, glancing at his watch, he said, 'It's almost lunchtime. Let's go back and see what our angels have been up to.'

The nursery in Rosa and Antonio's apartment was Nonno's former bedroom. The heavy teak furniture had been replaced by two cream-painted cots, a nursery table and a chest of drawers made of maple wood. On one of the walls, Rosa had painted an olive tree with branches reaching to the ceiling. On another wall hung Nonno's horseshoe-shaped mirror and cowboy hat. Rosa loved the room and was sure that Nonno, who had died three months before the twins were born, would have approved of it too. 'Your marrying my son is the best thing that's ever happened in my life — or his!' he had told Rosa.

'Ah, here are Mamma and Babbo,' Giuseppina said when Rosa and Antonio entered. She stood up, her cheeks pink and her laugh lines dancing on her face.

The twins were playing with their rubber train set on the floor, assisted by Ambrosio, who was chewing on the toy engineer. Lorenzo, the firstborn of the two, tried to stand but fell on his bottom, narrowly missing Allegra who was asleep next to him. Lorenzo had been named after Nonno. The second-born twin, Giorgio, had been given Antonio's middle name because there was no known maternal grandfather to name him after.

Lorenzo, who was fair like his father, started to cry. Rosa was surprised. He was usually more adventurous than his tawny-skinned brother and the fall would have been more of a surprise than painful. Giorgio tried to comfort his brother by offering his thumb, but when it was rejected began to cry himself.

'Ah!' said Antonio, covering his ears in mock anguish. 'What's happened to my sons' happy dispositions?'

'Here,' said Sibilla, standing up from the table where she had been drawing. She rushed to the twins to kiss them. 'I will make it better.' Her medicine worked. The twins stopped their tears and turned their attention back to their trains.

Rosa embraced and kissed each of the children. She pulled Sibilla onto her lap and they watched together what the twins were doing. Antonio got down on all fours and joined in with the boys' play, imitating the noise of a steam engine while pushing the toy along. The twins squealed with delight.

'I drew you and Babbo,' said Sibilla, reaching for her sketchbook and showing it to Rosa.

The picture showed Rosa in profile and Antonio facing forward. It was unusual for a child as young as Sibilla to draw figures in different orientations and with good proportions, but it seemed to Rosa that her daughter was advanced for her age in every way. She was self-disciplined and provided quick answers to questions. She was also showing an unusual ability for music.

'When I play the flute, Sibilla will hum along with me,' Rosa had told Antonio. 'She keeps time well and rhythmically.'

Rosa smoothed Sibilla's ebony hair. It was like silk between her fingers. Sibilla was so extraordinarily beautiful that people would often stop them in the street to admire her. They would study Rosa and Antonio, well dressed and good-looking, but the question on their faces was the one Rosa asked herself: where did such luminescent beauty come from? Certainly not from Osvaldo.

Sibilla slipped off Rosa's lap and went to show Antonio her picture.

'It's beautiful, darling,' he said. 'You've made me so handsome.'

'You are handsome,' she replied, tossing her head.

She knew that she had Antonio wrapped around her finger and that he couldn't resist her requests for anything.

'Sibilla's usually charming,' Giuseppina had confided in Rosa and Antonio when they'd asked her one day about the children's behaviour. 'But sometimes she can be haughty if she wants something and she's not getting it.'

Antonio had laughed it off as a stage in Sibilla's development. But Rosa had seen that characteristic too and it disturbed her. The haughtiness reminded her of the Marchesa Scarfiotti.

Ylenia walked into the room. 'I am wondering if you and Signor Parigi wish to have lunch on the terrace today?' she asked Rosa. 'The weather is beautiful. The children can eat here.'

Antonio struggled up from his undignified position. But once he was standing, he caught sight of the expression on his sons' faces: they were crestfallen because he had stopped playing.

'I think we might all eat in the nursery today, thank you, Ylenia,' Antonio said.

Rosa loved moments like these, when everyone was together. It was a peaceful and happy life. But the uneasiness she had felt on hearing the announcement of the attack on Abyssinia prickled her again. Dreams were fragile and dreamers woke up. Rosa closed her eyes, afraid that if she loved too much she might lose it all.

Antonio had been right when he predicted that the members of the League of Nations would impose sanctions against

Italy for its unprovoked attack on Abyssinia. By spring the lire had devalued and the gold reserves in the Bank of Italy were falling. To help the reserves and to encourage patriotism, Mussolini called on the people of Italy to sacrifice their wedding rings for the national cause. He termed it 'the Day of Faith'. Citizens were to take their rings to depots in the cities, towns and villages all over the country. Rosa and Antonio did not intend to help Mussolini kill innocent people. Rosa had read in the English press that the Italian military were defying international conventions of war and using mustard gas. She wept when she read the descriptions of blinded and burnt soldiers lying on the battlefield for hours, dying from the effects of poison gas, with no medical assistance because the Red Cross ambulances and hospitals were being targeted by the Italian airforce. 'The shame!' she cried. 'The shame!'

When the Day of Faith came the skies opened and it poured with rain. But nature's disapproval did not deter women from turning out in their thousands from seven o'clock in the morning until late in the evening to offer their wedding rings and other items of gold. Rosa and Antonio were on their way to an estate sale when they saw the lines of women outside the *comune*. They were middle- and working-class women, but the radio that morning had announced that the Queen of Italy, the princesses, and Mussolini's wife and daughter were all offering their rings. The churches and even the synagogues played the *Giovinezza* and called on women to donate their rings after the service.

Rosa heard a fishmonger greet a butcher with: 'To whom does Abyssinia belong?'

'To us! To us!' the butcher shouted enthusiastically, wiping his hands on his bloodied apron.

'It's like a football game to them,' Antonio whispered to Rosa.

While Rosa and Antonio had not donated their rings to the cause, they had taken them off and put them in the safe in their apartment. While they didn't agree with what was happening, it wasn't wise to openly oppose it. The patriotic zeal had been so worked up that things could go badly for anyone who questioned it.

'Do not allow Italy's march to victory to be hampered,' a Blackshirt volunteer was shouting through a megaphone outside a school where wedding rings were being collected. 'We will defeat the siege.'

The rain let up for a moment and Rosa caught sight of Signora Visconti coming out of the school. She was dismayed to see her husband's former paramour. Rosa was fashionable these days in her tailored clothes and with her hair centre-parted and swept back into an array of curls pinned into place at the nape of her neck. She even had a collection of pretty hats, including a flamingo pink one with silk roses on the brim. But Signora Visconti's beauty was as overwhelming as Sibilla's. With her peaked eyebrows, snood hat and golden skin, Signora Visconti looked as though her elegance needed no effort at all.

Rosa had seen Signora Visconti a few months earlier, when she was out walking with the children and Giuseppina. Signora Visconti had stepped in front of Rosa to block her way and her eyes had blazed with such anger that Rosa was frightened. Then the expression on that hard and beautiful face had changed to contempt and the woman had turned and walked away. Rosa had understood what Signora Visconti was telling her: You are his child-bearer but I am his great love.

Now, Signora Visconti caught sight of Antonio and fixed her eyes on him, but he took Rosa's arm and kept walking. He didn't say anything to Rosa even when they were several streets away.

'Antonio?' she ventured.

He looked at her. 'Yes?'

'Did you see Signora Visconti?'

'Yes.'

Rosa tried to read her husband's face. Did he still think of Signora Visconti? Perhaps when he was up late reading and

Rosa had already gone to bed? Or when he walked to the shop in the morning? Antonio's lips pinched. Rosa waited, and when she saw her husband didn't intend to comment further, she asked, 'Are you all right?'

Antonio grimaced. 'I had no idea she was such a fascist.'

Rosa's moment of insecurity passed and she laughed at Antonio's wry comment. She wondered why she needed her husband's reassurance when he never seemed to think of Signora Visconti at all. Was it her own 'unfaithfulness' she was afraid of? While Rosa loved and respected Antonio, she had never forgotten Luciano. He still held a place in her heart.

One afternoon in spring the following year, Rosa was in the vicinity of the Duomo and decided to go inside to light her daily candle for Luciano. She stood in the cathedral's cavernous Gothic interior and stared up at the frescoes of the Last Judgement on the interior of the dome. It was like looking up into heaven. She lit a candle and took a place in a pew to pray and contemplate. Rosa didn't believe in the political church. But she did believe in God. He was the only one who could save the Italian people from their folly.

While she was praying, Rosa noticed a woman pass by. There was something about her that was familiar. When the woman knelt down, Rosa caught sight of her elegant profile and the gold flecks in her hair under her veil.

'Orietta?'

The woman turned and Rosa's heart lifted at the sight of her old friend. Orietta returned Rosa's smile and indicated that they should move out to the aisle so as not to disturb the other worshippers.

'You are so beautiful,' said Orietta, embracing Rosa with genuine warmth.

Rosa was moved by the show of affection. She had not kept in contact with Luciano's family after she and Antonio had married and she had felt the loss deeply.

'What have you been doing with yourself?' she asked Orietta.

'I'm still working at the patisserie.' Orietta studied Rosa, guessing the next question on her mind. 'My brothers are fighting in Spain.'

'Spain?' Rosa's heart plummeted. She had been frightened for Luciano because of his anti-fascist activities in Italy. But the war in Spain was a bloodbath. 'Spain?' she repeated, feeling faint. 'They are fighting for the Republic?'

'Yes,' said Orietta. 'They left several months ago.'

Rosa thought she might be sick. The Spanish army, in league with the Church, landowners and Spanish fascists, had risen in revolt against the Republican government. Italy was supplying arms and troops to the battlefront to support the conservatives. Mussolini had ordered that any Italians fighting against their own country were to be shot if captured.

'Have you heard anything from them?' she asked.

Orietta shook her head.

Rosa swallowed. Everything was well beyond pamphlets now. The casualties amongst the Republicans in Spain were enormous.

'You came here to pray for your brothers?' she asked Orietta.

'Yes, I come every day.' Tears welled in Orietta's eyes.

'I light a candle for them every day too,' said Rosa. 'Let's pray for them together now.'

When they had finished praying, the women made their way outside the cathedral. Rosa noticed her friend looked thin and drained. Orietta's clothes, while clean, were worn. Life must be hard for her with her brothers away.

'Listen,' Orietta said, taking Rosa's arm and walking with her. 'You mustn't be a stranger because you and Luciano parted. I have always understood. Since he was a child, Luciano was not like other boys. Some men are meant to be alone.'

Rosa was grateful to Orietta for breaking the ice on that subject. She had to fight back tears. 'You and I were like sisters,' she managed to say.

Orietta nodded and smiled. 'We still can be. How is Sibilla? She must be a big girl now.'

Rosa was glad to have the diversion of talking about her children because hearing that Luciano was in Spain brought the reality of what was happening closer to her. She had a feeling that no matter how safe she tried to keep her family, Mussolini was about to bring calamity on Italy. The foreign press were referring to him as the 'worst of all European dictators'. The Italians should have stopped Mussolini when they'd had the chance.

It was a sign of Antonio's faith in Rosa that he didn't shrink from her suggestion that Orietta should work for him in the shop. She would earn more money there than at the patisserie. Rosa was busy with the children and organising the household and couldn't keep up with the catalogues or help with the sales as much as she used to do. Rosa didn't know of many men who would have tolerated, let alone welcomed, the sister of their wife's former lover. But Antonio was special that way.

'She has everything sparkling,' Antonio said when he came home for lunch with Orietta on her first day at the shop.

'Already?' Rosa said with a smile. 'You have a lot of furniture this month.'

Orietta blushed. 'I never knew there was so much to learn about tables and chairs but I am enjoying it.'

'She is quick,' Antonio told Rosa. 'She already knows her Louis XVI from her Louis XV and her walnut from her mahogany.'

The day was warm and the children, along with Giuseppina, joined them on the terrace for their gnocchi and peppers filled with rice and thyme.

'I'll come back at six o'clock,' Antonio told Rosa after lunch was finished. 'You remembered we are having dinner at the Trevis' home this evening?'

Rosa nodded. Of course she had. She had picked out her dress weeks earlier: it was in silver-lilac charmeuse with a bias-cut skirt and halter-neck. Her bag and shoes were silver lamé.

'Who are the Trevis?' asked Orietta, while Antonio was embracing the children before parting.

'Alessandro Trevi and his wife, Tullia, are old friends of Antonio's,' Rosa explained. 'I've met them before, at a party at the Uffizi gallery, but this is the first time I am visiting their home. Antonio says they have the most beautifully decorated apartment in Florence.'

'I would say this one was rather stylish too,' said Orietta walking towards the foyer with Rosa. 'Louis XVI!' she announced, patting the armchair in the hallway. 'Showing a more restrained elegance than Louis XV-style furniture and with cleaner lines.'

Both women laughed.

Rosa was impressed by the Trevis' apartment the moment she set eyes on its polished parquet floors, oriental carpets and majolica vases filled with calla lilies.

'Now let me show you some of the things your husband talked me into buying,' said Alessandro, leading Rosa to an ebony cabinet with pietra dura panels.

'It's beautiful,' said Rosa.

Tullia grabbed Antonio's arm. 'So you understand why we love him so much!'

Alessandro Trevi had white hair and vivid blue eyes. His wife, with her pointed nose and double chin, was not as handsome as her husband, but she was elegant and exquisitely dressed in a red chiffon evening gown.

Tullia glanced at Rosa's chain with the cross and key. Rosa was wearing the diamond bracelet Antonio had given her for their wedding, but she was loath to go anywhere without her charms.

'How unusual,' said Tullia of Rosa's jewellery. 'Do they have a meaning?'

'The key has been with me since birth,' Rosa said. 'It protects me.'

Rosa had thought she might be intimidated by the Trevis' wealth, but instead she found herself fascinated by the apartment. It was much better than an art gallery because everything expressed the personalities of the owners. Many of the pieces had been collected by Alessandro and Tullia on their travels. When Rosa and Antonio were led to the drawing room to meet the other guests, Rosa's attention was caught by the silk brocade sofas from China and an alabaster bust of a woman that Tullia informed her she had bought in Paris.

Tullia's sister, Margherita, was a thinner version of her sibling. 'Young people! How lovely!' she exclaimed, standing up to greet Antonio and Rosa.

Rosa had not thought of herself as a young person for a long time, but she realised that age was relative. Margherita introduced her husband, a German by the name of Herbert Kauffmann, and his brother, Otto.

'They are doctors,' Tullia said with a merry laugh. 'So if anybody chokes on the meatballs this evening they will be able to assist.'

The two Germans laughed but there was something uneasy about them. Rosa wondered if it was because they didn't understand Tullia's exuberant humour.

'Well, I think it's time we ate,' Alessandro announced after the second round of drinks.

The dining room was equally impressive as the rest of the apartment, with a solid oak table and a view of the Duomo. Tullia guided her guests to their places.

'Because you are the prettiest, I'm seating you next to my husband,' she told Rosa.

For Rosa, the dinnerware was of more interest than the food. She admired the Haviland Limoges plates, hand-painted with leaves and berries, and the crystal glasses with the silver stems.

The conversation moved from the World Trade Fair, which was to take place in Paris the following year, to Amelia Earhart's proposed crossing of the Pacific Ocean by aeroplane, to the Keeler polygraph.

'But how does it work?' Margherita asked Otto. 'Can it really tell us if a person is lying?'

Otto dabbed his lips with his napkin before replying. 'Well, you have a drum that rotates at a regular speed under some pens. Tubing is wrapped around the subject's abdomen and chest to measure his rate and depth of breath. When the subject is questioned, the polygraph measures his physiological responses.'

'How unnecessary!' exclaimed Tullia. 'I can always tell when Alessandro is lying. He goes red and sweaty and looks ridiculous.'

The gathering laughed at Alessandro's expense. He blushed but took the embarrassment with good humour.

'Are you looking forward to the Olympic Games?' Antonio asked the Kauffmanns. 'It must be exciting to have them in Berlin.'

'We won't see them,' Herbert answered, looking away. 'We will be here.'

The bitterness in Herbert's voice surprised Rosa. Antonio had not meant to upset him. She changed the subject in an attempt to make things light again.

'It's nice that you are having an extended visit with your sister,' she said to Margherita.

'I'm afraid it's for good,' replied Margherita. 'The laws passed by Hitler against Jews have made it impossible for us to continue to live in Berlin. Herbert and Otto can no longer treat Aryan patients.'

'For years it has been my pride to save people and they have been grateful,' said Otto. 'But these laws have stripped us of everything, including our citizenship. It's as if we are dirty outcasts.'

'That's terrible,' Rosa said.

Alessandro sighed and put down his knife and fork. 'The Germans used to be the most enlightened people in Europe: educated, tolerant, humane and reasonable. It's as if some sort of evil has been unleashed in the country.'

'The problem for me is not so much what the government did as how our friends reacted,' said Margherita, her eyes misting over. 'The women in my charity club stopped inviting me to functions; the grocer who I had visited every day for ten years put a sign in his window saying "No Jews"; German men who had been chivalrous suddenly pushed in front of me. I refuse to be reduced to a second-class citizen just to please the Nazis.'

Tullia turned to Antonio and Rosa. 'I've heard that not all the Germans behave like that. Some of them tried to defy the new laws and continued to shop at Jewish stores and associate with their Jewish friends, but they have been so intimidated by the Nazis that they are now as terrified as the Jews are.'

Rosa caught the apprehension in Tullia's voice. 'Could what happened in Germany happen here?' she asked.

Antonio was not a Jew by the Nazi definition of race, which classified someone as Jewish if they had three Jewish grandparents or practised the religion. But Rosa still felt afraid.

'Mussolini may be many things,' said Alessandro. 'But, thank God, he is not anti-Semitic. We are safe.'

After the dessert dishes had been cleared away, Alessandro rose from the table. 'What we need to do now is leave this gloomy talk behind,' he said. He smiled at Rosa and Antonio. 'I have something to show you that will impress you both, I'm sure: Antonio because of its structural beauty; and Rosa, because you are a musician.'

Alessandro and Tullia led the guests to the music room, which was as sumptuous as the rest of the apartment, with a gold Persian carpet and Savonarola armchairs with ruby red upholstery. Rosa's eye was immediately taken by the centrepiece of the room: an ebony Bösendorfer piano.

'Franz Liszt said the Bösendorfer was one of the only pianos capable of withstanding his energetic *fortissimo*,' said Alessandro.

Tullia laughed. 'It's crazy that we spent so much money

on something no-one in our family can play. But it was too wonderful to pass by.'

'It's beautiful,' said Antonio, opening the fallboard. The piano was sleek and unadorned. The only embellishments were the scrolled fretwork music desk and the decorative vine pattern on the inside of the fallboard. 'What do you think, Rosa?' he said, laying his hand on her back.

Rosa barely heard him. Her mind was spinning. *The piano suited her style perfectly: dramatic, rich and full-bodied.* She remembered the Marchese's tears when his sister's piano had been taken away. While there could be several Bösendorfers in Florence, Rosa knew from the tingling in her hands and toes that this one had been Nerezza's.

'It's been tuned and cleaned up,' said Alessandro, eyeing Rosa. 'Would you like to play something for us? The Englishman I bought it from played it for me but I wouldn't mind to hear how it sounds in this room.'

Rosa was trembling from head to foot. She wasn't sure if she could play. 'It's far too elegant an instrument for my poor talents,' she protested.

'Nonsense,' said Alessandro, pulling out the piano bench for her to sit on. 'By all reports you are most accomplished.'

The bench matched the piano in its simple elegance. Rosa pulled it closer to the instrument. She was surprised to find it heavy to move. She hadn't played the piano as often as she would have liked since the twins' arrival, so decided to play Chopin's Nocturne No 2 in E-Flat Major, which she knew very well by memory and wasn't too demanding for her out-of-practice fingers. She hoped the piece would suit the piano and the room.

Antonio and the others sat down to listen.

Rosa had a strange feeling in the pit of her stomach when she touched the keyboard — a queasiness like that she had experienced in the first months of pregnancy. She looked down at her hands and saw that they were not her own. The narrow palms and elongated fingers were the same but Rosa had not worn rings since the Day of Faith. Now on her right hand she saw a silver rose-cut diamond ring and on the left there was a gold locket ring and wedding band. Suddenly, as if in a dream, Rosa felt herself drawn away from the piano. Another woman sat in her place. Rosa knew who she was, although she was even more beautiful than she had imagined. Nerezza's dark skin was flushed and a spray of curls fell from her upswept hair and rested against her long, swan-like neck. She was fuller-figured than was currently the fashion but she was lovely. The vision faded and Rosa found herself back at the keyboard, playing the last line of the Nocturne. When she finished, she was out of breath and bathed in a perspiration.

The appreciative gathering clapped. '*Brava! Brava!*'

'So wonderful, we are indeed privileged,' said Alessandro.

Otto was smiling for the first time since the discussion about the Jews in Germany. 'Chopin himself could not have played it better,' he said.

Antonio sent Rosa a quizzical look. 'You have always been an accomplished pianist,' he whispered, 'but that was the best you've ever played.'

Tullia and Margherita both praised Rosa, and she did her best to respond with good manners. But she was shaken. This vision was not like those she had experienced before. She had seen animals and people, even the King of Italy, but none of those visions had inhabited her body the way Nerezza had. What did it mean?

Rosa stood up and moved the stool back again. She noticed the music drawer under the seat. There was something in it that was making the seat heavier than it should be.

'Rosa's noticed something unusual there,' Alessandro said to Antonio. 'You see there is a drawer with a lock in the stool. What do you make of that?'

The feature certainly was unusual. There were often locks on fallboards to prevent damage to the piano keys, but why would someone lock away their music?

'Do you have the key?' Antonio asked Alessandro.

'There was one for the fallboard but not the stool,' he answered. 'I did get a locksmith here to pick it, but he said it was too fine and was afraid he would damage it irreparably.'

'I told him to smash it,' said Tullia. 'I can't stand mysteries. There might be gold inside.'

Margherita laughed but Antonio and Rosa both winced. A beautiful stool was not something to be smashed. It was better to let the mystery stay hidden.

'How about a drink on the terrace?' said Alessandro, leading his guests from the music room.

Rosa was about to leave with them when a fancy seized her. She walked back to the stool. Her fingers reached for her throat. On an impulse she took the chain from her neck and placed the silver key in the lock. With one turn the drawer opened.

'My God, there's a coincidence,' Alessandro said, calling Antonio back to the room when he saw that Rosa had opened the drawer. 'Your wife's charm opened the lock.'

Rosa didn't think it was a coincidence. It felt more like witchcraft. A chill ran through her hands. Something wanted her to see what had been hidden in the drawer. She reached inside and found a thick notebook. Its cover was gold brocade. She opened the notebook and saw that the leaves were made of Japanese paper, and pasted and drawn onto them was a collection of sheet music, sketches, pressed flowers and poems.

'Well, I never,' said Alessandro. 'Your wife is an archaeologist as well as a musician. See what she's discovered.'

Rosa looked up at Antonio and Alessandro, not able to believe that she held the notebook of Nerezza Scarfiotti in her hands.

SEVENTEEN

Nerezza's notebook was a piece of art as well as a record of secrets. When Alessandro saw that it contained sketches of dresses, garden aspects, musical notes and opera tickets, he insisted that Rosa have it. Tullia supported him.

'That sort of feminine memoir bores me silly,' she said. 'But if you love history, you might find it interesting.'

'It is exactly the kind of thing Rosa revels in,' Antonio said, winking at her. 'I fell in love with my wife over her ability to tell the story behind a piece of furniture.'

Rosa thanked the couple profusely. They would never guess of how much interest the notebook was to her.

'If it turns out to be of any value or historical importance, we will return it to you,' Antonio told them.

'No, I insist that your wife keep it,' said Alessandro, with a twinkle in his eye. 'Rosa entertained us beautifully this evening and I want her to have it as a gift. I can see how pleased she is to have discovered it.' With a mischievous smile he added, 'Just let us know if you find anything scandalous in it. We love a juicy piece of gossip.'

Rosa wanted to read the notebook then and there. But

Alessandro turned everyone's interest back to drinks on the terrace and Rosa had no choice but to mingle with the other guests. When she and Antonio returned home, the children were already in bed and she went to the drawing room to read the notebook. But Antonio followed her and made amorous eyes.

'The notebook is not going anywhere,' he said, covering Rosa's neck with kisses.

Rosa put the notebook in the desk drawer and smiled at Antonio. She would wait until the morning.

The next day, once the children were settled with Giuseppina, Rosa disappeared to the drawing room with the instruction that she was not to be disturbed. She took out the notebook and studied the pages with fascination. Nerezza was certainly an artist. She had sketched exquisite gowns and labelled them: 'worn' along with the date; 'to be worn'; and 'envied'. One gown that caught Rosa's eye was made of black silk tulle over an ivory satin dress embroidered with gold peacocks. Nerezza had sketched it in meticulous detail, writing the fabrics used next to the design. There was a Chantilly lace wedding dress dated 1912, which Rosa assumed had been Nerezza's. One of the outfits labelled 'envied' was a Russian-style velvet evening coat with beaded passementerie panels. Rosa wondered who had worn it.

Rosa had been curious about Nerezza ever since she had seen the miniature opera sets in Clementina's room and realised that they had been made by the occupant of the unusual grave. She couldn't believe she had Nerezza's personal notebook in her hands. But even though the notebook was intriguing, something about it troubled Rosa. Her possession of it disturbed her in a way she couldn't define. It wasn't like an antique, something passed on after the original owner had died. The notebook seemed to pulse in her hands as if it were a living thing.

Other sketches included the Villa Scarfiotti, a scene from *Carmen*, and a self-portrait that showed Nerezza exactly as Rosa had seen her in her vision at the piano. However, Rosa soon realised that the notebook was more than a whimsical collection of special moments. It contained lists: of what Nerezza wanted to do when she went into Florence; of who to speak to at parties and who to avoid; of pieces of music she wanted to master. It was obvious that Nerezza had been an extraordinarily disciplined person. Her determination and her need to be admired jumped off the pages.

While at first Rosa interpreted the word 'envied' written under certain gowns as self-mocking, as she continued turning the pages she discovered 'envied' horses and carriages, holidays and diamonds. Nerezza had also written descriptions of 'envied' parties, including details of the food that had been served, the guests and the entertainment provided. Signor Collodi, the estate manager at the villa, had told Rosa that Nerezza's parties had been legendary. Rosa now saw that they had been the result of meticulous planning and observation. What Nerezza 'envied', Nerezza got — and improved on.

On the last page of the notebook was a date with a red line crossed through it: 13 March 1914.

Rosa's breath caught in her throat when she read the words under it: *I shall gain mastery over my heart*.

They were the words that had been written on the lapis lazuli in the Egyptian vault in the Marchesa's chambers. Why had both women been drawn to the same quote?

Rosa's fingers touched the back cover of the notebook and noticed something bulky there. The cover had a slip opening. Rosa reached inside and discovered two well-worn envelopes. She opened the first envelope and took out the letter. It was in French and was signed 'François'. Then she noticed the embossed letterhead: *The Baron François Derveaux*. She remembered the Baron with his gangly legs and winged eyebrows and the intrigued way he had looked at her. But why had he been writing to Nerezza? Then she remembered the vision she had seen of the young Baron and a dark-haired girl and she understood. Nerezza and the Baron had been childhood friends.

> *Paris, 1 May 1914*
>
> *My Dear Nerezza,*
>
> *You asked me how Paris is now and I will say that Paris is Paris and at its most beautiful in the springtime. The cafés are full of people, music drifts through the windows, and one smells the roses on every corner.*
>
> *Hélène and I were married last Wednesday. She was very pretty in her crocheted Irish lace gown. She sends her love and promises to write to you herself soon. We are very happy that you intend to come to Paris. I am intrigued by what you wrote, that you have 'news of great importance' to tell me.*
>
> *Now, as for your question about how I found Mademoiselle Caleffi, I'm afraid my response may not please you. Although she isn't the most buoyant of conversationalists I thought she had a certain she-devil charm. She is sharp and has something rather raw about her, but she's not afraid. I think she speaks her mind and, with the two of you vying for your brother's affections, I can only imagine that you would wish me to say otherwise. But I have never lied to you, Nerezza. My advice, if you wish to continue to enjoy a good relationship with Emilio, is not to push him either way. His flame for Mademoiselle Caleffi may well burn out on its own. But if it doesn't … your opposition will only push him further from you and closer to her.*

Rosa looked up from the correspondence. Mademoiselle Caleffi was now the Marchesa Scarfiotti. She shuddered. It was strange to read about the Marchesa this way, observed by people who knew her intimately. It was clear from the Baron's letter that Nerezza hadn't liked her.

The rest of the letter went on to describe the social life in Paris despite the threat of war. The Baron's tone was friendly and intimate, but the content was shallow. Rosa thought back to Clementina's garden party. Hadn't Miss Butterfield, his children's governess, implied that the Baron was frivolous? To be fair, the letter had been written over twenty years ago, when he was still a young man.

The second letter was written in Italian and signed 'Ferdinando'. Who was he? Reading the salutation, Rosa realised that he was Nerezza's husband, writing from Libya. The letter was dated a month after the Baron's letter and the tone was completely different.

> *Tripoli, 2 June 1914*
>
> *My Dear Wife,*
>
> *I do not understand this sudden urgency to see me. Should I be flattered? You should understand that the situation here is extremely unstable. I have lost my driver to a bomb attack and it is simply no place for a woman, although, as you pointed out, several of the army officers' wives have come here to be close to their husbands. I see no good reason for this except that the husbands have a need to flatter themselves that their wives cannot do without them, and the wives flatter themselves with the same foolish idea about their husbands.*
>
> *You and I know better. So put that thought out of your mind. I cannot spare anyone to take care of you as I go about my duties. I may, if I thought it would concern*

*you, tell you that I could be killed at any
time.*

*Now, for this matter you mention
regarding your brother's affection for
Signorina Caleffi, I have nothing but bad
news to report from my contacts. The
woman's father was respected but in his old
age fell for a woman of ill repute: a ruthless,
scheming personality not afraid to exploit her
own children for gain. And she certainly
intends to gain something by throwing her
daughter Emilio's way. Signorina Caleffi has
no moral character whatsoever. The man I
hired discovered that while she makes love to
your brother in Fiesole, she hedges her bets by
maintaining the interest of a rich young man
in Milan. Remember that it is your brother,
although younger, who will carry the title of
Marchese if he marries. What shame this
woman could bring on the whole family! You
must stop their union any way you can.*

Ferdinando ended his letter with nothing but his signature;
no affectionate salutation; no kisses. It was as if he had issued
an order.

Rosa leaned back in her chair and looked out the
window at the clouds moving across the sky. The letters she
had read were the only two in the notebook, but there must
have been many others given the nature of Nerezza's
relationship with the two men. Why had she kept only
these?

Rosa closed her eyes and thought of the cold, snake-like
Marchesa Scarfiotti. From these letters, the Marchese
seemed to have been very much in love with her, but his
sister and brother-in-law had been set against the marriage.
Rosa wondered if the Marchesa would have got her way if
Ferdinando hadn't been killed and if Nerezza hadn't been

pregnant and sick when she returned from Libya. She also wondered why Nerezza had disobeyed her husband and visited him when he had told her not to come.

The notebook raised more questions in Rosa's mind and answered nothing in return. She remembered Ada's face on that last day at the villa when she had seen the silver key around Rosa's neck. Antonio had explained that the key could probably open a variety of locks and the fact that it fitted the piano stool drawer was most likely a coincidence. But Rosa knew that wasn't true. The key she wore around her neck did belong with the stool, and the key had been found in her wrappings when she was left at the convent. She was certain now that she had come from the villa. But whose child was she? She had no way to contact Ada to find out, unless she wanted to be arrested for approaching the Villa Scarfiotti.

Rosa looked through the notebook again. Although Nerezza had possessed her when she was playing her piano, she didn't believe she was Nerezza's daughter. Ada had said that Nerezza's child had died. Rosa recalled Maria. Had Rosa been the child of a servant caught in a similar desperate situation? Her mind turned to Giovanni Taviani. Signor Collodi had said that he had got himself into some sort of trouble and that's why he'd been demoted as the estate manager. Rosa shuddered and put the thought out of her head. She simply could not be Giovanni Taviani's daughter because that would make her Luciano's sister!

Origin and heritage were everything. Rosa understood that. Ever since she was a child she had been burdened with the shame of not belonging. The discovery of Nerezza's notebook had not made things clearer; they had made them murkier still. She took the notebook and hid it under a pile of papers in the desk drawer. When Nonno died, Rosa and Antonio had grieved the loss and in time had found peace again. But Rosa lived with an emptiness inside her that even her happy marriage and the joy of motherhood had not managed to diminish. She sighed and thought of Suor

Maddalena. If not for the nun's dedication to her, Rosa's childhood would have been bleak. She remembered how comforting it was to find Suor Maddalena waiting for her in the kitchen after classes were over. The nun had been interested in every aspect of Rosa's day. She was the closest person Rosa had ever had to a mother. She was sure Suor Maddalena felt the same way.

It's as wrong for Suor Maddalena and me to be separated from each other as it is for a mother and child to be torn apart, Rosa thought. Surely now that years have passed and I am a respectable wife and mother, I should be allowed to see her.

Rosa wrote to the Badessa requesting permission to visit Suor Maddalena. She pinned all her hopes on a positive response. But the Badessa's reply cut her to the core: *While I am pleased to hear that you are settled in life and happy, I cannot allow you to see Suor Maddalena. Her duty to God in raising you has been completed. It is time for all to move on and not hold on to old attachments.*

Rosa cried as inconsolably as if she had been informed that her dear nun had died. She did her best to hide her grief from Antonio and the children, but Orietta saw straight through her façade when they went to church one evening together.

'Rosa, what's wrong?' Orietta asked.

The sympathy on her friend's face opened the floodgates for Rosa to express her grief. 'I'm a "No Name",' she told Orietta. 'I'm nothing but a black, empty space.'

Orietta listened with compassion to Rosa's story. 'You're not a "No Name",' she told her. 'You have a wonderful husband who adores you and you have beautiful children. Even your dog and cat love you. They follow you around everywhere.'

Rosa wiped at her tears and attempted to smile.

'Listen,' said Orietta, clasping Rosa's hands. 'I lost my mother before I could talk, and my father walked out on us.

But I try to concentrate on what I have, not on what I've missed out on. We can't change our pasts, Rosa. For your own sanity and the welfare of your children, you need to close the door on the mystery of your origins. You need to live in the present.'

Rosa did her best to follow Orietta's advice, and the years after the discovery of the notebook passed peacefully for her and her family. Without any firm evidence of her origins, Rosa did not mention to Antonio her suspicions that she had been born at the Villa Scarfiotti. Instead, she concentrated on her domestic happiness and managed to put her longing to know her past out of her mind. Then one morning in September 1939, she had a dream in which Luciano was shouting at her, 'Run!' She heard explosions and people screaming. But everything was in darkness. Rosa sat bolt upright, her heart pounding and her mind filled with dread that the peaceful life she had been living was about to change.

She turned on her side and pressed her cheek to Antonio's. His morning stubble prickled her skin. He murmured, kissed her, then fell back to sleep. She remembered their tender lovemaking of the night before and the way Antonio had looked into her eyes. They were passionate lovers but Rosa had not fallen pregnant again. She had obviously been fertile to conceive a child by Osvaldo, despite her terror and the deprivations of prison, and then to bear twins to Antonio so soon after their marriage. Why was her body suddenly refusing to bring another child into the world? Did it know something she didn't? And why, after all these years, had she dreamt of Luciano?

Later that morning, Rosa and Antonio sat at the breakfast table with the children and Giuseppina. Sibilla and the twins were eating boiled eggs while the adults nibbled rolls with marmalade and drank coffee. For some reason the newspaper hadn't arrived and so Ylenia had gone in search of a paperboy. Rosa was glad to have a break from the news. Tensions had been escalating in Europe since Germany had invaded Czechoslovakia.

The twins were laughing as they placed the salt and pepper shakers, bread basket and milk jug in order of size. Sibilla looked on with a benevolent smile, bending down every so often to pat Allegra and Ambrosio who were sitting near her feet. Suddenly she turned to Rosa.

'Mamma, was I born at home like the twins or in a hospital?'

'In a hospital, darling.'

'Which one?'

Rosa glanced at Antonio. Sibilla was seven years old and she liked to ask questions. Unfortunately, those questions were often about her birth and origins. She understood that Antonio was not her natural father, although she was now his legal daughter. Rosa would not have revealed that fact to Sibilla if she could have avoided it. Adoption was a rare and highly suspect event in Italy, where blood ties were everything. But it would be written on Sibilla's legal documents and Rosa and Antonio had decided it was better to tell her sooner rather than later. Luckily, Sibilla had taken it in her stride and called Antonio 'Babbo' anyway without prompting. But what could Rosa say about the father listed as 'unknown'? Sibilla was already showing signs of hypersensitivity. She would cry at the slightest reproach or if she couldn't do something perfectly. Her daughter's harsh self-criticism made Rosa want to protect her all the more. She couldn't tell her that she had been conceived from a rape.

'Well, it was a very old hospital,' Antonio explained. 'It's not a hospital any more. They use the building for something else now.'

'Where was it? I want to see where I was born,' said Sibilla.

Rosa knew Sibilla wasn't being difficult and was only exercising her natural inquisitiveness. But she wished her daughter would quell her curiosity, just as she had suppressed her own longings to know her origins.

'Well, maybe one day,' said Antonio. 'But, Sibilla, you are very busy. You are starting your ballet lessons soon.'

Sibilla clapped her hands with delight and began twirling around the dining room. Rosa sent a grateful look to Antonio. The mention of the much-anticipated lessons had proved a perfect distraction. Rosa guided her daughter back to her chair.

'Ballet takes a lot of strength, so you'll need to eat your eggs,' she said, kissing Sibilla.

Antonio had to leave early to go to an auction. Orietta was minding the store for the day. He kissed each of his children then embraced Rosa. 'Don't worry about Sibilla,' he whispered. 'It is natural for her to ask questions. It will soon pass. When she's older she will deal with it better.'

Rosa saw Antonio to the door and embraced him again. She was about to return to the dining room when the telephone rang. Ylenia hadn't returned yet so Rosa answered it herself. It was Orietta.

'Can you come and see me at the shop?' she said. Her voice was choked with tears.

A sick feeling gnawed at Rosa's stomach. She remembered her bad dream. 'What is it? What's happened?'

'Carlo returned last night. He has some terrible news ...'

Orietta broke down into sobs. Rosa waited a moment to hear if she could say anything more, but it was clear that she couldn't speak.

'I'll come straightaway,' Rosa told her.

She asked Giuseppina to mind the children and ran to the shop. She couldn't think clearly. Carlo had returned but not Luciano or Piero. Rosa could only anticipate with dread what Orietta's terrible news might be. In January, Franco's troops had defeated the Republican army in Barcelona. At the end of March, Madrid had fallen too. Despite Churchill's advice to Franco to show moderation in victory, thousands of supporters of the Republic were being summarily shot. Mussolini had told Franco to show no mercy to any Italians who had fought on the opposite side. Some had escaped into France, but were being interred under terrible conditions in camps that were riddled with disease. Many were dying.

When Rosa turned into Via Tornabuoni, she noticed people were spilling out of the cafés or gathered around radios inside the stores. But the blood was pounding too loudly in her ears to hear what they were saying. She arrived at the shop and found Orietta sitting with her head on the desk, sobbing. She steeled herself for the worst but knew that she would crumble when she heard it.

Orietta looked at Rosa with red-rimmed eyes. 'Piero and Roberto are dead,' she said. 'They were killed in Barcelona.'

The words hit Rosa like a blow to the chest. She covered her mouth with her hand and almost swooned. Piero! Kind-hearted Piero. She couldn't believe it. She saw in her mind the man who had been like a brother to her, saw him holding Sibilla on his lap and singing to her. Impossible! And Roberto too. Rosa hadn't liked him but she was sorry for his death. He had given his life for a noble cause.

Her eyes met Orietta's tear-stained ones. 'Luciano?' she asked, her lips trembling. The moment she spoke his name, she felt his warm flesh brush against her arm. She saw him standing by the Arno with the sunlight dancing around him. All her memories of him were imbued with life. It wasn't possible that he was dead.

Orietta shook her head. 'Carlo doesn't know. They were separated.'

Rosa took Orietta's hands and they sobbed together. At least they could mourn Piero and Roberto and be grateful for Carlo's return. But to have no word about Luciano was torture. From what Rosa had heard, a soldier in Spain would be better off dead than captured. The two women were still grasping each other when a customer walked into the shop. He started when he saw their stricken faces.

'So you've heard the news?' he asked.

Rosa recognised the man as Signor Lagorio, a friend of the Trevis. She couldn't comprehend what he was saying.

Signor Lagorio shook his head. 'This is the end of all Europe. Germany has marched into Poland.'

Rosa was in too much pain to take in anything more. She was stunned for a moment before she realised what Signor Lagorio had said. The British and the French will not stand for it, she thought. They had allowed Hitler to get away with Czechoslovakia but they would have to stop the tyrant now.

'Are we at war then?' asked Orietta, wiping her face.

'Not yet,' answered Signor Lagorio. 'Mussolini has declared Italy as non-belligerent.'

'But what about all the pacts Mussolini has been making with Hitler?' Rosa asked. 'It's impossible for Italy to remain neutral if Britain and France declare war on Germany.'

Signor Lagorio gave a sarcastic laugh. 'You would think so, wouldn't you? But no, that is not the nature of our leader. All this military posturing has been to bolster his ego. It's clear that Italy is not equipped to go to war. I'll tell you what he will do. Once the fighting begins, he'll look at which side is winning and join them just before victory is declared.'

Rosa was shocked that the world was collapsing into war, although she understood now that the domino effect had been occurring for years. But she was even more shocked that Signor Lagorio derided Mussolini openly. When she ran errands in the afternoon, she heard similar sentiments voiced at the post office and the bank.

'The Germans are a brutal lot,' she overheard one woman whisper to another in line at the post office. 'We are better off siding with the British and French. At least they are civilised.'

People cited Hitler's policies towards the Jews. They thought the British were better fighters and that Italy had more in common with France. The Italians had wanted glory, they had wanted an empire. But they did not want an alliance with Germany.

When Rosa reached the tranquillity of her home, she slipped into the drawing room before going to greet the children. She sat on the sofa and covered her face with her hands. She cried so much for Piero, Roberto and Luciano that her sides felt bruised and her throat became parched. She knew that she had to expend the grief she had inside her before Antonio came home. He would be understanding that she was upset about the unknown fate of her former lover and the death of her friends, but Rosa felt somehow that it would not be respectful and would hurt him even if he didn't show it. He had his pride, after all.

'Luciano!' Rosa wept. 'How foolish we have all been!'

Luciano and Roberto had been right to try to get rid of Mussolini all those years ago instead of waiting until disaster was on Italy's doorstep. But few people had supported the anti-fascists. Many had informed on them in the days when they had seen Mussolini as a god who was going to elevate them all. Now it was very clear that Mussolini was a devil, intent on dragging his people into hell.

EIGHTEEN

In April 1940, Germany invaded Denmark and Norway, and the following month entered Holland, Belgium and France. As Signor Lagorio had predicted, these rapid victories enticed Mussolini to declare war on the side of Germany in case he missed out on any of the spoils. Despite their abhorrence of Hitler, the Italian people took to the streets and cheered: '*Duce! Duce!* War! War!'

Rosa and Antonio watched the nightmare unfold from the seats of the Cinema Veneto in Florence. The newsreels had been sent from Germany and dubbed into Italian. Rosa wept at the sight of Belgian refugees fleeing in their cars or pushing wheelbarrows loaded up with frightened children and forlorn-looking pets. She couldn't help thinking of her own children as well as Allegra and Ambrosio. She and Antonio held each other as a Dutch child, no more than four years old, was shown searching amongst the ruins of her house for her family. 'The German people can be grateful that because of the Führer nothing like this will happen to us,' the commentator announced.

'My God!' cried Rosa through clenched teeth.

Antonio squeezed her hand. 'I know,' he said, tears choking his voice.

Rosa understood what he was trying to tell her. There were probably spies in the cinema, looking out for sympathetic reactions.

'Is feeling compassion for that child unpatriotic?' she whispered.

'Unfortunately, in Italy's eyes now, she is the enemy.'

On their way home, Antonio linked his arm with Rosa's and said, 'You know, many years ago I read an article about Mussolini and how heartbroken he was when his daughter contracted polio. He moved his office next to the bedroom where she was being treated and was unable to sleep or eat. I thought of Sibilla and how we suffered when she was ill. For a while there, Mussolini seemed almost human. But a human being with feelings couldn't do what he is doing.'

'How can he feel love for his own child and nothing for the children being killed or left as orphans because of his greed?' Rosa replied. She didn't understand that sort of coldness. Because she loved her own children and animals, she felt compassion for *all* children and *all* animals.

When they arrived home, Rosa and Antonio sat together in the drawing room. Giuseppina had put the children to bed and she and Ylenia had retired for the evening. Rosa was grateful. She was in shock, and being alone with Antonio meant she could give free rein to her fears.

'So it begins?' she said. 'We are in league with the Germans. We have blood on our hands, like them.'

'Mussolini is nothing more than Hitler's dupe,' said Antonio. 'He only introduced the laws against Jews teaching in universities and marrying Christians to please Hitler. I wish somebody had assassinated Il Duce before this.'

Rosa thought of her friend Sibilla. Brave people had tried and they had suffered for it.

'I'm worried,' she said. 'Your grandparents were Jewish and so was Nonno.'

'I'm not a Jew by anyone's definition,' said Antonio. 'My cousins only went to Switzerland because there was no intermarriage on their side of the family. They are pure Jews.'

'But the Germans are forever broadening their definition to include more people,' Rosa said. 'Conversions are not considered valid because it's about race not religion. What will Mussolini do next now that we are allies with Germany?'

Rosa could see in the way Antonio hunched his shoulders that he was concerned too, despite his attempts to reassure her.

'I've heard that in Germany, instead of having three Jewish grandparents, now one Jewish grandparent is all that is necessary to be outcast,' she continued. 'By that definition, not only was Nonno Jewish but so are you and the twins.'

Antonio sighed. 'If it comes to that, Enzo has said that we can stay with him and Renata in Lugano. It's a shame you never had a chance to meet my cousins. They are good people.'

Rosa stood up. Doing things sooner rather than later was the wisdom she had learnt from Luciano. 'I don't want to wait until it's too late, Antonio,' she said. 'I want you to go to Switzerland as soon as possible.'

'Not without you,' he replied. 'I'm not separating the family. If the children and I go, we all go.'

Rosa steeled herself. 'I will come later. We will need money. Who knows if we can get work in Switzerland, and Enzo and Renata will be in the same situation. They are older and we might have to support them. If the laws get worse, thousands of Jews will flee to Switzerland. The government there might close the borders. If I stay here, I can keep the shop going as long as possible and send more money to you.'

'No!' said Antonio, rising to his feet. 'It's out of the question! I'm not leaving you here on your own. Even if nothing happens with the Jewish laws, it's only a matter of time before the British start bombing Florence.'

Rosa rubbed her forehead. There was another reason she wanted to stay. She took Antonio's hands. 'We have to put the children first,' she said. 'Because of my record as an enemy of the state, it is unlikely they will let me out of the country. They will think I'm intending to join Giustizia e Libertà in Paris.'

Antonio shook his head. 'Then we'll obtain a false passport.'

'Please,' begged Rosa, swallowing the lump in her throat. 'I will jeopardise everyone's safety. You go with the children. I will do my best to follow you.'

Antonio walked to the window and stared out at the street. He didn't say anything for a long time. Finally, he turned back to Rosa. 'I will take the children to Switzerland. But as soon as I have settled them and organised their schooling, I will return to Florence. Whatever we face, Rosa, we'll face it together.'

Rosa had no choice but to agree. She didn't want Antonio to return because he was in danger as much as the twins. But perhaps she could persuade him to stay once he was in Switzerland.

Antonio pressed his palm to his forehead. 'Who knows, this might be all for nothing. The war might be over in a month.'

When Rosa watched her husband and children board the train for Switzerland that hot August day, she knew that her dream of a peaceful family life had vanished. No one could guarantee anyone's safety. Giuseppina had agreed to go with them, and was trying to balance Ambrosio in one arm while carrying Allegra in her cane basket in the other. The twins, who were under the impression they were only going away for the day, itched with a sense of adventure.

'Lugano!' said Lorenzo, pretending to be holding the reins of his rocking horse. 'We are going to see a big lake!'

Antonio had bought everyone a gelato at the café, which had been full of soldiers bidding farewell to their loved ones.

Giorgio, always the slowest eater, was still licking his ice-cream. 'Lugano!' he said, beaming at Rosa.

Sibilla, in contrast to the twins, looked stricken. No matter how gently Rosa had tried to explain it, Sibilla understood they were going away because of the war and that she would not see her mother for some time. Rosa knelt down to straighten her daughter's skirt.

'Zia Renata is a very kind woman,' Rosa told her. 'She will look after you well and you must do all that you can to help her. Babbo will organise a piano and ballet teacher for you. It will be fun. I've heard the city is beautiful. How fortunate you are to be able to see it! You must write to me and tell me all about the Swiss: what they are like and what foods they eat.'

Sibilla's chin trembled and then, with her characteristic self-mastery, she suppressed her tears. 'Yes, Mamma. I will do all that I can to help Zia Renata and I will work hard on my music and dancing.'

Rosa's heart ached. At what point did children learn to hide how they felt? Surely this was when they became adults; not when they reached adolescence?

Once the children, Giuseppina and the animals were on board the crowded train, Antonio turned to Rosa. 'The trains are running on slow timetables. I will send you a telegram as soon as we arrive. If anyone asks after me, say that I am away on a business trip and will be back soon.'

Rosa nodded. Antonio took out his handkerchief and dabbed at her tears before embracing her.

'I'll come back as soon as I can. We will get through this together.'

The train whistle sounded. Antonio held Rosa tightly to him then broke away to climb aboard the already moving train.

'Bye-bye, Mamma!' Giorgio shouted, waving his teddy bear out the window.

'Lugano!' cried Lorenzo.

Giuseppina waved and held Ambrosio to the window.

Antonio blew another kiss from the train door. Rosa caught sight of Sibilla standing next to him. She looked bereft. Sibilla's self-control had vanished when the train started moving. Tears were rolling down her cheeks. Rosa almost doubled over with the pain of saying goodbye to them all. She had done everything she could to keep her family safe but, when the train disappeared from sight, she was enveloped by a feeling of dread.

Rosa's suspicion that Mussolini would intensify his persecution of Jews after entering the war was correct. He had been openly friendly with the Jewish population in his early days, welcoming them as members of the Fascist Party and flaunting the Jewish mistress who had helped him rise to power. Suddenly he was claiming that Jews were anti-fascists and enemies of Italy. Even so, the country was still removed from the horrors taking place elsewhere in Europe.

Orietta arrived at the shop one day, looking pale.

'Are you all right?' Rosa asked her.

Orietta shook her head. 'I've heard the most appalling news.'

'Is there any good news these days?' Rosa asked. 'What's happened?'

Orietta checked there were no customers in the shop before answering. 'The Croatians have been slaughtering the Jews ... in the *thousands*. Men, women, children, old people. Everyone. Some Italian officers have been trying to help refugees into the Italian-occupied zones to protect them from the Ustaše.'

'How do you know so much?' Rosa asked. 'Are you listening to the foreign radio?'

Orietta shook her head. 'Carlo told me. He heard through his contacts with Giustizia e Libertà who got their information through British intelligence.'

Rosa sat back, trying to take in the news. This wasn't a war about territory. It was about race. It was going to be a bloodbath.

'Are Giustizia e Libertà still active in Florence?' she asked. 'Do they still need people to pass out pamphlets?'

'No, Rosa!' Orietta said, guessing what her friend was going to ask next. 'You have to think about your family. That's why Carlo won't come near you. Someone might recognise him from Spain and it would compromise you because of your record.'

'But I'm alone now,' said Rosa. 'I want to help. I wish I had done something sooner. I wish I had supported Luciano better.'

'No!' insisted Orietta. 'Luciano never asked that of you, and I'm not letting you get involved now.'

'But *you* are?' Rosa said. 'I know you are up to something. I can see the circles under your eyes. You're not getting much sleep.'

'I'm a single woman,' Orietta said. 'I'm not placing anyone else at risk.'

Rosa sighed. 'I *can't stand* being one of those people who complacently wait, doing nothing to help others and hoping that the war won't affect their lives too much.'

'You're not getting involved, Rosa,' Orietta said firmly. 'They don't send political dissenters to prison any more. They shoot them on the spot. I don't want your children growing up without a mother.'

Despite Rosa's protests for Antonio to stay in Switzerland after helping the children to settle, he returned to Florence at the same time the Italian army launched its blitzkrieg against Greece.

'The whole thing is a disaster,' Antonio told her. 'The Greeks have forced the Italian army back beyond their own territory. The British have been sinking our navy, and meanwhile the Ministry of War still closes two hours every day for a *siesta*!'

Rosa heard from Orietta that Mussolini had jumped into the war without a plan or preparation and was now leaving the battle strategies up to his generals. Meanwhile, he was romping around with his new mistress and was frequently out of contact because he was translating the novel *I promessi sposi* into German.

'You know,' said Rosa, 'I finally understand what the slogan "Mussolini is always right" means. If things go well, Mussolini takes the credit. If they don't, he blames the Italian people.'

To Rosa's amazement, despite the shortages of food and petrol that were growing worse, she and Antonio were able to keep the shop running. They weren't selling the large items of furniture but the smaller, luxurious ones: bronze and ormolu candlesticks; mosaic picture frames; majolica chargers; Murano glass hand mirrors; statues of angels and cupids. They were things people could fit into a car, a trunk or even a pocket. All the antiques on display in the store were Italian. Antonio had stored away the French trumeau mirror, the Louis XV side tables, the English walnut chest. It wouldn't have seemed appropriate to be admiring the enemy's craftsmanship.

'It's like I'm trying to hold onto the last bit of beautiful Italy,' one customer told Antonio and Rosa. She had purchased a magnificent Italian faïence urn with scenes of people in flowing robes sitting near a river. The handles were a pair of satyr figures. 'If I'm killed in the war, I want to be buried with this.'

Rosa showed the customer to the door and watched her walk down Via Tornabuoni. She had beautiful golden hair and skin like alabaster. In her gold brocade dress she was a piece of gilded art herself. What she had said reminded Rosa of a subversive cartoon someone had painted on the wall of the post office. In it, British aircraft were bombing Florence and the Italian people were rushing to the Uffizi gallery and crying over the paintings.

'Rosa?' said Antonio. She turned around and saw that he was holding up an empire-period charger with doves in the centre and an arrow and wheat motif border. 'I saved this for you,' he said. 'It's an anniversary present.'

Rosa took the platter in her hands. Peace in the midst of war and starvation, she thought. Then, looking at Antonio, she said, 'It's beautiful. You know what I like so well. But it's not our anniversary yet.'

Antonio didn't reply. Rosa saw the message in his eyes. These days it wasn't prudent to wait — for anything.

Although things had slowed down at the shop, Rosa and Antonio decided to keep Orietta employed for as long as she wished to stay. Rosa was left with little to do. She hated being in the apartment without the children and the animals there. She had once adored her lovely home but now she found it oppressive.

She gave blood, and she donated books to be sent to the military hospitals where wounded soldiers were being repatriated.

Rosa didn't see what she was doing as assisting the war effort. If she couldn't help the anti-fascists, then at least she could help people. She felt compassion for the soldiers' mothers. It had been hard enough for her to send Lorenzo and Giorgio to Switzerland to keep them safe. She could not imagine what it was like for a mother to see her sons sent off to war.

She had heard that the hospital was calling for volunteers to roll bandages and pack medical supplies for the battlefields, and decided to do that as well.

The Red Cross nurse at the hospital reception desk showed her to a room where a group of women were rolling bandages. At first Rosa thought she had walked into her own worst nightmare. Six of the women were wearing the black uniforms of the Fasci Femminili, the fascist women's group. The rest seemed to be wearing every fur they owned. Rosa closed her eyes to the rabbits, foxes and chinchillas running around the room until they disappeared. The sense of purpose she had been feeling drained away. An elderly woman stood up and for a moment Rosa saw a bear lumbering towards her, until she realised the woman's fur coat had been taken from the animal.

'*Buon giorno*,' said the woman in a falsetto voice. She reached out her wrinkled hand. 'I am Grazia Ferrara. It's icy in here and that's why we are wearing our coats. But we don't mind. The hospital has to ration its oil and the theatres and wards must be kept warm. We manage as best we can.'

Signora Ferrara dismissed the nurse with a nod of her head and urged Rosa towards a chair next to her own. She offered Rosa a sugared almond, which Rosa felt obliged to take although she didn't like them.

'We were discussing what's happened in Turin,' Signora Ferrara told Rosa. It was clear from the way the other women deferred to Signora Ferrara to set the topic of conversation that she was the leader.

'Not just Turin, Grazia,' said one slim woman who wore fingerless gloves. 'Also Genoa, Milan and Naples.'

One of the women in fascist uniform blew her nose loudly before turning to Signora Ferrara. 'We must insist that these bandages are used for Italian soldiers and are not going to be sent to the prisoner-of-war camps for Allied soldiers.'

The other women agreed except for a young woman by the unlit fireplace. She was studying Rosa carefully.

'Those murderers have been killing civilians,' said another woman, stroking her fox stole. 'They are nothing more than brutal terrorists; assassins of the innocent.'

Rosa was aware that the woman by the fireplace was still watching her but was careful not to give too much away by her expression. She didn't think the women were wrong for their sentiments. The Allies *were* killing women, children and old people because the men of military age in the bombed cities had already been mobilised. But hadn't Italy done exactly that to the Abyssinians? And what would these women say if British and French volunteers refused to roll bandages for wounded Italian soldiers in their prisoner-of-war camps?

'Those monsters are aiming deliberately for civilian targets,' said Signora Ferrara. 'They think they can demoralise us and turn us against Il Duce.'

The women murmured their agreement.

'They think we Italians are all romantics,' continued Signora Ferrara. 'I've heard that they say we have a temperament unsuited to war. We'll show them!'

Rosa glanced at the woman by the fireplace from the corner of her eye. Was she a spy or a kindred spirit? She wasn't wearing a uniform or a fur.

Later, Signora Ferrara sent Rosa and the woman to the supply room to collect the medical boxes to be packed for the front. 'You two are the youngest,' she said. 'It's better that you do the lifting.'

'That stupid Signora Ferrara,' the woman said while she and Rosa loaded boxes onto a trolley. 'The reason the Allies can bomb our cities is because Italy doesn't have an air defence plan. You don't hear her blame Il Duce for that!'

Rosa was careful to neither agree nor disagree. The woman had made an intelligent observation but, as convincing as she sounded, Rosa wasn't going to trust her and share her own opinion of Mussolini. The woman might well be a spy who would denounce her the moment she said anything subversive.

When they were back in the volunteer room and packing the boxes, it soon became apparent that there wasn't enough of anything to make a complete box each. They were in short supply of morphine, scissors and even soap. Rosa shuddered when she thought what the consequences would be when the field hospitals didn't receive those basic items. Signora Ferrara muttered that it was the League of Nations' embargo on Italy in 1935 that had caused the shortage, but Rosa suspected it was due to Il Duce's lack of preparation.

On her way home that afternoon, Rosa looked up at the sky. It was blue and cloudless. She had always gazed at the sky with wonder. No matter what country one lived in, everyone in the world shared the same sky. Now Rosa was fearful that when she looked at it she would see the shapes of planes approaching — and death and destruction would fall.

She returned to the hospital each morning to help with the bandages but the chatter of the women grated on her nerves. They did not see Italy's role in its own misfortune. The Red Cross also needed volunteers who could write and read letters on behalf of illiterate parents. Rosa went to the Red Cross office to enquire. On her way to the volunteers' desk, she passed a waiting room full of women. Some were staring at the ceiling while others were weeping. All had a look of devastation about them. At the volunteers' desk, she asked the receptionist who the women were.

'Those poor souls,' said the receptionist, lowering her voice and leaning towards Rosa. 'They are the wives and mothers of soldiers missing in action. They don't know if their men have been killed or are in prisoner-of-war camps.'

Rosa understood their pain. She and Orietta had heard nothing further about Luciano's fate. Not knowing was the worst thing of all.

'What do the volunteers do for them?' she asked.

The receptionist shook her head. 'Apart from being a nurse, I think that is the most unpleasant volunteer job you could apply for,' she said. 'That department has to decipher the lists that are sent and check them against birthdates and places of birth. The Allied officials misspell the names and you can imagine how many Luigi Rossis and De Lucas there are. You can't tell a woman her son is alive if he is dead and vice versa. That would be unforgivable.'

'Do they do anything else?'

'Yes, they are the ones who forward the deceased soldiers' belongings to the families. Honestly, you couldn't be doing anything more depressing. It would be much better to knit socks.'

'Who heads that section?' Rosa asked.

The receptionist's eyes flashed. She leaned forward again, keen to tell. 'It's run by a glamorous and rich widow.

She puts on airs of respectability but apparently she's led quite a racy life. Perhaps it's her penance.'

'Can I see her?'

The receptionist looked miffed that Rosa had ignored her advice and hadn't taken the bite at the juicy bit of gossip she had offered. 'Go to the waiting room and take a number,' she said, turning away from Rosa. 'She's there this morning. But it might take a while.'

Rosa felt the agony of the women who sat in the Dead, Wounded and Missing waiting room as if it were her own. There had been an Allied bombing of naval ships in the Mediterranean and that's why there were so many women there that day. Some of them sat stoically, the only sign of their inner turmoil the way their legs trembled when their name was called. Other women had collapsed and had been brought in by neighbours to receive — or await — further news.

'*Mio caro Orlando! Mio caro Orlando!*' one woman wailed, wiping at the tears pouring down her cheeks. She had saturated several handkerchiefs and was now using her sleeve. She was beyond the comfort of the two women who sat on either side of her holding her hands.

The section's secretary was a petite, grey-haired woman. 'I'm sorry you've had to wait so long,' she whispered to Rosa. 'The head of our department will not read out lists as they do in the other offices. She insists on meeting each woman individually to inform her about her menfolk.'

'Please, I will wait until last,' said Rosa. 'Make sure the others see her first.'

She could not imagine hearing about the fate of a loved one from a list read out by some official or posted on a noticeboard. It wasn't like a university examination where you could get another chance. Whoever this widow with the 'racy' past was, Rosa admired her sense of decency.

It was late in the afternoon by the time all the women waiting had seen the head of the section. Despite the fact that some of them had received the news they feared the most, while others had to continue their torturous wait, all of them seemed calmer for having spoken to the head of the section herself.

'The head is finishing writing a report,' the secretary told Rosa. 'She's had to tell a woman that she's lost her husband and two sons. It's been a difficult day.'

The secretary directed Rosa into a cramped office with overflowing filing cabinets and a scuffed pine desk covered with files and documents. The immobile ceiling fan was black with oily dust. After years of working with antiques, the first thing Rosa noticed about any room was the furniture. She then turned her attention to the woman, dressed in black silk, who was sitting at the desk and writing in one of the files. The secretary placed Rosa's file on the desk and left. The woman looked up. Rosa gave a start when she found herself standing in front of Signora Corvetto.

'So we meet again,' said Signora Corvetto with a smile. She indicated the chair opposite her desk for Rosa to take and glanced at her file. 'I see you are Signora Parigi now.'

Rosa blushed. She remembered the last time they had met, she had told Signora Corvetto that she was Signora Montagnani.

'Well, I am thankful that you have applied here,' said Signora Corvetto. 'We desperately need help and I have always had a good impression of you.'

Meeting Signora Corvetto again was awkward, but Rosa willed herself to speak. 'You must be very busy, Signora Corvetto. Your secretary says that you see each woman in person.'

Signora Corvetto sat back and folded her hands under her chin. 'I know some say it's not the most efficient way, but these are the wives, mothers and sisters of men who have given up their lives for Italy. There is no "efficient" way to deliver heart-wrenching news. I follow my conscience. Some of these women have to support young families or take care of elderly parents on their own. I have to make sure that somehow they leave here with the strength to carry on.'

Signora Corvetto seemed different from Rosa's first impression of her in the Marchese's car all those years ago. She was less frivolous than her elegant clothes suggested, and appeared resilient and compassionate. It made perfect sense that such a woman was Clementina's natural mother, not the Marchesa Scarfiotti.

'Just knowing that we care often helps them,' continued Signora Corvetto. 'Remembering their names and the names of their loved ones without them having to repeat them each time they come can make all the difference.'

The two women fell into an uncomfortable silence. Rosa knew that Signora Corvetto must be as surprised as she was to meet again. She wanted to help the women who were suffering, but how could she look at Signora Corvetto every day without being reminded of the Villa Scarfiotti? She wondered if it was better to be honest about that with Signora Corvetto or simply to apply for another volunteer position.

Signora Corvetto studied Rosa. 'When I came to your shop to buy that present for Clementina, I didn't know what you had been accused of ... *wrongly* accused of. It wasn't until Clementina was sixteen that she confided in me what had happened.'

There, thought Rosa, the small talk has ended. Now we get to the heart of what each of us is thinking. Signora Corvetto has not pushed these things to the back of her mind any more than I have.

'You can't imagine how it has tortured Clementina all these years,' Signora Corvetto continued. 'She wanted to find you but I told her it would not serve you. I already knew that you had a job and a baby. I told her that we should leave you alone to get on with your life.'

Rosa had no doubt that Signora Corvetto was being sincere but she had to tread carefully. She could never accuse the Scarfiotti family of anything without breaching the terms of her release. 'I was sent to prison,' was all she offered. She did not say whether her imprisonment was rightly or wrongly given. Signora Corvetto could work that out for herself.

Signora Corvetto's eyes widened. 'I don't think ... I don't think Emilio ... the Marchese Scarfiotti knew that. He thought you had been warned away. You see, if the Marchesa Scarfiotti had something against you, you would not want to return for your own good.'

Rosa stared at the floor. Was it really possible that the Marchese hadn't known her fate? It occurred to her that besides the Marchesa Scarfiotti, maybe no-one else at the villa did. Ada had returned the flute to the convent before Don Marzoli had found Rosa. Feelings she had not experienced for years came flooding back to her.

Signora Corvetto took out a cigarette and offered one to Rosa, who shook her head. Signora Corvetto lit the cigarette and looked at the ceiling. 'You poor woman. I had no idea. If it's any vindication, that awful Vittorio was sent to an insane asylum. He went raving mad about a year ago, telling everyone that the Marchesa Scarfiotti was not his sister. She was devastated by it. They'd always been close.'

Rosa didn't want to talk about Vittorio. He had been driven crazy by the previous war. It was his sister who should have taken responsibility for him. I want to be myself as I am now, she thought. I don't want to be dragged back to the past.

Sadness flickered in Signora Corvetto's eyes. Rosa was surprised to see it. Out of the two of them, Signora Corvetto was the better at hiding her emotions. As a mistress she must have practised it for years: seeing the man she loved — and then her daughter — possessed by another woman. But when it came to Clementina, she could not hide her love.

'Clementina has grown into a lovely young woman. Your influence on her has remained,' she said. 'She misses her father. He is commanding a division in Africa.'

The Marchese Scarfiotti was in Africa? That was one of the hardest-fought battlefronts of all. Rosa realised that Signora Corvetto felt herself every day what the women in the waiting room were going through. Did she see the Marchese in every list she received or package that passed through the office? Was that the secret of the zeal of her mission; the reason why she was so empathetic?

'Signora Corvetto, I can't talk about the Scarfiotti family without jeopardising all that I have gained in my life,' Rosa said. 'I want to work with you but only if we can leave the past behind.'

Signora Corvetto met Rosa's gaze. She hesitated a moment before she spoke. 'We won't talk of the past, you and I,' she said. She sat back and indicated the files on her desk. 'We'll have too much work to do anyway. Please say that you will help. I need someone with your fortitude.'

Rosa agreed that she would return the following day to commence work, but she knew in her heart that it would not be that simple to forget everything that had happened. The past was not something that could be wiped away with the wave of a hand: for either of them.

NINETEEN

Rosa's hours at the Dead, Wounded and Missing section were from eight o'clock in the morning until lunchtime. But there was so much to do that she frequently returned in the afternoon and worked until the evening. Her most difficult task was when the cases of deceased soldiers' belongings arrived and she had to pack them, along with a translation of the hospital chaplain's note, before sending them to the family. Occasionally a uniform was included, sometimes mud-caked and stiff with blood, but most often the items returned were Bibles and photographs. Rosa sometimes found notebooks, decks of cards, sheet music, rosaries and sketches. There were never compasses or binoculars unless they were broken; those were in short supply back on the battlefield. When Rosa touched the objects, visions and feelings flew through her. She saw the soldier on his wedding day, as a child in his mother's arms, running across a battlefield with cracks of gunfire in his ears. More than she liked, Rosa experienced their feelings at the moment of death: resignation, or cold, stark fear — like the hunted animals she sensed when she touched fur or skin. When the soldiers had died in a hospital rather than on the battlefield there were often feelings of relief or regret.

Whenever she considered it appropriate, she included a note of her own along with the official letter: a verse from a poem she thought might bring comfort or a quote from the Bible. Sometimes the soldier's death had been so tragic, the only thing she could think of to send was a pressed flower. By the end of each day she was drained, and yet somehow the following morning she found the strength to return to the section, ready to spend another day doing whatever small act she could to alleviate a woman's pain.

Some of the packages contained letters written by the soldiers to their families that had never been sent. Rosa was required to read them in case anything had slipped by the censor — quite often things had, whether by accident or on purpose. She learned more about the progress of the war from the correspondence of the deceased than she did from the censored press. She pieced together a war where Italian soldiers were being slaughtered because the army was badly equipped. *We don't have trucks to transport us*, penned one soldier. *We carry our supplies on mules*. A young officer wrote to his father that only two of his men understood Italian. When he ordered them to fight, the order had to be translated into several regional dialects.

It became the habit of Rosa and Signora Corvetto to sit together at the end of the day and unload their burdens to each other over a cup of tea.

'One widow has been coming to me for months for news of her son,' said Signora Corvetto one evening. 'She has cancer. Today I found out that he was killed in Greece. He's her only child.'

Rosa had thought all the tragic stories would make her numb after a while. But she never stopped feeling the terrible things that were happening.

'Italy wasn't prepared at all for this war, was it?' she asked.

Signora Corvetto threw up her hands. 'We are an

agricultural country,' she said. 'We never had France's or Germany's industrial capacity. We can't produce planes, tanks or automobiles as fast as they can. At harvest time, the Italian army had to send the conscripts back to bring in the crops otherwise the army as well as the civilians would have starved.' She poured them both another cup of tea. 'My late husband owned a merchant shipping fleet. No-one informed his company that Italy was about to enter the war. So when the declaration was made, the ships docked in Allied ports were immediately impounded. Those ships could have been used in the war effort. Instead, they are being used against us.'

Signora Corvetto glanced at the world map on the wall. Rosa followed her gaze to the outline of Africa. It was the one place that Italy had experienced some success. Everywhere else the war was a disaster.

'Italy is going to have to surrender,' said Signora Corvetto. 'There is no other way out of this.'

'Surrender?' A shudder ran down Rosa's spine. 'I've never believed Italy had a good reason for entering this war. But if we surrender what will the Allies do to us?'

Signora Corvetto bit her lip. 'I don't know.' She indicated the files scattered on her desk and the new crate of returned belongings that had arrived that day. 'But could it be worse than this?'

Rosa and Antonio had hoped to visit the children for Christmas. But, as Rosa had feared, as soon as the government official at the passport office reviewed her documents, he refused her request.

'Please,' she begged him. 'My children are very young. I haven't seen them for months.'

'Why did you send them to Switzerland?' the official asked her.

'So they would be safe.'

The official's eyes narrowed. 'Well,' he said, loudly enough for the people in the waiting area to hear, 'you obviously doubted Italy would win this war, so you are two times the traitor.'

He slammed down the shutter on his window and put up his 'closed' sign. It was still a quarter of an hour before lunchtime.

Rosa turned to leave. The people in the waiting area stared at her. Rosa remembered the times she had suffered public humiliation for being an unwed mother. But on this occasion she looked each of the people in the face.

'Was I wrong?' she asked them. 'Are we on our way to glorious victory?'

The onlookers averted their eyes. Rosa's subversive comment could incriminate them all, but she suspected that there was a stronger feeling prevailing among them than fear. They knew what she said was right and they were ashamed.

Rosa and Antonio argued that evening over whether he should go to Lugano without her.

'The children will feel abandoned if you don't go,' Rosa said. 'And I want you to see personally how they are.'

'Perhaps it's time to get that false passport,' suggested Antonio.

Rosa shook her head. 'That's one risk we will keep for when we know we are leaving and not coming back,' she replied. 'People are still buying from the shop. There seems to be a certain class of Florentine that doesn't realise there is a war on.'

Antonio nodded. 'The city does seem oddly safe. Perhaps the Allies are as sentimental about the birthplace of the Renaissance as we are.'

Rosa hid her heartbreak at not being able to visit her children by busying herself sewing clothes for them. She wrote each of them a long letter, asking Sibilla to read the one for the twins to them. *I'm so proud of you, my darling, amazing and lovely girl*, she wrote to Sibilla. *I hope you know that although I can't see you, I carry you and the boys in my heart always.*

Rosa wrote to Lorenzo and Giorgio about happy things — the change in the seasons, what Ylenia was cooking for them, what the neighbours were doing. But all her feelings could have been summed up in three simple words: I miss you. It hurt her to think of all the special moments with her children that she had been deprived of and could never have back again. She only hoped that when they were older the children would understand why she had been unable to see them and forgive her.

The night before Antonio was due to leave, Ylenia made them polenta with nettles and wild mushrooms. She'd had to piece together what she could from the rations, and Rosa refused to eat hedgehogs or guinea pigs. But they ate on their finest china and drank a bottle of the French champagne they had 'subversively' kept for a special occasion.

When they had finished dinner, Antonio leaned back in his chair and touched the rim of his glass. 'Do you ever think about him?' he asked.

'Who?' responded Rosa, looking up. Antonio had an unfamiliar expression on his face and she realised that he had meant Luciano. Antonio had never been the jealous type. Why was he bringing Luciano up now? She lowered her eyes. 'He's dead, Antonio. No-one has heard from Luciano since Spain. He would have contacted Orietta or Carlo if he were still alive. Yes, I think of him when I light my candle in the church, but I don't think of him the same way I once did. I pray to God every day that I may have half his courage and determination.'

Ylenia came in with some dried figs for dessert. When the maid left, Rosa asked Antonio, 'Do you still think of *her*?' She meant Signora Visconti.

It was Antonio's turn to be surprised. He shifted in his seat then looked Rosa in the eye. 'Every day. *Every day* I think of her.'

Rosa felt herself pale. She knew that Signora Visconti had been the love of Antonio's life, but ever since they had last seen her on the Day of Faith, Rosa had hoped that he'd forgotten her. It was a shock to hear from his own mouth that he hadn't.

'I see,' she said, trying to disguise her hurt feelings by holding Antonio's gaze. 'I guess she is rather unforgettable.'

'Exactly!' said Antonio, a smile dancing on his lips 'That is why I remember her every day when I see you and think, *Thank God I married Rosa*!'

It took Rosa a moment to comprehend Antonio's meaning. When she understood, she blushed with embarrassment but felt happy too. 'It's not nice to tease your wife that way!' she said, affecting an irritated tone.

Antonio stood up and placed his hand on Rosa's shoulder. 'Then suggest a nicer way for me to tease my wife?' he said.

In January 1941, the British launched an attack against the Italian strongholds in East Africa. After Keren fell, so did Asmara and Massawa. The Ethiopian capital was captured by the British. The Italian casualties were heavy. The Red Cross rounded up more volunteers for the Dead, Wounded and Missing section to help with the workload of informing relatives about the fate of their sons and husbands.

Rosa arrived one morning with the lists from the army telegraph office. She felt the unsettling presence around her that she experienced whenever she was reminded of the Villa Scarfiotti. Only she hadn't been thinking of the villa at all; rather, she had been disturbed to learn by letter from Antonio that the twins had colds. Still that presence was there — breathing, rippling and moving the air around her. The sensation grew stronger when she walked into Signora Corvetto's office to find the head of the section slumped over her desk and weeping. It was the first time Rosa had seen Signora Corvetto give way to her emotions but she understood. All the volunteers in the section were burnt out. Rosa was starting to see the faces of the women in the waiting room in her sleep. A human being could only deal with so much grief.

'I'll make you a cup of tea with sugar,' she said to Signora Corvetto. 'You're trembling.'

Signora Corvetto looked up. She had changed from a fresh-faced beauty to an old woman overnight. There were shadows under her eyes and grooves around her mouth. 'The list,' she said, holding out her hand. 'Give me the list.'

'The list can wait another five minutes,' Rosa told her. 'You can't help anybody if you aren't feeling well.'

Signora Corvetto sat back in her chair. 'He hasn't written,' she said, touching her fingers to her brow. 'Why hasn't he written?'

She was repeating the same lament Rosa heard every day from the women in the waiting room. For a moment she wondered if Signora Corvetto was suffering a breakdown. Then she remembered that the Marchese Scarfiotti was in Africa. 'I've already scanned the list,' Rosa told her. 'His name is not there.'

Signora Corvetto placed her hands on the desk as if she were trying to steady herself. Rosa pulled up a chair and sat beside her. She thought about all the women Signora Corvetto had comforted. Who would be there for Signora Corvetto now that she needed support?

'You have worked yourself into the ground,' Rosa told her. 'You know that you might not hear anything for months. There is no way that anything other than priority war correspondence will get through now.'

Signora Corvetto opened the desk drawer and took out a handkerchief from the plentiful supply she kept there. She wiped her eyes and blew her nose. 'When Rodolfo passed away, I thought Emilio and I could see more of each other,' she said, looking into the distance. 'We were happy together.' She lost her composure again and gave way to a new wave of tears. 'This damn war!' she cried. 'This damn war!'

'If he's not been on any of the lists so far, then that's a good sign,' Rosa said. 'Those in command are the first to be noticed missing.' But she was clutching at straws. Both she and Signora Corvetto knew that not being on the list did not necessarily mean a soldier wasn't dead. The Marchese and his unit could have been blown to bits, identity discs and all, and then no-one would know what had happened for months, maybe never.

That evening at church, while lighting her candle for the anti-fascists, Rosa said a prayer for the Marchese Scarfiotti as well. She had not been particularly fond of him, but two people she cared about were suffering over him. If Signora Corvetto was feeling the anxiety of not having heard any news, then Clementina must be in torment too. Rosa had tried to shut Clementina out of her mind for many years and lavish all her love and attention on her own children. But now her heart was breaking for Clementina.

One morning in early summer, long after Antonio had returned from his visit to Lugano, Signora Corvetto was called away to a meeting of the heads of the Red Cross volunteer divisions. Rosa and two of the new volunteers, an elderly couple by the name of Daria and Fabrizio Bianchi, sat at the front desk together. They were checking letters to be forwarded to Italian prisoners of war when the hospital librarian arrived with a box.

'This was sent to us by mistake,' he said. 'I thought it was some new books so I didn't look at it until now. But it's for your section. It's the belongings of a commanding officer.'

The Bianchis turned to Rosa; she dealt with the belongings to be returned because she could translate the Allied chaplain's notes. She stood up and took the box from the librarian. As soon as she touched it her heart plunged. The Marchese Scarfiotti is dead, she thought. Without even having to look at the contents she knew that they belonged to him.

'Excuse me,' she said to the volunteers. She took the box to Signora Corvetto's office and closed the door.

When she took the package out of the box and placed it on the desk she felt as if she had slipped away from time. She untied the string and opened the brown paper. Her fingers brushed the light grey *cordellino* uniform and what she had suspected was confirmed. She saw the Marchese as a boy playing in the garden at the Villa Scarfiotti. He was not the Marchese that Rosa had known because his gait was carefree and no shadows stalked him. The accompanying official letter said the Marchese had been killed on 15 March that year while defending the Sanchil Peak. Rosa gazed at the uniform to see if she could ascertain the Marchese's feelings when he died. She sensed light and sound fading. His death had been quick. He hadn't had time to think, although she felt fatalism in his last breath. She had the impression that he was at rest but, unknown to Signora Corvetto and Clementina, he had not wanted to stay in this world for a long time. He'd not found the courage to leave it until that final battle.

Rosa recalled Clementina's ninth birthday party. She remembered the arrival of Bonnie Lass and the delight on Clementina's face when she rode the pony with her father leading her. Rosa shook her head. The war was not some freak of nature. It was motivated by human greed and fear and that made it all the more tragic. She opened her notebook to record the contents of the package: there were no unsent letters, nor was there a wedding band or a Bible. However, there was the signet ring that the Marchese had worn the day he came to the convent and a silver-topped clothes brush. The Marchese's engraved map case had been included, although the Allied officials had removed the maps. Under the case was a book. Rosa picked it up and found it was a copy of Dante's *La divina comedia*. She opened it. On the title page there was a dedication from Nerezza. When Rosa saw the bold handwriting, the strange foreboding feeling returned to her.

For words that are yet to be said and for days that are yet to be lived it read. It was dated 12 October 1906. Perhaps it was a birthday gift.

Rosa was about to put down the book when she realised there were photographs wedged between some of the pages. The first was a portrait of Signora Corvetto. She looked beautiful with her softly lit face and her hair cascading over her shoulders in rolls. On the back of the photograph the Marchese had written: *Gisella, September 1937*. Rosa slipped it back between the pages and took out the next one. It was of a young woman in a tennis dress. She had large bright eyes and a broad grin and her hair was piled up in a fashionable style. At first Rosa thought it was another mistress of the Marchese's and was afraid of the pain that would cause Signora Corvetto, but then she realised the young woman was Clementina. She's grown lovely, Rosa thought.

There was a photograph of the Villa Scarfiotti with a couple and a young girl standing in front of it along with an infant in a pram. The light in the office was dim and Rosa took the photograph to the window so she could see it more clearly. There was no notation on the back, but Rosa assumed the child in the pram was the Marchese and the man and woman were his parents. The girl with them must be Nerezza. Rosa's fingers itched. She had seen the girl's face before. She turned the photograph to the light so she could view the features more clearly. Her heart dropped to her feet. The sculptured cheekbones and upward-slanting eyes … she could have been looking at a picture of her own daughter!

Rosa stayed on after the Bianchis had left so she could give the package to Signora Corvetto when she returned. She didn't want her to be alone when she received it. She wondered if she could remain strong for Signora Corvetto because her own mind was in turmoil. The resemblance between Sibilla and Nerezza was too striking for Rosa to have any doubt any more. She thought about the expression on Ada's face when she had seen the key from Nerezza's piano stool around her neck, and of the way Baron Derveaux had stared at her and said that from certain angles she reminded him of someone. She thought of the surround on the grave at the Villa Scarfiotti: she had never seen that statue face-on, only in profile. She went to the window and stared at her reflection in it, turning her head slightly. Is it possible? she asked herself. Isn't Nerezza's child buried with her in that grave?

Rosa returned to the Marchese's uniform to see if it would reveal any more secrets; after all, if what she suspected was true, then the Marchese had been her uncle. She rubbed her forehead. She didn't know what to think. She had heard that extraordinary beauty often skipped a generation and passed from grandmother to granddaughter. Still, there were enough resemblances between herself and Nerezza to make a link on their own. Both of them were musicians, each had a full figure, and Rosa had been taken to the convent around the same time that Nerezza had given birth to her child. Rosa pushed back her hair. Was she seeing more than what was there? If she was Nerezza's child, then why had she been taken to the convent and why had the Marchese been told that she had died? The Marchesa Scarfiotti's bloodless face appeared in Rosa's mind. Surely if there was any wrongdoing then she was involved. But why would the Marchesa have wanted to get rid of Nerezza's child? Rosa remembered Miss Butterfield, the governess, saying that the Marchesa was vain about her title. But Rosa was a girl. She wouldn't have had any claim on the title of Marchesa if her uncle had married. Was it simply spite? It seemed common knowledge that Nerezza and the Marchesa had hated each other.

'You're here very late,' said Signora Corvetto, walking in the door. She looked washed out. Her lipstick had vanished and her curls were falling flat. 'Was it an awful day? I tell you, that meeting was an eye-opener —' She stopped mid-sentence when she saw the package. Her face twisted into a terrible expression. 'No!' she screamed.

Rosa tried to help her into a chair but she stepped away. 'Just tell me!' she said, her eyes wide with fear. 'Just tell me!'

'The package was mislaid,' Rosa said. 'We only received it today. I'm sorry.'

Signora Corvetto sank to her knees. 'Oh God!' she said. It wasn't a dignified position, but there was nothing dignified about grief. Rosa thought it was like birth: you simply had to do whatever helped you bear the pain.

'This terrible war!' Signora Corvetto wept. 'When are they going to stop? When they've taken *all* the men?'

Rosa put her arms around Signora Corvetto. She thought that having to extinguish the light of a loved one was like tearing off a piece of your soul. Signora Corvetto rocked and trembled with the agony of it. After a few minutes, she muttered, 'I'm sorry that I won't hear his voice again or be able to listen to his lectures on Florentine architecture. All the things I shall miss when this war is over and we go back to our ordinary lives.'

Rosa wondered if they would ever have ordinary lives again. She thought of what she had felt when she had touched the Marchese's uniform and of Nerezza's dedication to her adolescent brother: *For words that are yet to be said and for days that are yet to be lived*. She was sorry for Signora Corvetto. She was grieving for a love that was a concoction of mirages and false expectations. From what Rosa knew of the Marchese at the villa and what she sensed from his uniform, by the time he had met Signora Corvetto, he had already given up hope for a happy future.

After more tears, Signora Corvetto gradually regained her composure. Her gaze fell to the package. Rosa helped her to stand up and passed it to her.

'Here,' she said, taking Signora Corvetto by the arm and leading her to her office. 'Take your time to look through his things and say goodbye. I'll be out here waiting for you if you need me.'

Rosa closed the door and sat at her desk again. At first there was only silence and then she heard Signora Corvetto sobbing. Rosa herself was experiencing a form of delayed shock. She took her coat from the cupboard and covered her legs with it. The lingering doubts she'd had about whether or not she was Nerezza's daughter seemed to have dissipated in the past hour. It was a strange sensation to have such an epiphany after living in limbo about her origins for so many years. Nerezza was my mother? Rosa tried to get used to the idea. She had thought that if she ever discovered the identity of her mother she would be overwhelmed by feelings of love, affection and belonging. Instead she felt numb. She found herself wondering what sort of mother Nerezza would have been, and recalled those endless lists in the notebook; her perfectionism. She might not have been any kinder to Rosa than the Marchesa was to Clementina. Rosa recalled Suor Maddalena singing her to sleep. She hadn't had all the material advantages that would have come with being the daughter of Nerezza, but she had been loved. She reminded herself that she didn't know everything there was to know about Nerezza. Maybe she'd had qualities that Rosa wasn't considering — she had loved her brother dearly, she loved music and art. I just don't know, thought Rosa, staring at her hands. I don't know what it would have been like if I hadn't been taken away to the convent. The chance to know was denied me by somebody else.

She stared up at the ceiling. She tried to keep the Marchesa Scarfiotti out of her mind but the woman forced her way in. She saw the woman as she remembered her from the villa: haughty, vain, superior and cruel. I was thrown in prison because of her, Rosa thought. Maybe I grew up with no name and no family because of her too.

It was almost eight o'clock in the evening before Signora Corvetto emerged from her office. Rosa had rung the apartment to tell Ylenia that she would be late and to serve dinner for Antonio.

'Signora Corvetto,' Rosa said, standing. 'Is there anyone I should call?'

Signora Corvetto took Rosa's hand and squeezed it. 'No, there is no-one to call.'

Rosa sensed how drained Signora Corvetto was through her skin, but she seemed more tranquil now she had expressed her grief.

'When you come in tomorrow, I'd like you to type an official letter to accompany the Marchese's things,' she said. 'We should be addressing it to the Marchesa Scarfiotti but I think we both know that would be a wasted effort. Address it to Clementina. I will take it with his belongings to her personally.'

'Certainly,' Rosa said.

Signora Corvetto smiled. 'Now, you have a husband who has been patient with your work here. I want you to go home. I don't know what I will do if you fall sick.'

'What about you, Signora Corvetto?' said Rosa. 'You are all alone.'

Signora Corvetto shrugged. 'It's the life that I chose,' she said, looking away. Then, turning back to Rosa, she said with a sad smile, 'Let's stop this formality. From now on I want you to call me Gisella.'

She took her coat from the cupboard and Rosa helped her with it.

'At least let me walk you part of the way to your apartment,' Rosa said.

'As you wish,' agreed Signora Corvetto.

The two women walked out of the building and onto the dark street. There was a blackout order but many Florentines had ignored it and left their curtains open. Rosa listened to the click her shoes made on the pavement.

'Signora Corvetto … I mean, Gisella,' she said. 'There is something I want to talk to you about.'

Signora Corvetto nodded for Rosa to continue.

'I know something about you. Don't ask me how I know. I just do. I know Clementina is your daughter.'

Signora Corvetto stopped and stared at Rosa in the dim light. Neither of them moved.

'How do you know?' she asked quietly. 'Did the Marchese tell you?'

Rosa shook her head. 'No-one told me. I sensed it.'

Signora Corvetto stared at her feet before turning to Rosa. 'You married your boss. I did too. Only my husband was forty years older than me and had already been married twice before. He'd outlived both his wives. People humoured him, "You won't outlive this one", but they despised me. It's easy to look down on people when you have money. Rodolfo wanted my youth; I wanted a better life. I was an orphan, you know. Even a baker I had taken a liking to looked down on me. What other woman in my situation wouldn't have married a rich man if she had the chance?'

'But Signor Corvetto was too old to father children?'

Signora Corvetto nodded. 'Poor Rodolfo was too tired to do anything. He didn't even approach me on our wedding night.'

'It must have been lonely,' said Rosa, 'for a young girl.'

'His family and his social circle would not even address me. It was as though I didn't exist. Not that we went out much.'

The two women continued walking.

'When I met Emilio, his marriage was miserable too,' said Signora Corvetto. 'We found solace in each other. But when I became pregnant, there was the risk of a scandal. Rodolfo would have been humiliated. We had to invent a suspected case of tuberculosis. I went away to a "sanatorium" in Switzerland. The Marchesa was often abroad in those days so it wasn't so difficult to pass Clementina off as her child, apart from the fact she's always been so thin. There's something wrong with her, did you know that?'

Rosa had suspected the Marchesa had some problem with her health. She hardly ate anything except nearly raw meat, and underneath the layers of make-up she had looked malnourished.

'Well, she can't have children so she agreed to take Clementina because at least she was Emilio's natural daughter. I thought she might be softer towards my daughter, but that was an impossible hope. I was glad for your influence on Clementina, and I am glad now that she is approaching an age when she can get away from the

Marchesa's clutches. There will be no-one to protect Clementina now that her father is gone.'

Rosa and Signora Corvetto fell silent, each lost in her own thoughts. They walked on further than they had agreed and stopped outside the door to Signora Corvetto's building and embraced before parting. Rosa watched the older woman enter the building and close the door behind her. She's an orphan too, she thought. Her own situation of being separated from her children made her sympathetic to Signora Corvetto's pain over Clementina.

After Rosa had finished the supper Ylenia had left for her in the kitchen, Antonio came in with the dictionary. '*Coincidence*,' he read aloud. '*A correlation of events without an obvious causal connection*.'

Rosa reflected on the definition. She was experiencing a correlation of events, but she sensed there was something behind them. Something had urged her towards Nerezza's piano and to try the silver key in the lock of the stool; and something had caused the Marchese's belongings to be mislaid so that she would see them before Signora Corvetto did. She longed to speak with Ada, who, she now understood, had recognised Rosa as soon as she had seen the key. Hadn't Ada said something was going on at the villa psychically after Rosa had arrived? But there wasn't much chance of speaking to Ada. Signora Corvetto had told Rosa that the Marchesa was entertaining fascist high officials at the villa and had even had Mussolini there as a guest. All the staff, and anyone entering the grounds, were checked by the secret police. Rosa sighed. Approaching Ada would have to wait until after the war. At least, with the way things were going, that wouldn't be too long away.

'Why did you ask me to look up "coincidence"?' asked Antonio, putting the dictionary aside.

Rosa shared everything with Antonio but she wasn't going to tell him her suspicions about her origins or the Marchesa until she had firm proof.

'It's a word that often comes up in my work,' she replied. 'I wanted to be sure I understood its true meaning.'

'Ah,' said Antonio. 'Perhaps what you mean then is more like "destiny": a course of events that leads inevitably to one's fate.'

Rosa stared at Antonio. She didn't know why but what he had said chilled her to the bone. Coincidence, destiny, fate: all these things tied her unequivocally to the Villa Scarfiotti. And no matter how she tried to avoid it, fate was leading her back there.

TWENTY

Signora Corvetto resigned from her role as the head of the section for the Dead, Wounded and Missing. She had filled her position with grace and compassion, but she was exhausted and if she didn't rest she was in danger of turning herself into an invalid. She was replaced by a retired army officer, Maggiore Valentini. Despite his brisk manner and military emphasis on efficiency, Maggiore Valentini was a kind man. Even with the increasing workload of the section, he did try to see at least the women in the waiting room whose men had been killed. The only problem was, when faced with an emotional woman, Maggiore Valentini stammered, which turned the breaking of the news into a drawn-out affair.

One afternoon in late June, Rosa, the Bianchis and a dozen of the new volunteers were packing boxes and deciphering lists when Maggiore Valentini told them there was to be an important announcement on the radio in one hour.

The volunteers exchanged nervous glances.

'What do you think it could be?' Daria whispered to her

husband. She wiped the sweat from her face with a handkerchief. All the desk fans were running but the office remained stifling in the summer heat.

'Who knows?' he replied. 'I only pray it's not another advance. We can barely deal with our work as it is.'

Rosa pushed a strand of damp hair from her forehead. Unlike the others, she was filled with hope at the thought of an important announcement. She'd heard through Orietta that members of the Fascist Grand Council were plotting to overthrow Mussolini and negotiate with the Allies for Italy's withdrawal from the war. Of course such a plan was high treason. There were spies all over the city trying to ascertain the chances of a popular revolt. Rosa was suspicious of the new postman who delivered their mail to the shop. He seemed to linger in the doorway longer than necessary, as if he was trying to eavesdrop.

'He's shifty,' Rosa told Antonio. 'I feel like he's watching me. Some of the letters from Renata and the children are being opened.'

'They're probably being checked by censors,' said Antonio. 'As for our *postino*, well, he's eighteen but for some reason hasn't been conscripted into the army. He might be slow — or he might only be dazzled by you.'

Rosa smiled when she remembered Antonio's compliment and brought her attention back to her work. She tidied her desk before tackling the next round of letters from soldiers to their families. What Orietta had heard about was a conspiracy amongst the elite; Rosa was disappointed that it wasn't the ordinary Italian people who were revolting. Mussolini's reaction to the bombing raids in the south and the reduced rations everyone was enduring was to say that they would make the Italian people stronger. Rosa didn't think the people on the streets looked stronger; she thought they looked demoralised.

When the hour had passed, the section's volunteers and staff gathered around the radio. The fans were turned off in order to hear the announcer. Rivulets of sweat poured down

Rosa's back. She remained hopeful that the news would be of a coup and that Mussolini had been deposed. Her mind drifted to what such an announcement would mean — the children coming home, lives spared, good food on the table again. Her imaginings were so vivid that she actually *felt* as if all those things had happened. It was a cold shock then when the radio announcer translated a message from Goebbels, the German minister of propaganda: Germany had invaded the Soviet Union.

Everyone looked at each other. No invader had ever captured that vast land and those passionate people. Why had Germany decided to open the war on two fronts? Did they really believe they could win?

'They haven't requested Italy to join them,' said Daria, looking half-puzzled and half-relieved.

'It's just as well,' said Rosa, unafraid to speak her mind. 'That's going to be a bloodbath.'

'What do you think, Maggiore Valentini?' one of the younger volunteers asked the section's leader.

Maggiore Valentini frowned. 'What I think stays in this section, all right? It's quite likely the Germans didn't ask Italy to join them because they have come to understand how ill-prepared this country was to leap into a war. We are a liability rather than an asset.'

When Rosa arrived at the shop later in the afternoon, Antonio and Orietta had already heard the news of the German invasion.

'It looks like the Germans haven't asked Italy to join them,' said Rosa. 'It's all for the best. Some of the volunteers are saying the Russians will slaughter the Germans. Perhaps Hitler will surrender then.'

Antonio shook his head. 'I'm afraid Mussolini won't want to miss out on any spoils. He will send the Italian army, no matter how many men it costs for him to get his hands on something.'

Antonio and Orietta exchanged a glance. Antonio stood

up and put on his jacket. 'I have a buyer to go see,' he said, kissing Rosa on the cheek and bidding farewell to Orietta with an embrace and kisses before heading out the door.

Rosa shifted uncomfortably. Antonio had departed from Orietta as if he didn't expect to see her again for some time. She turned to her friend. 'Orietta?'

'I'm leaving,' Orietta told her.

'What? Why?' asked Rosa, her heart sinking.

Orietta glanced at her fondly. 'You know I can't tell you.'

'Something to do with Giustizia e Libertà?' Rosa said, guessing the only reason Orietta would leave was because she had some mission to perform. 'What?'

Orietta smiled and shook her head.

'When will you be back?' Rosa asked the question although she knew from Antonio's manner of parting that it wouldn't be for a long time.

Orietta's eyes misted over. She stepped forward and embraced Rosa. 'Light a candle for me as well as the others,' she said.

Rosa held Orietta with all her strength. This was what she hated most about the war — not the rationing, not even the fear, but the separations. She missed her children and now she was losing Orietta too.

'I will,' she promised, crying. 'I will ask God every day to protect you.'

Without Orietta's friendship to distract her, Rosa missed her children more than ever. She realised how much she had come to rely on her 'sister' for comfort. She hated it when, out of habit, she walked into the shop expecting to see Orietta only to find that her desk was empty.

The war was escalating and the food shortages were growing worse. Rosa decided that her aim of trying to earn as much money as possible before joining the children in Switzerland was misguided. Security was nothing more than an illusion. To seek it was as futile as her attempts to keep Sibilla safe by avoiding becoming openly involved with the anti-fascists. If the Italians had got rid of Mussolini years ago, the situation would have been different. Any sane leader would have sided with the Allies.

'It's time we went to Switzerland,' she told Antonio. 'I'll take my chances on starting a new life.'

'I have found a forger to make you a passport,' Antonio informed Rosa the next day. 'He's Austrian. He's helped many Jews escape from Vienna.'

'When will the passport be ready?' she asked.

'Early next week.'

Rosa let Maggiore Valentini know that she was leaving the section but she didn't tell him the reason. 'You've served hard and well, Signora Parigi,' he told her. 'I hope we will see you again one day.'

Antonio and Rosa busied themselves packing the shop's remaining furniture and moving it to either the backroom or into the cellar under the shop. It worried Rosa to think that the most valuable piece she and Antonio had invested in — an eighteenth-century walnut and marquetry dining table — was too heavy to be moved. She covered it with a sheet and prayed that no-one would find it and think of chopping it up for firewood. She wrapped a Baroque scagliola panel, stopping a moment to admire the ballet-slipper pink cartouche of a couple riding in a boat drawn by seahorses. It was beautiful and dreamy, but there was no place for beauty or dreams in a war.

Antonio hid the accounts books in a safe concealed behind a cupboard. He was doing his best to be detached and methodical in going about his tasks, but Rosa knew it was breaking his heart. The shop had been his dream as a young man and he had worked hard to bring it to fruition. She remembered the first time she had seen Antonio in the shop, trying to sell the chairs with the swan-shaped armrests. He had not believed in Rosa's powers to see the source of things then. Even after seven years of marriage, he still didn't believe in them but he had come to respect that *she* did.

It was the thought of seeing the children again that helped Rosa through the next few days. She and Antonio taped the windows in the apartment and took the paintings off the walls. They did their best to hide things from potential looters, but nothing would save their much-cherished items if a bomb hit the building. They hoped it would never come to that. So far Florence had been spared.

The morning that Antonio was to collect Rosa's passport from the forger, she woke up with a knot in her stomach. It was understandable to be nervous, but many people were still getting across the border on false documents — and hadn't Antonio been assured that the forger had helped many Jews? Rosa went to the kitchen and made herself a cup of hot water with a slice of lemon because tea was scarce. Still, the cold fear would not leave her. She and Antonio had agreed to travel in separate compartments on the chance that if something happened to one of them, the other one would be able to reach the children. Rosa had insisted on this; Antonio had relented only after days of resistance. She took a sip of the hot water and shut her eyes, willing herself not to think of the children, afraid that her intense desire to see them might thwart the plan.

After Antonio had left to collect the passport, Rosa stood in the bare drawing room and contemplated how life had turned into a series of hurdles. Suddenly a simple thing like catching a train to Switzerland had to be meticulously planned. The only non-essential item Rosa was taking with her was her flute. She played Mozart to calm herself while waiting for Antonio to return. The ethereal beauty of the music made the disintegration of her life more bearable.

When Antonio had not returned by three o'clock, Rosa began to pace the floor. What could he be doing, she wondered. The train tickets were booked for that evening, they were already packed, and he hadn't mentioned any last-minute errands to be run. She walked to the window and looked out at the street, half-expecting the postman to be there, spying as she suspected. But the street was empty. 'Stop it!' Rosa told herself, trying to ease her mind. She thought about making dinner but then remembered there was no food in the house. They had got rid of it all to prevent rats and had intended to eat something at the station before the train departed.

By six o'clock she knew something was wrong. The train was due to leave at a quarter past seven. Even if Antonio returned now, they would most likely miss it. Rosa's pulse raced. 'Stay calm!' she told herself, scribbling a note to Antonio that she was going to the police station. Her hand shook so badly the writing was barely legible. She put on her hat, grabbed her bag and rushed out the door. She walked past the shop and looked between the gaps in the mesh shutter that covered the window. Antonio wasn't there.

The doors to the police station were heavy. They creaked when Rosa opened them, although no one in the waiting area heard — they were too busy arguing. There had been a crackdown on black-market profiteers, and an old woman wearing pince-nez and a wild-haired man in the waiting area were arguing the innocence of someone who had been arrested. Rosa was close to tears. She had never stepped inside a police station before and it brought back memories of the night she was sent to prison over Maria's death. A policeman, seeing the distress on her face, called her over to the counter. She explained to him that she was looking for her husband.

'He is not at the bar, signora? Could he not be with friends?'

Rosa shook her head. 'He never goes to the bar,' she said. She gave him Antonio's name and their address.

The policeman went to his file to check something. 'Come this way, please,' he said to Rosa, opening the counter and ushering her into a room towards the back of the station.

The policeman was polite but his averted eyes and stiff

walk told Rosa something was wrong. They were the same mannerisms Maggiore Valentini exhibited when he was about to tell a relative their loved one had been killed. Rosa was on the verge of fainting. The policeman asked her to sit down then he disappeared, returning a few moments later with the police sergeant, a heavy-set man with a florid complexion. He looked at Rosa gravely.

'Your husband has been arrested,' he said. 'He was caught purchasing a forgery.'

Rosa's thoughts crowded her all at once. Antonio arrested? That couldn't be! 'I should be the one arrested,' she told the sergeant. 'He has a legal passport. The illegal one was for me.'

The sergeant held up his finger to silence Rosa. She caught the glimmer of sympathy in his eyes. 'Yes, he has told me the story,' the sergeant said. 'I know that you have children in Switzerland and why it would be terrible for you if you were sent to prison. I understand. That's why we have agreed that he will go in your place.'

'What?'

Rosa had been relieved that Antonio was alive but this was dreadful. She knew prison life and still had nightmares about it. She couldn't bear Antonio to suffer; as much as she was terrified of prison, she would rather suffer herself. She began to cry. The sergeant was noticeably moved by her distress.

'Your husband told me the reason your passport was not approved,' he said. 'I will give you papers to go to see your children for one month. But you must come back, otherwise I will charge your husband with a more serious offence.'

Rosa pressed her fingers to her temples. How could this have happened? All she and Antonio wanted was to be with their children. They had closed up their shop, given away their lives. And now it was all for nothing.

'May I see him?' she asked.

The police sergeant turned and gave instructions to the policeman, who led Rosa to another room. It was not as clean as the previous one and the stench of sweat and vomit pervaded the air. In the middle was a table with chairs on either side of it. Antonio was brought into the room by a policeman and told to sit at the table opposite Rosa. He was still wearing his suit but the jacket was crumpled and the pants had dust on them as if he had been sitting on the floor. He looked shaken but pleased to see Rosa. She could not have loved her husband any more than she did at that moment.

'A fine mess,' he said with a wry smile. 'You were right about that postman. But it was me he was following. The forger managed to escape but I didn't.'

Rosa took Antonio's hand and pressed it to her cheek. 'Let me go to prison. Not you.'

He shook his head and whispered, 'Normally both of us would be thrown into prison. They are being lenient.'

Rosa's eyes filled with tears.

'Don't cry,' Antonio said gently. 'I won't have to wait long for a trial, and the police sergeant said it is most likely they'll put me in Le Murate so I'll still be in Florence. That's good luck not bad luck, Rosa. Others are being sent to Germany as forced labour — that would be a terrible position for someone with Jewish ancestry.'

'Why couldn't they just let you go?' Rosa asked, glancing at the policeman standing near the door. 'What you did is not such a great offence.'

Antonio shrugged. 'It's just the luck of the draw,' he said. 'They have to be seen to be doing *something* if they don't want to be shipped off to Germany themselves. But they have treated me well. To tell you the truth, they felt sorry that you were imprisoned for "anti-fascist actions" as a young woman. Even many of the fascists themselves are beginning to admit that they put their faith in a madman.'

The day of Antonio's trial, Rosa went to church and lit a candle not only for Orietta's and Carlo's work but also for herself and Antonio. *Please send him home to me*, she prayed. Antonio had told her to go to Switzerland and not come back, but Rosa had refused. She couldn't abandon him, especially if it meant he would be treated harshly. Her only hope was that God would intervene in some miraculous way.

The room where the trial was held was cramped and Rosa was not allowed to attend. She sat outside in the corridor, sick with anxiety and the heat.

Signora Corvetto arrived to give testimony on Antonio's behalf because he had been supportive of Rosa's demanding role with the Red Cross. 'I'm so sorry,' she said, taking Rosa's hands in her own. 'If there is anything I can do to help, please come and see me.'

The trial only lasted an hour but Rosa was seeing white spots dancing before her eyes by the time it ended. A group of officials piled out of the room, along with the police sergeant who did not look at her. Rosa stood up and nearly lost her balance when the dizziness rushed to her head.

'Where's my husband?' she asked.

Signora Corvetto moved quickly to Rosa's side. 'They were lenient,' she said. 'They gave him three years.'

'Three years!' Rosa could barely breathe. 'Three years for wanting to see our children!'

Signora Corvetto put her arm around Rosa's shoulders when her legs threatened to give way. 'It *is* lenient,' she said. 'The man before him was sent to fight in the Soviet Union.'

Rosa waited in the visitors' room at Le Murate prison. Being enclosed by prison walls unsettled her but she was determined to be courageous for Antonio. She had brought him two books to read that had been checked over by the guards. She had also brought him some ravioli that she had made herself. She had travelled to the countryside to purchase the vegetables, ricotta and eggs from a farmer because there wasn't enough of anything any more in Florence. Rosa took out her compact and checked her complexion in the mirror. *Devo fare bella figura*, she reminded herself. It was important that she maintain a brave face.

When Antonio was brought out to her, she was relieved to see that he still had colour in his cheeks and seemed to be keeping his spirits up.

'Ah, Spinoza,' he said, looking at the books Rosa had brought him. 'I've always wanted to read philosophy but I've never had the time — until now!'

Rosa felt such tenderness for her husband she thought her tired heart would break with it. 'I've put together a collection of books for you,' she told him. 'But I'm only allowed to bring you two at a time. You'll have to make those last for a while.'

'You're going to Switzerland tomorrow?'

Rosa nodded and did her best to smile. She was torn between her husband and her children. She couldn't bear the thought of leaving Antonio in prison with no-one to visit him, but her children were also fretting. Some days she thought she might go mad with it all.

'Rosa,' said Antonio, sensing her anguish, 'you must be strong. The children haven't seen you for a year and who knows when you will be able to see them again. For their sake — and ours — go and make them happy.'

After her visit to Antonio, Rosa walked across the Ponte Vecchio to the Convent of Santo Spirito. She sat in a shaded doorway, away from the oppressive heat that bounced off the cobblestones, and listened to the nuns singing. She had been forbidden from seeing Suor Maddalena but that did not stop her feeling the comfort of at least being near a place where she had once experienced maternal love. She was hungry for it. She didn't receive that sort of reassurance from Nerezza's notebook or even the silver key, unless she associated it with Ada. She tried to think of Nerezza as her mother, but she felt nothing. Perhaps it was because they'd never had a chance to bond.

On her way home, Rosa saw that posters with anti-Jewish slogans had been plastered on an apartment building and some nearby shops: *The Jews are the Enemies of Italy*; *Death to the Jews*. People were staring at the posters with horrified expressions on their faces.

'Who put these up?' Rosa asked one woman.

The woman shook her head. 'No-one knows. But my son thinks it was the German consulate. They did the same thing in Turin.'

Rosa wanted to rip the posters down but, with Antonio in prison and with her one chance to see the children in Switzerland, she couldn't take the risk of being arrested. She went home feeling as ineffectual as she had when Orietta wouldn't let her join Giustizia e Libertà.

Antonio had predicted correctly when he said that Mussolini would send soldiers to the Russian front whether he was invited to by Germany or not. When Rosa arrived at the station to catch the train to Lugano, she found it swarming with men in uniform. There were women too, crying or staring about them as if in shock. Rosa thought about the books she had given Antonio to read. Spinoza had said that governments that made having an opinion a crime were the most tyrannical of all because everyone has a right to their own thoughts. Rosa looked about the station and wondered what the people there were thinking. She imagined that she could listen in and hear their regrets, sadness and fears. She noticed a boy with curly hair looking up at his brother who was in uniform and wondered if he was regretting harsh words he had spoken to his sibling now that he may never see him again. She turned her attention to the father and imagined that behind his grim eyes he was puzzled as to his inability to praise his son, although he longed to do so. Was the young woman the soldier's fiancée? Rosa studied her doleful eyes. Was she wishing that she had shared one night of passion with her lover instead of insisting that they wait until they were married? Only the soldiers themselves and their mothers could be without regret. The mothers had sacrificed all they could for their children; and no matter what happened to the soldiers, they would be heroes in their family's eyes.

Rosa boarded the train. Her ticket was for a window seat. The luggage racks were overflowing and suitcases were stacked in the aisle. She had to place her luggage around her as best as she could. Once she was settled, she opened the book of poems she had brought to read on the journey. Steam wafted over the platform, sending a ghostly cloud over the people. For a moment they looked like spectres in a green-grey mist. Rosa squinted at them, then gave a start. 'It's impossible,' she whispered. No, there he was again. A man not in uniform moving amongst the soldiers. The strong shoulders, his height, the erect way he held his chin, were familiar to her. Rosa's heart raced. Was it Luciano? She pressed her face to the window, straining to see more clearly. The steam dissipated but there was no sight of the man.

No, she told herself, turning away from the window and closing her eyes. The train whistle sounded and the train lurched forward. I must have been dreaming, Rosa thought. Too much time has passed with no word. Luciano is dead. He perished in Spain.

TWENTY-ONE

Lugano was surrounded by mountains. Rosa's train reached the outskirts of the town a few minutes before ten o'clock. The sky was pure blue and the sun shone on the freshly swept streets. Window boxes brimming with geraniums and crimson begonias decorated the houses. Despite the town being only thirty miles north of Milan, the difference in mood was obvious as soon as she stepped onto the station platform. Even with the growing number of refugees who were fleeing there, Rosa did not sense in Lugano the fear and tension that seemed to be present everywhere in Italy these days. The town's ambience was as pleasant and light as the mountain air that permeated it.

Rosa looked around for Antonio's cousins, Renata and Enzo, hoping that she would recognise them. The photograph she had found in Antonio's album showing an elegant middle-aged couple was nearly ten years old.

'Mamma!'

Rosa's eyes darted amongst the people on the platform as she tried to determine from which direction the voice had come. Then she saw her: Sibilla. Her daughter was wearing a neatly pressed dress and standing with a couple who looked like the people in the photograph. In her free arm, she carried the Lenci doll that Rosa and Antonio had sent for her birthday. Sibilla had grown since Rosa had last seen her and her features were more defined. She was the image of Nerezza. Rosa's heart was torn in two directions: between her longing for her daughter and her painful alienation from her past.

Sibilla moved towards her and Rosa recovered from her inertia. She squeezed between people, apologising when she bumped or knocked them. Sibilla displayed no such patience. She darted between the passengers and shoved other children aside until she reached her mother and threw herself into her arms.

'How I've missed you,' said Rosa, embracing her. She relished the warmth of her daughter's body pressed against her own.

'Where is Babbo?' Sibilla asked. 'Zio Enzo said that he can't come this time?'

A pain jabbed Rosa's heart. She had prepared herself for this moment. 'Babbo is held up by work but will come as soon as he can.'

Sibilla gripped Rosa's hand and tugged her towards Renata and Enzo.

'The boys are with Giuseppina at the apartment,' Renata said, greeting Rosa with kisses. 'They are well and thriving.'

'Come,' said Enzo, welcoming Rosa with a warm embrace and taking her bag. 'It is not far to our apartment. Everything is close here.'

Renata and Enzo's apartment building faced an Italianate piazza with cobblestones and a linden tree in the middle with benches surrounding it. Rosa offered to help Enzo with her bag, which was awkward to carry up the narrow stairs, but he chivalrously refused.

Rosa was greeted by the excited voices of Lorenzo and Giorgio. If not for Lorenzo's resemblance to Antonio and Giorgio's to her, she would not have recognised them.

Despite the scarcities the war in Europe had imposed on the inhabitants of Lugano, the twins had grown rapidly. Their legs poking out from the pants of their sailor suits were sturdy. That Rosa had missed their development the past year struck her with such force she began to tremble. If not for Renata's reassuring hand on her back, she might have broken down. She dropped to her knees and clasped the twins to her as if she would never let them go.

'Come see!' said Lorenzo, breaking away and urging Rosa towards the table where Giuseppina had been giving them a drawing lesson. He held up a picture of an orange train filled with blue passengers. 'We drew you and Babbo coming to see us.'

'Babbo will come later,' Rosa told him, kissing his golden head. 'Meanwhile, we have so much to catch up on.'

She hoisted Giorgio onto her hip before kneeling again to pat Ambrosio, who had come to greet her with licks to her fingers, and Allegra, who sauntered over from her sunny spot on the windowsill to rub against Rosa's leg.

Rosa was so overwhelmed by seeing her children again that she didn't notice how small the apartment was until she went to the bathroom to wash her hands. Apart from the dining room, which also served as a piano room and sitting area, there was a compact kitchen, two bedrooms and a closet. There wasn't any room to spare. Rosa guessed that Giuseppina must be sleeping on the sofa in the dining room, and realised how generous Renata and Enzo had been to take in her children, their nursemaid and the family pets. Despite being over-populated, the apartment was spotless, with no dust anywhere and fresh towels arranged on the bath's edge.

When Rosa returned to the dining room, Giuseppina was making tea. Renata laid out plates and a platter of almond and chocolate biscuits on the table.

'Sibilla baked these,' she said. 'She often makes us treats.'

Rosa smiled at her daughter. 'I'm so proud of you,' she said, pressing her cheek to Sibilla's. Rosa was delighted and saddened at the same time: she had wanted to be the one to teach her daughter to cook.

The morning slipped by quickly while Rosa listened to her children's chatter about their year in Switzerland and the school they attended, Sibilla's ballet lessons, and the sojourns Enzo had taken them on into the mountains. The discussion continued until the lunch of polenta and bean stew Giuseppina had made was served. Afterwards, Enzo suggested that they should take a walk around the lake. Rosa sensed that he and Renata were keen to ask after Antonio.

'Parco Ciani,' Enzo explained to Rosa when they arrived at Viale Carlo Cattaneo, 'is one of the most beautiful parks in Switzerland.'

Rosa agreed that it looked like something from a postcard. The glistening lake with its backdrop of mountains was stunning enough, but the park was also landscaped with flowerbeds of azaleas and roses and shaded by laurels, oleanders and magnolia trees. Sibilla and the twins ran along the paths that crossed the green lawns and wove around statues and pavilions, pulling Giuseppina along with them. Ambrosio bounded after them, much to the dismay of the Swiss who walked their obedient Saint Bernards on leads.

'I didn't think they would react so warmly,' Rosa confided in Renata and Enzo. 'A year is a long time for children. I was afraid that they would be shy with me.'

Enzo directed the women towards a shaded path. 'We talk about you and Antonio every day,' he told Rosa. 'At dinnertime we take turns at guessing what you might have done that day, and every night before bedtime we say prayers for you. You and Antonio are always in our hearts.'

'Thank you,' said Rosa.

Renata linked her arm through Rosa's and walked in step with her. Rosa was taken with the older woman's stately beauty. She wore no jewellery, although her ears were pierced, and her dress, while stylishly cut, was not new. It wasn't artifice that gave Renata her graceful appearance, but something inside her.

'We've kept a diary of what the children have been doing each day,' she told Rosa. 'They grow so quickly at that age and we knew you and Antonio wouldn't want to miss a thing. You can take it back with you. I am sure it will comfort Antonio.'

Rosa was too moved to reply immediately. She was fortunate that her children were in the care of such a kind couple. She had heard of aunts and uncles, grandparents and even nursemaids and governesses trying to win the affection of children they were caring for at the expense of the children's relationship with their parents. But Renata and Enzo were not like that.

'I don't know how we will ever repay your kindness,' she said, finally able to look at Renata and Enzo without wanting to cry.

'Kindness doesn't ask for repayment,' said Renata.

She led Rosa to a bench to sit with her while Enzo went in search of Giuseppina and the children.

'But you've taken in my children, a nursemaid and a dog and cat,' said Rosa. 'You've sacrificed so much for us.'

Renata looked genuinely surprised. 'But I don't see it as a sacrifice at all,' she said. 'I find comfort in their company. And they are good children.'

'I'm glad to hear it,' said Rosa. 'They seem to have borne all that has happened well.'

'As long as their parents look at ease, children seldom worry,' replied Renata.

Enzo called the children back to the lawn in front of Rosa and Renata, and he and Giuseppina played a chasing game with them. Lorenzo squealed with delight when Enzo caught him, making Rosa and Renata laugh.

'My son is in the United States,' said Renata. 'He is a grown man with a family but I have some idea of what you and Antonio are feeling. Please tell me, how is our favourite cousin?'

The thought that Antonio was in a dank and dismal prison while she was enjoying this beautiful scenery tugged at Rosa's heart. How she wished that he could be here, sharing her joy in seeing the children again.

'He puts on a brave face,' she said. 'And I try to tell myself that at least he wasn't sent to the front.'

Renata clucked her tongue. 'We've always been fond of Antonio, although he is some years younger than Enzo and his father moved the family to Florence when he was only a boy.' She turned her gentle eyes on Rosa and smiled. 'And when he married you, we were so pleased. His father had been concerned about Antonio's happiness for years.'

'This terrible war,' Rosa said, thinking of Antonio's imprisonment again. 'They say it will be even worse than the last one.'

Renata picked up a leaf and spun it between her fingers. 'The difference about living in a neutral country ... well, we hear things that we never heard in Italy.'

There was something ominous in Renata's words.

'You mean what's happening with the Jews?' Rosa asked.

'In Italy they were only rumours, but the newspapers here report that in Poland and Austria Jews are being shot in the thousands.'

Rosa's stomach turned. In wars people were killed defending and attacking territory. But shooting civilians like that wasn't war, it was genocide.

'The Germans have been setting up posts in all the Italian cities,' she told Renata. 'We might be allies but it looks to me as though they intend to invade us. I tried to tell Antonio to leave Italy a year ago but he wouldn't hear of it. Now he is in prison and can't go anywhere.'

'When you return to Italy,' Renata said, looking Rosa in the eye, 'you must get rid of any evidence that Antonio has Jewish ancestry.'

Rosa saw that Renata understood the danger her husband faced. 'So you think so too?' she asked. 'You think Germany will take over Italy?'

Renata pursed her lips. 'I'm learning to live with uncertainty,' she said. 'Anything is possible. When Mussolini brought in those wretched racial laws, Nino tried to get us visas to go to America but our application was rejected. So we came to Switzerland instead. One can't forget that we are still next door to Germany.'

'Luckily Switzerland is neutral and likely to stay so,' said Rosa. 'You are much safer here than in Italy.'

Renata shook her head. 'Look at where this country is on the map. Switzerland is not some island in a faraway ocean. It will be impossible for it to remain neutral and avoid invasion. Germany may save us until last, but they will eventually get to Switzerland as a gourmand eventually gets to dessert — and then they will gobble us up whole.'

'Is that what the Swiss think?' Rosa asked. 'Is that what *you* think?'

Renata looked at her with pitying eyes. 'All we have on our side is time. Perhaps this attack on Russia has bought us some more.'

Rosa's month in Switzerland passed quickly. She tried to savour each moment with Sibilla and the twins. On her last night in Lugano, she lay awake agonising over whether she should take the children back with her to Florence. If what Renata had said was true, then Switzerland was in as much danger of invasion as anywhere else. If they had to face danger, wouldn't it be better that they faced it together?

Rosa turned over and gazed at the sleeping faces of the twins and Sibilla. They were crowded into one bed along with Ambrosio and Allegra. Renata had said that Switzerland had more time than Italy. Rosa brushed a strand of hair from Sibilla's forehead. Maybe time did count for something now that Hitler had decided to attack Russia. Hadn't those fearless Slavs repelled Napoleon?

By the next morning, Rosa had made her decision, although leaving the children behind gave her a bitter feeling in her blood. Lorenzo and Giorgio skipped along as the party made its way to the station, confident that their mother would return soon. Only Sibilla guessed the truth and cried floods of tears.

Rosa dried her daughter's face with her handkerchief. 'You've been so brave,' she told her. Her voice faltered but she remembered what Renata had said about the fortitude of children: that they would remain composed as long as their parents did. 'I love you, Sibilla,' she said, kissing her cheeks. 'I always have and I always will.'

Sibilla calmed with her mother's reassurance, but by the time they reached the station Rosa was feeling ill herself.

'Here, take this,' said Enzo, squeezing Rosa's arm and giving her a book of humorous stories. 'It will help pass the time.'

Time, Rosa thought. It was both a friend and an enemy. Time might save Switzerland from the Germans, but it would also rob her of sharing her children's most important years.

Before the train departed, Rosa glanced in the direction of the mountains and then at her children standing on the platform with Enzo and Renata. *Dear God, keep them safe*, she prayed. *Keep them safe for me*.

When the train reached the Italian border, the customs officer checked Rosa's papers and drew red lines over her travel pass before handing it back. 'No more trips abroad, signora,' he said. 'Italy is at war and things are getting worse. You will have to stay in your own country now.'

In Florence, it was apparent that the euphoric anticipation of a quick victory that had pervaded the population at the beginning of the war had dissipated. The tranquil autumn weather was at odds with the gloomy mood of the city.

'From what you say, it seems to finally be dawning on people that Mussolini's propaganda overestimated Italy's ability to wage war,' Antonio told Rosa when she went to visit him. 'Unless Il Duce can produce one of these secret weapons he's been boasting about, Italy is doomed.'

'I hope it won't come to that,' Rosa said. She and Antonio spoke in hushed tones but she sensed the guards had long ceased to care what they said to each other. 'It would be better for Italy to surrender than cause any more destruction.'

Rosa knew what had been meted out to Germany at the Treaty of Versailles, but this time Italy would have to bear the humiliation. Perhaps the Allies would consider that it was Mussolini who had foolishly led the Italian people into this war and punish him rather than the people themselves.

Despite his depressing predictions, Antonio was in good spirits. Rosa's stories about the children amused him and his face lit up when he saw the diary Renata and Enzo had made. He was also pleased with the book Rosa had brought him.

'I've always wanted to read *War and Peace*,' he said, grinning. 'But isn't it ironic? How did you get this past the guard? I didn't think Russian literature would be allowed.'

Rosa shrugged. 'I only thought of it as a classic. The guard looked at it but let me through. I've also brought you a novel by George Eliot, who was British. Maybe they no longer care what we do and read.'

'Something is in the air,' observed Antonio. 'Only a year ago you couldn't sneeze without someone having to put a fascist slant on it.'

Rosa reopened the shop for two afternoons a week and saw customers by appointment. Despite the pessimistic atmosphere, the ever-dwindling rations and the ever-increasing shortages, there were still people with enough money to fill their homes with fine things. The war seemed to have little impact on the privileged unless they had family members serving overseas.

Rosa tried to fill her time with reading, as Antonio did, but she was restless. She was only allowed to visit him twice a week and, with the children away, her days were long and empty. The nights of weary silence were worse. Ylenia had no family to go to and would have difficulty finding employment elsewhere, so Rosa kept her on although she hardly produced enough work to justify a full-time maid. Rosa needed something useful to do but didn't want to return to the Dead, Wounded and Missing office now that Signora Corvetto was no longer working there. When she passed by the hospital one day, she saw a notice calling for volunteer nurses to take up the places of those who had been sent with the military overseas. I could do that, she thought.

'What makes you believe you would be a good nurse?' asked the matron, looking up from Rosa's application form. 'Do you have any experience?'

'I have three children,' Rosa offered.

'You are married?'

'My husband is ... away.'

The matron ticked some boxes on Rosa's form and passed it over to her to sign. Being inexperienced and married would have made her an unlikely candidate in peacetime, but the hospital was desperate for help. Nevertheless, she thought she had better explain the enemy of the state classification on her personal documents in case the matron checked.

'I don't want to know,' said the matron, waving her hand dismissively. 'I don't care if my staff are fascists or not. I turned into an enemy of the state myself when they forced me to dismiss my Jewish nurses.'

Rosa couldn't believe what she was hearing. She'd been discriminated against for being an orphan, she'd suffered after Maria's death because of her supposed anti-fascist activities, and she'd been snubbed as an unwed mother. Suddenly, no-one cared what she was as long as she was useful to the war effort.

'You have training lectures twice a week,' the matron told her. 'Otherwise you start at six o'clock each morning.'

'When do I commence?' Rosa asked.

The matron raised her eyebrows. 'You start tomorrow.'

Rosa was puzzled. How could she help unless she went to lectures first? 'But I haven't been trained yet,' she said.

The matron sucked in a breath. 'Signora Parigi, someone will show you tomorrow how to sluice a bedpan.'

The work of a trainee nurse was arduous but Rosa was thankful for it because it kept her mind occupied. Many of the hospital's nurses were serving overseas and most of the orderlies had been conscripted, so the remaining staff were harried and put Rosa to work without hesitation. Even before she'd had her uniform made, she was cleaning bottles, scrubbing bedpans and washing soiled sheets. She performed all these activities without complaint but her favourite task was making up beds. There was something meditative about the feel of linen between her fingers as she stretched the sheets taut and mitred the corners. It reminded her of her time in the convent, where daily tasks were performed with reverence. It was a shield against her worries and distracted her from the danger looming from the outside world. But her menial tasks did not protect her from harsh realities for long.

'Nurse, could you come here, please.'

Rosa was folding linen and placing it in a cupboard. She looked up to see a doctor standing in the doorway of the ward where critical patients were nursed. The bombing of Milan and Genoa had left many of the hospitals in those cities inoperable — either as a result of being directly hit or because of the loss of gas, electricity and water supplies. Patients considered able to be moved were sent to Rome and Florence. The ward was full after the last bombing raid on Genoa.

Rosa was unused to being referred to as 'Nurse' and didn't realise that the doctor was addressing her.

'Nurse, this is urgent! Please hurry!' he said.

She closed the linen cupboard and followed the doctor into the ward. 'Excuse me, dottore, but I'm only a trainee …' Her voice caught in her throat when she saw the patient lying on the bed before her. It was a boy of about twelve years of age. He was missing part of one arm and both legs. The boy's head was bandaged but his eyes were open. Rosa could barely bring herself to look at his torso, which was a mass of black tissue oozing with fluid. Until then, her main contact with patients had been to help the nurses feed the elderly and the children. She hadn't witnessed an operation yet. The sight of the boy's wounds was a shock. It took all her strength to remain upright. The smell of charred and rotting flesh brought bile to her throat.

'You're only a trainee?' said the doctor, slipping on gloves and picking up a pair of scissors. 'Well, you'd better get up to speed fast. We are going to see more of this before the day is out. This boy is the only survivor of an entire street. Everyone and everything else was blown to smithereens.'

The doctor was young, in his thirties. He had a trim moustache and fine hands. Rosa saw from his tag that his name was Dottor Greco. He wasn't being arrogant with her, only matter-of-fact. When she realised that he intended to cut away at the dead flesh, she offered to administer the morphine.

'I have been trained to give injections,' she said.

Dottor Greco pursed his lips. 'That won't be necessary,' he said.

Rosa stared at him in horror. 'No morphine? Are we that short?' she asked.

He shook his head. 'Dealing with the dressings is going to be a daily matter. We can't give this patient morphine every time.'

Rosa's hands trembled when she passed the instruments to Dottor Greco as he called for them. The matron had said that the nurses should see things from a medical perspective, but Rosa could not forget that it was a young boy lying there in the bed, in dreadful pain, able to hear but unable to speak. She did her best to comfort him although she could see in the boy's eyes that every incision the doctor made caused him agony. Even the one arm left to him was so badly burnt that he couldn't move it. He was immobile, shut in a living hell.

When the ordeal was over, Dottor Greco rebandaged the boy's torso. Rosa was bathed in sweat. Dottor Greco looked directly at her for the first time when he had finished dressing the boy's wounds. His grim face showed the anguish he felt too, although his voice was steady. 'I'll get the sister to show you how to clean his eyes,' he said. 'I need someone diligent.'

At Dottor Greco's request, Rosa was transferred from auxiliary duties to working in the most difficult ward of all. But when the matron asked Rosa if she would prefer to be replaced with someone more experienced, she declined. In the weeks that followed, she gradually moved from being horrified by the lipless faces, fingerless hands and twisted flesh of the bomb victims to seeing the people beneath the wounds. With all the hell these disfigured patients had suffered, and would suffer for the rest of their lives, she made it her mission that at least none of them would lose their sight due to neglect. She cleaned the area around the patients' eyes every four hours with a saline solution, and impressed upon the night volunteer the importance of doing the same.

There were two senior nurses who worked with Rosa in the ward: Nurse Mazzetti, an extroverted woman in her late twenties; and Nurse Tommaselli, who was petite with a wide forehead, minute nose and a pointed chin. She looked like a mouse and twitched like one too.

One day when Rosa was helping Nurse Mazzetti remove stitches from a man's arm, the patient turned to them and said, 'Why aren't you two married?'

'Nurse Parigi is married,' Nurse Mazzetti told him, winking at Rosa. 'It's me who's looking for a husband.'

'Why is she here then?' the patient asked.

'My husband and children are away,' Rosa explained. 'I wanted to put myself to good use.'

'Well, no-one can change the sheets like you can,' the patient said to Rosa. 'You're the only one who doesn't make it feel like my skin is being ripped off again.'

'Changing sheets with the patient still in the bed is my speciality,' said Rosa with a laugh. 'I was awarded ten out of ten for my bed-making exam.'

Nurse Mazzetti glanced at Rosa and smiled. 'And Matron doesn't give perfect scores often,' she said in a tongue-in-cheek tone. 'In fact, until Nurse Parigi arrived it was unheard of.'

Rosa was glad for the camaraderie she felt with Nurse Mazzetti. It was a comfort because, despite the dedication of the nurses in the ward and Dottor Greco, they lost a patient a day. Some days they lost many more.

'It's septicaemia,' Nurse Mazzetti explained to Rosa one day when they were washing down a bed with carbolic acid. 'Despite all the care we take, infection in burns injuries is difficult to avoid.'

She flicked her head in the direction of the boy Rosa had seen on her first day on the ward. He couldn't speak to tell them who he was, so the nurses had named him 'Niccolò', after the patron saint of children. 'How's he progressing?' Nurse Mazzetti asked.

'His vital organs are intact,' Rosa said. 'He should be able to eat on his own soon.'

'Well, he's in good hands with you looking after him. Everyone admires your dedication. Even Dottor Greco commented on it.'

Rosa didn't tell Nurse Mazzetti, who scoffed at religion, that she prayed for Niccolò every day. Rosa intended that when the boy was better he would come and live with her. She couldn't bear to think that after all he had suffered, he'd be sent to an orphanage.

'The worst pain for the bomb victims,' the matron had told the volunteer nurses in one lecture, 'is not the horrific physical injuries they've suffered but the psychological ones.'

When Rosa arrived for work a few days later, she knew from Dottor Greco's averted eyes and the pained expression on Nurse Mazzetti's face that another patient had died overnight.

'Who?' she asked.

Nurse Mazzetti squeezed Rosa's shoulder. 'You know it's for the best.'

'Niccolò?'

Nurse Mazzetti nodded, and Rosa felt something inside her grow cold. The boy's death was for the best, she knew. Despite all the love and care Rosa and her family would have lavished on him, his injuries would have left him with a miserable life. But it wasn't fair that he should have suffered in the first place. What sort of army dropped bombs on civilians? Rosa looked around the ward. Most of these pitiful, mutilated people were doomed. What was Italy at war for? What was all this suffering accomplishing?

Rosa turned back to Nurse Mazzetti, fighting her tears. 'Has he been laid out?'

Nurse Mazzetti shook her head. 'We waited for you.'

Rosa's legs were leaden as she made her way to Niccolò's bed. The curtains around it had been drawn. She remembered the many mornings when she had approached the bed apprehensively, fearful that the boy had died overnight. She'd always been elated when she'd discovered him breathing. Now the day she had dreaded had come. Niccolò was covered with a sheet. Rosa gently lifted it and looked at his ashen face.

'You're with your Mamma and Babbo again now,' she whispered through her tears. 'With your brothers and sisters, aunts and uncles, your neighbours and friends, and your pets. They will be happy to see you again.'

Nurse Tommaselli appeared. 'I'll take him to the mortuary,' she said to Rosa. 'It might be hard for you. I know you were fond of him.'

Rosa was grateful for Nurse Tommaselli's kindness. Most of the time they were all so rushed off their feet there was no time to stop and support each other. The three nurses lifted the boy onto the trolley and Nurse Tommaselli wheeled him away. Rosa stripped the bed. It was her way of dealing with grief when a patient died. Only this time her emotions got the better of her and tears spilled from her eyes.

'When we finish our shift, we'll have a cigarette together,' Nurse Mazzetti said to her.

'I'll come with you to the canteen but I don't smoke,' Rosa replied.

'Lucky you!' said Nurse Mazzetti. 'When I worked with tuberculosis patients, the ward sister told me to have a cigarette after each shift to kill germs. Now I'm hooked. It's killing me because I can barely get a cigarette a day because of this confounded war. My mother has been drying oak leaves for me. Can you imagine? The smell is disgusting.'

Rosa could imagine. She didn't like Antonio smoking even normal cigarettes in the house or shop.

'Seriously,' said Nurse Mazzetti, 'you need to talk about this, Nurse Parigi. It's been a tough morning.'

When Rosa arrived at the canteen after reporting Niccolò's death to the matron, Nurse Mazzetti was already there with Nurse Tommaselli.

'None of this formal stuff,' Nurse Mazzetti said. 'We'll save that for the ward. I'm Gina and this is Fiamma.'

'You're doing very well,' Fiamma said, fixing her intense eyes on Rosa. 'I don't know how you manage to study on top of it all.'

'Without my family I have a lot of time on my hands,' Rosa told her.

'It's good of you to have volunteered,' said Gina. 'And then to have ended up in our ward after just a few weeks ...'

'Many experienced nurses can't take it,' agreed Fiamma. 'They can't stand the smell or the sight of the injuries, let alone changing the dressings ... It's like we are torturing our patients rather than helping them.'

'I remember when I came to the ward,' said Gina, lighting one of her oak-leaf cigarettes, 'I thought I'd seen it all. Then one day Dottor Greco was unravelling the bandages from a burn patient's head and the man's ears came off. I fainted.'

The women shook their heads and chuckled. There was nothing humorous about a man losing his ears, but the thought of Gina fainting in front of Dottor Greco amused them. They needed something to laugh at to stop them losing their sanity. The three women talked about the patients and staff. They didn't speak about the war. It was obvious things were getting worse. In some of the wards, rationing was so severe that the nurses handed out hot-water bottles to relieve the patients' hunger pains. The nurses were supposed to be given a free lunch each day. Lately Rosa, Gina and Fiamma had been sharing their food with their patients, unable to bear seeing the sick and suffering going without.

'You know, the worst thing I ever encountered,' said Fiamma, her eyes growing dark, 'was a young woman from Milan. Her arms and legs had been blown off in an Allied bomb attack. She'd lost the sight in one eye and all her teeth from the impact. I was on the night shift and every time I went to check on her, she begged me to end her life. "I'll never marry, I'll never have children. They'll put me in an institution." We had to drain her wounds every day and she was in agony. The woman was suffering so much that … well, one night when she was sleeping I nearly did put a pillow over her face. But that would be a sin, wouldn't it? Mercifully she died a few days later.'

Rosa shuddered. She still believed in God, but the war and working as a nurse had made her question some of the Church's teachings. Could it really be a sin to show mercy to another human being who was suffering that much?

In the visiting room at the prison, Rosa put on her brightest smile for Antonio. 'Ylenia made some gnocchi for you,' she told him. 'And I've brought Gorky for you to read.'

'I'll be fat and Russian by the time they let me out,' Antonio said, grinning at her. 'How are things at the hospital? Are you still enjoying what you are learning?'

Rosa told him about her training lectures. She did not tell him about Niccolò or the other patients who had died that week. She didn't tell him there was barely enough food to feed everyone and that she had heard from one nurse that in the mental asylums the inmates were being left to starve. Rosa kept her feelings to herself; she did not want to burden her husband. Then it occurred to her that maybe Antonio wasn't telling her everything either. He was cheerful when she came to visit him and clean-shaven. He assured her that he was being treated well and given sufficient to eat, but she could see that, despite the extra food she brought him, he was growing thin. Yet from his outward demeanour one could be fooled into thinking that his prison term was nothing more than an opportunity to catch up on his reading. Rosa knew it wasn't like that. We are both acting, she thought. Doing our best to paint a bright picture so as not to upset the other one.

When Rosa climbed into bed that night, she longed more than ever for her family. If she had Antonio near and could hug her children and pat Ambrosio and stroke Allegra, then somehow, she thought, she might even forget that there was a war on and embrace everything that was good about life again.

In December 1941, Japan, the third point of the axis with Italy and Germany, attacked Pearl Harbor and brought the United States into the war.

'That attack only served as a diversion,' Antonio told Rosa while they shivered one day in the prison visiting room at the beginning of 1942. 'Everyone knows the Germans are losing in the Soviet Union. After the initial successes the bitter Russian winter is slaughtering them.'

'There's a train of injured people from Genoa arriving today,' the matron told Rosa when she reported for duty. 'You are going to the station with Dottor Greco and some nurses from the casualty ward.'

It was the second trainload of new patients in the last week. Rosa wasn't sure how they were going to cope. The matron told her that some buildings in Florence had been selected to house patients who couldn't be treated in the main hospital, and that she was recruiting more volunteers.

When the train arrived, Dottor Greco instructed Rosa to attend to the last carriage. 'They have some Allied soldiers to be transported to the prisoner-of-war hospital. They'll need someone who can speak English to check them over.'

Rosa rushed past the stretchers and people on crutches to the last carriage, which was guarded by soldiers and police. Two other nurses who could speak some English came with her to help. Rosa heard a man moaning.

'Nurse?' a soldier in a blue uniform called out to her. His leg was bandaged and he stood on crutches near another man laid out on a stretcher. The prostrate man had an amputated arm and was writhing in agony.

'When was his surgery?' Rosa asked, kneeling down beside the man.

'Yesterday,' the soldier on crutches told her.

Rosa hesitated, not sure that she had heard him correctly. The hospital in Genoa couldn't possibly have sent out a patient so soon after major surgery! She didn't want to remove the man's bandage in these unhygienic conditions but from the shape of the cut it was a guillotine amputation, the kind that was performed in a hurry.

'I'm going to give your friend something for the pain,' she told the soldier on crutches.

She opened her kitbag and took out a syringe to draw the morphine. After a few minutes, the man with the amputation stopped writhing. The morphine wouldn't get rid of the pain completely but she could tell he was feeling relief. He was going to need further surgery. Rosa knew he had a slim chance of surviving.

'You're a good woman,' said the soldier on crutches. 'The nurses on the train wouldn't even give him a sip of water.'

Rosa wasn't supposed to engage in conversation with the prisoners beyond assessing their medical needs. But she looked up and noticed the soldier had a disarming smile. All the men in that uniform seemed to share the same square-jawed faces and tanned skin. They were about the same age as Rosa, perhaps younger. She looked over her shoulder. The police and Italian soldiers were occupied getting the patients on stretchers into the waiting ambulances.

'Which part of England are you from?' she asked the soldier. 'I don't quite understand your accent.'

The soldier laughed and his periwinkle-blue eyes seemed to turn even bluer. 'I'm from the very southern part of England,' he said. 'It's called Australia.'

Rosa understood the joke and smiled. 'Ah, Australia,' she said. 'Yes, I know it.' She remembered the woman with the Schiaparelli belt. 'You have kangaroos. When you go home, tell the people not to shoot them any more. They are beautiful. They should be taking care of them, not slaughtering them.'

The soldier's face turned serious. 'When I return home, I won't be shooting anything,' he said. 'I'll put my uniform and gun away forever. You can be sure of that. I've had a gutful of killing.'

An Italian policeman called out an order and Rosa and the Allied prisoner stopped talking. Two army orderlies picked up the man on the stretcher and the other prisoners who could walk were marched to the trucks. Rosa watched the soldier depart and wondered what kind of treatment he would get in the prisoner-of-war camps if the nurses on the train wouldn't even give his dying friend water.

She turned to signal to the other nurses to rejoin Dottor Greco who was still busy assessing the civilian patients. She was shocked when one of the nurses glared at her before spitting at her feet.

'English-lover!' the nurse growled. 'Whore!'

Rosa recoiled at the words. Had the woman lost her mind?

'You wasted morphine on that sheep farmer,' the nurse said, her eyes blazing, 'when there is a shortage of it for our own people!'

Rosa answered with genuine surprise: 'May I remind you that as nurses we have pledged to give aid to *all* who need it. That man was in agony.'

'Really?' the nurse retorted, her lips curling into a snarl. She pointed at the civilian patients. Most of them were women and children. One infant was wailing and the sound of its distress was sickening. The nurse turned back to Rosa. 'Do you know who those men are? They are the downed pilots who bombed Genoa. They've killed and inflicted unspeakable injuries on innocent women and children and you want to give them morphine to ease their pain! Why didn't you slit their throats!'

What happened at the station affected Rosa more than all the other horrible events that had occurred since the war broke out. Finally her veneer of cheerfulness in front of Antonio broke. She couldn't hide her tears. She had no idea how to reconcile her feelings of compassion for the Allied prisoners with her anger at what had happened to the children blown apart by their bombs. She had since learnt that downed Allied pilots were transferred to German prisoner-of-war camps where the conditions were harsher. The Australian pilot she had seen probably wouldn't survive the war.

'Rosa, what else could you have done?' Antonio said when she told him about it. 'It's your duty as a nurse to care.'

'I feel like I'm going crazy,' she said. 'They didn't look like cold-hearted killers. They looked like decent young men.'

'They probably are decent young men,' he answered. 'You've got to understand that we are doing the same to them. Their nurses are trying to put together innocent English children who have been blown to bits by *our* bombs — and we still expect the British to treat our pilots well!'

'The whole thing is a mess,' Rosa said.

Antonio reached out and touched her wrist. The guard didn't stop him. 'You know, once war breaks out there are no decent men and no morals any more,' he said. 'If people start thinking that way they will be defeated. What all the decent people need to do before war even breaks out is say "No!". That is the time to be decent. That's the only time it will do any good. But that's not what we Italians did. We either cheered Mussolini on for our material gain or tried to ignore him. Now we pay the price.'

Rosa sat back and thought of the things Luciano had said against Mussolini and the fascists all those years ago. He had been right. But the memory of it made her cry even harder.

In May the following year, Rosa arrived at the hospital to find the doctors and nurses milling around in shock. The Allies had just bombed Rome.

'I never believed that could happen,' said Fiamma. 'I thought all the Catholics around the world would object because of the Vatican. What next?'

Rosa realised that she and Fiamma were thinking the same thing: if the Allies could bomb Rome, then there was nothing to stop them bombing Florence. The tension amongst the hospital staff intensified when they realised that what had happened to the patients from Genoa and Milan could happen to them. The junior nurses changed the light bulbs to blue ones and checked the blackout curtains. When Rosa left that day, she saw volunteers sandbagging the hospital's ground-floor windows.

When she got home, she, Ylenia and the remaining neighbours in their apartment building stocked up the cellar with supplies and blankets, although Rosa knew from the patients she had been treating that a cellar wasn't much protection if a building was hit. When she climbed into bed that night she couldn't stop thinking of Antonio in Le Murate prison. He had assured her that the guards would move the prisoners to the cellars and bomb shelters if Florence was attacked, but Rosa didn't believe it. She was sure that if there was an air raid, the guards wouldn't release the prisoners. They'd be left in their cells like sitting ducks.

TWENTY-TWO

In July 1943, the Allies invaded Sicily, and Rome was bombed again despite the Pope's appeal to Roosevelt to spare the city. With the crushing defeats in Africa and the union strikes that were breaking out in the factories, it was clear Italy was crumbling. At the hospital, the staff and volunteers could no longer cope with the influx of patients from the other cities as well as the growing number of repatriated soldiers. While the shortages of everything were difficult, Rosa was horrified to discover that the only treatment many of the transferred patients had received before arriving was a dose of bismuth.

At the commencement of the war, the nurses' training course had been reduced from four to three years. With Italy's impending defeat, Rosa found herself performing the duties of a senior nurse well before her time, including training the auxiliary volunteers. There wasn't much scope for 'training' as such. The chaos in the hospital meant that Rosa had to show the volunteers once what she needed them to do and then leave them to it. Still, she felt herself in a better position than Fiamma, who had been transferred to triage, where incoming patients were coded with green, yellow or red cards depending on the severity of their condition.

'Consider yourself lucky!' the matron screamed at Fiamma one day when the nurse broke down at the announcement of another influx of patients. 'A military nurse in your position has it much tougher than you. She has to pass over critically injured men and attend to the ones most likely to be able to be sent out to fight again!'

The matron was showing signs of strain herself. In the past few months her hair had turned from salt-and-pepper grey to stark white. She wasn't the most even-tempered woman at the best of times and the war had pushed her beyond her limits. Still, she tried to help her nurses wherever possible.

'I've found some extra hands for you,' she told Rosa one morning. 'Nuns.'

Rosa wasn't surprised to have nuns as auxiliary nurses. Nuns had been attached to the hospital since its foundation and had been the original carers. They worked everywhere from the laundry room to the kitchen and Rosa found them resourceful and indefatigable. What surprised her was that the matron had found *more* nuns somewhere. Rosa had been convinced that any nun belonging to a charitable order must be fully employed in some sort of civil work. She had even seen nuns sandbagging buildings.

The matron told Rosa that the new recruits were waiting for her in the foyer. Rosa straightened her uniform and apron and donned her nurse's cape, which she thought gave her a look of authority despite the inexperience she felt inside. She flew down the stairs, past stretchers and nurses, and stopped in her tracks when she reached the foyer. She was stunned by the sight of the coifs, the black veils, the crosses and rosaries. The nuns waiting for her were not the usual sisters of charity who had professed vows of poverty, chastity, obedience and to serve humankind. These were religious nuns, those who had taken the solemn vows of enclosure from the world. Rosa found herself facing the nuns from the Convent of Santo Spirito where she had been brought up.

She approached the group as if in a dream. Most of the nuns were young and would have entered the convent after she had left. But there were some familiar faces too.

'Rosa!' an excited voice called out. It was Suor Dorotea who had helped Suor Maddalena in the kitchen.

Rosa felt short of breath. The appearance of the nuns had caused her to lose her bearings. She knew that some members of the order could voluntarily come out of enclosure under exceptional circumstances, and the demise of Italy must have been considered such a circumstance. She caught sight of Suor Valeria, the oldest of the group. The nun looked bewildered but determined. Florence must have changed since she had last seen it, when she had come out of enclosure during the Great War.

'Rosa! You are a nurse!' said Suor Dorotea, her eyes twinkling. 'We have come to serve the hospital. We have devoted all these years to prayer and now we are ready to help!'

'Suor Maddalena?' Rosa asked. 'Is she coming too?'

'*Madre* Maddalena,' Suor Dorotea corrected her. 'She is the Badessa now and will stay at the convent with the remaining nuns.'

The desperate situation at the hospital snapped Rosa out of her shock and back into action. She demonstrated the basics of patient care to the nuns. They took to their tasks in the convalescent ward without hesitation. Before the morning was out, they had the fundamentals of hygiene in hand. They were natural nurses in that they went about their work with an efficient calmness and had a positive effect on the patients.

That evening, Rosa sat up in bed and tried to take in what had occurred at the hospital. She was seized by a longing to see Suor ... no, *Madre* Maddalena again. Rosa thought it strange that despite her conviction that Nerezza was her natural mother, she was more impatient to see Madre Maddalena than she was to discover what had happened at the villa and why she had been sent to a convent. That, she had told herself, could wait. She took out some stationery and wrote Madre Maddalena a letter. She started by telling her that she was grateful that she had allowed some of the convent's nuns out of enclosure, and praised each one of them individually before adding:

> *With Florence in grave danger and the Allies rapidly approaching, you and I may never see each other again in this earthly life. I want you to know that I have not forgotten the love and faith with which you filled my childhood. Although my trust in God has taken many beatings, I have never lost it. It has brought me comfort in even my darkest hours.*
>
> *I have three children, Sibilla, Lorenzo and Giorgio, who have all been brought up in the Church. I am now a nurse helping those civilians and some soldiers who have been injured in this great tragedy. I rely on my faith daily to carry out my work.*
>
> *I would like to see you Thursday afternoon. As you may or may not be aware, I tried to visit you after I married but I was turned away by the former Badessa, who believed she had your best interests at heart. If your portress nun does not permit me entrance on Thursday afternoon, I promise that I will finally accept that it is not your desire to see me and I will never trouble you again.*
>
> *With love and fond memories,*
> *Your Rosa*

On the appointed Thursday afternoon, Rosa went to the convent after finishing her shift at the hospital. She stood before the weather-beaten door and braced herself. She was exhilarated and nervous at the same time. She touched the cross and key around her neck before ringing the bell. An image of Suor Maddalena placing a flute in her hands on her seventh birthday came to her. She remembered running to the kitchen after her lessons to find Suor Maddalena peeling potatoes and ready to hear all about her day. With such fond recollections, to think that the rich and beautiful Nerezza was her mother seemed like sacrilege.

When the portress nun answered the door, Rosa's breath quickened. She recognised the nun as the novice who had packed her bag for her on her last day at the convent. Though, of course, she was older now and no longer a novice.

'Good afternoon,' Rosa said in a hoarse voice. 'I have come to see the Reverenda Madre.'

The nun's face broke into a smile. 'Come this way, Rosa,' she said.

Rosa's heart leapt with joy. If it had been appropriate, she would have embraced the nun in gratitude.

On entering the parlour, she was assailed with familiar smells and memories. The blue-and-white décor had not changed, nor the smell of beeswax, incense and dusty Bibles. She took a seat and then noticed the portress nun had disappeared. Wasn't she supposed to stay to supervise the conversation?

Rosa squeezed her hands to control her emotions when she heard the familiar bell ring, signifying that the door to the outside world had been closed. The wooden shutter flew open and for a few seconds she and Madre Maddalena stared at each other. Rosa was so taken aback to see her childhood guardian's much-longed-for face that at first she felt she was looking at an apparition. She expected that Madre Maddalena, given her new position, might be aloof so was touched to see that she was also smiling and weeping at the same time. Rosa found it surreal that she and Madre Maddalena faced each other in their respective uniforms:

Madre Maddalena in her nun's habit, and Rosa in her nurse's outfit. Rosa Bellocchi was *Sister* Parigi now. It was a few minutes before either woman could speak.

'How good of you to come,' Madre Maddalena said finally, dabbing at her eyes. 'How good of you to remember me.'

'I wanted so much to see you,' Rosa replied. 'Many times.'

'It took this dreadful event to bring us together again,' Madre Maddalena said. 'Too many years have passed. And now look at you ... you are a wife and mother and you are serving God and your country.'

Rosa wanted to tell Madre Maddalena about Sibilla and the twins but tears choked her voice and she couldn't speak.

'I'm so proud of you,' Madre Maddalena continued. 'You're every bit as magnificent as I knew you would turn out to be.'

Rosa took a deep breath before speaking. 'But I thought ... I thought you believed that I ...' Madre Maddalena has never been ashamed of me, Rosa realised, weeping again. She has always expected the best of me. 'Your prayers were answered,' she told Madre Maddalena. 'Before this war I had a very good life.'

Madre Maddalena reached her hand towards the grille and Rosa rested hers against it. 'You will again, dear Rosa,' she assured her.

Rosa saw a picture of Madre Maddalena coming to her apartment once the war was over and having dinner with Antonio and the children.

'Will you come out of enclosure too?' she asked her.

Madre Maddalena shook her head. 'No, my place is here, and when the crisis has passed, my little flock of nuns must return too. This is our community. This is what we have chosen.'

Rosa and Madre Maddalena told each other about some of the things that had happened since they had seen each other last. Rosa learned of the death of the old Badessa and the new priest, Don Franchini, who had replaced the ailing Don Marzoli. Time passed quickly and soon Madre Maddalena had to return to her work. When they stood up to part, Rosa felt compelled to ask about Nerezza.

'She took music lessons here as a girl, didn't she?'

Madre Maddalena paused before she answered. 'It was before my time, although I do remember some of the others talking about her,' she said. 'I believe she was an exceptional musician. But, Rosa ... don't go anywhere near that family. I've never forgiven myself or Don Marzoli for allowing you to be sent there. And as for the Marchesa Scarfiotti, we've heard terrible stories.'

'What?' asked Rosa. 'I know that she's been entertaining fascists.'

Madre Maddalena turned pale. 'Worse than that. She's opened up her villa to some high-ranking German SS officers for "rest and recreation". Don Franchini has instructed the convent to accept no further donations from the Scarfiotti family.'

Rosa wasn't shocked. That sort of self-indulgent and arrogant behaviour was typical of the Marchesa. But, in the end, the Germans were Italy's allies, so the Marchesa could hardly be accused of frolicking with the enemy. But then Rosa noticed Madre Maddalena's hands were trembling.

'What is it?' she asked.

Madre Maddalena glanced away and shook her head.

A chill niggled Rosa's shoulders. Something terrible was going on at the villa. She could sense it.

'Please tell me,' she said. 'I worry very much for the girl, Clementina.'

Madre Maddalena turned to face Rosa. 'There were two servants at the Villa Scarfiotti who were investigated by the SS and found to have gypsy origins.'

The pulse in Rosa's temple began to pound and her legs became unsteady. All her instincts were telling her that something too horrible to imagine had occurred. She wanted to sit down but she willed herself to remain standing and listen to Madre Maddalena.

'A gardener who no longer works at the villa came to Don Franchini after a particularly debauched and drunken party had occurred there,' Madre Maddalena said. 'He told Don Franchini that the SS officers along with the Marchesa forced the two servants into the woods and ... hunted them like wild animals. They shot them for sport.'

Rosa covered her hand with her mouth. She could have screamed. No! It's not possible, she thought. That is cold-blooded murder! But then she remembered the things she had seen the Marchesa do: her cruel treatment of the man with the cowlick; sending away Nerezza's piano while her husband wept; and her order to destroy the Weimaraner puppy. Rosa realised that she *could* believe it. Then a worse thought came to her.

'Was it the cook and her assistant?' she asked. Rosa knew Ada and Paolina were witches but not whether they had gypsy blood.

Madre Maddalena shook her head. 'I don't know. I had the impression that the servants were men.'

Rosa thought quickly. She did recall two of the footmen had swarthy complexions. Why did God not strike the Marchesa down, Rosa wondered. She thought about the legend Ada had told her about Orsola Canova. Was the witch still there, lurking in the woods and waiting for justice? If so, she was losing. Evil and murder still reigned at the Villa Scarfiotti.

The story of the shocking deaths at the Villa Scarfiotti disturbed Rosa more than the news that the Allies were about to seize Rome and might be in Florence before the end of the month. She was starting to think that an Allied victory may not be the worst thing that could happen to Italy; what she feared most was the death and destruction that would be necessary to secure it if Italy continued to fight.

On her next visit to Madre Maddalena, Rosa confessed her suspicions that she was Nerezza's daughter.

'It's possible,' agreed Madre Maddalena. 'This convent has had a connection with the family for a long time. But the Wolf — who was he then?' she asked.

Rosa looked at the date in the back of the notebook again: 13 March 1914. Then she read out aloud the letter from Baron Derveaux, which mentioned that Nerezza had written about a matter of 'great importance' to tell him. It was obvious that they were close. Rosa also read the letter Nerezza had written to her husband and looked at the date.

'Nerezza never made that trip to Paris to tell Baron Derveaux what she had intended to,' she said to Madre Maddalena. 'Why?'

She laid out the notebook and the letters side by side. The date in March had been crossed out. Was it an unhappy memory? Nerezza had received a letter from the Baron in May and soon afterwards she had written to her husband, Ferdinando, wanting to see him although there was an obvious coldness between them.

Rosa sat back and sighed. She knew she had been brought to the convent in December 1914 as a newborn. She looked at the two dates again: March 1914 and December 1914, nine months apart. Her heart gave a jolt. Why had she not seen the obvious before?

'Oh!' she said, standing up and looking at Madre Maddalena. The knowing feeling in her stomach told her that she was right. 'The date that has been crossed out is the date I was conceived!'

'The silver key was in your wrappings,' said Madre Maddalena. 'If the villa's cook put it there, then it's possible you are Nerezza's daughter. The timing makes perfect sense. And the fact that the convent is well known to the Scarfiotti family could be the reason you were brought here.'

Madre Maddalena read the letters from the Baron Derveaux and Nerezza's husband again herself, but could make no more sense of them than Rosa already had.

When it was time to part, Rosa said, 'I can't tell you how happy I am that you agreed to see me. When I was separated from you, I felt as if part of my heart was missing.'

The nun's eyes misted. 'I'm glad of it too,' she said. 'And when the war is over, I want you to bring your husband and children to see me.'

'Truly?' Rosa asked. She was surprised. The only men permitted to pay personal visits to the nuns of Santo Spirito were blood relatives.

'Oh, yes, I intend for there to be changes around here,' said Madre Maddalena with a smile. 'I still believe in having a separate sanctuary in which to worship and pray to God — but we need to be of earthly use too.'

Rosa made her way to the hospital the following morning still feeling agitated by her discovery. Madre Maddalena had asked her to bring the notebook again the following week so they could put together more pieces of the puzzle. Until then, Rosa had to wrestle with her thoughts alone. If Nerezza's relationship with her husband had been antagonistic, she might have been less than thrilled to find herself pregnant with his child. Rosa was surprised to discover the idea did not hurt her the way it might have if she had learnt she was unwanted several years before. Now that she was reconciled with Madre Maddalena, her search for her roots came from a desire for understanding rather than her emotions. Or so she thought.

Rosa was so caught up in the mystery that she was halfway to the hospital before she realised something odd was happening around her. People were out on the streets much earlier than usual and they looked ... *happy*! Cafés were open again, although they had nothing to offer other than ersatz coffee and sugarless cakes. Rosa wondered what had happened to make the grim mood of Florence change so dramatically. Had Italy surrendered? No, that would have produced an anxious mood with people wondering what the Allies intended to do to them. What then? Had some miracle forced the Allies off Italian soil — like the closing of the Red Sea on Pharaoh's army?

Rosa stopped a policeman to ask him. He stared at her in disbelief. 'You haven't heard? Mussolini has been deposed!'

Rosa still hadn't taken in the news when she reached the hospital. But she knew it must be true when the matron embraced her.

'I've smashed all that bastard's pictures!' she told Rosa gleefully.

Even the patients who were without sufficient pain medication brightened with the news. One elderly patient wanted to waltz with Rosa until she convinced him she would be happier if he stayed in bed. Dottor Greco told Rosa that Mussolini had been ousted by the Fascist Grand Council, which included Galeazzo Ciano, the dictator's own son-in-law. King Victor Emmanuel, who Mussolini had reduced to a figurehead, had taken on the role of commander-in-chief of the Italian armed forces, and Generale Badoglio was now the prime minister in Mussolini's place.

'But that means the war will continue,' said Rosa. 'How could that be good news?'

'I don't think that the war will go on now,' said Dottor Greco. 'The Grand Council ousted Mussolini because he insisted that Italy continue to fight although the country is on the verge of collapse.'

Mussolini was imprisoned high in the Abruzzi Apennines. Rosa thought it justice for all the suffering he had caused those, including herself, who had been imprisoned while he was in power.

When she had finished her shift at the hospital, she rushed to Le Murate prison to see Antonio.

'I don't know what's going to happen now,' she told him. 'But the guard thinks that political prisoners and those who made only minor fascist breaches will be released.'

Rosa expected that Antonio would be delighted by the news. Instead he looked at her with reproach.

'What is it?' she asked.

'I wonder what Hitler will do when he finds out that the Italians have ditched their leader,' he said.

Rosa bit her lip. She had wondered about that too. 'The Allies are already in Italy and moving towards the north,' she said, repeating the opinion Dottor Greco had given her earlier. 'The Germans are retreating. Once Italy and the Allies make peace, the Italian army won't be standing in the way of the progress of the Allied forces. The Germans will be finished.'

'Yes, let's hope so,' said Antonio, looking unconvinced.

For the next few weeks, the mood of jubilation at Mussolini's demise continued. Although the fascists remained in power and the racial laws were still in place, political prisoners were being freed daily. Rosa took it as a sign that Antonio would soon be released too. But with the possibility of peace so close, why were the Allies still bombing Italian cities?

'Do you really think Italy will sign an armistice with the Allies?' a patient asked Dottor Greco while he and Rosa were changing his dressings. 'I've heard that Generale Badoglio has given assurances to the Germans that we are still on their side.'

'Generale Badoglio has to conduct the talks with the Allies in secret,' Dottor Greco replied. 'He doesn't want Italy to be walked over like the Allies did to Germany after the Great War.'

Although the general consensus was that things would soon get better, Rosa shared Antonio's fear that the longer it took to sign the rumoured armistice, the more chance the Germans had of regrouping and invading Italy. If people on the street were spreading rumours that the Italians were about to join the Allies, the German command must have the same suspicions.

Rosa was fearful for the safety of her children and their guardians too. If Germany invaded Switzerland, what would they do to the Italian refugees? She couldn't think about Nerezza and her mysterious past when the people she loved were in immediate danger. The only consolation was the good news one of the guards at the prison gave her.

'We are getting directions every day to free someone,' he said. 'I'm sure we will receive an order to release your husband soon. After all, he is one of the minor offenders.'

When Rosa told Antonio the news he was pleased. 'We will get the children, Giuseppina and our cousins out of Switzerland and take them south,' he said. 'Whatever happens, as long as I'm not in prison I can do something. I've been sitting here with my hands tied, unable to do anything to protect my family.'

Rosa brought out some of the items she and Antonio had hidden away in the apartment. More people were making appointments at the furniture shop and she had to enlist Ylenia to help her. As people became more confident that Florence would not be bombed, they once again turned their attention to furnishings and the finer things of life. Between the hospital, visiting Antonio, keeping the shop running and writing to the children, time passed quickly for Rosa — but not quickly enough. Why was it taking so long to get Antonio out of prison?

One evening when Rosa was playing the piano in the apartment she remembered the day that Nerezza had 'possessed' her while she was playing the Bösendorfer at the Trevis' home. Rosa stopped in the middle of her practice and went to the drawing room to look at Nerezza's notebook again. She was unable to believe that she hadn't figured out earlier what was so obvious. When Nerezza wrote her letter to Baron Derveaux telling him that she intended to visit him in Paris with news of 'great importance', she wasn't aware that he had married. She had written to him a few weeks after 13 March, when she would have had a suspicion that she was pregnant. From Ferdinando's letter, Rosa understood that he had been in

Libya for some time by then. It was impossible for him to have fathered Nerezza's child, while the Baron Derveaux had only recently gone to Paris. Rosa sat down, dizzy with the shock. When Nerezza found out the Baron Derveaux had married her friend, she had tried to see her husband as soon as possible so she could pass off the child as belonging to him.

Oh my God! thought Rosa, remembering Clementina's birthday party and the man with gangly legs and winged eyebrows. The Baron Derveaux is my father!

Rosa had always felt a yearning to know her mother but had not put as much emphasis on the identity of her father. It suddenly struck her as odd. But then maybe it was a result of having been brought up in a convent of 'mothers' and 'sisters' and being surrounded by paintings of the Christ child with the Madonna.

Now, instead of understanding her origins better, Rosa felt more confused than ever. All she knew of Baron Derveaux were the glimpses of him she'd seen at the villa, his letter to Nerezza, his polite manner, and Miss Butterfield's admonition that he was 'like a child himself'. It wasn't enough to piece together a true picture of the man.

Rosa rushed to the mirror and tried to find his face in hers, his limbs in her muscular arms and legs. But the reflection gave her nothing. The Baron Derveaux saw something in me, however, she thought, remembering the curious way he had looked at her. She understood clearly now what it had been: glimpses of Nerezza.

TWENTY-THREE

The hospital was still suffering shortages but, with the improved mood of the city, more volunteers were signing up to help. Rosa, Gina and Fiamma were sent to a palazzo on the outskirts of the city that was being used as a hospital for Allied prisoners of war of the officer class. Although Italy followed the Geneva Convention, the injured prisoners of war had most likely received lesser treatment than civilians in hospitals. With the Allies approaching, the Italians had to be seen to be doing more, which was why the hospital sent three of its qualified nurses to take over from the military medical staff at the palazzo.

'Well, they are faring better than I expected,' said Gina, after she, Rosa and Fiamma had inspected the medical charts of the patients and the conditions of the hospital.

Rosa had wondered if she would find those Australian pilots at the palazzo, but everyone there was from the infantry. The rule about no communication beyond medical subjects with the prisoners of war was enforced by the guards, but Rosa gleaned from the men's conversations with each other that they were expecting the Allies to arrive at any moment and repatriate them.

After a few days of working at the military hospital, it became apparent to Rosa why it was so clean and organised. Any patient who was capable of getting out of bed did something to help the others, whether it was folding sheets, rolling bandages or helping another patient to shave. Rosa found an American officer, the day after an operation on his abdomen, mopping the corridor with one hand while holding his saline drip in the other.

'Back to bed with you,' she scolded him. 'Do you want those stitches to open up?'

He smiled at Rosa's browbeating but did as he was told. 'It's unmanly to leave you nurses running around from bed to bed without pitching in,' he told her.

There was a New Zealander officer at the hospital who had lost both his legs. When Rosa was bathing him one day, and the guards were out of earshot, he asked her in his clipped accent, 'Do you think my fiancée will still want me?'

Rosa avoided meeting his gaze when she answered. 'If she's worth it, she will,' she told him. 'If she's not, you will find someone better.'

Rosa arrived one day at the hospital to find the guards celebrating with the patients. When the men saw her surprise, they laughed.

'Ah, here is someone who doesn't listen to the radio,' one of the guards said, holding up his wineglass. 'Generale Badoglio signed the armistice with the Allies! The war is over!'

Rosa tried to take in the words. 'It's really over?'

'What does the end of the war with Italy mean for me?' asked the American officer Rosa had found cleaning the corridor after his stomach operation. 'I'm not sick enough to be repatriated. I can still kick some German ass.'

'You will wait here until we receive instructions where to send you to meet up with your commanding officers,' the guard told him.

'But the Italians have been ordered not to hinder the Allies in any way,' protested the American. 'I can walk out of here right now.'

'You could,' the guard told him. 'But it would be wiser to stay here. We have orders to protect you in case the Germans come. You will be safer with your unit than you will be on your own.'

Rosa went to the window. The war was over? Across the street she could see youths and some housewives pulling down a fascist insignia on the building opposite and smashing it to the ground. Did the end of the war mean the end of fascism too? Rosa hoped so.

On her way to visit Antonio, Rosa witnessed more celebrations as the news spread. People cheered and danced in the streets. In one piazza, students piled fascist propaganda — black shirts, slogans, posters and books — onto a bonfire.

'Luciano,' Rosa whispered. 'If only you had lived to see Italy now. How things have turned! After twenty-one years of repression, we are free!'

The guard at the entrance to the prison grinned at Rosa. 'I have good news for you,' he said. 'Your husband will be released three weeks from today.'

Rosa almost danced on the spot. It was too good to believe: Antonio safe and at home again with her.

In the visiting room, she and Antonio gazed into each other's eyes. 'When they release you,' she told him, 'I'm going to hold onto you and never let you go.'

That evening, Rosa and Ylenia watched the celebrations from the apartment window before listening to the radio and the formal announcement of the armistice. Afterwards, they put clean sheets on all the beds in the apartment. As soon as things were settled and the Germans were ousted from the north, Rosa would fetch the children and their guardians from Lugano. She washed the dust out of Ambrosio's and Allegra's food bowls and placed them on the kitchen floor, imagining how wonderful it would be to have the cat and the dog under her feet again.

When Rosa awoke the next morning in the shadows of dawn, she realised that once her family was reunited she had other things to take care of as well. She would contact Signora Corvetto to see if they could arrange Clementina's removal from the Villa Scarfiotti. She needed to get away from the Marchesa. Signora Corvetto could persuade Clementina to attend finishing school in Switzerland or even to study in America. After that, Rosa intended to visit the Baron Derveaux and show him Nerezza's notebook. She would ask him if he knew what had happened the night she was born, but was undecided if she would tell him that he was her father.

Given the celebrations of the night before, Rosa was surprised to find a grim silence had settled over Florence when she stepped out onto the street. Signora Chianisi, who owned the dress boutique next to the furniture shop, told Rosa that the telephone lines to Rome had been cut and she couldn't get through to her sister. 'Something is happening,' she said.

Rosa had some accounts she needed to settle before she went to the hospital and she worked at the shop until mid-morning. As she was closing up, Signora Chianisi approached her.

'I found out what's going on,' she said, her eyes wide. 'The Germans are swarming through Italy. They have already occupied Bologna, Padova and Verona.'

The news was a slap in the face. Rosa hurried to the hospital, where she found that the patients who had sufficiently recovered were gone and, even worse, so were the guards and the military medical staff.

Gina was in the kitchen setting out the lunch trays. 'All those who were well enough to walk cleared out as soon as they heard the news,' she told Rosa. 'The Germans are spreading like a fire. They are heading towards Florence and will be here before we know it.'

'Germans!' Rosa glanced at the ward. There were about fifteen men left: amputees and those too ill to leave their beds. 'The guards were supposed to stay to protect them,' she whispered.

Gina shrugged. 'They were listening to the BBC radio with the patients when suddenly there was a mad panic to get away. The American officer is waiting for you in the cellar with a few of the others. You'd better see them before they go.'

Rosa found the American officer dressed in his uniform and sharpening a knife. A British and a Canadian officer were in their uniforms too.

'That damn Badoglio,' the American swore. 'The fool never closed the Brenner Pass. The Germans have been building up their forces all over Italy waiting for this moment. If that fool of a guard hadn't told us to stay, we could have got away days ago. Now I've heard that Badoglio and the King have fled Rome for the south without leaving any instructions for the Italian army.'

'Surely that can't be true!' Rosa cried. 'Surely the King and Generale Badoglio couldn't be so dishonourable as to abandon their people to the Germans! Not after having assured them of peace!'

The American officer didn't answer her. Rosa felt ashamed of her country.

'You can't leave in those uniforms,' she told the men. 'Let me fetch some of my husband's clothes for you.'

Rosa hurried to her apartment and returned with Antonio's pants and shirts. Gina drew maps for the men of the border crossings and marked where she understood the Allies to be, while Rosa wrote out Italian phrases that they might need: *Show me where the Germans are*; *Do you have food you can spare for me?*

Once they were ready, the officers went to the ward to bid farewell to their fellow soldiers.

'What about me?' asked the New Zealander officer whose legs had been amputated.

'I will stay here to look after you,' Rosa told him. 'You are protected by the Geneva Convention.'

When the American officer and the others were ready to leave, they each shook hands with Rosa, Gina and Fiamma and thanked them.

'Italian women are brave,' the Canadian officer told Gina. 'Even if their men are cowards.'

'I never knew your name,' the American officer said to Rosa. 'I am Lieutenant Edward Barrett.'

'And I am Sister Rosa Parigi.'

Lieutenant Barrett smiled. 'In my mother's garden in California she grows every kind of rose. Her favourite has always been *Rosa Toscana*, Tuscan Rose. That's how I will remember you, Sister Parigi: our brave Tuscan Rose.'

The nurses watched the soldiers depart. It was awful seeing them leave, despite their bravado. With the Germans at every point in the north, their chances of joining their armies were slim. But Rosa knew that if they had stayed, their chances of surviving German prisoner-of-war camps were even slimmer.

The sight of German tanks rumbling into Florence chilled Rosa. She sensed that this was a struggle in which she could no longer play a supporting role. Every Italian was going to have to choose a side and fight. When she saw the tanks position themselves in front of the Duomo, she made up her mind that the Germans were her enemy.

Rosa moved some of her things to the hospital and stayed there overnight with Gina and Fiamma. She left Ylenia what money and rations she could.

One afternoon, Rosa left the hospital early to close up Antonio's shop again. A young woman with a child in a pram and frightened eyes entered the shop while Rosa was packing away the accounts books.

'Can I help you?' Rosa asked her.

The woman reached under the baby's blanket and took out an ebony photograph frame. It had pietra dura floral plaques and was so exquisite it could have been a museum piece.

'It is beautiful,' Rosa said, admiring the craftsmanship.

'It was my mother's.'

Rosa studied the woman. She was no more than twenty-five but there were deep lines on her face. The terror in her eyes was unmistakable.

'You're Jewish?' Rosa asked.

The woman nodded.

'Do you have somewhere to hide?'

The woman started at Rosa's question but decided to trust her. 'My neighbours have a house in the country. They are going to hide us there.'

Rosa took out the cash book. 'I'll pay you for the frame and give you a receipt,' she told the woman. 'But I won't sell this. I'll put it in the safe. You can come and get it back again when … it's safe to do so.'

Rosa and the woman exchanged glances, realising that it may never be 'safe' again. The Allies had bungled their occupation of Italy after the armistice. They could have taken over quickly and outsmarted Hitler if there hadn't been so much to-ing and fro-ing with Generale Badoglio over the terms of the armistice.

Rosa watched the woman hurry down the street with the pram, looking over her shoulder at every corner. A terrible storm was coming to Italy and Rosa sensed it was going to be much worse than the bombings.

She was pulling down the grille over the window and securing it when Signora Chianisi ran up to her.

'Signora Parigi,' she cried. 'It's terrible. Have you heard?'

Oh God, what now? thought Rosa. She shook her head.

'They've rescued him.'

'Who?' asked Rosa, her mind racing to think if Signora Chianisi had any relatives fighting overseas and wondering why news of their rescue would be terrible.

'Mussolini!'

'What?' said Rosa, straightening.

'German paratroopers stormed the place where he was being held and rescued him. He is our leader again!'

Rosa sank back against the grille. She remembered seeing a film with Antonio about a vampire. Although his pursuers shot the monster and pushed him off a bridge, he could not be killed. He rose stronger and more lethal each time. Mussolini was like that vampire.

'What do you think will happen now?' asked Signora Chianisi. 'Should I close my shop?'

Rosa shook her head, thinking of Antonio in prison. Rosa had heard that there were whole units in the Italian army who didn't accept the armistice. They *wanted* to fight on the side of the Germans. They might take Antonio — or he might be sent as cheap labour to Germany.

'I don't know,' Rosa replied, feeling sick. 'I don't know.'

Signora Chianisi pursed her lips. 'We should have waited out the war on Germany's side and taken our medicine when it was defeated,' she said. 'Now both the Allies and the Germans despise us as traitors. Don't you agree?'

Rosa looked at Signora Chianisi. 'I don't think we should ever have entered this war in the first place. But if we did have to fight, it shouldn't have been on the side of a madman.'

A few days later, Rosa saw notices appearing on public buildings proclaiming that young men and returning soldiers must join the army of the Repubblica Sociale Italiana, the new government of Italy, to fight the Allies. Anyone who did not enlist within five days would be shot. At the same time, Rosa heard rumours of men hiding in the forests and hills around Florence — anti-fascists, communists, ex-soldiers, escaped Allied prisoners of war and young men avoiding conscription or being sent to Germany to work. These men wanted to fight the Germans. More notices appeared warning that anyone who assisted these rebels would be executed. What people hadn't expected was that innocent citizens would be rounded up and murdered each time a German soldier was killed by the partisans.

'I've heard it's ten Italians for each German soldier killed,' said Fiamma one day when she, Gina and Rosa were checking the supply cabinet. They had received no new instructions from the hospital and had not contacted them in case they were called back. The Allied prisoners of war at the makeshift hospital needed them, so the three nurses did their best to muster what supplies they could on the black market.

'The Germans are bluffing,' Gina assured her. 'They can't afford to alienate the Italian people otherwise everyone will turn against them.'

Rosa had heard shots ringing out across the city the previous night. She thought of the stories she had heard from the Allied prisoners who had fought in France. The first people the Germans usually shot in reprisal for resistance activity were those already captive in prison. There were only a few days left until Antonio was released from Le Murate. Rosa was sure she would not be able to breathe properly until he was free.

Besides reinstating fascist rule, the Germans brought their Nazi racial laws into practice. After Italy's milder racial laws had been introduced, records were kept of Jews living in Florence including those citizens of Jewish parentage. Because of Nonno's conversion, Rosa wasn't sure if Antonio was included in those records or not. But she didn't want to take any chances. The Italian soldiers returning from the east spread horror stories of mass killings of Jews.

'As you know we have a crypt under the convent,' Madre Maddalena told Rosa when she made her weekly visit. 'We have been approached by Rabbi Cassuto and have agreed to take several Jewish women and children and hide them there. When your husband is released from prison you can bring him as well.'

Rosa had never visited the crypt. She remembered as a curious child opening the door in the chapel that led to it and creeping down the cool and dark stairway. But she had been caught by Suor Dorotea who had scolded her so harshly that she had never ventured there again.

'Thank you,' said Rosa. She was grateful to Madre

Maddalena because helping Jews put the convent in danger. Hiding Antonio amongst the dead was not the homecoming Rosa had imagined for him, but there was nothing else to be done.

Later that afternoon, two German officers arrived at the prisoner-of-war hospital. Rosa was changing the sheets on the New Zealander's bed while Fiamma was working in the laundry and Gina was taking temperatures and checking dressings. Rosa almost flipped the New Zealander off the bed when she saw the two Germans looking at her. One was in his late twenties, the other slightly older. They both had the same flawless skin and grey-blue eyes. If not for the age difference, they could have been twins.

'Who is in charge of this hospital?' the first officer asked in Italian.

'I am,' said Gina, coming forward.

The officer frowned. 'Where is the doctor? Where are the guards?'

'They left a few days ago to join the militia,' said Gina.

She glanced at Rosa, who thought it was an excellent lie. She just hoped that the officers wouldn't check up on it.

'So who is guarding these men?' the officer asked.

He had a self-important air about him, but he spoke politely. Was his courtesy sincere or was it to trick them into revealing something? The second officer said nothing but looked around the room. Rosa wondered if it was because he couldn't speak Italian or because he was searching for something his fellow officer might miss.

'There is no need to guard these men,' Gina replied.

The officers glanced at the New Zealander's stumps and understanding dawned in their eyes. They exchanged a look and it seemed as if they were on the verge of leaving when the second officer pointed out the empty beds.

'And the others? They have fled? You helped them escape?' he asked Gina in English. Gina didn't understand him. He turned to Rosa.

'They were taken to the prisoner-of-war camp at Laterina once they were well,' Rosa said in Italian. She could have answered the question in English or German, but then Gina would not have understood and the soldiers might have cross-examined them.

The two officers stared at Rosa. She did her best not to flinch.

'Good!' said the first officer after a pause. 'That is all for now then.' The men left.

'This place is surprisingly well kept,' Rosa heard the second officer say to the first as they headed for the stairwell. 'Compared to the other shitholes for hospitals we've seen.'

Rosa had been struck by the Germans' proud posture and their assuredness. They gave the impression that Germany was sure to win the war. It occurred to her that Hitler had produced exactly the kind of soldiers he needed for European domination. The other thing she had noticed was the quality of the officers' uniforms and boots. Rosa thought of the men in the forest, including Lieutenant Barrett whose uniform was frayed after so many battles. Where could the partisans get weapons and equipment to match those of the Germans? She admired the courage of the men who had taken to the hills, but winter was coming and she feared that they were doomed.

The patients wanted to know what the Germans had said. Rosa explained it to them.

'That was quick thinking about the camp at Laterina,' said one of the Canadians, giving Rosa a nod of admiration. 'You would make a good spy — or a partisan.'

'Please don't even joke about it,' Rosa told him.

A few days later, Rosa, Gina and Fiamma were surprised to find that Red Cross parcels had arrived for the Allied soldiers at the hospital. They distributed the tins of food and packets of tea to the patients.

'It's like Christmas,' said Rosa, opening a tin of fruit for the New Zealander and handing him a spoon.

'You have some first,' he told her. 'I know that you have been giving your rations to me.'

Rosa squeezed his arm. Although his name was Alan, she always thought of him as 'the New Zealander'. She had trouble understanding him sometimes but she was as fond of him as an older sister would be of a younger brother.

There were no personal letters in the packages. Those had been removed. Although Mussolini had been rescued he was only the figurehead for the puppet government. It was the Germans who ran Italy now. All correspondence was banned. Rosa would not hear from her children now. She would rather have done without food than letters.

Rosa didn't sleep that night. She could hear bombing in the distance and gunfire. She had never been fond of fireworks displays, and this noise was far worse. The sound rang in her ears. With each explosion or crack of gunfire, she thought of the people who were being maimed and killed.

She visited the crypt with Madre Maddalena the next morning and was glad to find it wasn't as macabre as she had feared. The tombs were sealed and the area was covered in mosaic tiles. The nuns had set up camp beds behind vaults and secreted blankets and supplies in spaces in the walls. It was cold, however, and Rosa knew it would be an icebox in the winter. Afterwards, she rushed to the hospital to help with lunch and change bedding. She was due to pick up Antonio in the late afternoon. The inspector guard at Le Murate had told her that he would not be released unless she was present. 'You must take him within twenty-four hours to register for anything the Repubblica Sociale Italiana requires him to do.' Rosa was surprised that the new administration did not force prisoners to do that on release themselves, but was glad for it. She had no intention of taking Antonio anywhere except straight to the convent.

Rosa was putting the sheets in the laundry bag when a commotion broke out on the street in front of the hospital. She and Gina rushed to the window. They saw people with their hands on their heads being loaded at gunpoint by German soldiers onto a lorry. The prisoners looked like ordinary housewives and shopkeepers.

'It's a round-up!' said Fiamma, rushing in from the stairwell. She dropped the potatoes she had gone out to buy on a table. 'Some partisans attacked a convoy and now the Germans say they are going to hang thirty people in the Piazza della Signoria.'

One of the British soldiers moaned. Gina left the window to attend to him. Rosa saw a child, a girl of no more than ten or eleven, being pushed up onto the truck. She covered her mouth in horror.

'You'd better get away from the window,' Fiamma told her.

She was moving to lock the door to the stairwell when there was a rumble of footsteps. German soldiers stormed into the ward. They were nothing like the calm, methodical German officers who had come the week before. They were wild-eyed and their belts were laden with pistols and grenades. Rosa saw the SS symbols on their lapels.

Their officer shouted something in German that Rosa didn't understand. The nurses froze to the spot. He grabbed Fiamma and punched her in the face. She went sprawling onto the floor. For a terrifying moment Rosa thought the soldiers intended to rape her.

'Let her go,' shouted Gina. 'We are nurses.'

'You will come with us now,' the officer told Gina in Italian.

Rosa struggled to breathe. Had the Germans come to round them up too? The situation was so surreal that she didn't even feel fear for herself. She was more concerned about the patients. Who would take care of them if she, Gina and Fiamma weren't there? They'd be left to starve or die of infection.

'We can't leave these men,' she told the officer in German. 'We are the only staff at this hospital.'

The officer flashed his eyes at Rosa. She saw the killer

instinct in them. It was like staring into the soul of a beast. Then, to her surprise, he grinned.

'You speak German? I am impressed,' he said, stepping towards her.

Rosa flinched from the smell of wine on his breath but was even more unnerved by his sudden change of mood. She didn't like the way he was smiling.

'Such dedicated nurses,' the officer said, looking around the room. 'Albeit for the enemy.'

All the patients were awake now, looking nervously at the soldiers. Rosa felt sorry for them. None of them spoke German. They didn't know what was going on. She understood something of the powerlessness the men had felt after their amputations and debilitating illnesses. They had once been the strongest and bravest of their fighting forces; now they were helpless, with only three women to protect them.

The German officer cocked his head. 'I am impressed by your having learnt the fatherland's language and *very* impressed by your concern for these men,' he told Rosa. 'I want to do something for you.'

Rosa swallowed. The sense of menace that emanated from the officer turned her blood to ice. He was like a circling shark. She tried to see the source of him but all that came back to her was darkness.

The officer turned to his soldiers. 'I think we should relieve this good nurse of her worries,' he said.

Rosa saw him reach for his pistol and cried out. The soldiers opened fire on the patients, shooting them in their beds. The officer fired at the New Zealander, hitting him in the chest. Gina tried to shield the British soldier she was standing next to and both were shot in the face. Gina's lifeless body slipped to the floor. Fiamma's screams dissolved into sobs when the gunfire ceased. Within seconds the ward that the nurses had taken pride in keeping orderly was blood-spattered and bullet-ridden; the patients they had strived to keep alive were all dead. Rosa collapsed to her knees. The floor was covered in blood. She nearly fainted but was lifted roughly by one of the soldiers.

'Get your nurses' kits!' the officer shouted at Rosa and Fiamma. 'Put everything into them that you've been wasting on these soldiers.'

Rosa's hands trembled as she emptied the contents of the supply cabinet into the bags Fiamma held open for her. Fiamma looked haggard, as if she had aged ten years in ten minutes. Rosa saw that Fiamma's uniform was wet and then realised that her own stockings were damp too. They had urinated on themselves from the fright, but Rosa was too terrified to care about the humiliation. She dropped a vial of morphine. Luckily Fiamma caught it before it hit the ground, otherwise Rosa was sure the soldier who was guarding them would have shot her. Morphine was almost impossible to obtain. Gina had bought some vials on the black market and they were as precious as gold. Rosa stuffed everything they had collected into the bags, disgusted to think it was all going to be used by the enemy.

She heard the soldiers dragging the bodies of Gina and the patients down the stairs. Shooting defenceless prisoners of war and a nurse was a crime the officer might have problems justifying to his superiors.

When the soldier guarding them saw that Rosa and Fiamma had taken everything from the cabinet, he ordered them down the stairs. Rosa nearly slipped on one of the pools of blood on the floor. There was no sign of the lorry outside. Instead the women were pushed into an open-topped Mercedes. One of the soldiers jumped into the front seat next to the driver while the officer climbed in the back with Rosa and Fiamma, aiming his gun at them.

They were driven back towards the centre of Florence then in the direction of the Cimitero degli Inglesi. People on the streets stared in horror at the two captive nurses but quickly looked away. Rosa was convinced that she and Fiamma were going to be raped or shot — perhaps both. The onlookers probably assumed that too. The car turned onto the road to Fiesole. Rosa recognised the villa with the pietra serena columns that she had seen the day Giuseppe had driven her from the convent to her position in the Scarfiotti household. The windows were boarded up now and the magnolia and olive trees were dead. Fiamma reached for Rosa's hand and squeezed her fingers. Fiamma's touch, despite the horrific circumstances, comforted her. Rosa had always been closer to Gina, finding Fiamma's pessimism too intense at times. Now she experienced a profound love for Fiamma; a spiritual connection as they were both being driven to their deaths.

Rosa caught glimpses of Florence as the car sped uphill and raced around the hairpin bends. She would never see her city again. She wondered what would happen to Antonio now and prayed for his safety. Her mind drifted to her children. She had been upset to have missed their spurts of development. Now, she realised, she was going to miss every milestone in their lives. She would not be there. Lorenzo and Giorgio were young, they might forget her and think of Renata as their mother. It would be better that way, Rosa thought. She would rather be forgotten than be a source of pain to her sons. Then Sibilla's beautiful face loomed before her. Sibilla would not forget her mother. They had been through too much together. Rosa closed her eyes and hoped that her children would sense her love for them. She would have given anything for one more cherished moment in their presence.

The driver roughly changed gear and Rosa opened her eyes. Her heart gave a jolt when she saw that the car was descending down a narrow road bordered by stone walls. It was an overcast day and everything was shrouded in mist but those walls were familiar. Rosa's grief gave way to cold, silent terror when she saw the wrought-iron gates and the stone mastiffs appear in the distance and she realised where she was. The gate was guarded by SS soldiers who saw the car coming and opened it. Rosa's throat turned dry and she struggled to breathe when the ancient stone walls of the Villa Scarfiotti loomed up ahead.

TWENTY-FOUR

Rosa saw that the feeling of foreboding she had experienced the first time she had entered the villa gates had been a premonition of her demise. There was something lurking in the woods. She felt it. It was watching her. It crawled like a spider up her arm. The driver brought the car to a stop near the verdigrised fountain and Rosa gazed up at the windows of the villa for what she assumed would be the last time. She had been born here and now she was going to die here. But the villa had never been her home. Her home was the apartment she shared with Antonio and the children. Now she would never see any of them again.

'*Raus*!' the officer shouted at Rosa and Fiamma. 'Get out!'

Rosa wondered why he kept pointing his gun at their heads. How could they run when all the strength had been drained from them? Where would they go? The grounds were swarming with SS guards. A red flag with a swastika draped over the balcony signalled where the household's loyalties lay.

Rosa stumbled out of the car followed by Fiamma.

'This way!' the officer shouted, marching the women around the side of the villa.

Rosa was surprised to see Dono in his cage in the kitchen garden. An SS soldier was taking a picture of another soldier standing next to the bear. Dono was scrawny and his coat was dusty. From the mess on his cage floor it looked as though he was being fed nothing but scraps. When the officer pushed Rosa and Fiamma past the cage, Dono lifted his muzzle and looked Rosa in the eye. Did he recognise her after all these years?

The officer forced the women towards the cellar door. He knocked on it and it was opened by a guard.

'The nurses are here,' the officer said.

They were about to enter when Rosa saw two people coming from the path from the woods towards the house. One of them was an SS colonel, grey at the temples and with a toothbrush moustache. On his arm was a woman in a wasp-waisted dress with a sable-trimmed cape and matching hat and gloves. Rosa saw the little creature the fur had come from, sniffing the air and twitching its whiskers, sensing danger. The couple came closer and the woman's red hair against her pale skin made Rosa think for a moment she was looking at Signora Corvetto. But it was Clementina. The two women caught each other's eye. Clementina did not have the look of one coerced into the company of a Nazi. She had been gazing at the colonel with admiration. *Clementina, how could you?* Rosa remembered the bright-eyed girl with the pouch-like cheeks who had cleverly lampooned her classes at the Piccole Italiane. That girl was gone. She had caved in to the influence of the Marchesa. Rosa averted her gaze. She did not want to die with that shameful impression of Clementina on her mind.

The nurses were bustled down the stairs and past the room where Rosa had slept her first night at the villa. She remembered Signora Guerrini telling her it was haunted. There was a desk in there now, with what looked like a carpenter's toolbox on it. Rosa glimpsed blood on the handsaw. She and Fiamma were pushed through the cellar to one of the storerooms. The soldier guarding it opened the door. Rosa squinted, trying to adjust her eyes to the dim light. There was a thud and she turned to see that Fiamma had fainted. Indeed the smell in the room was foul. Rosa reached towards Fiamma, afraid of what the soldiers might do to her if she left her alone. But one of the soldiers dragged Fiamma back into the cellar.

'I thought nurses were supposed to have strong stomachs,' he laughed.

The SS officer grabbed Rosa's arm and urged her forward. He seized her face and held it up. Rosa's blood turned cold. Despite all the horrors she had seen as a nurse, she could not believe that the body that dangled before her was human. The naked man had not been hanged in the usual way, with a rope around his neck. No, his execution had been truly sadistic. A metal hook pierced his chin and jutted through his mouth. The man's body was covered in burn marks, his ears and nose were missing, and his genitals had been sliced off and now lay on the floor under his feet. The horror of the sight became worse when the man's body twitched and Rosa realised he was still alive.

'Partisans,' the SS officer told her. 'This particular unit is clever. They stole ammunition and supplies from a storehouse in broad daylight. Of course, we are keen to know where they are hiding out so we can retrieve our property.'

It was all Rosa could do to remain upright. She had tried her best to be a good, religious woman all her life. How could it be then that she was now in hell?

The officer indicated the mutilated man as if he were examining a painting in a museum. 'This one, while willing to talk towards the end, didn't know much that could help us. While his companion,' he turned to the corner of the room, 'knows a lot but has said nothing. You can imagine how much we would like him to talk as he is one of the band's leaders.'

Rosa turned to where the officer was pointing. She could see a dim figure chained to a support post. The officer dragged her closer. The man's head was slumped forward and his breathing was a laboured gurgle. The officer grabbed the man by the head and swung it upward. All Rosa's training — to be able to assess mangled tissue and see what organs could be saved — had not prepared her for the shock of the man's face. His eye socket had been smashed, by the butt of a rifle, Rosa assumed. His eyeball hung halfway down his cheek, held only by a loose thread of tissue. The man's teeth were gone and so were his fingers and toes. Rosa trembled, not because she hadn't seen worse in bomb victims, but because this man's injuries had not been inflicted by an impersonal weapon dropped from the sky but by the living, breathing man who now held her arm. How could any being made in the image of God possibly do such a thing?

'But we might get some information out of him when he watches us skin his friend,' said the officer. 'And if that doesn't work, then we will do the same to him.'

Rosa turned to the officer in horror.

'Oh, yes,' he said, relishing her reaction. 'We've called in a butcher — apparently one of your city's best. He doesn't mind if the meat isn't quite dead. He's skinned a live pig or two before. It means the flesh is fresh.'

Rosa could not speak. She had no words. Not for this officer, not for the Italian butcher. Not for any of them. All she could do was pray to God that this ordeal would be over soon.

'He's lost consciousness,' said the officer, kicking the partisan's feet. 'That's why we've brought you and your faint-hearted little friend. I want you to revive him.'

Revive him? Rosa could not believe what she was hearing. Was the SS officer mad or stupid? How could she revive him? The man was dying. He wouldn't be able to say anything. All that torturing him would do would be to make his inevitable end more painful.

The soldier at the door called to the officer and told him that he was wanted on the telephone.

'Is it urgent?' the officer asked, looking annoyed.

'It's Oberführer Bertling,' the soldier replied.

The officer pursed his lips before reaching up and pulling a cord. A light came on. 'Revive him,' he said to Rosa before storming out the door.

Rosa knelt down next to the partisan. The soldier guarding the door was speaking to another soldier and sharing a cigarette. Rosa tried to think clearly. She prayed, tears filling her eyes; still she did not know what to do. She reached for the morphine. It wouldn't revive the man, it would numb him, but she couldn't see anything else she could do. It was the only mercy she had to offer him. She remembered Alessandro Trevi saying that the German people had once been the most educated, tolerant, humane and reasonable in Europe. How had such monsters surfaced amongst them?

Rosa tapped the vial and filled the syringe before turning back to the partisan. She gave a gasp. The man was conscious again and looking at her with his remaining eye. *His sweet, blue, angelic eye.*

Carlo! Rosa wasn't sure if she had cried out aloud or not. She glanced at the soldiers who gave no indication of having heard her. Her tears fell fast now that she realised this tortured man was Luciano's dear brother. If not for that beautiful eye and the remnants of his blond curls she would not have recognised him. He had always been kind to Rosa and like an uncle to Sibilla. She took Carlo's bloodied hand and held it to her cheek. She could see through his agony that he recognised her too. She had to administer the morphine before the officer came back.

'Carlo,' she wept, strapping his arm and injecting the morphine. In a few moments his breathing eased. He looked at Rosa and closed his eye then opened it. He was a wounded animal begging for mercy.

The man on the metal hook twitched again. Rosa knew

that Carlo was doomed, that there was only more suffering for him. Even if the interrogators stopped the torture now, his injuries were too severe for him to survive. The rattle in his throat, the twisted position of his body, the bulge of his intestines all told Rosa that he had extensive internal injuries.

Oh God, have mercy on our souls, she prayed. She had six more vials of morphine in her bag. How many could she give Carlo before the officer came back? And after Carlo, could she do the same for the man on the hook? Maybe God had sent her for this task. Rosa thought nothing of her own safety or what the officer would do when he realised that she had mercy-killed the partisans. She glanced at the soldiers, who were still talking and smoking. She took out another vial of morphine and filled the syringe. Carlo seemed to understand what she was doing. He blinked again as if in gratitude.

'God and the angels are waiting for you in heaven, sweet Carlo,' Rosa whispered, her hands trembling.

She injected him and waited to see the reaction before taking out another vial. She heard the officer coming back down the stairs. If she injected this one she would be caught. She glanced at Carlo who had lost consciousnessness. His breathing was slowing down. Maybe he was numb enough to pass away now? But no, she had to take the chance. She injected the third syringe and just had time to throw it in her bag before the officer burst into the room. When he approached her, she was feeling Carlo's pulse in his neck. He was fading quickly and was only minutes now from death.

The officer grabbed Rosa's arm and yanked her up.

'He's dying,' Rosa said, suddenly finding the courage to speak to the fiend. 'There is nothing I could do to *revive* him.'

The officer's eyes narrowed. He spat in Rosa's face. He grabbed her by the hair and dragged her out through the cellar and up into the kitchen garden where he threw her down on her knees on the cobblestones. The sharp stones dug into her flesh. Dono let out a growl. The soldiers near the cage stopped taking photographs and turned to see what was happening. There was the click of a gun. Rosa closed her eyes, waiting for the bullet that would end her life. She was surprised to find that she was calm. After all she had witnessed in the last few hours she wasn't sure that she wanted to live any more. She said a quick prayer for the souls of Carlo and the other partisan, who she was sorry she had not been able to help, then one for herself.

'Obersturmführer Schmidt!' an Austrian accent called out.

The officer stood to attention but did not move his gun away from Rosa. She looked up to see that the speaker was the SS colonel, the one who had been holding Clementina's arm.

'Signorina Scarfiotti is in need of a nurse, and that other one you brought says that this one here is one of the highest-ranking nurses in Florence. Apparently it is a rather ... *delicate* matter.'

'She's a partisan sympathiser,' the officer said. 'She's too dangerous to have in the house.'

Rosa realised that the officer was a man who itched for blood. Having been deprived of the captured partisans, he had switched his bloodlust to her. He wanted to kill someone.

'Perhaps if you wish partisans to speak you shouldn't choke them so badly their vocal cords are crushed,' Rosa said.

It wasn't true — Carlo wasn't able to speak because his lungs were filling with fluid, not because his throat had been damaged — but Rosa's words had the effect she hadn't realised she had been aiming for.

The colonel gave a sarcastic smile and coughed. 'Is that so?' he said to Rosa, before turning back to the officer. 'Perhaps, Obersturmführer Schmidt, you should take the nurse's advice rather than killing her. It might make for more useful information gathering. I assume this means that we are no closer than we were last night to knowing where our weapons are and that we now have a well-armed partisan band in the immediate area?'

The officer gave Rosa such an evil look that she knew that Fiamma's lie about her skills had only bought her a few more hours to live. But she had struck a blow against him and for some reason that gave her satisfaction. A new, strange feeling was seething in Rosa: hatred. It was like a fire in her veins. She despised these SS soldiers so much that it had restored her will to live, even if only to do as much damage as she could before they cut her down.

The officer ordered her to stand up and pushed her towards the SS soldier accompanying the colonel. Rosa was then led into the house via the main entrance.

The décor of the Villa Scarfiotti had changed little since Rosa had last seen it, only now, to her trained eye, accustomed to discovering the beauty in fine lines, the white marble staircase and purple walls seemed gaudy. She caught her reflection in one of the mirrors. There was blood smeared on her face and on her apron. She thought it fitting that she was being taken to see Clementina in this unhygienic state. *Delicate matter?* What could be ailing that spoilt brat? Rosa could not believe that for all these years she had thought so fondly of Clementina. Signora Corvetto had said that Clementina had been distraught at Rosa's arrest and wanted to help. That may have been true of the young girl, but it was not true of the woman she had seen with a Nazi.

Rosa was led up the main staircase to what had once been the Marchese's quarters. She looked around to see if there were any familiar faces amongst the staff hurrying about on the landing, but she recognised no-one, except the woman poised at the door to the quarters. Rosa found herself once again staring at the scowling face of Signora Guerrini, although the housekeeper showed no indication that she recognised Rosa. Perhaps, with her nurse's veil and the blood on her face, Rosa was too different.

'This way,' said the colonel.

The soldier saluted and stayed by the door while Rosa followed the colonel into the Marchese's former sitting room. The mahogany and cherrywood furniture along with the framed antique maps and etchings of Italian castles gave the room a masculine atmosphere. The only feminine touches were the Aubusson cushions and the bowls of shell-pink roses on the side tables and mantelpiece. Clementina was reclining on a daybed and holding a compress to her forehead.

'I've brought the nurse as you requested,' said the colonel. Rosa shivered at the tone of voice he used with Clementina: affectionate and intimate. He was nearly three times Clementina's age and probably had a wife and children back in Austria. 'Obersturmführer Schmidt seems to think she is dangerous: a partisan sympathiser. Shall I have the private stay in the room with you?'

Clementina turned to him and smiled sweetly. 'I'd prefer that you didn't. You see, the problem is my ...' she said, lowering her eyes.

'Ah,' said the colonel, catching the hint that she had a female ailment. He blushed. 'Then perhaps the housekeeper should be present?'

'This nurse isn't dangerous,' said Clementina, still smiling but with a curt tone. 'She used to be my governess.'

The colonel glanced at Rosa suspiciously. He seemed confused. Rosa suspected that Clementina might often have that effect on him.

'Well, then,' he said, withdrawing. 'Please tell me whatever she says you need, my dear, and I will get it.'

When the colonel had left and shut the door behind him, Clementina sat up. 'There's nothing more repulsive to German men than women's bodily functions or something contagious,' she said.

Rosa realised that Clementina's illness was feigned. She had saved her life — or at least bought her a reprieve. Rosa wasn't sure whether to be grateful or not. The last few hours had shattered her view of the world. She couldn't believe that only that morning she had been in the convent's crypt with Madre Maddalena, discussing where to hide Antonio. Rosa's heart fell at the thought of her husband. He would be waiting at the prison now, wondering what was keeping her.

Rosa looked at Clementina, unable to hide her scorn. She couldn't separate the clever, vivacious girl she had loved from the young woman before her who consorted with sadistic murderers.

Clementina's eyes filled with tears, as if she knew what Rosa was thinking. 'The colonel is Mother's ... well ... I think you can guess.' She opened a silver case and took a cigarette in her trembling fingers. She offered the case to Rosa who declined.

'You were always a lady, Signorina Bellocchi,' Clementina said, lighting her cigarette and inhaling.

The sound of Rosa's former name transported her back to the days when Clementina was a child. She remembered sitting up with her and reading *Le tigri di Mompracem* to calm her nightmares. But Bellocchi was not Rosa's name any more. She was not the same person. She was a wife, mother and nurse. And she was no longer an orphan of unknown parentage, at least in her own mind. Rosa thought of Signora Corvetto; Clementina would not be keeping the company of Nazis if she knew who her real mother was. But that was Signora Corvetto's story to tell, and if she had not informed Clementina who she was after the Marchese's death, then she must have her reasons.

The colonel's voice came through the door. 'Is everything all right, my darling?'

For such a powerful, brutal man, he seemed to be wrapped around Clementina's finger. But that couldn't be true entirely, Rosa thought. Clementina had the look about her of an exotic bird locked in a cage. She could coo and preen but it was clear who was the true master.

'We'll be finished shortly,' Clementina called in return, sounding faint but with a contemptuous look on her face.

She turned back to Rosa. 'Babbo would turn in his grave if …' She stopped herself and swallowed. She swung her legs off the daybed and rushed towards Rosa.

'Listen, there isn't much time,' she said, her voice still lowered but hoarse. 'Downstairs they are holding eight people from a local village. They have been rounded up because of the partisans stealing that ammunition yesterday. A unit of German soldiers are on their way now to march those people back into their village square where they will be executed. The count is ten Italians for every German killed. No Germans were killed in the theft but the colonel is furious at having been made a fool of and is going to kill those villagers anyway. The partisans were so bold that they turned up at the storehouse in Italian army uniforms, saluted to the guards and took what they wanted. The colonel is looking for another two people to make it ten. It was supposed to be the partisans they caught, but now it's going to be you and your fellow nurse if you don't listen to me. No-one except the colonel and Mother ever leave this villa, Signorina Bellocchi. *Ever.* Not even the soldiers who guard it. Unless it's on the back of a truck with a bullet through their head. The only way I can save you is to pretend I have an ongoing illness and for you to stay here as my nurse.'

If there was anything redeeming about the day, it was that Clementina's heart proved not to have been completely hardened. Rosa did not want to die, but death in this case was preferable to living. She shook her head.

'Don't you understand what I'm saying?' said Clementina, grabbing Rosa's shoulders and looking horrified. 'They are going to shoot you!'

Rosa met her gaze. 'If I stay here, there will be more partisans. They will use me to help torture them.'

Clementina let Rosa go and strode towards the window. She snuffed out her cigarette on the windowsill. 'Maybe you can help them … suffer *less*.' She turned to Rosa, scrutinising her face to see if her words had any effect.

Rosa shook her head. She wouldn't be able to give them all morphine.

'Then you are going to have to decide between their lives and yours,' Clementina said. 'What good will you do them by sacrificing yourself? What good will it do whichever side wins if you are dead?'

Rosa looked at Clementina and pitied her. For all her wealth and privilege, she could not see what was obvious to Rosa. 'Is that how you think, Clementina?' she asked gently. 'Is that what you've decided to do?'

Clementina stared at Rosa, fighting back her tears. 'Isn't that the only way to think?' she asked. 'The only way one can survive in these circumstances?'

Rosa shook her head. 'I couldn't live with myself or face God with peace if I existed only for myself.'

Clementina stared at Rosa and winced as if she had been stabbed. 'God? Signorina Bellocchi, you must be the last person in the world who still believes in God.'

'Is everything all right?' the colonel asked, this time opening the door.

Clementina turned and did her best to smile at him. 'Yes, come in,' she said, lighting another cigarette and smoking it furiously. 'We're finished.'

The colonel walked into the room followed by his soldier. He looked at Clementina. 'Is it something serious?'

Clementina turned away. 'No, it's not serious. The nurse has given me advice about what to do for it.'

'So that's all?' asked the colonel.

Clementina glanced at Rosa and, when she realised that she could not change her mind, nodded.

The colonel seemed relieved. He indicated to the soldier who grabbed Rosa by the arm. Before Rosa was taken from the room, she heard Clementina say quietly, 'It's all very well to be a lady, Signorina Bellocchi. I just hope you are right.'

The soldier marched Rosa to the kitchen where a group of people were huddled around the fireplace. They were being guarded by the two young soldiers Rosa had seen with Dono. Fiamma was there too.

'Another nurse?' said an elderly man, a look of disgust on his face, when Rosa was made to sit with the group. 'I am old and of no use to anyone. But to shoot a nurse ... why, it's like shooting a nun.'

'Shh! Shh! They aren't going to shoot us,' said his wife, glancing at a young couple with a small child. 'That's only a rumour.'

Rosa counted the people: the elderly couple; an ancient-looking woman asleep in the corner; two middle-aged men in suits; the parents and their child; and herself and Fiamma. The little girl was included in the number to be executed. Rosa watched the mother cooing to the girl and tickling her cheeks and thought of Sibilla. The girl was laughing, innocent of the fate that awaited her. Rosa felt pity for the child's parents. There was a time when she would not have believed that anyone could kill an innocent child. But after what she had seen in the storeroom she could believe anything.

One of the suited men turned to the soldiers. 'It's wrong to shoot us,' he said. 'I've been a member of the Fascist Party since 1922. I lost a son in Africa. I hate the partisans. I wouldn't give one of them a crumb of bread even if he were starving. They should shoot the people who help them, not good citizens like us. If I saw a partisan or an Allied soldier, I would kick him in the face.'

'They don't understand you,' said his companion, clutching his fists to his face. 'The fucking Germans don't understand you.'

Fiamma and Rosa clasped each other's hands.

One of the soldiers guarding them looked at his watch. 'They should be here by now to take them,' he said. 'I can't stand this much longer.'

'Keep it together,' the other soldier told him.

'Are they really going to shoot these people?' the first soldier asked. 'They've done nothing wrong. I joined the army to fight for the fatherland, not to kill old people and children.'

'Shut up!' the second soldier ordered him. 'One of them might understand German. Do you feel sympathy for these people so much that you want to be shot along with them? Don't you know these people would cut your throat in your sleep if they could? As for that woman and child, be thankful it's not *your* woman. Not *your* child.'

Rosa heard voices out in the courtyard. The colonel was speaking with someone. She rose slightly and saw that a small detachment of Germans was standing there. The executioners had arrived. The door to the kitchen opened and a soldier told the prisoners to come out. Rosa looked at each of the people as they stood. Fiamma helped the geriatric lady, who turned out to be blind, to her feet. The father picked up his child in his arms and was followed out the door by his wife. When the girl smiled at Rosa, it was all she could do not to break down and cry.

The detachment waiting outside consisted of two officers and four soldiers. So these are the men who will end my life, Rosa thought. One of the officers was standing with the colonel. The other was in the rear of the group, his cap pulled low. Rosa despised him most of all. He was too ashamed even to show his face. He did not look one of his victims in the eye but kept his gaze averted.

'Report back to me,' the colonel said to the first officer, with no emotion in his voice. 'I'd like to know how many people in that village offer information on the hiding places of partisans when they see how we deal with those who don't.'

The officers and soldiers stood to attention. The officer near the colonel ordered the frightened group to march down the drive. As they walked by the cypress trees, a black car passed them on its way to the house. Rosa caught a glimpse of the Marchesa's pale face and red lips. She did not look at the group. They were invisible to her. Rosa cringed and turned away. The Marchesa had finally won. Rosa was doomed.

She stared at the autumn leaves, the golden fields, the hills they were being marched towards. Those things seemed to have taken on a strange beauty. She prayed for her family and for the souls of the condemned villagers. She did not pray for the German soldiers. She could not bring herself to do that.

'Where are we going?' the blind woman asked Fiamma. 'No-one tells me anything.'

'We are being taken to another village,' Fiamma told her. 'A safer one. But we must walk. Are you all right?'

'I'm all right,' the woman said. 'I'd still be helping my son in the fields if I wasn't blind. It was the sun, you know. All the years in the sun ruined my eyes.'

The group had been walking for over an hour when one of the suited men stopped and looked at the officer leading the group. 'You're not taking us in the direction of the village.'

'Be quiet! Shut up!' the officer shouted at him in Italian.

'They are going to shoot us and push us into a ditch,' the man's companion said to the group. His legs nearly buckled beneath him. 'They're going to shoot us in the forest like they've been doing to the Jews. Our families will never know where we are buried.'

The elderly woman put her hand on his back. 'It's better this way, Nando. It's better our families and neighbours don't see this. Imagine all the children in our village. What would it do to them?'

'I am a member of the Fascist Party,' the man said, weeping. 'I hung Mussolini's picture in my office. I've never been a communist. I hate the fucking partisans. They are the lowest scum in the world.'

Rosa noticed the officer at the front of the group glance at the other officer, the one with his cap pulled low. They exchanged a smile. Bile rose in her throat. Did they think a man begging for his life was amusing? Rosa could never bring herself to kill anything, not even moths and spiders. Antonio often laughed at her attempts to catch the creatures in a handkerchief so she could take them outside. She didn't believe in stomping out a life just because she could. All those creatures had was their lives, who was she to take that from them?

'I want the Germans to win!' said the other man in a suit. 'As for that leader of the local partisans — the Falcon or whatever they call him — I wish him a long, painful death. They say he is very clever, but if I ever came across him I would cut his testicles off and use them to make sauce for my ravioli!'

'Shut up!' the German officer growled at him.

Rosa saw the officer with the cap was doing his best not to laugh and despised him more. She noticed the grenade on his belt. She didn't know much about weapons but she believed that if she tugged on that grenade, she could blow him up. They could die together. She'd like to see him laugh when he realised what she'd done. She was contemplating her plan when he suddenly spoke, ordering the group to put their hands behind their heads and kneel on the ground.

The couple with the child kissed each other. The mother cradled her daughter in her arms. 'It's all right, Carlotta. It will soon be over. Don't be frightened.'

Fiamma helped the blind woman to the ground. She gave a look of hate to the officer and then one of farewell to Rosa.

'Get up!' Rosa heard the officer with the cap say behind her. She didn't realise he was speaking to her until she felt his gun in her back. 'Stand up and walk backwards.'

Rosa's heart thumped in her chest. So she was going to be the first to be killed. Perhaps it was better. She didn't know if she could stand watching the others being shot and waiting her turn.

'You too,' the officer said, kicking Fiamma's feet. One of the soldiers took Rosa and Fiamma to the side.

'Oh God,' whispered Fiamma. 'They are going to kill them and then make us check they are dead before killing us.'

Rosa wasn't listening. She was looking at the grenade on the officer's belt, wondering how hard she would have to pull it to make it go off. Surely it was worth a try.

'Listen!' said the officer with the cap to the main group, his German accent suddenly disappearing. 'I'm sorry you can't return to your village. But up there through those woods is a farm that will take you all in. I hope that in gratitude for your lives, you will do all you can to cooperate with the farmers who give you shelter and food. As for the partisans, I'm sorry that you were arrested because of us but I hope you will come to understand that we are your fellow countrymen and patriots fighting for the freedom of Italy. We are not Nazis and we are not fascists. We don't kill innocent children, women or old people, only Germans, fascists and *traitors*.' He emphasised the last category and clearly directed it at the men in suits as a warning. 'I hope you understand. Now get up, don't turn around, and start walking.'

'What about the nurses?' the old man asked protectively. 'What are you going to do with them?'

'We need their services. They are staying with us.'

The little group stood up looking dazed. 'They aren't going to shoot us,' the young father said, breaking down in tears and embracing his wife and child.

Rosa glanced at Fiamma. The whole scene was surreal. These men weren't Germans; they were partisans. The uniforms must have been stolen. And what about their accents? They had played the part so well they had fooled the colonel — again. Rosa's mind was too muddled to take it all in at once.

'Who are you?' the elderly lady asked, still obeying the officer's order not to turn around. She had linked her arm with the blind woman and was helping her along.

'I am the Falcon,' the officer with the cap said. 'And if

it's all right with you good people, I'd like to keep my testicles.'

The officer took his cap off and turned to Rosa and Fiamma to say something. The smile disappeared from his face and his eyes grew wide with surprise. Rosa felt that she must be dreaming. For standing there in a German uniform with his hair cropped short was Luciano.

TWENTY-FIVE

Luciano and Rosa stood staring into each other's faces. The brutality of what Rosa had experienced in the past few hours left her with a void as if her soul had been drained out of her. But Luciano's grey eyes took her back to a time when she had been a different person. For a few seconds, despite the danger they were in, she felt calm. How had Luciano returned safely from Spain? All this time she had thought he was dead. She had been praying for him in the past tense, as one prays for the deceased. His expression was full of something she couldn't describe. There was so much to say but there was no time.

As soon as the rescued villagers disappeared into the distance, the bushes around them began to move. Men of many different nationalities appeared in the clearing: partisans. The Italians were dressed in khaki shirts and pants, but there were other men — Allied soldiers — who either wore their army uniforms or ill-fitting civilian clothes. There were about thirty in total.

'The bridge is ready, Commander,' said a lanky Italian with an unshaven face and long black hair.

Luciano snapped out of his daze, changing in an instant from himself to the Falcon. The bird was known for its vision and speed. It soared in the sky to hunt and dived to stun its prey midair.

'Later,' he said to Rosa, giving her one last look before turning away.

An American soldier handed Luciano and the other men who had acted as Germans khaki uniforms. Without any thought to the women standing near them, the men stripped off and threw the German uniforms to the soldier. Fiamma averted her eyes from the naked men but Rosa looked at Luciano with curiosity. Her gaze travelled down his muscular back to the scar on his left thigh. He was older and leaner but not aged. The light that he'd always had in him was burning stronger than ever.

'You too,' said the soldier to Fiamma and Rosa, speaking in pidgin Italian. 'Hurry!' He pushed some trousers and shirts into their hands.

Rosa and Fiamma ran behind a bush and changed their clothes. The trousers were too wide for Fiamma. Rosa helped her tie a knot in them at the waist and to roll them up from her ankles. The soldier took their nurses' uniforms and carefully folded them into his backpack. Rosa thought he looked like a wardrobe mistress at the theatre. Did he intend to keep the uniforms for future masquerades?

'Quick march!' said the soldier, when he had put the uniforms away. He pointed his gun at them.

Luciano called out to him: 'It's all right, Blackbird. They aren't hostages. They are volunteers. *Staffette*. They won't cause trouble.'

Luciano sent a meaningful look to Rosa, who nodded. Fiamma indicated her assent too. *Staffette* were the women who assisted the partisans — as couriers, spies, cooks and nurses. Rosa was reminded of her time with the Montagnani theatre group: Luciano was difficult to refuse. After what she had seen, she knew that she would do anything to rid Italy of the Nazis, including sacrificing her life, but she had to get back to Antonio. There was no time to explain that to Luciano or the soldier. The group moved stealthily through the forest, Blackbird acting as guide for the two women. Rosa sensed the urgency was not so much to get away from the Germans, who would surely pursue them once they realised they had been fooled, but to reach a destination before nightfall. They never crossed open fields but stuck to riverbanks, woods and scrub. Rosa was impressed by their ability to move through foliage without making a sound and did her best to imitate their catlike strides.

The group reached the crest of a hill as the sun was setting. Rosa could see in the valley below a village with a bridge leading to it. The village consisted of a church, café bar and tobacconist along with a few houses. Its position was next to one of the main routes north. When the group of partisans reached the top of the hill, more swarthy and bearded faces popped up from the grass or slid down from trees.

'The explosives on the bridge are primed and ready, Commander,' said a fair-haired soldier with a British accent.

'Where are Plover and Snowfinch?' Luciano asked him.

'They haven't returned.'

Luciano frowned. 'They haven't returned?'

The British soldier shook his head. 'Woodpecker and Duck got the villagers out. They are in an abandoned farmhouse up the hill. Most of them were cooperative. Except the priest. He insisted on staying.'

'Fool,' muttered Luciano.

There was the rumble of trucks in the distance. 'Stay down,' said Blackbird, pushing Fiamma and Rosa into the grass. Through the quivering blades Rosa could see a German army jeep followed by two trucks heading towards the village. The partisans disappeared from sight into the grass or behind rocks and trees. Rosa noticed the British soldier squatting behind a boulder with a detonator. She put the scenario together in her head. Having duped the SS colonel twice — once in the guise of Italian soldiers and then as Germans — the partisans had anticipated swift and violent reprisals. The SS colonel was sending soldiers to do another round-up at the village and had fallen straight into the partisans' trap.

The jeep came to a stop before the bridge. The soldiers in it jumped out and checked the beams and scanned the hillside with binoculars. Rosa felt the partisans collectively hold their breath. She pressed herself as far as she could into the rocky soil. Fiamma did the same. Rosa heard the jeep start up again and then the trucks. She hoped that meant the Germans had decided it was safe to cross the bridge. Suddenly the ground vibrated and the sound of a loud explosion pierced the air. Rosa looked up to see the trucks toppling off the bridge into the ravine below. Soldiers were falling out of them like rag dolls. There were shouts and screams.

'Stay here!' said Blackbird to the women.

The partisans stormed down the hill, their machine guns firing. They didn't take prisoners but shot any German soldiers who were still alive. Despite the atrocities she had seen performed by the Nazis that day, Rosa was stunned to see men killed in front of her. The partisans lowered themselves into the ravine and worked quickly to strip the trucks of anything that might be of value. Rosa saw the priest run out of the village towards the bridge. Luciano met him, and a conversation with much gesticulating followed. The lanky, black-haired partisan stood next to Luciano, his gun still ready for action. Rosa guessed that he was the second-in-command.

Blackbird ran back up the hill. 'All right,' he said to Fiamma and Rosa, 'come quickly before more Germans arrive. We need to get back to our camp for an air drop.'

The women wasted no time in running after Blackbird, trying to keep up with his long, athletic strides. Rosa's lungs hurt. She was close to collapse but now was not the time to succumb to human weakness. They followed Blackbird to the village, where the partisans were loading the spoils from the trucks and guns from the slain soldiers onto a donkey cart. Luciano and the second-in-command were still speaking with the priest.

'But they were on their way to the other brigade,' Luciano was saying. 'One of your villagers must have informed on them. Who?'

'None of my people would have done that,' insisted the priest.

Luciano turned to his second-in-command. 'We have to send a search party for Plover and Snowfinch.'

It suddenly occurred to Rosa that they were talking about Carlo and the other partisan. Luciano didn't know his brother was dead. Rosa's legs froze. She would have to tell him. What would happen then? Knowing Luciano, he would order a raid on the Villa Scarfiotti. Rosa remembered what Clementina had said about no-one leaving that place alive. She closed her eyes against the memory of Carlo's mutilated face. How could she tell Luciano about that? But if she didn't tell him, the men on the rescue mission would be risking their lives for nothing. Then an even more sickening idea plagued Rosa. What would Luciano do when he realised that she had given Carlo fatal shots of morphine; that she had killed him?

'Luciano!' she called, walking up behind the men.

The shouts of the partisans loading the cart were too loud and Luciano didn't hear her and continued arguing with the priest. 'Luciano!' Rosa repeated, louder this time.

Luciano spun around and stared at her. The second-in-command glared and pointed his gun at her. Not understanding why they should be showing such animosity, Rosa continued: 'Luciano, I know —'

Before she could finish, Luciano seized her by the shoulders and shook her. 'No names!' he shouted, glancing at the priest before turning back to her. 'Do you understand? No names, ever! If you want to address me, you call me Commander.'

Rosa was shocked by Luciano's rebuke and lost the courage to tell him what she had to say.

He softened his grip and looked at her apologetically. 'We have to get out of here. We have to find the whereabouts of two of our men. Later we will talk.'

He was about to turn away again. 'I know where Carl —' Rosa stammered, before correcting herself. 'They are dead,' she said simply.

Luciano's eyes narrowed on her face. 'How do you know?'

'The Germans,' Rosa said, finding it difficult to breathe. 'That's why they brought us to the villa. They had tortured them for information and wanted me to revive them. But I couldn't, and I wouldn't have anyway. They had been beaten up too badly. I gave Carl ... him ... morphine to stop the pain. That's why they were going to shoot me.'

'How do you know they're dead?' Luciano asked.

'They passed away while I was there.'

Luciano reeled back. He staggered to a wall and leaned against it. Rosa could see the battle going on inside him — between Luciano the loving brother of Carlo, and Luciano the commander who was fighting a war. She had told the truth but not the whole truth. She had left out the nature of the torture and her role in Carlo's death. Was it really necessary for Luciano to know more?

'I'm sorry,' she said, trying to hold back her tears. 'I would have saved them if I could have.'

The second-in-command rushed to Luciano and grabbed his arm. 'How do you know this woman is telling the truth?' he said. 'She could have been sent by the Germans to muddle your mind. That's what women are good for. The SS might be trying to provoke you. So far you have been nothing but cool-headed. You've outsmarted them at every turn. Maybe this is their way of getting you to make mistakes, to lose your head.'

'She wouldn't do that,' Luciano replied, staring at the ground. 'I know her. She loved my brother.'

'What do you know of her?' insisted the second-in-command. 'I've never heard you mention a nurse. The war has changed everything and everyone. Remember Cuckoo?

His own wife turned him in to the fascists because he wouldn't enlist. That's what we know of women. You can't trust these sweet-talking Florentines. If you are going to throw yourself at a woman, at least let it be a strong, dependable one like Marisa: a woman who knows her place.'

The British soldier made a signal from the hill. 'Germans!' he shouted.

The warning snapped Luciano into action. 'Take the priest,' he said to his second-in-command. 'It's him I don't trust.' Then, turning to Rosa, he gave her a look of such pain that she felt her heart crumble to dust inside her.

Darkness was falling. The partisans, along with Rosa and Fiamma, moved like a pack of nocturnal animals. They passed a field and five men, led by the British soldier, broke away from the group without a word. Rosa understood it was to intercept the goods that were being dropped by air, presumably from the Allies. The rest of the group approached a farm with two barns. The partisans unloaded the contents of the cart and hid them under the straw in the barns.

'Watch him,' Luciano told Blackbird, pointing to the priest. He then signalled for Rosa and Fiamma to follow him into the house along with the second-in-command, who Rosa had learnt was called Starling, and a portly partisan who was called Partridge.

Inside the house, two women were laying out a table. The younger one, with a swarthy complexion and robust figure, glanced at Luciano before settling her suspicious black eyes on Rosa and Fiamma.

'Bread, soup,' Luciano said to her, before turning to Fiamma. 'Sit,' he told her. 'Marisa will get you something to eat.'

Starling opened a door to a room off the kitchen and lit a candle. The shutters were closed. Luciano indicated that Rosa should follow him inside. Partridge came too. Starling fixed himself against the door and Partridge leaned on a windowsill. Luciano placed a crate next to Rosa and told her to sit on it.

'So explain to us how you ended up at the Villa Scarfiotti,' he said. 'Wasn't that where you worked as a governess? The Marchese's daughter ... she was once your charge?'

Rosa felt sick in the stomach. Luciano was interrogating her. There was a time when he wouldn't have questioned her loyalty and integrity. Before, he had been an activist; now he was a soldier. Was that what Spain had turned him into? Rosa could only forgive his manner towards her because of what he must have been feeling about Carlo.

'We will ask your friend the same questions,' said Starling, nodding towards the kitchen. 'So we will know if you are lying.'

Rosa related her story again. She still couldn't bring herself to be truthful about the extent of Carlo's injuries and the fact that she had injected him with a fatal dose of morphine. How could she describe those things? How could she possibly explain them?

When Luciano had finished asking Rosa questions, Starling asked her exactly the same questions again, followed by Partridge. Rosa was afraid and exhausted but didn't contradict herself. Luciano glanced at Starling and Partridge, who both shrugged. Starling reluctantly conceded that Rosa was probably telling the truth.

'We need nurses,' said Partridge, resting his hands on his stomach. 'This could turn out to be good luck.'

'We need nurses,' agreed Starling, 'but they can stay at Vicchio. We don't need them here.'

'No, they will stay with us,' said Luciano. 'They need to move wherever we do.'

Rosa looked up. 'I can't stay,' she said. 'Antonio is in prison. I was supposed to collect him today. They won't let him out unless a relative is present.'

'So another relative can accompany him,' said Starling.

'There isn't anyone,' answered Rosa. A new thought stung her. What if the partisans didn't let her go? What would happen to Antonio?

Starling sent Luciano an exasperated look. Luciano turned away from him. Rosa wasn't sure if he was even listening to the conversation any more. Perhaps he was thinking about Carlo.

'Too bad then,' said Starling. 'Your husband will have to stay in prison.'

Rosa stood up. 'He's Jewish!' she said.

Luciano looked back towards her. If Rosa thought that getting down on her knees and begging would have helped, she would have done it. Antonio was in prison. He needed her. Rosa could not have begged the SS officer for her own life when he pointed the gun to her head, but she would sink to any level to save her husband.

'If you let me leave to get my husband out of prison, I swear on my life that I shall return,' she said. 'I will be your nurse. But please let me get my husband to safety first!'

The men said nothing. Luciano was looking at Rosa but she couldn't read his expression. Something inside her broke. Tears poured down her face.

'He's Jewish!' she wept. 'Don't you understand what will happen to him if he's left in prison? I swear on my life that I will come back!'

Starling shook his head. 'I told you we couldn't trust her,' he said to Luciano. 'The first sign of sacrifice and she's crying —'

'Her husband is Jewish,' said Partridge, cutting him off. 'Let her go. I believe she will come back to help us. Maybe her husband will join us?'

Rosa nodded. Yes, of course Antonio would. Both she and her husband had changed their views on what they were willing to do to fight the fascists. For a moment Rosa felt a light of hope but Luciano snuffed it out.

'It's too dangerous,' he said. 'Someone might recognise her.' He turned to Rosa. 'After what's happened, they'll be looking for you.'

Rosa knew that Luciano meant that she might be tortured the same way as Carlo had been to reveal information about the partisans. She could see the conflict in his eyes. He wanted to help her, but the same way as he'd had to master his emotions over Carlo, he expected her to master hers as well.

'I'll take the risk,' she told him.

'We won't,' said Starling. 'The first slap and you will be blabbing everything you know. You'll get us all killed. None of us can consider our own petty lives any more. Don't you think that the men in this band have wives and children — families who might be killed at any moment by the Germans or fascists? Can't you think beyond your own trivial worries —'

'Enough!' Luciano said, raising his hand to silence Starling. 'You are talking disrespectfully to a nurse. I'm sure she understands sacrifice.' He glanced at Rosa. 'You can't go but we'll send somebody. We have contacts in the city. They will pose as a relative and get your husband out of prison.'

Rosa could have kissed Luciano's hands to thank him for his mercy. She realised that she had created tension between him and his second-in-command and hoped that the rift would not last.

When Partridge led her from the room, she heard Starling hiss at Luciano: 'Who is this woman to you that you are willing to endanger one of our precious contacts and possibly our whole operation?'

Luciano said something in reply, but Rosa didn't hear what it was.

The following day, Rosa maintained a surreal calm while she went about performing the tasks placed before her. It was as if she and Fiamma had changed uniforms the way actors change costume and now they were playing new roles. They set up a makeshift hospital in one of the barns and wrote out a list of supplies that the unit planned to obtain during a raid on a fascist-supporting village.

'Do you know how to clean guns?' Partridge asked them.

Rosa and Fiamma exchanged glances, then shook their heads.

A smile came to Partridge's face. 'No, I don't suppose two nurses from Florence would know. Well, I'll teach you because it's rather important that our guns work.'

The idea of handling a device whose sole purpose was to end life was abhorrent to Rosa. She hated everything about guns — their weight, the metal smell, even the shape of them. What she had seen in the past days had left her with a disgust for the human race and their bloodlust. She understood why Madre Maddalena and the nuns of Santo Spirito desired to shut themselves away in order to be close to God. To be amongst humans was to be tainted by their murderous instincts. They killed animals for sport and each other out of greed. Still, the task of cleaning guns was given to them for a reason, and Rosa and Fiamma followed Partridge's instructions to his satisfaction.

'The Falcon won't approve,' he said, handing them a pistol each. 'But you are to keep these with you at all times.'

There was something in Partridge's manner that reminded Rosa of Friar Tuck. *The Merry Adventures of Robin Hood* had been one of Nonno's favourite books. Rosa imagined that if Partridge had not been fighting, he would have been at a bar somewhere indulging in wine and song. But from the way he could unload and reload the pistols within seconds, she also understood that he would be a formidable soldier in battle.

'You didn't trust me yesterday,' she said to him. 'Today you are giving me a gun. Things change quickly around here!'

Partridge smiled wryly but then his face turned serious. 'I don't believe in leaving women defenceless. The guns are for your protection only,' he said. 'If you are cornered by a German, the first bullet is for him. Should you miss, the second bullet is for yourself.'

*

The men left on a reconnaissance mission in the afternoon. The priest was taken with them, but whether that was to return him to the village or execute him as a traitor, Rosa didn't know. Priest or nun, no-one's position was sacred any more. Rosa had not seen Luciano all morning. Was he avoiding her? Maybe he had gone somewhere to mourn Carlo.

Rosa and Fiamma were sent to the farmhouse to help with duties there. Despite their savage lifestyle, the partisans took pride in their military discipline. Rosa and Fiamma were set to work by Marisa and the other older peasant woman, Genoveffa, cleaning uniforms and ironing them. They had to scrub their own nurses' uniforms and aprons to get the blood out of them.

Afterwards in the kitchen, Marisa held out two dead rabbits by their ears. 'Skin them!' she said to Rosa in a thick dialect. Her complexion was dark but had a healthy glow to it. She wasn't refined in any way and she smelled of stale sweat and garlic, yet there was an air of majesty in her face with its noble nose and full lips. She didn't slouch like most peasant women but held her chin high like a queen.

Rosa looked at the bloody corpses in Marisa's hand and had a vision of two rabbits following their kittens into their burrow. She shook her head. 'I'd rather clean the toilet,' she said.

Genoveffa laughed but Marisa scowled. She said something in dialect to Genoveffa that Rosa didn't understand. The older woman stopped laughing.

'Then clean it!' said Marisa, her eyes flashing at Rosa. 'If you think you are so superior!'

Rosa was unfazed. It was obvious from the looks Marisa had sent Luciano the previous evening and the disdainful way she regarded Rosa that she was his woman. He was a sensual man and being a loner did not mean that he wouldn't take comfort in such vital and attractive flesh. For her own part, Rosa viewed the situation between herself, Luciano and Marisa with impassiveness. When she had first recognised Luciano, she had felt immediately the warmth that had once existed between them. She knew then that she had never stopped loving him; she had only stopped being with him. But now there was Antonio and the children and that changed everything. It was her family that she had longed for the previous night when she lay down on the hard bunk in the attic, not Luciano.

Two days passed before the men returned from their mission. The soldiers seemed relieved, which made Rosa assume that the mission had been a success and the priest had been spared. But Luciano looked troubled. He would not meet Rosa's eyes. After the men had eaten and he had given them their orders for the following day, he entered the house and called for Rosa.

'I want to speak to you,' he said, still not looking at her. 'Come outside.'

Rosa felt Marisa's gaze burning into her back as she followed Luciano out into the yard and then to the storeroom he used as an office. He closed the door behind them.

'I have bad news,' he said, after clearing his throat. 'Antonio has been transported to Germany.'

Rosa nearly toppled over with the shock. The worst thing she could have imagined had happened! Cold chills ran over her. She sank to the floor and buried her face in her arms.

'Be brave!' said Luciano. 'As far as our contact could ascertain, it's a labour camp he's been sent to, along with other inmates from Le Murate. A camp for Italian forced labourers — *not* a concentration camp for Jews. The conditions will be harsh but the aim isn't to kill them.'

'But it's only a matter of time, isn't it?' Rosa asked, trembling so violently she could hardly get the words out. 'Before they discover he's Jewish?'

Luciano crouched down beside her. 'He's not a member of the synagogue and he has been a practising Catholic for all his life. He married you in a church so there is nothing outwardly to mark him as a Jew.'

Rosa was surprised Luciano's contact had been able to

find out so much so quickly. 'But the city records,' she said. 'His father and grandparents were Jewish.'

Luciano studied his palms. 'I think you have some luck there. When the mayor of Florence heard that the Germans were coming, he destroyed hundreds of documents regarding citizens' racial origins. The only way Antonio could be discovered to be Jewish is if someone denounces him.'

Rosa tried to be reassured by Luciano's words. She closed her eyes to calm herself but the picture she saw of Antonio's face in her memory made her cry. She had missed getting him out of prison and away from the Germans by a few hours.

She looked up and saw that Luciano had turned away from her, his jaw clenched. 'What is it?' she asked.

He stood up and moved to the opposite side of the room. 'The other nurse ... she said one of the partisans had been hung on a hook. You said they had been beaten. What she described was far worse.'

A pain gnawed at Rosa's side. 'Fiamma fainted from fear,' she told him. 'She doesn't know what she saw.'

Luciano clenched his fists and Rosa could see that he didn't believe her. The truth was going to come out sooner or later.

'How could I tell you?' she asked him. 'How could I describe what they had done to Carlo? It would have driven you mad. The Villa Scarfiotti is like a fortress. If you had known, would you have had the strength to resist getting yourself killed trying to avenge him?'

'What happened?' Luciano shouted, more in anguish than in anger.

Rosa's hands shook. She did her best to describe the scene in the storeroom and recounted all that had happened from the massacre at the hospital to the time when Luciano and the other men had rescued the villagers.

Luciano stood up and punched his fist into the wall. The storeroom shook with his rage. 'Carlo!' Luciano clenched his fists again and turned to Rosa. 'You said you gave him morphine. How much? Enough to stop the pain?'

'Enough ...' Rosa broke down in tears. 'Enough to end his suffering.'

The silence in the room was oppressive. Neither Rosa nor Luciano moved. It took a moment for the meaning of Rosa's words to register with Luciano. He rubbed his hands over his face.

'Carlo!' he said, turning to her again. 'You killed him? You overdosed him on morphine?'

'They were going to torture him again,' Rosa cried. 'They were going to ...' But she couldn't get the last words out, couldn't tell Luciano that they were going to skin his brother alive. Whatever Rosa had failed to do, at least she had spared Carlo that.

Luciano rushed at her. Rosa was sure he was going to strike her and flinched, waiting for the pain that would come with the blow. She was surprised when he dropped to his knees and took her hands. His flesh was cold and he was trembling. All traces of the Falcon had gone. He was his old self. Rosa pulled him to her and cradled his head against her chest.

'I'm sorry,' she wept. 'I would have done anything for Carlo.'

Luciano looked up at her with pain-stricken eyes. 'I know you would have,' he said, his voice catching in his throat. 'I'll never be able to thank you enough for having that kind of courage.'

As part of the military unit, Rosa and Fiamma were given codenames, unlike Marisa and Genoveffa. Rosa was Raven because of her dark looks and Fiamma was Nightingale in reference to her nursing. Despite Partridge telling them that they had to think like soldiers, however, they were provided with dresses to wear because the men didn't like to see women in trousers. When the Flock, as the unit termed itself, discovered Rosa's skill with languages even Starling was impressed.

'A band near La Rufina was wiped out when they were

penetrated by a German spy posing as a French Allied soldier,' he told Rosa. 'We have the British and American soldiers to interrogate people in English to catch any traces of an accent, but no-one who can switch from French to German to Italian to catch anybody out. You're useful to us but also to the other units around Florence.'

When word spread amongst the partisan bands that the Flock had two nurses and a translator in their midst, Rosa's and Fiamma's skills were in constant demand. But that put them in danger too.

One day Luciano received a visit from the commander of a neighbouring band.

'We want to take Raven with us on a reconnaissance mission,' he told Luciano. 'We believe there is a German-fascist command setting itself up a few miles from our camp. If we can get Raven close enough, she can tell us what the Germans are saying to each other.'

Luciano shook his head. 'I'm sorry, Lungo,' he said, using the commander's battle name. 'She's not skilled enough for that sort of mission. She'd only get herself and your men killed.'

After the commander had left, Rosa overheard Starling say to Luciano, 'You can't protect her like a little dove. You have a weapon there and sooner or later you will have to use it. We have a war to win, you know.'

Luciano's face remained expressionless and he did not look at Rosa. Since the night she had told him the truth about Carlo, he had not said anything further to her. She still had no idea what he had been doing since Spain. They had never had that 'later' talk. She was beginning to suspect that they never would.

Luciano must have taken Starling's words to heart because, the following month, Rosa was included in a mission. The Allies had made an arms drop to the Flock on the understanding that the weapons, ammunition and food would be distributed to the other partisan groups in the area as well. To avoid suspicion and the loss of a large stash of the precious equipment if they were caught, the partisans had to make several delivery trips. The men posed as farmers and the *staffette* as housewives. Marisa made a successful delivery of guns hidden in the donkey cart, which had been stacked with manure. Genoveffa cycled to the next town with hand grenades in her shopping basket. Rosa was to accompany Partridge and a few other men to a unit across the hills that needed someone who spoke German to help interrogate a suspected double agent, and a nurse to attend to a partisan with an infected gunshot wound. The men were to deliver machine guns and a radio.

The group set out just after dawn. It was the end of autumn and the cold air bit at Rosa's legs until she warmed up from the exertion of negotiating her way through the forest. The route involved passing within a mile of a German camp, and the group had to use caution to avoid being seen. They were making their way down a hillside — scattered rather than together, as the vegetation was thinning — when Rosa noticed there was an unusual amount of bird activity in the area despite the season. She saw a flock of snowfinches busily darting to and from a rock crevice. Snowfinch had been Carlo's battle name. Rosa had thought that the birds were only found at higher altitudes, but perhaps closer to winter they moved down the hillsides. She was watching the flock with fascination when she heard a 'click'. Her heart skipped a beat. Her first thought was that somebody had set their gun sights on her and she was about to be shot full of holes.

Before she had time to whistle the group's warning call, two German soldiers stood up from the bushes. They were as surprised to see Rosa as she was to discover them. The soldiers' guns were slung over their backs. One of them was holding a camera and the other a pair of binoculars. Rosa realised that the sound had been made by the camera.

'*Buon giorno*,' said one of the soldiers.

He and his companion smiled at Rosa. They were young, no more than eighteen or nineteen, with smooth skin and baby-blue eyes. Rosa realised that her dowdy woollen dress and stockings, mid-length coat and scarf had caused them to take her for exactly what she was posing as: a farmer's wife collecting firewood.

'We see many birds today,' the first soldier told her.

Rosa's head felt light. The soldiers were birdwatching. The moment was too bizarre to be real. Didn't these German boys know how dangerous the hills were? Hadn't they been warned?

The surreal moment could have ended there. Rosa could have nodded and walked on without things going any further. The young soldiers did not suspect her and they wished her no harm. But then Woodpecker and Duck burst from the trees, unaware of the situation. The German soldiers' eyes grew wide when the men in the khaki uniforms appeared behind Rosa.

'*Cazzo*!' swore Woodpecker when he saw the Germans.

The two soldiers, rather than reaching for their guns, backed away and started to run. Shots rang out in the air. They came from somewhere behind Rosa. The soldiers' bodies jerked and fell to the ground. The snowfinches fled. Rosa heard the crackle of twigs as the rest of the men arrived at the scene. Partridge lowered his gun. It was he who had fired. Woodpecker turned the soldiers over with his boot to make sure they were dead.

'Quick, drag them behind that rock,' said Partridge, 'and cover them before this area is swarming with Germans!'

The men obeyed the orders. Partridge stared at the bodies and wiped his brow. 'They were just boys,' he said to Woodpecker. 'Just ordinary soldiers. Not SS. I've got daughters that age!'

Duck and one of the other partisans took the German soldiers' guns and ammunition. Woodpecker picked up the binoculars but saw they were broken and tossed them into the makeshift grave.

'I had to shoot them,' Partridge said to Woodpecker, although his fellow partisan wasn't disputing the fact. 'They would have told their officers they'd seen us and where we were going. Every partisan in this area would have been compromised.' Partridge wiped his forehead again and looked at Rosa. 'Are you all right, Raven?'

Rosa had not moved from the spot where she had seen the boys. Her thoughts were indistinct. All she knew was that minutes ago the German soldiers had been alive, animated, enjoying the beauty of nature. Now they were dead. Partridge was right though. He'd taken a decision in a matter of seconds that she would not have been strong enough to make. She would have let the boys go. But then Rosa wasn't a soldier and couldn't think like one.

The men finished cleaning up and moved down the hill again. Partridge signalled for Rosa to follow. She thought of a volunteer in a Red Cross office somewhere sending letters to two mothers whose sons would never come home. *Just boys. Ordinary soldiers. Not SS.*

'*Cazzo!*' she said under her breath, before running after the men.

When Rosa refused to allow herself to think further about the death of the young German soldiers, she knew something inside her had changed. She had become hardened. Instead, she thought about what she had seen at the Villa Scarfiotti and about the stories of German and fascist atrocities that passed between the partisan groups, including the description of a young mother being beaten to death with her decapitated infant. Rosa was no longer a wife and mother. She was starting to feel detached from her family as if she were letting them go one by one: Antonio; Sibilla; Lorenzo and Giorgio; Allegra and Ambrosio; Renata, Enzo and Giuseppina. She rarely thought about Madre Maddalena. Was this distancing a kind of survival mechanism? The only way she could help them was to save Italy; it was as if the fate of her loved ones and the fate of her country were inextricably linked.

There was news of more horrors at the Villa Scarfiotti,

the latest being the murder of a group of terrified Jews who were shot as entertainment at a party the Marchesa hosted. With each new story that reached the Flock, Rosa watched Luciano's face grow darker. She sensed it was only a matter of time before he would insist on avenging the death of Carlo and everyone else who had been murdered at the villa.

Winter was descending rapidly. The Allies' progress was slowed and the battlefronts grew quiet. Rosa and Fiamma, with fewer wounded men to attend to, knitted socks and sweaters for the partisan army. Marisa took the socks the Flock didn't need into the local villages to be distributed amongst other groups by their wives and daughters. Before she left, Rosa heard Genoveffa warn her: 'Be careful you aren't caught. If they find you with socks they will hang you as surely as if you had been caught carrying grenades.'

Before the worst of winter set in, Luciano and his men went out on one final mission. Rosa and the other *staffette* didn't know where it was to take place or what it involved — missions were only discussed with those directly engaged in them — but Rosa noticed the partisans were packing large amounts of explosives. She assumed they intended to blow up a bridge or railway tracks. Whatever it was, she could see from the grim expressions on the men's faces that the mission was dangerous. When the unit was ready to leave, Rosa's heart dropped to her feet when Luciano turned around and looked each one of those staying behind in the eye. Was he bidding them farewell? Rosa was standing by the barn when the group passed by. To her surprise, Luciano stopped in front of her, his gaze resting on her face.

'You have to trust your husband, Raven,' he said, his breath making clouds in the cold air. 'You have to trust him that he loves you enough to do anything to survive so that he can come back to you.'

Rosa watched the men disappear down the road and through the trees. Luciano's words burned into her soul. If a man loved a woman, he would do all he could to return. Rosa believed that. But she wasn't sure if Luciano had been referring to Antonio — or himself.

TWENTY-SIX

A part from an Allied landing south of Rome, winter and the new year did not bring the partisans good news. Luciano and his men returned from their mission safely and with the information that Ciano and the other members of the Grand Council who had deposed Mussolini had been sentenced and shot.

'It's rumoured that the firing squad did a bad job of it too,' said Partridge, shivering. 'Somebody had to finish the wounded men off with a bullet to the temple.'

Parts of the mountains were snowed over and daily life, while still dangerous, was full of isolation and boredom. Rosa's convent upbringing and her earlier poverty and imprisonment had strengthened her for partisan life. Even Starling commented admiringly on her capacity to stay vital on small amounts of food and her ability to remain alert with little sleep. When the men were on their night missions, it was Rosa who kept watch over the camp.

One day when she was mopping down the makeshift hospital, Starling came to see her. 'Some Allied parachutists have come in,' he said. 'They are at a farm over near the ridge. One of them has broken his leg. I want you to come with me. I will teach you to shoot on the way. It's about time you learned to fire straight.'

Rosa did her best to keep a serious face. Starling was referring to the incident a few days earlier when her pistol had accidentally fired when she threw her kitbag down. The bullet had ricocheted off a rock, narrowly missing Starling's head. She knew his offer was a sign of how much his respect for her had grown since they'd first met. It was practical too. One of the women at least needed to know how to shoot a rifle if the men were away and the camp needed to be defended.

'I'll come with you,' Rosa told him. 'But I'm not shooting birds or rabbits. I'll only shoot targets that deserve it.'

'Understood,' said Starling, holding up some rusty cans on a string. He smiled. Rosa thought it was the first time she had ever seen his teeth bared at her without it being hostile.

'You're quite charming when you smile,' she told him, pulling on her coat.

'And you're quite charming when you shut up!' he replied.

The partisans didn't share much about their lives before they joined the Flock. Most of them had no idea what each other's real names were. It was a way to protect their families in case one of them was caught and talked under torture. Rosa guessed Starling was about twenty-five years of age. She also presumed, although she wouldn't say it, that he had been crossed in love. Why else was he so disparaging of women?

They walked into the woods and stopped when Starling found a fallen log. He placed the cans on top of it.

'Are you sure this is all right?' asked Rosa. 'I thought we weren't supposed to waste ammunition?'

Starling shrugged. 'Don't waste it then. Shoot straight.'

He showed Rosa the correct way to hold a gun, focus on her sights and aim at the target. 'If you keep your elbows tucked in, it will help to keep the gun steady,' he told her. 'And squeeze the trigger, don't pull or jerk it.'

Rosa fired. She hit the tin she was aiming for first go.

'Not bad,' said Starling. 'But you flinched. You have to get over that.'

'To tell you the truth,' Rosa confided, 'I loathe guns. I hate what they stand for.'

She had spoken without thinking and waited for Starling to explode with a diatribe on the weakness of women. Instead, he patted her on the back and said, 'That's all right, Raven. Just as long as you learn to hate Germans more.'

There was a faithful stream of supporters in Florence and neighbouring villages who risked their lives to bring the partisans food, clothing and news. The local farmers sheltered Allied soldiers and hid young Italian men avoiding conscription. Some village priests saved Jews from round-ups by slipping them into their congregations. Luciano saw the role of the Flock as being as much about protecting these civilians as it was to fight the German army and assist the Allies.

One day, one of the supporters from Florence, a man by the name of Signor di Risio, arrived on an oxcart. He'd disguised himself as a farmer, successfully Rosa thought, in his patched pants and worn hat.

'I'm sorry,' he said, greeting Luciano. 'But the Germans have requisitioned my truck. The journey's taken me longer than expected.'

The partisans were overjoyed when they saw what Signor di Risio had brought: woollen coats and sweaters, boots and shoes. The Flock had been lining their clothes with newspaper and cutting up rugs to use as insoles to keep warm.

'Here,' said Partridge, handing Rosa a magenta coat. She tried it on. The coat was tailored with a belted waist and shawl collar. The partisans whistled and Rosa gave them a twirl.

'You'll only be able to wear it at the camp, unfortunately,' said Starling. 'You don't look like a farmer's wife in it. You look like you've walked straight off Via Tornabuoni.'

'That's exactly where all this stuff came from,' said Signor di Risio. 'Many merchants there decided they'd rather give their goods to you than see them carted off by the Germans. The enemy have been raiding the stores by the lorry-load and sending everything to Germany.'

Partridge adjusted the camel-coloured trench coat he had put on. 'They aren't paying for them?' he asked, looking outraged.

'Some of the Germans pay, but with notes printed off in the Vienna Mint at an exchange rate that makes it worthless for us. Mind you, for the merchants who fled after the Allies bombed Florence in September, the Germans simply take what they want from their shops, closed up or not.'

Luciano shook his head. '*Bravo*,' he said. 'Thanks to Mussolini, the Italians are now the slaves of the Germans.'

Rosa thought of the furniture she'd had to leave stored at Antonio's shop. She pictured each piece — so lovingly chosen and cherished for its uniqueness — being carted off by barbarians who probably would not understand its true worth. Antonio might have thought that Rosa charming customers with her stories of the history of the piece was good selling, but he had never palmed off an ordinary piece of furniture as something more than what it was to even the most naïve customer, unlike other furniture dealers. Every piece had to be special. Now all that love was being brutalised and pillaged. Rosa shut her eyes. She couldn't think about Antonio or the shop. Survival for her had become a numbness of mind. She thought only of each task before her and never about the future. There was no knowing if the peasant woman who brought them potatoes, or Signor di Risio, or any of the partisans standing around the cart would be alive the next day. *Alive the next minute*.

Life had become ephemeral. Rosa could not allow herself to become too attached to anything.

The partisans thanked Signor di Risio and watched him on his way before returning to their duties.

'Raven, come with me,' Luciano called to Rosa.

She followed him to the storeroom. It was surprisingly cosy, with a blanket curtain across the door and a thick rug on the floor. The shutters were open to let in the weak winter light, but at night they were closed. Sometimes, when Rosa was on night watch, she saw Marisa tramp across the yard and knock on the door. But she didn't allow herself to think too much about what went on after that either.

Luciano pulled out a chair for Rosa and indicated for her to sit down. The storeroom was much warmer than outside but their breath still made steam in the air. Rosa pulled the tie of her coat closed and Luciano tucked his hands under his arms.

'Do you remember when we used to tour?' he asked. 'It was so warm some nights we couldn't sleep.'

Rosa recalled the hot night in Lucca when she was worried Sibilla would become dehydrated. She'd taken her to the hotel courtyard where it was cooler. In her memory she saw Luciano stepping out from the shadows, his braces down and his white singlet damp with sweat. The recollection made her warm despite the freezing air. She realised she was blushing.

Luciano smiled. 'I think of those days when I'm on night watch and my feet are turning to ice,' he said. 'I force myself to imagine that I'm standing on the burning cobblestones of one of the piazzas we played in, shimmering light all around me and sweat running down my back.'

Rosa laughed. The memory created a bond between them. Luciano asked her about Sibilla and the twins. He was relieved when she told him the children were in Switzerland.

'It's one less thing to worry about regarding reprisals,' he said grimly.

It was the first time since Rosa had joined the Flock that she and Luciano had spoken of personal matters. Although he had been grateful for what Rosa had done for Carlo, it had created a rift between them. Or perhaps their lack of conversation was simply because the world was upside down and the past didn't register with anyone any more. Rosa herself could barely remember giving birth to her children, being a mother. Deep down in her heart she loved them, but it was more with the memory of the love of the passionate person she'd once been and not the machine that she had become. Passionate people didn't survive wars. They lost their nerve and made mistakes. Rosa had striven to master herself. *I shall gain mastery over my heart.* She winced when she remembered the words she had seen in the Marchesa's chamber and repeated in Nerezza's notebook. She looked at Luciano and suddenly understood what it meant. To subdue one's emotions, one's hopes and dreams, and focus only on survival — and, hopefully, triumph. As long as there was a war to fight, she and Luciano could not revive old feelings.

Luciano shifted his gaze to the window, lost in thought for a moment. Something was bothering him.

'What is it?' Rosa asked.

Luciano lit a cigarette stub and blew out a puff of smoke. 'There is a *staffetta* coming to Borgo San Lorenzo,' he said. 'One of our best. She raises money from our supporters. I need you to go to the town to meet her and collect the money. You'll be watched. You have to be careful.'

'I'm going alone?' Rosa asked.

Luciano shifted uncomfortably. 'Woodpecker will take you to the stop before the factory where the other passengers get on. The driver is one of us. He'll support the story that you are coming from Florence if anyone questions him. But once you are in Borgo San Lorenzo, you'll have to find your own way. There's a restaurant there where the *staffetta* will meet you. It's a place favoured by Germans and fascist officials.'

Rosa's eyes widened. Now she understood Luciano's discomfort. He was sending a lamb amongst wolves. She wondered if this mission was the reason that Starling had insisted on training her not only in rifle shooting but also in firing her pistol at close range. Did he expect that she might need to defend herself?

'It's best in this situation to be right under their noses,' explained Luciano, rubbing his hand over his face. 'It's when strangers meet in secret that suspicions are raised. Signor di Risio has obtained you a suitable dress, perfume and so on. You can wear your new coat. There will be a man with the *staffetta* so it doesn't seem out of place for two women to be dining unaccompanied. Hopefully that will deter any amorous Germans from imposing on you.'

Rosa sucked in a breath. She was afraid. While she was at the camp she didn't feel danger for herself, only for the men when they went out on missions. But this was a war and she was part of the freedom army. She had to play her role if that's what she was asked to do. Obviously Luciano had his reasons for sending her, although she was touched to see that it distressed him to be putting her in danger. Because of that, she did her best to quell the cold fear in her stomach and put on a brave face.

'How am I going to recognise this *staffetta*?' she asked.

Luciano smiled. 'You'll recognise her,' he said. 'Orietta hasn't changed so much since you last saw her.'

Borgo San Lorenzo would have been an attractive town in peacetime, located on the left bank of the Sieve River and surrounded by hills. But the bombing by the British airforce the previous Christmas and the cold winter gave the place the melancholy air of a town that had lost two hundred people.

The bus driver struck up a conversation with Rosa, who sat directly behind him to avoid the other passengers seeing her face. He asked her set questions to which Luciano had given her the answers, about where she was coming from and who she was visiting, to throw any spies on the bus off her scent. But when the bus reached the station, the other passengers seemed more interested in hurrying to the safety of their homes than paying attention to the attractive stranger in the expensive coat.

At the bus station there was a dog standing to attention, looking hopefully at each passenger as they passed.

'Ah, Fido,' said the bus driver, pulling a piece of cheese from his pocket and giving it to the dog. 'His master saved him from a dangerous river when he was a stray puppy,' the driver explained to Rosa. 'Fido is quite a well-known character in town: he always accompanied his master to the bus station each morning and returned every evening to greet him when he came home from work.' The bus driver patted the dog on the head. 'Although poor Signor Soriano won't be coming home any more, Fido still comes every evening and waits for him.'

'The bombing?'

The driver nodded grimly. 'They were aiming for the German fortifications, but they blew up a lot of innocent people instead.'

Rosa cast her eyes down. When was all this killing going to end?

The bus driver nodded towards a long street. 'Now, if you walk straight ahead you will come to a piazza,' he told her. 'The restaurant you want is on the left.'

Rosa thanked the bus driver and patted Fido, who, the driver assured her, was being taken care of by Soriano's widow and the people of the town, before setting off on her way. The loaded pistol she carried in her bag weighed on her shoulder.

Rosa steadied her breathing when she found the piazza and spotted the restaurant with its canopied door and French windows. She recalled how the partisans had looked at her with envy when they saw her dressed up and being taken to the forest by Woodpecker, guessing she was being sent on an assignment. Their nerves were strained by weeks of inactivity.

They preferred risk to waiting. Only Marisa and Genoveffa were fully occupied with preparing food and other domestic chores, and Fiamma with three soldiers suffering from influenza. Rosa recalled Luciano's expression when she was leaving. He didn't utter a word but it was there in his eyes. *Come back*, he was saying. She understood then that what existed between them was only being held back by the catastrophe they found themselves in and by Rosa's love for Antonio. The image of Fido waiting for a man who would never return came to Rosa. But as quickly as the picture formed she pushed it from her mind. She couldn't afford to have those thoughts, particularly before a dangerous mission; that's why she preferred not to think at all.

She handed her coat and scarf to the coat-check girl as well as the overnight bag she had brought with her. She straightened her dress before entering the restaurant. It featured padded shoulders and a wraparound bodice, and it was simple and elegant: the kind of dress she might have worn before the war. Rosa had the sense she was slipping into a snake pit when she saw the number of SS officers and fascist officials seated in the restaurant. She had styled her hair so that a curl hid one side of her face in case she needed to turn away if she saw someone she knew. The women in the restaurant were mostly the diamond-clad German mistresses of the high command, but she did see one Italian woman feeding a German officer a fig. Rosa lifted her chin and did her best to hide her disgust. Not all Germans were bad people; she understood human nature well enough to know that. But all Germans were the enemy, and anyone who took one as a friend or a lover was a traitor as far as Rosa was concerned. Besides this, the SS officers were the worst of the worst. Rosa was surprised a partisan hadn't finished them off with a bomb thrown in the window one evening. But perhaps the thought of the reprisals the townspeople would suffer deterred them from action.

Orietta was sitting in a booth by the window with a man in a silk suit. She had chosen the most conspicuous spot in the restaurant for anyone passing by, but Rosa guessed that she had her reasons.

'My darling sister,' she said, rising to greet Rosa. 'I hope it wasn't too arduous for you to travel at night? I was worried the bus would be shot at or bombed if you travelled during the day.'

Rosa returned Orietta's embrace. 'Not at all,' she said, playing her part. 'I'm so happy to see you.'

'This is Emanuele,' said Orietta, introducing the man. 'He's been very keen to meet you.'

Emanuele was in his late thirties with a receding hairline and large, wide-set eyes. Rosa's heart dropped when she saw the fascist insignia on his lapel until she realised it was only for appearance. He rose from his chair to greet her and took her hand.

'I'm pleased to make your acquaintance, Signorina Gervasi,' he said, using Rosa's undercover name.

Rosa, Orietta and Emanuele sat down and made fictional chitchat about mothers and fathers, aunts and uncles who didn't exist. Orietta introduced Emanuele as a banker. Rosa wondered what he really did. He spoke with a slight lisp. Rosa was intrigued by the gold-and-ruby signet ring on his finger. He had smooth skin and good teeth. He didn't look like someone who was starving through the war, but perhaps that evening none of them did. Orietta was wearing a silk taffeta dress with a sweetheart neckline and looked the part of a wealthy young woman. Her code name in the Flock was the Canary.

The waiter brought them the dinner menus. Rosa had not seen so much food in years. The prices were black market but the variety was plentiful. She chose the carrot soup and the *tortelli di patate*, which was the speciality of the town. She thought it was sufficient to look like a healthy, feminine appetite without spending too much of the Flock's hard-won funds. Orietta also ate elegantly but modestly while Emanuele tucked into the beefsteak, the most outrageously expensive item on the menu, with gusto. Rosa wondered if it was what he thought necessary to keep his cover. Luciano had said that the best resistance work was done right under the enemy's nose.

When they were ready for dessert, the waiter returned with the menu. Rosa was dismayed when she saw all that was available were peach dishes: baked peaches, peaches in wine, peach cake and peach custard.

'The chef apologises,' explained the waiter. 'But all we have is tinned peaches.'

Before the war, there was nothing Rosa enjoyed more than to eat a peach picked straight from the tree. She loved the bright colour, the fragrant smell, the soft, moist flesh. She even liked tinned peaches in winter. But the standard Allied food drop to the partisans always included tinned peaches and eating the slimy, half-frozen fruit from the can in winter had nearly turned Rosa off them for life. But to maintain appearances she chose the baked peaches.

During dessert, more small talk ensued. Rosa was careful not to look around the room. She didn't want to catch anybody's eye and raise interest in herself. She continued to be intrigued by Emanuele. His manner was smooth, yet there was something about him that made her uneasy. But then, Rosa had to allow they were in the midst of the enemy. It would be difficult for even the most level-headed person to remain completely at ease.

Emanuele paid the bill and excused himself to go to the men's room. Rosa took out her compact and powdered her nose. Her heart skipped a beat. She saw the Marchesa Scarfiotti in the mirror's reflection. She was leaving the private dining room with a fascist officer and they were heading towards the coat-check. Rosa was out of their direct view, but then an official car pulled up outside the restaurant and in a moment the Marchesa and her companion would pass by the window to reach it. Rosa dropped her bag as an excuse to hide herself. A comb slid under the table. She fumbled around on the floor, pretending to be searching for it. Her hands were trembling.

'Can I help you, signorina?' asked the waiter.

'It's all right,' said Rosa, holding up the comb. 'I've found it.'

She straightened when the car outside the window pulled away. Orietta had sensed something was wrong but Rosa communicated with her eyes that the danger was gone. Yet somehow it wasn't. The sight of the Marchesa had caused a queasy feeling in Rosa's stomach that wasn't the result of over-eating. It was because of what she knew was going on at the Villa Scarfiotti, but was powerless to stop.

It had been arranged for Rosa and Orietta to stay in a hotel overnight and for them to part publicly at the bus station before daybreak the following morning. Emanuele walked them to the hotel, then bade them goodnight before continuing to his own accommodation.

The hotel room wasn't heated but its floral wallpaper and overstuffed furniture were homely. Orietta checked for listening devices and found nothing. But the walls were thin and the women spoke softly to each other. Despite the chill, Rosa washed herself in the bath with lukewarm water. She had not slept in a proper bed for months and the clean sheets and the soft pillows were luxuries to her. Orietta climbed into the same bed with Rosa; it was the only way to keep warm. The women intertwined their feet together.

'You've got to enjoy comfort when you've got it,' said Orietta, fluffing her pillow and looking up at the ceiling. 'That's what I've learnt. I seem to do most of my sleeping on crowded trains these days.'

Rosa turned to her. 'Who is Emanuele? Am I allowed to ask?'

Orietta shook her head. 'Honestly, the less you know about anyone the better it is for you and the network. He's been working for the partisans since September and has proved himself to be very clever. His only weakness is that he loves the high life and isn't good at depriving himself if the occasion calls for it.'

'I noticed that,' said Rosa.

'Now,' said Orietta, rubbing Rosa's frozen hands, 'tell me how Luciano is faring and how things are in the mountains.'

Rosa told Orietta about camp life, and described how Luciano had rescued her and the villagers. The women would have talked all night, but soon the comfort of lying in a bed and the tension of the dinner overtook them and they fell asleep.

In the morning, while they were dressing, Orietta gave Rosa the money for the partisans. It was hidden in a hollowed-out book.

'Now, I believe you have a fully loaded pistol with you?' she said. 'That's for me.'

Orietta's job was a dangerous one so Rosa wasn't surprised that Luciano had used her as a courier to deliver a weapon to his sister. Rosa was going to be met at the bus station by Woodpecker, so she'd have her own armed protection back to the camp and didn't require the gun. She handed it over carefully, the way Starling had taught her.

'Thanks,' said Orietta, tucking the pistol into a scarf and pushing it into her purse. 'Someone has been befriending Allied soldiers in the forest and telling them that he has a stash of weapons and food in a barn. When they follow him, they find the militia waiting for them. Whoever he is, he's slippery, but I'll find him.'

A chill ran down Rosa's spine. 'You're going to kill him? I thought you were only a *staffetta*?'

'If I have to, yes,' said Orietta, straightening her collar in the mirror and slipping on her shoes. 'This person knows too much about the Allied soldiers and the partisans around Florence. Sometimes a *staffetta* needs to become an assassin.'

'Does Luciano know you are doing such a dangerous thing?' Rosa asked.

Orietta laughed. 'Luciano has his old-fashioned views of women, but this is a war. Everyone has to fight.'

Rosa was shocked but didn't say anything. Orietta was right: this was a war and everyone had to do what they were called to do. A series of images of the former Orietta played in her mind: the woman who sewed an exquisite baby dress for Sibilla; played the violin beautifully; and polished Antonio's antiques to a high shine. This was what war did. It changed people. It had changed Rosa too. She'd almost triggered a grenade when she'd thought Luciano was a Nazi and she and the villagers were going to be shot. Starling had drilled her to be able to pull out and fire her pistol in seconds if she needed to defend herself. But Rosa wasn't sure that she had changed enough to hunt somebody down and kill him.

'Rosa,' Orietta said, as if reading her friend's thoughts, 'would it ease your conscience if I told you that this person who is helping the fascists capture Allied soldiers is the same person who denounced Carlo? An insider?' Orietta's face remained hard but her voice rose in pitch.

Luciano had informed Orietta about Carlo's death, but Rosa didn't know how much he had told her about the nature of his torture and she didn't want to bring it up.

'You and Luciano have lost so much,' she said quietly. 'Your family has sacrificed a lot to fight for freedom.'

'You too, Rosa,' said Orietta, brushing back her hair from her face. 'You've suffered too. What happened to Antonio broke my heart.'

Rosa sighed. 'Antonio will survive. He'll come back to me. That's what I tell myself, although I can hardly bear to think about it. A prisoner of war joined the Flock a week ago. He'd escaped from the camp near Orvieto. The conditions he described were terrible.'

Rosa looked out the window at the still-dark sky. If she was cold in a hotel room, what was Antonio enduring? She turned back to Orietta. Her heart jolted when she saw the expression on her friend's face. She looked aghast.

'You don't know?' Orietta asked. 'Luciano didn't tell you?'

The floor seemed to shift under Rosa's feet. Despite the chilly air, she felt hot and faint.

'My God, you don't know,' Orietta said, sitting down on the bed.

'What?' Rosa asked, struggling to keep her voice low. 'What don't I know?'

Orietta wrung her hands and looked at Rosa. 'Luciano asked me to find out what happened to Antonio after you arrived at the camp. I was to pose as your sister and get him out of prison. But when I went to Le Murate, Antonio and several other political prisoners had been sent to Germany.'

Rosa took a breath. It was what she already knew. But the pained look on Orietta's face told her that there was more. She dug her nails into her hands. 'What are you trying to tell me? Was he sent ... was he sent to a concentration camp?'

Orietta shook her head. 'I traced the train he was on. Luciano intended to somehow stop it by blowing up the tracks further up the line. He wanted to rescue Antonio. Starling told him that he was crazy and I had to agree. I was afraid that if they stopped the train, the guards would automatically start shooting the prisoners. But Luciano wanted to try. There were six hundred men on the train: Italian soldiers mostly. Luciano said if they were free, many of them would join the partisans.'

Rosa stared at Orietta. The blood was pounding in her ears.

'Before we could get anywhere near that train,' Orietta continued, 'the Allies ... You see, they didn't know it was a train full of Italians. They thought it was transporting German soldiers. They bombed it as it crossed a bridge. Several carriages tumbled into the river. The passengers couldn't get out. They were drowned.'

The room turned white. Rosa couldn't see. When her vision returned she realised she had stopped breathing. Pain ripped at her insides. She choked back a sob. 'All of them?' she asked.

Orietta stood up and clasped Rosa's hands. 'About one hundred Italians survived the crash. Those who could made a run for the woods. I've used all my network contacts to find out if Antonio was one of the men who escaped but his name or description has never come up once in my enquiries. He might have been one of the injured who were then sent on to Germany, but according to our intelligence reports many of those men later died from not receiving proper medical treatment.

Rosa sat down on the bed. The New Zealander she had cared for at the hospital had told her that he hadn't felt anything in the first moments after losing his legs. He'd simply heard a deafening noise and been blown backwards, landing in a ditch. When he looked down and saw his legs were gone his first thought was, *Oh dear, no more cricket.* Rosa was feeling that sort of dreamlike shock now.

'Antonio's still alive,' she said. 'He has to be. We all use false names, don't we?'

Orietta put her arms around Rosa and looked into her eyes. 'Most of the Germans were in the carriages that didn't fall into the river. They fired on the prisoners escaping. Only a few men made it to cover. It is very unlikely that Antonio is alive. If he was, I know he would be doing everything to find you.'

Rosa barely remembered her trip back to the camp. With each mile that passed, her invented hopes turned to dust. Antonio's train had been bombed and all but one hundred of the passengers had perished. Out of those, only the prisoners without injury had been able to make a run for the woods. Many of them were shot in their flight. What was the chance that Antonio was among the small number that remained alive? Orietta was right when she had said that if Antonio were alive he'd be doing everything possible to find her.

When Woodpecker and Rosa arrived at the camp, the partisans looked at Rosa with questioning faces. Had something gone wrong on her mission? Luciano ushered her to his office. Rosa stood in the corner, tired, cold and numb.

'Why didn't you tell me about Antonio?' she asked. 'Why didn't you tell me the train was bombed?'

Luciano pursed his lips and stared at his hands. 'The same reason you didn't tell me everything about Carlo. What good would it have done? You needed a reason to keep going. I wasn't going to extinguish your best one.'

Rosa sank to her knees. She felt Luciano's strong hands on her arms. It was as if she had tripped and was falling, and he had caught her.

'Have faith,' he told her. 'Antonio may still be alive. You've got to believe that.'

Rosa shook her head. 'I don't think I'm strong enough to deceive myself like that.'

Luciano shook her gently and forced her to look into his eyes. 'One hundred Italians survived the crash. From what I saw, at least half of those made a run for the forest. The others were sent on to Germany. Yes, many died but others are alive. You mustn't give up hope that Antonio is one of those who lived.'

'Why are you telling me this?' Rosa asked. She felt like a person who was about to lose consciousness being slapped awake by their rescuer. She wanted to be saved, she wanted to be comforted and to believe, but doubt was enveloping her.

The light caught in Luciano's eyes when he gazed at her. 'You thought I had died in Spain, didn't you? But I came back.' He didn't say it but Rosa imagined that she'd heard it: *I came back for you.*

Starling called from outside. Luciano touched Rosa's cheek before turning to go. 'Don't lose hope. It's all any of us have.'

The cold air rushing through the door when Luciano stepped outside made Rosa shiver. He was right. Hope was all they did have. The reality was grim. Rosa realised something else too: marrying Antonio, raising children and even thinking that Luciano was dead had not changed the love she felt for him. Luciano had once let Rosa go so that she and Sibilla could have a safe life. He had been prepared to risk himself to raid the train to save Antonio *for her*. Rosa finally saw the truth: no-one could ever love her like Luciano did. But I've seen it too late, she thought. There is nothing that can be done now.

TWENTY-SEVEN

In April, a young man avoiding conscription brought the Flock a terrible story. Communist partisans in Rome had exploded a bomb in Via Rasella while a column of German policemen were marching along it. The bomb had been hidden in a road sweeper's cart and several partisans had hovered nearby to keep passers-by from walking into the path of the explosion. Over thirty Germans were killed. The retaliation was swift and was ordered by Hitler himself to take place within twenty-four hours. Three hundred and thirty-five men — political prisoners, Jews, men and boys on the street — were rounded up and taken to the Ardeatine Caves.

The young man trembled as he repeated the story, told to him by a spy who had heard German soldiers discussing it. 'Because there was such a number to kill, the condemned were led into the cave five at a time and shot in the back of the neck rather than by firing squad. The soldiers in the killing squad were new to the task and several cases of cognac were provided to steel their nerves. One soldier refused to shoot and was forced to do so.

Another fainted. The killing took hours and, to save time, each successive group had to kneel on the bodies of the men killed before them. As the day went on the killing grew sloppy. Some of the prisoners had their heads blown off; others were not quite dead when the Germans threw grenades into the caves to seal off the entrance.'

When the young man finished his story, Rosa looked around at the faces of the partisans and also at Fiamma, Marisa and Genoveffa who were with them. In their eyes she saw growing determination. It occurred to her that the atrocities performed by the Nazis, intended to terrorise the Italian people into submission, were having the opposite effect. The Flock had doubled in size since spring had arrived and they'd had to move to another camp, higher up in the mountains. More civilians than ever were bringing them food and supplies, and the acts of union sabotage in Florence were increasing. The more the Germans killed people's husbands, wives, sons, daughters, friends and neighbours, the more reason they gave the Italian population to fight. If the Germans wanted obedience from the Italians, they should have made them comfortable and complacent and promised them the world. Attacking their families and friends brought out the soldiers in the race. An army was rising, still small in number compared to the general population, but with greater spirit than any Mussolini had imagined. It encompassed all ages, sexes and political and religious beliefs.

Rosa had experienced a metamorphosis herself. When she had returned from Borgo San Lorenzo and realised that the likelihood of Antonio being alive was slim, she had initially become paralysed. One night she dreamt that she was climbing the hills trying to find him. With effort she called out his name, and her scream awoke her. When she sat up, she found that her crippling grief had been replaced by rage. She raged against the Germans and against the fascists. She raged against Mussolini and everyone who supported him. She raged against the Allies for taking so long to reach Florence. And she raged against the Marchesa Scarfiotti.

'Get out of my country!' became thereafter Rosa's daily mantra. If Antonio was alive, he would not allow himself to be beaten and neither would she.

Rosa practised shooting her rifle every day. If ammunition was scarce, she practised without bullets, falling to her knee and taking aim in an instant. She ran, did push-ups and punched her fists into bags of corn husks, determined as any man to annihilate her enemy. She was fighting for Antonio, for Sibilla, for Lorenzo and Giorgio. They were no longer the background to her mission, but the heart. Rosa had come to accept that she loved Luciano with her soul. There was something that connected them at a deeper level than the physical world around them. It was as if he were the twin that made her complete. But her love for him did not diminish her love for Antonio, her husband and the father of her children. She couldn't fight what she felt for either man. She accepted it as another contradiction in the woman she had become: a pacifist prepared to kill; a religious Catholic ready to break a sacred commandment.

One day when the men were leaving for what Rosa anticipated would be a dangerous foray, she offered to go with them.

'No!' said Luciano.

'Why not?' asked Starling. 'Raven is as good a soldier as any. Probably better. She's fast.'

'No!' said Luciano, raising his voice to show that there would be no further argument.

The next day, however, Rosa was sent with Starling to take information and supplies to another partisan band close to Fiesole. At last the Allies were making progress up the peninsula, and for the past few weeks had been dropping pamphlets in the forests urging the partisans to step up their actions against the Germans by cutting their lines of communication and stealing their supplies. There was talk of the various bands joining forces so they could attack larger targets now that the Allies were more regularly supplying arms and ammunition by air drops. Starling was to begin talks with the group known as the Staff.

For much of their journey through the woods, Rosa and Starling caught glimpses of the view of Florence below. Rosa thought it was as though she was looking down from heaven on a life she had once lived. The sight of it brought back memories of the cobblestoned streets where she had pushed her children's prams and the furniture shop and apartment where she had shared her life with Antonio.

When they arrived at the camp, Rosa was astonished to see Ada and Paolina among the partisans and Allied soldiers. They were cleaning guns. When they recognised Rosa they froze on the spot. The women had more grey hairs than they had the last time Rosa saw them, but other than that they hadn't changed much.

'Goodness,' said Ada, stepping forward and embracing Rosa. 'You turn up at the strangest of times. But I *knew* we'd meet again.'

'I feared you were dead,' Rosa said, tears in her eyes. 'Terrible things have been happening at the Villa Scarfiotti.'

Ada's face turned dark. 'We left when the Germans came. Evil has been rising at the villa again, out of the ground and out of the tombs. But good is still there in the woods, and now the three of us are back —'

Ada stopped herself and Rosa turned to where she was looking. Emerging from one of the tents was another familiar figure: Giovanni Taviani, the gatekeeper from the Villa Scarfiotti.

'He's our commander,' whispered Paolina. 'Some of the staff wanted to stay, but Giovanni rescued us. Signor Collodi is here too, as well as some of the groundsmen and a few of the maids. There's a tunnel that goes under the villa to the gatehouse. I don't think anyone knew about it except him.'

Giovanni called Starling over to him. Rosa had hoped that she would be included in the negotiations for the joining of the partisans, but she was obviously too low in status. Starling signalled to her to wait outside for him. Although Giovanni glanced at Rosa, he did not appear to recognise her. There was still the sad look of resignation in his eyes but, for a man approaching seventy years of age, his body was as strong and broad-chested as a youth's. Perhaps being a partisan leader had restored some of his self-dignity. Rosa couldn't forget the way Giovanni had betrayed his family, but her judgement was tempered by the fact that he had rescued staff from the villa and that he hadn't slaughtered the Weimaraner puppy even though the Marchesa had ordered him to. Rosa thought of Luciano back at the Flock's camp. Was there any chance he would reconcile with his father? He'd obviously had no idea of the identity of his neighbouring partisan commander.

Ada glanced at Rosa as if she knew what she was thinking. 'The butler, Signor Bonizzoni, escaped with us but unfortunately was shot when we attacked a German convoy. I found out from him what had happened to Giovanni Taviani. He stole a valuable heirloom from the villa and sold it in Rome. The Marchesa knew and threatened to tell the Old Marchese about it. That's what she's had over him all these years. If the Old Marchese ever found out, the shame would have killed Giovanni. The Old Marchese looked on him like a friend, and asked his son to make sure he was taken care of after his death.'

Rosa saw everything clearly now. 'The Old Marchese and Giovanni knew each other before he went bankrupt. That's why the Old Marchese helped him by giving him a job,' she said, half to Ada, half to herself. 'When Giovanni stole that heirloom, he wasn't after the money for himself.'

Ada and Paolina looked at her quizzically.

'Giovanni wanted it to pay for his wife to go to hospital.'

Rosa repeated Donatella's story of a successful tailor who had made a risky investment and lost his entire fortune. The picture of the family being evicted from their home on Via della Pergola returned to her. Giovanni Taviani had made some tragic mistakes, but he'd tried to make up for them. It was more than could be said of a lot of people.

'Rosa, there is something important we need to talk about,' Ada said.

Rosa turned to her. 'I'm Nerezza's child. Is that it? The one who was supposed to have died? But I didn't, someone took me to the convent of Santo Spirito.' She touched the key around her neck. 'By some coincidence I happened upon Nerezza's old grand piano. The silver key fitted the lock on the piano stool.'

Ada gave a start. Her eyes misted over. 'I thought you had perished,' she said. 'I took that key from your mother's piano stool and tucked it in your wrappings for protection. I was the one who bathed and changed you after your feedings with the wet nurse. When the Marchese told me you had died, my heart broke.' Ada's voice trailed off before she regained her composure. 'I had thought you were too healthy and strong to die, but then I remembered everyone had always said the same thing about Nerezza.'

Although Ada had only confirmed what Rosa had already guessed, she felt overwhelmed. 'I am Nerezza's daughter for sure then,' she said. 'The Marchese was my uncle and Clementina is my cousin and I didn't even know it.'

Starling and Giovanni finished their talks and came out of the tent. Starling signalled to Rosa that he was ready to leave.

'I believe the Marchesa had me sent to the convent,' said Rosa. 'She didn't want me around. She told everyone that I had died.'

'But that's impossible,' said Ada.

Rosa looked at her, not comprehending.

'The Marchesa wasn't there when you were born,' Ada said. 'She remained in Egypt where they had been spending their honeymoon. Only the Marchese came back when he was told his sister was gravely ill. Nobody questioned it because everyone knew the two women hated each other. The Marchesa didn't come to the villa until a month after the funeral. She arrived late in the night so I didn't see her. She was sick too, with some Egyptian disease, and she stayed in her room for weeks with only her maid and Signora Guerrini attending her. After that, she always looked pale and ill and never ate properly.'

'Raven, we must leave now,' Starling called.

Apart from the fact that she was Nerezza's daughter, the scenario Rosa had put together had fallen apart. 'Then it must have been the Marchese who had me sent to the convent,' she said. 'But why would he have done that? Why would he have sent me away, and then collected me all those years later to be a governess to Clementina? It doesn't make sense. I never had any indication from him that he thought I was anything other than an orphan from the convent.'

'Raven!' Starling fixed his eyes on Rosa. She had no choice but to hastily bid farewell to Ada and Paolina and follow him.

'Come for a return visit,' said Ada. 'We'll talk more.'

As Rosa and Starling made their way back to the Flock's camp, Rosa turned and caught a glimpse of the road from Fiesole to Florence. Each time she had made that journey it had been significant. But would she ever know who had taken her down it that first time — and why?

Rosa waited until Starling had spoken with Luciano before approaching his tent herself. When she entered he was tracing a map of Florence with his finger. He smiled at her and Rosa remembered the first time she had seen him with the sun in her eyes that day by the Arno. What a journey they had taken since then.

Starling had told her that the Gatekeeper — Giovanni's battle name — had invited the leaders of the Flock to visit him the following day. Rosa thought she had better warn Luciano.

'Luciano, the Gatekeeper is —'

'The most capable partisan leader in the area,' Luciano cut in. 'He has managed some outstanding missions, which means the Germans are keen to find him. It's a danger, I know, but I have admired his leadership for some time. It's an honour that he is considering joining with us. Is that what you wanted to tell me?'

Rosa shook her head. Part of her was tempted to walk away and not say anything, but she had to tell Luciano. There was no way to soften the blow. She had to say it plainly.

'He's Giovanni Taviani,' she said. 'Your father.'

Luciano stared at her in disbelief. When the words sank in, he rose from his chair and turned away. Rosa was overwhelmed with pity. They were both people struggling with their pasts.

'Are you sure?' he asked. 'How do you know?'

'He was the gatekeeper at the Villa Scarfiotti. Many members of his band are from there. I found out that he was your father some years ago but there was no need to tell you then. I didn't want to cause you pain.'

Luciano had such a look of agony on his face that Rosa's own heart ached. She wondered, if Nerezza had lived and she was facing her for the first time, what they would say to each other. Joining the Flock was the most important thing Rosa had done in her life. But would her mother have been a fascist? If Rosa hadn't been sent to the convent, would she have shared those beliefs too? The possibility made her cringe. She looked back to Luciano. She could imagine a similar turmoil must be going on inside him, only for him it was real. For Rosa, it was only speculation.

'He's somebody else now,' said Luciano. 'Somebody I don't know. The Gatekeeper. The famous partisan. Not my father.'

'What will you do?' asked Rosa. 'Will you refuse to join with him?'

Luciano shook his head. 'He won't recognise me,' he said softly. 'I was ten when he left. I am a man now.'

'So you will still join with his band and share the command?'

Luciano closed his eyes, trying to master his pain. 'I have no choice. I have to think about winning this war and this is the only way we can do anything meaningful.'

Rosa wondered if it was possible that Giovanni would not recognise his own flesh and blood; and what would happen to his new-found sense of dignity if he discovered Piero and Carlo were dead — and how they had died.

The following day, when Rosa accompanied Luciano, Starling and Partridge to the Staff's camp, she wondered about Nerezza again. Had she been too hard on her mother by assuming that she would have been a fascist? She thought of the notebook and how she had been fascinated by Nerezza when she saw her opera sets. Nerezza was a great artist. Artists are sensitive people, Rosa conjectured, she couldn't have possibly behaved like the Marchesa. The Marchese wasn't a fascist, so maybe his sister wouldn't have been either. With that, Rosa began picturing how things might have been with her mother had she lived to bring up her child. Nerezza would have been strict, Rosa thought, but we would have shared a love of music and languages. I'm not beautiful like her. Would she have been disappointed by that or have loved me all the same? She flinched when she recalled that the date of her conception had been crossed out in her mother's notebook. But maybe that said more about what Nerezza had felt about Baron Derveaux than her? Rosa recalled how when she found out she was carrying Osvaldo's child she had been the opposite of delighted, yet once Sibilla was born, she loved her dearly. It would have been that way with my mother, she concluded. She would have adored me the way that I adore Sibilla. It's natural for a mother to feel that way. It is the most natural thing in the world.

Rosa felt her gut tighten when they approached the Staff's camp. Poor Luciano, she thought. Rosa had been included in the meeting because the Staff had several women partisans — not *staffette* but actual combatants. As well as

Ada and Paolina — who, Rosa realised, had been cleaning their own guns when she'd seen them the previous day — there were the maids from the Villa Scarfiotti, and two farmers' wives who had seen their sons hanged and their houses razed to the ground. With nothing left to lose, they had joined the partisans and could shoot as well as any man. Luciano, never comfortable with women as soldiers, wanted Rosa there to ease tensions if the need arose.

The atmosphere at the camp was friendly when the representatives from the Flock arrived. 'Welcome, comrades,' said the second-in-command, whose battle name was the Valet. Rosa wondered if the meeting would turn sour when Luciano saw his father for the first time. Giovanni emerged from his tent and Rosa studied his face for any sign that he recognised his son. She saw none. Just the sad resignation in his eyes that belied the determination in the set of his jaw and his proud stance.

Luciano shifted on his feet, but mastered his emotions and looked Giovanni in the face.

'So we meet,' said Giovanni, taking Luciano's hand and clasping him on the elbow. 'The Falcon — I am honoured.'

Giovanni ushered the delegation into his tent and was joined by the Valet and the Cook, who, of course, was Ada.

A young boy brought the group a bottle of wine and Giovanni poured it. He turned to Luciano and Rosa thought she caught a glimmer of something in his eye but it could have been a trick of the light.

'I have heard that you fought in Spain,' he said. 'And although the Republicans were defeated, you are remembered as an outstanding leader.'

'Spain made me what I am,' said Luciano. 'It changed me from a political activist into a fighter. I learned everything there.'

Giovanni raised his eyebrow and smiled, pouring Luciano a glass of wine. 'And what did you learn?'

'To not waste my energy on revenge. To not seek out and destroy the enemy simply to satisfy a weak human emotion.

Men and ammunition are only for useful purposes. We must solely attack targets that bring us closer to justice and freedom.'

Giovanni nodded his head, impressed. 'Then you have learnt well,' he said.

The Valet turned to Rosa. 'And you are the female partisan we have heard about — the one who runs like a deer in the forest?'

Rosa was embarrassed and blushed. Her training was supposed to have been secret. She'd had no idea she was being observed by other partisan groups. But when she looked at the Valet she saw that he'd meant it as a compliment not as a rebuke.

'We have many women soldiers amongst us,' said Giovanni, nodding towards Ada. 'They have proved the most successful soldiers because they have the element of surprise on their side. German soldiers do not expect a group of women gathering hay to suddenly turn guns on them.'

Luciano shifted uncomfortably. Rosa knew it was because he didn't believe that women should fight. It was the role of men to do that for them. In his eyes, a woman having to defend herself was a slight on the man who was supposed to protect her.

The discussion moved to strategy. As the front drew closer, the partisans needed to break into smaller divisions in order to remain hidden and move speedily, and yet maintain close enough communication and an effective chain of command so they could unite when the situation called for it. The group had been speaking for over an hour when the buzz of planes sounded from the sky overhead.

'Germans!' the Valet cried.

Giovanni was out of the tent in an instant, followed by the others. 'Take cover,' he ordered his band. 'They are headed this way.'

The camp's tents were already hidden under branches, and the partisans moved quickly to disappear into them.

Giovanni led the delegation into a makeshift wooden bunker half-buried in the earth.

The planes flew low over the camp but did not shoot. They disappeared up the hill.

'Stay where you are,' Giovanni shouted out to the camp. 'They may return.'

'Do you think they saw us?' the Valet asked him.

Giovanni shook his head. 'I don't know. But the sooner we break up and move from this camp site the better.'

Turning to Luciano, he said, 'I'm sorry our meeting has been cut short, but you had better get back to your camp and move your own men. I have an uneasy feeling about those planes.'

'So do I,' said Luciano.

No sooner had they stepped out of the bunker than the sound of shelling could be heard in the distance followed by gunfire. Luciano's face turned pale. 'It's coming from the direction of our camp! They are attacking the Flock!'

He bolted up the hill and disappeared into the trees. More explosions followed. Giovanni called out to his partisans and divided them into two groups: one to move the camp and one to follow him and Luciano. Ada passed Rosa a machine gun and they ran after the men, who were rushing towards the Flock's camp site.

When the partisans reached the forest on the outskirts of the camp, a terrible sight awaited them. The camp was surrounded by German storm-troopers. Rosa shivered when she recognised the skull-and-crossbones insignias on their helmets and jackets. This was the crack unit, sent only for special manoeuvres. But how had they discovered the camp?

Rosa could see that Woodpecker, who had been left in charge of the camp, had moved the partisans into the defence trenches. Marisa and Genoveffa were passing the ammunition along the line. The Flock were fierce fighters but sooner or later they were going to run out of ammunition and they had no way to escape. They were slowly being surrounded. The Germans fired a shell. It hit the old farmhouse that the Flock had been using to store its equipment. Another one struck the barn that was serving as a hideout and camp hospital. It burst into flames. Rosa flinched. Where was Fiamma?

She turned to Luciano, who was watching the disaster with horror on his face. Giovanni divided his partisans into detachments and ordered them to move towards the Germans. One of the squads hurried into the open as a distraction while the rest remained hidden in the forest. Rosa saw that they intended to fire on the storm-troopers from behind and in that way surround one side of the German attack force.

The storm-troopers were surprised to find themselves taking bullets from two sides. There were more partisans to fight than they had anticipated. They re-formed quickly to fire in all directions. However, they were outnumbered and exposed and outsmarted on this occasion by Giovanni. The partisans of the Flock now had a chance to turn their guns solely on the storm-troopers, attacking them from the rear, and, with Giovanni's partisans backing them up, the storm-troopers had no choice but to withdraw along the riverbed. But it wouldn't take long for such an elite unit to regroup and who knew when the planes would return. The partisans couldn't afford to be drawn out into the open for long.

As the partisans moved in on the withdrawing Germans, Rosa saw there were a number of injured men left behind in the trench. If the partisans had to suddenly flee, there would be no chance to save them. Fiamma stumbled out of the burning barn. She was too far away for the partisans to reach. If the troopers returned she was going to go down in a hail of bullets — or, worse, be captured. Rosa scanned the battle line. Two dead Germans lay by a machine gun they had been operating from behind a rock. Rosa looked at Ada who was thinking the same thing. If they could reach the gun, they could fire straight at the riverbed, cutting off the troopers' withdrawal. The Germans would then be forced to flee in several directions, delaying their ability to regroup.

'Cover me,' shouted Ada, slapping Rosa's back.

Before she knew it, Rosa found herself out of the forest and firing at the remaining German soldiers while running towards the machine gun. Ada reached it first, followed by Rosa, who rolled on her side fast enough to miss a bullet that whizzed past her head. She lifted herself onto her elbows. Ada had the machine gun and was firing towards the riverbed. The sound was deafening.

A trooper appeared from behind a tree near the women. Rosa's eyes widened as he hit the trigger on his gun but by some miracle it locked on him. Luciano took him out with a burst of gunfire while running towards the women.

'Get back into the forest!' he shouted, taking over the gun from them.

Rosa and Ada did as they were told, covering Luciano while backing into the forest. Rosa had no idea if she hit any of the troopers she was firing at, but at least she made them duck for cover.

Giovanni ordered the men forward. Starling reached Luciano and together the men moved the gun into a closer position. But the troopers were no longer firing, they were in full withdrawal. Rosa scanned the scene. Four partisans were dead from Giovanni's unit. Another three were injured. In the trench where the Flock had fought, there were ten dead that Rosa could see and another five injured. Fiamma was out of enemy lines now and Rosa ran towards her.

'Quick!' she shouted. 'The medicine chests!'

The women ran into the burning barn. Some beams were falling but the chests were not near the flames. They grabbed all they could and ran out of the building. The stretchers were hidden in the hay near the door, which fortunately had not caught fire. They dragged them out. Although the troopers were gone for the time being, the partisans had to hurry. Saving the injured was going to cost them time, but it was not in Giovanni or Luciano to leave their men behind. They would have buried the dead if they could have, but there would be no time for that.

Rosa fell into her role as nurse and directed the partisans to take the injured on stretchers as fast as they could into the forest. She was about to run after them when she saw Marisa, dead in the trench. Genoveffa was next to her, weeping. Although it was not the priority to take the dead and Marisa had disliked Rosa from the start, somehow Rosa couldn't leave the woman like that. She grabbed a stretcher and said to Genoveffa, 'We'll take her with us.'

Genoveffa gave Rosa a look of surprise and then nodded. Rosa took Marisa's limp shoulders while Genoveffa grabbed her feet. They carried Marisa's body into the forest, where two partisans took the stretcher from them. Rosa ran towards Luciano, who was talking with Giovanni.

'The wounded will slow you down,' she told them. 'There's a cave not too far from here. Leave me and Fiamma there with the injured men.'

'You'll be sitting ducks if the Germans find you,' said Luciano. 'There will be nowhere for you to run.'

'We'll all perish if you don't get away from here as soon as possible,' Rosa told him. 'Leave us overnight. If the Germans don't come by tomorrow, you can come back and collect us.'

Luciano was about to refuse when Giovanni stepped forward. 'What she's saying makes sense. From what I've seen, your Raven can take care of herself.'

Luciano reluctantly agreed to Rosa's plan, but ordered two of his men to guard the entrance to the cave with their machine guns and left them with a few rounds of ammunition. He turned to Rosa, about to say something, when the men bearing Marisa's body walked past.

'Stop!' said Luciano. He kept his face rigid but Rosa could see the pain in his eyes. He had not loved Marisa the way he loved Rosa, but she had been his partisan 'wife' and that meant something. Luciano's hands trembled when he touched Marisa's cheek. Rosa ached for him. For a man who had lost so much, each loss hurt more, not less.

'We'll take her with us to the cave,' said Rosa. 'If all is well, we can bury her tomorrow.'

Luciano looked at Rosa. 'Thank you,' he said, his voice hoarse. 'The Gatekeeper is right. You are a fighter. One of the best we've got.'

The night passed in the cave was full of tension. Rosa and Fiamma had to attend to the injured men before darkness fell as they would not be able to light a fire for risk of being spotted by the enemy. Fortunately the men had not sustained injuries to any vital organs, only their limbs. Rosa and Fiamma quickly cleaned and dressed the wounds. Rosa glanced at Marisa's body. They had not been able to spare a blanket for it and she was struck again by Marisa's queen-like profile. She had been quiet in life and was now silent in death, Rosa thought. She remembered Marisa ordering her to skin the dead rabbits and wondered what had inspired the simple peasant girl to join the partisans.

At dawn, Luciano came with a band from the Flock to move their comrades. First, they dug a grave for Marisa. Rosa and Fiamma placed wildflowers in her hair and a bunch in her hands before she was put in the ground. Rosa could not bring herself to look at Luciano's face, afraid of the pain she would see there.

Afterwards they moved through the forest towards the new camp. The injured were to be taken to the barn of a sympathetic farmer.

Luciano fell into step with Rosa. 'The double agent that Orietta has been tracking,' he said quietly, 'I believe he is the one who gave the Germans the location of the camp. I know that Orietta returned to Borgo San Lorenzo two days ago. I want you to go there and tell her what happened to the Flock. It might help her to pinpoint who the agent is.'

After the German attack, both the Flock and the Staff broke their bands into smaller divisions. While Fiamma stayed with the injured men near Vicchio, Rosa went to

Luciano's camp near a farmhouse in the Mugello Valley. The farmer's wife gave Rosa a floral dress for her mission into Borgo San Lorenzo. It was agreed that she should change her appearance in case anyone recognised her from her last visit. Rosa was touched because it was obviously the woman's prettiest dress and had been kept for special occasions. The woman's daughter cut Rosa's hair and bleached it blonde. She had been a hairdresser in Sesto Fiorentino but had come back to live with her parents when her husband joined the army. He was now a prisoner of war in Germany.

'Ah, Jean Harlow!' the women cooed when the final result was revealed. '*Bella! Stupenda!*'

There had been a time when bleached hair was the realm of prostitutes in Italy, but Hollywood had changed that. Even though American films had been banned during the war, it didn't stop young Italian women from imitating movie stars and dying their hair. Rosa had thought that blonde hair wouldn't suit her dark skin and eyes, but the colour was not unflattering and did make her look younger. She plucked her thick eyebrows into arches and transformed herself into a young coquette. She didn't wear make-up, but freshened her complexion by pinching her cheeks. The picture was completed when the farmer wheeled out Rosa's means of transport: a bicycle with a gelato cart attached to the back of it. On the canopy were the words *Luigi's Gelato*.

'Be careful on the road,' Luciano warned Rosa and the farmer, who was taking her part of the way in a donkey cart because his truck had been requisitioned by the Germans. The Allies were bombing vehicles on roads and gangs of bandits roamed the forest claiming to be partisans when they were nothing more than thieves and rapists. Luciano hated them with a passion because they turned the farmers against the partisans. 'If I catch any,' he vowed, 'I will hang them.'

The farmer dropped Rosa off some distance out of Borgo San Lorenzo. By the time she reached the town her thighs were raw and her calves were aching. Although the gelato cart was empty, it had been difficult to negotiate the hills and the holes in the road that had been caused by shelling. Unlike her first visit, this time there were two German soldiers patrolling the main road into town. Rosa wondered why. Fortunately, Borgo San Lorenzo was a large town and it would be easier for her to lie that she had a cousin she was going to help there than it would have been with the smaller villages in the valley. Rosa slowed down when she reached the patrol. One of the soldiers waved her on but the other one stopped her.

'What's in your cart?' he asked her.

'It's empty,' she told him truthfully. 'I will fill it when I reach my cousin's store.'

'What will you fill it with?' asked the soldier.

'With grenades,' said Rosa, smiling.

The soldier smiled back. Rosa's hunch had worked. He'd stopped her because he thought she was pretty, not because he suspected her. He was younger than she was and had a friendly face. He didn't look like he belonged in a brutal war.

'You sell gelato?' he asked.

'Only around the main streets and the piazza when my cousin can't find someone else to do it.' Rosa hoped the soldier's questioning would end there.

His face turned serious. 'I'm afraid business might be bad here today,' he said. 'I'd stay away from the centre of town, if I were you. There's something you don't want to see.'

The other soldier on guard coughed as if to remind his colleague that he wasn't supposed to be friendly with the local population. The first soldier stepped back and waved Rosa on, much to her relief. She was puzzled by what he had said. Why would business be bad today? It was a warm, spring day: a perfect day for enjoying gelato.

Her sense that something was wrong increased when she rode in the direction of the hotel where she had stayed with Orietta. The shutters on the houses were closed despite the fine weather, and the few people who were out on the streets moved in haste and with stupefied expressions on their faces.

Rosa caught the eye of a baker closing the grille of his shop. 'Don't go towards the town centre,' he told her. Behind him, Rosa saw his wife. She was crying into her apron.

The hotel was near the centre of town so Rosa had little choice but to head in that direction. She noticed as she approached it that there were more German soldiers and fascist militiamen out on the streets. She wondered if there had been a crackdown. In that case, Orietta might have already fled the town. She was considering what to do when she approached a street lined with trees. A policeman flashed her a sarcastic smile and waved her forward. Rosa cycled down the street and straight into a sight that would haunt her forever. Halfway down the street and onwards, from every tree dangled the corpse of an executed Italian. The victims had been hanged with wire. Rosa was too far down the street now to turn back without drawing attention to herself. The Germans had executed the victims as an example to the Italian population. Each had a sign hung around his neck: this man was a partisan; this man helped Jews; this man deserted the army. Some of them had lost control of their bladders and bowels when they were hanged. Some had nearly been decapitated by the thin wire. Their hands were tied but not their feet and it was evident that their deaths had not been quick. Rosa felt the darkness inside her heart grow with each corpse she passed.

Under one tree a family was gathered, weeping. A man lay prostrate on the ground under the corpse of a boy no older than fifteen. *Out after curfew* his sign read. Rosa felt her blood boil. The sight of the corpses did not frighten her; she had long got over the fear of dying. They made her murderous. The rest of the corpses belonged to partisans and those who had helped them. Soldiers and fascist militiamen paraded the street to stop anyone from cutting the bodies down.

Rosa was sure now that Orietta must have left the town. It was too dangerous for any partisan or *staffetta* to stay. She felt for the citizens who had helped the partisans or Jews and were now in danger of reprisals. She wondered if Orietta had discovered the identity of the double agent whom she had been tracking when Rosa last saw her. Surely much of this was the result of his work.

When Rosa was nearly at the end of the street, she slammed on the brakes of her bicycle. The last corpse was that of a woman. Her white skirt flapped in the breeze. One of her sandals had fallen off. The other was still on her foot. They were wedge sandals with bows on the ankle and peep toes: the shoes of a well-dressed woman. A picture flashed into Rosa's mind. She saw Orietta eating ravioli and wearing her silk taffeta dress the night Rosa met her to collect the money for the Flock. To be chicly dressed was part of her disguise.

'Oh God! No!' Rosa cried, edging towards the tree. She looked up. The ground shifted beneath her feet when she recognised the face of her beloved Orietta. Around her neck was the word *Spy*. Rosa stumbled backwards. She let go of her bicycle and it toppled over, taking the cart with it. A militiaman appeared next to Rosa.

'Did you know her?' he demanded. 'She wasn't from this town. Are you a *staffetta* too?'

Rosa had grazed her knees when she had fallen. She stood up and looked at the militiaman but was unable to answer. She had no words for him; she had no words to express this horror. The fascist took her dumbness for that of a simple girl with a weak stomach who had come across an unpleasant sight.

'Move along,' he hissed. 'Get out of here!'

Rosa barely felt her legs move beneath her as she tried to remount her bicycle. In the end, she ran along beside it until she turned a corner and was out of view of the fascist. She sat down on a step and collapsed against a door. Of all the terrible things she had seen, this would be the one that would break her, she was sure of it. She couldn't think clearly. She dry-retched into her hands. Orietta! Lovely, sweet Orietta!

'Well, you caught the famous *staffeta*,' she heard a man's voice say.

Rosa's spine tingled. She looked up. Her heart almost stopped when she realised she was leaning against the door to the police station. The voice had come from an open window. She grabbed her bicycle and had started to move away when the man spoke again. 'If it eases your conscience, you can be thankful that the Germans have paid you generously for your information.'

Rosa stopped in her tracks. Her shock subsided and the military discipline she had been training herself for took over. She smoothed her skirt and hair and put the stand down on her bicycle, pretending to adjust her cart while keeping her face hidden. She grabbed her handbag from the bicycle basket; her pistol was hidden inside.

The door to the police station opened. In her peripheral vision, Rosa saw a man in civilian clothes step out. She smelled musk aftershave and expensive cigarettes. The man passed her and she felt his shadow cross with her own. Glancing up she caught his profile: Emanuele. He walked down the street and turned the corner. Rosa released the stand and climbed on her bicycle, following him. *His only weakness is that he loves the high life and isn't good at depriving himself if the occasion calls for it.* Rosa's blood chilled when she recalled Orietta's words. She understood what had happened. Emanuele was the double agent and he'd been paid for informing on Orietta. Rosa knew now why the Germans had been able to find the location of the Flock. Emanuele had told them.

She dismounted her bicycle and leaned it against a wall, following Emanuele the rest of the way on foot. She would not allow him to slip away. If Italian patriots were to be made examples of by the Germans, then Rosa would show how partisans dealt with Italian traitors. She kept enough distance to see where Emanuele was going without attracting his attention. It helped that the shutters on the houses were closed and there was no-one on the street.

People had even taken their dogs and cats indoors they were so frightened. Rosa felt the gun in her handbag. She was a soldier now and she knew exactly what she had to do. If Emanuele had been a German, she might have worried about reprisals being taken out on the townspeople. But he wasn't. He was nothing better than scum. And he had to be silenced.

Emanuele stopped in front of a house at the end of the street. He took a key from his pocket and opened the door, disappearing inside. Rosa crept under the front window, straining to hear if any other voices came from inside. A wife? Children? She heard nothing. Taking the pistol from her bag, she hid it under her arm and knocked on the door. A few seconds later it was opened by Emanuele. He grinned, pleased to see a pretty woman on his doorstep.

'Did they pay you well for your soul?' Rosa asked him.

Emanuele's smile faded. Recognition flashed in his eyes. He stank of sour wine. He'd been drinking. 'Your friend knew what she was doing was against the law,' he said.

'Whose law?'

'The law of the Repubblica di Salò,' Emanuele answered maliciously. 'The true government of Italy.'

'There is no Italian government any more,' Rosa answered. 'Mussolini is nothing more than a figurehead. We are ruled by the Germans. And you are their whore.'

Emanuele made a grab for the shelf near the door where he had a gun. But Rosa was faster. She fired her pistol. The bullet struck Emanuele between the eyes. He fell backwards, blood oozing from the wound over the tiles. Rosa kicked his feet inside and shut the door. She checked the street both ways but no-one had come out. She ran for her bike and pedalled furiously for the road out of town.

The young German soldiers on patrol waved to her as she passed them. 'Good luck selling your gelato!' the one who had been friendly to her shouted.

Rosa raised her hand as if to bid him farewell but kept her face turned. She rode with all her strength away from the street of horrors where her beloved Orietta had been slain; and away from the scene of her first assassination. The spring sunshine and the green forest seemed to have different qualities. They no longer seemed bright and joyful. No birdsong came from the trees. The world had taken on a grim haze. Rosa was seeing things differently now. She was not the same person she had been before. She had become a killer.

TWENTY-EIGHT

Rosa returned from Borgo San Lorenzo in the early evening. Giovanni and the Valet were at the camp discussing tactics with the Flock's leaders.

'What happened?' Luciano asked Rosa, noticing her torn dress and grazed knees.

'I shot the double agent,' she told him. 'It was Emanuele. The Canary's friend.'

'Did you question him?' asked Starling. 'Did you find out what information he'd given the Germans?'

Rosa shook her head. 'There wasn't time. He would have got away. I followed him and shot him.'

'Slow down,' said Luciano, grabbing Rosa by the shoulders. He turned to Woodpecker. 'Bring her some water.'

Giovanni stepped forward and put his jacket over Rosa's shoulders. She was shivering although the evening was warm. The terrible image of Orietta hanging from the tree came back to her and she began to cry.

'It's better that Raven killed him straightaway,' said Partridge. 'There might be some good Germans but there are *no* good fascists.'

'What made you so sure he was the double agent?' asked Luciano. 'Did the Canary tell you?'

Rosa looked up at Luciano. She shook her head. His eyes turned dark but he said nothing, waiting for her to speak. Woodpecker brought her a tin of water. She took a sip but it didn't quench her parched throat. Nothing would bring her relief or make telling Luciano any easier.

'Where is she?' asked Luciano, scrutinising Rosa's face.

Rosa trembled. 'She's dead,' she said through her tears. 'The Germans paid Emanuele to inform on her.'

Luciano's face blanched. He staggered backwards. Giovanni caught him.

'Who was this *staffetta*?' Giovanni asked.

At first Luciano looked as if he had gone deaf and blind to the world. The colour had drained from his face with his grief and shock. His lips moved but no words came out.

When Giovanni repeated his question, Luciano's mouth twisted with bitterness. He wrenched himself away from Giovanni and shoved the older man backwards. 'You don't remember her because she was only a year old when you walked out on us! Carlo wasn't even born. But Piero and I suffered every day that you didn't come home!'

Giovanni's face turned ashen. He had the same expression of disbelief in his eyes that Emanuele had when Rosa shot him.

'You didn't recognise me!' said Luciano, pointing an accusing finger at Giovanni. 'You didn't recognise your own son! You forgot us!'

'No,' said Giovanni, shaking his head. 'No. I've never forgotten.'

Rosa and the other partisans looked on, unable to do anything to calm the scene that was unfolding before them.

'If you didn't care about us, I could forgive you,' Luciano snarled. 'But I'll never forgive you for what you did to Mother! She died of a broken heart!'

'No!' said Giovanni. 'You don't understand!'

The two men circled each other. It hurt Rosa to see Giovanni cower; it was like watching a wild animal reduced to a ghost of itself in a zoo. His dignified posture disappeared and once again he looked like the wounded, humiliated man she had first seen at the Villa Scarfiotti.

'I knew you, Luciano,' Giovanni said quietly. 'From the moment you arrived at my camp. You see, you look just like your mother. But there was no way to make amends for my terrible, cowardly actions. I hoped for your sake that *you* hadn't recognised *me*. I prayed that somehow I could be the father to you that I should have been by fighting by your side.'

Luciano paused for a moment, as if he were trying to comprehend what Giovanni had said. But then his grief over Orietta stabbed him again and he was determined to take it out on his father.

'I don't want anything to do with you!' he said, turning away. 'Once a coward always a coward!'

Giovanni seemed to age with Luciano's harsh words. His eyes looked empty, drained.

'We'd better go,' said the Valet, grabbing Giovanni by the shoulders. 'There's nothing to be gained by staying here.'

Rosa handed Giovanni's jacket back to him. 'I remember you too,' he told her. 'What a fine fighter you've become.'

Giovanni allowed himself to be led by the Valet away from the camp. Nobody knew who to pity more: Luciano or Giovanni; or themselves for seeing the two greatest commanders of the partisans break apart from each other.

Luciano glared at the members of the Flock who were watching. 'Get back to work!' he said, struggling to regain his self-control. 'All of you!'

The news that the Allies had liberated Rome brought a sense of euphoria to the Flock but also apprehension. The Allies were supposed to have cut the German army off before Florence but that strategy had failed. The battle front was now moving towards them. Every day Rosa awoke to the sounds of planes flying low in the sky and bridges being bombed. It was rumoured that Florence would be an open city, handed over to the Allies in a knightly way. Rosa doubted it. If the German army had been brutal towards the Italians before the Allied victory, what would they do now? If the Germans lost the war they had so believed it was their right to win, Italy's changing sides was a significant contributor. The broadcasts over British radio of thousands of Romans cheering in the Piazza Venezia to welcome the Allies would not endear the Germans to the Florentines, who were yet to be liberated.

The Germans mined the roads and bridges. One day, when Rosa was out on a food mission with Partridge, she nearly stepped on an S-mine. Fortunately she saw the edge of the device where the earth fell away from it and jumped back at the last moment. Partridge probed for the mine with his pocket knife and disarmed it by inserting a sewing pin into the safety catch.

'You know, Raven,' he said, unscrewing the mine's sensor and gazing at her thoughtfully, 'very few of the partisans who joined bands in 1943 are still alive today. The average life span of a patriot fighter is less than a year. When do you reckon our numbers will be up?'

Rosa looked at him. She was trying to catch her breath after the shock of nearly having detonated a device designed to launch into the air when triggered, sending shrapnel flying in all directions.

'It's up to God,' she said. 'The Falcon survived Spain against all odds. He fought fascism long before that and he always goes on the most dangerous missions. And he is still here.'

'Yes, but the Falcon isn't quite mortal. Not like the rest of us.'

Rosa and Partridge climbed to a vantage point where they could view the road heading north. Dozens of German lorries were leaving Florence.

'They are moving their auxiliary forces,' noted Partridge. 'It may be that they intend to blow up the whole of Florence before the Allies arrive.'

Following the lorries were dozens of private cars that, Rosa knew from intelligence reports, belonged to fascists too scared to stay in the city without the Germans. Her gaze shifted to the direction of Fiesole and the Villa Scarfiotti. Starling had been keeping his eye on the villa. According to him, the Marchesa was still there along with her SS colonel. Rosa was glad to hear it. The Marchesa was one fascist she did not intend to let get away.

When they returned to camp, Rosa could feel the excitement in the air. Starling was putting away the radio.

'We've listened to a broadcast from the commander-in-chief of the Allied forces,' he said. 'He promises that the Allies are on their way and asks all Italian patriots to cut army communications, destroy roads and bridges, railways and telegraph wires. We are to ambush Germans trying to escape but to take prisoner any who surrender.'

Rosa wondered about the last command. How were they going to guard German prisoners of war as well as feed them? The farmer she and Partridge had visited had only been able to give them two bags of corn. Everything had been taken by the Germans at gunpoint. Rosa and Partridge had taken less than the farmer had offered them because they could see that he had barely enough for his own family. Rosa looked over at Woodpecker, who was repairing one of the tents. She had learnt from Starling that Woodpecker's wife and one of his daughters had been raped by the Germans and their house set on fire. She wouldn't want to be a German prisoner of war left in his hands.

Rosa spotted Luciano sitting on a log outside his tent. Although she and Partridge had just returned, she anticipated that Luciano would send them out again to pass on General Alexander's message to the partisan groups without access to radios. Instead he continued to sit, drawing diagrams in the dirt with a stick. Luciano was still one of the finest and most daring commanders in the region, but since Orietta's death, Rosa had seen the light go out of him.

'*Ciao*!' she said, taking a seat on the log next to him.

'*Ciao*!' he replied, glancing up at her for a moment before looking back to the ground.

She waited for him to say something but he continued to draw shapes in the dirt. 'This is it,' he said finally. 'This is the big moment. A new Italy is about to be born and Piero, Carlo and Orietta aren't here to see it.'

Rosa put her hand on his arm. Partridge had been correct when he had observed that the life of a partisan was short. Apart from herself and Fiamma, Luciano, Starling, Partridge and Woodpecker, few of the original Flock were still alive. The Allied servicemen had left to try and join their battalions, but who knew how many of them had made it. The Flock had been replenished mainly by young men of conscription age and members of the Italian *carabinieri* who had fled their police posts when they were ordered to wear black shirts like the fascist militiamen. They had always been mainly pro-partisan and saw no reason to be shot because of a lack of differentiation between them and the fascists.

'Your brothers and sister will see it,' Rosa told Luciano. 'Their spirits live on in you.'

She realised that death was something you accepted when you became a partisan. You lived with its constant presence — and you dealt it out. She shivered when she remembered Emanuele's staring eyes and thought about her near miss with the mine that morning. She had told Partridge that the time of one's death was up to God. It was the first time she had mentioned God since she had shot Emanuele. One of the young partisans who had been killed had left behind a Bible. It was given to Rosa who had, until Emanuele's assassination, read it faithfully each night. But since she had become an agent of death, she couldn't bring herself to open it. She felt like a hypocrite. She remembered what Clementina had said and wondered if maybe *the last person in the world who still believes in God* had lost her faith.

'Commander,' she said, looking into Luciano's eyes, 'I think you had better tell the Gatekeeper about the broadcast. You are the two most capable partisan leaders. You have to work together.' She gently took the stick from Luciano's hand. 'What your father did was nearly thirty years ago. He's a different man now. You can't forget that he saved the Flock. Our band would have been annihilated by the storm-troopers if he hadn't acted quickly and sacrificed some of his men. Your father has found his courage — it might be too late for you, but it's not too late for Italy. You can't change the past but you can win this country back together. I think Piero, Carlo and Orietta ... and your mother would be proud if you did that.'

Luciano still didn't answer. She had no idea if he had even heard her. A formation of Stukas roared overhead, pursued by American fighters. They disappeared in the direction of Florence. A chill ran over Rosa. She had the same uneasy feeling she experienced when she sensed a storm was coming.

When the Flock had been divided into smaller groups, Genoveffa had moved to one of the brigades further up the mountains, leaving Rosa and Fiamma to cook for Luciano's camp. Now it was summer the food situation had improved slightly and they had been successful in thinking of different ways to serve beets, artichokes, chestnuts, potatoes and rice. Rosa was happy on that diet, but the men demanded meat. They hunted rabbits and birds and brought them to Rosa to skin or pluck but she wouldn't touch them. To her they were still alive. Her affinity with the source of things had grown stronger with the war. Even when she passed the dead bodies of soldiers or civilians when she went out on food searches, she still saw them as whole people and mourned the potential of what might have been. It was all senseless waste as far as she could see, but she was caught up in it. She remembered what Antonio had once told her: *if you want to be moral, the only time to do that is before a war actually starts. Afterwards, it's too late. If you think morally, you will be defeated.*

'Those in this camp who want to eat flesh have to cook it themselves if Nightingale isn't here. Raven is not required to do it,' Luciano told the men when they grumbled. 'We're lucky to have a nurse, a cook and a *fighter* amongst us.'

One day when the men were out on patrol and Fiamma and Rosa were guarding the camp, a peasant appeared with a lamb in his arms.

'For you,' he said, putting the lamb on the ground. 'For all you have sacrificed for Italy.'

A lamb was quite a gift for a poor man to bestow, although Rosa had heard the peasants preferred to give their animals to the partisans than have them taken away by the Germans. Fiamma thanked him and the peasant nodded.

'I pray that some kind person will feed my son in Germany,' he said. 'That someone will take pity on him too.'

The man quickly left, not wanting to be seen. Rosa and Fiamma looked at each other and then at the lamb. She was perfectly formed, with neat little hoofs, a pink nose and gentle eyes.

'Baa! Baa! Baa!' she bleated, nudging Rosa.

'She thinks I'm her mother,' said Rosa, touching the lamb's soft wool. 'She thinks I'm going to feed her.'

'What are we going to do?' asked Fiamma. 'No-one has brought us a live lamb before.'

Rosa looked at the lamb, pure white and innocent like an angel. Although she had shot a man between the eyes, she could not imagine what sort of person could rip a knife across such a trusting animal's throat. Since Emanuele's death, Rosa had thought of herself as a murderess. She realised how wrong that was. She still had her abhorrence of violence and unnecessary killing. If morals and compassion were fatal flaws in wartime, Rosa's number was going to be up shortly.

'Baa! Baa! Baa!'

'God!' said Fiamma. 'She's like a baby. I guess we'll just have to wait until the men come back. One of them will have to do it.'

'They won't be back until this evening,' Rosa said. 'Can you watch this lamb all day knowing that later someone is going to slit her throat?'

Fiamma bit her lip and shrugged. 'I suppose you're right. And the men will be tired and hungry when they come back. They'll be angry that we haven't dealt with this ourselves. I might have suggested that we draw straws but I know you won't be able to do it.'

Fiamma went to the box where they kept the knives and selected one.

'It's not sharp enough,' Rosa said, her heart in her throat. 'She'll die slowly and in agony.'

Fiamma touched her thumb to the blade and saw that it was blunt. 'I guess that you and I are two hopeless town women,' she said, sharpening the knife on a stone.

The lamb nudged Rosa's leg again. Rosa couldn't look at its trusting face. Did it expect mercy from a human being of all creatures? Couldn't it see what they were?

When Fiamma had finished sharpening the knife she placed it in her belt and picked up the lamb. 'I won't do it in front of you,' she said. 'I'll go into the forest.'

Rosa watched Fiamma disappear with the lamb into the trees. She had to turn away when she saw the lamb wagging its tail happily, as if this were some sort of game. The lamb was like a woolly dog. Rosa felt sick. Killing it would be like killing Ambrosio.

Rosa distracted herself by repairing some of the men's clothes and tidying the hospital tent. She cut up the vegetables and began preparing a stew. When Fiamma hadn't returned after an hour, she grew uneasy. Had she been caught by Germans? Had she stepped on a landmine?

She regretted that because of her Fiamma had felt obliged to go away into the forest. Another hour passed and Rosa took her gun, checked it and reloaded it. She was alone in the camp now and had a strange sense that she was being watched. She couldn't leave the camp unguarded — but where was Fiamma?

Another hour passed and there was still no sign of Fiamma or the men, who Rosa had expected to have returned by now. The sky was turning dark. She scanned the trees nervously. Suddenly she heard bleating and the lamb appeared from the forest, bouncing towards her. Rosa stood up, sure now that something had happened to Fiamma. She picked up the lamb and heard a crackle of twigs. She took her gun and slid down into the trench, staring into the dim light. She heard another sound, this time from somewhere behind her. She remembered the day the storm-troopers had surrounded the Flock and was sure she was finished. At least the rest of the partisans weren't there to be killed along with her.

A hand grabbed her shoulder. Rosa spun around and found Fiamma crouching down next to the trench. 'I couldn't do it,' she said. 'All I could see was your unhappy face.'

Rosa clutched her chest. 'You gave me a fright!' she said. 'Why didn't you call out when you approached the camp?'

Fiamma had a wild look in her eyes. She didn't respond to Rosa's question. 'Then I thought about it,' she said, tucking her hair behind her ears. 'I didn't want to kill the lamb either. I was going to kill her because I thought the men would be displeased with me if I didn't. Then suddenly it occurred to me: to hell with that! Why should I be living my life to please men all the time? You and I are risking our lives, and many women like the Canary and Gina have lost theirs, and this country wouldn't even give us the vote. Yes, darling, no, darling, I'll kill a lamb and cook it for you, darling. No more!'

Rosa was puzzled. This was a side of Fiamma she hadn't seen. She was normally so placid, so willing to please.

'I tell you,' said Fiamma, looking at Rosa with burning eyes, 'if after this war is over we still don't get the vote, I'm going to live in America.'

Rosa was considering reminding Fiamma that under Mussolini men hadn't had the right to vote for the past twenty years either, when she heard the crackle of twigs behind her again. She put her fingers to her lips. 'Shh!' she told Fiamma.

'Don't shush me,' Fiamma replied. 'I've been put in my place enough!'

Rosa pointed to where the sound had come from. 'Someone's watching us.'

Fiamma climbed into the trench with Rosa and took out her pistol.

'Who's there?' Rosa called out.

'Nervous lot, aren't you?' answered a familiar voice. It was Ada's. 'You've made this new camp difficult to find!'

'*Dio Buono*!' cried Rosa. It was the second near heart attack she'd had in five minutes.

Ada and Paolina had come to the camp to give them the message that the Germans were holding three hundred hostages in Florence and had threatened to shoot them if any more Germans were killed. 'They've also brought some guns up from the front and have situated them around the city. The Allies are now forty-five miles away,' said Ada.

'The Germans' "scorched earth policy" has taken a turn for the worse,' added Paolina. 'They are raping whole villages of women and children and slaughtering livestock even when they have no intention of eating it themselves.'

Rosa shivered when she remembered what Osvaldo had done to her. It was so long ago now. But she would not wish that terror on others.

'They are not going to make it easy for the Allies to march through the north and then take Germany,' Ada said. 'They have destroyed factories and laboratories in Florence and stolen artworks. We are going to be left paupers.'

'It sounds to me as if they are an army terrified of the

people around them,' said Rosa. 'And it's a sign that they see the defeat of Germany as inevitable now.'

'No,' said Ada, shaking her head. 'That's exactly the opposite of what they think. They keep talking about a secret weapon Germany has been developing — something so terrible the world has never seen the likes of it before. They are going to use it on Britain first.'

'They place a lot of weight on it,' agreed Paolina. 'Everything they do is to try to buy time.'

Rosa looked from Ada to Paolina. Was there any truth in the speculation or was it just propaganda? She had also heard the rumours about a weapon so powerful it would bring entire nations to their knees in a matter of hours.

As well as the news, Ada and Paolina had brought food. 'The farmers around us have been generous,' Ada said. 'The Gatekeeper said we should share it.'

Rosa opened the sack Ada had brought and found loaves of bread. 'We haven't seen this much bread ... well, since before the war.'

'It's a peace offering from the Gatekeeper,' said Ada. 'We'd have a much better chance of getting the Germans out of Florence if our bands were together again. Do you think you could talk to the Falcon?'

'I've tried,' said Rosa. 'But I will talk to him again. Maybe when he hears what you've told us he will come around.'

Among the other things Ada had brought was some milk, which the women all agreed they would give to the lamb.

'But we don't have a bottle,' Rosa said.

'You don't need one,' replied Ada. 'What you do is dip your finger in the milk then let her suck on it until she learns to drink on her own. She's old enough to do that.'

The women watched the lamb, who they had decided to call Speranza, which meant 'hope', drinking her milk and wagging her tail.

'The men will want to eat her when they see her,' said Paolina.

'Too bad,' said Fiamma. 'She's Raven's pet now.'

Darkness was falling and with it came the sound of renewed shelling. Some of the explosions, although far away, vibrated through the earth underneath them. Rosa wondered if the mountains would collapse from the shocks.

'You'd better stay here for the night,' she told Ada and Paolina.

They were all glad when the men began returning in small groups from their mission.

'They are evacuating the houses along the Arno,' Luciano told Rosa. 'They are about to declare the city in a state of emergency and all residents are to stay indoors. The Allies must be close. A partisan from Florence told us that it's a New Zealand battalion that's clearing the route to the city.'

Rosa thought of the New Zealander she had nursed at the officers' prisoner of war hospital. How proud he would have been.

Luciano noticed Ada and Paolina. Ada was adding some wild herbs she'd collected to Rosa's stew, while Paolina came over to relay to him the information dispatched by Giovanni. Luciano saw the ample bread the men were being served with the stew and realised that it had been sent by Giovanni too.

'I will go with you when you return to your camp tomorrow and speak to the Gatekeeper,' he told Paolina. 'The partisans in Florence have asked us to help take back the city and welcome the Allies when they arrive.'

Starling eyed Speranza, who was tied to Rosa and Fiamma's tent. 'When are we going to eat that?' he asked.

'Don't even think about it,' Fiamma warned him. 'It's Raven's pet.'

Starling rolled his eyes. 'No, seriously, if you're not going to eat it what do you intend to do with it?'

'Wait until it grows bigger,' answered Rosa, glancing at Fiamma. 'Then we'll shear it and make socks from the wool.'

'Are you serious?' Starling asked.

'Of course,' replied Rosa. 'You don't *need* to eat lamb to live but everybody *needs* a pair of woolly socks, don't they?'

Starling stared at her, mulling over her words. 'Yes, I suppose so,' he said.

When the men had settled down for the evening, Rosa and Ada, having had the least strenuous day, stayed up to keep watch. The sounds of shelling and cannons whistled and boomed through the night. There were six or seven massive explosions intermingled with the continuous crackle of gunfire.

'I've been thinking about the night you were born,' Ada told Rosa. 'Who was where and what happened and when. I think the Marchese honestly believed you were dead. He loved Nerezza so much he would have brought you up as his own, not sent you to a convent anonymously. You've seen the grave? It's the monument of a broken-hearted man. After Nerezza's death, he dismissed most of the old staff, which is not something a nobleman in the right state of mind does to loyal workers. It's dishonourable. It was as if he couldn't bear anything that reminded him of the days when he and Nerezza were growing up. He even had her portraits taken down. Some of them were great pieces of art.'

'Yes, I've thought that too,' said Rosa. 'The other possibility is that Baron Derveaux took me to the convent.'

'Why would he have done that?'

'Because he's my father. Perhaps Nerezza confessed that on her deathbed. Maybe he was afraid of a scandal — or wanted to protect me from the Marchesa.'

Ada's eyes grew wide with surprise. 'He's your father? I don't think he knew. He was in Paris when Nerezza died. He was her childhood friend but for some reason he wasn't told how gravely ill she was. I am sure he would have rushed to see her if he had known. He is a bit of a gadabout but he's not cold-hearted.'

Rosa and Ada lapsed into silence, thinking over the matter.

'We can't ask the Baron Derveaux what happened anyway,' Ada said eventually. 'He fled with his family to France when war was declared. Their villa is being used by Germans as a fuel storage unit. The Baron would be horrified to see what they've done to his furniture.'

Rosa sighed. Although Ada had told her the Marchesa was in Egypt when Nerezza died, she couldn't help thinking that she'd had some role in her being sent to the convent. But who then was this 'Wolf'? And had he been trying to save Rosa or simply doing the Marchesa's bidding?

Ada looked at the sky. 'Lately, I've been thinking of Orsola,' she said. 'You see, I think she was dormant until you came to the villa. Then all sorts of mischief started happening. She's been there for centuries. She knows what happened to you as a baby.'

Rosa sat up at the mention of Orsola's name. 'Yes, I think of her too,' she said. 'But not as darkly as I once did. I don't think she is after revenge, Ada. I think she is a spirit seeking justice.'

Ada nodded. 'You may be right. It's as if she wants to sweep away the evil at the villa, but she needs human hands to do it.'

After their watch was over, Ada and Rosa headed to the women's tent. Fiamma had taken Speranza inside, afraid if she left her unguarded one of the men would steal her. The lamb was peacefully asleep, tucked under Fiamma's arm. Ada drifted off quickly but Rosa was restless. It was a hot night and the extra bodies in the tent made the air oppressive. She took her blanket and slipped outside, intending to sleep in the open air. She was about to settle down when she caught sight of Luciano some distance away, surveying the valley below. He wasn't wearing a shirt and his torso bathed in the moonlight gave off an ethereal sheen. The sight of him was like a magnetic pull. She remembered one summer's night in Montecatini Terme when it had been too warm to sleep.

'It's gone quiet,' she said, stepping up beside him.

Luciano turned to her. 'The calm before the storm, I guess.'

Rosa felt the warmth of his body although she didn't touch him. She breathed in his scent, fresh like the forest, earthy and full of life. She moved away, afraid of the desire that was rising in her.

Luciano caught her by the arm. Her skin burned where he touched it. His arms encircled her waist.

'Don't,' whispered Rosa. 'I can't resist you.'

But it was not Luciano who moved. Before Rosa knew what she was doing, she had clutched him to her. His hands ran over her back. They yielded to a force that neither of them could resist any longer. They kissed as if they were thirsty for love. Rosa was breathless. They pulled away for a moment, and then embraced again, tugging at each other's clothes until skin found skin and they lay down in the woods together.

'I've missed you!' Luciano whispered, kissing her neck.

Behind him, the fir trees rose to the sky and the stars glistened. Those celestial lights meant magic to Rosa. She cried when Luciano entered her: tears of grief, of abandonment, of love. They loved each other so much that it caused them agony and at the same time it transported them to a place far away from the battle for Florence, far from the war, far from death.

When the first wave of passion passed, they made love again. This time tenderly, slowly. The smell of the pines and the warm summer air enveloped them. Rosa gazed into Luciano's eyes. The light had returned to them. It seemed in that moment that all the war had numbed in Luciano and Rosa had come back to life; they were a forest regenerating after a fire, fresh shoots and leaves bursting from dead trees. The sun began to rise on the horizon and bathed their skin in golden light. They rested in each other's embrace. Despite the shelling of the previous night, the birds twittered in the trees. All was hope: the birds; the new day. Rosa felt safe in the dawn's tranquillity, even though she knew the woods were being surveyed by the Germans and she and Luciano were hunted creatures. But in her lover's arms at that moment, she felt nothing bad could happen to them.

'It's strange that we should be reunited this way — in the middle of a battle,' Luciano said, kissing the top of her head. 'And yet it was somehow meant to be.'

Rosa pressed her cheek to Luciano's chest. His heartbeat was steady, serene. It lulled her. If they had been discovered by the enemy and shot at that moment, Rosa was sure that she would die in peace.

Luciano, Rosa and selected members of the Flock, along with Ada and Paolina, were preparing to leave for the Staff's camp later that morning when Partridge came running towards them from the forest.

'The Germans have blown up the bridges!' he shouted. 'They did it last night. All of them except the Ponte Vecchio.'

Rosa followed the others as they ran up the hill to their lookout. A cloud of smoke was floating over Florence.

'Some of the houses collapsed from the shock waves,' said Partridge.

Although they couldn't see the Arno from their vantage point, the cloud of smoke was ominous enough. Rosa felt part of her life had been blown away. The Ponte Alla Carraia. The Ponte Alle Grazie. The Ponte Santa Trinita.

'Why couldn't those barbarians have spared the lovely Ponte Santa Trinita?' she said out loud.

'They spared the bridges in Rome and lost men because of it,' said Partridge. 'They weren't going to take that chance again.'

Luciano turned and rushed back to the camp, ordering the partisans to prepare to move. They were going to join the Gatekeeper's band and move nearer to Florence. Together they would attack select German targets from the rear to take the pressure off the Allies. Rosa caught up with him and he turned to her. He looked as if the sun was shining from within him.

'This is the moment. This is it,' he said, embracing her.

Rosa felt joy despite all the dangers. She was happy to see the fire in Luciano's eyes again.

Luciano, Rosa, Partridge and Starling went with Ada and Paolina to the Staff's camp, leaving the others to pack up the Flock's camp and follow later.

When the group arrived at the camp, Giovanni was looking at a map with the Valet. As soon as he saw them approaching, he stood up. He hesitated and so did Luciano. But the moment was too important. Nothing mattered in the face of this event in history. It was larger than any individual strife and was a chance to be a part of something that would change the destiny of Italy.

'I'm glad you came,' said Giovanni, moving towards Luciano.

Luciano wavered then stepped towards his father. The two men embraced. Rosa's heart soared to the clouds. The reunion of father and son was a far greater victory than any battle the Allies and Germans had fought. The past didn't matter now; they were all standing on the brink of triumph.

'Come,' said Giovanni, signalling to Luciano's men to partake of some food. 'There are other bands that will join us. We will meet together and start to move into Florence this afternoon.'

A short while later, the rest of the Flock arrived at the camp. Fiamma was leading Speranza on a length of rope intertwined with golden wildflowers.

'Nobody is to touch the lamb,' Luciano told his father. 'She's our mascot; our symbol of hope.'

Giovanni's eyes sparkled when he smiled. 'And what a beautiful mascot she is,' he said, reaching down to caress Speranza's head. 'I've had many wonderful animal companions in my life. They've all passed on from old age now.'

Rosa's fingers tingled and a strange sensation fell over her. She shrugged it off. Why would Giovanni patting the lamb move her more than anyone else doing the same thing?

'We have two hours,' said Giovanni, turning to his men. 'Rest well now, for tonight will be one hell of a battle.'

Suddenly a woman's cry sounded from the forest. The partisans grabbed their guns. Rosa turned in the direction of the trees. Something flashed between them: a green silk dress; a woman. One of the Staff's partisans appeared, holding a woman at gunpoint in front of him. The woman's hair had come loose from its pins and was hanging over her face: a beautiful golden-red colour. The pair approached the camp and the partisan pushed the woman into the clearing. She fell to her knees. He pointed his gun at her head and toyed with the trigger.

'A spy,' the partisan announced. 'I found her observing the camp from the trees.'

The woman caught her breath and looked up. Rosa was shocked to see Clementina.

'Signorina Bellocchi!' she cried. 'I'm not a spy. I ran away from the villa. I … *bribed* a guard. I told him I wanted to meet my lover. Then I came looking for you.'

'Who is this woman?' Luciano asked. 'Raven, do you know her?'

Rosa nodded. She was too taken aback by Clementina's appearance to elaborate.

'She's the daughter of the Marchesa Scarfiotti,' said Giovanni.

A clamour rose up amongst the partisans at the mention of the Marchesa's name.

'The Villa Scarfiotti,' said Starling, sending a gob of spit towards Clementina. 'The murderers!'

Clementina's eyes grew wide with terror. 'I'm not a murderer,' she said. 'I never killed anyone. I was afraid. I was a prisoner there.'

'A very nicely dressed prisoner,' said Starling, moving menacingly towards her and poking the end of his rifle under her chin.

Clementina looked at Rosa with pleading eyes. Rosa

raised her hand. 'Stop it,' she said to Starling. 'When I was taken captive at the villa, she tried to help me.'

Starling removed his rifle but kept it pointed at Clementina's head. Rosa stared at Clementina and tried to read her face. She was torn between the memory of the precious little girl she had once loved and the pragmatic young woman who had associated herself with the German high command.

'What is it you were coming to tell me?' she asked.

Clementina swallowed. 'When they were mining the bridges they searched the houses and buildings around the Arno. They entered a convent and found that the nuns there had been hiding Jewish women and children in their crypt.'

Rosa's heart gave a jolt. 'Which convent?' she asked.

'The Convent of Santo Spirito.'

'What did they do with the nuns and Jews?' asked Giovanni, stepping forward. 'They'd have trouble transporting them north now.'

Clementina's hands trembled. 'They've brought them all to the villa.' She turned to Rosa with tears in her eyes. 'The colonel says he and the Marchesa are going to shoot them all before the Allies enter Florence and hang their bodies from the lampposts as a welcoming present.'

Rosa stepped back as if someone had punched her in the stomach.

'Mother is urging him to do it,' Clementina said, tears pouring down her cheeks. 'She's evil. Evil! I wish I had never been born!'

Rosa stared at Clementina. She's not your mother, she thought. Rosa knew in her heart she had grown hard. The war had made her so. But still something in her wanted to believe Clementina. She was not the child of someone evil. She was the daughter of the compassionate Signora Corvetto who had ruined her health trying to help others.

'Signorina Bellocchi, you have to save them,' Clementina continued. 'Ever since you were rescued by the Falcon, the colonel has been obsessed by you both. He knows you are the partisan called the Raven. I have overheard his rants about the escapades of the Flock in the mountains.'

Luciano and Giovanni exchanged a look.

Partridge stepped forward. 'Perhaps we can save the hostages after we've freed Florence,' he said. 'I'm sure the Allies will despatch a unit to help us.'

'It will be too late by then,' said Luciano. 'They intend to kill the hostages when the Allies reach the city so they can flee in time.'

'It's already too late,' said Woodpecker. 'We go to fight in Florence today. This is the moment we have been waiting for — a chance to engage our enemy face to face and take back the city.'

Luciano glanced at him and then looked away.

'Come on,' said Woodpecker. 'We will never succeed in getting those women out of the Villa Scarfiotti. It will be suicide.'

Luciano took a deep breath and turned to Woodpecker. 'There are other partisans who can fight for Florence,' he said. 'These are women and children as well as holy nuns. It is our duty to protect the innocent as much as it is to assist the Allies.'

Starling turned to Luciano. 'You are right. But there aren't enough of us to do such a thing. We'll be slaughtered. How will we ever get past the guards and into the villa?'

'There's a tunnel, isn't there?' Luciano asked Giovanni.

'I took the servants out that way,' said Giovanni, 'when the Germans came. We hid the entrance and exit points when we left, but after so many of us disappeared they must have searched for an escape route. It's probably best we assume that it's been filled in now — or even booby-trapped — and not rely on it.'

'We have to make a reconnaissance mission then,' said Starling. 'To find another way.'

Luciano shook his head. 'The Allies are rapidly gaining ground. The longer we leave it, the less chance we have of getting them out alive.'

'*Cazzo!*' said Woodpecker, jerking his head towards Clementina. 'How do you know this bitch is telling the truth? How do you know it's not a trap to lure the Falcon and Raven to the villa? Maybe we should torture her and find out!'

'No!' said Rosa, stepping in front of Clementina. 'We will not act like them!'

She looked at the young woman. She couldn't read her face at all. What if it was a lie? They'd be killed. As the possibility of defeat became a reality and the secret weapon that had been promised did not appear, the Germans seemed to be sinking into madness. Their frenzied acts of rage would get worse. But the partisans had no choice but to believe Clementina. They couldn't take the chance of leaving the nuns and the others in the hands of the Nazis.

Luciano glanced at Rosa as if he had read her mind before turning to the partisans.

'Everyone who comes on this mission must volunteer freely,' he said. 'Don't come if you have any doubt about sacrificing yourself. We are going to get every last woman and child out of there — or die trying. This isn't about striking targets of military importance. These women and children won't make a difference to the outcome of the war. There aren't going to be medals and accolades from the Allies for this. But this isn't about any of that. This is about honour.'

As Luciano spoke those last words, Rosa was blinded by a light. She saw an angel standing next to Luciano. The light was too intense to see the angel's face but Rosa knew it was the same one that had appeared in her dream the night that Sibilla's fever had broken. We will not be alone on this mission, Rosa thought. The angel is coming with us. She remembered what she and Ada had discussed about Orsola and her companions. They were not forces of darkness but spirits of light who had been waiting for them to fulfil their destinies. The vision faded but not the feeling of a divine presence.

'God is with us,' Rosa said.

She looked at the partisans and, to her amazement, none of them showed signs of having seen the angel. But something had changed amongst them. Every one of them was willing to go, including Woodpecker. In that moment Rosa's heart burst with love for them. Often on missions she wished that she had been blessed with steady nerves. Yet at that moment, a sense of peace fell upon her and she realised that she was being called too.

'Luciano,' she said, 'I know the villa very well. I also know the nuns of Santo Spirito. I am coming with you.'

'No!' he said, turning to her. 'It's too dangerous.'

'I'm coming,' she said.

Again Luciano shook his head. But Rosa persisted.

'Do you remember once you told me you had a sense of being born for a divine mission in life? Well, this is mine. Everything that's happened to me has been leading up to this moment — my upbringing, my visions, my time as Clementina's governess, prison, poverty, marriage and children, and the war. All of it. It was all to prepare for this moment. I have a connection to the Villa Scarfiotti that I can't explain yet. You will have to trust me.'

Luciano was about to refuse her again but he must have seen the fire in her eyes. He hesitated and then said: 'All right. I can't stand in the way of a calling.'

The partisans murmured their approval.

'It would have been a mistake to leave our bravest soldier behind,' said Starling, resting his hand on Rosa's shoulder.

Now the partisans had agreed to the mission, the leaders went to Giovanni's tent along with Rosa, Ada and Paolina — who knew the layout of the villa first-hand — to discuss strategy. The partisans were used to stealth and sabotage. Until now they had orchestrated skirmishes, ambushes and moonlight raids. But penetrating an ancient and well-guarded villa to save a group of nuns, women and children was another matter.

Starling brought Clementina and guarded her at gunpoint. She told them there were about fifty prisoners being held in the cellar.

'How many soldiers are there?' Giovanni asked her.

'Most have already left,' she said. 'There is the colonel's personal division of about thirty men in the villa as well as the guards.'

'Have the woods been mined?' asked Ada.

Clementina shook her head. 'I don't think so. Dono wanders there and I haven't heard any explosions. Some of the officers wanted to hunt him so they let him out of his cage. But he got away from them.'

Giovanni knelt and began making a crude model of the villa on the tent floor, using pieces of string for the driveway and blocks of wood for the buildings. Starling showed him where the gun posts had been the last time he'd observed the villa. 'But there's no guarantee they haven't moved them now the Germans are fleeing.'

'And don't forget they are using the Derveaux villa as a fuel storage facility,' said Ada. 'There is a reserve force nearby that could be at the villa in fifteen minutes if they hear the guns being fired.'

Rosa glanced at Clementina. It occurred to her that they were relying on information from a witness none of them trusted. Normally a dangerous mission like this would need thorough reconnaissance but there was no time. They had no choice but to strike that night.

Starling took Clementina away to be guarded by another partisan and returned so the group could discuss their plan.

Giovanni turned to Luciano. 'This is your mission,' he said. 'You have full command. I will obey whatever orders you give me.'

Luciano looked at his father steadily and nodded. It was no small thing for Giovanni, the more senior commander, to hand over control to Luciano. But it was a sign of his regard for his son and the point wasn't lost on those present.

'Despite the Germans withdrawing north, the colonel is still well protected,' Luciano said. 'But the Derveaux villa could be to our advantage.'

Luciano used a piece of paper to represent the Derveaux villa. 'If we can create a diversion here and cut the telephone lines to the villa at the same time, the colonel may assume the fuel supply is being attacked and send his force from the villa to there. Then we can attack that force and at least weaken it. At the same time we will need to neutralise the machine gun posts near the gates.'

'But we wouldn't attempt to take the villa from that direction,' said Starling. 'The reserve force might be on our heels before we even make it to the villa.'

Luciano nodded. 'That's right. That's why we will have two groups suppress the machine gun posts at the rear and side of the villa and we will storm the house from the woods. But getting into the villa is one thing. Getting out again with fifty women and children is another.'

Luciano outlined a plan where he would divide the partisans into three groups. Giovanni's group would be responsible for creating a mock attack on the fuel store at the Derveaux villa and ambushing the soldiers the colonel would send from the Villa Scarfiotti to defend it. By laying mines on the road they would also slow down the reserve force that would arrive when alerted to the attack on the villa. It was also this group's responsibility to suppress and then take over the guard post near the gates. The assignment would call on every skill the partisans had learned in their years of fighting. Giovanni nodded his approval, pleased with his role.

The next group would be led by Starling. Their job was to suppress and neutralise the gun posts at the rear and side of the villa once the colonel had sent off his soldiers in response to the mock attack. That achieved they would then storm the villa and pick off any remaining soldiers and servants who got in their way. They were to take the Marchesa and the colonel captive — or to shoot them if they resisted.

'The third group will be the smallest,' Luciano said, 'and will be led by Raven and myself along with Partridge.'

Rosa's heart leaped. She was being given a leading role? Luciano must have truly believed what she had said about her calling.

Luciano explained that it would be the responsibility of the last group to get the women and children out of the villa and take them through the woods to safety. The majority of Luciano's group were to secure the escape route and wait in the woods with Woodpecker for the hostages while Luciano, Rosa, Ada and Partridge entered the villa to rescue the hostages from the cellar. Nobody voiced it, but it was the most dangerous role of all. Once Luciano's squad were in the lower part of the villa, they would be trapped if Giovanni's group couldn't hold back the reserve force long enough. Although their mission would need nothing short of a miracle to succeed, Rosa believed in the angel. Whatever happened, they were called to do this.

After the group had agreed on the plan, they lapsed into silence, each absorbed in his or her own thoughts. The danger was brought home again when Luciano reminded each partisan to reserve a bullet for themselves in case they were captured by the Germans.

The plan was to attack at night, so the partisans spent the afternoon cleaning and checking their weapons as well as giving orders to their own squads. Those who could sleep, did. Others wrote letters of farewell to their wives and parents, which would be left with Fiamma and some of the *staffette* who would be waiting at the edge of the woods to receive the hostages and any injured. Rosa and Luciano left to tell the priest of a nearby village to warn the inhabitants to hide in case there were any German reprisals if the partisans did not succeed.

They walked back to the camp as the sun was setting.

'Rosa,' Luciano said, using her real name for the first time since she had joined the Flock. 'Promise me something before we go on this mission.'

Rosa turned to him. 'What is it?'

'Promise me that if I order you to withdraw, you will. That whatever I tell you to do on this mission, you will obey my command.'

With Luciano's eyes intently upon her, Rosa had no choice but to agree. He took her hand and squeezed it. They had not spoken of their feelings since they had made love. They didn't need to. Rosa hadn't allowed herself to think about the future — or the past. She only allowed her mind to dwell in this present moment. All she knew was that she and Luciano must fight together, and that occupied her full concentration.

When they reached the camp, Luciano called Partridge over. 'Witness this,' he said, before turning back to Rosa. 'Raise your right hand,' he told her. Rosa did as he asked.

'By the powers awarded to me by the National Liberation Committee for Northern Italy, I hereby swear you into the rank of lieutenant,' Luciano said.

'Lieutenant?' Rosa repeated. 'That's a high rank.'

'You've earned it,' he said.

Rosa, Luciano and Partridge shared a piece of bread together before gathering their equipment. The partisans set off for the villa as the sun was sending its last rays through the trees. Rosa had a final word for Clementina who was being guarded by two *staffette*.

'I hope you know that if you are lying, you are sending your countrymen to their deaths,' she said. 'And our neighbouring partisans will not be generous in their treatment of you once the Allies arrive.'

Clementina stared at Rosa then turned away. 'You'd better hurry,' she said. 'They'll notice I'm gone when I don't come down for dinner. You're lucky they eat late at the villa these days.'

As the partisans departed the camp, Rosa looked at the men and women with whom she had fought for the past year and blessed each one in her heart. Their mission depended on the element of surprise. It was a flimsy foundation. All it would take would be for one thing to go wrong and everything would be lost. She sensed that God was with them, but she didn't know if that was because they were marching to victory — or to their deaths.

Darkness had fallen by the time they reached the woods bordering the villa. Giovanni's group prepared to depart. He and Luciano embraced.

'I'm proud of you, my son,' Giovanni told Luciano.

Luciano couldn't bring himself to speak and did not take his eyes off his father until the group disappeared around a bend in the road. After that, the rest of the partisans made their way through the woods. Rosa walked with Ada and Paolina, appreciating how her time as a partisan had improved her night vision. As they moved stealthily through the trees, she became conscious of three figures cloaked in black moving next to them. They were not earthly beings. Ada and Paolina were aware of their presence too.

'It's Orsola and her companions,' whispered Ada.

Rosa silently prayed. She didn't know what was going to happen to her, but she knew that she was surrounded by beings of light. The figures of the three witches moved closer to each other until they formed one large mass. Rosa became aware of the strong earthy smell of a large animal and realised it was not three figures she was looking at any more but Dono. He was striding along beside them.

'*Buon Dio*!' said Starling in a strangled whisper. 'It's a bear!' He raised his gun but wasn't able to shoot without giving the whole mission away.

Rosa pulled down the barrel of his gun. 'He doesn't intend us harm,' she said. 'He's escorting us through the woods.'

'When that woman said "Dono",' whispered Partridge, 'I thought she was talking about a dog!'

The villa appeared before them and the partisans crouched down behind the trees. The place was quiet except for soft music coming from the Marchesa's quarters. It was the Intermezzo from the opera *Cavalleria Rusticana*. Rosa remembered the time she had stumbled across the Marchesa listening to it while looking at Nerezza's opera sets. There had been tears in her eyes. She recalled what the Marchesa had said to her — *When two opponents meet, there can only be one winner* — and realised that she was not only on a mission to save the nuns and Jewish women and children, but also to seek justice for herself.

Starling signalled to his men who crept into their positions ready to fire on the machine gun posts. Starling had selected four partisans who were famous for their perfect aim to lob the grenades into the posts once the fire attack was under way.

The lower floors of the villa were lit up and Rosa saw servants moving about in the rooms. She shivered when she spotted Signora Guerrini in the dining room. The housekeeper was no doubt giving orders in her usual imperious manner, oblivious to the mayhem that was about to unfold. Two guards stood in the kitchen garden; if they didn't move when they heard the explosions go off then they would be amongst the first to be shot.

Luciano's group waited in silence, their breathing measured and shallow. But with her strained nerves, everything sounded too loud to Rosa. Their whole mission could be given away by the clink of a gun against a belt, a cough or a sneeze. She looked for Dono but he had disappeared. Luciano squinted at his watch. Something was wrong. The explosions Giovanni's team was to set off as a diversion should have gone off ten minutes ago.

Luciano set his gun sights on the two guards in the kitchen garden. Rosa wondered what would happen if Giovanni's bombs didn't detonate. The summer heat played havoc with explosives. Starling's and Luciano's groups would have to attack the villa without a diversion, and that would simply be suicidal. Rosa tried not to think about the women and children in the cellar and the nuns. Madre Maddalena would be with them too. She prayed they were all unharmed.

Suddenly there were booms like thunder. Giovanni's bombs had detonated! The two guards ran into the house. There was a commotion and a few minutes later three trucks sped down the driveway. Luciano and Rosa looked at each other. The colonel had done exactly what they'd hoped he would do; he had sent his soldiers to defend the fuel store. They had no time to wallow in their first victory. Gunfire crackled. Starling's fire support team was attacking the machine gun posts. The skirmish team managed to suppress and take over the positions. Everything was moving like clockwork now — and quickly. The rest of Starling's group sprang one at a time over the low hedge into the kitchen garden. There was a burst of gunfire in the kitchen. Rosa saw two SS guards fall. The other partisans kicked down the door that led to the rooms underneath the villa. The SS officer who had captured Rosa from the hospital ran forward firing a gun, but he was cut down in a hail of bullets. There were more shots. Then one of the partisans ran out and gave the signal to Luciano.

'Move! Move! Move!' Luciano commanded Rosa, Ada and Partridge. They ran after him towards the villa, stepping over the bodies of the guards the partisans had shot and entering the lower part of the house. Luciano kicked open the cellar door and the group burst inside. The women and children had heard the gunshots and had pressed themselves as far away from the door as possible. Some had hidden themselves behind barrels and crates. They screamed when they saw the partisans, thinking they were coming to execute them.

Madre Maddalena recognised Rosa and stood up. She had black bruises under her eyes. Someone had broken her nose. It made Rosa angry to see the injuries but there was no time to think about it.

'We are here to rescue you,' Rosa told her. 'We have to get everybody out quickly.' Giovanni and his men would hold the road against the reserve unit that would surely be sent but they couldn't do so forever. Soon the place would be swarming with soldiers.

Madre Maddalena called to her nuns to help get the women and children moving. But they seemed dazed, as if they had prepared themselves to die and now couldn't believe that God had sent them rescuers instead.

'I thought we were forgotten,' said Suor Valeria, grabbing Rosa's arm. 'I thought we had been forsaken.'

'You've not been forgotten nor forsaken,' Rosa told her. 'But please, you must hurry. Go up the stairs to where the partisans are waiting for you.'

Rosa had not anticipated that it would take so long to get the hostages to move. Not all of them were Italians. Some were foreign Jews who had fled to Florence for safety. Rosa tried to communicate in Italian, then English and then French to one terrified woman who was huddled in the corner with a small child in her arms. Finally, she realised the woman was Czechoslovakian and picked her up and pushed her towards the door.

The hostages moved out of the room on unsteady legs. Rosa saw them being lifted into the kitchen garden. Other partisans were helping them into the woods. Out of the corner of her eye, Rosa caught something move in an upstairs window. It was a guard with a machine gun. Her heart stopped when she saw that he was about to mow down the women and children struggling towards the woods. But Starling returned to the kitchen garden and saw him too. The guard collapsed in a crackle of gunfire. Rosa wondered where the Marchesa had gone. Had the partisans managed to capture her?

Luciano and Ada guarded the cellar door while Partridge, Rosa and Madre Maddalena searched the cellar to make sure nobody had been left behind. They found four small children wedged under a wine rack. No matter what Rosa said, she couldn't coax them to come out.

'Their mother was shot by the Germans when we got here,' Madre Maddalena explained.

The longer the children stayed there, the more time was running out. It was inconceivable to leave them to their fate, but Rosa and Partridge couldn't move the heavy wine rack without the risk of crushing them. A thought suddenly came to Rosa. She spoke to the children in German, telling them that if they came out the nuns would look after them and they would be safe. The children understood her. The eldest came out first, followed by his siblings. The youngest was three years old: too young to run on his own. Partridge lifted him onto his back.

'The Germans even kill their *own* children simply because they are Jews,' Rosa said to Madre Maddalena. 'It's unbelievable!'

'Go! Go! Go!' Luciano shouted, pushing his group out of the door.

They reached the exit to the kitchen garden at the same time Giovanni and his men raced up the driveway, pursued by two lorries full of SS soldiers. The reserve corps had reached the villa faster than expected. It was the first thing to have gone wrong. Giovanni's men were withdrawing and defending, the hardest manoeuvre of all. Luciano and his group couldn't get out of the villa now. They were in the firing line of the Germans.

Starling, who had moved everyone else into the woods and sent them fleeing, turned and stared at Luciano and Rosa. Grief welled in his eyes when he realised he couldn't help them.

'Go!' shouted Luciano. 'Quick! Save the others!'

Giovanni and his men were driven back to the kitchen garden but did their best to pick off the SS soldiers, defending both the hostages fleeing into the woods and Luciano's group trapped in the villa.

'The tunnel!' Giovanni shouted to Luciano. 'It's your only hope! There are more trucks coming!'

Where were all these reinforcements coming from? Rosa wondered. Weren't the Germans supposed to be withdrawing north?

'Quick, this way!' called Ada, directing the group to the room where Rosa had first stayed. 'The tunnel's here,' she said, pushing aside the heavy bed with the help of Partridge.

By some miracle the entrance had not been nailed shut. Or was it a trap? There was no choice but to try it and hope that Giovanni's men could hold off the Germans until they reached the end.

Partridge jumped inside first. Ada and Madre Maddalena passed the children down to him and then followed themselves. Rosa and Luciano climbed in and pulled the bed back into position. The tunnel led down some stairs. Rosa tugged her flashlight from her belt. Partridge, Ada and Luciano had turned on theirs too. The tunnel was much larger than Rosa was expecting and had stone walls. She wondered what its original purpose had been. Signora Guerrini had told her that the room above it had been used for plague victims. Perhaps the tunnel had been a way of transporting their bodies out of the grounds without infecting the rest of the villa.

They were able to run upright in it, two abreast, but it twisted and turned in all directions. Sometimes it seemed to be descending deeper into the earth and at other times there were steps and ladders. Madre Maddalena struggled up them in her long habit. The group ran as fast as they could, exhausted but driven by fear. Suddenly they heard the sound of running and shouts behind them. The Germans had found the tunnel.

'Faster!' Luciano said.

One of the children tripped and began to cry. Rosa picked her up and ran with her, but it meant that she couldn't use her gun if she had to. They came to a section of the tunnel that had gaps in the top. Moonlight streamed inside and Rosa could see the outlines of trees. They must already be on the outside of the villa gates. More lights bounced from somewhere behind them and the footsteps grew louder. The Germans were gaining ground.

Luciano turned around and aimed his gun, ready to fire on them. *Withdraw and defend, the hardest manoeuvre of all.* The girl in Rosa's arms began to wail. Partridge, Ada and Rosa looked at each other. The truth was obvious. Madre Maddalena and the children would never be able to outrun the soldiers. Rosa passed the girl to Ada.

'Run! Take them!' she said to Partridge and Ada.

She gave Madre Maddalena her flashlight, before turning and dropping to her knee beside Luciano, aiming her gun in the direction from which the soldiers were coming. It was a fatal decision, but there was no other choice but to try and slow the Germans down in order to save the others.

'Withdraw.'

Rosa looked at Luciano. In the glow of his flashlight, she saw that he was regarding her with the same tenderness he had that morning after they had made love.

'Withdraw,' he repeated.

She didn't comprehend at first. She shook her head. She and Luciano were soldiers and lovers, they must fight side by side. 'No!' she said.

'Withdraw, Lieutenant. As your commanding officer, I order you to withdraw!'

Luciano's face was burning with love. It was so full of light that the tunnel seemed to be illuminated with it.

'Withdraw!' he said. 'You have been called to save the children and the nuns, not me.'

His words shattered inside Rosa because she knew he had spoken the truth. She was being called to live and he was being called to stay.

'Luciano!' she cried, tears pouring down her cheeks.

He grabbed her and kissed her, then pushed her away. The sounds of the Germans approaching were growing louder now. They would soon be within their sights.

'If you love me, Rosa, run!' Luciano said.

Rosa's heart fell to pieces as she turned and fled. Only out of love for Luciano, not fear for her life, did she run with all her strength. Through the darkness she could see up ahead of her that the exit was only a few feet away. Partridge was lifting the others up the ladder and out of the tunnel. She reached the ladder too.

'Raven! Give me your hands,' Partridge shouted when he saw her.

Rosa turned back to where Luciano was waiting. His silhouette was illuminated in the flashlights of the Germans.

He was holding up a grenade. Rosa knew the pin had been pulled. She saw the angel wrap its wings around him. An explosion shook the tunnel. The walls began to collapse. Dust flew up around Rosa and mixed with the tears on her face. She lost consciousness for a few moments before she felt hands pulling her out of the ground. The warm summer air floated around her. She opened her eyes. The stars were twinkling in the sky up above her. But they no longer held any charm for Rosa now that Luciano was gone.

TWENTY-NINE

When Rosa arrived with Partridge and the others back at the camp, it was apparent that many of the partisans had perished in the raid and most of the casualties had been in Giovanni's group. Rosa was consumed by a sickening grief in her stomach and her legs were shaking beneath her. But the sight of Fiamma and the nuns tending to the injured brought back her nurse's discipline. Somehow she had to find the strength in her to help them; it was what Luciano would have wanted her to do.

'How many?' she asked Fiamma, almost collapsing into her arms.

'We've got the injured out; the ... dead we had to leave. There are about twenty with gunshot wounds.'

'The hostages?'

'Only one casualty: the elderly nun. She wasn't shot. Her heart simply gave out.'

Rosa looked to where Fiamma was pointing and saw Suor Valeria lying on a stretcher. She knelt beside the nun and kissed her forehead. 'Not forgotten nor forsaken, dear Suor Valeria,' she whispered.

It took everything Rosa had to pull herself together. The light was breaking in the sky. She washed her hands in a basin and looked for the most seriously wounded partisans, the ones the *staffette* and nuns weren't qualified to help.

She caught sight of Madre Maddalena kneeling next to Giovanni and rushed to them. Madre Maddalena looked at her with wide eyes. 'The Wolf!' she said.

Rosa was puzzled and turned to Giovanni, who was struggling to breathe. She remembered the Weimaraner puppy and the animals he had saved and suddenly understood what Madre Maddalena was trying to tell her. Why had she not realised it before? It was him. Giovanni was 'The Wolf'. He had taken her to the convent all those years ago. But why?

She drew back the blanket that was covering him. Giovanni had a wound to his stomach but it was the rasping in his chest that worried her. His lungs were struggling to take in air. She loosened his shirt and saw that several bullets had gone through his chest. She realised that they were going to lose him.

'This is the child you rescued,' Madre Maddalena said, clasping Giovanni's shoulder. 'This is the girl you brought to me. See what a heroine she has become.'

Giovanni rested his eyes on Rosa. Despite his pain, he smiled at her and struggled to explain. 'She told me to get rid of you,' he said through gritted teeth. 'And to bring back your heart to prove I'd killed you. But I couldn't do such a thing. I took you to the convent and stole a dead child's heart from the university's anatomy department.'

'The Marchesa?' asked Rosa, stroking Giovanni's forehead. 'The Marchesa told you to do it? After Nerezza died?'

Giovanni nodded. 'She killed Nerezza. Poisoned her,' he wheezed.

So the Marchesa *was* there. Rosa had long suspected that the woman had tried to get rid of her but not that she had murdered her mother too. Giovanni had been told to kill

Rosa but hadn't had the heart to do it, any more than he had to slaughter the puppy or any of the other animals the Marchesa had considered ... *imperfect*. Suddenly it all made sense. But even such an earth-shattering revelation meant little to Rosa at that moment. Giovanni was dying and she did not want his last thoughts to be of the Marchesa.

She pressed his hand to her cheek. 'Thank you, kind man, for saving me. Thank you for your mercy.'

Giovanni squeezed her hand with his waning strength and turned his head. 'My children,' he said.

Rosa realised he was looking at the German children they had saved from the cellar. For a moment, their faces blurred and she saw in their place a young Piero, Carlo, Orietta ... and Luciano.

'You're going home to them,' she said, fighting back her tears. 'They are waiting for you.'

Giovanni nodded and his face shone. 'We'll never be separated again,' he said.

The light faded from his eyes. Madre Maddalena murmured a prayer. Rosa didn't think it was possible to feel any more pain than she was already experiencing but her heart turned blacker. Another person she loved was gone.

When Rosa had done all she could to help the injured, she slumped down next to a tree. The depth of all that had been lost finally hit her. Luciano was gone. She didn't know where Antonio was but it was most likely that he was dead too. Her children were all that she had left but she'd had no contact with them for over a year. Were they safe?

She felt someone standing beside her and looked up to see Fiamma.

'Luciano gave his life for ours,' Rosa wept.

Fiamma knelt down beside her. There was a piece of paper in her hand. 'He gave me this,' she said. 'He told me that if he was killed and you survived, I was to give it to you.'

Fiamma embraced Rosa then left her on her own. Rosa held the paper between her fingertips, the way one would hold a delicate leaf. She took a deep breath before opening it.

> *My Dearest Rosa,*
> *The sudden turn of events means I cannot tell you all that is in my heart in this brief message. But if you receive this, it means that I am dead. Do not grieve for me, Rosa. I loved you and adored you. In your arms I found my greatest happiness. Know that I have died happy and content to have loved you. It is the most I could have ever asked: the chance to see Italy free and to hold the whole world when I embraced you in my arms.*
>
> *Find Antonio, for I know that he is out there somewhere looking for you. And when you find him, love him with all your heart — but sometimes, when you look at the stars, think of me and smile.*
>
> *In memory of Piero, Carlo and Orietta, teach Sibilla and your sons to love freedom and truth and to never allow themselves to become slaves.*
>
> *Farewell, my love. One day we shall meet again.*
> *I am your beloved,*
> *Luciano*

Rosa reread the letter, lingering over each word as if by doing so she could hold onto Luciano a little longer. The sentiments he had expressed had been written down less than a day ago ... and now he was gone. But she knew what he was telling her. It was the same message she had been given in the tunnel: that she was to live and, in doing so, to be a witness to all that had happened. Her mission was not over. It had just begun.

A church bell started ringing. Rosa looked up. Then more bells sounded, one set after another.

Starling, who was carting water from the river, put down his buckets. 'It's coming from the direction of Florence,' he called out to the partisans. 'The city is free!'

'The Germans are gone,' Starling told Rosa, two days later. 'We have secured the Villa Scarfiotti. It would be better to move the injured there and get them out of the elements. We've checked for mines and booby-traps. It looks like the Germans didn't have time to set them before they fled.'

'What about the colonel and the Marchesa?'

'The colonel resisted and was shot,' Starling said. 'We have the Marchesa captive at the villa. We'll keep her under guard until we can hand her over as a war criminal. The housekeeper, Signora Guerrini, was killed during the raid. She started firing on my men. The rest of the servants are in the village gaol.'

Rosa agreed that it would be best to take the injured to the villa where there was running water and an ample supply of beds and linen. They would then inform the Red Cross in Florence that they were using the villa as a hospital. Clementina had been sent with a *staffetta* to the city, where Signora Corvetto was waiting for her. Rosa gazed at her hands. The injured needed her and Fiamma to nurse them but she wasn't sure if she had the strength to return to the Villa Scarfiotti. Starling guessed the reason for her hesitation.

'The tunnel has collapsed,' he said. 'We couldn't retrieve Luciano.'

Rosa remembered the grenade and shook her head. 'No,' she said, 'I think he would have preferred it like that. He died like a soldier: in battle.'

When they arrived at the villa, Starling, Fiamma, Rosa and the nuns converted the ballroom into a hospital ward.

Partridge left for Florence to inform the Red Cross that they needed supplies and also to offer the rest of the villa as a hospital or accommodation for the Allies if it was needed.

Rosa couldn't bear to go anywhere in the villa other than the ballroom and kitchen. It wasn't that Luciano had died at the villa alone that made her feel the way she did. It was the thought that she would be sharing the same roof as her mother's killer. Another person might have been enraged enough to want to face such a murderer immediately, but Rosa had lost so much in her life because of the Marchesa that she couldn't even bear to breathe the same air as the woman, look at the same walls, climb the same stairs. The Marchesa had murdered Rosa's mother, tried to kill Rosa, left her an abandoned orphan, had her falsely accused and sent to prison — and, finally, was responsible for the death of Luciano and the partisans because of her collaboration with the Germans. Rosa couldn't even use the word 'hate' to describe her feelings for the Marchesa. Her loathing was such that there were no words for it. She knew that one day there would be a confrontation, but she could bide her time for that. She needed to build her strength. Until then, the Marchesa could wait.

Ada and Paolina took over the kitchen. The nuns helped them by restoring the kitchen garden. The Jewish women and children worked in the orchard. The Convent of Santo Spirito had been destroyed when the bridges were mined and the nuns had nowhere else to go. Rosa appreciated how difficult the destruction of their community was for them, especially those who were committed to enclosure. But she was also grateful that they all pitched in to do what they could.

One morning Rosa stepped out into the kitchen garden to find Dono on the edge of the woods. He sniffed the air and lumbered towards her. The women and children fled indoors but Rosa wasn't afraid. Dono pressed his nose to Rosa's shoulder. His cage was still there in the kitchen garden. For his own safety, he would be better off there than wandering around the woods where some poacher might shoot him. Rosa hating making him a captive again, but he seemed to understand when she led him to his cage. She gave him a bowl of water and some artichokes and he sat there contentedly eating them.

After that, she took Dono out of his cage twice a day so he could stretch his legs. The sight of Rosa walking down the driveway with a bear sent the partisans clambering behind rocks or running into the summerhouse. The only people, besides Rosa, who weren't afraid of the bear were the German children.

'What's his name?' Karl, the eldest, asked Rosa. The others were called Alfon, Hannah and Erhard.

'Dono,' she replied. 'It means "gift".'

They took turns in patting the bear's head. Because the German children had lost their parents, they followed Rosa around like ducklings. She didn't mind. She liked their company. It took her mind off her pain.

In early September, the battlefield moved north and, with the villa secured, it was time for the partisans to return to their families and to rebuild their lives. Rosa embraced each member as they set off, wishing them a safe journey. Starling and Woodpecker and a few of the other men insisted on staying to protect the villa and guard the Marchesa.

'We'll leave when you do,' they told Rosa.

'What about your wives and children?' she asked.

'I'm a single man,' said Starling.

'My brother moved my wife and children to our mother's home in Sant'Anna di Stazzema. It's an isolated hilltop village,' Woodpecker told Rosa. 'They will be safe there until I collect them.'

Rosa thanked the men. She wondered what news Partridge would bring from Florence when he returned. She hoped that he would be able to find supplies. They were running out of morphine. Rosa was having to ply some of the patients with wine from the cellar to ease their pain. She couldn't bear to go there herself, so Ada went instead, always bringing back the finest vintages.

'What do you give the Marchesa?' Rosa asked her.

'Vinegar with water,' Ada replied.

One day, Rosa ventured into the woods to see if she could find more berries for Dono. He liked the peaches from the orchard and the vegetables she gave him but berries were a special treat. Rosa found that looking after him soothed her heart. He needed healing and care and so did she. She walked the path to the gatehouse, her gun slung in its holster over her back, and crept stealthily about. Although the Germans had left, there were looters and poachers in the vicinity. The woods were different in the daylight, peaceful. It saddened Rosa to think that the last time she had passed by these trees Luciano had been by her side. She felt a breeze brush over her. She couldn't see anything but she sensed it was Orsola. The witch hadn't completed her work; justice had not yet been done. Rosa's mind turned to the Marchesa, but she didn't want to think about that now.

She found some wild strawberries and picked them and put them in her bucket. She was about to straighten up when she saw two sets of boots and legs in grey pants standing before her. Her heart skipped a beat. Germans! She looked up and against the light through the trees saw two figures. She seized her gun.

'Don't shoot! Don't shoot!' the soldiers shouted, raising their hands in the air. 'We surrender!'

Rosa stood up. The men were unarmed but instinctively she looked around to see if there were other soldiers, in case it was a trick.

'It's the gelato girl,' said one of the men.

Rosa recognised the two soldiers from the day she had cycled into Borgo San Lorenzo and discovered Orietta had been killed. Rosa's blonde hair was growing out but she had hidden the dark roots under a scarf.

'How can you surrender?' she asked the soldiers. 'We're

not fighting. You are deserters. You should have gone with your army. If they find you now, they will shoot you.'

'Please,' said the soldier who had flirted with Rosa. 'The German army does terrible things. We don't want to be a part of it.'

Starling froze when he saw Rosa marching the two German soldiers out of the woods.

'*Cazzo*!' he said, running towards her. 'What's this?'

'They are our prisoners.'

'You captured them?'

'Yes.'

Starling looked at her. 'It's obvious they are deserters,' he said.

'Yes,' she replied. 'But I suspect it was obvious to them that I was a *staffetta* when I went to Borgo San Lorenzo — and they let me go.'

'Where the hell are we going to keep two German prisoners?' he asked her. 'Who will guard them?'

'I will,' said Rosa. 'Until the Allies come and collect them. We need help getting the grounds into shape. They can assist the sisters in the garden with the heavy work. And there is a field of corn that needs to be harvested.'

'*Cazzo*!' Starling said again. 'Raven, one day you will be the death of me! You and Nightingale!'

'Nightingale?' repeated Rosa. 'What's she done?'

'She's found another sheep that we aren't allowed to eat,' replied Starling. 'She says they are social animals and Speranza needs a friend.'

Rosa looked over to the kitchen garden where Speranza was tied to the fence so she wouldn't devour all the herbs. There was another lamb with her.

'Will you talk to her?' Starling pleaded. 'There's a good stock of food in the villa but the men would like some fresh meat.'

'Of course,' said Rosa, waving to Fiamma. 'What's the new lamb's name?' she called out.

'Pace,' Fiamma replied.

Rosa turned back to Starling. 'There,' she said. 'His name is Pace — "peace". Do you really want to slaughter two animals called Hope and Peace?'

The day after the German prisoners came to the villa, Partridge returned from Florence with disturbing news.

'The Allied command wants to assume power over Florence,' he said. 'The Tuscan Committee of National Liberation has only consultative powers and barely those at that.'

'I'm sure the intention is to hand the government back to Italy when the state of emergency is over,' Rosa assured him.

'That may be so,' said Partridge. 'But we are expected to surrender our weapons, and war criminals captured by the partisans are being set free.'

'That can't be,' said Starling. 'They can't possibly be letting traitors like the Marchesa Scarfiotti go.'

'It's chaos in Florence,' Partridge explained. 'Some fascists were shot, but other people have taken advantage of the situation for personal vendettas — knocking off people they didn't like and even members of their own families. But not one person of the Marchesa's status has been brought to justice. From what I've witnessed, they never will be.'

Rosa's mind travelled back to the time when she had been accused of assisting Maria with an abortion. She was innocent and yet, because of the Marchesa's powerful connections, she had been wrongly imprisoned as a scapegoat for Vittorio. The war had not changed a thing. The rich and powerful would still get away with their crimes.

Starling's face twisted. 'Surely if we hold her until the justice system is reinstated she will be brought to trial.'

'That's going to be months, maybe years, away,' said Partridge. 'We won't be able to keep her under arrest all that time. The Allies will take over the villa and she will be free to escape to Brazil or somewhere else.'

Starling gritted his teeth. 'Then we will execute her ourselves. Now!'

Partridge shook his head. 'If we shoot her now, without an official tribunal, we are in danger of being charged with unlawful murder ourselves later on.'

'I'll hang,' said Starling, 'before I see someone like that walk away from what she's done.'

Rosa's head was swimming. It was as if she were looking at all the people who had died because of the Marchesa, either directly because of her sadistic 'hunting' expeditions or by her willingly allowing the villa to be used as a base for the Nazis. Letting the Marchesa go unaccountable for her crimes made a mockery of all those people's deaths.

'The Marchesa is a criminal,' she said. 'Someone who has committed heinous acts. She's not some petty informer who can be bumped off with a bullet. She is a disgrace to this country and that should be set down on public record. Surely she will stand trial!'

Partridge shook his head. 'Raven, that's not going to happen. It hasn't happened in Naples, Sicily or Rome.'

Starling looked from Rosa to Partridge. 'If justice won't be done, then we will carry out a military execution now,' he said. 'We'll backdate it. Everyone here is in agreement about the Marchesa Scarfiotti's crimes.'

Rosa saw tears in Starling's eyes and knew he was thinking of Luciano as well as the other partisans who had died.

'Yes, but to make that decision we need someone of high rank from the National Liberation Committee for Northern Italy,' said Partridge. 'And they are still too busy fighting the Germans to be concerned with this.'

'You are the leaders of the division,' said Rosa. 'You are the representatives of the committee here in the mountains. You can make that decision.'

Starling shook his head. 'Only Luciano was properly appointed, on account of his status from Spain. The rest of us haven't been officially sworn in. In the heat of the war, we didn't care about rank. It wasn't important to us at the time. We played our roles, obeyed Luciano and that was it.'

'Given the circumstances,' said Partridge, 'it looks like we have no choice but to let the Marchesa Scarfiotti go. We don't have anyone who has official status with the committee.'

'Yes, you do,' said Rosa, looking him in the eye. 'You witnessed Luciano swearing me in as a lieutenant before the raid. I have the power to order the execution of the Marchesa.'

'Raven,' said Partridge, 'think about what you are saying. There could be consequences. The Allies see the war here as over. Our role has finished.'

'The Marchesa is a war criminal,' Rosa said. 'If there is no-one else to oversee her execution, then I must do it. How else will all the innocent people she's killed ever be at peace?'

It was still uncertain whether what the leaders of the Flock were planning was legal. But as the country was under martial law, they did what they could to document in military terms the crimes of the Marchesa and the reason for their sentence. Rosa, Partridge and Starling met in the schoolroom where Clementina and Rosa had once discussed the great composers and Chinese culture. When Rosa described what she had found in the cellar when the Nazis brought her to the villa, and how Carlo and the other partisans had been tortured, Partridge covered his eyes. I will describe it, thought Rosa, no matter how painful it is for us, because we must bear witness so their deaths are not in vain.

'We will execute her tomorrow, at dawn,' Starling said. Then, turning to Rosa, he added, 'You must officially inform her of the sentence to be carried out.'

Ada did her best to assemble a uniform for Rosa. She found a khaki skirt in one of the cupboards and Rosa combined it with a bomber jacket and beret that one of the farmer's wives had been wearing. Starling gave her his scarf to tie around her neck and she wore her own ammunition belt and gun holster. Her hands were steady but her throat was dry.

'Do you want me to come with you?' asked Starling.

Rosa shook her head. 'I have to face this woman on my own,' she told him. She might have added that she and the Marchesa had been fighting a duel her entire life, and there could only be one victor.

Rosa climbed the main staircase to the Marchesa's quarters. She had come a long way since her days as a governess at the villa. The realisation that she been sneaking around a house that was rightfully hers seemed ironic now. The Marchesa had got away with murdering Nerezza and trying to dispose of her child. But things had come full circle now. The 'little people' had finally got her.

Woodpecker was guarding the door to the Marchesa's quarters while Paolina was sitting in the corridor inside. Paolina looked Rosa in the face to give her strength, before moving to the landing to wait with Woodpecker.

The Marchesa was sitting in the room with the portraits. The shutters were open but the curtains were half-drawn, diffusing light over the Peking rug. She was dressed in an ice-blue brocade dress and matching open-toed shoes. Despite the absence of staff and her captive status, the Marchesa's impeccable grooming had not wavered. Next to her was an ashtray full of half-smoked cigarettes but no books or papers. Rosa was struck by the Marchesa's stillness. She did not appear to be brooding over the past or fearful of the future. Nor did she give the impression of someone waiting for death. She was simply sitting. Rosa wondered how a person who had committed the horrors the Marchesa had could be so composed.

'You have been tried for your crimes,' she told the Marchesa. 'And I have come to announce your sentence.'

The Marchesa barely glanced at her. 'Ah, the governess gets her revenge,' she said, rubbing her forehead with her finger before taking another slow puff of her cigarette.

'It is not about revenge,' replied Rosa. 'It's about justice. You are a traitor to your country and will be executed as such.'

She read out the Marchesa's crimes and the sentence of death.

The Marchesa watched Rosa with impassive eyes. Her haughty manner was intolerable under the circumstances. Rosa felt the pent-up hatred she harboured towards the woman rise in her blood. How many people had suffered because of the Marchesa? How many more would continue to suffer? When Rosa, Starling and Partridge had attempted to document the Marchesa's crimes and the reasons for her execution, they couldn't name every one of her victims or say where they had all come from.

'There is something else,' said Rosa, 'although we don't have the authority to try you for it. But if the civil courts were in order you would be charged with the murder of Cristina Lancia, formerly Cristina Scarfiotti, and affectionately known as Nerezza, as well as the attempted murder of her daughter.'

The Marchesa's face remained expressionless but something flashed in her eyes at the word 'attempted'. The faintest outline of a frown creased her forehead. It seemed to Rosa that the Marchesa was watching her in a peculiar way. Of course, she thought, she thinks that Giovanni Taviani killed me and that she has my heart.

The Marchesa slowly stood up and walked to the window. 'Are you Nerezza's daughter?' she asked.

'Giovanni Taviani never killed me,' said Rosa, her official manner giving way to her excitement. 'He took me to the Convent of Santo Spirito. The heart he gave you was from the university's anatomy department.'

The Marchesa looked out of the window. 'I should never have trusted that thief,' she said. 'I should have strangled you myself.'

Rosa's heart jolted. It was extraordinary to hear confirmed what she had long suspected.

'When you are executed tomorrow,' she told her, 'take it that it is also the penalty for the murder of Nerezza. My mother.'

The Marchesa turned from the window and this time she looked Rosa in the eye. To Rosa's surprise, she began to laugh. It's because she hated Nerezza so much, Rosa thought. And now Nerezza is having her revenge she is in hysterics.

The Marchesa stepped towards Rosa, her eyes ablaze. 'I didn't kill Nerezza,' she said. Her voice was hollow, and Rosa experienced an uneasiness; an attack of the anxiety she had often felt without being able to pinpoint the exact cause. The Marchesa placed her hand on her chest. 'I am Nerezza. It is Luisa Caleffi who is dead.'

Rosa wondered if she had imagined the moment; if she were asleep and this were all a dream. 'You killed Luisa Caleffi?' were the only words she could manage.

'I didn't kill Luisa Caleffi,' said the Marchesa, turning back to the window. 'My stupid brother did, in a jealous fit on their honeymoon. She had another lover. The harlot! I warned Emilio about her but he wouldn't listen. The scandal could have brought down the Scarfiotti family.'

A sickening realisation was falling upon Rosa. She involuntarily looked at the Marchesa's foot: slim with a longer second toe.

The Marchesa flung the curtains open. 'You people look but you see nothing,' she said. The light fell across the paintings and sculptures. 'Is this woman me?' she asked. 'Look closely. It isn't, but you all saw what you wanted to see! Even that stupid fool Baron Derveaux and his insipid wife! It was lucky for my brother that getting rid of a body in Egypt is not so difficult.'

Rosa was struggling to breathe. 'The Baron Derveaux is my father.'

'An indiscretion on my part,' said the Marchesa. 'The man is a buffoon.'

Rosa thought she might faint. The Marchesa grabbed her arm. Her touch was cold, like something dead.

'Do you know what it took to become someone else?' she said. 'The mastery to deceive even one's friends? But I did it. I fooled them all!'

The pieces of the puzzle Rosa had long been trying to solve started to fall rapidly into place but not in the way she had expected. She saw it all before her eyes: the Marchesa's heavily painted face; the way she starved herself; her reaction when Baron Derveaux had placed his cigarette on the Bösendorfer piano.

'No! It's not true!' she cried out in a final act of resistance to what was becoming obvious. 'What about Vittorio?'

'What a stroke of luck that was,' said the Marchesa, looking amused, 'that he came back from the war like a zombie. It was only when he started to recover that I had to have him committed. Until then he was the perfect associate.'

'And the woman who came to visit you and Vittorio at the summerhouse? That was Luisa's mother?'

'A wonderfully callous woman of the most mercenary kind. She was happy to be silent on the fate of her daughter in return for money. All around it was a very successful collaboration with the Caleffi family, I think.'

Rosa looked at the Marchesa, seeing beyond the make-up and starved figure to the woman underneath. Yes, this was Nerezza — disciplined, jealous and vengeful. She knew that from the notebook. But what about the young woman who had played beautiful music and created lovely opera sets? Rosa suddenly understood what Giovanni's dying words had meant: playing Luisa Caleffi had *poisoned* Nerezza. For Luisa had had no talent, no appreciation of beauty or art. The suppression of her genius had driven Nerezza insane.

'If you are my mother,' Rosa asked, 'why did you get rid of me? The Marchese would have kept me.'

'Why?' said the Marchesa, letting go of Rosa and stepping back. 'Because I never wanted you. Because you were the child of a dimwit. I'd have to look at you every day and remember my stupid mistake. Besides that, you could never have been passed off as Ferdinando's. He was dead by the time I got to Libya, and it was only a matter of time before people would find out that we had never met. I was nearly four months pregnant anyway. But people don't ask so many questions about the dead. Nobody wishes to think ill of them, especially babies.'

The Marchesa was a monster. Rosa shouldn't have cared. She'd been treasured by Madre Maddalena; her children adored her; she'd been loved by Luciano and Antonio. But this rejection from her birth mother stung her far more deeply than she could ever have imagined. She was taken straight back to the convent when the other children taunted her: 'No Name! No Name!'

'If you didn't want me then why did you adopt Clementina?' Rosa asked.

'After we had been "married" a while, people expected a child,' replied the Marchesa matter-of-factly. 'But I couldn't bear one with my brother, could I? And a girl was an infinitely better choice than a boy. If Emilio died and the boy married, I could have lost my title. I resented that it passed over me in the first place. I should always have been the Marchesa Scarfiotti. Not *her*.'

Rosa slumped against a wall. This was Nerezza's vanity: she would sink to all this just to keep a title. Rosa understood it now. Nerezza had pretended to die from an infection after Rosa was born; then she returned, masquerading as an ill Luisa so she could stay in isolation to complete her transformation. That's why the Marchese had got rid of the old staff and kept only those who were loyal to Nerezza or hired new ones. It was also why the Marchese always looked sad. He was living a terrible lie. That was the shadow that Rosa had seen around him.

The Marchesa gave Rosa a treacherous smile. 'Rather paradoxical, isn't it?' she said. 'When you put me in front of the firing squad tomorrow, so eager to punish a "war criminal", you will be executing your own mother. What will your fellow partisans think of that?'

Rosa wanted to get out of the room, to flee from this monstrosity that was her mother. For so long, she had yearned to know her origins. And this was the answer! To be an orphan — a 'No Name' — was better than this. She ran for the door, but before she reached it her strength came back. She turned around and faced the Marchesa.

'You thought it was a scandal for your brother to have killed his unfaithful bride in a fit of passion. What is it then to have been responsible for the deaths of innocent people! The Scarfiotti name will be cursed!'

'But no,' said the Marchesa, still smiling. 'I can easily support your claim that you are my daughter and all this will belong to you when I am dead.' She waved a hand, indicating the villa. 'From tomorrow, millions in lire, a house in Paris, jewellery, furs ... they could all be yours, my daughter. You, not Clementina, should be the rightful Marchesa Scarfiotti. Just think of that. A nothing from a convent is suddenly a rich marchesa!'

Rosa raised her chin. The Marchesa was deceitful to the end. She didn't want to bestow her wealth on Rosa. She wanted her convicted of murder when civil law was restored. There was no way for Rosa to prove she was Nerezza's daughter. It would look like she had made the whole thing up to get her hands on the Scarfiotti fortune. But even if that hadn't been the case, Rosa didn't want anything from the Marchesa.

'My name is Rosa Parigi,' she said. 'Wife of Antonio Parigi, the fine furniture dealer of Via Tornabuoni. Mother of Sibilla, Lorenzo and Giorgio. My battle name is Raven. I will oversee your execution tomorrow as a lieutenant in the army of the National Liberation Committee for Northern Italy. The Scarfiotti name means nothing to me.'

With that, Rosa turned and left the room.

Madre Maddalena and Suor Dorotea led the Marchesa out of the villa the morning of her execution. Two partisans followed behind as the group made their way to where Rosa and the other partisans were waiting. The Jewish women and children had been sent to the gatekeeper's cottage with the rest of the nuns. The site chosen for the execution was a field some distance from the house where there was a stack of hay to absorb any bullets that missed their target. The partisans were not following the tradition of having two guns containing blanks so no-one would know who had fired the fatal shot. There was no time for that sort of ceremony. The firing squad — Starling, Woodpecker and Partridge — were all using live ammunition. Rosa knew from nursing that death by shooting was rarely instantaneous. Sometimes the heart continued to beat for another two or three minutes. It could even take up to ten minutes for the person to die, in which case they were bleeding to death. That was why the lieutenant of a firing squad always carried a pistol to finish off the job if the volley of bullets did not hit the prisoner's heart directly. That was why Rosa was holding her pistol now.

The nuns approached the field with the Marchesa, who, despite the warm weather, was wearing a black woollen dress trimmed in panther fur. Rosa stared at it, willing herself to see the majestic jungle creature that had been slaughtered to make the outfit. But the animal didn't appear. Rosa had lost her ability to see the source of things. She knew it was gone forever now. Perhaps she no longer possessed it because she had finally discovered her own origins.

Traitors were traditionally shot in the back. But Rosa had not arranged for that. She had not even ordered that the Marchesa have her hands tied for the execution. It was not for the sake of the Marchesa's dignity that Rosa had neglected these arrangements. It was for her own. Although the Marchesa was a war criminal who had been sentenced to death for her crimes, Rosa could not forget that she was about to execute her mother.

'The blindfold,' said Madre Maddalena, offering the Marchesa a white cloth.

The Marchesa shook her head. 'I don't need it,' she said. 'I'm not afraid of death.'

For a fleeting moment Rosa saw Nerezza once again: proud, defiant, beautiful. *I shall gain mastery over my heart*, she had written in her notebook and on the lapis lazuli stone Rosa had found in her private chamber. Nerezza had succeeded. But at what cost? Rosa was sure that she heard music from somewhere: Chopin's Nocturne No 2 in E-Flat Major. The piece she had played for Signor Trevi and his guests before she discovered the notebook; the night that Nerezza had 'possessed' her. From the way the Marchesa cocked her head, it seemed that she too heard the music. At the moment of death, mother and daughter shared a passion for a few seconds that they had never shared in life. The music faded.

'Do you have any final words?' Madre Maddalena asked the Marchesa.

The Marchesa lifted her chin. 'Long live Mussolini!' she replied. 'He will see that my death is avenged.'

Rosa's mother did not look once at her daughter but simply stared straight ahead at the three partisans who were to shoot her. Rosa knew it was her final snub. Madre Maddalena and Suor Dorotea moved away behind the partisans who were serving as witnesses. They included Ada and Paolina. Fiamma was there as well, to check for a pulse after the Marchesa had been shot.

Rosa raised her arm. Her fingers trembled. 'Ready!'

The men cocked their rifles. The Marchesa did not move a muscle. Not one part of her flinched.

'Aim!'

When Rosa dropped her arm and gave the command to 'Fire!', she saw the partisan who had been tortured and hung like a piece of meat in the villa's cellar; she saw Carlo and Orietta; she saw Luciano, Giovanni and all the partisans who had never seen Florence liberated. She remembered everyone who had suffered because of the Marchesa's collaboration with the Nazis.

The bullets struck the Marchesa in the chest. She sank to her knees, still looking straight ahead. Then she collapsed backwards, her arms outstretched and her eyes staring at the sky. Fiamma rushed forward, followed by Rosa clutching her pistol.

'There's no need,' Fiamma told Rosa, feeling for a pulse in the Marchesa's neck. 'She's dead.'

Rosa nodded to the squad who put down their guns. The last legitimate Scarfiotti was gone. Rosa knew that the witches would leave the villa now. Justice had been done. But Rosa, standing over the bloody body of the mother she had never known, felt no closure; only desolation.

A few weeks after the Marchesa's execution, Rosa and Fiamma were sitting in the garden with their patients when Rosa noticed a black car weaving its way up the driveway towards the villa. Starling saw it too and picked up his gun. Then Rosa glimpsed the Red Cross flag on the bonnet. So, they have finally come to requisition the villa for Allied soldiers, she thought. The car came to a stop near the fountain and Rosa's face broke into a smile when she recognised the driver: Signora Corvetto. Clementina was beside her in the passenger seat.

Signora Corvetto, in a black dress with red cherries on it, rushed from the car and embraced Rosa. 'Thank God you're alive!' she said, tears welling in her eyes. 'I've lost so many friends!'

Rosa glanced towards Clementina.

'She is becoming her cheerful self again,' Signora Corvetto said, grimacing slightly. A serious look fell across her face and she lowered her voice. 'You know when Clementina said that she had "bribed" a guard so she could come and see you ... it was more than that. You know what they were like. You know what he would have expected.'

Rosa flinched. No, she hadn't realised. She hadn't given any thought to what Clementina might have suffered in order to warn her about the hostages at the villa. Rosa remembered how harshly she had spoken to Clementina and was sorry for that now.

'Does she know?' she asked Signora Corvetto. 'That you are her mother?'

Signora Corvetto's face lit up. 'When I told her, Clementina said that she had often wished that I was her mother instead of the Marchesa Scarfiotti! Do you think we will be all right? Do you think I will be a good mother?'

Rosa reached out and clasped Signora Corvetto's hand. 'You will be wonderful,' she said.

The question made Rosa think of her own children. With all that had happened, she believed that she and Antonio had done the best they could in sending Sibilla and the twins to Switzerland to keep them safe. But having not heard from her all this time, they might view her as a stranger when she went to collect them.

Signora Corvetto squeezed Rosa's hand in return. 'I think it's been a relief to Clementina to know that she is not the daughter of that … *monster*. What a terrible burden that would be to bear! No-one will mourn that woman, no-one at all.'

Rosa knew that Signora Corvetto meant well, and she had only confided her feelings in Rosa because she had no idea who the Marchesa Scarfiotti had really been. Rosa herself had to agree with the sentiment: Clementina *was* lucky not to have the burden of that parentage.

'What are your plans now?' she asked.

'The war is still raging in the north,' Signora Corvetto said, 'but when it's over, I will take Clementina to Switzerland. We'll make a new start there.'

'That would be for the best,' agreed Rosa. 'But what about the villa? It belongs to Clementina now.'

Signora Corvetto turned towards the car and waved to Clementina to join them. 'She wants to tell you about that herself,' she said.

Clementina walked towards them. She was fresh-faced in her polka-dotted dress and bore no resemblance to the coquettish young woman Rosa had seen on the colonel's arm.

Clementina lifted her eyes to Rosa. 'Signorina Bellocchi,' she began.

'Signora Parigi,' her mother corrected her.

'Signora Parigi, I mean,' said Clementina, blushing. 'The villa has been a place of horrors but I want that to change. I want this villa to be a place of kindness and generosity.' She took Rosa's hand. 'I intend to donate the villa so it can be used as a home for war orphans: not a horrible, impersonal institution but a place where children feel safe and loved. I know that you are the right person to make that transformation.'

'We understand that you will be returning to your busy family life,' Signora Corvetto added. 'But we would be honoured if you would chair the board to decide on the running of the villa. We hope to find a suitable director, and if you have any recommendations we would be grateful to receive them.'

At that moment, Madre Maddalena walked out of the villa with a group of children behind her. She was going to read them a story in the sunshine. The sisters of Santo Spirito no longer had a convent, but they certainly had a new home if they wanted it. If they decided not to return to enclosure and obtained permission from the Pope, then this would be the perfect place for them.

'I know exactly the person for the role,' Rosa said.

Clementina nodded, understanding who Rosa had meant. Rosa thought of the times she had spent with Clementina as her governess, with no idea that the bubbly girl was her cousin. Rosa had not been alone in the world; she'd had a blood relation. And she would still have her, although she would not tell Clementina about the Marchesa being her mother. She and Clementina were going to organise the orphanage together. Their work for the good of the children would be the bond between them.

'Would you be offended if I suggested we change the name of the villa?' Rosa asked.

'Not at all!' said Clementina, her eyes wide. 'It needs a new beginning. We don't want any associations with the past. Do you have an idea of what we should call it?'

Rosa saw Speranza and Pace grazing on Ada's freshly planted flowers, oblivious to the scolding they would receive when Ada discovered them. Rosa had to stifle a laugh when she thought of the times the affection she and Fiamma held for the sheep had confounded the partisans.

She turned back to Clementina. 'I have the perfect name,' she said. 'How about La Villa della Speranza e della Pace: the Villa of Hope and Peace?'

'Yes!' said Clementina, turning from Rosa to Signora Corvetto, who nodded enthusiastically. 'That's perfect! That's exactly what we should call it!'

Signora Corvetto and Clementina turned to go. Rosa walked with them to the car. Clementina opened the passenger door, and then ran back to Rosa.

'Can you forgive me?' she asked, tears in her eyes. 'Can you forget that I stayed here and didn't join the partisans? I'm so ashamed.'

There was nothing to forgive as far as Rosa was concerned. In her eyes, Clementina was once again the charming girl she had known. They all had to put the war behind them now.

'You were a confused young girl,' she said, stroking Clementina's hair. 'But you have emerged from the terrible experience as a beautiful and wise woman. What more could a governess ask?'

Clementina covered her mouth and burst into sobs. 'Signorina Bellocchi ... I mean, Signora Parigi ...' Clementina was too choked up to say what she wanted. Instead, she smiled and shrugged. 'You will always be Signorina Bellocchi to me.'

Rosa embraced her. 'And you will always be lovely Clementina to me,' she said.

When Signora Corvetto and Clementina had left, Rosa walked through the woods towards the villa's cemetery. After the execution, the partisans had decided to place the Marchesa's body in the grave with the surround. When they had opened it, they found it empty except for some paintings of Nerezza.

'Should we donate them to the city of Florence?' Partridge had asked Rosa. 'Some of these are by famous artists.'

'No,' Rosa had replied. 'Leave them where they are.'

After Partridge and Starling had removed the cover of the tomb, Rosa had been able to see the statue front on for the first time. It was the image of Nerezza as she had been when she was young and uncorrupted. Rosa looked at the beautiful woman before her and then at the bloody corpse of the Marchesa, which Starling and Partridge were lowering into the tomb. What an incredible waste.

Now, Rosa sat by the grave and studied the statue of the child-angel fervently praying to the image of its mother. Signora Corvetto had been right when she said that Clementina was better off not bearing the burden of having had a monster for a mother. But she had been wrong when she said that no-one would mourn the death of the Marchesa. Rosa wept her heart out for all that could never be.

Rosa had registered Karl, Alfon, Erhard and Hannah with the Red Cross to find out if they had any living relatives, but so far had not heard anything. She'd already decided that if no-one claimed them, she would take them into her home. She'd always wanted a large family.

She was playing with them inside the villa one day when she became aware of a commotion outside. She looked out of the window and saw the two German prisoners of war, Hartmut and Klaas, in the orchard. They were cowering but she couldn't see beyond the trees to tell what was threatening them. Not Dono: he was still in his cage. Rosa had been able to persuade the local chief of police to let the German prisoners stay at the villa where they were needed, rather than be transferred to a camp where Rosa had heard the conditions were terrible. Had the chief of police changed his mind? Then, through the trees, Rosa glimpsed Woodpecker brandishing a gun at the Germans. Starling and Ada were there too, trying to appease him.

'Stay here!' Rosa told the children.

She ran to the orchard. What was Woodpecker doing back at the villa? She had sent him away after the execution of the Marchesa to return to his family.

'What's happened?' asked Rosa, arriving at the scene. Woodpecker's face was deathly white.

'Dirty German scum!' he screamed, his gun swinging between Hartmut and Klaas. 'Filthy murderers!'

Starling and Ada looked at Rosa with frightened eyes. Without thinking, Rosa rushed to stand in front of the two Germans, directly in Woodpecker's gun sights.

'What's happened?' she asked, looking from Woodpecker to Starling and Ada.

Ada sucked in a painful breath. 'The German army carried out a massacre in Sant'Anna di Stazzema. Woodpecker's family are all dead.'

Rosa's hands dropped to her sides. 'But I thought the hilltop town was safe?' was all she could manage. She knew Woodpecker had moved his family there after the Germans had attacked his village.

Starling clenched his fists. 'They killed them all — villagers and refugees. The victims were women, children and old people. The men had already left to avoid reprisals. Some of the victims were shot in their homes but many were killed outside the church, where they had gone for protection. The Germans even killed the priest who begged them to take mercy on the children.'

'They cut open a woman in childbirth and shot the baby!' screamed Woodpecker. 'My wife and children were locked in a barn. The Germans threw grenades inside.'

'Oh God!' cried Rosa, holding her hands to her face. Was there no end to this?

She looked to Hartmut and Klaas, who were frozen on the spot, before turning back to Woodpecker. 'Listen,' she said, her heart in her throat, 'these two men weren't there. They deserted the army at the risk of being shot. They didn't want to do what their army has been doing.'

Woodpecker didn't hear her. Tears were streaming down his face. 'And do you know what the Germans did after four hours of killing?' he said. 'They sat down and ate lunch and sang songs. One of them played the harmonica.' He raised his gun again. 'You'd better move, Raven,' he said. 'Don't make me shoot you too.'

'Woodpecker!' Rosa screamed. 'Listen to me! These men were not there! You'd be killing innocent men!'

Woodpecker gritted his teeth and cocked his head in Hartmut's and Klaas's direction. 'They surrendered because they knew the Germans were going to lose the fucking war! They didn't give themselves up in 1943, did they? For the last time, get out of the way, Raven!'

The pain in Woodpecker's eyes was palpable. Rosa felt crushed by it. If he shot her, she didn't care. She moved towards him, blinded by her own tears. To her surprise, Woodpecker put down his gun. Starling grabbed it. Rosa threw her arms around Woodpecker, embracing him as she would a terrified child. His body was racked by sobs. They both collapsed to their knees.

When Woodpecker's breathing calmed he looked at Rosa and said, 'My youngest child was a baby.'

Ada crouched down next to Woodpecker and put her arm around him. Starling knelt too. Hartmut and Klaas kept a respectful distance. Woodpecker was a brave soldier but a crushed and broken man. Rosa could see what the war did: it destroyed people. How could things ever be the same? 'Stay with us, Woodpecker,' she said. 'There are children here who need your love. We'll be your family now.'

By mid-autumn, Rosa knew it was time for her to return to Florence. Signora Corvetto had made enquiries about

Antonio, but so far no information had turned up. It didn't appear as if he had ever made it to Germany. But Rosa had to face her city and find out what had happened to the shop and the apartment. When the war was finally over, she would bring her children back. No correspondence was coming through from Switzerland, but she had to trust that they were safe.

The Jewish women wanted to stay at the villa with their children until Germany had been defeated; a cautionary measure Rosa could understand. Signora Corvetto and Clementina agreed without reservation that the women could remain as long as they wished. Rosa told them that she would leave the running of the villa to Starling and Fiamma along with Madre Maddalena until she had completed what she had to do in Florence and could return to help them.

The morning Rosa was leaving for Florence, she went to see Hartmut and Klaas, who were repairing a retaining wall in the kitchen garden. Nobody bothered guarding them any more. One day they would return to Germany, but they were such a part of the villa now that Rosa was only willing to let them go when she knew they could return home safely. She had heard that many German prisoners of war had been killed in acts of revenge.

'I have one final thing for you to do,' she said, showing the men a diagram of a deep ditch she wanted them to dig near the summerhouse.

Hartmut trembled when Rosa explained the width and depth she wanted the ditch to be. 'A mass grave?' he asked, his eyes wide with terror. 'You want us to dig our grave?'

Rosa was astonished for a moment before she understood. 'No,' she said, pointing in the direction of Dono's cage. 'You see our poor bear there? He has been in that cramped cage for years. I want you to dig him a proper bear pit with a cave for him to shelter inside. Can you do that?'

It was Hartmut's turn to be dumbfounded but Klaas

understood and smiled. 'Yes, we can do that,' he said. 'We'll do an excellent job. We are Germans. We'll figure it out.'

Rosa explained to the men that she was going away for a while and that they would probably be gone by the time she returned. Hartmut and Klaas each shook her hand. It occurred to Rosa that it was an odd thing to be doing: two German soldiers and an Italian patriot parting on such amicable terms. But she had come to the conclusion that while most Italians — and probably many Germans — had not wanted war, they had chosen a path of greed and pride and the result had been war. For where else did violence begin but within each individual human heart? It started with violence of thought and action, jealousy of others and loathing of oneself. It had its beginnings in the daily choices one made, including the indifference towards the suffering of animals in what one selected to eat and wear, and towards the poor and oppressed. From there it escalated into a collective consciousness of competitiveness, selfishness, pettiness, spite and greed. Violence of even the most seemingly innocuous kind begat more violence. That was the origin of war. Rosa could no longer tell where food, clothes or items of furniture had come from, but she saw clearly the source of conflict. What the Germans had done was an extreme form of what any human being was capable of, if they *chose* to do so. Hartmut and Klaas had chosen differently.

She was at the kitchen door when Klaas called after her. She stopped and he ran towards her.

'I want to know why you didn't let your fellow partisan shoot us,' he asked. 'If the Italian army had done to the Germans what we have done to you, I would want to kill every Italian I could lay my hands on.'

Rosa plucked a rose from the garden and placed it in Klaas's buttonhole. 'There's been enough killing,' she said. 'I might have let him shoot you if I had honestly thought that it would have done any good. But it wouldn't have. If there is one thing I've learnt it is that revenge never brings the peace you hope it will.'

Klaas nodded. 'Good luck,' he said, shaking Rosa's hand again. 'I hope the future is good to you.'

'And I wish the same for you,' Rosa replied.

Madre Maddalena, Starling, Woodpecker, Fiamma, Ada and Paolina walked Rosa and Partridge to the end of the driveway when they were ready to depart. Partridge was accompanying Rosa to the outskirts of Florence before returning to his own home in Bagno a Ripoli.

'Don't eat my sheep,' Rosa told Starling. 'I want them to be here when I get back.'

Starling rolled his eyes. 'Mankind has been eating animals for centuries.'

'We have been murdering each other for centuries too. Do you think that's something we should also continue out of habit?'

Starling's face broke into a grin. 'If there's one thing about you, Raven,' he said, 'it's that you always manage to get the final word.'

Rosa saw a look pass between him and Fiamma that made her smile. In the past few weeks she had noticed a growing intimacy between them. Wherever Fiamma was, Starling was never too far away. Rosa had a feeling that Starling didn't intend to be a single man for much longer. The partisans embraced and Rosa and Partridge began their journey home.

It felt strange to be in Florence again; Rosa had been away for more than a year. The autumn weather was clear and sunny. Bands were playing in some of the piazzas. There were flags hanging in store windows — Italian, American, British, Canadian. There was a sort of carnival atmosphere about the city but it wasn't sincere. The bands sounded tinny and empty. After hiding in the mountains for so long, after living the life of a soldier, Rosa felt like someone who had been away in a foreign country. She looked at the people's faces as she passed them on the street. Everyone was busy going about their lives. Some people were smiling, and some scurried along with their eyes averted. Everyone walked close to the buildings, a habit cultivated during the outbreaks of gunfire that had occurred between the Germans and the partisans during the last days of the occupation. Rosa had fought for her country, but many of the people around her hadn't. She was no longer surrounded by comrades, but was moving amongst people who had cooperated with the fascists in some way and may even have collaborated with the Germans. There were still revenge killings happening on a daily basis and women with shaved heads being paraded in the streets. The wounds in Florence ran deep and who knew when they would heal.

The palazzo where Rosa's apartment was located had suffered some shell damage but a plasterer and tiler were at work repairing the roof. She didn't meet anyone on the stairs and wondered what had happened to her neighbours. Had they been sucked into a void like so many others from the city? The door to her apartment had been ripped off its hinges so her anxiety about no longer having the key had been unnecessary. She slipped through the doorway and into the foyer. The tiles were littered with her and Antonio's personal letters and documents. The looters had found where they had stashed their artwork and most of the paintings were gone, except a work in oil of the Madonna, which had been urinated and defecated upon. The charger that Antonio had given Rosa for their anniversary was smashed to pieces on the drawing room floor. Rosa picked up the centrepiece with the peace doves still intact on it and slipped it into her pocket. She looked about her home with the same dazed fatigue that someone would look at their neighbourhood after an earthquake or other natural disaster. She remembered the furniture that had once pleased her eye and appealed to her senses. It was mostly gone now, and in its place obscenities had been scrawled on the walls. In the bedrooms, the sheets had been ripped to shreds and the children's books were torn and strewn about the floor. Sibilla's baby dress, the one Orietta had made for her, was crammed behind a door. Rosa picked it up and discovered it was stiff with blood, as if someone had used it to staunch a wound.

Rosa sank to the floor. She noticed that Nerezza's notebook had been used to balance a bed that had a wobbly leg. It seemed bizarre that her mother's notebook was the only thing that had been left intact in the apartment. She covered her face with her hands, about to give way to tears, but then rallied herself. This was the last battle, wasn't it? The battle to rebuild her life and the lives of her children. To not let what had happened destroy them. She lifted her eyes and looked around the apartment the way she had once examined burns patients — seeing what was savable beyond even the most horrific injuries. She had to make a home for her children again.

Rosa walked into the bathroom. The putrid smell sent her reeling. The toilet was brimming with excreta. She turned on the taps and found one relief — there was still hot and cold running water. She filled a bucket and decided that she would start with the kitchen.

'Signora Parigi?'

Rosa turned around to see Ylenia standing behind her with a broom and mop.

'I was coming to clean the apartment,' she said, looking like she had seen a ghost. 'I had to flee when it was taken over. I've been staying with the neighbours.'

'The Nazi bastards,' said Rosa, shaking her head.

'Oh, they were bad,' agreed Ylenia. 'But this damage was done by the Goums. They seem to think that looting and raping are their rewards for fighting in Italy. I suggest that you and Signor Parigi get the door fixed and reinforced as soon as possible.'

Rosa's eyes filled with tears. 'I don't know where Antonio is.'

Ylenia frowned.

'He was taken away to Germany,' Rosa explained. 'And I've been in the mountains since last August.'

Ylenia gave a little cry. 'No, Signora Parigi, your husband was here this morning, looking for you. When I saw you here just now, I assumed that you had found each other.'

Rosa's heart leaped in her chest. It hurt her. It must have been weakened by the war. 'Antonio was here?' she asked, her voice rising with excitement. 'Are you sure?'

'Yes,' said Ylenia. 'He gave me money to buy bread and vegetables and he asked me to mind your flute.'

'Do you know where he is now?'

Ylenia shook her head. 'He said he's been going to all the hospitals searching for you.'

Luciano's words filled Rosa's mind. *You have to trust your husband, Raven. You have to trust him that he loves you enough to do anything to survive, so that he can come back to you.*

'Where has he been?' Rosa asked.

'He was taken away by train the day you were to collect him from the prison,' she said. 'But the train was bombed. He escaped and came back to Florence to find you but you had disappeared. He worked with the underground here but eventually had to flee north to join the partisans,' Ylenia said.

Rosa thanked Ylenia and went running out into the street. *Hurry! Hurry!* she told herself, heading in the direction of Via Tornabuoni. But her heart ached and she had to stop every so often to catch her breath. It seemed to her that the air was echoing with the sounds of rebuilding: scraping, chiselling, hammering. Some of the shops were untouched while others had been badly damaged. Rosa saw the sign for Parigi's Fine Furniture and Antiques. The grille was still over the window but when she looked inside she saw that, like the apartment, nearly all the furniture was gone. There was no sign of Antonio.

'Rosa?'

In the reflection of the window, Rosa could see Antonio standing behind her. He was wearing his favourite trench coat and hat and looked the way he used to when he went to work each morning before the war. It was such a beautiful vision that she was afraid to turn around in case she was dreaming.

'Rosa?'

Slowly she turned. Her eyes met Antonio's. He leaped towards her and clasped her in his arms. 'Rosa!' he cried, kissing her lips and face. 'Rosa! Is it really you? They told me you had been taken away by the Germans!'

'I heard the same thing about you!' she said.

Antonio stepped back, taking her face in his hands. He gazed at her as if he were holding a precious treasure. His skin was darker than Rosa remembered. He was still handsome but had a haggard look of exhaustion about his eyes.

Antonio gazed at her with wonder and then embraced her again. 'The children are safe,' he told her. 'I made contact with them when I was up north. As soon as the Germans are routed, we will go and collect them.'

For a moment the world stood still while Rosa took in the news she had yearned for. She saw a picture of her treasured children playing with Ambrosio and Allegra. The image of Sibilla and the twins was like a flame, thawing her loneliness. How she longed to be with them again — to watch them sleep, to hear their laughter, to comfort them: all the joys of motherhood that the war had denied her.

The door to the shop was warped from having been forced when the looters entered it. Antonio kicked it open and took Rosa's hand, helping her inside. The shop had not been vandalised the same way that the apartment had been, but still the missing furniture and the smashed vases and light fittings brought back the feeling to Rosa that her life had been violated. The only item the looters had left behind was the eighteenth-century walnut dining table that had been too large for Antonio and Rosa to hide. She remembered how beautiful the shop had once looked and how hard Antonio had worked to build his dream. Tears she had held back began to fall down her cheeks.

'Rosa,' said Antonio, squeezing her hand. 'We have each other. We have the children. We have everything. We can start again!'

Rosa wanted to embrace that optimism but a dark feeling overcame her. Like a nightmare, it all flashed before her: the people she had seen killed; her assassination of Emanuele; the terror in which she had lived. Even the one light she had known in the past year — her love of Luciano — pushed her further from her husband. How could she ever explain that to him? She thought of the way Antonio had said her name: as if she were still his graceful, sweet-hearted wife. He had searched for her in the hospitals, but that person didn't exist any more. She was a stranger. Rosa stepped away from Antonio.

'What is it?' he asked, his eyes full of concern.

Rosa tried to gather her thoughts. The pain in her heart was engulfing her. 'I'm not the same person,' she said, struggling to get the words out. 'I'm not the Rosa I was before the war ... I've seen and done things ... terrible things.'

'None of us are the same after the war,' replied Antonio. 'Not one of us is unblemished.'

Rosa tried to say something but tears choked her voice. Then she confessed it all. She told Antonio everything that had happened to her during her time with the partisans: the things she had done and the people she had killed. She told him about Luciano. If they were to begin again, then Rosa couldn't build her new life with Antonio on lies. She dared not look him in the face when she recounted the story of the Marchesa and how she had been her mother. Would Antonio still want her after all she confessed? She glanced up at him, expecting to see at least reproach, if not resentment, in his eyes. But Antonio was looking at her with the same loving regard he had always shown her. He stood up and went to the walnut dining table, feeling for its quirks and faults.

'Do you remember when you first came to work for me what I taught you about antiques, Rosa?' he asked.

She stared at him, not comprehending. He smiled and continued. 'The patina is the history of an object and shows what has happened over time. A crackled finish, a nick, a scratch — all these things give a piece character. The patina is what makes the piece truly valuable. The Germans didn't see this table for what it is. They left the rarest and most expensive piece of furniture behind.'

Rosa covered her mouth with her hand. Her heart was too full to speak.

'I want you, Rosa,' Antonio said, turning to her. 'I want you with your scars and your suffering. You are my wife and everything that has happened to you only makes you more precious to me.'

Rosa felt a wave of pain rush through her. It was as if she were suffocating. A burning sensation radiated out from her chest, causing her shoulders and arms to ache. The agony was so overwhelming she thought her heart might seize up with it, that she would stop breathing. She looked at Antonio standing in the ruins of their former life, beseeching her with his eyes to find the strength to begin again. *Despite all that she had confessed, he still loved her.* Could she do it? Could she draw up the strength when she felt she had none left? The pain in her heart subsided. It was replaced by a feeling of tenderness. She saw Luciano in the tunnel, his eyes full of love. He had died to save her. What would that sacrifice mean if she didn't do something with her life? Her calling had been to live. *Find Antonio, for I know that he is out there somewhere looking for you. And when you find him, love him with all your heart — but sometimes, when you look at the stars, think of me and smile.* Rosa knew what she had to do and that she would find the courage.

'Yes!' she said, rushing to Antonio and throwing her arms around him. 'Let's bring back the children and then decide what to do next. It doesn't matter where we live as long as we are together.'

Antonio brushed his fingers down her cheek and looked

into her eyes. 'We'll be all right, Rosa,' he said. 'Whatever we face in the future, we will face it together.'

Rosa saw that was the truth. There was so much to be conquered, so much suffering to be overcome. But she and Antonio had each other. They had their family. It was all that they needed.

AUTHOR'S NOTE

Dear Reader,

Tuscan Rose is a fictional story set in a historical period. The events that occur in the novel in terms of fascism and the Second World War are true. Florence has also been researched (and delightfully absorbed) to re-create the city as it was at that time.

However, all the characters are fictional and are not based on any real living or deceased person. Except for Fido, the faithful dog of Borgo San Lorenzo. I will mention more about him later.

The Convent of Santo Spirito is a fictional convent, however I undertook research on convent life and also on the treatment of unwed mothers and illegitimate children to create a situation true to the times. The women's prison in Florence in the 1930s was Santa Verdiana, which was attached to the men's prison, Le Murate. However, I didn't name the prison Rosa was sent to because I wanted to have some leeway with the characters there and did not want them to be mistaken to represent any of the nuns or guards serving at the prison at that time. However, my fictional prison is true to the era based on my research on women's prisons in Italy and the treatment of female political prisoners during the Mussolini years. I also took this approach with the hospital and some other institutions in Florence.

The events I describe as taking place in Borgo San Lorenzo, while true to the conditions of the war in terms of the viciousness of reprisals and the horrific examples that were made of those Italians who helped the partisans, did not occur in Borgo San Lorenzo. I used the town because it was close to the location of the fictional partisan group, the Flock.

However, as mentioned above, Fido the faithful dog is based on a true historical character. For the convenience of the storyline I moved him from his small Apennine village of Luco to the larger town of Borgo San Lorenzo. As described in *Tuscan Rose*, Fido was rescued as a stray puppy by the bricklayer Carlo Soriano. Every morning Fido would accompany Carlo to the stop where the bricklayer would catch a bus to his workplace in Borgo San Lorenzo. Sadly, Carlo was one of the victims of the bombing described in the novel in which many innocent civilians were killed. For the next thirteen years, Fido continued to wait at the bus-stop every evening for Carlo to come home. Some years after the war, the Mayor of Luco declared Fido belonged on the list of the village's honoured citizens as an example of fidelity. Fido was then able to live tax-free as the only legally unlicensed dog in Italy. A statue commemorating Fido can be found in Piazza Dante in Borgo San Lorenzo. As Fido's name means 'faithful' I thought he was the perfect symbol for this part of the story. I also kept Carlo's name as Fido's master in the book. I wanted them to be as inseparable in fiction as they were in real life. I decided to include this wonderful story because for me it is just another example that animals do have feelings and attachments, and no scientist will ever convince me that they don't so therefore it is acceptable to abuse them.

To give the novel a sense of place, I used Italian terms, titles, phrases and idioms where I felt they added flavour to a scene. Although in the 1930s and 1940s many Italians would have still been favouring their regional dialects, I decided to use standard Italian to avoid confusion for modern readers who may have knowledge of the language.

The exception to this was the use of 'babbo' rather than 'papà' as this is a word still used by Florentines today and which distinguishes them from other regions.

I hope that you enjoyed reading *Tuscan Rose* as much as I enjoyed writing it. I also hope that you will take away with you and share the core message of the novel — that peace on a world scale is determined by each of us creating peace in our own hearts and minds first, and doing our best to live in harmony with the people and other living creatures around us. When we can each do that, I believe together we will then become a force powerful enough to create positive change on a scale never before conceived.

ACKNOWLEDGEMENTS

Each book I have written has taken me on a journey of learning about another country and culture and another time in history. *Tuscan Rose* is no exception. I'd sincerely like to thank those who have not only made that journey possible but who have also been delightful travelling companions:

Professor Alessandro Fantechi of the University of Florence for so generously helping me with some tricky historical and cultural questions about the city.

Gianluca Alimeni, Associate Lecturer in Italian Studies at Macquarie University and President of the Tuscan Association of NSW, for reading the manuscript to check the Italian references. This was of invaluable help to me. To Melinda Gallo who so kindly helped me check facts about Florence and Florentine culture.

Pauline O'Kane of Ku-ring-gai Library who helped me find even the most obscure books for my research and managed to obtain all of them on inter-library loan.

To my brother, Paul, for his excellent explanations of military tactics and Second World War history. His illustration of how to correctly storm an enemy stronghold — using oranges, avocados and a banana on the kitchen counter to demonstrate — is a memory that will always make me laugh.

Thank you again to my lovely and gracious publisher, Linda Funnell, for her tremendous support for me and her enthusiasm for *Tuscan Rose*. I'd also like to express my appreciation to my talented editor, Nicola O'Shea. Nicola has worked with me since my first book, *White Gardenia*, and I always know my story and characters are in safe hands with her.

I'd like to thank Kate O'Donnell, Senior Editor at HarperCollins *Publishers* Australia, for her expert coordination of the editing process. She is always courteous and accommodating and her efforts are very much appreciated.

Thank you to the wonderful team at HarperCollins *Publishers* Australia who greet each new book with enthusiasm and verve. I'd especially like to thank Michael Moynahan, CEO; Shona Martyn, Publishing Director; Karen-Maree Griffiths and Jim Demetriou; and the dynamic sales, publicity and administrative departments.

Finally, I would like to thank my wonderful family and friends for all their support; especially my father, Stan, Johnny (Giovanni Battista), Melinda Hutchings, and Fiona Workman.

Thank you to you all.

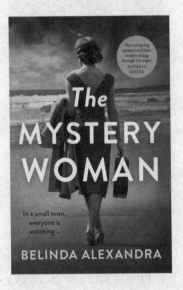

Rebecca Wood takes a job as the postmistress in a sleepy seaside town, desperate for anonymity after a scandal in Sydney. But she is confronted almost at once by a disturbing discovery – her predecessor committed suicide.

Her hopes for a quiet life are further threatened by the attentions of the dashing local doctor, the unsettling presence of a violent whaling captain and a corrupt shire secretary, and the watchful eyes of the town's gossips. Yet in spite of herself she is drawn to the enigmatic resident of the house on the clifftop, rumoured to have been a Nazi spy.

Against the backdrop of the turbulent sea, Rebecca is soon caught up in the dangerous mysteries that lie behind Shipwreck Bay's respectable net curtains.

'Belinda Alexandra is a master at keeping the pages turning'
Herald Sun

Paris, 1899. When Emma Lacasse receives a request from her estranged older sister Caroline, to visit her in New York, she is intrigued.

Caroline lives a life of unimaginable luxury as one of New York's Gilded Age millionaires and Emma is soon immersed in a world beyond her wildest dreams — a far cry from her bohemian lifestyle in Montmartre. Emma hopes for an emotional reunion, but instead she finds herself in the vice-like grip of her charismatic and manipulative sister, who revels in the machinations of the ultra rich.

As Emma begins to question her sister's true motives, a disaster strikes, and New York society is stripped bare — beneath the glittering exterior lies a seething nest of deceit, betrayal, moral corruption ... and perhaps even murder.

From the bestselling author of *Tuscan Rose* comes a mesmerising tale of two sisters and the dangers and seductions of excess.

'Reading her novels is like going on holiday for a long time. You don't want to come back' *West Australian*

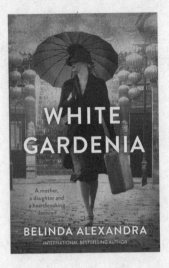

'Mama, Mama,' I said to myself, 'keep safe. You will survive, and I will survive, until we can find each other again.'

In a district of the city of Harbin, a haven for White Russian families since Russia's Communist revolution, Alina Kozlova must make a heartbreaking decision if her only child, Anya, is to survive the final days of World War II.

White Gardenia sweeps across cultures and continents, from the glamorous nightclubs of Shanghai to the harshness of Cold War Soviet Russia in the 1960s, from a desolate island in the Pacific Ocean to a new life in post-war Australia. Both mother and daughter must make sacrifices, but is the price too high? Most importantly of all, will they ever find each other again?

'Captivating' *Daily Telegraph*

'A passionate and powerful family saga' *Australian Women's Weekly*

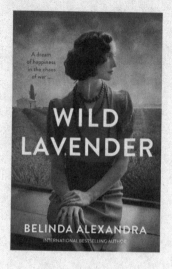

'*Nothing is wasted, Simone. The love we give never dies.*'

At fourteen, Simone Fleurier is wrenched from her home on a Provençal lavender farm and sent to work in Marseilles. Her life there is hard and impoverished, but Simone discovers the music hall and a dream: to one day be a famous dancer and singer. But when war threatens, Simone makes a decision that will lead to great danger — yet ultimately prove that love, just like wild lavender, can grow in the least likely of places …

Belinda Alexandra has created a tale of passion and courage that moves from the backstreets of Marseilles to the grand music theatres of Paris, from the countryside of Provence to decadent pre-war Berlin and jazz-age New York.

'Filled with glamour, heartbreak, drama and suspense'
The Age

'Rich in detail, and the story fairly rattles along'
Choice magazine

Love Belinda Alexandra?
Sign-up to her newsletter!

Each season Belinda shares her insights into the writing
process and her creative journey, seasonal reflections and lots
of fun content along with events and special offers.

Sign up for Belinda's newsletter at
www.belinda-alexandra.com